The Dove Code

A Novel

Chatan N. Kallah

Cover Painting: *The Second Sabbath*
by Patricia White

The Dove Code

by Chatan N. Kallah

ISBN 978-158169-2990

For Worldwide Distribution

Printed in the U.S.A.

Publisher

Ghost Writers from on High

JOHN 14:26

But the Comforter, which is the Holy Ghost, whom the Father will send in my name, he shall teach you all things, and bring all things to your remembrance, whatsoever I have said unto you.

The Dove Code

Table of Contents

Chapters

OnLine Resources:

http://www.TheAncientChest.com

Dedication

Dedicated to the brave sons and daughters of the Most High God that have sailed the seas of love. Their experiences have made this writing possible.

Psalms 107:23
They that go down to the sea in ships,
that do business in great waters;

This novel is based on both fictional and real experiences and places. Some of the real events have been time compressed or time expanded. Also some locations have been changed for the purposes of the novel. The type in parts of some of the scriptures has been bolded or highlighted for the purpose of emphasiing the thought being discussed.

Chatan N. Kallah

Introduction

The setting is RSU located in the mid US. Sarah and Kim, two University students struggle with determining their purpose, their destinies, and how they will find their future mates. Kim is a biophysics major and encounters controversy as she discovers conflicts with her faith in some of her science classes.

In the meantime, Sarah has been contemplating some spiritual discoveries and new insights into scriptures she has made after opening an ancient chest. Some of these "discoveries" initially took her breath away—to the point that she was almost afraid to share them with her best friend, Kim.

Through the eyes of Sarah, Kim and their friends, this novel examines a variety of questions ranging from the identity of Mary Magdalene and her relationship to Jesus, what is true spiritual love, would God be pleased with a woman Chief Justice of the Supreme Court to—stunning revelations [and courtroom trial controversies] about the earth's creation as described from scientific and biblical viewpoints.

The voice of joy, and the voice of gladness, the voice of the bridegroom, and the voice of the bride ... *Jeremiah*

Chapter 1

For, Lo, the Winter is Past

"It was like one of those first recognized childhood memories that remain forever etched within," Kimberly related. "I looked down and saw the little toy cars crawling like ants on I-75. I picked out one and wondered about who was driving and what their concept of direction in life was. I saw little towns dotting the landscape here and there. Suppose I graduate from college and go to this little town or that one, who would I meet and what would my life be like?"

"Whoa, wait a minute," said Sarah, a friend of Kimberly from the fifth grade on. "Aren't you becoming the philosopher on me? What brought on these deep thoughts during a routine flight from your first spring break back to Nashville?"

"Yeah, I suppose those are strange thoughts," Kim said, "but we will be graduating and going out into the world in a couple of years. I'm feeling like a person who could get on her horse and ride off in many directions. Will I live in that little farm house with the tin roof or end up in a large city with its many apartment buildings? All of these decisions affect whether I marry and have children or become a career girl or whatever. My thoughts were that I could go in many different directions, but are there some invisible, eternal magnetic lines of force that determine what finally happens to us in the end?"

"You mean like do you have a destiny that's already predetermined," Sarah mused, "or do you have a choice of destinies?"

It was one of those story book springtime days. Sarah and Kimberly sat on a huge rock overlooking the river. In the distance one could see a paddle wheel tour boat churning its way up river against the powerful current. The maples and the oaks were sunning themselves in the soft breeze, the wild flowers were blooming, and the soft cooing of the turtle doves could be heard. A blue crested heron glided over the river toward the eastern sandbar shore.

Sarah and Kimberly reflected on the rhetorical question about their destinies for several minutes. A pair of doves glided down onto the outward part of the cleft of the majestic limestone bluff rocks just below them and began their little dance of cooing and cuddling.

As Sarah watched Kim reflecting about her future, she pondered about Kim being a dreamer. She thought, *Kim wants answers yesterday concerning life events that could be years away. I fear her immediate reactions to future events may cause her to choose the wrong path. I hope she learns to let her feelings settle in her spirit until God stirs them.*

"Look at those doves," said Kim. "They have found each other, and their decisions in life are already made. I wonder if I will ever find my true love and we will cuddle and coo like that? How sweet, and oh, so romantic!"

Kimberly's words would have startled Sarah had she not known her friend so well. Sarah struggled not to show her true thoughts on the outside. Dare she tell Kimberly about the secret documents that she found in the ancient wedding chest that Uncle Andy and Aunt Myra had bought in Trinidad? The chest was now resting at the foot of the bed in her uncle and aunt's house. Even though Kimberly was her almost lifelong friend, these documents touched on things that not many people would understand.

In fact, they had really thrown Sarah for a loop for about a year until she began to understand that her Uncle Andy and Aunt Myra had collected some unusual documents and penned some very unique insights before they passed on. Most of these were never shared or published and those that were published were given very limited distribution. Was there some purpose from on high that these writings had ended up in Sarah's possession?

Sarah decided not to reveal her secrets about the doves to Kim until she had some time to think things through. She had to develop a suitable way of presenting the concepts because she didn't want Kim to freak out. Sarah was pursuing a teaching degree with a particular interest in high school students. She regarded the high school years as a period when students' concepts were still pliable as they searched for truth and were not yet fired in the furnaces of tradition into a hard mold. She planned to get a year of teaching experience and then return to RSU for an advanced degree in education.

Kim, on the other hand, was deep into the sciences, and she loved biogenetics. She planned to get her basic degree at RSU and then get a masters and hopefully a doctorate at Baylor. Kim was quite analytical, and Sarah was very intuitive—perhaps they hit it off so well because their talents were complementary to each other. Sometimes they even traded places and Sarah became the left-brained voice of reason and Kimberly became the right-brained romanticist, such as when they were watching the courting ritual of the doves.

"How do you think these doves got together?" questioned Kim. "Did they sort of collide in midair and become aware of each other? Or, did they watch each other from a distance and think about how handsome or how beautiful the other one is. Did they wonder *Am I destined to marry that one or is this just a fling?* How did their first date go and did they have a long engagement?"

Kim's questions added to Sarah's turmoil within. She agonized about whether she should tell Kim about the Dove Scrolls. Sarah disliked keeping secrets from her friend. They had always shared everything, passing notes back and forth in school, giggling about a new boy in math class, and discussing what colors they would like for their wedding. *But this is different,* Sarah thought. *Once Kim has a dream, she has trouble waiting for the right time. Would she read the documents and run out and tackle someone she thought might be her God given mate? Or, would she try to digest the information and allow the Spirit of God time to make the scriptures alive in her?* Sarah really admired Kim's discipline in her scholastic studies. *She is exceptionally bright, but does she have enough discipline in matters of the heart?*

After basking in the warm spring sunlight for a while longer, they mounted their bicycles and rode back to the RSU campus. Kim and Sarah were standing in the cafeteria line in the basement of McKinny Hall chatting with their friend Tiffany—when they ran into Nancy. Nancy was hardly five feet tall, but she had tremendous energy and drive. Among the students in the College of Criminal Justice, she was considered a real mover and shaker. Her fellow students thought she might rise to become a Supreme Court lawyer or even a Supreme Court judge. Nancy was known as an organizer, and this night she was proposing a trip to the movie theater. The movie theaters near the university had gone out of business and one had to drive out to the bypass to visit the new 14 theater cinema.

"Hey, Tiff, Kim and Sar—how about going to see The Empty Quarter Frontier? It's a real adventure movie. Won three Oscars. Floyd is working at Campus Pizza tonight so I can borrow his car."

Tiffany, Kimberly and Sarah agreed and they were off to the cinema in Floyd's old Malibu. They all chipped in for a giant box of popcorn and settled down for a romantic adventure into the unknown. After fifteen minutes of the inevitable previews and advertisements, the movie finally began.

After the movie, they drove to Barney's Barn for hamburgers and shakes. As Kim, Nancy, and Sarah rehashed the movie, they noticed that Tiffany was unusually quiet.

"Tiff—what was your take on the movie? You've hardly said a word." asked Nancy.

"Its not the Empty Quarter movie that bothering me. It was the previews." said Tiffany. The Towers of Magdala preview stirred up some very deep stuff inside. I really sort of want to see it —but then I don't want to see it."

"Oh—you mean the story about Mary Magdalene? Well, nobody knows yet what will be in the movie—so how can you be disturbed about it? It might be a good movie." queried Nancy.

"Well, I don't know, maybe it's more on a personal level." Tiffany said. "All this stuff about the relationship between Mary Magdalene and Jesus is very upsetting to my upbringing. It sort of brings everything that happened in my family to the surface!"

"Well, its not just you," Sarah said. "We all have those kind of thoughts. The life of Jesus has been portrayed as that of a single man. And all of a sudden, Plop! Into the middle of it is dropped the idea that he may have been married or even fathered a child."

"Or worse yet," said Tiffany. "Some won't come right out and say it, but the implication is there that he may not have been married when he fathered a child. I was born out of wedlock, and my mother received no support from my father. She made a promise to God that if He would help her, she would raise me in the church and bring me up in God's teachings. And I have been in the church regularly from the first Sunday after my birth. I learned about the values of love, self-control, and chastity. And here, all of a sudden, the ideas are advanced that Jesus may not have adhered to the very values that are written in the Bible! That's what's really bothering me."

"I know what you mean," said Kim. "It's like you're playing the game, and it has certain rules. And then somebody moves the goal posts. Sex before marriage—it's on every girl's mind and are there now no restrictions? I like to be able to reason things out, so changing the rules in the middle of the game bothers me."

"Well, life for my mother would have been much easier had she waited and not been a single mom," replied Tiffany. "But who knows, maybe I wouldn't even be here if that had not happened."

"Well, this discussion is getting awfully deep and personal," said Nancy. "Maybe we should go back to the campus before I start blabbing about my secret life and hidden thoughts."

And so they drove back in silence, dropped the Malibu off for Floyd at Campus Pizza. Sarah and Kim left the group to walk back to their dorm on the beautiful, starlit night. They found the North Star and rehearsed what they had learned from the movie about the empty quarter. There was a quadrant of the night sky that seemed like a coal bin compared to the abundance of twinkling stars in the other sectors of the sky.

Kim and Sarah immersed themselves in their studies until the following weekend and decided to once again bicycle out to the rock by the river. This time they went to the shady glen just north of the main rock where they could be much closer to the river. There was a ring of rocks for sitting almost like some Indians had brought them there in order to have a council around a campfire. Even though the temperature was much warmer, the shade of the stately oaks was refreshing as was the pleasant breeze coming in from up the river.

Two students from the local seminary came hiking by and stopped to ask if Kim and Sarah would be interested in attending a free concert at the river seminary on the following Wednesday. Kim politely took the free tickets and chatted with the boy named Everett just a bit. And then the boys went on their way. Noting Everett's attentiveness toward Kim, Sarah teasingly queried her about whether she thought Everett considered Kim to be a POI—a person of interest.

"Well, it would probably be safer to date one of them than some of the wild types that we ran into at Joe's last fall," said Kim. "Hopefully, one would not end up like Tiffany's mom. We probably shouldn't ever mention to our folks that we went to Joe's. After all, we were just college girls trying our wings once we had left home. Maybe our parents live far enough away that they've never heard of the reputation of Joe's Rendezvous."

"I agree—I'll never tell." said Sarah, "You know—I think that Tiffany's opening up her soul the other night might've got to you just a bit. Are you still stewing over the Jesus and Mary Magdalene relationship?"

"Yeah, I guess so," said Kim. "When Tiffany started talking about Mary Magdalene and Jesus, it brought a lot of stuff back to the surface that I suppressed and did not want to face. When I left you that night and rode home with that guy from Joe's, I felt very guilty about it, and then shoved it back into the recesses of my mind. You've heard of WWJD (What Would Jesus Do?)—now I'm wondering WDJD (What Did Jesus Do?)."

Just then there was the whirring of wings, and two doves lit on the rock directly across the imaginary campfire circle from Sarah and Kim. They began their little courtship dance of cooing and cuddling. *Oh no!* thought Sarah. *Here we go again! Is this a sign from heaven that I'm supposed to tell Kim about the Dove Scrolls? These scrolls answer a lot of the questions about the relationship between Jesus and Mary Magdalene. But it took me a year to sort it out. I'm not sure that Kim can handle it. And once you start into it, your questions are answered, but then you have more questions. Dare I open Pandora's box and discuss this with Kim?*

Kim studied Sarah's face. "You look like you're thinking something about the doves and not telling me. I've known you since the fifth grade, and when you get that look on your face, something is brewing."

Sarah was dismayed at Kim's intuitiveness. Should she risk sharing with her? *Well, fasten your seat belts, here we go!* thought Sarah.

"Kim, you know me too well—your questions about Mary Magdalene and Jesus and the stage right arrival of the doves is unreal. I've been fighting the idea of even discussing this with you, but you flushed it out into the open."

"Ha! Trying to keep secrets from me!" exclaimed Kim. "What on earth could these doves have to do with Mary Magdalene and Jesus? Yeah, I know that a dove descended on Jesus when he was baptized. So? You're being your usual cryptic self before you tell me a secret that you know you're going to tell me anyway. Come on, spill it!"

"Remember last weekend when we were here at the rock, and you were trying to figure out how doves met each other, dated, courted, got engaged, then married, and mated?"

"Yeah, I remember—you accused me of being a philosopher trying to figure out my destiny just before the doves came and lit on the rock cleft."

"OK, what do you really know about the lives of doves?" questioned Sarah.

"Not really that much. Come on, get to the point and tell me what I should know about doves."

"Let's start out with the fact that there are always two eggs in a dove's nest. And one of these eggs always contains a male dovelet and the other always contains a female dovelet."

"So," said Kim. "It is interesting that we have always have a brother and sister in the dove's family. That's neat, but it still doesn't really explain anything."

"Would it shock you if I told you that the brother and sister in the nest were spousal mates for life? Doesn't that really simplify the process of choosing one's partner for life?"

"Yeah, that is really surprising. I didn't know that. But wouldn't that be inbreeding? And you're still being very mysterious about how this relates to Jesus and Mary Magdalene. We certainly know that they were not brother and sister. I don't think Jesus even knew Mary until he was over thirty years old."

"Maybe," said Sarah, "as far as inbreeding, it doesn't seem to be a problem with the doves. That's the way they were created to reproduce, and they've been around for thousands of years. Let me ask you this—have you ever sung the hymn with the lines about Jesus being 'the fairest of ten thousand'?"

"Yeah, I remember it from back when we were in the Junior Choir."

"Then, would it surprise you to find Bible verses referring to '*my sister, my love, my dove*' and also referring to 'the chiefest among ten thousand' one having '*eyes of doves*'?" questioned Sarah.

"I can see the chiefest among ten thousand having the *eyes of doves*, but this thing about *my sister, my love* throws me for a loop. Are you sure that's in the Bible?"

"Not only that," said Sarah, " but the phrase '*my sister, my spouse*' is in the Bible multiple times. When we get back to the dorm, I'll show you the scriptures"

"Where are you getting all this knowledge? Did it just come out of the blue and hit you in the head?"

"Promise me that you won't think I'm weird, but I got it from some documents entitled *The Dove Scrolls* that were in the possession of my uncle and aunt. I found them in an old chest in their closed up house. You know, the ones that were down in Brazil that probably met some kind of tragic end?"

"Yeah, I remember how you grieved for them. But do these documents have anything to say about Jesus and Mary Magdalene being married? Were they married or were they not?"

"That question is difficult to answer without some qualification. But, if you demand a yes or no answer like our lawyer friend Nancy would, the answer to whether they were married is yes and no."

"You can be soooo frustrating sometimes," said Kim. "Your answer reminds me of the unmarried girl being questioned about being pregnant and she said, 'I'm only a little bit pregnant.' You're either pregnant or you aren't—there's no in between! Now, were Jesus and Mary Magdalene married—or not?"

"You made your point!" said Sarah, "However, there are concepts that may not have even entered your mind. Let's go back to the dorm where we can find a Bible and *maybe* I'll let you look at the scrolls."

Sarah and Kim made it back to their dorm room, and Sarah took out her Bible to show Kim the verses that she had mentioned earlier. After further discussion, they decided that they should go down to Campus Pizza to get cherry floats to quench their thirst. They found a quiet table and began discussing the romance of the doves as described in Song of Solomon.

SONG OF SOLOMON 4:9-12 *Thou hast ravished my heart,* **my sister, my spouse***; thou hast ravished my heart with one of thine eyes, with one chain of thy neck. How fair is thy love,* ***my sister, my spouse!*** *how much better is thy love than wine! and the smell of thine ointments than all spices! Thy lips, O my spouse, drop as the honeycomb: honey and milk are under thy tongue; and the smell of thy garments is like the smell of Lebanon. A garden inclosed is* **my sister, my spouse***; a spring shut up, a fountain sealed.*

"See," said Sarah. "In four verses, the phrase 'my sister, my spouse' is used three times."

Sarah felt a tap on her shoulder, and it was Fred.

"My," said Fred, "I am so impressed to see you two reading the Bible. What brings on this burst of spiritual activity?"

"Oh," said Sarah laughingly, "I've decided to become a preacher and I'm just boning up on my scriptures."

"Well," said Fred, "while you're doing all your boning up, you will probably read somewhere in the Bible that we shouldn't have woman preachers and particularly not have women teach men!"

Unbeknownst to Fred, Nancy, the criminal justice major, had walked in and was in earshot when she overheard Fred's last statement.

She walked up beside Fred, put her hand on his collar, and said, "Fred, old buddy, if you don't like women preachers, what is your thinking about women lawyers or even women judges? Who knows, my colleagues voted me the most likely to become a Chief Justice of the Supreme Court someday. It's a joke, I'm sure, but wouldn't you love that?" Her brown eyes were flashing playfully as she looked up at Fred.

Fred sputtered with surprise for a few moments and then said, "Well, Nancy, I really like you personally, but women should not judge men! I would advise you to set your sights on a different goal more in line with a woman's true role in society. Now you know it's nothing personal!"

Nancy eyed Fred cooly and with her legal background, began framing a reply to Fred's criticism of her professed career.

Sarah chuckled to herself, as she remembered something written in the correspondence between her Aunt Myra and Uncle Andy. Could she remember where it was in the Bible and spring the trap? She quickly checked her Bible, found the verses, and decided to give it a try.

"Fred, do you think God would be upset if a woman were selected to be Chief Justice of the United States Supreme Court?"

"Oh, I know God would be displeased with that," responded Fred. "He would not want a woman setting in judgement over men!"

"Fred, I know you believe in the Bible. Right? So, I'm sure that you would not mind explaining these verses from the book of Judges to me concerning God's displeasure with a woman chief justice sitting in judgment over an entire nation. Fred, please read this out loud and then explain it to me," said Sarah.

JUDGES 4:4-5 And Deborah, a prophetess, the wife of Lapidoth, she judged Israel at that time. And she dwelt under the palm tree of Deborah between Ramah and Bethel in mount Ephraim: and **the children of Israel came up to her for judgment.**

Fred picked up the Bible and slowly began reading the first of the two verses that were pointed out by Sarah. *"And Deborah, a prophetess, the wife of Lapidoth, she judged Israel at that time."* Fred looked sheepishly at the three smiling girls and said, "You're just trying to trick me. You're probably taking this out of context!"

"Come on, Fred, it's in the Bible. Just read the next verse to be sure you get the context of it," said Sarah.

"And she dwelt under the palm tree of Deborah between Ramah and Bethel in mount Ephraim: and the children of Israel came up to her for judgment," read Fred haltingly. And then his face brightened and he said, "I can explain the answer to this. Deborah was elected judge over Israel by men.

She wasn't set in place as a judge by God. That's your answer."

Nancy's legal mind sprang into action and she said, "Fred, old personal friend, since I am just a mere upstart of a lawyer, would you please show me chapter and verse for your conclusions?"

"Well, I'm sure it's in the Bible; I just need some time to find it," said Fred.

"Before you start looking for the verses that prove your conclusion, Fred, I wonder if you would read this verse to us and tell us who set the judges in place over Israel?" questioned Sarah. "It's in the book of Second Samuel, chapter 7 somewhere...here it is...verse 11."

Fred picked up the Bible again and began to read:

2 SAMUEL 7:11 And as since the time that **I commanded judges to be over my people Israel**, *and have caused thee to rest from all thine enemies. Also* **the LORD** *telleth thee that he will make thee an house.*

"Now, Fred, who was it that commanded judges to be set over Israel? Was it God or man? I think when you read the context of this verse, it is perfectly clear that the LORD is doing the talking and *He* commanded the judges, even Deborah, to be the chief justices over Israel. Please explain this verse to us," requested Sarah.

"Well—uh—uh—you see—uh, you sprang this on me all of a sudden, I'll need some time to check this out. I'm sure my pastor knows the answer, " stammered Fred. "Let me—uh—get back to you later." And with that, Fred hurried to the counter, picked up the pizza he had ordered, paid his bill and left.

With that, the girls looked at each other, smiled, and then enthusiastically gave each other high fives. Nancy was very impressed with learning that Deborah was the chief judge of Israel and profusely thanked Sarah and Kim for the enlightenment. She told them that she liked what was in Sarah's version of the Bible and that Chief Justice Deborah had now become her role model. She even wondered if Deborah's position was more like a combination of say—the presidency and chief justice offices.

After the high fives, Nancy departed to the counter to pick up her pizza. Kim had been taking in all of this discussion and looked at Sarah in amazement. "How did you know all that about the judges of Israel and the Chief Justice? I don't remember this from Sunday school. Hmm, yeah, I bet that's what it is. You got this from your Aunt Myra and Uncle Andy?"

"You guessed it," said Sarah. "It was in some of the email correspondence that was on a diskette Andy had stored in his old roll top computer desk. It was written while Myra was in Brazil on a contract medical study, and Andy was still in the States. Andy missed Myra very much and they discussed all kinds of things, many of them spiritual, by email."

"You sure surprised Fred. And I don't think Nancy is much into spiritual things, but I think you made a friend for life with her. She liked what was read out of *Sarah's* Bible, as she put it."

"Yeah, once Fred started beating us poor, inferior women over the head, it was hard to resist doing it," said Sarah. "And I think Nancy has spiritual interests, she just represses them most of the time."

"This has been a lot of spiritual excitement," said Kim. "Let's finish our floats and we'll go back to the dorm. And, would you puleeeze, pretty puleeeze, let me take a peek at the outside of the Dove Scrolls—my curiosity is running rampant. You can finish all of your explaining so I won't think that you're weird before you actually let me read them."

As they walked past the park lake on the way back to the dorm, Sarah noticed some swans swimming gracefully in the lake. She told Kim that not only doves, but swans and pigeons were also spousal mates from birth. And as if on cue, two pigeons were seen on the sidewalk of the boulevard. The male pigeon with his beautiful indigo colored breast was strutting and cooing in a little courtship dance around the female.

"Yeah," said Kim, "I thought you were a little weird in talking about the doves, but it is even more weird that nature seems to be setting a stage of God's creation for us to see."

Sarah paused, took Kim by the arm, and said, "You think this is strange, let me read you the verses from Song of Solomon that perfectly describe what we saw when we first watched the doves on the rock." And she read.

SONG OF SOLOMON 2:10-14 *My beloved spake, and said unto me, Rise up, my love, my fair one, and come away. For, lo, the winter is past, the rain is over and gone; The flowers appear on the earth; the time of the singing of birds is come, and the voice of the turtle is heard in our land; The fig tree putteth forth her green figs, and the vines with the tender grape give a good smell. Arise, my love, my fair one, and come away.* **O my dove, that art in the clefts of the rock, in the secret places of the stairs**, *let me see thy countenance, let me hear thy voice; for sweet is thy voice, and thy countenance is comely.*

Kim was shocked and amazed to hear these verses from the Bible. She thought that it was surreal that not only was there a cleft in the rock where they first saw the doves but there were also stairs faintly etched in the rock. It was difficult to know if these stairs had been hewn by man or were placed there by nature. Had God really set the stage for them?

Sarah smiled and nodded in recognition of Kim's revelation and said, "For, Lo, the winter is past."

Sarah and Kim continued to walk along the tree lined boulevard observing nature's lesson as they watched the birds and bees, and as it were to smell the roses. There were neatly kept lawns fronting on the boulevard and quite a few students stayed in the private homes rather than the dorm. Shimmering streams of light parted their way through the leafy branches of the pin oaks and the maples. As they walked, Kim pondered how her very own roommate could be drawing from such a deep and hidden well of spiritual knowledge. How had she kept it so well hidden from her? It was like suddenly discovering that your very own sister had been an undercover agent for some spy agency for the last two years. Her curiosity about Sarah's aunt and uncle deepened.

Chapter 2

Opening the Secret Chest

"Sarah, you will have to tell me more about your uncle and aunt and their secret chest," said Kim. "I know you told me that they were missing when they took a car trip from the mouth of the Amazon heading southeast along the coast. That's been over three years ago. Was anything ever resolved?"

Sarah unfolded the story to Kim that nothing was really resolved concerning their disappearance. The local authorities did find their rental car, and one of their credit cards ended up in Rio where a street kid tried to use it. However, they didn't think the street kid was involved—he was a young teen and had no way to be that far north. Their two children, Mike and Marie, had both enlisted in the military medical services and were overseas at the time and still are. When they came back on leaves, they asked Sarah's parents to keep the house closed up and intact in case anything broke on the case.

"So how was it that you went through the chest and found the Dove Scrolls?"

Sarah related that Michael and Marie, being overseas with a long enlistment to pay back the government for their med school training, were not in a position to sort through the house. Their grandmother did not live close by, and it was too big a task for her. After much time went by, they had asked her to spend the summer going through things and cataloging them. She explained that the reason she disappeared from time to time during the previous summer was that she was preparing items for an eventual estate sale.

"And that's why you were going through the closets, desks, and chests and found all these writings and private correspondence?" asked Kim.

"Right. I talked to Mike and Marie about it on a conference call, and they insisted that I catalog the private papers and said I could read any of them or the writings that I liked. They even gave me permission to make copies of the writings if they interested me."

"It still floors me," said Kim. "How could you have figured this out all by yourself without someone to tutor you? Obviously, your aunt and uncle weren't around to help you. You must have gotten some help from somewhere. Or could it have been inspiration from God?"

"Could be," replied Sarah. "God speaks to us in many ways and sometimes through a still, small voice."

Sarah and Kim reached the arched stone doorway of hallowed old McKinny Hall and continued down the hallway to their room. Kim had an overpowering feeling of being just like an Indiana Jones archaeologist on the verge of making some great discovery. She wondered if Sarah would show her copies or the real thing. Sarah went to her closet and removed a small chest with a velvet cover and inside lining. She explained that the chest had been an insert in the bigger chest at the foot of the bed. It contained a number of writings and scrolls. She had brought it along with her from home, intending to read through the various papers for cataloging. Her problem was that she would get immersed in the scrolls and not want to do her studies. She handed the chest to Kim who sat it down on the bed beside her.

"I can't get it open," said Kim. "It's locked."

"I know," said Sarah. "Remember that you promised me that if I let you look at the scrolls, that we would do quite a bit of talking before you actually read them. This is for your own protection, because I know how it affected me. It was over a year before I really gained a perspective on what was written. It even affects how I look at finding my true love—whoever he is or wherever he might be."

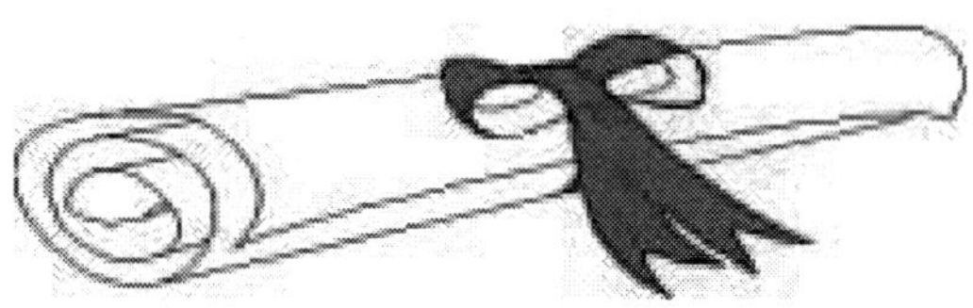

"OK, OK, I promise. Do you want it written in blood? An arm, a leg and a pint of blood as security?"

"Not necessary, I'll trust you," said Sarah as she removed from her purse a small key with jewels in its handle and handed it to Kim. "Here's your key to filling your empty quarter."

Kim took the ornate key and slipped it into the keyhole of the velvet chest. She heard a reassuring click and lifted open the chest lid. Inside were a number of small booklets, scrolls, and loose sheets of paper. On the very top was a smaller, ancient looking scroll with a red ribbon tied around it. It looked like the graduation scroll that one would get from college. She reached out and gingerly touched it. "What is it?"

"It's like a marriage certificate for doves," replied Sarah. "It isn't the main Dove Scroll; that's deeper in the chest. You can touch them if you like, but don't open them up yet. We must do some more talking before that happens."

"OK, OK," said Kim. "Let's get on with it. I'm ready for Dove Scrolls 101 or whatever you want to call it, oh, great, mighty, wise, and all-knowing education major."

As Sarah locked up the chest and put it away in the back recesses of her closet, she checked herself to make sure she could slow Kim down. She thought, *That run away train is on the track and its whistle is about to blow. Kim just has to exercise enough discipline to deal with the strong meat of concepts within the small chest and then wait on God's timing.* She remembered her aunt and uncle's email exchanges with their stories of how some people ran with the dove themes and really made a mess of it.

Taking a deep breath, Sarah then took a blank piece of paper and sat down at the study table with Kim. "Kim, *who* are you?"

"What do you mean, who am I? We've known each other since the fifth grade, and you're asking who am I?"

"Maybe I should say, who *really* are you and *what* are you?" said Sarah. "Do you have any plans for marriage, you know like the doves that really love each other?"

Kim shook her head in bewilderment. Then Sarah began to draw some stick figures on the blank sheet of paper. First, she drew a girl with a skirt and then a boy with pants. They were facing each other.

"Maybe, we should send you back to Art 101." Kim laughed. "That art has all the quality level of my sister's four-year-old kid."

"Now, now," rejoined Sarah. "You haven't answered my question yet about who you really are, but we will skip on to another question: "Why do some marriages succeed and others fail?"

"Well, I don't know, " said Kim, "maybe values, religion, interests, attractiveness, culture, money, health, war, and peace can affect the success of a marriage."

"Very good!" said Sarah. "You're putting on your thinking cap. A long time ago, a very wise king with the wisdom of Solomon, actually it was Solomon, wrote: '*a threefold cord is not quickly broken.*' How would you interpret that scripture in relationship to the success of a marriage?"

"That's not too hard." said Kim, "If they have a lot of common interests, the marriage is much stronger. Three cords in a rope are much stronger than just one strand. You know that TV advertisement for e-happiness.com —'we determine your compatibility so you can find your soul mate.'"

"Very good!" replied Sarah. "You're an excellent student. It almost makes teaching easy. You mentioned 'soul mate.' Would the soul compatibility be one of the three cords?"

"I think so," said Sarah. "If two people think alike in their soul, then they are much more compatible. And I suppose that another cord might be physical attractiveness. I've heard it said that a lot of marriages are only skin deep. When the bloom comes off the rose, the second stop is e-divorce.com. Now, tell me, what is the third cord?"

"I don't know," said Kim. "I would really have to think about that."

"Don't feel alone in trying to identify the third cord. Most of the world goes merrily along thinking that all there is to life is the physical body and the reasoning power of the mind, the soul, or as the Greeks call it "the psyche"—hence, our modern day psychology and psychiatry. In fact, some of the religions go no further than the interaction of the soul with what they call 'the Great Soul.' Some call their soul the 'Higher Self.' Have you ever heard the phrase, 'a marriage made in heaven'?"

"Yes, many times," replied Kim.

"Then, what part of our being would be made in heaven rather than from the dust of the earth?"

"I don't know. You're asking questions that I haven't thought about."

"Now, we're back to my original question about *who* you are and *what* are you? I will open the scriptures and ask you to read the answer that was written by a scholar named Paul."

Kim began to read, "1THESSALONIANS 5:23 *And the very God of peace sanctify you wholly; and I pray God your whole* **spirit** *and* **soul** *and* **body** *be preserved blameless unto the coming of our Lord Jesus Christ.* Oh, I see, the third cord would be our spirit. I'd never really thought of it that way. But, that makes sense, there is something much deeper than just the body and soul. So, just finding your body mate and soul mate aren't enough to have a threefold cord that is difficult to break! Ah, the light is dawning in the morning sky!"

"Right on," agreed Sarah, "and now read this scripture." Sarah opened the Bible again to the writings of Solomon: "*Then shall the dust return to the earth as it was: and* **the spirit shall return unto God who gave it.**" She pointed to this verse, paused while Kim read it, and asked, "Now, can you tell me who you are and what you are?"

Kim stroked her cheek and looked deeply at Sarah. "I am a spirit, made in heaven, I have a soul and I have a body which was made from the dust of the earth."

"Excellent. A+ for you!" exclaimed Sarah. "And now we are ready to connect the dots, or should I say the cords on my little stick drawings." Sarah wrote the word "soul" near the head of the boy and also the head of the girl. And then, she dropped down to near the thighs and wrote the word "body."

"The part about the location of the spirit is a little tougher." said Sarah. "You've heard the phrase, 'What do you feel in your gut?" The human spirit seems to be located somewhere in the heart-bowel midsection of the body. It is our 'heart of hearts.' If we let it, our spirit will rise from our belly like living water and water the thought seeds in the garden of our mind or soul. Now, Kim, please connect the dots."

"Thanks, Teach," said Kim. "That I can do." She took the pencil and began drawing in the cords.

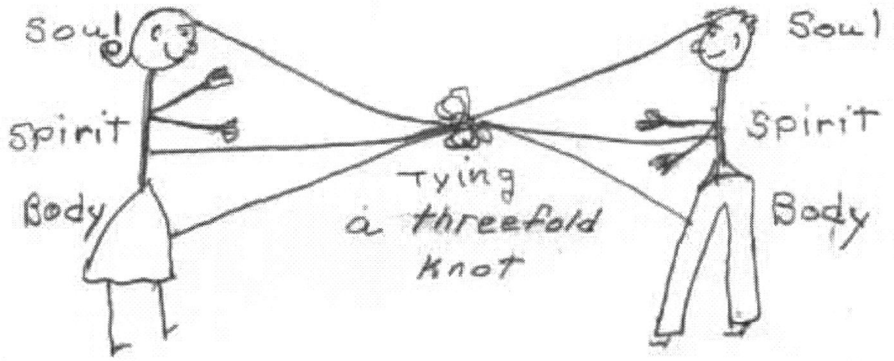

"You're really making this easy," observed Sarah. "You've identified the first cord as the physical or body attraction, and the second cord as the soul attraction. We know that soul attraction means enjoying and sharing each other's thinking. A two-cord marriage based on both ties between the physical and mental would be much stronger than one just based on good looks and sex. What do you think the third cord could be that would make the marriage even stronger?"

"You know, I can really see how much trouble I could have gotten into if I had continued that fling with the 'hunk' that we met at Joe's. I was a freshmen trying her wings," said Kim. "That would have been a one-cord marriage for sure! That guy had more hands than an octopus. Please accept my apologies for cutting out on you and leaving you to drive home alone in the car we borrowed from Floyd."

"Consider it just a learning experience," said Sarah. "Now, let me ask you a question: Do you believe in the hereafter?"

"You know I do," said Kim. "As our forefathers have said, I believe that there is a heaven to be gained and a hell to be shunned."

"Then, if you believe in the hereafter, do you believe in the heavenbefore?" questioned Sarah.

"Heavenbefore—what's that? Is there a heavenbefore?"

Sarah nodded, "Yes, think about it. Your spirit returned to God—therefore it must have come from God in the first place. Did God just strike a match, and say 'Here, divine spark, go to earth and be a Kim? Or maybe God struck two matches and said, 'Here, divine sparks, go to earth and be a Kim and a *whatshisname*. Of course, God knows who whatshisname really is."

"If He struck two matches at the same time, then we would be twins like the doves. But, I don't remember anything from the Bible about there being twins."

Sarah reminded Kim of the pastor's story about the kid that wrote home from college and asked his parents for $100. They wrote back and said, "You will find your answer in Matthew 6:30-34." The kid wrote back saying he didn't need Bible verses, he needed $100. And his parents replied telling him to read Matthew 6. Disgusted with his parents stubbornness, he opened up the Bible to Matthew 6 to look for the cryptic message his parents were giving him and found a $100 bill.

"Would you like to read a few verses about twins from the Song of Solomon?"

"O.K., I'm guessing that you have some verses already marked, or you wouldn't be asking me about them," said Kim. "Give me the references."

SONGS 4:2 Thy teeth are like a flock of sheep that are even shorn, which came up from the washing; whereof every one bear **twins**, *and none is barren among them.*

SONGS 4:5 Thy two breasts are like two young roes that are **twins**, *which feed among the lilies.*

SONGS 6:6 Thy teeth are as a flock of sheep which go up from the washing, whereof every one beareth **twins**, *and there is not one barren among them.*

SONGS 7:3 Thy two breasts are like two young roes that are ***twins***.

"OK, you've made your point. I don't remember reading these verses, but I must say they certainly are romantic. You have to admit that these verses say nothing about the '*heavenbefore*', as you call it," observed Kim.

"There was another Teacher who was confronted with the same question about there being a 'heavenbefore' and if you will turn to John 8, I will show you."

Sarah hesitated and then continued, "And please don't stone me for talking to you about the 'heavenbefore.'"

JOHN 8:57-59 Then said the Jews unto him, **Thou art not yet fifty years old, and hast thou seen Abraham?** *Jesus said unto them, Verily, verily, I say unto you,* **Before Abraham was, I am. Then took they up stones to cast at him***: but Jesus hid himself, and went out of the temple, going through the midst of them, and so passed by.*

"Rest easy, I won't stone you," said Kim. "And I can see that Jesus isn't saying that He lived in an earlier incarnation on earth in order to appear to Abraham."

"A good observation," said Sarah. "I think that we can agree that as written in the book of Hebrews, Jesus participated in the creation of the earth. So we know He was around at that time. And I suppose that, like the angels, if Jesus wanted to appear in the form of a man to Abraham, He could well do so without having to be born through a woman in the earth. Do you agree?"

"Yes," said Kim, "but it does sort of turn my thinking topsy-turvy to even consider the possibility that the two divine sparks knew each other as spirits in heaven before they ever were dispatched to the earth. Maybe that's why some romances are so romantic. It is a recognition of a long lost relationship renewed. Amazing! I always thought that God just created the human spirit the very instant it was to be sent to earth, and twin spirits never even entered my mind. Now, I'm reconsidering."

Sarah went on to tell Kim about the different kinds of bodies. She enumerated the body terrestrial that we have now, the resurrection body, and the body celestial. She directed Kim to preview John 20, but told her not to get into details about the types of bodies just yet. First, she would need to read The Dove Scroll.

JOHN 20:16-18 *Jesus saith unto her, Mary. She turned herself, and saith unto him, Rabboni; which is to say, Master. Jesus saith unto her,* **Touch me not; for I am not yet ascended to my Father:** *but go to my brethren, and say unto them, I ascend unto my Father, and your Father; and to my God, and your God. Mary Magdalene came and told the disciples that she had seen the Lord, and that he had spoken these things unto her.*

"Now, you've really put my poor brain on overload," said Kim. "I thought Jesus had it all body wise, after He was resurrected. Now, I see there was another step He had to take."

"Well, you'll never really understand it by reasoning with your brain or soul alone," replied Sarah. "The understanding will come from deep within—from your 'gut' or spirit. However, quit worrying about it; it took me a year to get the gist of it from deep inside into my mind. I would say you're doing just great."

"When can we open the scroll?" said Kim excitedly. "Am I ready?"

Sarah and Kim discussed the timing for opening the scroll. With Sarah's Integral Calculus test coming up and Kim's Genetics test on Thursday, it was decided to wait till the weekend. Sarah cautioned that this would be like opening up Pandora's box. It would answer some of Kim's questions but generate many more. They needed time when they were not distracted to do things properly and to give the material time to settle into their spirits.

"All right, I can hardly wait. But, you're right. Time has flown by. It's already nine o'clock. Next weekend will be fine."

Sarah and Kim immersed themselves in their studies, and soon it was Thursday night. In the early hours of Friday morning, Kim had a dream. She was in her father and mother's home alone doing her studies.

She went to the bookcase to find a dictionary and noticed an old looking book with an ornate leather cover and golden engravings on it. She opened it and began reading. There was a knock at the door, so she put down the book and went to open the door, but there was no one there. She returned and picked up the book and the doorbell rang. She checked the door but, once again, no one was there. Puzzled, she returned to reading her book. Once again, the doorbell rang. This time, rather than going to the door, she pulled the curtain slightly ajar and peeped out. There was no one in sight, but on the sidewalk was a dove. The dove seemed to look straight at Kim with its beautiful eyes and then flew away into the afternoon sky.

The dream abruptly ended and Kim awoke. She knew that she just had an unusual dream with a spiritual meaning. The colors in the dream were very vivid—the grass and trees were greener and the sky was bluer than normal, and the color of the flowers was breathtaking. She wanted to wake Sarah immediately to share her dream and see how Sarah would interpret it, but she thought better of it. *Sarah cautioned me to be more disciplined in the things of the spirit; this is a good opportunity to practice. It can wait till morning.*

She lay awake in bed until light began filtering into the window and she heard Sarah stirring. "Sarah, Sarah, I had the most unusual dream. There was a dove in it and an old ornate book. I remember reading in the book, but now I can't remember what I read."

Sarah gave Kim a sleepy smile and said, "Let's hear your dream." And she listened intently as Kim provided the details of the dream.

"Kim, I'm not going to try to interpret the dream for you. You can do that yourself. But I am going to give you a few scriptures that will interpret the dream for you. Let's see, your first set of scriptures is in the Song of Solomon. You will understand why you looked out the window lattice rather than the door. Also, your dream experience is like that of Samuel's when he thought he heard Eli the priest's voice in the night, only to find out that it was the Lord speaking to him rather than Eli.

SONG OF SONGS 2:8-11 *The voice of my beloved! behold, he cometh leaping upon the mountains, skipping upon the hills. My beloved is like a roe or a young hart: behold, he standeth behind our wall,* **he looketh forth at the windows, shewing himself through the lattice**. *My beloved spake, and said unto me, Rise up, my love, my fair one, and come away. For, lo, the winter is past, the rain is over and gone.*

1 SAMUEL 3:8-9 **And the LORD called Samuel again the third time**. *And he arose and went to Eli, and said, Here am I; for thou didst call me. And Eli perceived that the LORD had called the child. Therefore Eli said unto Samuel, Go, lie down: and it shall be,* **if he call thee, that thou shalt say, Speak**, *LORD; for thy servant heareth. So Samuel went and lay down in his place.*

Kim read the scriptures eagerly, and she did not have to stretch her mind to understand the meaning. The Spirit of God was showing her dove relationships through symbols. She knew that something was written in that ornate, leather bound book concerning her destiny, but she just couldn't remember it. It was like revisiting your first grade room and reopening one of your primer reading books. Well, whatever it was, perhaps it would be revealed in the timing of the Lord.

Sarah told her that the reason the grass, the sky, and flowers looked so sharp and beautiful is that the dream took place in the spirit realm which is invisible to the human eye. The frequency of light in this spectra is much higher and wavelengths much shorter than in the very limited human visible spectrum. Sarah told Kim that she learned this from her Uncle Andy who was a radar operator in the Marines at one time. Sarah compared it to going from 200 x 160 pixels to 1000 x 800 pixels on a computer monitor.

Opening the Secret Chest

The old monitors from the 90s had low pixel, fuzzy pictures. Uncle Andy's free hand drawing was not all that great either, so when Sarah showed the three-fold marriage sketch to Kim, she drew it just like Uncle Andy did for her when he was passing out words of wisdom for a young girl beginning her junior year of high school.

Aunt Myra, on the other hand, had her specialty. She had a doctor's degree in Neurology and also did work as a medical illustrator. Before the incident, she had been based in Belém and was a consultant being retained by the Brazilian government to determine the source of some unusual neurological problems being encountered by the natives. While she was alive, Aunt Myra had taught Sarah much about the temple of the body as it related to neurology.

TGIF! thought Kim. *I wonder when we can get down to business and open the Dove Scrolls?*

However, when she got back to the dorm from classes, Sarah wanted to delay the opening of the scrolls until Saturday morning. "Lets go down to the old stone church that sits high on the hill overlooking the river. We can find one of the quiet Sunday school rooms, open the scrolls, consult our Bibles, and have enough privacy for a long discussion."

That night it had rained. In the morning it was a beautiful, clear spring day as in Kim's dream. Sarah opened up the velvet chest and retrieved the Dove Scrolls. She carefully put them in her briefcase, and they departed to the stone church with their Bibles.

The old stone church was set back from the river about three or four blocks on a hill overlooking the river. It was built by the settlers, and there are fifth generation families that still attend the church. While most of the worshippers had gone to the newer churches out on the bypasses, the old church had been maintained, and its steeples, arches, carvings, and stained glass windows were wonderful examples of the construction skills of a bygone era. The church doors were usually open and people could go in and pray, look through the library books, or just find a quiet place to sort out their thoughts. Finding an empty room with an old wooden plank table probably over a hundred years old, they sat down and Kim eagerly awaited the opening of the scrolls.

"Kim, you're ready," Sarah said. "It would be best if I let you read some of the pages first, and then we can discuss the questions that you will have. Here is a note pad—I'm sure you will have questions. Make notes of your questions as you read, and we can discuss them over a period of time."

In her briefcase were three scrolls, each tied with a red ribbon. She set the small scroll labeled Dove Marriage Archives aside. Then, she removed one of the larger scrolls that was also bound with a red ribbon. She handed this one to Kim and said, "Untie the ribbon, it is yours to examine."

Kim untied the ribbon and unfolded the scroll. The scroll was actually a number of pages, beautifully bound, and rolled up. On the first page was beautiful art work with two doves, a picture of a scroll, and a bride and groom. She opened the next page and found it bordered with roses.

"You will find that some of the things that I told you are essentially quotes from The Dove Scroll," observed Sarah. She left the third, unopened scroll in the briefcase. "Now that you've seen The Dove Scroll, I will set it aside as it is a somewhat fragile document. Instead, I'll give excerpts, which I have lifted from it using my scanner, that summarize the dove concepts. The Dove Scrolls have a lot more information to digest, but let's not try to climb Mount Everest on our first mountain climbing try. We need to do a lot more talking before delving into the entire scroll. Don't look disappointed; you'll get to look at the entire scroll later."

Kim settled down and began reading. Every now and then she scribbled on the note pad and then continued reading. Sarah wandered off though the old church, marveling at its artwork and innate beauty. The old stone church was pleasantly cool, even though the outside temperature was in the 80s. She returned to find Kim still immersed in her reading.

"I see what you mean," said Kim. "This has themes that I never even thought or heard about. I'm glad that you prepared me for what I'm reading."

Sarah smiled at Kim, sat down, pulled out her Ed Psych book and began studying, waiting for Kim to reach a pausing point.

Editor's Note: The complete texts of The Dove Marriage Archives and The Dove Scrolls are given in The Ancient Chest section at the back of this book.

On-line copies, In FULL COLOR, may be accessed at: http://www.TheAncientChest.com/DoveScroll

Chapter 3

The Dove Scroll

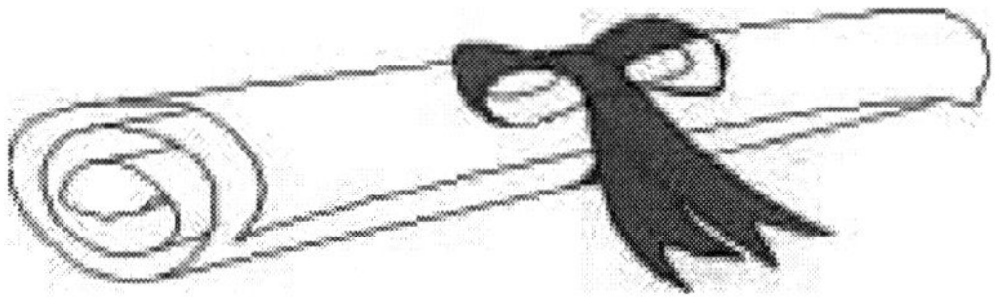

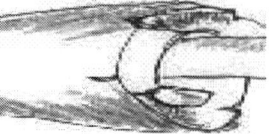

My Love, My Dove

From an ancient people of old, the story of the doves is told. For in the story of the doves is the secret of love's beginning and never ending.

It is a very simple story and yet very profound. Did you know doves are unique and for each other created? You see that in the dove's nest, there are always two eggs. One would think that in these two eggs might be contained two brothers, or possibly two sisters, or even a brother and sister. But *all* of these combinations do *not* occur. The dove is heaven's symbol of love. And one egg always contains a male dove and the other egg always contains a female dove. For these two doves in the nest were uniquely created for each other from birth.

> *My beloved spake, and said unto me, Rise up, my love, my fair one, and come away.*
>
> *For, lo, the winter is past, the rain is over and gone;*
>
> *The flowers appear on the earth; the time of the singing of birds is come, and the voice of the turtle [dove] is heard in our land;*
>
> *The fig tree putteth forth her green figs, and the vines with the tender grape give a good smell. Arise, my love, my fair one, and come away.*
>
> *O my dove, that art in the clefts of the rock, in the secret places of the stairs, let me see thy countenance, let me hear thy voice; for sweet is thy voice, and thy countenance is comely.*

But we know in this earth those who come into a marriage relationship may not even meet each other until they have matured and are ready for courtship. Others may know each other from childhood and then fall in a more serious love in their later years. But if we say a marriage is made in heaven, then when does the recognition of that spark of heavenly love come? It is as penned by the prophet:

> ISAIAH 60:8 Who are these that fly as a cloud, and as the *doves to their windows*?

And the ancient king records his description of that wonderful moment when one looks through heaven's window and finds:

> My beloved is like *a roe or a young hart*: behold, he standeth behind our wall, *he looketh forth at the windows, shewing himself through the lattice*.
>
> My beloved spake, and said unto me, Rise up, my love, my fair one, and come away.
>
> For, lo, the winter is past, the rain is over and gone;
>
> The flowers appear on the earth; the time of the singing of birds is come

My beloved is like a roe or a young hart

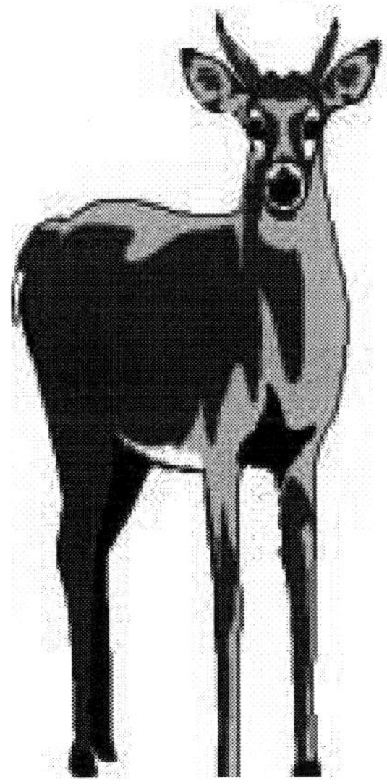

he looketh forth at the windows

"Whoa!" exclaimed Kim. "This is amazing. It is just like the dream that I had where I saw the dove looking at me through the window, or as the Bible says, a lattice. And, I think that I'm beginning to remember a few words of what was written in that ornate leather book inscribed with gold letters. But where have I seen that book before?"

"It goes back to my question about *who* are you?" said Sarah. "Remember that you told me that you are a spirit, you have a soul, and you live in a body? What part of you is remembering some of the words that were written in, as you say, your book of destiny?"

"Well, my spirit must have seen it because my mind or soul just doesn't remember anything like it. And my body didn't even exist yet," replied Kim. "But when? When did my spirit see this book? Was it before God sent my spirit to earth that I was given a glimpse of what God created me to do or to be? Or maybe He just sealed up the message inside of me and all I can remember is that, as one of the writers put it, I have a purpose driven life."

"You're coming face to face with some of the soul searching—or should I say spirit searching—that I did when I first came across this material. Welcome to the club!"

"Yeah, but you've worked your way through a lot of it, and you're here to help me work my way through it," observed Kim. "Sarah, you amaze me. Yes, I can see that you were thrown for a loop when you began to read the material in the secret chest. But your aunt and uncle were already dead by then, so you couldn't talk to them and ask them questions. I just can't fathom how you learned so much just by reading the writings and correspondence. You are kind of unreal—like an angel standing before me that suddenly matured into some great teacher. Where did that playful high school Sarah go to get all this spiritual maturity?"

"Yes, I will admit that I did get some help," agreed Sarah. "You see, when I began to read about all this, it soon became much more than just a romantic story. It had its roots so deep in theology. I went to my parents and described what I had found. They were not totally surprised and simply characterized the concepts as something much deeper than you would find in the everyday church. About five years ago, they had even discussed some parts of Andy and Myra's beliefs with Pastor Williams. He listened politely, but Dad said the pastor wasn't able to fit it into his standard seminary theology. Although he considered it interesting, he was not inclined to pursue it. And I think, at that time, my parents more or less put it on the shelf because they were extremely busy with their own professional activities."

"So, you were sort of out there by yourself," said Kim. "Have you ran across anyone, anywhere with similar concepts? How did you find a tutor?"

Sarah continued, "I couldn't let it go, and I guess my parents got tired of me bugging them about it. They said that my grandma knew more about this than they did. Grandma was always a very spiritual person. However, one summer when Uncle Andy and Aunt Myra attended summer semester, they left their kids with Grandma. I think Mike and Marie were only about four and five years old at the time. Grandma said that everything was more or less routine until Mike and Marie began to ask her what she remembered about heaven. She told them about what she had been taught about heaven and read a few scriptures out of the Bible about it.

"But, MeMa, don't you remember being in heaven and seeing Jesus?" asked Marie.

Then Mike chimed in and said, "We talked to Jesus and he told us about earth. We sat by a beautiful river with pretty fish while he talked to us. He told us about you. Don't you remember heaven, MeMa?"

"Needless to say, MeMa was shocked right out of her socks by the innocent questions coming out of the mouths of babes," said Sarah. This opened up a whole new spiritual vista for both Grandpa and Grandma. Only my grandma is still alive now. So, I borrowed the car and made a quick trip to Grandma's to learn more. But, let's get back to the pages from The Dove Scrolls before discussing this further. OK?"

And the eyes are the window of one's soul. They are the gateway of the beautiful light when one of heaven's spirits first recognizes their dove twin upon the earth. And the ancient king describes his beloved.

My beloved is unto me as a cluster of camphire in the vineyards of Engedi.

Behold, thou art fair, my love; behold, thou art fair; thou hast doves' eyes.

... behold king Solomon with the crown wherewith his mother crowned him in the day of his espousals, and in the day of the gladness of his heart.

Behold, thou art fair, my love; behold, thou art fair; thou hast doves' eyes within thy locks:

You have encouraged me, O my sister, my bride; you have stolen my heart with a look on one of your eyes, with one necklace of your neck.

And his bride to be looks through the window and returns the recognition of the sparkles in the eye seen in the windows of heaven's remembrance.

His eyes are as the eyes of doves by the rivers of waters, washed with milk, and fitly set.

SON 7:4 Thy neck is as a tower of ivory; *thine eyes like the fishpools in Heshbon*, by the gate of Bathrabbim ...

Beautiful is the mystery of the doves meeting one another and looking into the deep pools of each other's eyes. But it is said solving one mystery simply leads to another mystery. And the additional mystery is this: How can it be that one can be both a sister and a spouse to her husband at the same time? Not likely - but how is it the ancient scriptures speak of a sister and a spouse as being one?

Thou hast ravished my heart, *my sister, my spouse*; *thou hast ravished my heart with one of thine eyes*, with one chain of thy neck.

How fair is thy love, *my sister, my spouse*! how much better is thy love than wine! and the smell of thine ointments than all spices!

Thy lips, O my spouse, drop as the honeycomb: honey and milk are under thy tongue; and the smell of thy garments is like the smell of Lebanon.

A garden inclosed is *my sister, my spouse*; a spring shut up, a fountain sealed.

I am come into my garden, *my sister, my spouse*: I have gathered my myrrh with my spice; I have eaten my honeycomb with my honey; I have drunk my wine with my milk: eat, O friends; drink, yea, drink abundantly, O beloved.

I sleep, but my heart waketh: it is the voice of my beloved that knocketh, saying, Open to me, *my sister, my love, my dove*, my undefiled: for my head is filled with dew, and my locks with the drops of the night.

Could it be the twin spirits of the doves were created as sister and brother in the heavens and then at a time and place written upon the pages of destiny, they meet each other in the earth and enter into a spousal relationship? To pursue this second mystery, we must look into the very genesis of creation.

GENESIS 1:26-27 And God said, Let us make man in our image, after our likeness: and let them have dominion over the fish of the sea, and over the fowl of the air, and over the cattle, and over all the earth, and over every creeping thing that creepeth upon the earth. So God created man in his own image, *in the image of God created he him; male and female created he them.*

And how did the created beings look before woman was separated out of man? To attempt to draw this could prove rather difficult. Instead, we will return to our allegorical example of the doves. Those who handle eggs know from time to time there occurs an egg which is slightly larger than usual and this egg may also have twin yolks inside. God is one God and yet has male and female characteristics. And the beings created were in this same image and were male and female.

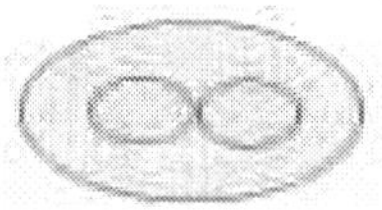

In the heavens, we can think of these two twin spirits created in the image of God as represented by the double-yolked dove egg. The ancient king and poet wrote that for those coming into the earth, their spirits would return "unto God who gave it." Therefore, the spirits on earth must have at one time previously been in the heavens.

Or ever the silver cord be loosed, or the golden bowl be broken, or the pitcher be broken at the fountain, or the wheel broken at the cistern.

Then shall the dust return to the earth as it was: *and the spirit shall return unto God who gave it.*

Then, could it be that these twin dove spirits were separated from each other in the heavens where they were brother and sister and a veil of forgetfulness placed over their remembrance of their creation before they were sent into the earth?

Now, let us trace the path of the twin dove spirits which were created in the heavens in the image of God. We will follow this path of events taking place that results in their being born in the earth and ultimately recognizing each other once again. Let us consider the yolks as representing the twin spirits, and white of the egg as being the soul or sum total of the mental capabilities of the couple. Then the shell would represent the outer covering or celestial body. And we will say, that similar to Adam and Eve, the surgeon's sword of the Lord separates these twins from one egg into two eggs.

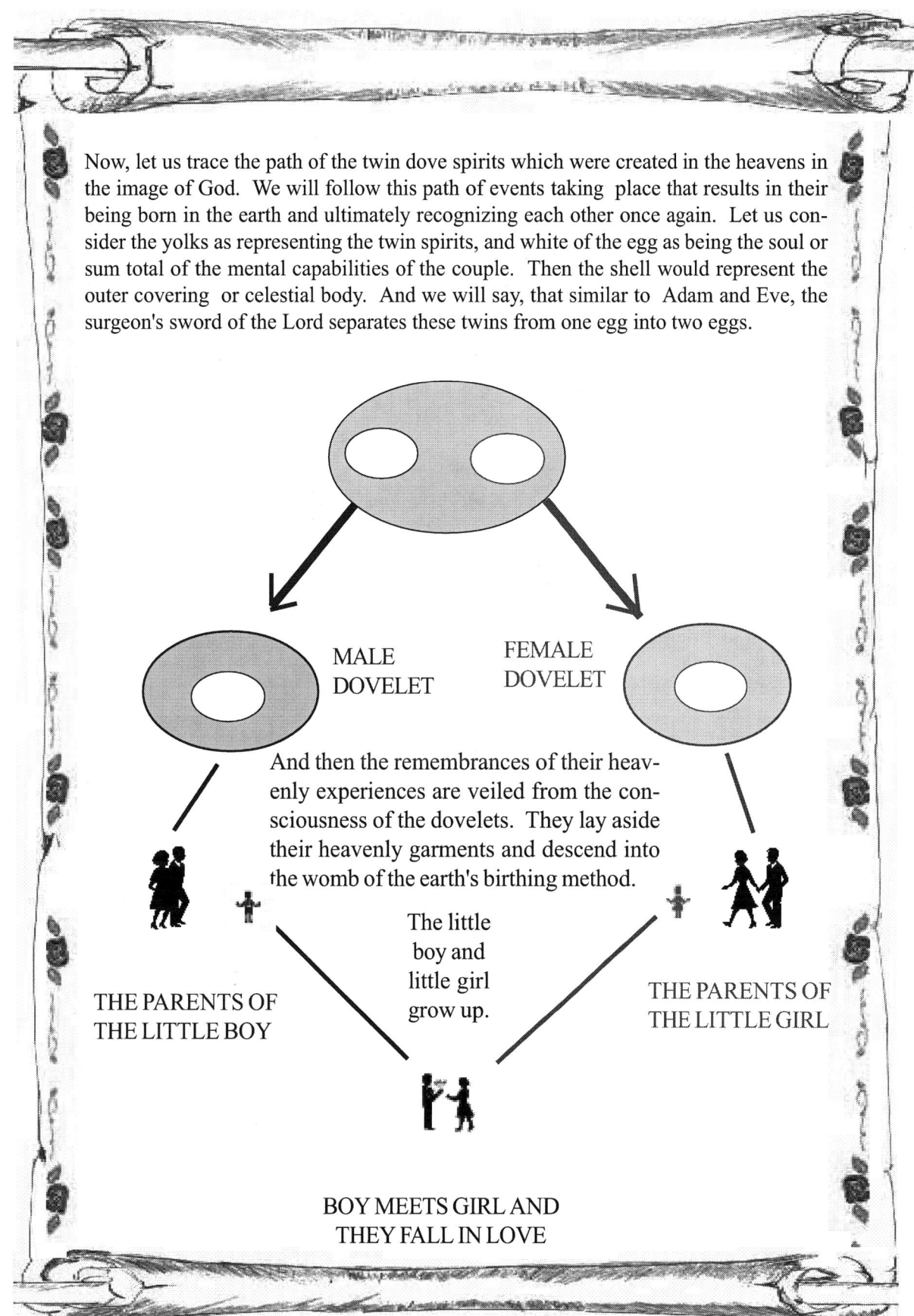

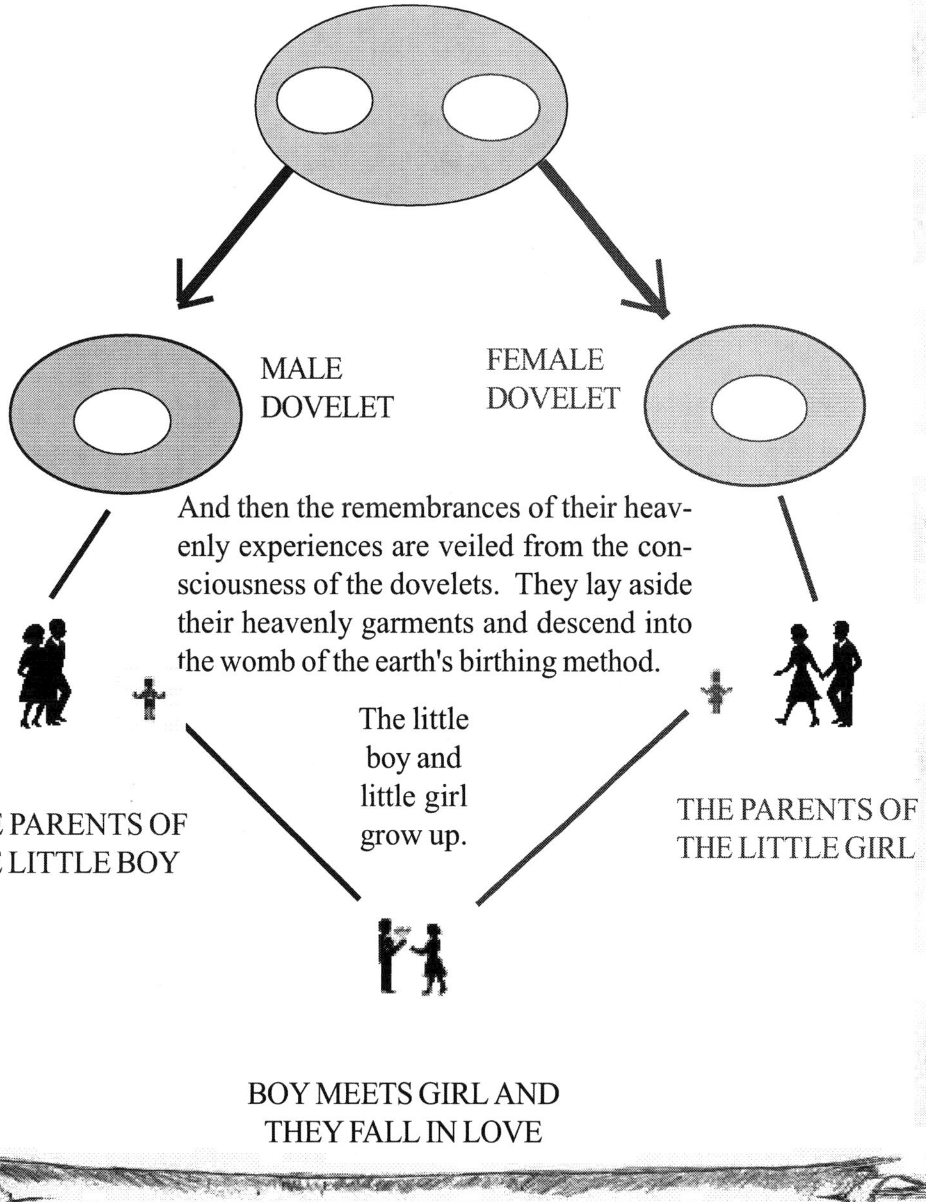
MALE DOVELET
FEMALE DOVELET
And then the remembrances of their heavenly experiences are veiled from the consciousness of the dovelets. They lay aside their heavenly garments and descend into the womb of the earth's birthing method.
The little boy and little girl grow up.
THE PARENTS OF THE LITTLE BOY
THE PARENTS OF THE LITTLE GIRL
BOY MEETS GIRL AND THEY FALL IN LOVE

Sarah glanced up from her Ed Psych book from time to time as Kim continued to read. She contemplated Kim as she read from the pages of The Dove Scroll. Kim is no plain Jane but is neither a Naomi Camble. She has a slender stature, delicate features, and reddish blond hair. Her deep green eyes are like the glistening of a tide pool. Because Kim does not create a presence when entering a room, some might think this is a handicap. But when she begins to speak, one realizes that she has a depth and strength to her personality. In spiritual aspects, Sarah wondered if Kim would be like the Joseph of the Old Testament. Joseph was given wonderful dreams, but his exuberant personality and natural abilities got him into a lot of trouble before he settled down to the mission that God gave him. Was she making a mistake in awakening Kim's Joseph type personality at this stage in her maturity? Sarah considered Kim's scholastic abilities far above hers, but she hoped that Kim would be able to proceed with discretion when it came to matters of the heart.

Sarah watched Kim's eyes dance as she read. She remembered how Kim had fallen head over heels for Larry in high school. She and Larry were absolute soul mates during the last semester of high school. They were making plans how they would be together and live happily ever after. Then, while Kim was away for a six-week, summer workshop for gifted math students at UT, it turned out that Larry found another girlfriend. Sarah remembered being at Kim's house when the news of Larry's betrayal arrived. Kim flew into her father's arms, and her being literally shook with earthquake sobs as her father consoled her. Sarah thought, *Kim is spiritually excited about what she is reading but has questions. I fear the questions will be personal instead of spiritual. I just hope she makes the spiritual concepts part of her being—before she starts on any personal quest. I remember that Uncle Andy and Aunt Myra in their emails agonized over the question of whether everybody has a dove.*

Kim turned over the last page that Sarah had given her and said, "This is sooo interesting. It answers some of my first questions, but now I have more."

"Imagine that," laughed Sarah. "When I first read this material, I didn't know how to put it in any kind of context. Only after getting with my parents and then with Grandma, did it really begin to fall in place."

"Well, good," said Kim. "You can answer my questions and be a 'grandma' figure to me. But before we get into the questions, please tell me more about your grandma—what's she like?"

"Umm! Let me see. My grandma's name is Sarah, I am her namesake. We have always been very close. I went to the farm as often as I could growing up. Grandma is short, although she never seemed short. She was always loving and a comfort to me. When I was ten years old, we were the same height. Her hair is white now, but when she was young it was a deep, dark brown like my mom's. Her complexion is darker now because of all the years she has spent working the gardens on the farm. Grandma would spend hours in the fields with my Grandpa Albert. She would ride the tractor with him and made sure he drank enough water in the hot summer days.

Thinking about them now, they may have been doves. They were always together and loved each other very much. It was very hard on Grandma when Grandpa died of lung cancer. He never smoked, but the doctors said the many years of farm dust and chemicals probably caused the cancer.

Grandma goes once a week to have her hair done. She says a girl cannot be too old or slow to look her best. She always wears an apron when she's home and never leaves the house without her hat and gloves.

Grandma was a registered nurse in her younger days. She completed her nurse's training at Rockview and graduated at the top of her class. She was an ER nurse, cool as a cucumber in heated situations at Memorial Hospital. She was always asked to handle the most difficult, life- threatening cases.

When she was young she started attending the local community church. She met Grandpa who was quite a Bible student. She still attends the local church from time to time, but her and grandpa's beliefs deepened over the years to much more than what was taught there.

Grandma is a marvelous cook, but it took some time for her to substitute more healthy oils for lard. Her cakes and cookies are to die for; she makes the best donuts from biscuits. Her pot roast dinner, which she made almost every Sunday, was so good that everyone always overate. I can smell the aroma of the vegetables stewing in the gravy right now.

Grandma and Grandpa grew in their spirituality as they got older. They had a remarkable understanding of the strong meat of the scriptures. After Grandpa died, she started spending more time in the scriptures. She understood the secrets of The Dove Scrolls and explained them to me. It was very interesting how she taught me. 'Slowly!' I can hear her saying to me, 'It's not important how fast you learn, but that you get it into your spirit so it will be part of your life.' That's Grandma for you."

"Wow, she seems to be quite a character," said Kim. "I can almost see you and your family riding along singing, 'Over the river and through the woods to grandma's house we go.' But that's not what really interests me. Did she learn this through her experiences with her daughter Myra and her son-in-law Andy or did she have some deep spiritual experiences of her own? And is there anybody else around that shares these beliefs or does your Grandma live on some isolated spiritual, country island?"

"Perhaps, you will get a chance to meet her—maybe this summer," replied Sarah. "Grandma did tell me about an experience that she and Grandpa had when they visited Callaway Gardens near Atlanta. They were walking through one of the most beautiful parts of the garden when the azaleas and rhododendrons were in bloom. When they looked up from admiring the flowers, they saw an elderly couple walking toward them. The old gentleman had white hair, an ornate walking cane, and twinkling eyes. He was stocky and wore knee length pants suitable for the tropics. The lady had white hair, and yes, she had some wrinkles, but her features were strikingly beautiful for her age. Grandma said that the couple reminded her of a scene from an English garden book where the country gentleman and his wife tour their garden."

"I've been to Callaway Gardens and can appreciate how serenely beautiful it is in spring," said Kim. "What happened next?"

"This is difficult to explain," Sarah replied. "But Grandma said the lady looked directly at her with twinkling eyes and a deep smile as she and the gentleman passed by. Both she and Grandpa were in awe over the experience. It was as if they had just climbed some high mountain. Grandma said she understood at that moment the depth of Sarah's courage when she had to tell Abraham to send the bondwoman, Hagar, and her son away. And as they compared their experiences, Grandpa related knowing the depth of Abraham's love for the Lord. He knew Abraham's agony about almost losing Isaac until the ram caught in the thicket was provided as a substitute. And also his agony when he was told by the Lord to listen to his wife's counsel about sending his son, Ishmael, away even when it grieved him to do so."

"You're really confusing me," said Kim. "Are you saying that your grandparents saw some reincarnation of Abraham and Sarah as a country gentleman and his lady?"

"Not at all," said Sarah. "Here's where the story gets really, really interesting. Let me see if I can pull up the scripture on my computer. Have you ever thought about why Joseph insisted on having his bones brought back to the promised land at a future time when the Hebrews would leave Egypt?"

GENESIS 50:25-26 *And Joseph took an oath of the children of Israel, saying, God will surely visit you, and* **ye shall carry up my bones from hence**. *So Joseph died, being an hundred and ten years old: and they embalmed him, and he was put in a coffin in Egypt.*

"I think that God can gather up one's bones from most anywhere, including Egypt, when it comes to the resurrection, but Joseph seemed to know that some future event would take place in the promised land. He wanted to be there to be part of it," continued Sarah.

Now, Kim, let's look at another scripture, and you tell me your reaction to it."

HEBREWS 13:2 *Be not forgetful to entertain strangers: for thereby* **some have entertained angels** *unawares.*

"Oh, I believe in angels," said Kim. "But I just don't get the application here. Are you saying that two angels took on the appearance of Abraham and Sarah, and that's why your grandparents reacted the way they did?"

"No, I'm not. But my grandma does believe that it was actually Abraham and Sarah that appeared to them, and that they were dressed in an appropriate manner to fit in with today's society and dress codes."

"Sarah, you said that you wanted to prepare me in advance before opening the secret chest so I wouldn't think that you're weird. I think that the part about the boy and girl dovelets is very romantic. It's this story about your grandma that seems weird to me. I don't think that you're weird, but your grandma...hmm? Don't you know that Abraham and Sarah are lying in the grave somewhere over in Israel awaiting the blowing of the last trump and the resurrection of the dead? How could they be walking around appearing to your grandma?"

"What makes you think that they are still awaiting the resurrection?" asked Sarah.

"Well, *everybody* knows that to be true. OK, you've become a very accomplished Bible student, *prove it* to me from the Bible!" challenged Kim.

"You requested proof from the Bible—how about this?" asked Sarah as she searched for the keywords "saints" and "graves." "And by the way, there is even evidence* that Abraham was resurrected before this—I have even added a little footnote to that effect. Maybe this was the *first* trump, not the *last* one."

MATTHEW 27:51-53 *And, behold, the veil of the temple was rent in twain from the top to the bottom; and the earth did quake, and the rocks rent; and the graves were opened; and* **many bodies of the saints which slept arose, and came out of the graves after his resurrection, and went into the holy city, and appeared unto many.** *(See also LUKE 20:36-38)

"Oh! Oh, my gosh!" I never thought of it in that way!" exclaimed Kim. "Maybe your grandma was right! Abraham and Sarah were certainly saints and *many*, not just a few, were resurrected. Maybe Joseph was also in the group that was resurrected, and that was why he wanted his bones brought to Israel just to be part of it. But those that were resurrected, did they die again? I think that Lazarus probably died at some much later period of time after Jesus called him out of the grave."

"I think there is quite a difference between those whom Jesus raised from the dead after they had been dead just a short while and those saints and patriarchs who had lived full and complete lives. Jesus proved that he could be resurrected from the dead and not die again, why would it be any different for those who participated in the same experience with him?"

"Good point," observed Kim, "But wouldn't those that had received their resurrection bodies be somewhat different than the angels?"

"Yes and no." replied Sarah. "The saints that arose, unlike the angels, had already experienced life as the offspring of man. However, their resurrection bodies were not really that much different than the angels. Remember how Jesus answered the question about whose wife of the seven husbands she was?'"

MARK 12:23 *In the resurrection therefore, when they shall rise,* **whose wife shall she be of them? for the seven had her to wife.**

MARK 12:24-25 *And Jesus answering said unto them, Do ye not therefore err, because ye know not the scriptures, neither the power of God?* **For when they shall rise from the dead, they neither marry, nor are given in marriage; but are as the angels which are in heaven.**

"OK, as usual, you've made your point. And I suppose, like Jesus, those in their resurrection bodies could walk right through walls if they wanted to, or appear as a gardener, or even as a country gentleman or his wife?"

"That's right. Let's not limit their powers. Remember that Jesus showed the disciples his hands and feet and ate regular food in front of his disciples to prove to them that he was not a ghost."

LUKE 24:39-43 *Behold my hands and my feet, that it is I myself: handle me, and see;* **for a spirit hath not flesh and bones**, *as ye see me have. And when he had thus spoken, he shewed them his hands and his feet. And while they yet believed not for joy, and wondered, he said unto them, Have ye here any meat? And they gave him a piece of a broiled fish, and of an honeycomb. And he took it, and did eat before them.*

"Do you think that some of these same saints still walk around the earth today and appear and disappear like the angels when God sends them on a mission or wants them to deliver a message to someone?" asked Kim.

"What do you think, Kim?'

"I'll have to admit, you've really got me to thinking about it," said Kim. "Now, I can't just dismiss your grandma's experience as the result of eating the wrong kind of mushrooms. It still boggles my mind that this could be happening. So these saints that were resurrected don't die anymore?"

"Grandma told me about different religions and their beliefs. She found it amazing that some religions talk about overcoming death and achieving immortality and in the same breath glorify going through cycle after cycle of death. She quoted to me several scriptures about Jesus' purpose in coming to earth."

JOHN 10:9-10 *I am the door: by me if any man enter in, he shall be saved, and shall go in and out, and find pasture. The thief cometh not, but for to steal, and to kill, and to destroy:* **I am come that they might have life,** *and that they might have it more abundantly.*

HEBREWS *2:14 Forasmuch then as the children are partakers of flesh and blood, he also himself likewise took part of the same; that* **through death he might destroy him that had the power of death, that is, the devil.**

"So, your grandma was saying that if a religion glorifies cycle after cycle of death, leave it alone. Jesus came to bring life and not death?" asked Kim.

"Death is a horrible thing," replied Sarah. "Why be like a freshman that is so dumb he wants to take the same class over and over and over again? Jesus gives life once and for all! Jesus brought good news for us and bad news for the buzzards and the devil."

"I agree," said Kim. "But what about your grandma—is she part of some group of people?"

"Well, Grandma explained it to me this way. She is part of the little country church that she attended as a child, but she is much more than that in the depths of her beliefs. She visits various churches from time to time as directed by the Holy Spirit, and sometimes she remains secluded for long periods to receive what the Lord wants to teach her before going out again.

Grandma thinks that God is about to make some type of transition on the earth much like that when Paul was given the apostleship for the Gentiles. After his Damascus Road experience, Paul was taken out to the desert to receive his instructions and was away from the church in Jerusalem for three years. Do you remember the scriptures?"

GALATIANS 1:15-19 *But when it pleased God,* **who separated me from my mother's womb, and called me by his grace**, *to reveal his Son in me, that I might preach him among the heathen; immediately I conferred not with flesh and blood: Neither went I up to Jerusalem to them which were apostles before me; but I went into Arabia, and returned again unto Damascus.* **Then after three years I went up to Jerusalem** *to see Peter, and abode with him fifteen days. But other of the apostles saw I none, save James the Lord's brother.*

"So, yes, Grandma does have friends that believe like her, but they do not seem to be organized in the sense of the church denominations that you and I have experienced. I just think of Grandma as a spiritual resource to help me find my way up the mountain."

"Thanks for telling me about your grandma," said Kim. "Your explanations have helped me a lot in putting this in some kind of context. And we've been so busy discussing your grandma, I still haven't had a chance to ask question one about the romantics of The Dove Scrolls. You have given me a lot of food for thought.

"Speaking of food," said Sarah. "Kim, look at the time! We've gotten so absorbed in the spiritual food that we have just about missed eating lunch. Let's wind this up, and get something to eat. Then we can come back and discuss the Dove Scrolls in detail."

"Great idea!" said Kim, "Lets do it."

"Do you want to go to Wimp's? No, let's try something different. How about going low cal for a change?"

"Let's get a sub," said Kim. "They're having a special promotion for students—the second one is only a dollar. All we have to do is show our RiverRoc State University ID card."

"Let's go; I'm famished!" agreed Sarah.

Chapter 4

The Patrix and The Matrix

EXODUS 13:12 *That thou shalt set apart unto the LORD all that openeth the matrix ...*

Kim ordered a spaghetti meatball sub and Sarah ordered the new Angus steak sub. They found a quiet table near the back and proceeded to refresh themselves after a morning of work. It was not physical work but spiritual work which can be even more demanding and sometimes very tense and nail biting. Sarah did not want Kim to think her weird, and she was somewhat wary about revealing secrets.

Sarah had been particularly reluctant to discuss her grandma , but in the end, Kim seemed to be OK with Grandma's spiritual experiences—at least those that Sarah had related to her. Sarah was thankful for the pause that the lunch provided before they started in once again on Kim's questions. Kim is so goal oriented, Sarah thought. When she picks out a goal, she goes right to it, and then sets another goal. Of course, she has the natural ability to achieve difficult goals. She was able to skip all the freshmen math and science classes and even one sophomore physics class when she began college.

After contemplating Kim, Sarah's thoughts turned to herself. I, on the other hand, consider myself above average but not as smart as Kim. She is the brains between the two of us. My hair and eyes are ordinary, brown! My stature is tall—too tall I think. But, I'm glad I'm not lanky. Volleyball and basketball are my favorite sports—but I'm not inclined to become a Phys Ed major. I keep my hair shoulder length to camouflage my long neck—and around my face to enhance my features. Kim tells me that my neck is very graceful and is an asset to my appearance, but I simply do not agree. When I look at myself in a mirror I see a head set on a stick like a lollipop. My complexion is medium and I tan easily in the summer time—I like my attributes best in the summertime. The sun adds beautiful red highlights to my hair and the tan somehow gives me confidence. I guess it is true that feeling good about yourself boosts your confidence.

My personality is assertive. I have an ability to lead a group of people without too much effort. I do not know how I do it, but it comes natural to me. I do not have to think about what I am going to do, I simply step on a stage, stand up in front of a group, or clear my throat. I believe it must be a gift God has given to me. I try to be a good person and obey the commandments, but not like the Pharisees. They seemed to bend the commandments to suit their wishes. I would rather be like the good Samaritan that helps those in need. Lord, you know all my secret faults, help me to overcome them!

Sarah was jarred out of her self contemplation as the hyperactive little boy at the next table knocked his lemonade on the floor. Sarah and Kim scrambled to help the mother, holding her young baby get everything back in order and to replace the lemonade for the crying boy. Their child-handling skills were excellent. Kim had an older sister and a younger brother and sister. Sarah, while an only child, was the most popular baby-sitter in the neighborhood in her younger days.

When things settled down, Kim finished her sub and said, "You know, what I've read about the doves so far has given me some insight into a very important part of my life—do I have a mate out there somewhere waiting for me? But there are other things on my mind too. How would I relate to that mate once married? You remember our little incident with Fred at the pizza parlor? Suppose my future mate is someone like Fred, and he convinced me that God wanted me to be a timid little mouse. If that becomes the case, why am I studying genetics, advanced calculus, geology, and biophysics?"

"So," observed Sarah, "You would like to find your dove mate, you wonder how you and he will get along, and you wonder about your profession—be it a biophysicist, a housewife, or both. I think most every girl of your age has these same type of questions."

"It's in the profession area that I feel most spiritually stretched out," continued Kim. "It's one thing to listen to the preacher in church and then when I enter a biology or geology class, it seems that it is a completely different universe. They want me to check my faith at the door. The professors and some of the students are almost meticulous in trying to label my beliefs as archaic myths. If I want to learn their so-called 'real science,' I am told to lay my personal beliefs aside and parrot the ideas presented in the class."

"Maybe science is in your calling," said Sarah. "Have you ever thought that part of your life's mission statement is to discover secrets of creation and reconcile the breach between God and man? Paul spoke to Timothy about science. I think he called it *the oppositions of science falsely so called.* There does seem to be a breach between man's concept of science and God's concept of science. Grandma told me one time that she thought I had a calling to 'repair the breach' and she told me to memorize Isaiah 58:12."

And they that shall be of thee shall build the old waste places: thou shalt raise up the foundations of many generations; and thou shalt be called, **The repairer of the breach**, *The restorer of paths to dwell in.*

"Since I found the writings, I have thought maybe my calling was to be part of the healing of the breach that has existed between men and women since the fall in the garden."

"Sarah, do you think I have a calling on my life?"

"Kim, you certainly do. Maybe your calling does involve science. I don't think it is any accident that you are gifted in science. But you're right in observing there is a breach between man's concept of science and God's concept of science. Look at these scriptures. Maybe the breach that you will heal is between the persons and things not seen (God, angels, spirit) and the material world as we know it.

HEBREWS 11:1-3 *Now faith is the substance of things hoped for, the evidence of things not seen. For by it the elders obtained a good report. Through faith we understand that the worlds were framed by the word of God,* **so that things which are seen were not made of things which do appear.**

"I've asked God many times to help me sort this out," replied Kim. "Maybe He will. But we're digressing from my questions about The Dove Scrolls, and I left my pad of my questions back at the church."

Sarah and Kim returned to the church and they settled down for the questions of the afternoon. Kim picked up The Dove Scroll pages once again and then glanced at her note pad of questions.

"Wow! This is such romantic story about the doves." exclaimed Kim, as she laid aside the scroll. "Do you think my dove is out there somewhere, and I just haven't found him yet?"

"Could be," remarked Sarah. "Every since I read the scroll, I've been looking for my Abraham. But, I've remembered the story about Abraham and Sarah getting impatient about having a child, so I have been content to wait."

"Would my dove and I be born in the earth on the same day?" asked Kim.

"It could be, but most likely not," said Sarah. "Consider the actual story of Abraham and Sarah. Did you know that Sarah was Abraham's half-sister? Here, let me show you."

Sarah flipped through the first book of her Bible and after a minute of scanning said, "Abraham told a half truth about Sarah because he wanted to hide the fact that they were married from the king—who had eyes for Sarah. Then God told the king in a dream to keep his hands off Sarah. See—read it for yourself."

GENESIS 20:5-13 *Said he not unto me,* **She is my sister?** *and she, even she herself said, He is my brother: in the integrity of my heart and innocency of my hands have I done this. ... And Abimelech said unto Abraham, What sawest thou, that thou hast done this thing? And Abraham said, Because I thought, Surely the fear of God is not in this place; and they will slay me for my wife's sake. And yet* **indeed she is my sister**; *she is the daughter of my father, but not the daughter of my mother;* **and she became my wife**. *... whither we shall come, say of me,* **He is my brother.**

Sarah continued, "Abraham and Sarah were certainly doves. However, look here, Abraham was ten years older than Sarah."

GENESIS *17:17 Then Abraham fell upon his face, and laughed, and said in his heart, Shall a child be born unto him that is an* **hundred years old?** *and shall* **Sarah, that is ninety years old**, *bear?*

"Gee," Kim mused, "that must mean that if they were created as twin spirits, Abraham departed into the earthly womb ten years before Sarah did. Maybe Abraham did tell the truth after all—Sarah must have been his twin spirit sister. I wonder what she did in the heavens while awaiting her flight departure to be born in the earth? Do you think that the spirit of Abraham and the spirit of Sarah actually conversed with each other after God created them and before Abraham departed for earth? Did they know that they would be married on earth?"

"Kim, you're very perceptive in your questions," replied Sarah. "You're wanting to open a second box of mysteries, which is in another writing that I found in the chest. Yes, they may have even known their destiny while in heaven, and then a veil was placed over the remembrance when they came to earth. Please confine your questions to the puzzle we have just opened—let's not open another puzzle, just now."

"OK, but I am making a note of it right now so we will cover it at sometime in the future. Right? Agreed?" asked Kim.

Sarah replied, "Deal, and you can mark it with this note: *'Then said I, Behold, I have come! In the roll of the scroll it is written concerning me.'* These were the recorded words of a spirit that had just departed the heavens and had descended into that frequency we call earth. Now, would you like to open the two smaller scrolls that are included in The Dove Scrolls?" Kim nodded and Sarah handed her the two remaining scrolls.

She unrolled the first and exclaimed, "Why, it just like a marriage license that records the marriage of a dove couple. How beautiful!" She then unrolled the second, puzzled about it for a minute, and said, "It seems to be a dialog between doves. What is its meaning?"

Sarah replied, "It is a recording of marriage vows for doves, taken from the Song of Solomon. It could be used as a wedding ceremony. Maybe if my Abraham—whoever he is—agrees, it will be used in my wedding ceremony." [**Note:** The contents of the *Dove Marriage Archives* are available in the Ancient Chest part of this book. The *Dove Marraige Archives* and the *Dove Marriage Vows* are available online and in color.]

"Well, who knows," said Kim. "Maybe, I'll use it too. Now, one of my notes has to do with the relationship between Jesus and Mary Magdalene. After reading The Dove Scrolls, I can see a lot of possibilities that I hadn't thought of before."

Kim continued, "But the scrolls do not specifically mention Jesus and Mary Magdalene in any relationship. How could the answer to whether they were married be both yes and no? Well, OK, I think you said a 'qualified' yes and no."

"Let me try these scriptures out on you." said Sarah, "You are part of the bride of Christ, and so was Mary Magdalene."

REVELATION *21:9-10 And there came unto me one of the seven angels which had the seven vials full of the seven last plagues, and talked with me, saying,* **Come hither, I will shew thee the bride, the Lamb's wife.** *And he carried me away in the spirit to a great and high mountain, and shewed me that great city, the holy Jerusalem, descending out of heaven from God,*

"Sarah, I ought to whap you! Of course, I'm part of the bride of Christ and so is all of his church," protested Kim. "You know that's not what I'm talking about. I want to know if Jesus and Mary Magdalene were actually married on a one-to-one basis."

"I know." Sarah grinned as she teasingly scooted the old chair across the stone floor just out of Kim's reach. "We will find that spiritually there are three levels of marriage, and you have made it rather plain the one-on-one is the marriage in which you are interested."

"Explain, please."

"OK, you're a math whiz. I know, you've helped me with my calculus. So, think of this like a matrix that has twelve stones around its perimeter. If we were to measure inside the stones, we would have a ten by ten matrix. See? Measuring the outside which is 12 X 12 gives a good biblical number of 144. However, a long time ago, an angel told the Apostle John to: *Rise, and measure the temple of God, and the altar, and them that worship therein.* So, we not only measure the outside, but those *lively stones,* as the Bible calls them, that are within. And the measurements within would be 10 X 10 or 100."

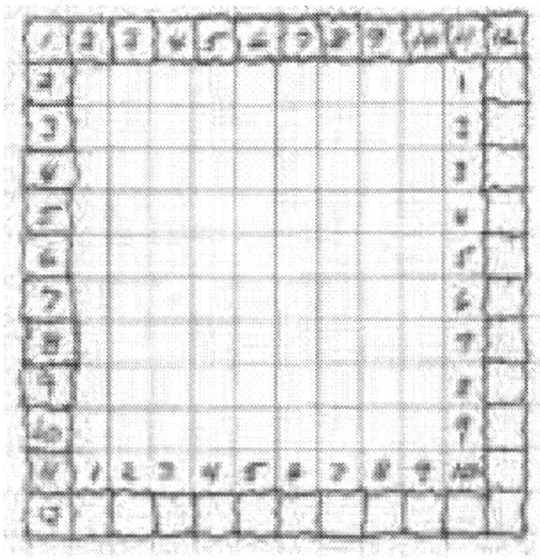

Plan view of the stones in the top row of the altar—as described by Ezekiel in chapter 43. The inside space of the altar measured ten cubits by ten cubits and was ten cubits deep.

"Ok, I'm following." said Kim. "I'm beginning to feel like I'm looking over King Solomon and also King Hiram's shoulders as they were preparing to build the temple and the altar. Is there some kind of a code to this that your aunt and uncle deciphered?"

Sarah replied, "I believe there is—I would call it the dove code. It's very strange, but most of the spiritual secrets are hid in plain sight in the Bible. You just need to have the scales removed from your eyes in order to begin to understand the secrets. And then, once you see it, you begin to wonder why many others haven't seen it before. And even stranger is that many of those who have deciphered the code relating to stone work cannot understand what the stones and their geometry truly represent."

"You're getting very mystical again," complained Kim. "Maybe I'm just dumb or have scales over my eyes, but, tell me what those stones represent."

"The stones represent people as a many membered body of believers, but they also represent the human body on an individual basis. We'll go into this much deeper, but consider the transition that Jesus made from stones to the body.

1PETER 2:5 **Ye also, as lively stones**, *are built up a spiritual house, an holy priesthood, to offer up spiritual sacrifices, acceptable to God by Jesus Christ.*

There are many churches and organizations that, even today, are too blind to make this transition from wood and stones to living beings: *Jesus answered and said unto them, Destroy this temple, and in three days I will raise it up. Then said the Jews, Forty and six years was this temple in building, and wilt thou rear it up in three days?* **But he spake of the temple of his body.**

Aunt Myra was a neurologist, and she recognized that the tree and stone symbols were only that—symbols. They actually represent part of the nervous system of the body—the electrical energy part of which is the human spirit. Uncle Andy had a near death experience in his early years after enlistment and felt the pins and needles as his spirit was leaving his body. And then he experienced the tunnel of light. But we're digressing from our subject. I suppose you want to get back to Jesus and Mary Magdalene?"

"Right, but let's put a tag on this for later discussion. It is all so very interesting."

"OK, but we will first need to complete our little math discussion. I know you wonder why the math, but trust me, it is necessary so you will understand how the puzzle fits together." Having asked for trust, Sarah pulled out her PDA and entered the following numbers into the mini-spreadsheet.

10 X 10	**100**	**1000**	**10,000**	**100,000**	**1,000,000**	**10,000,000**	**100,000,000**
12 X 12	**144**	**1440**	**14,400**	**144,000**			

"Kim, you already know about the 144,000 in the book of Revelation that ascend upon Mt. Zion with their harps. There are several denominations that have this as almost the entire doctrine of their members. They say that they are the 144,000 that are the elite ones, and the rest of the world will go through a hellish tribulation at about the time of the second coming of Jesus. Remember Franklin, the freckled redheaded boy in high school who wanted us to be 'sealed' to be one of the 144,000?"

Kim nodded.

"OK, the numbers concerning the doves are the 10 X 10 series of numbers, particularly the 10,000 and ultimately the 100,000,000 number. You know from math that opening a matrix is like the opening of a womb. Let's look at a grand matrix of 100,000,000 as detailed in the book of Revelation. Yes, it is really there—10,000 X 10,000 is 100,000,000. See in Revelation 5:11 ... *and the number of them was ten thousand times ten thousand, and thousands of thousands;"*

"I can follow the math, but where is this leading? I can't see what this has to do with Jesus and Mary Magdalene. Are you stalling on me?"

"Great question. You're timing is perfect," said Sarah. "Now I will begin to show you that 10,000 is the number of the doves. Please take the Bible and turn to the Song of Solomon and start with these verses in chapter five, verses 9 through 11. Please read it Kim, and you will have answered your own question."

SONGS 5:9-12 *What is thy beloved more than another beloved, O thou fairest among women? what is thy beloved more than another beloved, that thou dost so charge us?* **My beloved is white and ruddy, the chiefest among ten thousand.** *His head is as the most fine gold, his locks are bushy, and black as a raven.* **His eyes are as the eyes of doves** *by the rivers of waters, washed with milk, and fitly set.*

"You made your point," said Kim. " But this is talking about maybe a bridegroom being '*the chiefest among ten thousand,'* and he does have the '*eyes of doves'*. And I will admit that you did ask me to remember that we used to sing that Lily of the Valley song about Jesus being the fairest of ten thousand. But if there are ten thousand male doves, so to speak, where are the ten thousand female doves to match them? Wouldn't there be twenty thousand altogether—you know, two dove eggs in every nest, a male dovelet and a female dovelet?"

"Again, your timing is wonderful," encouraged Sarah. "Now please turn to the Psalms and read these verses, and you will see your twenty thousand doves. Read these verses."

PSALMS *68:13,14,17 Though ye have lien among the pots,* **yet shall ye be as the wings of a dove covered with silver, and her feathers with yellow gold.** *When the Almighty scattered kings in it, it was white as snow in Salmon. ...* **The chariots of God are twenty thousand**, *even thousands of angels: the Lord is among them, as in Sinai, in the holy place.*

"OK," agreed Kim, "it does mention doves and the number is twenty thousand. But how do we know that there are 10,000 male doves and 10,000 matching female doves? Are there two armies? Besides, when I think of chariots, I think of horse drawn carts in an army, not doves."

Sarah replied, "Back to the Song of Solomon we go, and please read these verses. Again, I think you will answer your own questions."

SONGS 6:9-13 **My dove**, *my undefiled is but one; she is the only one of her mother, she is the choice one of her that bare her. The daughters saw her, and blessed her; yea, the queens and the concubines, and they praised her.* **Who is she that looketh forth as the morning, fair as the moon, clear as the sun, and terrible as an army with banners?** *I went down into the garden of nuts to see the fruits of the valley, and to see whether the vine flourished and the pomegranates budded. Or ever I was aware,* **my soul made me like the chariots of Amminadib**. *Return, return, O Shulamite; return, return, that we may look upon thee.* **What will ye see in the Shulamite? As it were the company of two armies.**

"Wow!" exclaimed Kim, "You really led me into that one. It does mention not just one army, but two armies. And one army is led by a dove!"

Sarah pulled a folded sheet of paper out of her brief case. "Sometimes, this is easier to visualize graphically. I'll show you a picture. What's the old saying about one picture being worth twenty thousand doves? - er—maybe I misquoted it just a bit." She laughed. "First let's look at the 10 X 10 matrix of those who are worshipping inside the temple. We will put 100 in each of the 100 individual squares, and this will give us a matrix of 10,000. Now, imagine that this little 10,000 matrix is just—as Ezekiel described it—the *first of all the firstfruits* of the 9,999 other matrixes just like it waiting to be opened. Then we would have the *ten thousand times ten thousand* or the 100,000,000 that the Apostle John wrote about.

10,000 x 10,000 = 100,000,000

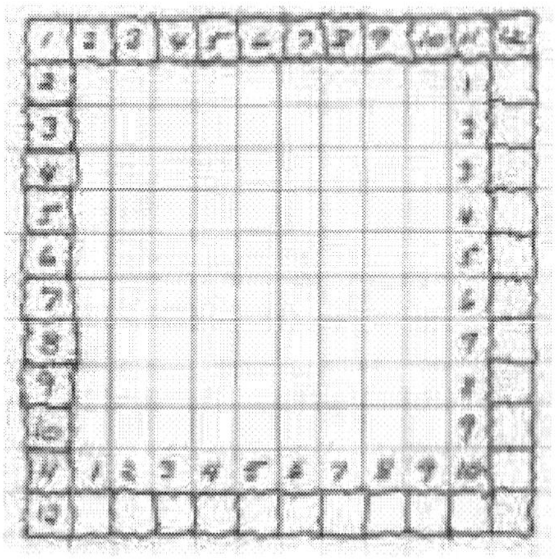

Sarah then unfolded the sheet of paper and inside were two doves within two arrays. "You've seen that there are two armies—one army is male and the other army is female. So, we are going to call the male dove army the 'patrix' and female dove army the 'matrix.'

"That's a new one on me," said Kim. "I don't think my math teacher taught me about a patrix. Maybe, all you have to do is to change the polarity of a matrix to have a patrix—like the two poles of a magnet."

"You've heard about men being from Mars and women from Venus," said Sarah. "There is some evidence that identical twins have instantaneous communication with each other—how I don't know."

"Gee, I almost feel like this describes the quantum physics experiment where twin electrons communicate with each other at faster than light speeds. Of course, quantum physics has some really weird things."

The Patrix	***The Matrix***

10,000 Male Doves	***10,000 Female Doves***

"Good analogy," said Sarah. "Now, let's fold the sheet of paper along the line in the middle so that on one side of the folded sheet we will have the patrix, and on the other side we will have the matrix. Now, let's scotch tape the ends together, and then we will roll it up like a scroll and put a ribbon on it. Here, Kim, put your fingerprint as a seal on the sticky part of the scotch tape, and we will put a seal upon it."

"OK," said Kim. "But you realize that CSI could examine this and find out that I was the one that sealed it."

"You're right. And now to be sure that CSI has lots of fingerprints, put six more scotch tape seals on the scroll. Don't give me that funny look, just trust me and do it."

"I don't see the point of it. I suppose you have some method to your madness; so being the nice person that I am, I will do it just to humor you." Kim then launched into the repetitive labor of adding six more seals. "OK, it's done. Now what?"

Sarah replied, "In the old days they usually had their information in scrolls rather than in books. So, we have a scroll, with writing on the front and back sides, and it is sealed with seven seals. Now, I want you to read these verses from Revelation."

Kim took the Bible already opened to the book of Revelation and began reading:

REVELATION 5:1-5 *And I saw in the right hand of him that sat on the throne* **a book written within and on the backside, sealed with seven seals**. *And I saw a strong angel proclaiming with a loud voice, Who is worthy to open the book, and to loose the seals thereof? And no man in heaven, nor in earth, neither under the earth, was able to open the book, neither to look thereon. And I wept much, because no man was found worthy to open and to read the book, neither to look thereon. And one of the elders saith unto me, Weep not: behold, the Lion of the tribe of Juda, the Root of David, hath prevailed to open the book,* **and to loose the seven seals thereof.**

"So that's why you had me put seven seals on it. And I can see why you folded the sheet so that the patrix was on the back and the matrix was on the inside. And Jesus can loose the seals and open the matrix."

"That's right." said Sarah, "And one of the last seals on the womb of the matrix is the knowledge of the morning of the creation of spirits. This matrix was sealed up a long time ago, and now it is being opened by Jesus—a member of the priesthood of Melchisedek. See, look at these verses in the Psalms. And did you know the same Hebrew word for **womb** is sometimes translated as **matrix** in other parts of the Old Testament?"

PSALMS *110:3-4 Thy people shall be willing in the day of thy power, in the beauties of holiness* **from the womb of the morning**: *thou hast the dew of thy youth. The LORD hath sworn, and will not repent,* **Thou art a priest for ever after the order of Melchizedek**.

Kim remarked, "This is amazing! There it is—*the womb of the morning or maybe I should say matrix of the morning.* Now, I can see that Jesus was the chiefest of ten thousand of the male doves. But, where does that fit in with Mary Magdalene—was she Jesus' dove?

"Let me put it this way," said Sarah. "The first patrix bridegroom company of 10,000 is married to the first matrix bridal company of 10,000. So, in that sense, Mary Magdalene was part of Jesus' corporate bride. I know! I know, I haven't answered your nagging question yet. But, there's more foundation needed to make it easier to understand."

"I feel a little lost!" exclaimed Kim. "So what are the other things I need to understand?"

"It's getting late," said Sarah. "We've been at it for a long time. So what I will do is give you some questions to think about before we talk again. OK?"

"Proceed."

"The first question I will warn you is a trick question. It has twists and turns that aren't at all obvious. You remember our friend and Supreme Court Chief Justice staffing advisor Fred and his girl friend Katie. They were having a discussion on Valentine's Day about whether they should hurry up and get married before Jesus returns because they were afraid that their bodies would be changed, and they wouldn't be marrying each other or having sex after the second coming. So the first question is:

1. If Jesus and Mary Magdalene were married, would they be married throughout all eternity? And your text scripture is here in LUKE *20:28-36 Saying, Master, Moses wrote unto us, If any man's brother die, having a wife, and he die without children, that his brother should take his wife, and raise up seed unto his brother. There were therefore seven brethren: and the first took a wife, and died without children. And the second took her to wife, and he died childless. And the third took her; and in like manner the seven also: and they left no children, and died. Last of all the woman died also. Therefore in the resurrection whose wife of them is she? for seven had her to wife. And Jesus answering said unto them, The children of this world marry, and are given in marriage:* **But they which shall be accounted worthy to obtain that world, and the resurrection from the dead, neither marry, nor are given in marriage:** *Neither can they die any more: for they are equal unto the angels; and are the children of God, being the children of the resurrection.*

So, were Fred and Katie's concerns about possibly not experiencing the joys of marriage and sex valid? Are all marriages dissolved after the resurrection, and there is no marrying after that?"

"I know your tactics," scolded Kim mockingly. "You warn me that something is going to happen like a trick question, and then you pull it off, and your excuse is 'I warned you!' like that makes it all right."

"Me—guilty of that? Never!" smirked Sarah. "And now, moving on to the second question which concerns translations from source texts.

2. "Did the word 'angel' always mean an angelic, nonhuman being when it was translated, say in the King James Version or some of the other more modern versions? Your assignment, Miss Kimberly, should you decide to take it before this message self destructs, will be to check this out using an original language concordance. I will give you a hint. In some cases the word 'messenger' is translated as 'angel.' However, a 'messenger' could be a human messenger or an angelic messenger. Then again, the translation to the word angel could be from something else entirely. Your source text for this is PSALM 8:4-5 *What is man, that thou art mindful of him? and the son of man, that thou visitest him? For thou hast made him a little lower than the* ***angels****, and hast crowned him with glory and honour.*

If you check this out in the concordance, you will find that 'angels' should have been translated 'elohims'. And if you do further checking you will find that there is an Elohim in the sense of God, with a capital E and capital G, and then there are little elohims under the powerful Elohim. A second source text for this is PSALMS 82:1 *God standeth in the congregation of the mighty; he judgeth among the gods.*"

"You're right, it does mention God standing in a congregation of little 'g' gods. I never even thought about that. I wonder who these little gods are?" questioned Kim.

"In order to answer who the little gods are, we will need to break the code. I will call it the dove code. Part of the code concerns the names of God. Yes, don't look puzzled, there are a number of names for the Godhead which are used in the Bible. God is one God, yes, but God has different attributes, depending on the purpose of the interaction with us humans. For example, your father is a Mississippi Basin Timber Company botanist, the husband of your mother, a softball coach, and a house owner. Is he four different persons or just one?

"I see what you're driving at," said Kim. "My father interacted differently with me when I was three years old than he would have during the same period with a 30 year old bio-tech who he was responsible for supervising. I doubt whether he ever picked up his researcher and hugged him like he did me. Or yes, he had my mother do some of the hugging and nurturing while he was away at work."

Sarah said, "Kim, you're right on! You need to think of the Godhead in terms of parents. Now, if you were to paint an image of me, would it look like me?"

"If I had taken another year of art, it probably would." Kim laughed. "OK, yes, the image would at least resemble you."

"Then consider these scriptures that describe the image of God and tell me what are the characteristics of God."

GENESIS 1:26-27 *And God said,* **Let us make man in our image, after our likeness***: and let them have dominion over the fish of the sea, and over the fowl of the air, and over the cattle, and over all the earth, and over every creeping thing that creepeth upon the earth.* **So God created man in his own image, in the image of God created he him; male and female created he them.**

Surprised at what she had read with true understanding for the first time, Kim exclaimed, "You're right—my oh my—man was created in the image of God as male and female, so God must be male and female. Are our father and mother together in God? If that is the case, what are the names of the Papa and Mama parts of God? And who is this *'us'* that does the creating?"

"I'm going to give you the code as to what part of the Godhead is acting in the various scriptures in the Bible. It's really not all such a big secret, most Bible scholars have known about it, but very few understand the names. The translation has its roots in the Hebrew names for the Godhead. Here, look at these notes."

Most High God or Most High = El Elyon = Supreme All in All

God = Elohim = Parents = (Yahweh and El Shaddai together)

LORD = Yahweh = Father = Male Elohim

Almighty = El Shaddai = Mother = Wisdom = Female Elohim

"When you do your homework in a concordance, you will find in the King James Version of the Old Testament that 'LORD' almost always refers to *Yahweh*; 'Almighty' almost always refers to *El Shaddai*; 'God' almost always refers to the '*Elohim*'; and Most High God almost always refers to *El Elyon*."

"Wow!" said Kim. "I never really thought of an attribute of God as being a mother. Are you sure about this? And, also, Almighty seems to be an unusual name for a mother."

"Remember that 'Almighty' is a translated word from the Hebrew word El Shaddai. Besides, if you ever messed with a bear cub, you would find that Almighty is a good name for a protective mother bear caring for her young! OK, O Kimberly Ann, doubter of Motherhood in the Godhead, explain these scriptures to me."

JOHN 3:4-5 *Nicodemus saith unto him, How can a man be born when he is old?* **can he enter the second time into his mother's womb, and be born?** *Jesus answered, Verily, verily, I say unto thee, Except a man be born of water and of the Spirit, he cannot enter into the kingdom of God.*

.IONS 4:26 *But Jerusalem which is above is free, which is* **the mother of us all**.

u can see the previous two scriptures definitely refer to motherhood," said Sarah. "But how do you expla.n the scriptures from Proverbs about wisdom? Wisdom is definitely female and apparently has existed back in time before the earth was even created. So, please explain these scriptures to me."

PROVERBS 8:1 *Doth not wisdom cry? and understanding put forth* **her** *voice? ...*
[Yahweh]
22 The LORD possessed me in the beginning of his way, before his works of old.

23 **I was set up from everlasting, from the beginning**, *or ever the earth was.*

"I'm not sure that I can." replied Kim.

"See where I penciled in the name of Yahweh after the word 'LORD' so you know that mother Wisdom was the companion of Yahweh before the earth ever was. Also, the word *shad* in the Hebrew means breast. Now, the third part of your assignment is to take the verses I will give you and pencil in the Hebrew words that describe the various parts of the Godhead."

Sarah looked in her Bible and began to write out question number three:

3. The Names of God:

Psalms 91:1 He that dwelleth in the secret place of the most High [________]

shall abide under the shadow of the Almighty. [__________]

2 I will say of the Lord [_________], He is my refuge and my fortress: my

God [__________]; in him will I trust.

"See, Kim, how easy it is," encouraged Sarah. "All you have to do is use the code I have given you and pencil in the Hebrew names that go with Most High, Almighty, LORD, and God."

"That doesn't look all that hard," observed Kim. "But I still don't have a feel for how these natures of God interact with us."

Sarah smiled and brought out an old parchment that had been folded. "When Myra was in Bele'm, she went to a street flea market and bought an old Portugese Bible for about $R15 Reais—whatever that is—and took it home to look at the interior artwork. She found this old parchment folded up inside the Bible and managed to get someone to translate it. [**Editor's note**: See Appendix C for picture of parchment and its translation—also see *The Ancient Chest*; *Song of the Ancients* section for a well used copy of *The Song of Melchisedec*]. Strangely enough, it was about this Melchisedek—king and priest—that mysteriously shows up to bless Abraham. The Bible says he was king of Salem. I wonder if there was a queen of Salem? The book of Hebrews also mentions Jesus and the order of Melchisedek. This order of Melchisedek is kind of baffling to me but when you look at the translation, it is very enlightening about understanding the names and natures of God and how they interface with us humans."

"Gee, this thing is really, really old. I'm almost afraid to touch it," said Kim.

"The Bible it was in apparently came from the northwest coast of Portugal. You can look at the parchment in detail when we get back to the dorm, but let's not dwell on it now," said Sarah.

"Prof, you've loaded me up with homework," said Kim. "The first item has to do with Jesus and Mary Magdalene and the resurrection. The second has to do with the translation of angels and little elohims, and the third is about the Hebrew names of the Godhead. Right?"

"Right, you are, Kim. I'm just trying to make what's coming understandable to you, so don't fuss at me. Actually, I'm amazed at how fast you're picking this up. I was much slower."

"Yeah, but you didn't initially have a teacher to help you, other than what you were able to read from the chest and emails. I'm not fussing at you; you are truly a dear friend for taking me into your confidence."

"The email files had some equations and computer programs I didn't quite understand," said Sarah. "Maybe, you can teach me about them when we go to the old house this summer."

"Do you remember the subject matter of these particular files?" asked Kim.

"I remember some of it," replied Sarah. "I think it has something to do with the patrix and the matrix. Uncle Andy was using a particular and a somewhat puzzling scripture to come up with four dimensions. Let me find it."

EPHESIANS 3:17-19 *That Christ may dwell in your hearts by faith; that ye, being rooted and grounded in love, May be able to comprehend with all saints what is the* breadth, and length, *and* **depth**, *and* height*; And to know the love of Christ, which passeth knowledge, that ye might be filled with all the fulness of God.*

"The puzzling thing about verse 18 is that it has the three dimensions of breadth, length, and height, but it adds a dimension of depth which would seem to be redundant. However, in the original Greek, the word *depth* seems to have its roots in *profound* and *mystery*. Anyway, Uncle Andy had two five dimension arrays in a program called gwbasic. One array was the matrix which had breadth, length, and width in it along with time. Then he added female polarity to get five dimensions."

"This sounds like something out of my physics class," said Kim. "Where did he go from there?"

"He did a second five dimension array for the patrix just like the matrix, but used a male polarity. He and Myra sent emails back and forth with a lot of discussion of these scriptures."

JOB 38:33 *Knowest thou the* ordinances of **heaven**? *canst thou* **set the dominion thereof in the earth?**

2CORINTHIANS 3:18 *But we all, with open face* **beholding as in a glass** *the glory of the Lord,* are **changed into the same image from glory to glory**, even as **by the Spirit of the Lord**.

HEBREWS 11:3 Through **faith we understand that the worlds were framed** *by the word of God, so* **that things which are seen were not made of things which do appear.**

"Uncle Andy tried to combine the matrix and patrix into various configurations like a scroll written on both sides. He had the matrix and the patrix as mirror images of each other."

"This is really fascinating," responded Kim. "The ten dimensions seem like something out of my quantum physics class; except they say there are four dimensions we can see and six dimensions that are somehow 'curled up' and can't be seen. And now, they think there may even be one additional dimension. This would result in four **seen** dimensions and seven **unseen** dimensions, giving a total of eleven dimensions.

"Curled up?" asked Sarah. "What do you mean, I don't think I have ever ran across this concept before. I can look at this table and say it is 6 feet long, 4 feet wide, 32 inches high, and it had these dimensions one minute ago, and that it has these same measurements now. Are these seven, unseen dimensions curled up like hair, or a window shade. or a scroll?"

"Yeah, sort of like that. Curled up means it's invisible to the eye," explained Kim. "But where did your Uncle Andy get the idea for five arrays mirroring another five arrays?"

"He got the five mirroring arrays out of Solomon's temple," replied Sarah. "Let me see if I can find it."

1KINGS 7:48-49 *And Solomon made all the vessels that pertained unto the house of the LORD: the altar of gold, and the table of gold, whereupon the shewbread was,* **And the candlesticks of pure gold, five on the right side, and five on the left, before the oracle**, *with the flowers, and the lamps, and the tongs of gold,*

"OK, I see the five candlesticks—five on the right and five on the left," said Kim. "Were these candlesticks like the little dish with a candle in it that we used to have around the camp fire in girl scouts?"

"Oh, no," replied Sarah, "these were very special candlesticks. Let me see if I find some information in one of the internet writings. Ah, let's try this. See the candlestick is actually seven candles. It has a main branch with three branches out of one side and three branches out of the other side. It represents the Seven Spirits of God named in Isaiah chapter 11. The main shaft of the candlestick is the envelope of the Spirit of the Lord. This is the white light which embraces the six branch lamps. It is like the colors of the rainbow combined in white light which is the Spirit of the Lord."

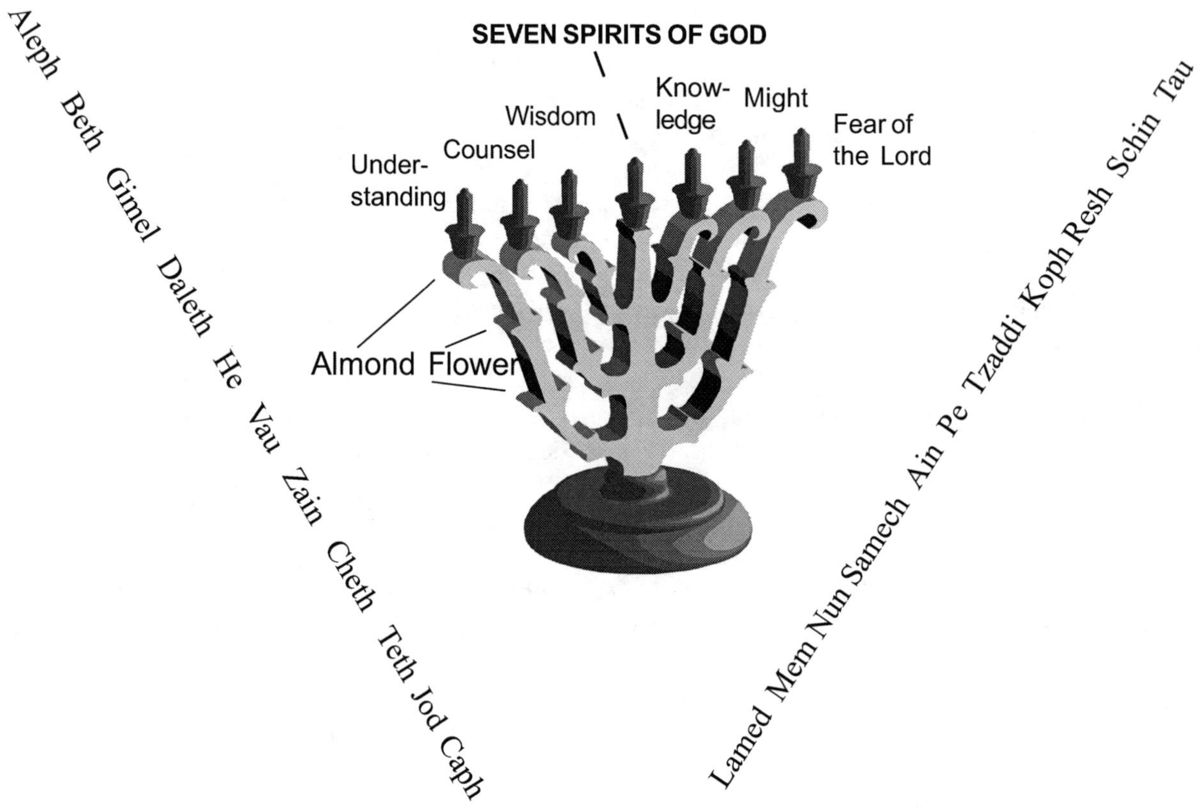

"Wow, this is exciting!" exclaimed Kim. "Since these are spirit dimensions—my oh my, my oh my—these might be the seven invisible, curled up dimensions our astrophysics and quantum mechanics friends have been so diligently seeking. This is like finding the seven cities of Cibolo or maybe even the Holy Grail of physics! This is one of the bridges between faith and science I've been searching for!"

"Kim, I confess I'm lost when you start using astrophysics or quantum mechanics terms on me," said Sarah. "But I can clearly see that you're very excited about this. Do you think these seven curled up realms were described in the scriptures by the prophets long before our present day scientists even thought about them?"

"Well, let me put it this way...how can I phrase it?" said Kim. "This is so exciting—it doesn't shake my faith; it shakes my unfaith in the Bible. The mathematicians have been predicting these unseen dimensions for some time, but the physicists are just now on the verge of finding them. But what are those funny little words printed on each side of the candlestick?"

"Oh, those," replied Sarah. "You see the candlestick has twenty-two almond flowers engraved on it. Six branches have three flowers apiece, which gives eighteen, and then there are four on the main shaft. That gives a total of twenty-two. The almond rod was what Moses used to part the Red Sea. You know what the twenty-two flowers represent, don't you?"

"Not a clue—tell me."

"Right in the middle of the Bible is Psalm 119. It is an acrostic, and each of the twenty-two letters of the Hebrew alphabet have eight verses that begin with that letter," said Sarah. "Those little words that you see are the twenty-two letters of the alphabet."

Kim's jaw dropped and she gasped, "I can't believe it! Not only do you have the seven curled up, invisible, dimensions in the candlestick, but you also have the twenty-two Hebrew alphabet letters. These must be the building blocks of creation!"

"Oh, there's a lot more," said Sarah. "I'll show you some of Uncle Andy's and Aunt Myra's emails on this subject. They discuss how the things we see were framed by faith from the unseen things of the spirit. Andy was even pondering Job going through a whirlwind time warp worm hole in the scroll when God showed Job about the creation of the earth. Then there were the wheels within wheels in Ezekiel that he put alongside Calibi something or other shapes. He pondered the meaning of King David's harp of ten strings. Aunt Myra joked the patrix man had been trying to understand the matrix woman for a very long time. However, Uncle Andy countered that it was really the relationship between the invisible spirit world and the visible world that we see. Anyway, I got lost in their equations and programs. I'll show you some of the emails, but we're not here to discuss technical stuff, or we'll be here all day. Let's get back to the doves. [Editor's Note: see Appendix A for email references to candlestick.]

"This is all very intriguing," said Kim. "I can't wait to get into it. But, OK, let's go back to the doves. Something is really bothering me—does everybody have a dove?"

Sarah chided Kim that she had a knack for picking out the difficult questions. Her Uncle Andy and Aunt Myra had exchanged quite a number of emails on this very subject. They discussed Paul's writings about the virtues of celibacy versus marriage. They discussed what the scriptures say about the eunuchs and tried to determine if this applied only to terrestrial relationships. They considered the "be fruitful and multiply" scriptures. They talked about priests and nuns. They discussed whether doves might still be doves but never marry in the earthly, physical sense and so on. She asked Kim whether she should continue or give her the short answer.

"Give me the short answer," requested Kim.

"After all their discussions, their short answer was very simple. They said: 'We don't know if everybody has a dove,'" replied Sarah.

"I can appreciate their candor," said Kim. "If you don't know, it is better to say so, rather than try to promote a bunch of made-up theories."

"Kim, I know we have answered some of your questions, and I know you have a lot more questions. I have made a complete copy of The Dove Scrolls for you to study at your leisure. I think using the introduction we've had today, you will be able to handle the whole writing," said Sarah, as she handed the complete writing to Kim. "Are you about ready to head back to the dorm?"

"Let's go," replied Kim. "And Sarah, I really, really appreciate your help in answering my questions and sharing some things that maybe you were afraid to share with me. Thank you for trusting me."

"You're welcome, Kim. I hope that it blesses you."

Editor's Note: The complete texts of The *Dove Marriage Archives* and *The Dove Scrolls* are given in The Ancient Chest section at the back of this book. On-line copies, IN COLOR, may be accessed at http://www.TheAncientChest.com/DoveScroll. The *Dove Marriage Vows* are available only from the online resource.

Chapter 5

The Towers of Magdala

Sarah and Kim resumed their studies and got back into the flow of routine class attendance. Kim was preoccupied with completing her semester paper on avian anatomy, but from time to time, she would drag out Sarah's concordance and check out the translations of various words and also the various names of God. However, when it came to answering Sarah's trick question about if Jesus and Mary Magdalene were married, would they be married for all eternity, Kim was hitting a brick wall.

"Sarah, how about a clue on the marriage for all eternity even after Jesus was resurrected?" bugged Kim. "Please, just one little clue to get me started."

"OK," Sarah relented. "Just one little clue. Actually, I have already given it to you. Remember, when we were going over the three cord marriage diagram? I told you then there was more than one type of body that could be involved in the body cord and to make a note of it. You will need to study the different types of bodies."

"Oh wonderful!" said Kim. "And how do I do that? Give me a little clue to get started."

"Being the generous person that I am, I will give you three clues. Study the 11th chapter of John, the 14th chapter of I Corinthians, and the 1st chapter of Hebrews."

"Thank you, oh Ed Psych guru. Actually, wouldn't it be a lot easier to just tell me how it could be—you know—if those with a resurrected body are no longer married, then how could Jesus and Mary Magdalene still be married? That is, if they were even married in the first place. Come on, give me more clues. Pretty pleeeeze?"

"Nope. Dig it out for yourself. However, maybe you should refocus on the problem. Suppose God hired you as a counselor."

"Yeah, like He needs my advice."

"Well, play like He did, and you were given this problem. In older days divorces were not common, and single mom and dad situations were even less common. Now, you have all these live-ins, multiple marriages, divorces, children from affairs, etc. Suppose Joe has been involved in all these things, been married three times with children from each marriage, and in the final five years of his life had a spiritual awakening. What would Joe's relationships be like on the other side when he passed on?"

"It would be a mess to sort out," said Kim.

"Exactly," said Sarah. "You've got the picture. What is your advice to God, counselor? Or, do you think that over some extended age of time, Joe and his true dove would spiritually progress 'on the other side' from resurrection bodies to celestial bodies and eventually be reunited? Uh, oh! It's almost 10:00 o'clock. We have a general assembly at Rotunda Hall. Grab your stuff. Let's go."

Sarah and Kim made their way to the middle balcony of the assembly hall where their little group of friends usually sat. Nancy, Tiffany, and Floyd were there along with others they knew. The dean and registrar droned on for 45 minutes about the newest on-line summer and fall registration and class selection protocol, and then they were dismissed.

As they were walking out through the brass plated theatre type doors, Sarah felt a tug on her elbow. It was Tiffany.

"Sarah, I need to talk to you about something," whispered Tiffany.

As Sarah paused to talk to Tiffany, Kim motioned, "Hey, I'm off to my bio-lab. See you later."

"Is this confidential or something?" said Sarah. "Why the whispers?"

"It's not exactly confidential. I just don't want to hurt Nancy's feelings. She wants me to go to *The Towers of Magdala* movie with her when it opens on Friday evening, I'm not sure I want to go."

"I understand," said Sarah. "There has been a huge amount of controversy about it. You're not the only one with very mixed feelings about it."

"I don't want to be like a hot house plant and be sheltered to the extent that I can't survive out in the real world. I think my mom is a little over protective. On the other hand, I can see that there is no point putting your head down on the rail and waiting for the train just to see what it feels like to lose your head. And I don't want Nancy to think that I'm a prude."

"I know where you're coming from," agreed Sarah. "So what is it that you want from me?"

"Do you think I should go the movie with Nancy? She needs a ride, and I have Mom's car."

"I can't make that decision for you, Tiff, but we can look at what the Bible and other historical sources have to say about Mary Magdalene. Then, you can decide."

Tiffany felt an urgency to meet with Sarah that evening to delve into the Magdalene study, but Sarah put her off until the following evening. Sarah wondered if Tiffany would mind having Kim join the study because of Kim's interest in that subject. Tiffany agreed but asked Sarah not to say anything about Nancy's request.

Sarah and Kim both dug into their studies that night for tests that they had the next day. Later, at lunch the next day, Sarah told Kim that Tiffany wanted to come over to do some research on what the Bible and some other sources had to say about the relationship between Mary Magdalene and Jesus. Sarah considered Tiffany to be remarkably adaptive. Her background was biracial—Sarah did not realize this until scholastic achievement awards were given in assembly. The parents, if available, accompanied those receiving the awards to the stage as part of the ceremony. Sarah was not displeased with her own figure, but Tiffany was the type that would look good in any dress, even if it were a flour sack. Yet, both she and her mother had a special dignity about them as they came forward to be presented with Tiffany's Excellence in Social Sciences award. It was clear that a strong mother-daughter bond existed between them.

Kim was quite pleased with the opportunity to research the Mary Magdalene questions because she too had questions about the upcoming Magdala movie. Sarah and Kim agreed, however, not to say anything to Tiffany about the secret chest or the things that were discussed in the old stone church. Later that evening, there was a knock on the dorm door. Sarah opened it and invited Tiffany in to join Kim and herself in having Blue Bunny fudge bars before beginning discussions.

"So, you two want to do some serious study of Mary Magdalene," began Sarah as they moved to the round study table. "My question to you is how you would unhang a hung jury?"

"What do you mean?" said Tiffany, "What jury is hung up?"

"Well, we have *three* juries of scholars. **1.** Some say that Mary Magdalene was the sinful woman that anointed Jesus' feet with the alabaster box in the pharisee's house. Others disagree and say that Mary Magdalene could not have been this person. Then there are, shall we say, very heated arguments about even the implication that Mary Magdalene was a harlot. **2.** Some say that Mary Magdalene and Mary of Bethany—you know, Martha's sister—are one and the same. Others disagree. **3.** And we haven't even yet discussed the subject being deliberated more recently by a third jury—was Mary Magdalene Jesus' girl friend or even his wife? That's what I mean by hung juries. So, how would you unhang a hung jury?"

"If I were the judge, I would order them to reexamine the evidence and try to arrive at a verdict," replied Tiffany.

"OK, the judge does that, and you are a member of the jury—where to now?" asked Sarah.

"Well, maybe we should use some of the CSI and Numbers' probability techniques: draw time lines, add evidence, opportunity, and MO's and also look at motives," volunteered Tiffany.

The group decided that even though they were not skilled in CSI techniques—they would wing it with what they knew. It was agreed to change the meaning of CSI from Crime Scene investigation to Christ Scene Investigation. Tiffany thought that Nancy, if she were with them, would have been proud of the group using some of her law methods and suggested maybe they should title their investigation Jerusalem CSI.

"Hey, maybe we can get some DNA in here somewhere, too," suggested Kim. "Let's go with our Christ Scene Investigation team. Lay out the evidence for us, Sarah."

"One of the techniques that works best is to break a large complex problem down into solvable parts, and then look at the overall problem again," said Sarah. "So let's start by looking at the first hung jury's problem only. Who is this Mary Magdalene, where did she come from—does she have an AKA [*also known as*] as the sinful woman who anointed Jesus' feet in the house of the Pharisee?

Sarah opened her laptop and found the icon for her Bible software and opened the program up to the book of Luke. She related that Luke has most of the background information on Mary Magdalene. The starting place would be the woman with the alabaster box who was labelled a sinner.

LUKE 7:36-40 *And one of the Pharisees desired him that he would eat with him. And he went into the Pharisee's house, and sat down to meat. And, behold,* **a woman in the city, which was a sinner**, *when she knew that Jesus sat at meat in the Pharisee's house,* **brought an alabaster box of ointment,** *And stood at his feet behind him weeping, and* **began to wash his feet with tears, and did wipe them with the hairs of her head, and kissed his feet, and anointed them with the ointment.** *Now when the Pharisee which had bidden him saw it, he spake within himself, saying, This man, if he were a prophet, would have known who and* **what manner of woman this is that toucheth him: for she is a sinner.** *And Jesus answering said unto him, Simon, I have somewhat to say unto thee. And he saith, Master, say on.*

Sarah asked the team to tell her the location of this incident.

"It doesn't give the name of the city here, but we know the meeting was in Simon the Pharisee's house. Can you back up and find out where Jesus generally was traveling when he came to this city?" asked Kim.

"OK, let's look. Looking, looking ... "

LUKE 7:11 *And it came to pass the day after, that he went into* ***a city called Nain****; and many of his disciples went with him, and much people.*

"There, you have your city."

Tiffany went to the large flip chart on the wall near the table and wrote "Nain" and "Simon the Pharisee's house." She wondered if Nain was close to Magdala where Mary Magdalene was from.

"You're jumping ahead, counselor," admonished Sarah. "Magdala is not yet in the evidence. Next, we need to look at the MO—that is, ministry of operation."

"OK, the woman broke an alabaster box and anointed his feet with the ointment," replied Tiffany. She wrote MO: Used alabaster box ointment, anointed feet, kissed feet, cried, wiped tears off feet with hair."

"What else do we know about this woman?"

Tiffany scribbled on the flip chart that the woman who broke the alabaster box was a sinner and had a poor reputation with Simon the Pharisee.

"Now you know the story that Jesus related to Simon, and it is summed up in the following verses."

LUKE 7:45-47 *Thou gavest me no kiss: but this woman since the time I came in hath not ceased to kiss my feet. My head with oil thou didst not anoint:* **but this woman hath anointed my feet with ointment**. *Wherefore I say unto thee,* **Her sins, which are many, are forgiven; for she loved much**: *but to whom little is forgiven, the same loveth little.*

"What can we say about motives?"

Kim thought it probable that the woman had heard about Jesus' message of love and forgiveness somewhere, and was extremely grateful to Jesus for giving her hope of a new life. Tiffany wrote: Grateful and Loved Much. For Simon, she wrote: Judgmental and Loved Little. Sarah then scrolled down to the next set of scriptures.

LUKE 7:48-50 8:1-3 *And he said unto her, Thy sins are forgiven. And they that sat at meat with him began to say within themselves, Who is this that forgiveth sins also?* **And he said to the woman, Thy faith hath saved thee; go in peace.**

And it came to pass afterward, that he went throughout every city and village, preaching and shewing the glad tidings of the kingdom of God: and the twelve were with him, **And certain women, which had been healed of evil spirits and infirmities, Mary called Magdalene, out of whom went seven devils,** *And Joanna the wife of Chuza Herod's steward, and Susanna, and many others, which ministered unto him of their substance.*

"Oh, look at that!" exclaimed Tiffany. "I didn't realize that Luke's account had the woman with the alabaster box and his first mention of Mary Magdalene so close together in scripture. Two verses after Jesus tells the woman to go in peace, Mary Magdalene is mentioned. And then there's Joanna and Susanna, too. Now, that Mary Magdalene is 'entered into the evidence'—as you say—can we look at the map and see how close Magdala and Nain are together?"

"Your timing is admirable." grinned Sarah. "Let's do it. I will type in Nain and Magdala and let's see what we get on the map software. There it is. See the two round dots."

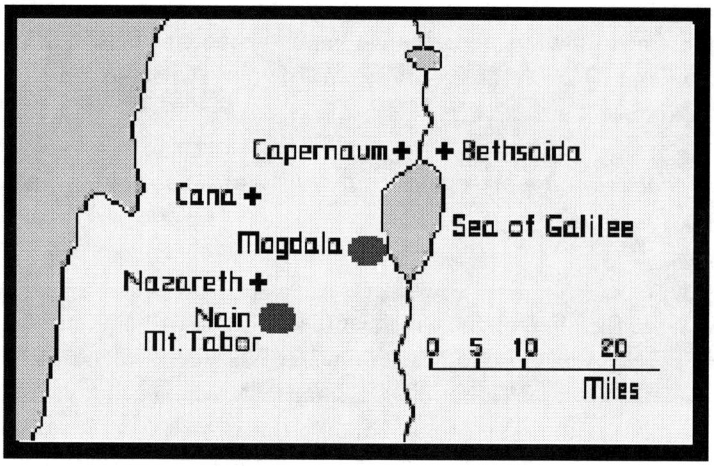

Kim thought it a little puzzling that Mary Magdalene was placed in a a group of women *that ministered to him of their substance.* She wondered if Mary Magdalene had substantial wealth to help finance Jesus' ministry and his travels. Did her *substance* come from inheritance, professional abilities, or industry ownership—such as fishing boats? She pointed out the village of Magdala is on the shores of the Sea of Galilee and that Nain is near Mt. Tabor. She judged that they might be about 15 miles apart. The group wondered what path Jesus was taking on this journey. They searched earlier scriptures in Luke to determine his path.

LUKE 7:1 *Now when he had ended all his sayings in the audience of the people,* **he entered into Capernaum.**

Kim proposed that since Capernaum is above the Sea of Galilee, it was likely he traveled downward along the Sea of Galilee and then over to Nain. She thought he probably would have come right through Magdala. The woman with the alabaster jar might have been from Magdala and followed him when Jesus went to Nain.

Tiffany put on the flip chart: opportunity for Mary Magdalene: she had the opportunity to be at Nain, and it looks like she followed Jesus from Nain.

"Also, we can add motive in that she was plagued with seven devils, so she would want to get rid of them and did through the ministry of Jesus," added Kim. "I wonder what it means to have seven devils removed and to receive Jesus' healing ministry to repair the damage? Strange?"

"Well, you remember Jacob's ladder with the bottom on the earth and rungs going upward," said Sarah. "Repeatedly the Bible mentions the Lord as being the God of Abraham, Isaac, and Jacob. If you take Eve, and add Sarah, Rebecca and the four wives of Jacob, you get seven women. Remember the prophet Isaiah said that seven women would take hold of one man? The seven devils being cast out are symbolic of the cleansing of the seven matrices— or garments—of the soul."

Tiffany looked startled. "I don't understand; what are you talking about?"

"You're right, I am digressing from our subject. We need to refocus on who Mary Magdalene is and what was her relationship to Jesus," Sarah replied. "Now that we have both opportunity and motive down on the sheet, it is time to consider our first question: Could the sinner that broke the alabaster box and shed her tears on Jesus' feet be Mary Magdalene?"

Kim glanced at Sarah as if reading her thoughts that Sarah had almost said too much and opened up a new subject about the matrices that she really didn't want to get into with Tiffany, at least not now.

Tiffany thought it a puzzle that Luke the physician didn't just come out and say that the sinner who shed tears on Jesus' feet was Mary Magdalene, if that's who she was. She related an incident about her then sixteen-year-old niece who her church helped get off the street and off drugs. When Tiffany and her mother visited her grandmother's church in Ohio last year, her mother was asked to teach Sunday School. She told about how a sixteen-year-old girl in her church was rescued from a sinful life. However, Tiffany considered her mother very wise not to give the name of the girl because it could have been an embarrassment for the girl with her Ohio relatives.

Kim agreed with Tiffany that even today, physicians are discreet about discussing the ailments of their patients. Maybe Luke the physician, in regarding Mary Magdalene as a fellow believer and perhaps even a fellow apostle, didn't want to embarrass her about her earlier life. She wondered if one of the earlier gospels let the cat out of the bag, so to speak, so Luke did go ahead and mention the casting out of the seven devils.

Sarah remembered that Mark was the earliest gospel written and ran the phrase "seven devils" on the computer to see if Mark wrote about it. She found a reference in Mark.

MARK 16:9 *Now when Jesus was risen early the first day of the week,* **he appeared first to Mary Magdalene, out of whom he had cast seven devils.**

"Yes, you're right, there it is in Mark. So maybe Luke just confirmed the part about casting out seven devils but reported generically on the sinner who kissed Jesus' feet."

"I think that we may be ready for our jury to reconsider whether Mary Magdalene and the woman who anointed Jesus' feet in Simon's house are one and the same," said Tiffany.

"Time line is our first consideration. This shows that **NW** (*Nain woman*) and **MM** (*Mary Magdalene*) could be identical. So, we check this yes?" asked Kim. Tiffany and Sarah nodded.

"Evidence: Magdala and Nain are within walking distance. We know **MM**, Joanna, and Susanna followed Jesus after he left Nain. Evidence is not conclusive, but it could be **NW** and **MM** are the same. Likely or possible?" Tiffany and Sarah nodded.

"Opportunity: Mary Magdalene was in Nain about the time Jesus was there. Yes, no doubt, she had opportunity," said Kim. "Now, modus operandi, this is difficult to evaluate, since **NW** used anointing oil, and we don't know much yet about **MM's** MO, or ministry operation as you suggested, Sarah. What do you think?"

"Maybe, we should just put down an unknown." said Tiffany. Sarah nodded in agreement.

"Motive?" said Kim. "One was a sinner and the other had seven devils to contend with. I would say that **NW** (*Nain Woman*) and **MM** (*Mary Magdalene*) both had an almost identical motive. Check it yes?"

Again, Tiffany and Sarah nodded in agreement.

Now, let's sum it up," said Kim. "Time line—Yes; Evidence—Likely; Opportunity—Yes; MO—unknown; Motive—Yes. We have three yeses, a likely, and one unknown."

"OK," questioned Sarah. "Do you think this would be enough to unhang a jury and have them agree that the alabaster woman and Mary Magdalene are one and the same?"

"If I were on the jury, I would vote yes," said Tiffany.

"I think I would abstain at the point," said Kim. "There's quite a bit of evidence, but I'm just not convinced yet. However, I would admit that if this were a civil jury requiring only a majority, it would probably go the way of NW and MM being the same person."

"OK, take off that chart and stick it on the wall. We will start considering the next question before our hung jury: Is Mary Magdalene and Mary of Bethany one and the same person? You will find that the next time line references to Mary Magdalene in the four gospels are involved with the crucifixion. Jesus' interaction with Mary of Bethany—the one who sat at Jesus' feet while her sister Martha complained about kitchen duty—was in the time period leading up to the crucifixion."

"Yeah, my heart goes out to Martha." said Tiffany, "I often thought about her when I was cleaning up the dishes down at Shannon's Steak House. Tonight, I feel more like the Mary who got to discuss spiritual things."

"Before we start looking at Mary of Bethany, I need to put in another scripture, so we don't get out of sequence on the time line." stated Sarah, "Dalmanutha ... Dalmanutha—searching—searching—uh—here it is." Sarah pointed at the laptop screen.

MARK 8:10-12 *And straightway he entered into a ship with his disciples, and came into the parts of* ***Dalmanutha.*** *And the Pharisees came forth, and began to question with him, seeking of him a sign from heaven, tempting him. And he sighed deeply in his spirit, and saith, Why doth this generation seek after a sign? verily I say unto you, There shall no sign be given unto this generation.*

Kim and Tiffany read the scriptures and returned a blank look to Sarah.

"What does this have to do with Mary Magdalene?" questioned Tiffany.

Sarah explained this event happened on a later tour of Jesus when he once again came through the sea of Galilee area. Some say that Dalmanutha and Magdala are the same town. Others say that Dalmanutha is a little village adjacent to Magdala.

"Gee!" said Tiffany, "How did you know that? I'm impressed."

"Well, I'm not really all that smart," replied Sarah. "My grandma showed this to me, when she was telling about the sign from heaven the Pharisees requested. Actually, they really had been given a sign."

"What sign were they given?" asked Kim.

"We are not told this in Mark, but we can find it in some of the other gospels," replied Sarah. "Let's see...Jonas...here it is."

LUKE 11:29-30 *And when the people were gathered thick together, he began to say, This is an evil generation: they seek a sign; and* **there shall no sign be given it, but the sign of Jonas** *the prophet.* **For as Jonas was a sign unto the Ninevites, so shall also the Son of man be to this generation**.

"I can see a analogy between Jonas' preaching and Jesus' preaching. Is there more to it than this?"

Sarah clicked on the word "Jonah" and then clicked on the pull down for the Bible dictionary and said, "Look, the meaning of '*Jonah*' in the Hebrew is '*dove*.'"

Kim looked at Sarah quizzically and wondered if Sarah would open up the subject of doves with Tiffany. Strange that the Pharisees rejected Jesus and most likely his follower, Mary Magdalene, in Mary's own city. She wondered if the sign of the dove given to the Pharisees was Mary Magdalene herself.

"Oh, I see," said Tiffany. "The Pharisees not only rejected Jesus, but they were also rejecting the Holy Spirit which came down on Him in the form of a dove when He was baptized."

"That is one way of looking at it," agreed Sarah. "So, on our time line on the next sheet, let's put down our data."

Tiffany wrote: Dalmanutha, MM's hometown, rejection of Jesus by Pharisees, Jonah—sign of dove.

"Great summary, Tiff," said Sarah. "Now let's move forward to Mary of Bethany—the sister of Lazarus who was raised from the dead. Before getting into the scriptures about Mary of Bethany, let's consider what some of the early church fathers had to say about Mary of Bethany and Mary Magdalene. Let's see...let me try the internet. Here it is—a reference from one of the encyclopedias":

> '**Tradition as early as the 3rd century** (Hippolytus, in his *Commentary on the Song of Solomon*) **identifies Mary Magdalene with Mary of Bethany and the woman sinner who anointed Jesus's feet.**'

"Let's see—let me do a search for Origen, another early church father who wrote a commentary on the Song of Songs. Whoops! Wrong one—here's the book index—finding Mary. Here's the quote from Origen (184-254AD)." said Sarah.

> 'What difference, therefore, does it make whether it is the Bride in the Song of Songs who anoints the Bridegroom with ointment or the disciple Mary in the Gospel who anoints her Master Christ, hoping, as we said, that by that ointment the odour of the Word and the fragrance of Christ will be returned to her, so that she too may say: We are a good odour ... unto God?'

"Hmm—I wonder if Origen's reference to Mary as a disciple put her on a par with the other twelve disciples, or is he writing in a more generic sense that we are all disciples of Christ?" mused Kim.

"We'll add early Christian writings and Hippolytus and Origen's commentaries on Song of Songs to our chart," suggested Tiffany. "Now, what can we say about Mary of Bethany's ministry?"

"Here are some Mary of Bethany scriptures. We'll call her MB for short," said Sarah.

"Great, now we've got **NW** (*Nain Woman*), **MM** (*Mary Magdalene*), and **MB** (*Mary of Bethany*). We can talk in code!" laughed Kim.

Sarah pulled up several Mary of Bethany scriptures on her computer.

JOHN 11:1-5 *Now a certain man was sick, named* **Lazarus, of Bethany, the town of Mary and her sister Martha. (It was that Mary which anointed the Lord with ointment, and wiped his feet with her hair,** *whose brother Lazarus was sick.) Therefore his sisters sent unto him, saying, Lord, behold, he whom thou lovest is sick. When Jesus heard that, he said, This sickness is not unto death, but for the glory of God, that the Son of God might be glorified thereby. Now Jesus loved Martha, and her sister, and Lazarus.*

LUKE 10:38-42 *Now it came to pass, as they went, that he entered into a certain village: and a certain woman named* **Martha received him into her house And she had a sister called Mary, which also sat at Jesus' feet,** *and heard his word. But Martha was cumbered about much serving, and came to him, and said, Lord, dost thou not care that my sister hath left me to serve alone? bid her therefore that she help me. And Jesus answered and said unto her, Martha, Martha, thou art careful and troubled about many things: But one thing is needful: and* **Mary hath chosen that good part, which shall not be taken away from her.**

Sarah said, "We need a map to see where Magdala, Nain, and Bethany are. Searching ...ah, we have our map. See Bethany is down near Jerusalem and Magdala is near the Sea of Galilee."

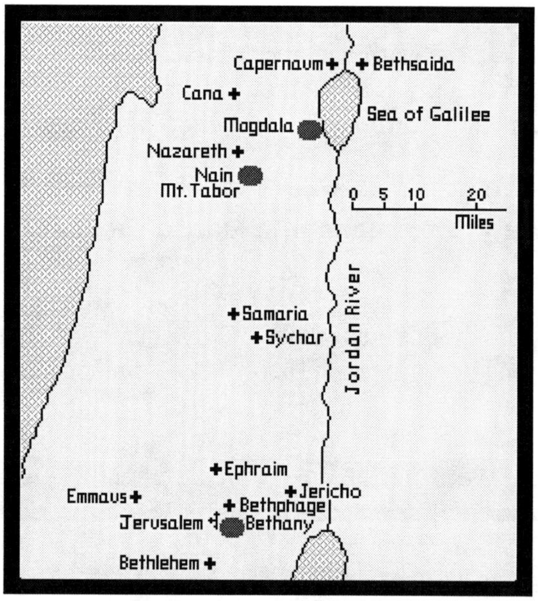

Kim mused, "It is possible that Martha and Mary were originally located at Magdala and then, following Jesus, later moved to Bethany. But, that would only be supposition."

"Wow! We have a gold mine of information to add to our charts," exclaimed Tiffany. "First, we can add that MB was Lazarus' sister. Then, for MO, we can say that MB was the one who anointed the feet of Jesus and wiped his feet with her hair. This is just about identical to the MO that we had for NW—the woman sinner who broke the alabaster box and anointed the feet of Jesus in Simon the pharisee's house in Nain. Keep going, Tiff."

"We can show on MO that Mary of Bethany—uh MB—loved to sit at the feet of Jesus. And for evidence we can say MB is Martha's sister and is staying at Martha's house."

"One thing is so clear from this," observed Tiffany. "Mary treasured sitting at the feet of Jesus and learning from him. I remember the old saying—it isn't in the Bible—that cleanliness is next to godliness. Busy Martha chose second best, and Mary chose godliness."

The group knew the story about Lazarus well, so they skipped the part about Jesus delaying to come to Bethany until Lazarus had been dead for about four days and went on to these scriptures.

JOHN 11:17-27 *Then when Jesus came, he found that he had lain in the grave four days already. Now Bethany was nigh unto Jerusalem, about fifteen furlongs off: And many of the Jews came to Martha and Mary, to comfort them concerning their brother. Then Martha, as soon as she heard that Jesus was coming, went and met him: but Mary sat still in the house. Then said Martha unto Jesus, Lord, if thou hadst been here, my brother had not died. But I know, that even now, whatsoever thou wilt ask of God, God will give it thee. Jesus saith unto her, Thy brother shall rise again. Martha saith unto him,* **I know that he shall rise again in the resurrection at the last day.** *Jesus said unto her, I am the resurrection, and the life: he that believeth in me, though he were dead, yet shall he live:* [26] **And whosoever liveth and believeth in me shall never die. Believest thou this?** [27] *She saith unto him, Yea, Lord: I believe that thou art the Christ, the Son of God, which should come into the world.*

"Kim, we have discussed the 11th chapter of John before," said Sarah. "How would you interpret verse 26, and do you think that Martha even understood it or did it go right over her head?"

Kim remembered that studying the 11th chapter of John was part of her homework on determining the different types of bodies. She saw Sarah give her a slight but knowing smile. "I doubt Martha even understood it," said Kim. "However, I would rather overcome death than die and have to be resurrected."

Tiffany seemed puzzled by the exchange between Sarah and Kim.

So Sarah quickly changed the subject. "OK, let's see what happens next."

JOHN 11:28 *And when she had so said, she went her way,* **and called Mary her sister secretly, saying, The Master is come, and calleth for thee.**
29 *As soon as she heard that, she arose quickly, and came unto him.*
30 *Now Jesus was not yet come into the town, but was in that place where Martha met him.*
31 *The Jews then which were with her in the house, and comforted her, when they saw Mary, that she rose up hastily and went out, followed her, saying, She goeth unto the grave to weep there.*
32 **Then when Mary was come where Jesus was, and saw him, she fell down at his feet**, *saying unto him, Lord, if thou hadst been here, my brother had not died.*

Tiffany proposed the relationship between Jesus and MB was a deep relationship, because Jesus wanted to talk to MB privately. She wrote: Jesus & MB deep relationship.

"And look, " said Kim, "There MB is at the feet of Jesus again. It seems to be a pattern."

"You know the story of how Jesus raised Lazurus from the dead," said Sarah, "so we won't go into it here. But after Lazurus is resurrected, there is another tidbit about MB. Here it is:"

JOHN 11:44-47 *And he that was dead came forth, bound hand and foot with graveclothes: and his face was bound about with a napkin. Jesus saith unto them, Loose him, and let him go.* **Then many of the Jews which came to Mary, and had seen the things which Jesus did, believed on him**. *But some of them went their ways to the Pharisees, and told them what things Jesus had done. Then gathered the chief priests and the Pharisees a council, and said, What do we? for this man doeth many miracles.*

"I see the tidbit," said Tiffany. "MB apparently had told the Jews about the ministry of Jesus. Maybe Origen was right in calling her a disciple. Let's put down MB—a minister for Jesus. Probably the Pharisees were upset at her, too."

"Yes, that's true." agreed Sarah, "There is an incident concerning the Pharisees that happened just before NW broke the alabaster box and anointed Jesus' feet at Nain. Maybe we should look at it now because it shows the Pharisee's attitude."

LUKE 7:34-37 **The Son of man is come eating and drinking; and ye say, Behold a gluttonous man, and a winebibber, a friend of publicans and sinners!** *But wisdom is justified of all her children. And one of the Pharisees desired him that he would eat with him. And he went into the Pharisee's house, and sat down to meat.* **And, behold, a woman in the city, which was a sinner, ...**

"Gee," said Kim with a knowing glance at Sarah. "Do you think that if Jesus were in River City today, he would visit the pool halls—'starts with P and rhymes with T and spells Trouble'—or maybe even minister to those down at Joe's Rendezvous? If Dr. Simon Starchy, pastor of the River City Aloof Church, heard about it, he would probably be quite upset. He wouldn't want those trashy people coming to his church!"

Sarah, Kim, and Tiffany all had a big laugh. Kim was on a roll with her witticisms.

"That's the type of place where we found my adventurous niece—in front of Manny's Main Street Bar. She felt that her life was hopeless and one of the scriptures that my mother gave to her—Sarah, find it on your word search on the computer—it was something about harlots and the kingdom."

Sarah nodded:

MATTHEW 21:31 ... *Verily I say unto you, That* **the publicans and the harlots go into the kingdom of God before you.**

"You know," reflected Tiffany, "I'm beginning to get a different view of Jesus. If He came to this river city like in biblical times, I think He would spend more of His time with the poor white, black, or whatever trash, than He would in the majestic church buildings."

"I think you've seen a great truth," agreed Sarah. "Now, let's look at another set of scriptures that have their setting somewhere in Bethany. However, they don't say that it was Mary of Bethany or even Mary Magdalene."

MARK 14:3-10 *And* **being in Bethany in the house of Simon the leper, as he sat at meat, there came a woman having an alabaster box of ointment of spikenard very precious; and she brake the box, and poured it on his head.** *And there were some that had indignation within themselves, and said, Why was this waste of the ointment made?*

For it might have been sold for more than three hundred pence, and have been given to the poor. And they murmured against her. **And Jesus said, Let her alone**; *why trouble ye her? she hath wrought a good work on me. For ye have the poor with you always, and whensoever ye will ye may do them good: but me ye have not always.*

She hath done what she could: she is come aforehand to anoint my body to the burying. Verily I say unto you, **Wheresoever this gospel shall be preached throughout the whole world, this also that she hath done shall be spoken of for a memorial of her.** *And Judas Iscariot, one of the twelve, went unto the chief priests, to betray him unto them.*

Kim suggested other clues for the flip chart: MO—amazingly identical—the woman has an alabaster box of ointment. Anoints head instead of feet. Jesus establishes a memorial for her and the location is Bethany instead of Nain.

"Yeah," said Tiffany. "And look, it is in the house of Simon, but in this case he is a leper. Do you think the Simon the Pharisee in Nain was stricken with leprosy and had to move to another place?"

"Might just be coincidence," analyzed Kim. "The name Simon in the first century may be like Smith or Jones today."

"I agree." concurred Sarah, "The same is true with the name Mary. Have you ever thought about why we commonly call 'Marys' by two names? For example, Mary Lou, Mary Ellen, Mary Lee, Mary Lynn, or Mary Anne. I would think it is because there are so many Marys that it helps in distinguishing them. This is probably part of the problem we are having in distinguishing between Mary Magdalene and the other Marys. I read an article about the names of women inscribed in burial sites at the time of Jesus. It was said that about one out of four women had the name Mary. And, as Kim says, Simon was also a very popular name. Perhaps Simon the Pharisee did 'touch the Lord's anointed. There is some precedent for this sort of thing," said Sarah. as she searched: "Verses...Moses...Miriam...leprous... searching...here it is. See."

NUMBERS 12:1-3,10 **And Miriam and Aaron spake against Moses because of the Ethiopian woman whom he had married**: *for he had married an Ethiopian woman. And they said, Hath the LORD indeed spoken only by Moses? hath he not spoken also by us? And the LORD heard it. (Now the man Moses was very meek, above all the men which were upon the face of the earth.) And the cloud departed from off the tabernacle; and, behold, Miriam became leprous, white as snow: and Aaron looked upon Miriam, and,* **behold, she was leprous.**

"Wow! You're right! It doesn't pay to criticize the Lord's anointed," said Tiffany. "I didn't know Moses' wife was an Ethiopian. I thought maybe she was of Arab type descent, you know, in the desert."

"You're thinking about Zipporah—she was a Midianite of the desert," replied Sarah. "The Bible doesn't give details on Moses' first wife, but it does refer to the book of Jasher twice, and the book of Jasher describes the Ethiopian wife."

"I don't remember the book of Jasher," questioned Tiffany. Are you sure it's mentioned in the Bible?"

"Oh, yes, "replied Sarah. "Let me run the references on the computer. Jasher verse references? There it is: JOSHUA 10:13 and II SAMUEL 1:18. Believe me now?"

"Did you learn this from your grandma, too?" questioned Tiffany.

"Oh, no," laughed Sarah. "I learned it from my uncle. There are instances of leprosy suddenly striking a person in the Old Testament. It was King Uzziah who was the Lord's servant until he became proud and criticized the priests. When he transgressed the Lord's anointed, he became leprous in his forehead and fell into disgrace. Then, there is the story of a Syrian king's servant who had leprosy and received instructions from Elijah to dip seven times in the Jordan river. There's the seven matrices of cleansing again. The servant was cured of his leprosy, but Elijah's servant wanted to pick up some change as payment for Elijah's ministry on the sly. The Lord showed this to Elijah, and his servant was stricken with leprosy."

"It seems like the woman breaking the alabaster box and anointing the head of Jesus was a breaking point for Judas, also. Jesus did not appreciate Judas criticizing the woman. At the same time, Judas was ticked about Jesus defending the actions of the woman. Was Judas jealous of the woman anointing Jesus and simply snapped? After this, he scurried out to find the chief priests and schemed to betray Jesus."

"Kim, you're very perceptive," said Sarah. "We can only speculate, but there is some evidence that Simon the leper and Judas may have been related. Look at these verses from the book of John:

JOHN 6:70-72 *Jesus answered them, Have not I chosen you twelve, and one of you is a devil? He spake of* **Judas Iscariot the son of Simon: for he it was that should betray him**, *being one of the twelve.* 13:26 *Jesus answered, He it is, to whom I shall give a sop, when I have dipped it. And when he had dipped the sop, he gave it to* **Judas Iscariot, the son of Simon**. *And after the sop Satan entered into him. Then said Jesus unto him, That thou doest, do quickly.*

"Gee, that does really make you think. I never connected Judas with being the son of Simon," said Tiffany. "We've got a lot of details here, and we've fallen behind on getting them on our Christ Scene Investigation chart."

Just then the phone rang, and Kim and answered it. "Hello...Hi Mom. Really? When? What's her name? Just a minute." Kim put her hand over the mouthpiece and said, "It's Mom...my sister Wanda just had her baby about two hours ago!" Resuming the conversation, she said, "Mom, I'm back. How's Wanda doing? What did it weigh?"

Sarah motioned to Tiffany and suggested they call it quits for the night. She knew that Kim tended to have long conversations with her mother. Tiffany agreed and thanked Sarah for having Kim participate in the discussions and adding her insights. She picked up her things to leave.

"I'll walk with you down to the lobby," said Sarah. As they continued walking Sarah asked, "Tiff, one thing I don't understand is why Nancy wants to go to the movie with you. She knows you have reservations about it."

"She's not trying to bug me," said Tiffany. "The problem is Floyd is going out of town and has a date for both Friday and Saturday night. Nancy wants me to borrow my Mom's car and take her."

"Well, Floyd could take her on the following weekend."

"Not really." said Tiffany, "You know how Floyd is, science is his god and he told Nancy that he wouldn't waste his time or money going to see a movie about Christian myths."

"OK, I see the problem."

"Sarah, I don't know what to do. Should I risk offending Nancy by saying no, or should I risk spending money to support a movie that might desecrate Christ? I don't know about this movie."

"Neither do I," said Sarah. "I have a suggestion for you. You and your Mom are really close and can talk to each other. Why don't you have a heart to heart talk with her and decide?"

"Thanks, Sarah, I will," said Tiffany. She gave Sarah a hug and opened the door. "Bye."

Sarah returned to the dorm room and found Kim still chatting away. After a while, Kim hung up the phone and said, "Guess What?"

"What?"

"Wanda's baby is named Mary Beth. It was born at 7:59, weighs 7 lbs, 8 oz., and is 21 inches long."

"Mary Beth…interesting name, huh?"

Kim apologized for interrupting the CSI but observed they probably couldn't have finished the study that evening anyway. She wondered out loud how Tiffany was reacting to the content of their study session.

"As far as I can tell, she seems to be coming along very well," said Sarah. "I did not want to get deep into the subject of doves with her, but that may come in due time. Who knows—maybe you will be the one to tell her about it, Kim."

"Yes, I appreciate you taking your time with me. I probably would have choked if you had dropped all this on me at one time," said Kim.

Sarah then related to Kim the story her aunt had told her about a church pastor in Trinidad. He had apparently received a number of revelations from the Lord and began to blab all of them in a short period of time to his church. And as one might guess, it caused controversy. He had a dream in which he was giving his three month old baby a bottle of milk. There was some steak left over on the table from lunch, and he heard the Lord say, 'Give the baby some steak.' 'I can't do that Lord!' he said, 'It would choke the baby!' 'Yes, it would,' said the Lord. 'Quit choking my little ones until they have been prepared for meat.'"

"Interesting story. I suppose the pastor was caught up in spiritual pride because God had chosen him for special revelations," observed Kim.

"Most likely," responded Sarah. "Unfortunately, when some people receive special revelation, shall we say at a college level, they want to go back and burn down the high school, the grade school, and the kindergarten. But God needs these beginning grades for the young ones coming along till we all come in the unity of the faith and full knowledge of the Son of God. However, sometimes we have a grade school teacher who thinks his denomination knows it all and does not want anyone to graduate to high school."

GALATIONS 4:1-2 *Now I say, That the heir, as long as he is a child, differeth nothing from a servant, though he be lord of all;* **But is under tutors and governors until the time appointed of the father.**

"God has placed those in our lives to tutor us," continued Sarah. "When we are spiritual babes, we need the milk of the word. As we mature, we need the meat of the word, and then later the strong meat of the word—all to be digested with the help of the Spirit. It is very important that we give due honor to those that God has placed there to tutor us. At the same time, there is something wrong with the picture of a forty-year-old man taking milk from a baby bottle. So, let us pray those teachers that God has placed along our way will promote us from grade to grade as we are ready, but not before we are ready."

Kim asked Sarah about what happens if the tutors and governors abuse their position. Sarah told her about the concept of God's woodshed. She used the example of Moses who struck the rock in anger when he was in the desert. The people needed the water from the rock to drink, so God chose to punish Moses at a later time, rather than right in front of the people. Later on the leadership of Moses was replaced by the leadership of Joshua who took the Hebrews into the promised land.

"Sarah, thanks for not choking me. What do you think about this new movie *The Towers of Magdala*? How do you think they will treat the life of NW, MM, and MB? And why do they call it the towers?"

"Hard to tell what Hollywood will do. As far as the towers, here let me show you on the computer what the Bible Dictionary says about Magdala."

The Towers of Magdala

Magdala (tower) In most of the MSS. the name is Magadan. Christ came into the limits of Magdala after the miracle of feeding the 4,000 on the other side of the lake. Now called El Mejdel, on the W shore of the Sea of Galilee, close to the water, about 3 miles north of Tiberias, at the SE corner of the plain of Gennesaret. There was a watch tower here that guarded the entrance to the plain. Here was the home of Mary Magdalene. Dalmanutha in Mark.

"I can see why they might call it the tower of Magdala, but why towers?" asked Kim.
"I was afraid you would ask that," replied Sarah. "Here is your answer."

SONG OF SOLOMON 8:10 *I am a wall, and my breasts like* **towers***: then was I in his eyes as one that found favour.*

"Oooh! I can see what you're talking about," surmised Kim. "How do you think they will handle this delicate allegory in the movie?"
"It depends on the motives of those making the movie," replied Sarah. "Actually, breasts are translated from the Hebrew 'shad.' One of the Hebrew encyclopedias refer to the feminine part of the Godhead—El Shaddai—in the terms of the hills and mountains (breasts) of God or the breasted one of God. Perhaps, Mary Magdalene, after her conversion was a symbol of this, particularly as a teacher of the gospel. So, I hope and pray that Hollywood doesn't mess this one up."
Kim and Sarah went through their Wednesday and Thursday classes uneventfully. That evening Kim had gone to the library, and Sarah, tired from the classes, decided to take a nap. The phone rang, it was Tiffany.
"Hi, Tiffany. Have you had your talk with your Mom?"
"Yes, I did," said Tiffany. "My Mom is a very wonderful person, and we talked for a long time."
"What did you decide?"
"Mom thought I was well prepared to judge things for myself, so she thought it would be OK to go to the movie and check it out. So I called Nancy and told her I would pick her up tomorrow."
"OK," noted Sarah. "At least you can quit worrying about offending Nancy. Actually, I think Nancy would completely understand if you had told her you didn't want to go and why. But maybe this is something you were supposed to work out within yourself."
"That's not all," said Tiffany.
"What do you mean?"
"It was on the evening news tonight. There is a big controversy about the foreign rights to the showing of *The Towers of Magdala.* A federal judge has issued a restraining order on the showing of the movie. Its opening will be delayed a minimum of two weeks and maybe more if the parties do not show 'substantial progress' in reaching an agreement."
"So, do you still plan to go when it opens?"
"I think so. We'll see when it actually does open. In any case, I want to thank you for the wonderful evening that I spent with you and Kim. I know a lot more about NW, MM, and MB than I ever did before. My mother was very interested in this also. We talked for a long time, and she pointed out that Mary Magdalene, and some other women brought sweet spices to anoint the body of Jesus. I guess that's part of her MO. Talking this over did something deep down, my mother and I bonded like never before. Again, I want to thank you so much," said Tiffany as she and Sarah said their byes.

Editors Note: Express your thoughts.
See http://www.TheAncientChest.com/Women

Which statement best expresses your thinking?

☐ 1. The woman at Nain who broke the alabaster box and Mary Magdalene were two different women.

☐ 2. The woman at Nain who broke the alabaster box and Mary Magdalene are the same woman.

☐ 3. Haven't reached a conclusion yet.

☐ 4. Leaning toward choice #1

☐ 5. Leaning toward choice #2.

Chapter 6

For This Cause Came I into the World

"Sarah, last night when Tiffany was here, you highlighted for me a verse in the 11th chapter of John. I've been mulling over this verse, and some others you said would give insight into the different types of bodies. Here's a list that I've come up with so far. Let me show you on your computer."

JOHN 11:25-26 *Jesus said unto her, I am the resurrection, and the life: he that believeth in me, though he were dead, yet shall he live: And* **whosoever liveth and believeth in me shall never die**. *Believest thou this?*

1CORINTHIANS 15:40-41 *There are also celestial bodies, and bodies terrestrial: but the glory of the celestial is one, and the glory of the terrestrial is another. There is* **one glory of the sun**, *and* **another glory of the moon**, *and* **another glory of the stars**: *for one star differeth from another star in glory.*

"Could there be three types of bodies, like the sun, moon, and stars?" asked Kim.

Sarah encouraged Kim that she was on the right track. She explained that there is an earthly body, which we know about; and there is a body angels have, which is like the resurrection body. *For in the resurrection they neither marry, nor are given in marriage, but are as the angels of God in heaven.* But the resurrection body is like that of the angels. She didn't see any scriptures on Kim's list from the first or second chapter of Hebrews where it says that Jesus and eventually those with Him will be higher than the angels. She suggested Kim consider Jacob's ladder. Also, consider Paul spoke about one—was it Paul himself or someone else—being caught up to the third heaven?

Kim wondered what it was that Jesus meant when He stood before Mary Magdalene in His resurrected body. Was He telling her that He had to ascend first or what was it He told her in the garden?

Sarah found these scriptures to describe the dialog at the tomb.

JOHN 20:16-17 *Jesus saith unto her, Mary. She turned herself, and saith unto him, Rabboni; which is to say, Master. Jesus saith unto her,* **Touch me not; for I am not yet ascended to my Father**: *but go to my brethren, and say unto them, I ascend unto my Father, and your Father; and to my God, and your God.*

"Kim, I think you are beginning put together some pieces of the puzzle, but remember I told you this was a trick question about Jesus and MM. Let's leave this one for further study and go on to another subject. Remember we were talking about the 'heavenbefore,' and we put a tag on whether the doves knew about their script or destiny before they ever descended into the earth realm and veil of forgetfulness was placed over them?"

"Yeah, I remember it." said Kim.

"Well, it's sort of like in our English Lit class when we read Shakespeare's *As You Like It.* Googling it... Here it is."

"All the world's a stage, And all the men and women merely players: They have their exits and entrances; and one man in his times plays many parts, His acts being seven ages. At first the infant, Mewling and puking in his nurses arms. And then the whining schoolboy ..."

"Kim, remember the seven seals that you scotch taped on? One of those is an understanding of the heavenbefore, so you can understand the here and the hereafter. It's time to remove that seal so you can go on to other things. Jesus put it this way..."

JOHN 18:37 *Pilate therefore said unto him, Art thou a king then? Jesus answered, Thou sayest that I am a king.* **To this end was I born, and for this cause came I into the world**, *that I should bear witness unto the truth. Every one that is of the truth heareth my voice.*

"Remember you had the dream about the dove knocking at the door and finding an old ornate book you started reading, but couldn't remember what was in it?"

"Yes."

"It's time to begin to open that book and see what your manifest destiny is."

After some discussion, Sarah and Kim agreed on getting together once again in the old stone church on the following Saturday to begin opening the book of destiny. Then it was time for lunch at the cafeteria. Kim got a baked potato with broccoli and cheese, and Sarah dug into a turkey sandwich. As they were munching away, they saw Fred coming from the serving table with his plate of roast beef. Katie, Fred's fiancee, was still in line while Fred searched for a table for them.

"Uh, oh, here comes Fred," whispered Kim.

"Hi girls," said Fred, smiling brightly. "I just wanted to tell you I researched our discussion about the Supreme Court justice, and I have some answers about Deborah being a judge. Also, I would like to talk to you some time about what the New Testament says about women teaching men in the church."

"OK," said Sarah, "When?"

"Katie and I are going on a church retreat on marriage this weekend. Would it be all right, if I called you next week and set up a time?"

"That's fine, Fred. Give me a call. Tell Katie 'Hi.'"

Kim and Sarah waved at Katie as Fred hustled off to join her.

"Sarah, you're a glutton for punishment!" said Kim. "You know what Fred will do. He will clunk you over the head with Paul's *But I let not a woman to teach men* scripture, smile at you, and say 'How do you explain that, Sarah?' He would dearly love to give you payback on the Judge Deborah incident that happened down at Campus Pizza."

"Oh, I know," said Sarah. "I'm expecting that."

"Aren't you worried about explaining it to Fred?"

"Not at all," said Sarah. "Can I let you in on somewhat of a secret?" offered Sarah.

"OK, I'm all ears."

"I need to ask you some questions."

"I should have known," complained Kim. "Go ahead and torture me instead of just telling me the secret. Let the torture begin."

"OK, consider this—the LORD God cursed the ground so that Adam had to till the ground by the sweat of his brow to have food. Adam even had to hoe out the thorns and thistles. Do you think the ground will be cursed forever?"

"I don't think so," said Kim. "It would seem to me that God would remove this curse and the earth would flourish during the thousand year reign when Jesus returns."

"Good answer. Now, next question: The woman was told that in sorrow, she would bring forth children. Do you think this will go on forever?"

"Oh God! I hope not. I remember my sister's first child. She was screaming to high heaven!"

"OK, then you would agree that fighting thorns and thistles and screaming in pain during childbirth are not good and desirable things?"

"Oh, definitely!"

"Then," asked Sarah, "What about the other part that the LORD God told the woman? Remember she was told her desire would be toward her husband, and he would rule over her?"

"Gee, I would have to think about that," said Kim. "I always thought that was the way it was supposed to be."

Sarah told Kim about a conversation with her grandma that helped her put some of the seeming paradoxes in the current church age in their proper perspective. Grandma related how the Pharisees, representing the law given in the wilderness, were in total shock when Jesus began preaching. He taught about something beyond the law of outward appearances—fulfilling the inner law—grace, love, forgiveness, and mercy. Grandma asked why it should be any different at the dawning of the new millennium. Would the church system of today be in for any less of a surprise? The scriptures give a marvelous destiny for the daughters of Zion and the daughters of Jerusalem, but very little has yet been fulfilled. Grandma quoted that Paul told the New Testament Church that they only knew *in part* and *saw through a glass darkly.* No doubt the Pharisees of Jesus' day thought their way was 'the way it was supposed to be' and didn't want to change.

"Talking about a script—how would you like to have Eve's script?"

"Wow! She gets blamed for almost everything," said Kim. "She made one little, or maybe big, slip up and everything came crashing down on her. Even Adam said, 'The woman made me do it.'"

"Do you think that she was subject to vanity?"

"Well, probably so. She wanted to be wise and beautiful."

"When we get back to the room, I will show you a scripture that will make you really think about the roles of Adam and Eve. Let's head back."

They returned to their room and Sarah opened the large Bible sitting on the coffee table to Romans 8 and pointed to verses 20-23.

20 For the creature was made subject to vanity, ***not willingly****, but by reason of him who hath subjected the same in hope, 21 Because the creature itself also shall be delivered from the bondage of corruption into the glorious liberty of the children of God. 22 For we know that the whole creation groaneth and travaileth in pain together until now. 23 And not only they, but ourselves also, which have the firstfruits of the Spirit, even we ourselves groan within ourselves, waiting for the adoption, to wit, the redemption of our body.*

"Now look at verse 20. I ask you this question: Were Adam and Eve willingly made subject to vanity?"

"Sarah, you're blowing my mind! Gee, maybe things from God's view are much different than I thought. *The creature was made subject to vanity,* ***not willingly ...*** Does this mean what I think it does?"

"Food for thought. Maybe your mind or soul needs to be blown so you can hear from your spirit," said Sarah. "Come Saturday, we will look at what our spirits might have known about our fate before we ever came to earth. To this end we were born and for this cause came we into the world."

That night was dark and stormy, and the emergency alert system sounded. All the students were hustled into the basement of the dorm at 2:30 am because the Doppler weather system had picked up tornadic wind circulation. The lightning flashed and the thunder shook even the old stone building. Most were nonchalant about it, but underneath there were quite a few silent prayers to let the system pass without damage.

Finally, the red and purple splotches on the Doppler TV pattern moved toward the east, showing the storm had passed over without harm to the city. Some of the TV news people were saying that "tornado alley" had moved eastward from Oklahoma. When the thunder and lightning was so violent, Kim and Sarah had noticed quite a few white faces there in the basement.

"That's kind of the way life is," observed Sarah. "Most events are not that important. It is just day to day stuff. But I think the big events are written in the book of our life. Take Job, he was paddling down the river of life very serenely until catastrophes struck, and he didn't understand it until he was caught up in the whirlwind."

"The whirlwind?" questioned Kim. "What do you mean?"

"Here, let me show you," replied Sarah. "See Job's sudden awakening by the Lord scriptures in chapter 38."

JOB 38:1-4 **Then the LORD answered Job out of the whirlwind**, *and said, Who is this that darkeneth counsel by words without knowledge? Gird up now thy loins like a man; for I will demand of thee, and answer thou me.* **Where wast thou when I laid the foundations of the earth?** *declare, if thou hast understanding.*

"So, Kim, where were you when the LORD laid the foundations of the earth?"

"I never even thought of that," said Kim. "I suppose we will get into this on Saturday."

"It will keep till then," said Sarah. "Let's get back to bed. We have classes in a few hours."

Band after band of showers came Friday with street flooding in some low lying areas. Then came Saturday morning with a beautiful, clear blue sky, brilliant sunshine, and the greenest of grass. The birds were singing, the flowers blooming and it was a great day to be alive.

Sarah and Kim split a Texas omelet and gathered up their study materials to head for the old stone church. A group of girl scouts were meeting in a number of the rooms, so they wandered back behind the altar and found an unoccupied room where the choir robes and communion utensils were stored. The assistant pastor, noting they had a Bible, gave them permission to use the room.

Sarah's question about where Kim was before the foundation of the world bothered Kim. Her concept was that she was no older than the day she was born or maybe when she was conceived. Now, she pondered if her spirit might be older than she thought. She decided to ask Sarah about when spirits came into being.

"Good question. Actually new spirits are being created all the time. However, some spirits are much older than others." Sarah flipped open her laptop saying, "Look at this and tell me what the difference might be between old spirits and young spirits. By the way you will read the answer later in the old booklet that I will show you."

ACTS *2:16-17 But this is that which was spoken by the prophet Joel; And it shall come to pass in the last days, saith God, I will pour out of my Spirit upon all flesh: and your sons and your daughters shall prophesy, and* **your young men shall see visions**, *and* **your old men shall dream dreams***:*

"Oh, I remember this," observed Kim. "This is what Peter said about the day of Pentecost. Hmm...I think...no wait...old men dream dreams...young men see visions. Could it be the younger men, or should I say younger spirits, weren't there when earlier events happened? Maybe the vision is like a DVR recording of an event that has already happened."

Sarah thought so. A vision could also be of something in the future, so an ancient spirit could also have a vision of something that is to happen in the future. Job, in his spirit, saw future and past. If Job had been present to watch the creation of the earth, over 2000 years of earth time would have elapsed before he sat in the dust and scraped his boils. Yet Job seemed to have watched the creation of the earth. How could he have written this back in the days when most of the people thought the earth was flat? Job's view seemed to be one of a NASA astronaut viewing the compass of day and night on the earth. A compass draws a circle. How could Job have possibly viewed the edge of day and night as it made a circle around the entire globe?

JOB 26:7-10 *He stretcheth out the north over the empty place, and* **hangeth the earth upon nothing**. *He bindeth up the waters in his thick clouds; and the cloud is not rent under them. He holdeth back the face of his throne, and spreadeth his cloud upon it.* **He hath compassed the waters with bounds, until the day and night come to an end**.

"Wow!" exclaimed Kim. "The earth does hang in space on nothing. And the astronauts did see the earth's light and the darkness, or day and night, from the moon. Maybe Job actually did see creation!"

"I remember the shocked look on your face when I asked you where you were when the foundations of the earth were laid," said Sarah. "Don't you think Job was just as shocked when the LORD spoke about the timing of Job's birth?"

"Did he do that? He must have been talking about the birth of Job's spirit."

"Yes, he did. Some translations give it as a question, and others give it as a statement. I'm going to pull up the *King James* translation and the *Young's Literal Bible* translation, and you can look at them both."

[KING JAMES VERSION] JOB 38:21 *Knowest thou it, because thou wast then born? or because the number of thy days is great?*

[YOUNG'S LITERAL] JOB 38:21 **Thou hast known - for then thou art born And the number of thy days {are} many!**

"Ooh, you're right," agreed Kim. "Which translation do you think is right?"

"More than likely the *Young's* translation, since it tries to do a word for word translation even if the sentence in English is a bit more broken."

"I see what you mean. The LORD could have been telling Job that his spirit—not his body or soul—was there and saw creation," said Kim.

"Now, I want you to consider a possibility, which is a real shocker—we don't know this for sure—but do you think that Job's spirit made an agreement with God that he would go to earth and endure many tribulations and that agreement was made before he came into the earthly womb?"

"If he did, what a fool he was!" exclaimed Kim.

"What if **God** asked you to do the same thing?" questioned Sarah. "Would you do it?"

Kim looked dumbstruck and struggled to answer.

"That's OK, Kim. Don't try to figure this out just now. I think you are ready to read something else that I found in the chest. It is called *The Scrolls of the Ancients*."

"The Scrolls of the Ancients—have I heard that before?" asked Kim.

"You probably have, you just didn't realize its significance," responded Sarah. "It is based on a New Testament scripture, which is a quote from Psalm 40's roll of a scroll, or a book as we call it. The volume of the book or the roll of the scroll is also mentioned in the book of Hebrews. Here is the reference from Hebrews."

HEBREWS 10:5-7 **Wherefore when he cometh into the world**, *he saith, Sacrifice and offering thou wouldest not, but a body hast thou prepared me: In burnt offerings and sacrifices for sin thou hast had no pleasure.* **Then said I, Lo, I come (in the volume of the book it is written of me,) to do thy will, O God.**

Sarah and Kim discussed whether these were the words spoken by the spirit of Jesus as he stripped himself of His heavenly garments and descended into the frequency of the earth to be carried to birth by the Virgin Mary. Kim turned over the possibility in her mind that not only did the spirit of Jesus speak these words, but other spirits, as they came from heaven to earth, spoke the same words about coming to do the will of God. Sarah reached into her briefcase and pulled out an old writing. Some of the pages toward the front were damaged or torn off, but what was left was readable.

"My aunt had this writing for many years," said Sarah. "There is an interesting story about how she found it. It goes back to just before she got married in the eighties."

"That is a while. How did she find it?"

"At that time, she was head over heels in love with Uncle Andy. The only problem was that he was in the Marines and stationed on a ship at sea most of the time. He tried but couldn't get leave to the States."

"Knowing your Aunt Myra, I'm sure she was quite resourceful," said Kim.

"Yes, she certainly was. They had figured out Uncle Andy would be in a port of call situation in Trinidad for a week. So Andy managed to get five days off from his commander in order to get married, but he could not leave Trinidad."

"And your aunt, did she fly down there to get married?"

"She certainly did," said Sarah. "Apparently Grandma about had a hissy fit, but she couldn't talk Myra out of it. After all she had saved some money, and it was hers to spend as she liked even if it was airplane fare to Trinidad. She and Andy wanted a Christian wedding so they found a church near the port area and made arrangements with the minister to get married."

"Do you think they were doves?" asked Kim.

"I don't think they could have known all these things if they weren't," replied Sarah. "Myra had taken a wedding dress with her and when she was dressing for the wedding in a side room, she noticed this booklet laying on the table. As she glanced at it, it really caught her attention."

"I would think her attention would be more on getting married," said Kim.

Sarah related that after the ceremony, when Myra went back to the room to change into street clothes, the booklet was still there. The pastor's wife came in to help her get things together. She picked up the book and asked the pastor's wife about it. "Oh, that was left over from a conference that was held last month. You can have it if you like," she replied. So, Myra slipped it into her bag.

"She read the book on her honeymoon?" questioned Kim.

"Oh no, I'm sure she and Andy were preoccupied with other things. However, on the plane on the way back to the States, she noticed the writing in her bag again and began to read it. She found it somewhat overwhelming and even cried, realizing her romance with Andy had been planned for a long, long time."

"How did you know about all this?" asked Kim. "Did Myra tell you?"

"Oh, no, she kept the book a secret. I only knew from Grandma about Aunt Myra's surprise trip to Trinidad. The other part I found out from a letter she had written to Uncle Andy about the unique booklet that she had found and read on the plane trip back. The letter was inside the back cover of the booklet, apparently saved by Andy as a love letter written just after the honeymoon."

Kim was very impressed with Sarah's detective work, but she wanted to stop talking about the book and actually look at it and hopefully read it.

Sensing Kim's impatience, Sarah told her she would indeed get to read the book and explained that some of the pages were missing or torn. However, in order to preserve the original, she had made copies for Kim. Sarah started to hand the copied pages to Kim and then pulled them back. "There is something else that I must tell you before you start reading the entire book," said Sarah. Noticing Kim's wince, Sarah continued, "No, I'm not trying to be melodramatic. This will help you understand something within yourself. and this booklet is an excellent laboratory for doing it."

"OK, Sarah," said Kim. "You have the full attention of your eagerly awaiting lab assistant."

"Kim, I'm amazed at how fast you are able to grasp these type of concepts. I can't decide whether you, in your spirit, are of the tribe of Benjamin, or if you are just going through a Benjamin experience right now."

"Benjamin—was Jacob's youngest son and Joseph's little brother. Right?"

"Right, the curious thing about Benjamin was that he was ambidextrous. His mother, Rachel, called him the 'son of sorrow,' but his father called him the 'son of the right hand.' But the unique thing about the Benjaminites was the scriptures say that they could fling a stone lefthanded with amazing accuracy. Now, let me ask you this question: Do you think you are predominantly left brained or right brained?"

"Gee, I don't know," replied Kim. "I suppose from all the detailed studies that I do and my interest in biochemistry and genetics, I am left brained. But when I get around you, I seem to be more of a right brain dreamer like Benjamin's brother Joseph."

Sarah elaborated on how Kim seemed to be able to figure out detailed left-brained soul or mind activities and yet to be very intuitive and know right brain things out of the blue from deep in her spirit. The Apostle Paul was a Benjaminite. In his left brained role, he was a Pharisee of the Pharisees and insisted that every jot and tittle be in place, or in more modern language, every *i* be dotted and every *t* crossed. He held cloaks while Christians were stoned. Then, after he had his Damascus road experience, he went out into the Arabian desert for three years to learn what he later wrote. She then brought up scriptures written by Paul about spirit versus word. Words (letters) usually are formulated in the left brain.

ROMANS 2:28-29 *For he is not a Jew, which is one outwardly; neither is that circumcision, which is outward in the flesh: But he is a Jew, which is one inwardly; and* **circumcision is that of the heart, in the spirit, and not in the letter***; whose praise is not of men, but of God.*

2CORINTHIANS 3:6 *Who also hath made us able ministers of the new testament;* **not of the letter, but of the spirit***: for the letter killeth, but the spirit giveth life.*

"Now, let's build a model of what we know. I know you know anatomy because you were dragging *Grey's Anatomy* book around for a semester. Let's suppose that the human spirit located in the mid section of a being—the belly and heart area—would like to speak to the soul or mind which is located in the head. But unfortunately, this spirit in the heart is gagged by a flesh covering and can only groan or whimper once in a while. You know what I mean by the flesh?"

"Oh yes, I know," replied Kim."The Bible uses the word 'flesh' to mean the lower natures of man. When man behaves like a reptile or a beastly animal, he is said to behave in a fleshly way."

Sarah concurred with Kim, pointing out another word for flesh is "carne," and when man behaves in a carne or carnal way, his behavior is said to be in the flesh. So when someone is saved, this gag is removed from their spirit and their spirit begins to whisper to their mind or soul the thoughts of God, rather than the thoughts of their lower, carnal nature. Acknowledging Jesus as Savior, asking forgiveness, and being baptized is equivalent to the circumcision of the flesh gag from around the mouth of the human spirit.

"Sarah, the Israelites practiced circumcision for the male offspring only. Does this mean the **human spirit is male**?" asked Kim.

"Kim, your Benjaminite thinking is amazing. OK, figure this out. If the human spirit is male, then what part of the makeup of the human anatomy is female? Where is the womb where thoughts are conceived?"

"Sarah, that's too easy. It's like one of those 'who's buried in Grant's tomb' questions."

"That's not as easy a question as you might think," quipped Sarah. "Actually, Grant and his wife are buried in Grant's tomb. Ha! Ha! Now answer the question if it's so easy."

"OK, here it is. *The husband is the human spirit and the wife is the human soul or mind where thoughts are conceived,*" replied Kim.

"Next question: Do men have minds (or souls)?"

"That's debatable!" snickered Kim. "OK, yes men do have minds or souls, else they could not conceive thoughts."

"What if the soul doesn't want to listen to her spirit husband?" asked Sarah.

"Well, I suppose she wants to do her own thing. Ooh, I'm beginning to understand something!" exclaimed Kim. "*Maybe men as well as women have to learn to obey their husbands!*"

"I think you've grasped it," observed Sarah. "The reason we are going through this little exercise is that the excerpts I have copied from the book are best received by the spirit. The other pages you will read later are there to help the mind or soul to understand it. You will see the difference as you read the spirit pages and the letter or soul pages."

"Good. I would like to try my wings in discerning the difference."

"Now Kim, don't get upset at me. I'm not trying to delay giving you the booklet, but I can see that we need to cover just a few more things before you start in the booklet. Remember the Samaritan woman who came to Joseph's well and Jesus offered living water to her?"

"Yes, I remember. It was the woman who had five husbands, and Jesus offered her living water out of the well so she would never thirst again."

"OK, look at the scriptures below and tell me who the woman is and where the well is located in the human anatomy."

JOHN 7:38-39 *He that believeth on me, as the scripture hath said,* **out of his belly shall flow rivers of living water.** *(But this spake he of the Spirit, which they that believe on him should receive: for the Holy Spirit was not yet given; because that Jesus was not yet glorified.)*

ROMANS 8:16 **The Spirit itself beareth witness with our spirit**, *that we are the children of God.*

Kim turned it over in her mind thinking, OK, the woman is the soul, and the husband spirit is located in the belly. So once a person's spirit is ungagged, the Holy Spirit can begin a deeper work with the human spirit and flow out of the belly and rise up to the mind or soul. She then posed the question to Sarah, who agreed with her evaluation.

"But one thing is puzzling me," queried Kim. "Why did this woman have five husbands? Was she a sinful woman, did they all die, or what happened?"

Sarah told her that a lot of people have pondered the same question. She then brought up a set of scriptures that dealt with the Apostles returning and expressing some indignation that Jesus was talking with a lowly Samaritan woman at the well."

JOHN 4:27-32 *And upon this came his disciples, and* **marvelled that he talked with the woman***: yet no man said, What seekest thou? or,* **Why talkest thou with her?** *In the mean while his disciples prayed him, saying, Master, eat.* **But he said unto them, I have meat to eat that ye know not of.**

Kim thought it typical that men look down upon women. But Jesus seemed to be saying that there were concepts that the disciples didn't know about—maybe some future thing? She wondered out loud what this had to do with the woman having five husbands.

"Kim, you're looking at this in the natural. Look at it as an allegory. Yes, there really was a woman who had five husbands, but you're thinking of five men. Look at the verse below and tell me who the five husbands of the soul were."

EPHESIANS 4:10-12 *He that descended is the same also that ascended up far above all heavens, that he might fill all things.) And he gave some,* **apostles***; and some,* **prophets***; and some,* **evangelists***; and some,* **pastors** *and* **teachers***; For the perfecting of the saints, for the work of the ministry, for the edifying of the body of Christ:*

Kim held up her hand and began to count start with the thumb: "**1.** Apostles **2.** Prophets **3.** Evangelists **4.** Pastors **5.** Teachers. You're right, there are five, and I can see how these might be the five husbands of the soul."

"Yes, but what do you think the meat is that the disciples didn't know about?"

"I don't know," replied Kim, "but I suppose it refers to some deeper truths or strong meat that were yet to be revealed."

"Good answer, Kim. Now, let me ask you, have you ever heard the saying that a thousand years is as a day with the LORD?"

"Oh yes, I've heard that. I think that it's in the Bible."

OK, Kim, you're good at math. Here's a difficult one for you. If one day is equivalent to one thousand years with the LORD, how many years is two days?"

"Let me borrow your calculator for such a difficult problem," Kim laughed. "Of course, it's two thousand years."

"I'm impressed!" chuckled Sarah. "Now, tell me how you would interpret these scriptures."

LUKE 13:31-32 *The same day there came certain of the Pharisees, saying unto him, Get thee out, and depart hence: for Herod will kill thee. And he said unto them, Go ye, and tell that fox, Behold, I cast out devils, and* **I do cures today** *and* **tomorrow**, *and* **the third day I shall be perfected**.

"After two days, or two thousand years, a perfection will begin to dawn," replied Kim.

"Now Kim, tell me, how many years has it been since Jesus walked the earth?"

"About two thousand years since his birth and a little less than 2000 years since His crucifixion. Ooh, I see, something much greater than what the five husbands knew about is about to happen. It is the **dawning of the millennium.**"

"Exactly!" replied Sarah. "This is the strong meat which the disciples did not know about."

"Sarah, please pull up that scripture about the woman's five husbands. I need to ponder it some more."

"OK, and let me pick out a few more that go with it."

JOHN 4:18-26 *For thou hast had* ***five husbands****; and* **he whom thou now hast is not thy husband***: in that saidst thou truly. But the hour cometh, and now is, when the true worshippers shall worship the Father* **in spirit** *and in truth: for the Father seeketh such to worship him.* **God is a Spirit***: and they that worship him must* **worship him in spirit and in truth**. *The woman saith unto him, I know that Messias cometh, which is called Christ: when he is come, he will tell us all things. Jesus saith unto her, I that speak unto thee am he.*

"I can see from these scriptures that Jesus is truly speaking about freeing the human spirit to give living water to the soul. But who is this sixth person: *he whom thou now hast is not thy husband.* There are so many soap operas around today, one would almost think it was her live-in boyfriend. OK, OK, don't give me that look. But, if the sixth isn't a ministry, what is it and why isn't she married to him?"

"An astute question, Kim. I'll give you a short answer, otherwise we will be here all day."

"Give me the short answer. I can see I'm the one causing the delay now with my questions."

Sarah explained that John the Baptist said he was not the bridegroom but was a friend of the bridegroom. Then John said concerning himself and Jesus that *"I must decrease and he must increase."* John knew he wasn't a bridegroom and a husband to be, but his ministry was to prepare the way for Jesus.

"I understand, but that was about 2000 years ago. What is the sixth ministry that Jesus spoke about to the woman at the well?"

Sarah told her about the prophet Ezekiel who wrote about the sixth ministry in his ninth chapter. There were six men, and *one of the six had a writer's inkhorn*. He was to go through the city and place a mark on those men that are truly seeking God. This same sixth ministry is described in Psalm 45.

"You mean toward the end of 2000 years since Jesus walked the earth, the writers will be the sixth ministry that *prepare the people for the new millennium*?"

"Right, and this sixth ministry will not try to be a husband and lord it over the people but will point the people to the true husband, which is Jesus working in a person's very own heart or spirit."

JOHN 4:25-26 *The woman saith unto him, I know that Messias cometh, which is called Christ: when he is come, he will tell us all things. Jesus saith unto her,* **I that speak unto thee am he**.

"Now, I can see what you mean," said Kim. "The day will come when we will all have that living water flowing into our soul, and we will never thirst again."

"How do you think the living water gets from the belly to the soul?" asked Sarah.

"Gee, I don't know...through a pipe I guess."

"And did you find a pipe in your anatomy book? Did an iron pipe show up in the x-rays?" asked Sarah laughingly.

"No, I don't think so, but is the living water actually water that flows from the spirit to the soul, or is it something else?"

Sarah related her Aunt Myra was a neurologist and very well known in medical circles. She had articles that were published in both *JAMA* and the *New England Journal of Medicine*. She would have said the living waters are the river of thoughts. These seeds of thought are generated in the husband spirit and conceived in the womb of the feminine soul as the waters described in Ezekiel.

EZEKIEL 47:1 *Afterward he brought me again unto the door of the house; and, behold, waters issued out from under the threshold of the house eastward: for the forefront of the house stood toward the east, and* **the waters came down from under from the right side of the house, at the south side of the altar.**

"Now, one of the great mysteries that Aunt Myra and Uncle Andy stumbled upon is how all these descriptions of houses and temples in the Bible are merely symbols of something much greater. Jesus pointed the way when He more or less told the Pharisees to forget about the stone temple and instead concentrate on the temple of the body, which He resurrected in three days.

"I think the movie *The Raiders of the Lost Ark* popularized this and raised a lot of curiosity among those who had never given much thought to the Bible. For example, do you know where the altar, the mount of Olives, the serpent, and the heel of the woman are in the anatomy of the body?"

"No, I don't," replied Kim. "But I thought the mount of Olives was over in Israel?"

"The mount of Olives is in Israel and that's where the garden of Gethsemane is located. But get away from the mere shadows of the natural representations and look at from within your heart or spirit."

"Professor, I'm stuck—help me out."

"OK, consider this scripture:"

GENESIS 3:14-15 *And the LORD God said unto the serpent, Because thou hast done this, thou art cursed above all cattle, and above every beast of the field; upon thy belly shalt thou go, and dust shalt thou eat all the days of thy life: And I will put enmity between thee and the woman, and between thy seed and her seed; it shall bruise thy head, and* **thou shalt bruise his heel.**

"Now, let me ask you. If the woman, or soul, is located in the head, where would the heel be?"

Kim studied for a few moments and said, "If this woman has to fit within the skull, I suppose her feet would be somewhere at the top of the neck. Right?"

"Right, and then where would the head of the serpent be?"

"I suppose it would be the spinal cord. Uh oh, here we go again!" exclaimed Kim. "I've seen pictures of the spinal cord in my anatomy book, and it does look like a serpent!"

"Yes, and the medical folks call the very top of it the 'olive' because it is swelled up like an olive."

Kim asked, "Do you mean we have a mount of Olives right inside us? And, isn't there a scripture that when Jesus returns, the mount of Olives will be split in two?"

Sarah confirmed the internal split of the mount of Olives. But she admonished Kim to hold on to her spinal cord because she would need it until her terrestrial body was changed into a celestial body.

She then revealed a flash of insight that the top of the spinal cord (the olive) is the altar where we must sacrifice the fleshly desires of the lower natures. She reiterated Ezekiel's insight that the spirit bubbles up and flows out of the right side of altar and into our right brain.

"Wow, and all this has been in the Bible, literally right under our very noses! Why haven't we seen this before?"

"It wasn't time for it to be revealed," replied Sarah. "Now, we could go on for hours and hours on the subject of the Bible and anatomy. Much of it is coded in the tent tabernacle Moses built in the wilderness, and even more of it is encoded in Solomon's temple. We need to get off the anatomy subject so that we can look at the booklet on the ancient scrolls. So, I tell you what, I will give you a copy of the secret temple code that I put together from Aunt Myra's writings for your future reference. Here it is:

Temple Code

1. Central Nervous System - 12 gates of Jerusalem - 12 paired nerves - 24 elders of the mind - located in head
2. Peripheral Nervous System - 31 paired nerves in spinal cord - serves body from neck downward - 31 kings smitten by Joshua in battle for promised land -
3. Spinal cord - serpent enters garden of the soul
4. Top of Spinal Cord - altar - head of serpent - olive - mount of Olives - Gethsemane
5. Pomegranates - cells of the brain
6. Jachin - right pillar in front of Solomon's temple - right eye
7. Boaz - left pillar in front of Solomon's temple - left eye
8. Three courts of temple - three levels of brain (reptilian, animal, and cerebrum)

"Wow!" said Kim, "There's a lot of code here to digest. I remember in our physiology book that humans have three levels in their brain. The lower brain is called the reptilian brain because it is the same as that of reptiles. The middle brain or cerebellum is called the animal brain because animals also have it. Only man has the cerebrum which is the highest and third level of the brain. And you said there were three divisions in the tabernacle and also in Solomon's temple. OK, OK, I'll put it away for another time. Where do we go from here?" [Editor's Note: *See Appendix E for Myra's Discussion of the Temple Code*]

"Well, the buildup for studying the ancient scrolls is longer than I had anticipated, but I guess it was supposed to happen that way. The reason we went through all this is so you can better discern between what is of the spirit and what is of the soul (or psyche). You know that the soul can have lovers other than the spirit of Jesus with our human spirit, and this is where all the medium related dis-incarnate spirits and traffic of that type enter in. However, let's not get into that subject now."

"All right, go on."

Sarah explained the pages from the booklet to be read were curious. One can read them intuitively within their spirit by starting at page 10 and reading the poetry or prose on every even numbered page until page 30 is reached. And if one's spirit finds the poetry to be true, they will know it deep within their spirit without having to reason it out in the soul mind. Sarah related she found some of the concepts in this book very jarring to her traditional views, even though she felt in her gut or spirit they were true. Fortunately, the odd numbered pages in the book were there, replete with supporting scriptures so that her mind could begin to grasp the concepts. If the supporting scriptures had not been there, she might have trashed the book early on.

"This book upset your apple cart that much?" asked Kim.

"It most certainly did," replied Sarah. "So I am giving you the spirit oriented pages first, in order to upset your apple cart. Then, after a few days, you can read the left brained and soul oriented odd numbered pages with the supporting scriptures to satisfy yourself that these concepts are really in the Bible. The soul demands proof and logic! But, on the other hand, if you can receive it in your spirit, further reading may be unnecessary."

"Sarah, you've got me so curious to find out what on earth, or in heaven, you're talking about that I'm beside myself. Please give me the pages without further ado."

Sarah gingerly handed the packet to Kim. Kim looked it over and noted the title page and then page 10. Then, she started reading.

Sarah was quite thirsty and went down the hall past the girl scout classes to find a soft drink machine. Getting a drink for herself and one for Kim, she returned to find Kim intently absorbed in the packet of pages from The Scroll of the Ancients. She reminded Kim to skip over the supporting explanations—even those containing scriptures—which had been Xed out. The explanations and the extremely important supporting scriptures would be there for her reading the second time through. Summing it up, Sarah observed that the true scriptures are—as Paul said—*written not with ink, but with the Spirit of the living God; not in tables of stone, but in fleshy tables of the heart.*

Needing some time to reflect on the conversations of the morning, Sarah walked out the back of the church and toward the overlook of the river. She found a park bench under a shade tree and pondered about Kim reading back in the church. *If I know Kim,* Sarah thought, *she will read the poem part of the booklet and be somewhat accepting of it. Then, a day or two later, she will start turning it over in her mind and have to go back and make sure some scripture hasn't been misinterpreted. Her left brain thirst for 'proof' and 'logic' will absolutely bug her until she does it. But, so what—the spirit is supposed to seed the soul, and the soul has to have time to conceive its thoughts.*

Sarah remembered her Aunt Myra and Uncle Andy having an email discussion about the intuition of the spirit versus the reasoning of the soul. The problem they were discussing was a high brick wall surrounding a secret garden. The gate to the garden had been locked for years. Somewhere, hidden in that wall behind an imperceptibly loosened brick, was the key to the gate of the garden. In his earlier days, Uncle Andy would have labored to check each brick starting with brick number one and ending with brick twenty thousand in an effort to find the key. He then learned how Aunt Myra could look at the wall, and with the Holy Spirit working through the intuition of her own spirit, point to a certain brick and tell Uncle Andy to look there to find the key. Uncle Andy learned a lot about how to flow with the spirit rather than work by the sweat of the brow in order to find the key to the secret garden of the mind.

After their discussion, Sarah walked on toward the old courthouse—found another park bench— and began to watch the perspective of the little toy like cars crawling like ants crossing the river bridge in the distance. She contemplated how succinctly Aunt Myra had summed up the relationship between the spirit and soul. The words of an email replayed within her:

The soul is the glory of the spirit. For the spirit did not come out of the soul but the soul came out of the spirit. The soul should be covered by the spirit—so that the spirit is open to God and can share and interpret messages with its soul.

Editors Note: The even numbered pages from The Scroll of the Ancients are given in chapter 7. Those who would like to read the entire booklet with supporting scriptures will find it in The Ancient Chest section in the back of this book. The well worn sheet music for the song: *The Volume of the Book* may be found in the Songs of the Ancients section of The Ancient Chest.

The booklet, IN FULL COLOR, is also available on-line at http://www.TheAncientChest.com/destiny You may download and share this booklet freely with your friends.

Chapter 7

The Scrolls of the Ancients

10

Verse One

A LONG TIME AGO WHEN WITH MY SAVIOR FACE TO FACE

I DID AGREE TO THE VOLUME WITH HIS HELP AND GRACE

THE VAILS ARE BEING BROKEN AND I SEE HIS THRONE

THE DAWN BREAKS THROUGH AND I WILL KNOW AS I'M KNOWN

LO, I COME TO DO THY WILL, O GOD

PSA 90:1 **Lord, thou hast been our dwelling place in all generations.**

2 **Before the mountains were brought forth, or ever thou hadst formed the earth and the world**, even from everlasting to everlasting, thou art God.

Can there be any doubt that the spirit of the writer of the above Psalm dwelt with the Lord before the foundation of the earth? For time in the spirit realm is different than time as we know it in the earth realm. And when was it that our spirits were chosen in Him for our mission upon this earth?

EPH 1:3 Blessed be the God and Father of our Lord Jesus Christ, who hath blessed us with all spiritual blessings in heavenly places in Christ:

4 **According as he hath chosen us in him before the foundation of the world**, that we should be holy and without blame before him in love:

5 Having predestinated us unto the adoption of children by Jesus Christ to himself, according to the good pleasure of his will,

6 To the praise of the glory of his grace, wherein he hath made us accepted in the beloved.

7 In whom we have redemption through his blood, the forgiveness of sins, according to the riches of his grace;

Can there be any doubt that we were chosen in Him *before* the foundation of the world and our predestined adoption was recorded in the volume of our book?

The volume of our book is an outline of the manifest destiny for our lives so what was predestinated in the heavens would be manifested upon the earth in the fullness of times.

EPH 1:9 **Having made known unto us the mystery of his will**, according to his good pleasure which he hath purposed in himself:

10 **That in the dispensation of the fulness of times** he might gather together in one all things in Christ, both which are in heaven, and which are on earth; even in him:

11 In whom also we have obtained an inheritance, **being predestinated according to the purpose of him who worketh all things after the counsel of his own will:**

Did we see God face to face when our spirits were with Him? Our remembrance of this was obscured by the veil that was placed over our spirits when we came into the earth. And yet part of the very light of God remained within us, but it was as if we saw through a glass darkly.

1CO 13:12 **For now we see through a glass, darkly; but then face to face**: now I know in part; but then shall **I know even as also I am known**.

JOH 1:2 The same was in the beginning with God.

4 In him was life; and **the life was the light of men**.

5 **And the light shineth in darkness**; and the darkness comprehended it not.

A LONG TIME AGO WHEN WITH MY SAVIOR FACE TO FACE
I DID AGREE TO THE VOLUME WITH HIS HELP AND GRACE

"Sarah, this is really upsetting my apple cart. Do you realize the total implications of this? Does it mean that before my spirit was dispatched to be born in the earth, I might have talked to Jesus about what He wanted me to accomplish in the earth? It's one thing, to think that we might have seen Jesus in heaven, but to have talked with Him about our destiny! That's almost too much."

"I agree," replied Sarah. "It does seem like almost too much. But, if it's true, it doesn't matter how we think about it—it's still true."

"But, what about some of the bad things that have happened to me? You know, those things in my life that I would like to take a big eraser and just cut them out of my script. I wish I could go back in time and have them never happen."

Sarah related that to some extent, you can take a time travel device back in time and correct some of the things you would like to erase, both things that others have done to you and things that you've done to others. It's called "forgiveness." We glibly recite the Lord's prayer and ask him to "*forgive us our trespasses,*" but most of the time we leave out considering the next part which requests God to forgive our trespasses "*as we forgive others their trespasses.*" Forgiving others is key to our spiritual growth and releases God's forgiveness in a greater measure to ourselves. So, perhaps, some of the so-called 'bad' things in our destiny were intentionally put there as learning experiences for us. They should not be considered *strange*. Peter wrote about fiery trials and suffering.

1PETER 4:12-13 **Beloved, think it not strange concerning the fiery trial** *which is to try you, as though some* **strange** *thing happened unto you: But rejoice, inasmuch as* **ye are partakers of Christ's sufferings***; that, when his glory shall be revealed, ye may be glad also with exceeding joy.*

"But, we would have to be fools to agree to the bad things! I don't want bad things to happen to me. Did I agree to my high school 'going steady' with fickle hearted Larry? Then, he betrayed me by finding another girlfriend when I was gone for such a short time. Was that in my script?" asked Kim.

"Did you learn from the experience?" asked Sarah.

"Well, yes."

Sarah continued, "Then, the experience may have been in the volume of your book. By, the way, if you haven't forgiven Larry by now, you should go ahead and forgive him."

"Well, Larry's betrayal was a big deal to me. But compared to what Job went through, I suppose it was only a blip on the radar screen," said Kim. "I know the Job question has come up before, but I must ask it now. Do you think that Job's spirit agreed to a script before he was ever born in the earth?"

"Yes," replied Sarah.

"What a fool he was! Why would anyone agree in advance to that kind of suffering? I wouldn't sign that contract."

Sarah elaborated that Job's experiences, as written in the book of Job, have given consolation to millions of Christians. It has helped them to understand that we partake of Christ's suffering; but in the end, everything works out OK. It's an interesting question to consider. If before coming to earth, one were presented with a Job-like script of suffering, should they accept it? Or, if Jesus personally asked them to take that script, should they?

"I'm not sure that I could withstand what Job went through," replied Kim. "Right now, I think that I'm happy with whatever I agreed to when my spirit was still in heaven."

"Good observation," said Sarah. "There is a scripture that says that God '*knows our frame,*' and I don't think He would send us out on a mission if He didn't think we could complete it. Since you seem intrigued with Job's decision, I'm going to give you some extra pages of mainly scriptures at this point to help you consider what Job may have agreed to."

With that, Sarah handed Kim the additional pages about Job.

When we came into the earth the veil placed over our spirits caused us to forget our previous experiences of the heavens. And this forgetfulness extended even to forgetting who we were to the extent that we do not really know our own identity. But the day will come when we will know ourselves as we were once known. We will look in the mirror of the Spirit and recognize our own faces.

1JO 3:1 Behold, what manner of love the Father hath bestowed upon us, that we should be called the sons of God: **therefore the world knoweth us not, because it knew him not**.

2 **Beloved, now are we the sons of God, and it doth not yet appear what we shall be: but we know that, when he shall appear, we shall be like him; for we shall see him as he is**.

3 And every man that hath this hope in him purifieth himself, even as he is pure.

2CO 3:16 Nevertheless when it shall turn to the Lord, **the vail shall be taken away**.

17 Now the Lord is that Spirit: and where the Spirit of the Lord is, there is liberty.

18 **But we all, with open face beholding as in a glass the glory of the Lord, are changed into the same image** from glory to glory, even as by the Spirit of the Lord.

But is there any record in the scripture of a man remembering the things that he saw in his spirit before he came to this earth? Consider the words of Job that were penned in a day when man truly believed that the earth was flat. Where did Job receive his inspiration?

JOB 26:7 He stretcheth out the north over the empty place, and **hangeth the earth upon nothing.**

8 He bindeth up the waters in his thick clouds; and the cloud is not rent under them.

9 He holdeth back the face of his throne, and spreadeth his cloud upon it.

10 **He hath compassed the waters with bounds, until the day and night come to an end.**

Look carefully at the description penned by Job. This is something that one would expect aa astronaut to write, but not someone like Job whose body was limited to the terra firma of earth. An observer from the moon would view the earth as hanging "upon nothing." The observer would see the bounds where "the day and night come to an end." And he would note how the earth "compassed the waters." In other words, Job, in his spirit, knew the earth was circular long before Galileo.

And yet Job considered himself one of the most miserable of all people until he encountered the whirlwind. When one is taken up in a whirlwind, they are changed or accelerated from one dimension to another. Enoch was taken up in a whirlwind and so was Elijah. And so it was when Job had reached the end of himself, the Lord spoke to him out of the whirlwind.

JOB 38:1 Then **the LORD answered Job out of the whirlwind**, and said,

2 Who is this that darkeneth counsel by words without knowledge?

3 Gird up now thy loins like a man; **for I will demand of thee, and answer thou me**.

4 **Where wast thou when I laid the foundations of the earth**? declare, if thou hast understanding.

Verse Two

WAS I THERE WHEN PLEIADES AND ORION WERE MADE?

WAS I THERE WHEN THE FOUNDATION OF THE EARTH WAS LAID?

WHEN INTO THE EMPTY PLACE THE EARTH HE HUNG

AND THE SONS OF GOD SHOUTED WHILE THE MORNING STARS SUNG

LO, I COME TO DO THY WILL, O GOD

PRO 8:25 Before the mountains were settled, before the hills was I brought forth:
26 While as yet he had not made the earth, nor the fields, nor the highest part of the dust of the world.

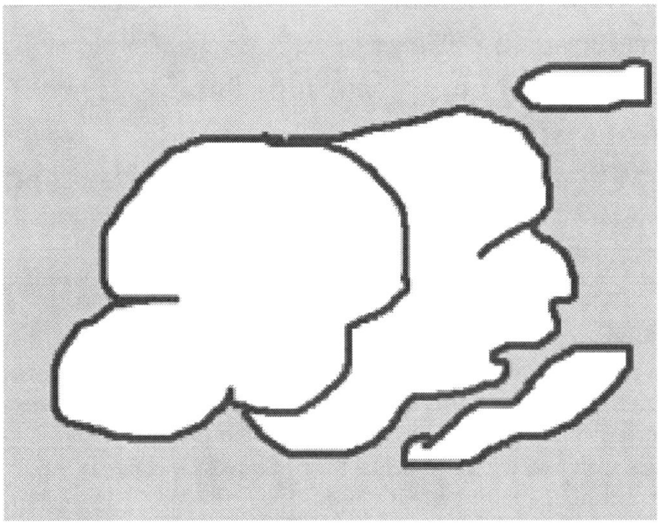

PSA 90:1 Lord, thou hast been our dwelling place in all generations.
2 Before the mountains were brought forth, or ever thou hadst formed the earth and the world, even from everlasting to everlasting, thou art God.

JOB 9:8 Which alone spreadeth out the heavens, and treadeth upon the waves of the sea.
9 Which maketh Arcturus, Orion, and Pleiades, and the chambers of the south.

JOB 38:31 Canst thou bind the sweet influences of Pleiades, or loose the bands of Orion?
32 Canst thou bring forth Mazzaroth in his season? or canst thou guide Arcturus with his sons?
33 Knowest thou the ordinances of heaven? canst thou set the dominion thereof in the earth?

JOB 26:7 He stretcheth out the north over the empty place, and hangeth the earth upon nothing.
10 He hath compassed the waters with bounds, until the day and night come to an end.
13 By his spirit he hath garnished the heavens; his hand hath formed the crooked serpent.

13

The Lord Questions Job

JOB 38:1 Then the LORD answered Job out of the whirlwind, and said,
2 Who is this that darkeneth counsel by words without knowledge?
3 Gird up now thy loins like a man; for I will demand of thee, and answer thou me.
4 Where wast thou when I laid the foundations of the earth? declare, if thou hast understanding.
5 Who hath laid the measures thereof, if thou knowest? or who hath stretched the line upon it?
6 Whereupon are the foundations thereof fastened? or who laid the corner stone thereof;
7 When the morning stars sang together, and all the sons of God shouted for joy?

The Lord asked Job where he was when the foundations of the earth were laid. And if each of us were asked the same question, how would we reply? Then the Lord put forth the astounding concept that the sons of God and the morning stars watched the earth being formed. Now, in conventional theology, we would say (other than Jesus) that the sons of God came down through the genealogy of Adam, who is referred to as a son of God in Luke 3:38. But Adam, at least in his dust body, did not exist until after the earth was created and the dust was taken to make a body for him (Gen 2:7).

But stand back and look at the above verses from a different perspective. It says that the sons (plural) of God shouted when the foundation of the earth was laid. If the sons of God were not yet created before Adam, then how could they have shouted when the foundation of the earth was laid? The only truly satisfactory explanation is that spirits of the sons of God existed before Adam was ever given a dust body in the earth. How else could anything have existed to shout with the joy of watching creation come forth?

The Lord continued to quiz Job.

JOB 38:18 Hast thou perceived the breadth of the earth? declare if thou knowest it all.
19 Where is the way where light dwelleth? and as for darkness, where is the place thereof,
20 That thou shouldest take it to the bound thereof, and that thou shouldest know the paths to the house thereof?
21 **Knowest thou it, because thou wast then born? or because the number of thy days is great**? (KJV)

JOB 38:21 **You know, for you were born then,** And the number of your days is great! (RSV)

Sometimes a truth is so overwhelming that even the translators have a problem believing it. But after the understanding of Job was elevated in the whirlwind, the Lord,, in effect, said to Job that the number of his days was great and that he watched creation take place. How else could Job have penned the words of Job 26:7-10 about the earth hanging upon nothing and being encircled by waters?
And who are the morning stars (plural) that sung when the foundation and cornerstone was brought forth in creation's youth? See Psalm 144:12 for a clue.

Kim finished looking at the scriptures about Job and said, "This really helps in putting things in context. My admiration for Job has increased greatly. And I just love all the scientific oriented information about the creation of the earth. I wonder if Job ever had the satisfaction of knowing that he had completed his script or his book?"

Sarah nodded with a smile and found these scriptures to answer Kim's question.

JOB 19:23-26 *Oh that* **my words were now written! oh that they were printed in a book! That they were graven with an iron pen** *and lead in the rock for ever!* **For I know that my redeemer liveth,** *and that he shall stand at the latter day upon the earth: And though after my skin worms destroy this body, yet* **in my flesh shall I see God:**

Sarah related watching a story on one of the docudrama type programs about a teenage boy who lost both of his legs on a train track. The boy was very strong in spirit and was determined that this accident would not deprive him of a purposeful life. Somehow the boy, after being fitted with artificial legs, learned to walk more or less normally. He went on to be sort of a cheer leader to inspire those who had lost limbs to rise above their circumstances. He became well known. Then the interviewer asked him, "If you had it to do all over again, would you have taken a different path that day to avoid the accident?" The boy thought it over and said, "No, if the accident had not happened, I would not be who I am today."

"Ohh—what a tough decision that would be!" exclaimed Kim.

Kim then expressed concern about the "sons of God" that had fallen. She had read several books about being wary of the doctrine of the fallen sons. Sarah then took a blank piece of paper and, just out of Kim's view, nicked it with her pencil lead. She asked Kim what she saw on the paper. Kim replied that she saw a fly spec. Sarah then asked her about the rest of the sheet of paper that had no fly specs on it. Wasn't the rest of the paper clean and pure and white? Kim agreed that we tend to focus on the negative and conceded that not all of the sons of God fell. Sarah asked Kim to keep the references to the sons of God (and daughters, too) in context of those who are worthy to be called the sons of God. She said it was true that some fell as described in Genesis 6, but one should focus on those sons *who remained loyal to God.* Sarah pointed out that Genesis 6 did not say anything about the daughters of God falling. As John put it: *"now are we the sons of God, and it doth not yet appear what we shall be: but we know that, when he shall appear, we shall be like him."* Kim agreed to keep that in mind.

Sarah continued, "Maybe it was necessary for you to look at the Job scriptures at this point so you could get your mind wrapped around the concepts. But now, in the following pages, I'm asking you to just read the poetry and prose and consider it in your spirit. *Don't get bogged down in the scriptures and explanations just yet.* In fact, I've taken a ruler and red lined them out. You can go back in a few days and sort things out by reading the supporting scriptures if you need to."

With that, Kim turned over the page to verse three of the poem.

Editor's Note: See http://www.TheAncientChest.com/destiny
Express your thoughts:
Does each person have a God given book containing the will of God for their lives?

___ Yes

___ No

If yes, how does this book manifest itself in our lives?

____

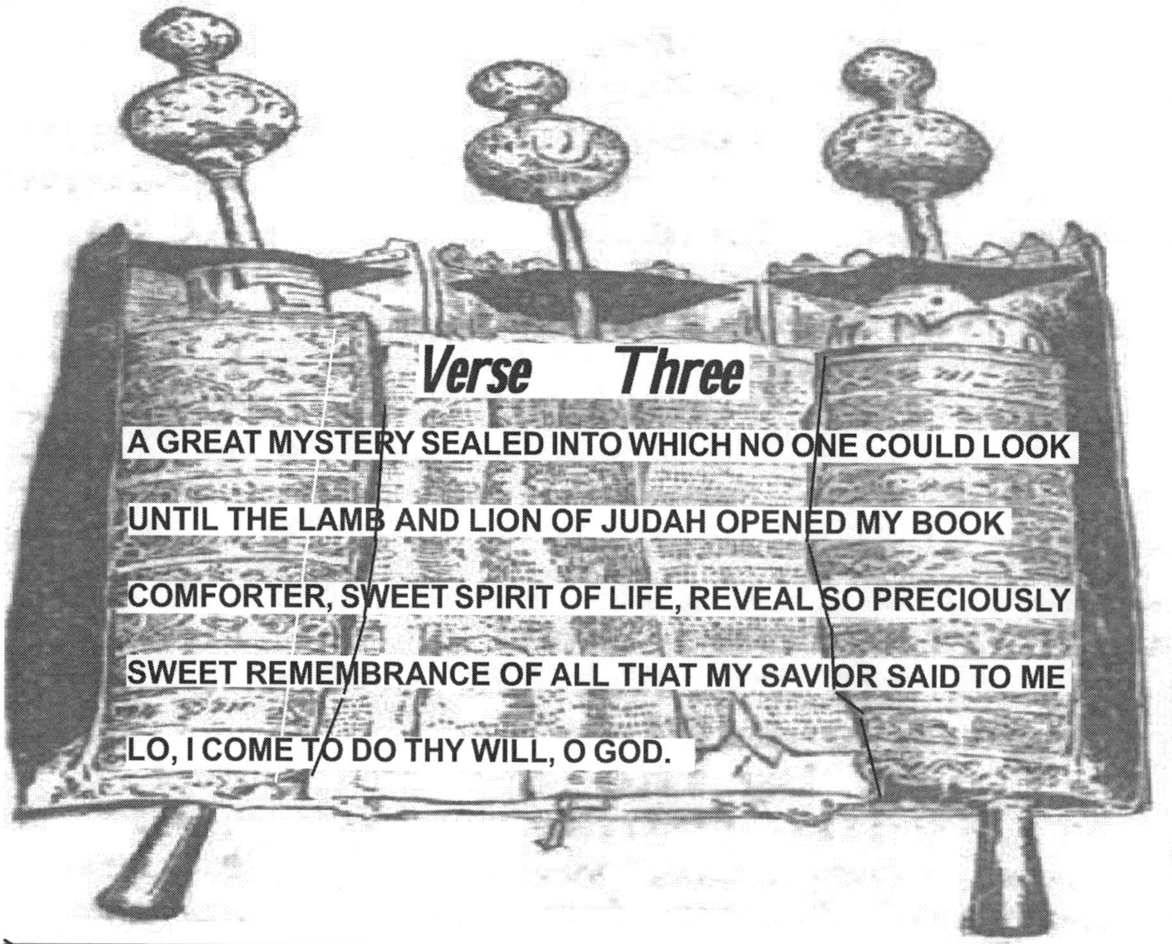
Verse Three
A GREAT MYSTERY SEALED INTO WHICH NO ONE COULD LOOK
UNTIL THE LAMB AND LION OF JUDAH OPENED MY BOOK
COMFORTER, SWEET SPIRIT OF LIFE, REVEAL SO PRECIOUSLY
SWEET REMEMBRANCE OF ALL THAT MY SAVIOR SAID TO ME
LO, I COME TO DO THY WILL, O GOD.

**REV 5:1 And I saw in the right hand of him that sat on the throne a book
written within and on the backside, sealed with seven seals.
2 And I saw a strong angel proclaiming with a loud voice, Who is worthy
to open the book, and to loose the seals thereof?
3 And no man in heaven, nor in earth, neither under the earth, was able
to open the book, neither to look thereon.
4 And I wept much, because no man was found worthy to open and to
read the book, neither to look thereon.
5 And one of the elders saith unto me, Weep not: behold, the Lion of the
tribe of Juda, the Root of David, hath prevailed to open the book, and to
loose the seven seals thereof.
6 And I beheld, and, lo, in the midst of the throne and of the four beasts,
and in the midst of the elders, stood a Lamb as it had been slain, having
seven horns and seven eyes, which are the seven Spirits of God sent forth
into all the earth.**

16

Verse Four

FOR LO, HE DID COMMAND AND SIFT AMONG THE NATIONS

HIS CHILDREN AS GOLDEN GRAIN, THE WINDOWS OF SALVATION

AMONGST EVERY KINDRED, TRIBE, AND PEOPLE THEY WERE GIVEN BIRTH

NOT KNOWING THAT THEY WERE KINGS AND PRIESTS TO REIGN UPON THE EARTH

LO, I COME TO DO THY WILL, O GOD

AMO 9:9 For, lo, I will command, and I will sift the house of Israel among
all nations, like as corn is sifted in a sieve, yet shall not the least grain fall
upon the earth.
11 In that day will I raise up the tabernacle of David that is fallen, and close
up the breaches thereof; and I will raise up his ruins, and I will build it as in
the days of old:
13 Behold, the days come, saith the LORD, that the plowman shall over-
take the reaper, and the treader of grapes him that soweth seed; and the
mountains shall drop sweet wine, and all the hills shall melt.

Verse Five

IN THE BOOK WERE ALL MY MEMBERS WRITTEN LONG AGO

BEFORE HE FORMED ME IN THE WOMB, HE LOVED ME SO

MY SPIRIT TO EARTH CAME FROM PALACES OF IVORY

HE BREATHED AND LO, THE BREATH OF LIFE ENTERED MY BODY

LO, I COME TO DO THY WILL, O GOD

**PSA 139:13 For thou hast possessed my reins: thou hast cov-
ered me in my mother's womb.
14 I will praise thee; for I am fearfully and wonderfully made:
marvellous are thy works; and that my soul knoweth right well.
15 My substance was not hid from thee, when I was made in
secret, and curiously wrought in the lowest parts of the earth.
16 Thine eyes did see my substance, yet being unperfect; and
in thy book all my members were written, which in continuance were fashioned, when as yet there was none of them.
17 How precious also are thy thoughts unto me, O God! how
great is the sum of them!**

A question occurred to Kim. "Sarah, the stanza about the little baby in its mother's womb raises a lot of personal questions for me. I remember the scripture about Jacob's ladder and the spirits descending and ascending on it. What do you think happens to little babies that for various reasons just don't make it?"

Sarah responded, "I think we can take comfort in how Jesus regarded little children. Didn't he say *Let the little children to come unto me, and forbid them not: for of such is the kingdom of God.* But, why do you regard this as a personal question?"

"I think I may have told you, I am a twin.. My younger twin sister had a heart defect and did not live through her first day. When I think of it—there is always an emptiness like part of me is missing. Do you think I will see her in heaven someday—or, perhaps God will grant her spirit permission to re-enter the earth to complete a fuller mission?"

"Kim, how do you ever manage to come up with such hard questions? My, oh my, how can this one be answered without asking Jesus, himself? I can tell you that Uncle Andy and Aunt Myra speculated about this. They pondered if the spirits of aborted babies or innocent children who died before reaching accountability would still be given a chance to complete a fuller mission in the earth realm and rung of Jacob's ladder. They concluded that they didn't know and left the question before the Lord. They also considered scriptures about the prophet who translated into the chariot of fire and then many years later his spirit was present in the earth realm. But this was a rather unique case–by translating he bypassed death. Bypassing death does not fit in at all with the standard, death intensive theories. Kim, lets not pursue this any further—you know these earthly theories also have a very dark side. Lets not go there."

"Sarah, please quit treating me like a babe in the woods. How will I learn to find my way unless you provide some guideposts so I can avoid the pits?"

"Well, Ok, we will touch on it just a bit, but this question should be put on the shelf until both of us have reached a greater maturity in our discernment of good and evil. We do not want to throw out the baby with the bath water. On the other hand, the baby should not be left in the woods unprotected from the predators. You want to avoid the pits, then consider the account of the demon possessed men coming out of the tombs of the 'other side' in the country of the Gergesenes. When Jesus came near, the demons responded by detesting the Lamb and the atonement blood they knew he would shed for sin. Let me find the verse.

MATHEW 8:29 And, behold, they cried out, saying, What have we to do with thee, Jesus, thou Son of God? **art thou come hither to torment us before the time?** [30] *And there was a good way off from them an herd of many swine feeding.*

You remember the rest of the story. The evil spirits begged Jesus to let them enter a herd of swine. And then the swine ran over the cliff into the sea. So, these were the spirits of men—some were giants—who had once inhabited the earth and were living as *parasites* in host humans. These dis-embodied entities push aside the human spirit and endulge their pleasures in the body of their host. Then, there also may be others that have met some tragic, unexpected death—that like ghosts—have not yet left the earth realm to take their next Jacob's ladder step. We need the gift of discernment to be able to tell the difference between false spirits and those that are sanctioned by God. Each rung of the ladder is a frequency range—the *third heaven* is higher, the earth rung has natural eyesight light between infared red and ultra violet, and the lower frequency hells descend to what the Bible calls the *lowest hell.* Paul in his letter to the Philippians tells us that even *things under the earth* will eventually bow their knee to the Lord Jesus Christ. The evil spirits knew that their time in the earth realm would be coming to an end.

Kim mulled over Sarah's admonition about the need for discernment and then replied, "I see what you mean. I look forward to completely being in the presence of Jesus. These spirits were *tormented* by his mere presence. I get all creepy and crawly when I even think about them."

"That is a good evalution. Now, we can quit dwelling on it and put it back on the shelf." replied Sarah. With that Sarah was happy to change the pace by going outside into the brilliant sunshine while Kim continued her reading.

Verse Six

HE PUT MY TEARS IN BOTTLES AT MY GETHSEMANE

WHY DID I AGREE? FOR NOW THY VOWS ARE UPON ME

MY LIFE I HAD PLANNED AND MY RACE I BEGAN TO RUN,

UNTIL, NOT MY WILL BUT THINE BE DONE

LO, I COME TO DO THY WILL, O GOD.

LUK 22:42 Saying, Father, if thou be willing, remove this cup from
me: nevertheless not my will, but thine, be done.
43 And there appeared an angel unto him from heaven, strengthening
him.
44 And being in an agony he prayed more earnestly: and his sweat was
as it were great drops of blood falling down to the ground.
45 And when he rose up from prayer, and was come to his disciples, he
found them sleeping for sorrow,

The Volume of the Book

I have a beginning, I have an ending, and I have another beginning, saith the Lord. Yea, you have heard my word even as you have come into this place, saith God. Yea, in this day, I will send you forth now into a new day. For you have sung about it, you have taught it, you have spoken it, you have thought about it, and now it is time to do it, saith the Lord.

Yea, I say unto thee, Sons and Daughters, this is my day. You are my day. You are my love. You are my life. You are my beginning and ending. You are my all, and in all. For I have invested my very life in you, and I trust you—I know you. I've known you from the beginning, and I'll know you to the end, and to the new beginning. And I know what you're capable of, I know what you'll do, I know how you'll handle it, and you will make it, saith the Lord.

Yea, for surely I have stripped thee. Did you not hear the word that I created the waster to destroy, saith the Lord? Yea, I hardened that loved one that lives right within the walls of your own home, saith the Lord. I direct thy every move, saith God. Thy every circumstance, saith the Lord, is ordered by my hand. And you knew it, when we agreed upon it before the foundations of the earth. We talked about it; we discussed it; we agreed upon it

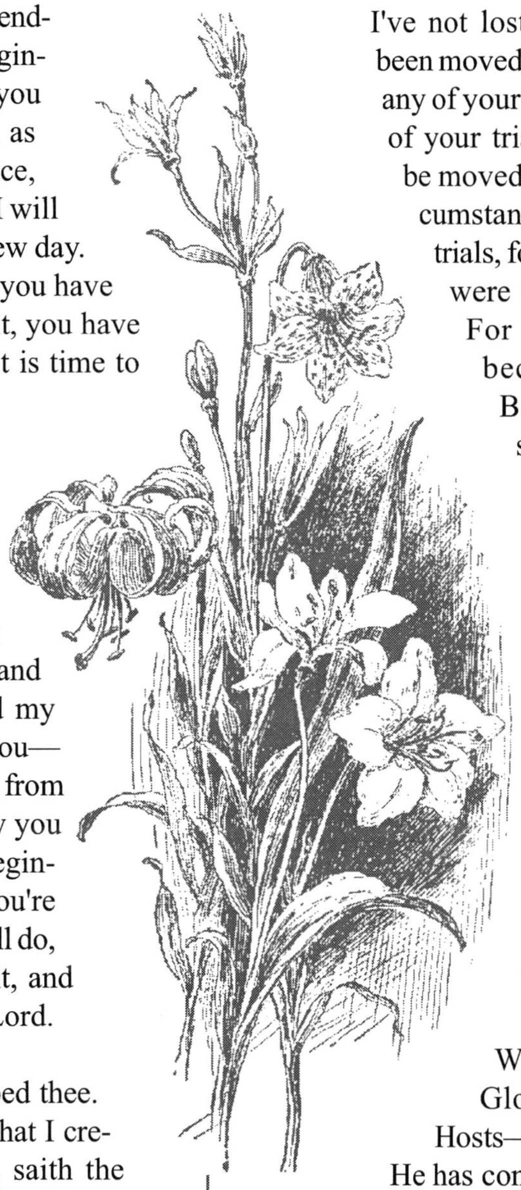

I've not lost control. I've not been moved off of my throne by any of your circumstances, any of your trials, nor will I ever be moved by any of your circumstances, by any of your trials, for I sent them! They were right out from me. For I am making you because I love you. Because I want to show you my love. I do these things for you, not against you.

I do these things because I chose you. You are my beloved. So lift up you heads, oh ye gates. Even lift them up, ye everlasting doors. For the King of Glory has come in.

Who is this king of Glory? The Lord of Hosts—the Lord of armies. He has come in. Arise, shine, for the glory of the Lord has arisen upon thee, my children. The glory of the Lord has arisen upon thee my children! My glory is upon thee and the world shall see.

The gross darkness, yea, it will cover the people but not thee for my glory is upon thee. It radiates from thy very being.

Verse Seven

TO HOLD MY PEACE WHILE MEN SUFFER WILL BE AMISS

AM I CALLED TO THE KINGDOM FOR SUCH A TIME AS THIS?

WILL THE KING HOLD OUT HIS SCEPTER WHEN I ENTER THE DOOR?

WHAT SURPRISES AWAIT ME OR HAVE I BEEN THIS WAY BEFORE?

LO, I COME TO DO THY WILL, O GOD

EST 4:11 All the king's servants, and the people of the king's provinces, do know, that whosoever, whether man or woman, shall come unto the king into the inner court, who is not called, there is one law of his to put him to death, except such to whom the king shall hold out the golden sceptre, that he may live: but I have not been called to come in unto the king these thirty days.
12 And they told to Mordecai Esther's words.
13 Then Mordecai commanded to answer Esther, Think not with thyself that thou shalt escape in the king's house, more than all the Jews.
14 For if thou altogether holdest thy peace at this time, then shall there enlargement and deliverance arise to the Jews from another place; but thou and thy father's house shall be destroyed: and who knoweth whether thou art come to the kingdom for such a time as this?

26

The wedding of the spirit and soul

Note in the illustration above that the man has a bride in his mind which represents the soul. Paul said that our mind was to be presented as a chaste bride.

2CO 11:2 For I am jealous over you with godly jealousy: for I have espoused you to one husband, **that I may present you as a chaste virgin to Christ.**

3 But I fear, **lest by any means, as the serpent beguiled Eve through his subtilty, so your minds should be corrupted from the simplicity that is in Christ.**

Note also in the illustration above that the woman has a bride in her mind or soul. So she, too, has the battleground of the soul in the garden, even as Jesus struggled with His soul.

JOH 12:27 **Now is my soul troubled**; and what shall I say? Father, save me from this hour: but for this cause came I unto this hour.

LUK 22:42 Saying, Father, if thou be willing, remove this cup from me: **nevertheless not my will, but thine, be done**.

Verse Eight

TO HIS OVERCOMERS ALL THINGS WORK TOGETHER FOR GOOD

AS THE AUTHOR AND FINISHER OF OUR FAITH KNEW IT WOULD

FOR HE AND WE FOREKNEW OUR MANIFEST DESTINY

FORGOTTEN AND VEILED, YET TO IT WE DID ONCE AGREE

LO, I COME TO DO THY WILL, O GOD

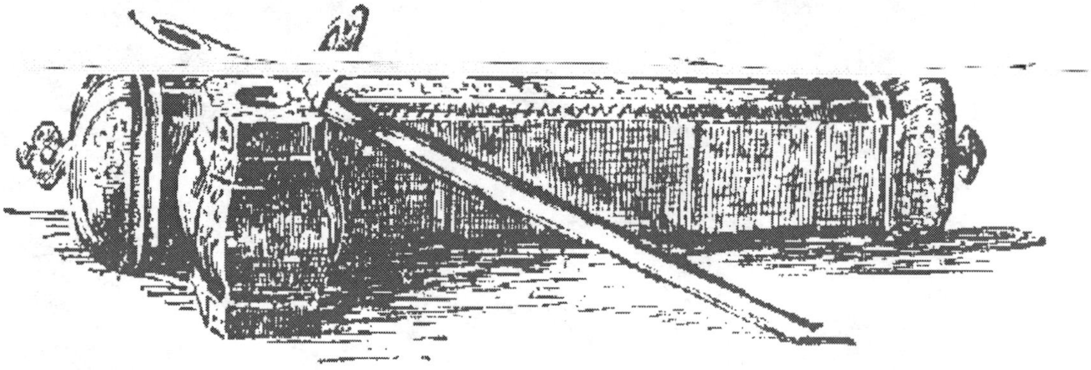

Scribe's Ink Pen

**HEB 12:1 Wherefore seeing we also are compassed about with so great a
cloud of witnesses, let us lay aside every weight, and the sin which doth so
easily beset us, and let us run with patience the race that is set before us,
2 Looking unto Jesus the author and finisher of our faith; who for the joy
that was set before him endured the cross, despising the shame, and is set
down at the right hand of the throne of God.
5 And ye have forgotten the exhortation which speaketh unto you as unto
children, My son, despise not thou the chastening of the Lord, nor faint
when thou art rebuked of him:
6 For whom the Lord loveth he chasteneth, and scourgeth every son whom
he receiveth.
7 If ye endure chastening, God dealeth with you as with sons; for what son
is he whom the father chasteneth not?**

30

Verse Nine

HE SENT MY SPIRIT FROM HEAVEN TO EARTH AND LO!

FOR OF HIM, AND THROUGH HIM, AND TO HIM WE GO

FOR THE AUTHOR WROTE FOR US A WONDERFUL STORY

OF HOW THE FIRSTBORN LEADS SONS AND DAUGHTERS TO GLORY

LO, I COME TO DO THY WILL, O GOD

The Transfiguration

HEB 2:9 But we see Jesus, who was made a little lower than the angels for the suffering of death, crowned with glory and honour; that he by the grace of God should taste death for every man.
10 For it became him, for whom are all things, and by whom are all things, in bringing many sons unto glory, to make the captain of their salvation perfect through sufferings.
11 For both he that sanctifieth and they who are sanctified are all of one: for which cause he is not ashamed to call them brethren,

Editor's Note: See http://www.TheAncientChest.com/destiny for an online Color copy of The Scrolls of the Ancients.

Chapter 8

Mary the Magdalene

Sarah wandered back to the old stone church, and Kim was on page 28 of the booklet.

"I'll be finished in about ten minutes," said Kim. "I see what you mean, the poetry and prose part is easy to read. But if I start trying to put all the scriptures together, my mind says, 'Whoa, I have to check that out.'"

After a little while, Kim put down the pages and said, "I have a question. What if I am called to do something very significant in the volume of my book, and I fail to do it? What happens then?"

Sarah suggested that their friend Shakespeare would tell them that God always has an understudy. King Saul disobeyed God, and King David was raised up in his place. Esther was an understudy until Queen Vashti refused to appear before the king. The Gentile woman begged for crumbs off of the table, and Jesus had compassion for her daughter even before the time of the Gentiles. It seems that if anyone really seeks after God, He provides the opportunity for an understudy to play a major role in His timing.

"I can see that," responded Kim. "But maybe God already knew in advance that King David would replace King Saul."

"Yes, that is true," agreed Sarah. "But King Saul brought the tragic circumstances of his death on himself. Look at it this way, there are many roads that you can take from here to Springfield. Some take longer than others, but you can get there whether you take the interstate or back country roads."

"But what if you are supposed to get to Springfield, and you have a head-on collision and are killed."

"Good point. Let me pull some scriptures from my chance file on this subject."

ECCLESIASTES 9:11 *I returned, and saw under the sun, that the race is not to the swift, nor the battle to the strong, neither yet bread to the wise, nor yet riches to men of understanding, nor yet favour to men of skill;* **but time and chance happeneth to them all**.

LUKE 13:4-5 *Or those eighteen, upon whom the tower in Siloam fell, and slew them,* **think ye that they were sinners above all men that dwelt in Jerusalem?** *I tell you, Nay: but, except ye repent, ye shall all likewise perish.*

Sarah observed that time and chance happen to everyone. "Doesn't God s*end rain on the just and on the unjust.?* However, you've heard the old saying, 'I guess it wasn't my time, yet.' So, if the Most High has something else for us to do, and we are willing to do it, miracles do happen. Even corpses are sometimes found alive in funeral homes. Remember the scripture: *With men this is impossible; but with God all things are possible?'"*

"Gee, do you think that God deals with probability and chance? Maybe there are some applications here for my probability and chaos theory course," mused Kim.

"You might say that," replied Sarah, "but, consider this. Let me find it...keyword 'lot'...searching... searching...here it is in Proverbs. The lot refers to the stones in the high priest's breastplate which were used to determine an answer. Somehow, out of pure chance, God is in control of the final outcome."

PROVERBS 16:33 *The* **lot** *is cast into the lap;* **but the whole disposing thereof is of the LORD.**

"Maybe, when we get our new bodies, we won't have to worry about time or chance," said Kim. "Won't that be great? We can walk through all kinds of situations, unscathed."

"It depends on what kind of body that you have," replied Kim. "Even after the return of Jesus to rule and reign for 1000 years, there will be some that still have natural bodies. Even when the lion, wolf, and lamb are on friendly terms, there is still some chance of death. Isaiah, the prophet talked about this.

ISAIAH 65:20 *There shall be no more thence an infant of days, nor an old man that hath not filled his days:* **for the child shall die an hundred years old**; *but the sinner being an hundred years old shall be accursed.*

It dawned on Kim and Sarah the age span seemed to be like it was before the flood when people got married and didn't have children until they were 150 years old or so. Kim began giving more thought to the homework that Sarah gave her about the different types of bodies. She articulated in her mind what the types of bodies might be.

"I think its like this," said Kim. "We have a natural body which is subject to death. Then, there is a resurrected body which can not be killed. It can walk right through walls, just like Jesus did, after he was resurrected."

"OK, good. Keep going."

Kim continued, "The resurrected body has its limitations—it is a spirit body like that of the angels. The angels cannot marry, and neither can those that have resurrected bodies. Right?'

"Right."

"Then I found these scriptures in Hebrews1:9-11 that say man will ultimately be higher than the angels and rule over them. Right?"

"Right, you're on track."

"Then, I began to consider the scene where Jesus spoke to Mary Magdalene in the garden after the resurrection. It would seem to me that Jesus was in his resurrection body then. OK? Pull up that scripture on the computer and let's look at it again."

"Here it is."

JOHN 20:16-17 *Jesus saith unto her, Mary. She turned herself, and saith unto him, Rabboni; which is to say, Master. Jesus saith unto her,* **Touch me not; for I am not yet ascended to my Father**: *but go to my brethren, and say unto them, I ascend unto my Father, and your Father; and to my God, and your God.*

"Then it must be Jesus had to take a step up, as you say, Jacob's ladder to the realm of the Father to receive something more. Could it be that He received His celestial body, then?"

"And what might be the difference between the celestial body and the resurrection body?"

"I don't know," Kim replied. "I haven't been able to specifically find it anywhere. But I do wonder if those who achieve transformation from the resurrection body to the celestial body are able to marry in the celestial realm. If that is the case, then would Jesus be both a dove, have a celestial body, and be eligible for marriage in the celestial realm?"

"Isn't Jesus the bridegroom to the bride of Christ? Don't you want to be part of the bride of Christ?"

"There you go again," complained Kim. "You know that isn't the question I want answered."

Sarah deferred Kim's frustration by mentioning that Aunt Myra put it this way in one of her emails to Uncle Andy. She asked, if given a choice, would it be preferable to be a spirit with a resurrected body or to climb higher and be a full son or daughter by overcoming all things, even death, and reach immortality by being transfigured? Aunt Myra had used these scriptures to outline the choices.

1CORINTHIANS 15:52-54 *In a moment, in the twinkling of an eye, at the last trump: for the trumpet shall sound, and the dead shall be raised incorruptible, and we shall be changed.* **For this corruptible must put on incorruption**, *and* **this mortal must put on immortality**. *So when* **this corruptible shall have put on incorruption**, *and* **this mortal shall have put on immortality**, *then shall be brought to pass the saying that is written,* **Death is swallowed up in victory**.

"Then, it would seem that the corruptible body has passed through death and becomes a resurrection body. And the mortal body becomes the immortal or celestial body?" questioned Kim.

"I think so," said Sarah.

"Wait a minute…wait a minute!" exclaimed Kim. "Jesus didn't achieve the celestial body without first going through death, so how do explain this?"

"Well, wasn't Jesus transfigured before he went to the cross?" replied Sarah.

"You've got me there. Yes, He was."

Sarah again referred to her Aunt Myra's explanation: **"Jesus overcame all things while He was alive and walking in His natural flesh body. When He overcame all things, He was transfigured. He became an example for mankind that it is possible to achieve a celestial body without dying. Then, remember, He laid aside his transfiguration victory over death and told Pontius Pilate that Pilate would have no power over Him unless it had been given from above. Jesus' remaining mission was to prove that those that were already dead, or even those that would die in the future, could be resurrected from the dead. And He became the example of how victory over death could be achieved."**

"Now I begin to understand why you kept highlighting the dialog between Martha and Jesus after Lazarus had died," said Kim. "Martha didn't understand it at the time, but now I think that I do. Pull it up on the screen for me."

JOHN 11:24-26 *Martha saith unto him, I know that he shall rise again in the resurrection at the last day. Jesus said unto her, I am the resurrection, and the life: he that believeth in me, though he were dead, yet shall he live:* **And whosoever liveth and believeth in me shall never die. Believest thou this?**

"There it is in verse 26," Kim pointed out. "**Jesus is saying that there is a path that overcomes death without going through a death of the natural body.** I think I understand it."

"The timing of this is difficult to determine," observed Sarah. "Some think it will only occur at the second coming of Jesus, and others think that there have been a few in each generation that have overcome death without going to the grave. True, it is appointed to man to die and then the judgment. However, wouldn't it be wonderful if someone else kept your appointment at the dentist for an abscessed tooth?"

PSALMS 102:19-20 *For he hath looked down from the height of his sanctuary; from heaven did the LORD behold the earth; To hear the groaning of the prisoner;* **to loose those that are appointed to death;**

"Appointment? Do you realize how long we have been here?" said Kim, "Let's go down to the River Dog Cafe and get lunch and then do some shopping. I need to get a congratulation card for Wanda and her husband on their new daughter."

That evening, Sarah went to the gym to work out and Kim was busy writing a letter and wrapping a gift for her new little niece, Mary Beth. There was a knocking on the dorm door, and when Kim answered it, it was Tiffany.

"Hi, Tiffany, come on in."

"Hi, Kim, is Sarah here?"

"No, she's working out at the gym."

"Well, I'll stay just a minute. But I would like to ask a favor of you. Those flip charts we used for the CSI on Mary Magdalene—do you think Sarah would mind if I borrowed them? Mom and I have been talking some more about MM, and she is very interested in what we put together."

"I don't think that Sarah would mind at all—go ahead and take them. Studying the scriptures falls into the same category as motherhood and apple pie," replied Kim. "Here, they are yours to borrow."

"By the way, Mom has hinted that she would really like to meet you and Sarah and maybe even sit in on our next Mary Magdalene session when we finish looking at the MM scriptures."

"Hey, Tiff, I will pass the hint on to Sarah in my usual diplomatic way," smiled Kim.

"Thanks, Kim, I'm not sure what that means, but anyway, thanks...I think. Bye."

"Bye."

When Sarah returned, Kim apprised her of Tiffany's visit and her Mom's hint.

"I like Tiffany's Mom—she's quite a lady. It's amazing how she has risen above her circumstances of growing up in poverty and become such a great mother to Tiffany. I'll give Tiffany a call, and we will set up something. Where have you hidden our roladex phone file?"

Kim listened as Sarah phoned Tiffany. "... Yes ... Yes ...Tomorrow night? ... Seven will be fine. ... See you then."

"That was quick," remarked Sarah. "But it's better to get together on a Sunday night than to try to work something in during the week when we're so busy with classes."

Sunday evening came with a beautiful gold and red sunset, and promptly at seven, Tiffany and her Mom were at the dorm door. Tiffany introduced her Mom to Sarah and Kim. Her first name was Velda. Sarah and Kim gave her a warm hug and invited them to their study table. With the greetings completed, Kim and Tiffany rehung the flip charts on the wall in preparation for resuming the Mary Magdalene relationships study.

"I really appreciate the opportunity to join in this study," said Velda. "When Tiffany described the Nain woman's situation, I think that you called her NW, and how Jesus defended her and how He was friends with the downtrodden, it sort of got to me."

"Our code is **NW** for *the sinful Nain Woman*, **MM** for *Mary Magdalene*, and **MB** for *Mary of Bethany,*" reviewed Kim.

"Mom Velda, were there any other thoughts or reactions you would like to share before we start looking at more scriptures?" asked Sarah.

"Yes, I really wondered about the family situation in which Martha, Mary of Bethany, and Lazarus found themselves in. The Bible doesn't mention that they were living with their parents, and I wondered if they had come from a broken family. They seem to have had their own house. Maybe it's because I'm seeing my own family situation in this. My father was killed in Vietnam, my mother had a nervous breakdown when the news came, and my older sister and my little brother and I were left to fend for ourselves."

"I can see your point," said Kim. "I've read that story a number of times and the thought never crossed my mind about why the two sisters and a brother were occupying the house, and there was no mention of it being their parent's house. What happened when you were left without parents?"

Velda related the story of her trying childhood: Her mother never recovered; in biblical terms, you might say she was vexed with a devil. She eventually died in an asylum. Her older sister was a real Martha who held the family together. They both loved their little brother, and he chose to stay with them rather than go to live with an aunt. Velda was the dreamer in the family until she reached her middle teenage years. Then she became the prodigal daughter and wouldn't listen to anybody and did her own thing. She hopped a bus to Houston and got in with the wrong crowd in the bars around the ship channel. Finally, pregnant and broke, she could not cry out to her natural father—he was dead. So she cried out to her heavenly Father for help. When she had poured out her heart, she saw a Salvation Army shelter in the next block and began the way back to her Father's house. She was given a bus ticket and returned to her sister's house, and she welcomed her with open arms. However, her little brother was sick, so she found a job to help pay his medical bills and also to prepare for the birth of the love of her life, Tiffany. The Lord blessed her in her employment.She was able to support Tiffany and herself and also help out with her little brother's education.

Tiffany dabbed at her moist eyes, walked over to her Mom and gave her a hug. "I love you so very much, Mom, thank you for loving me."

"I can see how you might relive some of your own experiences through the lives of NW, MM, and MB," observed Kim.

Mary the Magdalene

"I don't really know if my story is just like what happened to these three women or perhaps one woman, but that's how it affected me," said Velda.

"Thank you, Velda, that is a really touching story," said Sarah. "Now we need to kind of review just a bit to get a foothold on where we are. We've pretty much finished NW (Nain Woman), and maybe have just a little bit more on MB (Mary of Bethany). Most of the earlier time line scriptures that we have looked at on Mary Magdalene came from Luke. There is also one from Mark about the same incident, and then there is one from Matthew where Jesus is dealing with the Pharisees near the Sea of Galilee and discusses seven unclean spirits that return to a swept house."

LUKE 8:2 *And certain women, which had been* **healed of evil spirits and infirmities, Mary called Magdalene,** *out of whom went seven devils,*

MARK 16:9 *Now when Jesus was risen early the first day of the week, he appeared first to* **Mary Magdalene, out of whom he had cast seven devils.**

MAT 12:43-45 When the unclean spirit is gone out of a man, he walketh through dry places, seeking rest, and findeth none. Then he saith, I will return into my house from whence I came out; and when he is come, he findeth it empty, swept, and garnished. **Then goeth he, and taketh with himself seven other spirits more wicked than himself, and they enter in and dwell there:** *and the last state of that man is worse than the first. Even so shall it be also unto this wicked generation.*

"I never thought of this applying to Mary Magdalene," said Velda. "But I can see how it might. I remember how I felt very guilty about prostituting myself with the sailors coming into the ship channel. I found a little church and talked with the pastor. He helped me clean out some of my unclean thoughts.

"Then, I thought I could get my life back on track and got a job as a waitress. However, when I couldn't pay my rent and was about to be evicted, I went right back to my old habits and fell even further into despair. It wasn't till I knelt on the street and asked my heavenly Father and Jesus to get me out of my pig sty that I felt clean and was able to resist the temptations of the lower natures. I don't know what casting out 'seven devils' means, but it seemed like there were at least seven recurring thought patterns that kept running around in my mind. Things like 'you're rotten, the people in any decent church won't accept you; if you want love, you will have to get it through sex; you'll die like your mother,' and so on.'"

"Well, we can only theorize about what happened to Mary Magdalene. However, a person having gone through an experience can much better understand a situation than one who only has a theory. Perhaps you can feel the depth of Mary Magdalene's despair and her gratitude to Jesus much more than the rest of us can really know," said Sarah.

Tiffany squeezed her mother's hand. Then, she made a flip chart with the seven devils' experience on it and sandwiched it in between the time of NW and when Luke recounted that MM began following Jesus along with Joanna and Susanna.

"You know, our charts are getting a little confusing in trying to keep up with our time lines. Maybe, we should devote one chart just to time lines," said Tiffany.

"Let's do it," agreed Kim. "We can make it kind of general because some things may have to be shifted back and forth as we get new information."

1. **Jesus Near Sea of Galilee**
   - Nain Woman breaks alabaster box and wipes Jesus' feet with hair (Simon the Pharisee's house)
   - Mary Magdalene, Joanna and Susanna follow Jesus (MM had seven devils cast out)
2. **Jesus at Bethany**
   - Mary B sits at Jesus' feet while Martha serves
   - Mary B and Martha ask Jesus to come—Lazarus is dead
   - Mary B anoints Jesus with ointment
3. **Women at crucifixion of Jesus**
   - ? ? ?

"Now, I think we are ready to take our time line forward to the crucifixion," said Sarah. "There are a number of scriptures about MM being at the crucifixion. Let's pull them up and look at them."

JOHN 19:25 *Now there stood by the cross of Jesus his mother, and his mother's sister,* **Mary the wife of Cleophas**, *and* **Mary Magdalene**.

MARK 15:40-41 *There were also women looking on afar off: among whom was* **Mary Magdalene**, *and* **Mary the mother of James the less and of Joses, and Salome;** *(Who also, when he was in Galilee, followed him, and ministered unto him;)* **and many other women which came up with him unto Jerusalem.**

Kim's analytical mind was racing and she said, "It's not what we see in these scriptures, it's what we don't see. We don't see Mary of Bethany mentioned here. There is Jesus' mother Mary, Mary the wife of Cleophas, Mary the mother of James, and MM herself. The *omission of Mary of Bethany* here is very significant, possibly resulting in equating MM and MB as being the same person."

"Oh, here's another scripture about the women at the tomb," said Sarah. "Let's look at it.

LUKE 23:49-56 *And all his acquaintance, and the women that followed him from Galilee, stood afar off, beholding these things. And he took it down, and wrapped it in linen, and laid it in a sepulchre that was hewn in stone, wherein never man before was laid. And that day was the preparation, and the sabbath drew on.* **And the women also, which came with him from Galilee, followed after, and beheld the sepulchre, and how his body was laid. And they returned, and prepared spices and ointments; and rested the sabbath day according to the commandment.**

"No, Mary of Bethany is not mentioned her either," said Kim.

"Right," agreed Tiffany, "and we do see these women did follow Jesus to Jerusalem. Sarah, how far did you say Bethany and Jerusalem were apart?"

"OK, I'll pull up Bethany on the Bible Dictionary: It looks like...here it is...'Bethany—located about 1.5 miles from Jerusalem on the eastern slope of the mount of Olives.'"

"Gee, that's what you would call greater Jerusalem, today it's kind of like St. Louis and Clayton, where I stayed last summer. OK, here goes a flip chart on the crucifixion," said Tiffany as she began to write down the Marys and the omitted Mary of Bethany and their motives and MO's. *Note: It appears at least four Marys were present at the crucifixion.*

"The next happening on our time line would be the description of Mary Magdalene and the other women after the crucifixion when they followed the body to the tomb." continued Sarah, "This was when Joseph of Arithmathea begged Pilate for the body, and it was given to him."

MATTHEW 27:59-61 *And when Joseph had taken the body, he wrapped it in a clean linen cloth, And laid it in his own new tomb, which he had hewn out in the rock: and he rolled a great stone to the door of the sepulchre, and departed.* **And there was Mary Magdalene,** *and the* **other Mary**, *sitting over against the sepulchre.*

Mary the Magdalene

MARK 15:46-47 *And he bought fine linen, and took him down, and wrapped him in the linen, and laid him in a sepulchre which was hewn out of a rock, and rolled a stone unto the door of the sepulchre.* And **Mary Magdalene** and **Mary the mother of Joses** *beheld where he was laid.*

Tiffany set up another flip chart for the tomb and showed Mary Magdalene and Mary the mother of Joses as being present. She made a note that the 'other Mary' was not Mary of Bethany. Sarah directed the group to look at the announcement of the resurrection, since it is the best known passage involving MM. Mary Magdalene went to the tomb twice. First, she saw an empty tomb; and then later she returned with the disciples, and they did not find Jesus. The first visit is in these verses.

JOHN 20:1-3 **The first day of the week cometh Mary Magdalene early, when it was yet dark,** *unto the sepulchre, and seeth the stone taken away from the sepulchre.* **Then she runneth, and cometh to Simon Peter, and to the other disciple,** *whom Jesus loved, and saith unto them, They have taken away the Lord out of the sepulchre, and we know not where they have laid him.* **Peter therefore went forth, and that other disciple, and came to the sepulchre.**

The disciples ran to the tomb, they found the tomb empty, but did not find Jesus. So, the disciples returned home.

JOHN 20:4-10 *So they ran both together:* **and the other disciple did outrun Peter, and came first to the sepulchre.** *And he stooping down, and looking in, saw the linen clothes lying; yet went he not in. Then cometh Simon Peter following him, and went into the sepulchre, and seeth the linen clothes lie, And the napkin, that was about his head, not lying with the linen clothes, but wrapped together in a place by itself. Then went in also that other disciple, which came first to the sepulchre,* **and he saw, and believed.** *For as yet they knew not the scripture, that he must rise again from the dead.* **Then the disciples went away again unto their own home.**

Sarah pointed out these scriptures don't say why MM went to the tomb on the first day of the week, but other scriptures say she went there to anoint the body of Jesus with spices.

"Here it is," said Sarah. "On MM's first trip to the tomb, she had Mary, who was James and Salome's mother, with her. You have your MO again, and Mary Magdalene did have in mind to anoint the body of Jesus with spices."

MARK 16:1 *And when the sabbath was past,* **Mary Magdalene**, *and* ***Mary the mother of James***, *and Salome,* **had bought sweet spices, that they might come and anoint him**.

"Now, drum roll, please," Sarah continued. "The stage is set, the disciples have left, and Mary Magdalene is still at the tomb."

JOH 20:11-16 **But Mary stood without at the sepulchre weeping***: and as she wept, she stooped down, and looked into the sepulchre, And seeth two angels in white sitting, the one at the head, and the other at the feet, where the body of Jesus had lain.*

And they say unto her, Woman, why weepest thou? She saith unto them, Because they have taken away my Lord, and I know not where they have laid him.

And when she had thus said, she turned herself back, and saw Jesus standing, and knew not that it was Jesus. *Jesus saith unto her, Woman, why weepest thou? whom seekest thou? She, supposing him to be the gardener, saith unto him, Sir, if thou have borne him hence, tell me where thou hast laid him, and I will take him away.*

Jesus saith unto her, Mary. *She turned herself, and saith unto him,* Rabboni*; which is to say, Master.*

Kim thought it strange the disciples looked in the tomb and saw nothing. And then Mary Magdalene looked in the tomb and saw two angels. Then, Jesus suddenly appeared out of nowhere but in a form Mary could not recognize. Kim supposed that resurrection bodies and angels, too have a lot of capabilities like appearing or disappearing, or even walking through walls.

"They certainly do," said Sarah with a knowing glance at Kim. "Now, as our friend Paul Harvey would say, "Let's look at the rest of the story."

JOHN 20:17-18 *Jesus saith unto her,* **Touch me not; for I am not yet ascended to my Father***: but go to my brethren, and say unto them, I ascend unto my Father, and your Father; and to my God, and your God.* **Mary Magdalene came and told the disciples that she had seen the Lord***, and that he had spoken these things unto her.*

JOHN 20:19-20 Then the same day at evening, being the first day of the week, **when the doors were shut where the disciples were assembled for fear of the Jews, came Jesus and stood in the midst,** *and saith unto them, Peace be unto you. And when he had so said, he shewed unto them his hands and his side. Then were the disciples glad, when they saw the Lord.*

"You know, this has always bothered me," said Velda. "If I were Mary Magdalene, and my Savior, who I thought was dead, suddenly appeared alive, I would hug the bejeebers out of him for joy."

"Well, she probably wanted to," said Kim. "But, if Jesus said, 'No,' I think we would honor his wishes."

"Didn't Thomas get to thrust his finger into the wounds in his side?" asked Tiffany, "That would be touching him."

"Let's look and see." replied Sarah, "Here are some scriptures, but it was eight days later when doubting Thomas was finally satisfied that it was Jesus."

JOHN 20:24-27 *But Thomas, one of the twelve, called Didymus, was not with them when Jesus came. The other disciples therefore said unto him, We have seen the Lord. But he said unto them, Except I shall see in his hands the print of the nails, and put my finger into the print of the nails, and thrust my hand into his side, I will not believe.* **And after eight days again his disciples were within, and Thomas with them***: then came Jesus, the doors being shut, and stood in the midst, and said, Peace be unto you. Then saith he to Thomas,* **Reach hither thy finger, and behold my hands; and reach hither thy hand, and thrust it into my side:** *and be not faithless, but believing.*

"I don't understand this," said Tiffany. "I don't think Jesus had ascended up into the clouds at this point. The ascension came later. Maybe he ascended to the Father and then came back within the eight-day period, and then later he ascended from the earth within the forty days after his crucifixion?"

"A very good question, Tiffany, I've wondered the same thing myself," said Kim with a questioning glance at Sarah. "Why could Mary Magdalene not touch him and yet Thomas could?"

"Well, as our professors say when confronted with the hard questions, that is beyond the scope of our study tonight, so we will leave it to be pondered," said Sarah. "Now, we have essentially finished with the Bible references to Mary Magdalene, can anyone think of where we might go next?"

"No, please tell us," said Kim.

"How about going back to Bethany for the ascension?" replied Sarah.

"The ascension? It was on the mount of Olives—why go back to Bethany?"

"Isn't Bethany on the side of the mount of Olives?"

"Oh."

LUKE 24:49-51 *And, behold, I send the promise of my Father upon you: but tarry ye in the city of Jerusalem, until ye be endued with power from on high. And he led them out* **as far as to Bethany**, *and he lifted up his hands, and blessed them. And it came to pass, while he blessed them,* **he was parted from them, and carried up into heaven**.

"Wow! You're right," exclaimed Kim. "Do you think he went to Bethany in honor of Mary of Bethany?"

"Could be," said Sarah. "And where do you think we might go next to find the women that had followed Jesus?"

"He told them to tarry in the city until they were endued from power on high. And we know Pentecost occurred ten days later. But were the women included in that group?" asked Tiffany.

"Let's take a look," said Sarah.

ACT 1:13-14 *And when they were come in, they went up into an upper room, where abode both Peter, and James, and John, and Andrew, Philip, and Thomas, Bartholomew, and Matthew, James the son of Alphaeus, and Simon Zelotes, and Judas the brother of James. These all continued with one accord in prayer and supplication,* **with the women, and Mary the mother of Jesus**, *and with his brethren.*

"The women are included," said Tiffany. "For some reason I thought the 120 were all men. Dumb ol' me."

"Don't put yourself down, Tiffany. There is a lot of power in words," admonished Sarah. "God wants you to be endued from on high with power just like his women disciples were. Now, let's put some of the latest info on our charts."

With that, Tiffany and Kim finished the time line and added an MO for Mary Magdalene anointing the body of Jesus.

Sarah told of additional references to Mary Magdalene in what are called the non-canonical gospels and the Gnostic gospels. The non-canonical gospels are those which were not included in the Bible. The Gnostic gospels are in this group, and their validity has been questioned. The Pharisees tended to ritualize everything, and their ceremonies were quite literal, and every jot and tittle had to be in place. Jesus severely scolded them for this:

MATTHEW 23:23-25 **Woe unto you, scribes and Pharisees, hypocrites!** *for ye pay tithe of mint and anise and cummin, and have omitted the weightier matters of the law, judgment, mercy, and faith: these ought ye to have done, and not to leave the other undone. Ye blind guides, which strain at a gnat, and swallow a camel. Woe unto you, scribes and Pharisees, hypocrites!* **for ye make clean the outside of the cup and of the platter**, *but within they are full of extortion and excess.*

Sarah said, "Those who wrote the Gnostic gospels, on the other hand, tended in the opposite direction to spiritualize things, even to the degree some denied Jesus was a literal human being who walked the earth. They said His crucifixion was only a spiritual crucifixion. The pendulum swung so much in this direction that John, the beloved apostle, was compelled to write these words:"

1 JOHN 4:2 Hereby know ye the Spirit of God: **Every spirit that confesseth that Jesus Christ is come in the flesh is of God:"**

"John went on to say that if a spirit could not declare that Jesus came in the flesh then that spirit was not of God."

1JO 4:3 *And every spirit that* **confesseth not that Jesus Christ is come in the flesh is not of God:** *and this is that spirit of antichrist, whereof ye have heard that it should come; and even now already is it in the world.*

Sarah continued, "I'm sure each of you have a firm foundation—you believe that Jesus is the Son of God, that your sins are covered by the blood that He shed on the cross—that is, if you ask forgiveness for sins. I think each of you have repented and received baptism. So, the question is: Do you want to look at some of these other gospels or would you rather stop here?"

"Do you have them?" asked Tiffany.

"Yes, my Uncle Andy collected a set of this type of books. His approach was to eat the grapes and spit out the seeds. I would treat them more like history books rather than as sacred scriptures. As you very well know, history books tend to be slanted toward the viewpoints of the historian. If you like, I have access to them through the internet. I could print out a sheet for you which relates only to Mary Magdalene's activities. Why don't you think about it for a few days, and if you decide you want this printout, I will give it to you."

Tiffany and her Mom looked at each other and nodded. "That seems like a good plan. We will think it over, and if we want to look at the material outside of the regular Bible, we will let you know," said Tiffany.

"OK, let's all look at the charts one more time and wrestle with several questions: First, are the Nain woman and Mary Magdalene one and the same? And second, are Mary Magdalene and Mary of Bethany one and the same?" asked Sarah.

1. **Jesus Near Sea of Galilee**
   - Nain Woman breaks alabaster box and wipes Jesus' feet with hair (Simon the Pharisee's house)
   - Mary Magdalene, Joanna and Susanna follow Jesus (MM had seven devils cast out)
2. **Jesus at Bethany**
   - Mary B sits at Jesus' feet while Martha serves
   - Mary B and Martha ask Jesus to come; Lazarus is dead
   - Mary B anoints Jesus with ointment
3. **Women at crucifixion of Jesus** *Note: It appears at least four Marys were present at the crucifixion.*
   - [1] Jesus' mother, Jesus' mother's sister, [2]Cleophas' wife Mary, [3]Mary Magdalene, [4]Mary the mother of James the lesser and of Joses, other women which came up to Jerusalem with him
4. **At the tomb for the burial**
   - Women who came with Him from Galilee, Mary Magdalene, the other Mary (Joses' mother)
5. **First day of week—first visit to tomb**
   - Mary Magdalene and 'other' Mary (probably Joses' mother) to anoint body; tomb empty
6. **Second visit to tomb**
   - Mary Magdalene, Peter, and 'other' disciple (probably John)
   - Male disciples leave; Mary Magdalene stays, sees angels in tomb, Jesus appears to MM
   - MM told not to touch, Mary Magdalene leaves tomb to tell disciples she has seen Jesus
7. **Jesus appears to disciples**
   - Disciples see wounds; Thomas absent but thrusts hand into Jesus' side eight days later
   - Jesus goes out to Bethany, ascends 40 days after crucifixion; Pentecost 10 days later

"OK, I'll go first in expressing my opinions," said Velda. "Initially I thought NW and MM were one and the same, but now I have reservations. However, the Nain woman was a sinner—that's all we know. But all have sinned and come short of the glory of God. So we don't know if she was involved in something like prostitution, or maybe she was just a publican like Matthew the tax collector, or maybe just a despised Samaritan woman. On the other hand, Mary Magdalene had been healed of seven evil spirit and infirmities. But the key seems to be that she was **HEALED and FREE from whatever was tormenting her** and so very thankful! I guess that I'm struggling within myself about even suggesting that Mary Magdalene might have been a prostitute because I know from my own experience how awful and degrading that label can be."

"And what about Mary Magdalene and Mary of Bethany being the same person or two different persons?" asked Sarah.

"I think it is significant that Mary Magdalene is consistently mentioned among those at the cross, at the tomb for the internment, and at the resurrection, and the name of Mary of Bethany is consistently omitted," replied Velda. "It seems to me that Mary of Bethany was so close to Jesus that wild horses couldn't have kept her away from His crucifixion, entombment, and resurrection. And both of them were anointers with their ointments and spices. I'm leaning toward saying they are the same."

"And what about you, Kim?"

"I'm kind of like the king who told Paul that Paul had almost persuaded him to become a Christian. I tend to believe that NW, MM, and MB are the same woman, but, in modern-day terms, I have reasonable doubt. So, if there are some other early church accounts or histories, I would like to see them before making up my mind."

"I think we have covered most of the easily available references.," remarked Sarah, "However, to go much deeper, we would have to do a lot of researching and digging into the ancient accounts we have talked about— the Dead Sea scrolls, Gnostic gospels, archaeological findings, etc."

"That's OK; I still like to look at everything before making up my mind," replied Kim.

"And what about you, Tiffany?"

"I still think the Nain Woman and Mary Magdalene are one and the same, just from the proximity of Magdala and Nain. It was right after the Nain woman burst the alabaster box and anointed Jesus' feet and wiped them with her hair that Mary Magdalene shows up on the radar screen. I think Luke was just being polite in not naming the sinful woman as Mary Magdalene. As for MB and MM being the same, it bothers me the same author, Luke, would not consistently call Mary Magdalene, Mary Magdalene all the way through his gospel. Some of the material we covered tonight is new, and I need time to digest it."

"OK, folks, let's leave it there and wind it up for the night."

"And what about you, Sarah?" sounded a chorus of three voices.

"I'm just the moderator," smiled Sarah. "Since you all haven't made up your minds, I don't want to try to influence you one way or the other."

"Would you mind if we borrowed the flip charts again?" said Tiffany. "Mom and I need to hash out our viewpoints a little more so we can see where we agree or disagree."

"By all means, take them," replied Sarah. "Otherwise, I would have to take them down and put them in the closet."

Tiffany and Velda gathered up the charts and, as they were leaving, Velda gave Sarah and Kim a big hug and thanked them for including her in the Sunday night session.

"I think Velda really enjoyed tonight," said Kim. "But why didn't you go ahead and give them the information on the non-canonized gospels? You *know* I will want to read them."

Sarah told of the frog experiment where the frog is sitting happily in the pan of room temperature water. And then the temperature is raised ever so gradually until the frog has the characteristics of an intense sunburn and doesn't even know it. Kim agreed if things were done in a slow and gradual way, a lot of movement can occur when it appears everything has remained the same. Sarah felt they needed to proceed cautiously because of the diversity of 'spiritual' writings. Some were very good, some were in the middle, and other writings amounted to idol worship or even worship of demonic entities. She felt the book of Thomas was mostly a collection of the sayings of Jesus, many of which are present in the canonical gospels. She thought Tiffany and Velda may not yet be prepared to plunge into these documents. She was glad she gave them the choice, and if they asked, she would give them just a few passages that related directly to Mary Magdalene.

"Since you're here to help me if I get too far out in this swamp, " requested Kim, "how about showing me some of the MM passages from the books of Thomas and Phillip."

Sarah responded, "You and I have had a chance to develop some background on concepts which are discussed in the gospel of Thomas, so it won't be as confusing to us as it would be to Velda and Tiffany."

"OK, I'm ready, I think...maybe I am...can we do it now?"

"We'll use my computer file where I stored some pertinent passages from Scholar's Version Translation of the Gospel of Thomas that was on-line. We'll start here and not all of these verses are related to MM.

"These are the secret sayings that the living Jesus spoke and Didymos Judas Thomas recorded. 1 And he said, **"Whoever discovers the interpretation of these sayings will not taste death."** 2 Jesus said, "Those who seek should not stop seeking until they find. When they find, they will be disturbed. When they are disturbed, they will marvel, and will reign over all. [And after they have reigned they will rest.]"

"Gee," responded Kim. "This looks like the scripture that Jesus spoke to Martha. You know, the one that says—I'm paraphrasing...'Whosoever lives and believes in me shall never die.' Do you believe this?"

"It does, doesn't it?" replied Sarah. "I believe that the key here must be the belief and the timing because there are many saintly people who believed in Jesus and still have died."

"The gospel of Thomas does seem secretive. What next?"

"These passages bear on the subject of the types of bodies." said Sarah, "Here they are."

37 His disciples said, "When will you appear to us, and when will we see you?" Jesus said, "When **you strip without being ashamed**, and **you take your clothes and put them under your feet like little children** and trample then, then **[you] will see the son of the living one** and you will not be afraid."

"This is baffling." said Kim, "Is he saying our celestial bodies are different than our earthly bodies?"

"Yes, let me put it this way. Has anyone in your family ever bought a car that was a real lemon?"

"Oh, yes," replied Kim, "my uncle bought a car that had repeated transmission trouble and he returned it to the dealer multiple times. Finally, he invoked the 'lemon law' and got a different, trouble-free model."

Sarah explained why voyeurism is so rampant today. When Adam and Eve sinned, they were ashamed that their bodies had changed and wanted to hide it from God. So they covered themselves with fig leaves to hide their shame—they had fallen bodies and reproductive organs like the animals. The animals, even today, run around without clothes and are not ashamed. It's only humans that cover their private parts— that is, unless they are strippers. Then she asked Kim if she remembered the woeful old refrain: *"When from the Celestial to the terrestrial tree man did stoop, He was dismayed at the emergence of pee and poop."*

Sarah continued, "There are no waste products from the celestial fruit. Why does man hide behind the bush or the bathroom stall today? Why is mankind so embarassed by unflattering flatulence? Or why do satanic cults break into Christian places of worship and desecrate them by urination, defecation, and lurid sexual acts? It is like they want to block the way back to the celestial realm—if they are miserable, everybody should be miserable!"

"So—I get it—the serpent sold Adam and Eve a lemon, and he's trying to make lemonade out of it by promoting sexual exhibition as something desirable and good. And today the strippers display and the peeping Toms peep at the same type of private parts that Adam and Eve covered with fig leaves."

"Yes, that's right. However, the Bible does say the marriage bed is undefiled. There is a balance between being a prude and an exhibitionist, but today exhibitionism is rampant. The scriptures also say that we are 'fearfully and wonderfully made,' so don't get down on yourself. OK, let's continue on."

82 Jesus said, "Whoever is near me is near the fire, and whoever is far from me is far from the kingdom." 83 Jesus said, "Images are visible to people, **but the light within them is hidden in the image of the Father's light.** He will be disclosed, but his image is hidden by his light." 84 Jesus said, "When you see your likeness, you are happy. But **when you see your images that came into being before you and that neither die nor become visible,** how much you will have to bear!"

"I think he's talking about our *spirit* as being *the* light or image," conjectured Kim. "Our spirit came into being before 'we' did, it is not visible and does not die. Our spirit is made in the very image of God."

Kim continued: "Those that have had near death experiences say that the doctors and nurses in hospitals walk right through them without knowing they are there."

"That's right," replied Sarah. "The body and soul can die, but not our spirit. If we are totally depraved sinners, our earthly body is dead, our soul dies, and our spirit becomes like a silver coin that is eventually cast into the fire to remove the impurities and then stamped as new coin, minus its previous evil personality. Remember, Peter said that Jesus preached unto those peoples disobedient before the flood—the scriptures describe them as '*spirits in prison'*. Don't you think he gave them a fiery sermon that led to their conversion?"

"What does he mean about those being near him are near the fire?"

Sarah delved into the concept of fire. She said, "We talk about 'hell fire' but is it really different than the fire that came down on the day of Pentecost? Didn't John the Baptist say the fire would separate the wheat from the chaff? The Bible says judgment begins at the house of God. Peter talked about the fiery trial believers would encounter. So, like the transmission service ad, everyone will come to God sooner or later. Christians choose to come sooner and are rewarded for it. Sinners eventually come, but with much consternation because when they die and see what could have been, they have much to bear."

"That is a different viewpoint. Does the Bible put it the same way?"

"Oh, yes," replied Sarah, "there are different levels of salvation, depending on whether it is the spirit only having been regenerated by grace, or additionally the soul being rewarded by its works. Then the third salvation is the body being transfigured and overcoming death. Let me go back to the Bible for a moment. See?"

1 CORINTHIANS 3:11-15 *For* **other foundation can no man lay than that is laid, which is Jesus Christ.** *Now if any man build upon this foundation* **gold, silver, precious stones, wood, hay, stubble;**
13 *Every man's work shall be made manifest: for the day shall declare it, because it shall be revealed by fire; and* **the fire shall try every man's work** *of what sort it is. If any man's work abide which he hath built thereupon, he shall receive a reward.* **If any man's work shall be burned, he shall suffer loss: but he himself shall be saved; yet so as by fire.**

"Hmmm—I never thought of it this way—but it does look like there will be some that just barely make it inside the door of heaven with their spirit and have no works reward from their soul."

"My next verse from Thomas bears that out," said Sarah. "Remember the threefold cord of marriage and we said some just operate in the carnal mind only."

87 Jesus said, "How miserable is **the body that depends on a body,** and how miserable is the soul that depends on these two."

"Hey, I'm getting better at this," said Kim. "*This means that if a person totally operates in the body or flesh, he will be miserable*; **and** *if only the soul and body are active, they are still miserable. One needs the foundation of their spirit in order to be happy.* OK, Prof, did I get this one right?"

"Yes, very good. The verses in my Thomas file are not in order, but we need to look at this one."

18 The disciples said to Jesus, "Tell us, how will our end come?"

Jesus said, "**Have you found the beginning, then, that you are looking for the end?** You see, **the end will be where the beginning is.**

Congratulations to the **one who stands at the beginning: that one will know the end and will not taste death.**" 19 Jesus said, "Congratulations to **the one who came into being before coming into being.**

"Oh," enthused Kim, "this is just like what we read in the Scrolls of the Ancients booklet. *If we know our heavenbefore, we then can find our hereafter.* This is amazing! I can see why you said it was necessary to break one of the seven seals in order to know your beginning."

Sarah continued her dissertation by pointing out verses where Mary Magdalene asks a question of Jesus. She said, "This will sail right above your head, unless you realize the ones who can take off their clothes and not be ashamed have already been transfigured into their celestial bodies. *The celestial body can not be taken away by robbers—but robbers can take away the earthly body by bringing death. The field is the body and the house is the soul. When Jesus' disciples take off the clothes of the earthly body, they are not naked because they are clothed with a celestial body and have entered the kingdom as little children.*" Remember John wrote *The thief cometh not but for to steal, and to kill, and to destroy.*

21 Mary said to Jesus, "**What are your disciples like**?"

He said, They are like **little children** living in a **field** that is not theirs. When the owners of the field come, they will say, "Give us back our field." **They take off their clothes in front of them in order to give it back to them, and they return their field to them.**

For this reason I say, if the owners of a house know that a thief is coming, they will be on guard before the thief arrives and **will not let the thief break into their house** (their domain) and steal their possessions.

As for you, then, be on guard against the world. Prepare yourselves with great strength, so the robbers can't find a way to get to you, for the trouble you expect will come.

"I see what you mean," said Kim. "If I had read the book of Thomas a month ago, this would have made no sense to me. I might have even been shocked."

"And if we had not had our discussion about the marriage of the spirit and soul together and the 10,000 matrix—10,000 patrix, these verses would not have made any sense to you at all." said Sarah.

22 Jesus saw some babies nursing. He said to his disciples, **"These nursing babies are like those who enter the kingdom."**

They said to him, "Then shall we enter the kingdom as babies?"

Jesus said to them, "When you make **the two into one**, and when you make the inner like the outer and the outer like the inner, and the upper like the lower, and when you make male and female into a single one, so that the male will not be male nor the female be female, when you make eyes in place of an eye, a hand in place of a hand, a foot in place of a foot, an image in place of an image, then you will enter [the kingdom]."

23 Jesus said, "I shall choose you, one from a thousand and **two from ten thousand, and they will stand as a single one.**"

Kim said, "I remember the scripture in the Bible about entering the kingdom as little child. But this confuses me. How do you explain it?"

Sarah asked Kim to look at it in a different way. The thought presented is the marriage between the spirit and the soul. Doesn't the Bible describe the mystery of marriage as two becoming one? The marriage between the human spirit and the corresponding soul is sacred. It means that the soul has renounced all other lovers that would try to plant the seeds of not only evil thoughts, but even thoughts mixed with good and evil, into the womb of the mind. Once a soul has married its spirit husband, it should not be unfaithful to that husband. Then, the true spirit husband and the soul can parent a child.

LUKE 18:17 *Verily I say unto you, Whosoever shall not receive the kingdom of God* **as a little child shall in no wise enter therein.**

EPHESIANS 5:31-32 *For this cause shall a man leave his father and mother, and shall be joined unto his wife,* **and they two shall be one flesh. This is a great mystery: but I speak concerning Christ and the church.**

"I can see the spirit and soul must first get married, "responded Kim, "and I can see why God hates unfaithfulness. An unfaithful soul would break the wedlock and go back to her good and evil spirit lover."

"That's right," said Sarah. "That's what happened in allegory to Eve when she received '*another spirit.*' Look at the scripture in 2 Corinthians. There are hints concerning the soul only having one husband. I think it should be clear the husband should be Christ in our spirit—but another husband can be chosen of a different spirit."

2 CORINTHIANS 11:3-4 *But I fear, lest by any means,* **as the serpent beguiled Eve through his subtilty, so your minds should be corrupted from the simplicity that is in Christ.** *For if he that cometh preacheth another Jesus, whom we have not preached,* **or if ye receive another spirit, which ye have not received,** *or another gospel, which ye have not accepted, ye might well bear with him.*

"This is a lot clearer to me now. A faithful marriage between the spirit and soul is a necessary prerequisite—but what is all this eye, hand, foot, image business?" asked Kim.

"Look at the verses very carefully, this time," said Sarah. "After the marriage of the spirit and soul, can there be a baby? But what baby is being discussed here? Is that baby really the birth baby of the celestial body?"

22 Jesus saw some babies nursing ...

Jesus said to them, "When you make the two into one, and when you make **the inner like the outer** and the outer like the inner, and the **upper like the lower**, and when you make **male and female into a single one**, so that the male will not be male nor the female be female, **when you make eyes in place of an eye**, **a hand in place of a hand**, a foot in place of a foot, **an image in place of an image**, **then you will enter [the kingdom].**"

Sarah explained that *once there has been a marriage of the spirit and soul, that person is eligible for the marriage supper of the Lamb.* The next part of the verse is a description of the replacing of the terrestrial body with the celestial body. The terrestrial eye is replaced with a celestial eye, the terrestrial hand is replaced with a celestial hand and so on until finally the terrestrial, Adamic image is replaced with the celestial image in the likeness of Christ. *The process being described here is the birthing of one's celestial body***.** That is why one must enter the kingdom as a little child. When matured, these bodies will be able to come and go as the wind. Jesus answered Nicodemis' question about being born of the spirit.

JOHN 3:5-8 *Jesus answered, Verily, verily, I say unto thee, Except a man be born of water and of the Spirit, he cannot enter into the kingdom of God. That which is born of the flesh is flesh; and* **that which is born of the Spirit is spirit**

Marvel not that I said unto thee, Ye must be born again. The wind bloweth where it listeth, and thou hearest the sound thereof, **but canst not tell whence it cometh, and whither it goeth: so is every one that is born of the Spirit.**

"Remember the cleft in the rock? Some of the basic steps were easily seen, but others were hidden."

"I'm beginning to understand," said Kim. "The process is like stair steps. We take one step at a time."

"This next verse is a bit different," said Sarah. "But since we are going through the book of Thomas, we might as well get it now. What do you think this means?"

> 19 Jesus said, "Congratulations to the **one who came into being before coming into being**. If you become my disciples and pay attention to my sayings, these stones will serve you.
>
> **For there are five trees in Paradise for you**; they do not change, summer or winter, and their leaves do not fall. **Whoever knows them will not taste death.**"

"OK, I think the first part speaks about our spirit being with God for some period of time before we came to earth. The stones and the trees, I don't really understand. Understanding the trees must be important if a knowledge of them avoids tasting death."

"Forget about the stones for the time being, remember I told you that there were twelve paired nerve trees in the central nervous system. These twelve paired nerve trees are your twenty-four elders. The five trees are symbolic of five of these cranial nerves. Remember, the man in the Bible that saw men as trees walking?

MARK 8:24 *And he looked up, and said,* **I see men as trees, walking**.

This is what it is all about. But don't worry about it now. All this can come later, when we get into Aunt Myra's study on the nervous system."

"I can see why you were reluctant to get into the gospel of Thomas with Tiffany and her mom. This has my head spinning," said Kim. "By the way, what verses would you have given them out of this gospel?"

"Only the last verse in the book, and there is even some controversy about whether it is really part of the book of Thomas. Here it is."

> [Saying added to the original collection at a later date.] 114 Simon Peter said to them, "**Make Mary leave us, for females don't deserve life.**" Jesus said, "Look, I will guide her to make her male, so that she too may become a living spirit resembling you males. For every female who makes herself male will enter the kingdom of Heaven."

"I would interpret it to mean Mary Magdalene will have her spirit become the husband of her soul—the same process as for the disciples," said Kim. "However, Peter seemed to have an attitude problem! Do you think Peter thought that God doesn't have daughters?"

"There are some sons teaching daughters that they have to be changed into sons. But I think they are misguided. Look, God not only has sons but he has daughters, also."

2 CORINTHIANS 6:17-18 *Wherefore come out from among them, and be ye separate, saith the Lord, and touch not the unclean thing; and I will receive you, And will be a Father unto you, and* **ye shall be my sons and daughters**, *saith the Lord Almighty.*

"And how do you think Tiffany and her Mom would interpret Thomas verse 114?" asked Sarah.

"I think they would rejoice that Mary Magdalene is included in Jesus' inner circle and leave it there," said Kim.

"I believe you're right," replied Sarah. "Now, I will make a printout of the gospel of Thomas for you so you can look through it at your leisure."

"What about the book of Phillip?" questioned Kim, "You mentioned it, too."

Sarah accused Kim of being a glutton for punishment. It was 11:00 PM. They agreed to look at one more verse and call it an evening. Sarah reiterated these books are outside the regularly accepted books of the Bible. She admonished Kim to check to see if the verses agreed with the Bible, and if not, to leave them alone. She explained the only reason she would include a verse from the book of Philip on the printout for Tiffany and Velda is that they would know about it from the popular press. Then she found the pertinent verse from the book of Philip. She indicated that where brackets [ ] were found, the words had been filled in by the translator.

59. The wisdom which (humans) call barren is herself the Mother of the Angels. (Ph 40) And the **Companion° of the [Christ] is Mariam the Magdalene**. *The [Lord loved] Mariam more than [all the (other)] Disciples,* **[and he] kissed her often on her [mouth]**.[1] *The other [women] saw his love for Mariam,*[2] *they say to him: Why do thou love [her] more than all of us? || The Savior° replied,*[2] *he says to them: Why do I not love you as (I do) her? (Prov 24:26, S-of-S 1:2, Ph 35 36 40;* [2]*asyndeton; Th 61b; interlinear)*

Kim asked, "Was the word [mouth] filled in by the translator?"

"Yes."

"So it could be on the mouth or on the cheek. I suppose the translator for some reason thought it was the mouth. I've always though the kiss of death Judas gave Jesus was on the cheek. You know, when my boyfriend, Larry, picked me up on prom night, he greeted me with a kiss on the mouth right in front of my parents; nobody thought anything of it."

"I agree," said Sarah. "Of course, there is a difference between a kiss on the mouth and a lip lock. Customs may have different in those days, too. See the footnote to Proverbs 24:26, *Every man shall kiss his lips that giveth a right answer.* The background here is that a wise man gives a true answer and is not a respecter of persons. There are a couple more verses following after this one. Let's look at them."

60. (While) a blind (person) and one who sees are both in the dark, they do not differ from one another. When the light comes, then he who sees shall behold the light, and he who is blinded shall remain in the darkness.

61. The Lord says: **'Blest is he who is before he comes into Being!' For he who is, both was and shall be.**

"Oh, there it is again," exclaimed Kim. "The heavenbefore affects the hereafter."

"The book of Philip is somewhat difficult to fathom, but it is still fascinating to contemplate."

Sarah closed her computer, looked at her watch, and said, "Kim, there are a number of other early books that mention Mary Magdalene, but we could be here all night. We have classes tomorrow. Let's turn it for the night.

"You're right," said Kim. "My head is still spinning; I hope I can get some sleep."

Kim and Sarah went through their nightly ritual of preparing for bed, and when all was done the lights were turned off.

"Night."

"Night"

After about 10 minutes had elapsed and Sarah was just drifting into a light sleep, she heard the words, "Sarah, Sarah, I've got a question in my mind. Sarah—are you awake?"

"I am now. What is your question?"

"Do you think Mary Magdalene and Jesus knew each other in the heavens before either one of them was born in the earth? And did they agree to the volume of the books of their destinies?"

"Kim, why don't you sleep on that question. In the meantime, I will sleep on it, too."

"Maybe I need to get out the book again on The Ancient Scrolls. Good night."

"Night."

Editor's Note: Express your thoughts:
See http://www.The AncientChest.com/Women

Which statement best expresses your thinking?

- ☐ 1. Mary Magdalene and Mary of Bethany were two different women.
- ☐ 2. Mary Magdalene and Mary of Bethany are the same woman.
- ☐ 3. Haven't reached a conclusion yet.
- ☐ 4. Leaning toward choice #1
- ☐ 5. Leaning toward choice #2.

Chapter 9

Women! An Insider's View

The alarm clock bleeped and Sarah hit the five minute snooze alarm. In five minutes, the alarm rudely bleeped again so Sarah shut it off. She looked for Kim, but she was asleep in the other room curled up on the sofa with the printout of *The Gospel of Thomas* lying lightly against her face.

"Oh, well," she thought. "Kim doesn't have a class till nine, I'll reset the alarm for her."

Sarah had agreed to meet Kim at the classroom door after Kim's biophysics class, and they would head to lunch. As students were streaming out of the classroom, Sarah noticed Kim and Dr. Gordon Harper were having a somewhat serious discussion near the lectern. Sarah waited patiently, and after a few minutes Kim and Professor Harper came out of the classroom laughing.

"Looks like you are one of Dr. Harper's favorite students." Sarah laughed as she and Kim walked down the old marble inlaid floor of the hall."

"Ooh, that Dr. Harper," complained Kim, "he is so intellectual and overbearing. He has an answer for everything. Granted, the guy is smart, but unless you agree with him, he will try to overwhelm you with what amounts to technical gibberish. He does this when his argument is weak."

"At least you had him laughing," recalled Sarah. "You must have kind of a squabbling, sibling type relationship."

"Well, the jerk took off 20 points on our lab experiments becausewe did it just like the lab book said rather than what he said we should have gotten out of his lecture. In effect, he told me how much smarter he is than the author of our lab book."

"Then, how did you guys end up laughing?"

"I told him I was going to place an ad in the campus newspaper to sell my lab book, I apparently didn't need it anymore."

"What did he say to that?" asked Sarah.

"He asked why. I told him I was like the guy who placed a want ad in the paper to sell a new set of encyclopedias with the explanation he didn't really need them because his wife already knew everything."

"And ... ?" laughed Sarah.

"He was a little shocked at first but saw the humor of it and laughed. The guy probably thinks he's God's gift to women and to science. The only problem is he acts like he is God so he can generously give of himself to us poor students."

"Kim, you're good at using humor to neutralize conflicts. But, I suspect Dr. Harper will try to figure out some way to get the last word."

"Maybe so, but he did give me my 20 points back after that."

That evening Kim and Sarah attended a dinner for Dr. Stansel who had been the University sponsor of the Campus Christian Center for the past 20 years and was retiring. Dr. Stansel was greatly loved by the students and admired for his willingness to counsel with them when they had problems. With his shock of white hair and kindly face, Sarah thought he must have resembled the patriarch Abraham. Sarah had been elected vice president by the CCC, and she added her contribution to the accolades given Dr. Stansel after the dinner. As Kim and Sarah were leaving the banquet room, they saw Katie's smiling face.

"Kim, Sarah, so good to see you here. The tribute for Dr. Stansel was just wonderful."

"I agree," said Sarah. "And how was your weekend marriage prep seminar with Fred?"

"It was great. I learned a lot of what is expected of a wife and how she should interact with her husband."

"Katie, best wishes for a happy marriage for you and Fred," said Sarah as they were heading down the steps.

"By the way, Sarah, Fred said he would be in touch with you. He's worked out a whole set of scriptures on submission of the wife to the husband, and he wants to discuss them with you."

"Very good Katie, have him get in touch with me," replied Sarah. "Bye"

"Bye."

As they walked back to the dorm, Kim said, "Well, I told you so, get ready to get clunked over the head with the '*I suffer not* ...' or maybe it's, '*I let not women to teach men*' or something like that scripture."

"Well, Paul said Christians must go through suffering, so I suppose I should get ready, huh?"

Kim thought that after their long, long discussions on the husband being the spirit and the woman being the soul, she could see what the scriptures are saying about the soul. The soul has a tendency to be deceived by man's wisdom and should not be teaching the husband spirit, endowed with God's wisdom, in the church. But she wondered how Sarah could possibly explain this to Fred.

Reading her thoughts, Sarah said, "I will have to show Fred a more excellent way."

"And how will you do that?"

Sarah promised to show Kim her strategy when they could access the appropriate scriptures. Arriving in their dorm room, Sarah opened her laptop and pulled up the last verse of Paul's first letter to the Corinthians chapter 13, often referred to as the 'love chapter.'"

1 CORINTHIANS 13:10-13 *But when that which is perfect is come, then that which is in part shall be done away.* **For now we see through a glass, darkly; but then face to face***: now I know in part; but then shall I know even as also I am known. And now abideth faith, hope, love, these three; but the greatest of these is love.*

Sarah noted, "Paul wrote these verses about two millennia ago, but now a new millennia is beginning. There is a scripture where Jesus told Herod, *I do cures to day and tomorrow, and the third day I shall be perfected.* If a day as a thousand years, now is the beginning of the third day. Is this the dawning of *when that which is perfect is come*—the wonderful day that we will be perfected?"

"So, you are saying that Paul was describing something much greater than he or the other disciples could see clearly at that time?"

"Yes, now I've told you about a more excellent way. Let me illustrate by asking you a question. What do you think of the ten commandments?" questioned Sarah.

"What do I think about the ten commandments? That's a strange question. The ten commandments were given by God and are a moral law to live by. They are pretty much the basis of both western law and of the Mideast. A huge controversy is going on about whether the ten commandments are too religious oriented and should be taken out of public buildings."

"Uncle Andy, in one of his emails to Myra, wrote about hearing a sermon that Christians should 'hang' the ten commandments. How would you react if Reverend Smith on Sunday morning preached that?"

"I would be shocked. I suppose there is some rhyme or reason to such thinking?" questioned Kim.

"The ten commandments were regarded as the law, or at least a portion of the law by the Hebrews. Remember what Jesus said about the law? Let me find it." continued Sarah, "Ah, here it is. Jesus said:

MATHEW 5:17Think not that I am come to destroy the law, or the prophets: **I am not come to destroy, but to fulfil.**

Now, you've helped me a lot with my calculus course. Right?"

"Right, but why do you get changing the subject?" inquired Kim.

"You'll see. Is calculus a more powerful and excellent tool than algebra?" questioned Sarah.

"Yes, that's true. You can do computations in mathematical expressions of exquisite beauty and simplicity in calculus, which would be very unwieldy in algebra, Calculus basically includes algebra and much more."

"So then, you could say that calculus fulfills the weaker areas of algebra?"

"Yes...I think I'm getting a glimmer of where you're going with this," mused Kim..

"OK, if we equate calculus to the more excellent way and algebra to the weaker law, we can understand some of Paul's comments. Paul was given the task of taking the Old Testament law and the teachings of Jesus and presenting them to the Gentiles in a form that they could understand."

GALATIONS 3:24-25 **Wherefore the law was our schoolmaster** *to bring us unto Christ, that we might be justified by faith. But* **after that faith is come, we are no longer under a schoolmaster.**

Sarah recounted the scene where the Nain woman washed Jesus' feet with her tears. Instead of looking at the very whitewashed, pious, ritualistic exteriors of the Pharisees, Jesus used a more excellent and powerful law and looked at the thoughts and intents of the heart. The woman who broke the alabaster box had a heart much more oriented toward God than the hypocritical Pharisees. Sarah described Christian church law, Hebrew law, Sharia law, and secular law as only able to change one on the outside. It would take the Christ Spirit and the Holy Spirit working from inside the heart to really change one's behavior. Sarah stated, "However, Mr. Law, the schoolmaster, is still there for the lawless, helping them to realize the futility of trying to keep the law without having the inward working of Christ."

"And what is this more excellent and powerful law that would lead one to 'hang' the ten commandments? I hope you mean hang it on the wall rather than hang it in a noose," questioned Kim.

"I thought you would never ask," smiled Sarah. "It seems Jesus told us the real secret in an incident where he was being questioned by a lawyer. Here it is."

MATTHEW 22:35-40 *Then one of them, which was a lawyer, asked him a question, tempting him, and saying, Master, which is the great commandment in the law?*

Jesus said unto him, **Thou shalt love the Lord thy God with all thy heart, and with all thy soul, and with all thy mind.** *This is the* **first and great** *commandment.*

And the **second** *is like unto it,* **Thou shalt love thy neighbour as thyself. On these two commandments hang all the law and the prophets.**

"Don't worry about hanging the ten commandments in a noose. You can see if you fulfill the first two commandment with the higher law of love, the other eight are automatically fulled. Would you kill, steal, adulterate, covet, or break any of the commandments if you kept the first two?" questioned Sarah.

"You are absolutely right!" exclaimed Kim. "I never thought of it that way! The two commandments of love have such exquisite beauty and perfection...if...if...we follow them, we have fulfilled the law."

Sarah continued, relating to Kim that her grandma had summed up Paul's love chapter of first Corinthians as: *Love trumps doctrine, and the soundest doctrine is love.*

"Ohh, that makes it so simple yet so profound," said Kim. "Sometimes, I feel so conflicted in circumstances, but now I know to ask if my proposed course demonstrates the love of God and of my neighbor."

Sarah described her Uncle Andy's email detailing that both he and the congregation were shocked when this old preacher from the hills of Georgia proposed hanging the ten commandments. But then, after they heard the sermon, they realized that a person could be taught the positive nature of the first two commandments and never even have to deal with the negative nature of other commandments if they only followed the law of love. *The law of love did not do away with the other eight commandments; it fulfilled them, supported them, and gave them something from above on which to hang.*

"I can see that, but back to our friend, Fred. What has this to do with your almost certain discussions with him? I'm surprised you haven't gotten a phone call from him already so he can make a date to give you his list of scriptures."

Sarah told Kim not to worry. Fred would call soon enough. But, the more excellent way has everything to do with what Fred is struggling with. They then talked about how when our husband spirit is circumcised, the spirit is no longer gagged by the flesh and begins to woo the bride, which is the feminine soul or mind. This comes with the basic salvation when one accepts Jesus, repents, asks forgiveness, and is baptized. Then when the church was formed on the day of Pentecost, the Holy Spirit began to witness within the spirit of the 120 in the upper room. This event suddenly and essentially rewired their soul or mind to a great extent and some even appeared to be drunken because the change was so great. *Not only was the husband spirit ungagged, but the feminine soul allowed the spirit to speak directly without trying to edit or understand what it was saying.* Paul described the event.

1CORINTHIANS 14:14-15 *for if I pray in an {unknown} tongue, my spirit doth pray, and my understanding is unfruitful. What then is it?* **I will pray with the spirit**, *and I will pray also with the understanding;* **I will sing psalms with the spirit**, *and I will sing psalms also with the understanding;*

"You mean what was happening there was the human spirit was allowed to speak, and the woman (or mind) stood aside and let it speak words it was getting from the Holy Spirit?" asked Kim.

Sarah confirmed this and reminded Kim one of the gifts given by the Holy Spirit was the gift of discernment to look beyond the exterior of someone and see inside what are the interior thoughts and motives of the heart. The criticism Jesus had of the Pharisees was in the way they used the law. The law could only see and judge the external acts of a person. So, the Pharisees tried to whitewash the outside and hide their motives on the inside. Some of them tried to operate just on the lawful side of unlawful to gain an advantage. If one thinks the ten commandments are tough, **the internal law of love is even tougher!**

"So what you saying is, as Christians, we must learn to submit to the discernment provided by our husband spirit and the Holy Spirit in our heart in order to know how to handle a situation."

"Exactly. *Jesus saw what was on the inside of people and whether they were motivated by God through their spirit or if their spirit was bound and gagged by religious ritual.*"

MATTHEW 23:26-27 *Thou blind Pharisee,* **cleanse first that which is within the cup and platter, that the outside of them may be clean also.** *Woe unto you, scribes and Pharisees, hypocrites! for ye are like unto whited sepulchres, which indeed appear beautiful outward, but are within full of dead men's bones, and of all uncleanness.*

"Oh, I see," observed Kim. "We discern what the situation is with our spirit and then listen to our husband spirit and the Holy Spirit to act in such a way that we fulfill the first and second commandments: Love God and love your neighbor."

"You've got it right."

"Hmm," said Kim, as her eyes brightened with the inspiration of an idea. "I can take your algebra-calculus example and expand upon it. Suppose God gives you ten stakes or commandments and a rope and tells me to lay out a circular foundation on the ground. Could you do it?"

"I suppose so," replied Sarah, "but it would probably look more like a ten sided polygon than a circle. But maybe, with a little tweaking here and there I could get it almost round. Oh, I see what you're talking about—trying to make the circle perfect is like adding the stakes of the hundreds of Hebrew laws! Just a little tweak here and there, and the circle will be round—but it never is. Would I need an infinite number of stakes to get a perfectly round foundation?"

"Exactly!" agreed Kim. "But let me show you what God's formula is for a perfect circle of love. Take one stake—the first commandment—and put it in the very center of God's love. Let the radius of the rope be God's love and the marker at the end of the rope be us and our neighbors—the second commandment of love if you will. Then, as the marker completes one revolution, God's love has drawn a perfect circle! The circumference of a perfect circle is 2*Pi*R and knowing that, I can calculate the radius of love."

"Kim, this is a wonderful example, You have just had a seed of inspiration from your husband spirit blossom and grow in your female soul. You have conceived an example of God's love."

"Yes, I suppose I am a litte shocked. But back to Fred, I still don't know how you will convince him. He has some very set ideas about women and submission. Even your Uncle Andy struggled at times—remember his email you showed me?" [See Appendix D].

Sarah told her that after church was formed at Pentecost, the place of the Holy Spirit operating within the spirit of man was slowly eroded. And today, many of the so called church rules and teachings have become just like the legalisms of the law as practiced by the Pharisees.

Sarah said, "It is best to wait and see what Fred has to say. And second, if he says what we think he will say, we will put a number of situations in front of him illustrating the weakness of a system that is based on external appearances."

"I can see it," said Kim, "but, again, it will be hard to convince Fred. By the way, does external appearances mean whether a person looks like a man or a woman?"

"Well, let's sleep on that one." Sarah smiled. "It's getting late."

The next day flew by. Kim received accolades from the other three members of her biophysics lab team. They had chosen her to talk to the elite Dr. Gordon W. Harper about the 20 points he had knocked off their lab report. Being sucessful, Kim was now their hero because the 20 points would likely be the difference between an 'A' or a 'B' lab grade. Sarah had a late class and when she got back to the dorm, she saw a message by the phone. Kim confirmed that Fred had called and wanted Sarah to return the call. Sarah made an *Oh Joy*! kind of face and then picked up the phone and called Fred. They chatted for about ten minutes.

"Well?" questioned Kim, "Are things about like what you thought?"

"Pretty much," replied Sarah. "Fred wants to get together and trade information on Thursday evening. I hope you are available then."

"I wouldn't miss it for anything," said Kim. "This is so very interesting—almost like a chess game."

"He wants us to meet him at Campus Pizza at six on Thursday evening. We'll have a pizza while we trade information. I had rather Fred came by himself because I think he will be grandstanding with Katie there. But apparently Katie plans to come, too."

Wednesday had its usual heavy schedule of classes and labs. Sarah managed to spend about 45 minutes on Wednesday evening preparing some information for Fred. Then she hit the books for her Calculus test on Thursday.

That evening, Kim and Sarah arrived a few minutes early at Campus Pizza and Fred and Katie were already there waiting for them. They conferred and decided to split the huge "BIG DADDY" pizza with multiple toppings to suit everyone's taste. After placing the order, the group took their drinks and retired to the far end of the pizzateria to begin chatting. Thursday night business was relatively light, and there were only a few customers in the table area.

Fred then updated Sarah and Kim on the marriage seminar that he and Katie had attended the last weekend. He reported they had a wonderful time and learned a lot of new things about each other. They were given a questionnaire and told to go down by the lake and fill it out. He and Katie both surprised each other by some of their answers about attitudes and feelings. The take-away lesson emphasized by the seminar leader was husbands were to love their wives as much or more as they loved themselves. And wives were to likewise love their husbands."

"I've heard it's a great seminar," said Sarah. "Did you get your sheet of scriptures that you want to give me about the role of women at the seminar?"

"Oh, no. That list is something I've been working on for a long time to be sure I know how to be the head of the household. You sort of blindsided me with your comments about a woman chief justice, but I have all of that put in context now," said Fred as he opened his Bible and gave the sheet to Sarah.

Man as Head of Woman Scriptures

I Corinthians 11:3-5 But I would have you know, that the head of every man is Christ; and the head of the woman is the man; and the head of Christ is God. Every man praying or prophesying, having his head covered, dishonoureth his head. But every woman that prayeth or prophesieth with her head uncovered dishonoureth her head: for that is even all one as if she were shaven.

I Corinthians 14:34-35 Let your women keep silence in the churches: for it is not permitted unto them to speak; but they are commanded to be under obedience as also saith the law. And if they will learn any thing, let them ask their husbands at home: for it is a shame for women to speak in the church.

I Peter 3:1-7 Likewise, ye wives, be in subjection to your own husbands; that, if any obey not the word, they also may without the word be won by the conversation of the wives; While they behold your chaste conversation coupled with fear. Whose adorning let it not be that outward adorning of plaiting the hair, and of wearing of gold, or of putting on of apparel; But let it be the hidden man of the heart, in that which is not corruptible, even the ornament of a meek and quiet spirit, which is in the sight of God of great price. For after this manner in the old time the holy women also, who trusted in God, adorned themselves, being in subjection unto their own husbands: Even as Sara obeyed Abraham, calling him lord: whose daughters ye are, as long as ye do well, and are not afraid with any amazement. Likewise, ye husbands, dwell with them according to knowledge, giving honour unto the wife, as unto the weaker vessel, and as being heirs together of the grace of life; that your prayers be not hindered.

JUDGES 4:4-6 And Deborah, a prophetess, the wife of Lapidoth, she judged Israel at that time.
5 And she dwelt under the palm tree of Deborah between Ramah and Bethel in mount Ephraim: and the children of Israel came up to her for judgment. And she sent and called Barak the son of Abinoam out of Kedeshnaphtali, and said unto him, Hath not the LORD God of Israel commanded, saying, Go and draw toward mount Tabor, and take with thee ten thousand men of the children of Naphtali and of the children of Zebulun?

Context: God couldn't find a suitable man to judge Israel so he had to resort to choosing a woman—Deborah—to judge Israel.

Notes compiled by Fred Ridgemon

"Now, you'll have to admit," emphasized Fred, "these are all scriptures in the Bible [patting the open Bible with his hand] right there in black and white, and it is very clear the man is the authority figure for the woman. He's kind of like an umbrella for the woman, if she gets out from under the man's umbrella of protection, she becomes very vulnerable."

"I see," said Sarah, as she scanned over the scriptures in the list. "I will take these and study them. Now, I promised I would give you some material to read also. So, I will give you—"

"Oh, here comes the pizza!" exclaimed Katie, "Look, it's Floyd bringing it."

"Hi Floyd," chorused the group.

"Hi guys," replied Floyd. "This BIG DADDY pizza is huge. I could barely get it out of the oven. Here, you will need to move your stuff, Bible and all to the side. There we go."

"We're having a little Bible Study," said Fred. "Would you like to visit with us?"

"Oh no," replied Floyd. "I'm busy preparing some "to go" orders in the kitchen, and besides, the Bible just isn't my cup of tea."

"Why is that?" questioned Fred. "Studying the Bible is a good thing to do."

"Well, since you asked, I think most of it is based on myths, and it is full of errors and inconsistencies. It just doesn't stand up under scientific examination."

"Do you have an example of an error or inconsistency which is bothering you?" asked Sarah.

"OK, I'll give you one. In fact, Dr. Harper and I were discussing this the other day. The creation account is all out of sequence. We know the sun and its light in our part of the universe was formed first and then the earth and various planets fell into an orbit around the sun. Look in the first book of the Bible and read me the sequence."

Fred opened up his Bible to the book of Genesis and began to read:

GENESIS

1:1 In the beginning God created the heaven and the earth.

2 And the earth was without form, and void; and darkness was upon the face of the deep. And the Spirit of God moved upon the face of the waters.

3 And God said, Let there be light: and there was light.

4 And God saw the light, that it was good: and God divided the light from the darkness.

5 And **God called the light Day, and the darkness he called Night. And the evening and the morning were the first day**.

"Stop for a moment. See," said Floyd. "There is light and morning and evening and the sun hasn't even been created yet. Now, Fred, continue reading."

6 And God said, Let there be a firmament in the midst of the waters, and let it divide the waters from the waters.

7 And God made the firmament, and divided the waters which were under the firmament from the waters which were above the firmament: and it was so.

8 And God called the firmament Heaven. **And the evening and the morning were the second day.**

"This firmament thing sounds strange to me," said Floyd. "But I suppose it is talking about separating land and water under the sky to make continents or whatever. But look, here we have light because it was the second day, and do you see any mention of the sun yet?"

The rest of the group looked at the text and did not reply.
"That's right. No mention of the sun. Fred, continue reading," said Floyd.

9 And God said, Let the waters under the heaven be gathered together unto one place, and let the dry land appear: and it was so.

10 And God called the dry land Earth; and the gathering together of the waters called he Seas: and God saw that it was good.

11 And God said, **Let the earth bring forth grass, the herb yielding seed, and the fruit tree yielding fruit after his kind**, whose seed is in itself, upon the earth: and it was so.

12 And the earth brought forth grass, and herb yielding seed after his kind, and the tree yielding fruit, whose seed was in itself, after his kind: and God saw that it was good.

13 **And the evening and the morning were the third day**.

"Now, isn't this just peachy?" exclaimed Floyd. "We have vegetation growing, fruit trees growing, and no sun yet. What a miracle!"

14 **And God said, Let there be lights in the firmament of the heaven to divide the day from the night; and let them be for signs, and for seasons, and for days, and years**:

15 And let them be for lights in the firmament of the heaven to give light upon the earth: and it was so.

16 **And God made two great lights; the greater light to rule the day, and the lesser light to rule the night: he made the stars also.**

17 And God set them in the firmament of the heaven to give light upon the earth,

18 And to rule over the day and over the night, and to divide the light from the darkness: and God saw that it was good.

19 And the evening and the morning were the fourth day.

"Aha!" said Floyd. "Finally! On the fourth day we get the sun to shine. You see, folks, this is why I have such a hard time believing the Bible."

"And just why do you think this sequence is wrong?" questioned Sarah. "Were you there to watch it?"

"Of course not!" said Floyd. "And Sarah, were *you* there to watch it?"

"Who knows?" replied Sarah, "I just might have been."

"Floyd. Floyd," a voice rang out from the pizza counter. It was the pizza manager waving Floyd back to the kitchen for something.

"Guys, I have to go. But I think I made my point about why you can't trust the Bible."

"Well, that is debatable," said Sarah.

"Then lets' debate it." said Floyd. "You would end up on the losing side. Guys, I've got to go, before my boss gets on my case for spending too much time away from the ovens."

"Wow, that Floyd is something else," exclaimed Fred. "It's easy to see he doesn't believe God is all powerful and can create things in any order He so desires."

"He's really such a nice guy, too," said Katie. "It's too bad he has let some of the professors corrupt his mind with all this humanistic stuff."

"Sarah, do you realize Floyd has challenged you to a debate?" questioned Kim. "I don't know why it is, but it seems like everyone wants to debate you, and you're such a nice person."

"Maybe it's something about the atmosphere inside Campus Pizza." Fred laughed. "Last time I was in here, we had our friendly and spirited discussion about a woman chief justice for the Supreme Court."

"Speaking of that," said Sarah, "we did agree to exchange notes. You've given me your notes and then we were interrupted by Floyd. Fred, here's my set of notes and scriptures for you to look over."

Fred took the sheet from Sarah and scanned down through it. He frowned, "I don't see what this has to do with our subject. It's about Jesus' agony in the garden of Gethsemane and about the meaning of the word 'soul'?"

Sarah assured Fred she had listed these particular scriptures for a reason. It was her opinion that the gender of the soul is feminine. She reported some languages like Hebrew and Greek make much greater use of gender by giving gender indication to what we would consider as neutral gender nouns. An example in the English language might be a decision whether to call a ship "she" or "it." The Hebrew noun for soul is *nephesh* and the Greek noun is *psuche*. Sarah requested that Fred research the gender of these two nouns. If he did not agree the soul has a feminine gender, then he should correct Sarah the next time they got together."

"OK," said Fred. "I have a friend who reads directly from the Hebrew Old Testament and the Greek New Testament. I will ask him about it."

"That would be great," said Sarah. "Just look over the scriptures I gave you and when we get back together, we can compare notes. And beside, folks, the pizza is getting cold!"

Then the conversation relatively subsided as the group chowed down for the evening.

On Friday, Kim came back from her biophysic's lab with a big smile on her face. "Guess what, we got an 'A' on our bio-labs, and the lab team is taking me out to dinner tonight to celebrate."

"That's wonderful!" said Sarah. "Where are you going?"

"We're going to Houston House, and I get to choose the best steak on the menu. And there's something else."

"What?"

"I think Red is the one who arranged it. His real name is Rufus, but we call him Red. I think that he has eyes for me because I notice him looking when he thinks that I don't see him. But there is one of those convex safety mirrors in the hall entrance to the lab so I do see him."

"What's he like? Is he a nice guy?" asked Sarah.

Kim described him as like a character actor she had seen in a Shakespeare play—very tall, kind of awkward, and somewhat shy.

Kim said, "One can picture him as a body guard for the king with a Hershey's kisses type cap with the button on top, stripped shirt, ruffled sleeves, and linen hose. He comes into the lab wearing his funny cap like a sports car driver or something."

"Hmmm...maybe he has been looking at you looking him over. Mirrors reflect both ways you know."

"Oh, shut your mouth—it's nothing. He hasn't even asked me for a date."

Sarah was already in bed when Kim returned late from her dinner engagement with the lab group. Both were very tired from an exhausting week, so they slept till noon and then began studying for finals, which would begin week after next. Kim said little about her dinner the previous evening other than she had a wonderful prime rib and had fun with the group. Sarah really wanted to ask how things went with Rufus the Red, but she decided maybe Kim was a bit sensitive about it, so she would play the waiting game.

That afternoon the phone rang twice. The first call was a wrong number, and the second was Fred saying he had looked over the notes Sarah had given him but he still didn't see how it related to men having headship over women. And, of course, Fred asked if Sarah had really studied the scriptures he had given her. Fred wanted to get together that evening to resume the discussion, but Sarah put him off until Sunday afternoon in order to devote the rest of the day to preparing for finals.

"Our friend Fred?" asked Kim.

"Yes, I or we—if you want to go—will get together with him Sunday afternoon at the picnic table at Council Rocks."

Notes for Fred

(Greek and Hebrew Words for 'soul' and 'spirit' In Parentheses)
Compiled by Sarah

MATT 16:24-26 Then said Jesus unto his disciples, If any man will come after me, let him deny himself, and take up his cross, and follow me. For whosoever will save his life [*psuche*) shall lose it: and whosoever will lose his life [*psuche*] for my sake shall find it.
For what is a man profited, if he shall gain the whole world, and lose his own soul [*psuche*]? or what shall a man give in exchange for his soul [*psuche*]?

MATT 26:38 -41 Then saith he unto them, My soul [*psuche*] is exceeding sorrowful, even unto death: tarry ye here, and watch with me. And he went a little farther, and fell on his face, and prayed, saying, O my Father, if it be possible, let this cup pass from me: nevertheless not as I will, but as thou wilt.
And he cometh unto the disciples, and findeth them asleep, and saith unto Peter, What, could ye not watch with me one hour? Watch and pray, that ye enter not into temptation: the spirit [*pneuma*] indeed is willing, but the flesh is weak.

1CO 15:45 And so it is written, The first man Adam was made a living soul (*psuche*); the last Adam was made a quickening spirit [*pneuma*].

GEN 2:7 And the LORD God formed man of the dust of the ground, and breathed into his nostrils the breath of life; and man became a living soul [*nephesh***].

HEB 4:12 For the word of God is quick, and powerful, and sharper than any twoedged sword, piercing even to the dividing asunder of soul [*psuche*] and spirit [*pneuma*], and of the joints and marrow, and is a discerner of the thoughts and intents of the heart.

1TH 5:23 And the very God of peace sanctify you wholly; and I pray God your whole spirit [*pneuma*] and soul [*psuche*] and body be preserved blameless unto the coming of our Lord Jesus Christ.

1PE 3:4 But let it be the hidden man of the heart, in that which is not corruptible, even the ornament of a meek and quiet spirit [*pneuma*], which is in the sight of God of great price.

JOH 4:21-24 Jesus saith unto her, Woman, believe me, the hour cometh, when ye shall neither in this mountain, nor yet at Jerusalem, worship the Father. Ye worship ye know not what: we know what we worship: for salvation is of the Jews.
But the hour cometh, and now is, when the true worshippers shall worship the Father in spirit [*pneuma*] and in truth: for the Father seeketh such to worship him. God is a Spirit [*Pneuma*]: and they that worship him must worship him in spirit [*pneuma*] and in truth.

PRO 20:27 The spirit of man [*neshamah***] is the candle of the LORD, searching all the inward parts of the belly.

** Old Testament Hebrew rather than New Testament Greek

"I believe he thinks he has you on the ropes and can't wait for the knockout. However, did you notice Fred was much more friendly after you stood up to Floyd?" asked Kim.

Sarah agreed. "Sometimes, it takes opposition from the outside to keep Christians from fighting among themselves. And some of the doctrinal disputes have very little to do with the path of salvation. I guess that's why we have denominations. A denominator is a divisor. It's a shame we can't all just be Christians and forget the divisive labels."

"I concur," said Kim, "but the denominations are probably here to stay until Jesus returns."

The afternoon air was warm, but the breeze off the river and the shade given by the tall white oak trees made the picnic tables at Council Rocks a comfortable and refreshing location for a lazy Sunday.

"Hey, I'm impressed, you brought your laptop. I have to do it the old fashioned way," said Fred as he laid his Bible and notes out on the picnic table.

"Well, I have to have something to keep up with you and Katie," smiled Sarah. "Otherwise, you would overwhelm me."

Kim opened the ice chest and dug out a round of frozen fruit popsicles for everyone, and they settled down for the task at hand.

"Do you want to go first?" asked Sarah.

"No, ladies first," replied Fred. "Please start with any questions you have."

"Fine," said Sarah. "The first question I have for you is do you require your women to keep silent in the church? I know you and Katie aren't married yet, but when you are, will you require her to keep quiet and ask any questions that she might have when you get home? You know the scripture I'm talking about—here it is on the screen."

1 CORINTHIANS 14:34-35 **Let your women keep silence in the churches:** *for it is not permitted unto them to speak; but they are commanded to be under obedience as also saith the law. And if they will learn any thing, let them ask their husbands at home: for it is a shame for women to speak in the church.*

"During a formal meeting, we do ask the women to be quiet while the men teach. And the woman are encouraged to discuss their questions with their husbands, off-line, so to speak," replied Fred.

"But do you have women teachers teaching girls or other women in the church, say like a girls Sunday School class?"

"Oh, yes," replied Fred. "Women teaching girls or women or even young boys is perfectly OK."

"So, in a church setting, then it is OK for women to teach other women or girls in silent sign language, but they still have to be silent in the church. But since we are outside of a church building, it's OK for me to be speaking now."

"You're being ridiculous!" exclaimed Fred. "You're taking it completely out of context. No one is expecting women to be completely silent in the church building."

"I'm just taking at face value what you have given me," said Sarah. "I think it's ridiculous too, and that's why I think you have to look at the context the *women keep silence* scripture was given in order to know how to interpret it."

"Speaking of context," said Fred. "I think you took the Deborah being judge scripture out of context. This situation was somewhat of an aberration because God couldn't find a suitable man to be judge over Israel, so he chose a woman."

"Do you know that from scripture, or is that just something somebody told you?" questioned Sarah.

"Well, the Bible says in the time when God placed judges over Israel, every man did that which was right in his own eyes. So, God must have decided that the men were doing their own thing, and he chose a woman instead."

"I see," said Sarah. "It was really just an unusual circumstance? Deborah was *not only a judge*, she was a *prophetess*, also. Let's see if there are some other unusual circumstances where women were used to give judgement or religious counsel to men. What about Huldah the prophetess?"

"Huldah?" questioned Fred. "Are you sure she didn't just teach women?"

"Let's look and see." said Sarah. "Huldah...searching...searching ...here it is."

2 KINGS 22:14-15 **So Hilkiah the priest**, *and Ahikam, and Achbor, and Shaphan, and Asahiah,* **went unto Huldah the prophetess**, *the wife of Shallum the son of Tikvah, the son of Harhas, keeper of the wardrobe; (now she dwelt in Jerusalem* **in the college**;*) and they communed with her. And she said unto them,* **Thus saith the LORD God of Israel, Tell the man that sent you to me**....

"I can see I'm going to have to get Bible computer software to keep up with you," said Fred. "OK you found another instance where the priests consulted with a woman. But this is just Old Testament accounts. What about the New Testament?"

"Before, we go on to the New Testament, let me just mention that Miriam, the sister of Moses, was a prophetess, too. OK, here we go. You wanted examples from the New Testament. Searching...searching... searching."

LUKE 2:36-38 *And there was one* **Anna, a prophetess**, *the daughter of Phanuel, of the tribe of Aser: she was of a great age, and had lived with an husband seven years from her virginity; And she was a widow of about fourscore and four years,* **which departed not from the temple**, *but served God with fastings and prayers night and day.* **And she coming in that instant gave thanks likewise unto the Lord, and spake of him to all them that looked for redemption in Jerusalem.**

"That's not really totally New Testament," observed Fred. "Jesus hadn't come into His ministry yet and was still a child. It's OK for women to prophesy to children. There probably weren't any men there."

"Let's look and see the context," said Sarah. "Oops, it does look like Joseph was there and most likely Simeon who came also and gave a prophetic word concerning Jesus."

Since Fred wanted New Testament examples, Sarah searched on the computer and found the incident where Jesus talked to the lowly Samaritan women about living water at the well and His disciples were upset about it. Then she preached the message to the men in the town, and they came to Jesus. Fred thought Sarah embellished the account about the woman preaching to the men.

"OK, if you think I embellished it, let's look at it." replied Sarah.

JOHN 4:27-30 *And upon this came his disciples, and marvelled that he talked with the woman: yet no man said, What seekest thou? or, Why talkest thou with her?* **The woman then left her waterpot, and went her way into the city, and saith to the men**, *Come, see a man, which told me all things that ever I did: is not this the Christ? Then they went out of the city, and came unto him.*

"This is the woman that had five husbands and then was living with a sixth, not her husband. She was just a sinner and had just been converted. She did not know the rules of the church yet," said Fred.

"Fred, Fred, Fred!" Kim interjected. "Let him who is without sin cast the first stone! Doesn't the Bible say *all have sinned and fallen short of the glory of God?*"

"Fred, honey, don't you think Jesus is pleased when we talk to others about him?" questioned Katie.

"Wait a minute, girls, hold on! Uh, uh. That isn't what I meant," grimaced Fred. "Of course, we are all sinners and must come to Jesus for forgiveness, and Jesus is pleased when we share with others about Him. What I'm saying is this wasn't a church building where formal church is held."

"Isn't it true many of the New Testament churches met in houses rather than church buildings?"

"Well, yes."

"What do you think the rules would be in this house church type setting where we have four New Testament prophetesses?" asked Sarah.

ACTS 21:8-9 *And the next day we that were of Paul's company departed, and came unto Caesarea: and we entered into the house of Philip the evangelist, which was one of the seven; and abode with him. And the same man had* **four daughters, virgins, which did prophesy.**

"It doesn't say house church," objected Fred. "And besides, as long as these four prophetesses didn't minister to the men it would be OK."

"Well, something spiritual was going on in this house. Look at the context. In the next verses, there is a prophet named Agabus who came and prophesied to Paul about what would happen to him. Do you think these four daughters might have prophesied in their own house?"

"Yes, I see." replied Fred. "But, it doesn't say the four daughters ministered to Paul. It was perfectly all right for the male Agabus to prophesy."

"Oh, I see your point," said Sarah. "In a church setting, when something spiritual is going on, the women should keep silent. Right?"

"Right."

"Fred, where was the first church actually formed?"

"Why everyone knows the church was first formed in the upper room on the day of Pentecost," replied Fred.

"Fred, were there women in the upper room?" asked Sarah.

"I don't know. I never really thought about it. I thought it was mainly the disciples and maybe some others," replied Fred. Fred stroked his chin and frowned, "Where are you going with this?"

"Let's go to the upper room where God's church was first formed by the Holy Spirit and see who was there," said Sarah as she clicked on the books of Acts. "Fred, does it say that women were there?"

ACTS 1:13-14 *And when they were come in, they went up into an upper room, where abode both Peter, and James, and John, and Andrew, Philip, and Thomas, Bartholomew, and Matthew, James the son of Alphaeus, and Simon Zelotes, and Judas the brother of James.* **These all continued with one accord in prayer and supplication, with the women, and Mary the mother of Jesus**, *and with his brethren.*

"OK, OK, it does say women were there. But it doesn't say that they spoke, does it?"

"Well, let's see what happened when the Holy Spirit fell."

ACTS 2:14-17 *But Peter, standing up with the eleven, lifted up his voice, and said unto them, Ye men of Judaea, and all ye that dwell at Jerusalem, be this known unto you, and hearken to my words: For these are not drunken, as ye suppose, seeing it is but the third hour of the day. But this is that which was spoken by the prophet Joel; And it shall come to pass in the last days, saith God, I will pour out of my Spirit upon all flesh:* **and your sons and your daughters shall prophesy**, *and your young men shall see visions, and your old men shall dream dreams:*

"Gee, Fred, it sure looks to me like the women were part of the sons and daughters that prophesy."

"Yes," said Kim, " and it was right in the middle of the church as it was formed by the Holy Spirit."

"Fred, honey," Katie asked, "didn't you say that church was wherever two or three were gathered together in his name? I don't understand why there is one set of rules for a church building with a steeple on it and another set of rules for when we had a Bible study at Brother Edwin's house. Brother Edwin encouraged me to read scripture references for the Bible study."

"OK, OK, OK," said Fred. "You can say what you like, but I still go back to the scripture about women being silent in the church, and explain to me why we shouldn't require women to keep quiet in the church. Pull that up on your screen."

1CORINTHIANS 14:34-35 **Let your women keep silence in the churches**: *for it is not permitted unto them to speak; but they are commanded to be under obedience as also saith the law. And if they will learn any thing,* **let them ask their husbands at home: for it is a shame for women to speak in the church.**

"See," said Fred. "There it is in plain English, or Greek, or Hebrew—whatever it was spoken in. How do you conclude anything different than that?"

"Actually, men are to keep quiet in the church, too," said Sarah.

"What? Then how could you have a church service? That can't be."

"Oh, yes it is," said Sarah. "Look."

1CO 14:28 *But if there be no interpreter,* **let him keep silence in the church**; *and let him speak to himself, and to God.*

"Oh, that one." said Fred. "You're taking it out of context. That's not talking about men keeping silence in the church, it talking about spiritual gifts and to keep quiet if there is no one in the church to interpret a message given in a tongue that is not the commonly spoken language of the church."

"Then, if I've taken the scripture for men to keep silent in the church out of context, then maybe you've taken the scripture for women to be silent in the church out of context."

"How do you mean?" asked Fred.

"Look at the verses on each side of it," said Sarah. "Isn't this whole chapter about spiritual gifts, not about gender of the person using the spiritual gifts.?"

1CORINTHIANS 14:27-34 *If any man speak in an unknown tongue, let it be by two, or at the most by three, and that by course; and let one interpret.* **But if there be no interpreter, let him keep silence in the church;** *and let him speak to himself, and to God. Let the prophets speak two or three, and let the other judge. If any thing be revealed to another that sitteth by, let the first hold his peace. For ye may all prophesy one by one, that all may learn, and all may be comforted.*

32 **And the spirits of the prophets are subject to the prophets**. *For God is not the author of confusion, but of peace, as in all churches of the saints.* **Let your women keep silence in the churches:** *for it is not permitted unto them to speak; but they are commanded to be under obedience as also saith the law.*

"Now, Fred, Let me ask you this. Are prophets supposed to speak out of their spirit or their soul?"

"Out of their spirit, of course, it says so in verse 32," said Fred. "I will agree the soul cannot be trusted."

"Great, Fred," said Sarah. "This is something we agree on. Now, if you will take the sheet of notes I gave you, please look at the first set of verses. Would it be safe to say Jesus is saying that we must give up our psuche, as the Greeks call it, or maybe I should say psyche in modern day terms, in order to save it?"

MAT 16:24-26 Then said Jesus unto his disciples, If any man will come after me, let him deny himself, and take up his cross, and follow me. **For whosoever will save his life** *[psuche]* **shall lose it: and whosoever will lose his life** [*psuche*] **for my sake shall find it.**
26 For what is a man profited, if he shall gain the whole world, and lose his own soul [*psuche*]? or what shall a man give in exchange for his soul [*psuche*]?

"I think Jesus makes it pretty clear," replied Fred. "Jesus wants us to make decisions from within our spirit rather than our soul."

"Very good," said Sarah. "You and I are on a roll, now. Let's go on to the next set."

MAT 26:38-41 Then saith he unto them, **My soul** (*psuche*) *is exceeding sorrowful, even unto death*: tarry ye here, and watch with me. And he went a little farther, and fell on his face, and prayed, saying, O my Father, if it be possible, let this cup pass from me: nevertheless not as I will, but as thou wilt. And he cometh unto the disciples, and findeth them asleep, and saith unto Peter, What, could ye not watch with me one hour? Watch and pray, that ye enter not into temptation: **the spirit** (*pneuma*) indeed is willing, but the flesh is weak.

Sarah questioned Fred if he would agree Jesus took his very advice and was willing to put his very own soul (*psuche*)—where his fleshly desires and reasonings were manifesting—to death. But at the same time, he was wanting his willing spirit (*pneuma*) to keep him from giving in to temptation. After all, his soul was telling him that crucifixion would be painful and what's the point of being a sacrificial lamb, anyway.

"I can't argue with that," replied Fred. "I think the scriptures make that clear."

"Good. Now, I'm going to say something that will probably shock you at first. Jesus had woman trouble," tendered Sarah.

"Woman trouble. What do you mean? He did not have woman trouble! He always conducted himself in a proper manner and was without sin."

"Sarah, you've gone over the line, now," exclaimed Katie. "Jesus did *not* have woman trouble! He was tempted just like we are, sure, but he did not have woman trouble! How could you *even think* of saying such a thing?"

"I had a feeling you would react this way. You're thinking of a woman as like a girlfriend or as a wife. But, let me ask you where thoughts are conceived. Katie, you're a woman—what do you think?"

"Well, I suppose thoughts are conceived in the mind," replied Katie.

"And Fred, you're a man—where does the male seed of thoughts come from that are implanted and conceived in the mind?"

"Well, hopefully, they would come from within one's spirit if they are truly spiritual thoughts. If they are devilish thoughts, they come from somewhere else," replied Fred.

"*Oh, you mean our soul is like a feminine lover*?" asked Katie. "*It can accept seed to conceive heavenly thoughts or accept devilish seed to conceive hellish thoughts?*"

"That's right," said Sarah.

"Goodness gracious!" said Katie. "I never thought of us having a woman as a soul which conceives thoughts."

Kim pointed out Sarah had warned them that they would be shocked. Kim had been around her long enough to know when she warned you about something, then she will probably do exactly what she warned you about. One has trouble believing Jesus had woman trouble, until a certain verse is highlighted and revelation comes that *the woman is a symbol of the soul.*

"Show me the verse," requested Fred.

JOHN 12:27 **Now is my soul troubled**; *and what shall I say? Father, save me from this hour: but for this cause came I unto this hour.*

"All right," said Fred. "I will grudgingly admit if the woman is a symbol of the soul, Jesus' soul was troubled."

"I think your grudging admission is very gracious," smiled Sarah. "Thank you for it."

"You're welcome." Fred laughed.

"Now, you and I had one scripture that was included in both our notes we exchanged. The verse was from the third chapter of I Peter. In looking at this scripture, is our spirit portrayed as a male or female?"

1PETER 3:4 But let it be **the hidden man of the heart**, in that which is not corruptible, even the ornament of a meek and quiet spirit *(pneuma),* which is in the sight of God of great price.

"It's obvious it is male," observed Katie. "It calls it the hidden man—not woman—but man of the heart. I think that the center of our spirit is located somewhere in our heart, or shall we say the 'gut' area."

"Very good, Katie. Fred, do you agree?" asked Sarah.

"Yes, I agree," said Fred. "But I'm not sure I like the direction this is going."

"And why is that, Fred?" asked Sarah.

"I'm afraid you're going to say our *spirit is the husband* and our *soul is the wife*; and the wife (or soul) must submit to the husband (or spirit) if we want to advance spiritually."

"Fred, Fred, you're just paranoid. You need to get your paranoids taken out, then you can trust me more. But since you brought this up, let's look at the context of this scripture and see if what you just said fits."

1 PETER 2:25.3:1-4 *For ye were as sheep going astray; but are now returned unto the Shepherd and Bishop of your souls. Likewise, ye wives, be in subjection to your own husbands; that, if any obey not the word, they also may without the word be won by the conversation of the wives; While they behold your chaste conversation coupled with fear.* **Whose adorning let it not be that outward adorning** *of plaiting the hair, and of wearing of gold, or of putting on of apparel; But let it be* **the hidden man of the heart,** *in that which is not corruptible,* **even the ornament of a meek and quiet spirit, which is in the sight of God of great price.**

"Peter is saying *the hidden man of the heart is the ornament that should be worn by the woman.* Think of *the woman as being the soul that conceives thoughts*." continued Sarah.

"I can see the soul should be in submission to the spirit." said Fred. "However, I can also see that the wife can win an unbelieving husband by following the leading of the spirit within."

Sarah concurred Fred was right on both counts. The secret to a happy marriage is when the physical husband and the physical wife both have their souls in subjection to their spirits. She chose these scriptures to elaborate on submission of the soul to the spirit.

1 PETER 3:5-7 *For after this manner in the old time the holy women also, who trusted in God, adorned themselves, being in subjection unto their own husbands: Even as Sara obeyed Abraham, calling him lord: whose daughters ye are, as long as ye do well, and are not afraid with any amazement. Likewise, ye husbands, dwell with them according to knowledge,* **giving honour unto the wife, as unto the weaker vessel**, *and as* **being heirs together** *of the grace of life;* **that your prayers be not hindered.**

"Gee," said Katie, "am I supposed to call Fred, lord Fred?"

"Do what ever you are comfortable with," replied Sarah. "However, before you jump off the deep end, you might want to consider this example of how Sarah handled a delicate situation with Abraham and remained in obedience to God. Look at what happened here and tell me if Sarah adorned her female soul with her husband spirit."

GENESIS 21:8-12 *And the child grew, and was weaned: and Abraham made a great feast the same day that Isaac was weaned. And Sarah saw the son of Hagar the Egyptian, which she had born unto Abraham, mocking.* **Wherefore she said unto Abraham, Cast out this bondwoman** *and her son: for the son of this bondwoman shall not be heir with my son, even with Isaac.* **And the thing was very grievous in Abraham's sight** *because of his son. And God said unto Abraham, Let it not be grievous in thy sight because of the lad, and because of thy bondwoman; in all that Sarah hath said unto thee,* **hearken unto her voice; for in Isaac shall thy seed be called.**

"It looks to me like Sarah heard from God through her spirit and gave God's message to Abraham," said Katie. "I wonder if I would be that bold if I thought God wanted Fred to do something."

"Kim, Sarah, don't be fooled by Katie's sweetness and meekness," said Fred. "When she thinks God is wanting us to do something, she can be a real fireball."

"I imagine Abraham's Sarah was a real fireball when she was convinced of what God wanted," said Kim. "Fred, would you want Katie to be any other way if she thought God wanted you to do something?"

"Well, it would probably really grind on me," said Fred. "But you're right, for my own good, I shouldn't try to change Katie from being a fireball in the spirit. Could it be she would want me to send away the Hagar part of my soul? Now, if Katie gets in the soulish flesh, I would have a few reservations about that."

Katie gave Fred a sugar sweet smile and squeezed his hand. "Thank you, Honey."

"Katie and Fred, there's a lot more we could discuss, but it's getting late. Could we pause for a period of time before going over the rest of your material, Fred?"

"That sounds like a good plan," said Fred. "Katie and I have a lot of talking to do anyway about how we should relate to each other."

"I agree," said Katie. "Fred and I appreciate your spending time with us."

"Good. With finals coming up, we need to get back to our studies," said Sarah. "And just to set your mind at ease, Fred, we are not suggesting that women go out and burn their bra. I think we would all agree that at certain times, like in pregnancy, the woman is very vulnerable to outside pressures and particularly needs the extra love and support of her husband."

"And, although, there may be some exceptions," added Kim, "women are generally the weaker vessel and should enjoy the physical protection of men rather than being the victims of their control as in rape cases."

"Would it be OK if we end this on a set of scriptures which will help all of us?" asked Sarah.

"Go ahead," said Fred. "I'm sure the scriptures will be good for us."

MATTHEW 22:35-40 *Then one of them, which was a lawyer, asked him a question, tempting him, and saying, Master, which is the great commandment in the law? Jesus said unto him, Thou shalt love the Lord thy God with all thy heart, and with all thy soul, and with all thy mind. This is the first and great commandment. And the second is like unto it, Thou shalt love thy neighbour as thyself.* **On these two commandments hang all the law and the prophets.**

EPHESIANS 5:32-33 *This is a great mystery: but I speak concerning Christ and the church.* **Nevertheless let every one of you in particular so love his wife even as himself; and the wife see that she reverence her husband.**

Then, Fred, Katie, Kim, and Sarah gave each other hugs, and Sarah and Kim headed back to the dorm. Fred and Katie joined hands and walked along the banks of the river enjoying the cool of the evening.

"Meeting at the river was a great idea. I love this place." said Kim.

"It was actually Fred's idea. He didn't want to meet in a church building."

"Don't you think Fred favors the letter of the law and is a little legalistic? Imagine not wanting to meet in a church building because he might be taught by a woman," asked Kim.

Sarah thought Fred was quite legalistic: "It was the proper thing to do to respect his beliefs and meet him where he is spiritually. He's thinking things over now. Hopefully, he will come to grips with the scripture about the legalistic letter of the law killing but the spirit of the law giving life. God looks at the thoughts and motives inside the heart and not so much at external acts or even whether the plumbing of a person is male or female."

"Did you learn most of this from your grandma or from Uncle Andy and Aunt Myra?" asked Kim. "I didn't think that you would be able to handle Fred's arguments. You've never been married, you know, so I was impressed with your way of handling the situation."

"My aunt and uncle wrote quite a bit about husband-wife relationships. It was like turning on a light in a dark room when I learned some of the concepts. Fred and Katie are walking along the river now in the glow of romantic courtship. But a lot of the ideas Fred has will be tested by real life situations when they get married. It is then that he and Katie will learn the great power and simplicity of love and guidance from their spirits with the help of the Holy Spirit. Hopefully, they will keep their souls in submission to their spirits. This is much more powerful than a long list of rules like what the Pharisees set up."

"I wonder what Fred would have thought about Lydia. Like we discussed—she was the leader of a group of women who were Paul's very first converts to Christianity in all of Europe. She was a merchant women who traveled and sold dyes—particularly purple. I suppose she was like one of the *women of substance* supporting Jesus. Her house was a meeting place for the 'brethren". And—*by the way*—you didn't use the scripture about the lady deacon Phebe in your discussions with Fred," queried Kim. "I thought the example was *so totally neat*; I couldn't wait for you to use it."

"I had planned to use it if and when Fred brought up the verse in First Timothy about *'But I suffer not a woman to teach, nor to usurp authority over the man, but to be in silence.'* but Fred didn't refer to First Timothy, so I must have forgotten about it." replied Sarah.

"Phebe must have been a real miracle working women to hold the office of deacon in a church building and keep her mouth shut when around men. Show me those scriptures again about the duties of a deacon."

Sarah opened her laptop once more and pointed to these scriptures where Paul highly commended three women for their contributions to the church.

ROMANS 16:1-6 *I commend unto you* **Phebe our sister, which is a servant** *[diakonia]***of the church** *which is at Cenchrea: That ye receive her in the Lord, as becometh saints, and* **that ye assist her in whatsoever business she hath need of you***: for she hath been a succourer of many, and of myself also. Greet* **Priscilla** *and Aquila my helpers in Christ Jesus:* **Who have for my life laid down their own necks***: unto whom not only I give thanks, but also all the churches of the Gentiles.* **Likewise greet the church that is in their house.** *Salute my wellbeloved Epaenetus, who is the firstfruits of Achaia unto Christ.* **Greet Mary***, who bestowed much labour on us.*

1TIMOTHY 3:10-13 *And let these also first be proved; then let them use* **the office of a deacon** *[diakoneo], being found blameless. Even so must their wives be grave, not slanderers, sober, faithful in all things. Let the deacons be the husbands of one wife, ruling their children and their own houses well. For they that have used the office of a deacon well purchase to themselves a good degree, and great boldness in the faith which is in Christ Jesus.*

"I can understand the classroom theory of submission in Fred's church, but in the real laboratory of New Testament churches, Phebe is a deacon and Priscilla, along with her husband Aquila, have church in their own home," said Kim. "I suppose the church leaders of that time used the remote to mute Phebe during the deacon's meeting, and Aquila muted Priscilla during the house church meeting."

"Now, now, Kim," admonished Sarah. "You're leaving the high plains of friendly persuasion and descending into the swamps of satire."

"Oh, I know," agreed Kim. "It's just that it seems women are sometimes treated like property—no different than cattle, sheep, goats, or chattel—whatever chattel is. Moo, moo. Baa, baa. It just really irks me. *Now,* I feel better since I've vented."

"Good. Now that you've got it off your chest, what say let's grab a Cafe N'Orleans sandwich and then get back to the dorm?"

Kim and Sarah decided to split one of Thibadeau's *e'norme* Cajun sandwiches. Kim wondered if Fred would have second thoughts about their discussions of the day.

"Oh, I have a feeling that we will hear from Fred and Katie again," replied Sarah. "We just need to give them some space to mull things over."

Chapter 10

A Spiritual Journey With Grandma

That evening Kim asked Sarah if she had contacted her grandma about getting together after their classes were finished. Sarah admitted she hadn't yet, there were just too many things running through her mind, with finals and everything coming up. Little did Sarah realize that events of the final days of the semester would set the tone and course for spiritual searchings during the summer.

Monday morning came with a light rain and Sarah equipped herself with an umbrella as she went to her early classes. When she left her last class and was walking across campus to meet Kim for lunch, she saw a circular rainbow. This was quite unusual she thought, for the only time she had seen the full circle rainbow before was on a plane flying out of Memphis. She came to the door of Kim's classroom, but Kim was not there waiting as usual. Peering inside, she saw Kim engaged in a conversation with a tall, red headed student.

"Hey, Sarah, come on in," waved Kim. "I want you to meet Red—he's a member of my lab team."

"Hi Red, good to meet you," said Sarah. "Kim told me you guys managed to get an 'A' out of the course and celebrated with a dinner on the town."

"Hi!" responded Red. "It was nip and tuck for a while on our grades, but the dinner was the really fun part. Kim has told our lab team about you; it's really good to meet you in person, Sarah."

Dr. Gordon Harper was passing by, and he heard overheard Red mention Sarah's name. Dr. Harper was of medium build, his amber blond hair laid on his head in small waves just beyond his slightly receding hairline. Sarah imagined this guy must get his hair coiffed at the Narcissus beauty shop every week. She thought he had a "ski jump" nose like Bob Hope's. No doubt that Dr. Harper could be charming—he had a soothing kind of smile—but how much was real and how much was a facade? His dress was dapper.

Kim had been filling in Sarah on Dr. Harper's personality for some months, and they had decided to play one of their favorite games and psychoanalyze him. In the end, they decided Dr. Harper's more private Mr. Hyde personality was really the best part of him. Mr. Hyde was an excellent laboratory investigator, helpful to his students, and insightful in interpreting experimental results. It was Mr. Hyde's ability to write excellent papers about experimental lab data that had been very helpful in advancing Dr. Harper's career.

It was the public persona of Dr. Harper's Jekyll personality that was most troubling. His Jekyll side should have been in politics—he loved a large classroom audience. He was a name dropper and twisted things around for self promotion. Jekyll was the one that gave grades. Kim said she could tell when Jekyll was "out" because, when stressed, Jekyll would rub his thumb and forefingers rapidly together. Kim related she had heard a quote in her statistics class that fitted Dr. Harper: "... statistics have proven that two out of every one person is schizophrenic." Sarah, reacting to Kim's descriptions of Dr. Harper, thought it a shame Robert Louis Stevenson had not met him. His book title might have changed to the "Strange Case of Dr. Jerkyll and Mr. Hyde."

Kim had responded by saying, "Maybe we should call it 'Strange Case of Charm Quark and Strange Quark.' Seeing Sarah's puzzlement, she said, "Oh, never mind, it's an insider quantum mechanic's joke."

"Ah, are you Sarah, Kim's friend?" asked Dr. Harper in his 'wonderful to finally meet you' tone.

"Hi, Dr. Harper. Yes. I'm afraid that's me," replied Sarah.

"Well, great," said Dr. Harper. "Floyd has told me quite a bit about you."

"Floyd? Why would Floyd be telling you about me?" questioned Sarah as a puzzled look crossed her face.

"Oh, you know," responded Dr. Harper, "he said that you and he were going to have a debate on whether the earth or the sun was set in place first."

"What?" queried Sarah. "What debate? All I said to him was his statement about the creation scriptures being in error was debatable.

"Well, he certainly thinks you're going to have a debate. He was asking me about the sequence of formation of the solar system last week."

"Hmm...I'm not sure if he wants to debate me or bait me," said Sarah.

"I suppose that's up to you," said Dr. Harper. "It takes two to debate. However, if you don't have the strength of your convictions, I suppose you could just tell him no."

"Are you baiting me, too, Dr. Harper?" asked Sarah.

"Oh, no," Dr. Harper laughed. "It might be unfair for a professor to join in on the side of a student. After all, I do have a minor in astrophysics. However, I must tell you I agree with Floyd. This whole thing reminds me of the debate Galileo had with the church centuries ago. Galileo won, you know."

"I think that Floyd and I need to talk," said Sarah. "Thank you for the information, Dr. Harper."

"You're welcome, Sarah."

"How do you do it, Sarah?" asked Kim. "You seem to end up being a lightning rod for the most controversial subjects."

"I would say you're definitely on Dr. Gordon Harper's radar screen," volunteered Red.

"Lucky me," said Sarah. "I'm glad I'm not in his class. Let's go to lunch before the line gets long."

"Would it be OK if I invite Red to join us?" asked Kim.

"Oh no, you can't do that," laughed Sarah. "I will invite him instead. Red, would you please join us for lunch?"

Sarah bit into her chicken salad sandwich, chewed vigorously, and complained, "You know I need this like a hole in the head. Here it is, the week before finals, and the good doctor Harper and Floyd want to debate the formation of the solar system. And all I said was Floyd's comment about the scriptures being in error was debatable. Why me, Lord?"

"Careful," said Kim. "He may answer you."

"Maybe it will be like when I was on board ship," laughed Red. "A voice will come over the loud speaker saying, 'Now hear this Sarah, Now hear this, Sarah, the reason I want you to debate Floyd is ...'"

Sarah, Kim, and Red all enjoyed a good laugh.

"Were you in the navy?" asked Sarah.

"Oh, yes. I was stationed at Norfolk, but my ship traveled all over the Atlantic, even into the polar regions."

They finished up their lunch, and Sarah went back to the dorm while Kim and Red walked to the library. Sarah found Floyd's number in the campus directory and called. His roommate answered and said that Floyd wasn't there, he had gone over to Nancy's to study for a Medieval Philosophy final.

Sarah decided not to disturb Nancy and then changed her mind and dialed her number. Nancy answered. After exchanging pleasantries, Sarah asked to speak to Floyd.

"Floyd, we need to talk. Somehow, people have the idea we are going to have a formal debate over how the solar system was formed."

Floyd did a crayfish-like backtrack, but admitted he had talked with 'several' people about having an organized debate with Sarah. Sarah thought she and Floyd should first review any supposed debate 'agreement' before making any anouncements

Sarah and Floyd reviewed their schedules and agreed to get together at Wimp's on Thursday evening. Sarah wanted to talk face to face rather than try to discuss details over the phone. Nancy had overheard part of the conversation and asked if she could talk to Sarah again. When all was said and done, they had agreed to meet at 6:00 PM. Also, if Kim were available, she would come with Sarah.

Floyd complained to Nancy that it was strange—Sarah seemed upset and thought he had been going around trying to promote a full scale debate. That was not his intention at all. He thought it would just be a little discussion with maybe a few friends present. Even though Sarah had a very weak case, he hoped he didn't insult her with his comments at the pizza parlor last week He wondered if she was one of these religious zealots.

"Floyd, you need to realize Christians hold what they consider to be Bible truths very sincerely," responded Nancy. "I think you should be more considerate of their beliefs. Some of your statements about Christianity just being a bunch of myths and the Bible being full of errors are upsetting to them."

"OK, OK, maybe you're right," said Floyd. "But you see I know all about Christianity. I was very active in the Campus Christian Center when I first came to college. But when I really dug into my science courses, the Bible just didn't square up with what I was learning. I was only expressing my belief so that others could see the light. Look, I only pointed out just one of the errors in the Bible."

"You and Sarah need to talk. She has the impression you have been actively promoting a debate like one would a prize fight. Apparently Dr. Harper is even involved."

"Dr. Harper? How would he be involved? I did ask him about the sequence of the formation of the solar system to be sure I had my facts straight. Hmmm...he did ask me about why I wanted to know, and I told him I was gathering information because I was debating this with one of Kim's friends. But I don't think I ever said that we were having a big, formal debate."

"In any case, you and Sarah can talk it out when you get together. I'm just telling you, as a good friend, when it comes to religion, you need to be more diplomatic," said Nancy.

In the meantime, Sarah had googled up a number of articles about the formation of the solar system. Most started with the sun being a fireball and spinning off accretion disks, which formed into asteroids and planets. The articles cited astronomer's views of other solar systems in various stages of formation.

When Kim came in, Sarah told her about her phone call to Floyd and the meeting that had been arranged at Wimp's for Thursday evening.

"You seem a little disturbed about this whole situation," observed Kim, "Having watched you debate with Fred, I wouldn't want to debate you."

"Yeah, but this is different."

"How so?"

"In the discussions with Fred, I had already gone over Uncle Andy and Aunt Myra's material and was well prepared. And there's a lot more I could have told them, but I didn't want to overwhelm them. In this case, I don't think Andy and Myra ever wrote about the sequence of formation of the earth and sun. They did get into time space continuums, stretching out the heavens, hyper expansion, string and harp string theory, rolling up heavens, and similar subjects. Why did Floyd have to pick the one subject I don't feel confident about? Sure, I can say God can do anything He wants to and in any order, but I don't think that is the answer."

"You remind me of the story that my great aunt used to tell about the nutrition and vitamin pill lecturer."

"Oh, what's that?" asked Sarah.

Kim could not remember all the details of the story so she decided to wing it. It seems this vitamin pill manufacturer had accumulated a lot of money and fame as a source of healthful diet information. So, his board asked him to tour throughout the country promoting the products. And he was driven from town to town by his chauffeur, lecturing as he went. After a while, the chauffeur said, "Boss, I've heard your lecture so many times, that I could give it myself."

"Oh, really, well, I'll tell you what. The next town is an isolated town and no one knows us there. We'll trade places. I'll put on the chauffeur's cap and you do the lecturing." offered the boss.

At the next town, the chauffeur gave the lecture with perfect precision, even including all his boss' jokes and he wowed the audience. At the end of the lecture, as was customary for his boss, he asked if there were any questions. After answering a few, a question came up that had him really stuck. No one had asked that question before, and he didn't know the answer. He hemmed and hawed at bit and finally had an inspiration.

"You know," he told his questioner, "the answer to that question is so simple, even my chauffeur can answer it." And then he asked the chauffeur to come up and answer the question.

Sarah and Kim enjoyed a good laugh.

"Yeah, I feel just like the chauffeur," said Sarah. "I wish I could just call on Uncle Andy and Aunt Myra to come to the debate and advise me on what to say. Well, there is grandma—we can consult her—but I don't think she's into astrophysics. Hopefully, it will just between me and Floyd, with maybe a few friends there; or maybe there won't be a debate at all. We're too busy with finals, and then the semester is over."

Kim proposed maybe God was taking Sarah out to the end of the dock and saying it was time for her to learn to swim on her own. Could be Floyd and Dr. Harper were just players on the stage of life written in the volume of Sarah's book.

"Kim, that's very unfair. You're using my own tactics on me. Now you've got me wondering if I have God to blame for setting me up like this."

"Shh, be quiet." Kim laughed. "God might be listening. He wouldn't want you to blame Him."

"And how did things go with you and Red at the library?" asked Sarah.

"Are you changing the subject on me?" questioned Kim. "Everything went just fine; Red and I got a lot done. Now, back to you—what do you plan to do—will you debate Floyd?"

"I don't know," replied Sarah. "One part of me wants to wade into Floyd for coming out—right in front of God and everybody—and saying the Bible is in error. The other part just wants to be left alone."

Early Thursday morning Sarah roused into the zone between sleep and wakefulness. She had finished her semester psychology paper on stages of teenage growth the previous night and had continued to prep for her finals. The get together with Floyd floated in and out of her cognizance. Finally, she said deep within her being, "God, I don't know what to do about debating Floyd—you do what you want to do." and turned over and went back to sleep.

That evening, Nancy called. Then Floyd and Nancy came by the dorm in Floyd's old Malibu, and they headed to Wimp's. Everyone was laughing and on very friendly terms. The surface of the lake was so smooth and peaceful, one would never guess some monster debate might be lurking under the surface.

"We could have gone to Campus Pizza," said Floyd. "But when you work in a place and get all the pizza you want, it just isn't fun anymore. I'm going to have the Big Wimp burger with all the lettuce, tomatoes, pickles, and ketchup they can get on it."

After everyone had gotten their order and pretty well had munched away most of it, Sarah began to tell Floyd about her encounter with Dr. Gordon Harper and his sneering comment about her maybe not having the strength of her convictions. Floyd told Sarah he had consulted Dr. Harper just to be sure he had his facts straight, and that he had no idea that Dr. Harper would be in contact with Sarah. Floyd did admit that he had told Dr. Harper Sarah's name and that she was Kim's friend.

"Look, Sarah," said Floyd, "you and I are good friends. If I've upset you, I apologize. However, if we do debate this, I will not pull any punches. I will lay it out just like I see it, and I would expect you to do the same. At the end of it, if neither one has persuaded the other one, can we at least agree that we have disagreed on this subject and not let it stand in the way of our friendship?"

"I think that's very fair," responded Sarah. "After all, the Bible does tell us that love and friendship are very good virtues. But I'm not sure about the debate. I suppose this is to be just between you and I with a few friends in the dorm room rather than have Dr. Harper involved?"

Nancy suggested putting the debate off till the fall semester. The delay would give them both time to think things over and decide if they wanted to have a debate and even what type of debate.

"I think that's a great idea," replied Sarah. "I need to be thinking about finals and not about debating the formation of the solar system."

"I agree," chimed in Floyd. "This is just too important of a subject just to rush into, and I have the same problem with the finals next week."

"Great, then it's settled. We will revisit this subject next fall and decide then," said Nancy. "And I've been thinking about something else."

"What's that?" questioned Floyd.

"Well, if you guys decide between yourselves you want a more public forum than the dorm room, I can offer it to you. You see in the CJ department, we're always looking for cases or subjects where our prelaw students can observe courtroom debating skills."

"Ohh, courtroom—this is getting wild," exclaimed Sarah. "What do you have in mind?"

Nancy explained Criminal Justice and Prelaw had taken over the old courthouse that was there since sometime in the 1800s. This was a move both for historic preservation and to give the students a real taste of court room drama. The concept had been tested on the regular campus by having senior citizens who were looking for ways to pass their time to serve as jurors and at skimpy juror pay. Even so, they really seem to enjoy it. Then, a number of retired judges had volunteered to add to the realism of the court atmosphere. Next fall, a retired Federal court judge would be available for presiding over trials. And those training in law enforcement even get the experience of escorting mock prisoners to and from the courtroom and also serving as court bailiffs.

"Gee, you mean this will all be conducted in a real courtroom?" asked Kim.

Nancy told them it was indeed a real courtroom and it had been used in past trials, even from pre-civil war days.

"The atmosphere is just like in the movies and the history of the place will add to it," said Nancy. "The prelaw and criminal justice students just love the concepts, which have already been tried in the classroom. When they complete their course of study, they will have experience and not just theory from books under their belt. And the nice thing is when the court is not in session, it can be used as a classroom."

"I think we had better think about it later this summer and not right now," said Sarah. "I'm not sure I like the idea of a courtroom instead of a dorm room."

"I agree," said Floyd. "I'm not sure I'm ready to become a lawyer. I would really like Nancy if only she didn't want to become a lawyer."

"Wait till you need me," laughed Nancy. "People never appreciate lawyers until they need one."

"Would you like to hear my latest lawyer joke?"

"No."

After the group concluded their meal they headed back to campus.

The sprint to the last final seemed like a blur to both Kim and Sarah. Then, there came that wonderful day when they decompressed—no more classes for the summer. It was time to savor the moment!

Escaping the classrooms and the dorm, they headed for the outdoors. The sun was shining, the sky was blue, the fluffy clouds were white, and a soft breeze blew through the campus shade trees on the terraces adjacent to Rotunda Hall. Kim and Sarah sat and tickled their toes through the soft blades of Kentucky bluegrass. Sophomore year and all its courses were finally over. Hooray for the summer!

"Sarah, what do you think of Red?"

"You're right—he is on the tall, awkward side, but I think it adds to his charm. But I hardly know him. You know much more about him than I do. Why do you ask?"

Kim complained she couldn't get the Dove Scrolls book out of her mind. She liked Red's looks and thought they could be soul mates because they thought alike. She and Red loved country bluegrass music and their majors were nearly the same. They could talk for hours, but hadn't really discussed anything spiritual, yet. Neither he nor she had brought up spiritual subjects, yet questions of the spirit were out there.

"Grandma used to say if you plant a potato, don't pull it up every few days to see if it has sprouted. Continually digging to look for sprouts disturbs the growth process. Some potatoes will rot in the ground, and others will sprout and grow. So, let time take its course and see if your relationship with Red rots or grows."

"Oh, I know you're right," responded Kim. "Ever since we got into the dove and volume of the book concepts, my mind has been in overdrive; I suppose I should just relax and let my heart sort it out. My spirit is looking at the living word in a new light, but my my mind insists on trying to reason it out."

Sarah agreed, "At first, I thought maybe some of the scriptures quoted in the books weren't in the Bible because I didn't remember reading them before. But the more I struggled with them, the more my eyes were opened to see the same concepts in the 'new' scriptures and also the scriptures I thought I was already familiar with." Sarah laughingly observed that Uncle Andy wrote in one of the emails that having to document spiritual themes by adding all the supporting scriptures was a distraction, but a necessary one. Otherwise, particularly those people who were covered with moss grown tradition, would attack saying these things really weren't in the Bible.

Kim lay back on the grass, looking at a fluffy white, sail boat shaped cloud, navigating its way across the heavens.

"This is really great. We're done with our finals one day ahead of expected, we have no books with us, not even a Bible. I so much enjoy just having a heart to heart talk."

"I agree," said Sarah. "My namesake, Sarah and her husband Abraham really didn't have a Bible in those days. They were writing with their lives some of the very words that would go into the Bible. I think that pen, ink, and paper is one thing, but more important is the Living Word that resides inside us."

Kim had been bugging Sarah about setting up a trip to meet Sarah's grandma. She was very curious about this lady who had so many spiritual experiences and had firsthand knowledge of the adventures of Myra and Andy. Finally, the semester was over, and the visit was about to come in focus. Sarah phoned Grandma to set up the details and found to her surprise Grandma had already planned a trip of her own, which was to be a surprise to Sarah and her parents. Grandma had already surprised Sarah's parents about the trip.

Grandma Fidellus lived alone on the old family farm that had not been seriously farmed since her husband had passed away in the eighties. Only sharecropping was now done there. In the previous year, a forest fire had burned right up to the property line fence and left a few scorched posts before the wind changed and the fire blew back on itself. Concerned about this timber being lost in a future forest fire, Grandma had arranged with the state forestry service to advise her on managing the timber. The areas of virgin timber on the original farm were to be left intact, but some of the border areas of the fields had grown up with a fine stand of walnut, hickory, and oak timber. The sale of the larger trees from this area had brought in much more than Grandma had expected. She sought the Lord concerning the use for this unexpected blessing.

It had always bothered Grandma that Sarah's Mom and Dad had such a tough time getting established after their marriage and could not even afford a honeymoon. Now Grandma was relatively well off and had a cache of timber money in the bank, she wanted to bless them with funds for the honeymoon that they didn't get. The gift was to be a honeymoon river trip on a paddle wheeler from Hannibal to Chattanooga. But Grandma was an adventurer too and liked to travel. What to do? Having a mother along on a honeymoon didn't seem such a good idea, but they had been married 25 years and had one daughter. The solution? Grandma and Sarah would get a room on the opposite side of the boat from Sarah's mom and dad.

"By the way, Grandma," Sarah related, "my roommate here at RiverRoc had gotten very interested in spiritual things and would really, really like to meet you."

"Oh, I know that." said Grandma. "I knew there was someone—a friend of yours that wanted to meet me."

"Grandma, how did you know?" asked Sarah. "I never told any one about it."

"Don't ask me how," replied grandma. "I just knew it would happen. Why don't you ask your friend to come with us on the river trip—a cabin for three doesn't cost much more than a cabin for two. Your mom and dad have arranged for a one-way rental car drop, and we will pick you up on the way to Hannibal."

Sarah said her phone good-bye to Grandma and excitedly went into the bedroom to tell Kim she was invited on a trip down the Mississippi and up the Ohio and Tennessee rivers. Kim was very excited until she found out the dates and discovered schedule conflicts. A surprise party had been planned for her older sister Wanda and the new baby Mary Beth. Kim felt very impressed that she must be present for her new, little niece's party. The problem was the paddle wheeler would have left Hannibal by the date and be on the way to St. Louis. So, Sarah called her grandma back and told her about Kim's scheduling problem.

"Oh, don't worry," said Grandma. "The Lord's just shuffling the deck to be sure everyone has the hand that he wants them to have."

"What deck are you talking about Grandma? Surely not some physical deck of cards," asked Sarah.

"Oh, no. It's just the deck of circumstances and events so everything takes place when it should. When things seem to be on hold or all messed up, He's just doing some shuffling of the cards. Sleep on it. Everything will fall into place."

Sarah related her grandma's message to Kim, and they decided to quit struggling with the schedule and sleep on it. In the morning Red dropped by to see Kim and then offered a ride home in his Mini Cooper. He would only have to go fifty miles out of his way to drop them off in their hometown.

Kim explained she needed to go by her sister Wanda's house first for the surprise party. Since Wanda's house was not far from Red's hometown, maybe the offer of a ride would work out just fine. And by the way, Sarah didn't need a ride, her folks were coming through and picking her up for a surprise river boat trip from Hannibal down the Mississippi.

"Lucky Sarah," observed Red. "It should be an adventure—you know, Tom Sawyer, Huck Finn, and all the river boat lore."

"Sarah invited me to go, too." bemoaned Kim, "But I would miss the boat leaving Hannibal by just one day because of Wanda's surprise party. And I can't miss the party. I want to see my new little niece."

"Doesn't the boat stop over for sightseeing in St. Louis?" asked Red.

"I suppose so," replied Kim. "But I don't know for how long."

"Well, then, maybe you have no problem. Ride with me back to see your sister and niece, and then catch a Southwest flight out of Nashville to St. Louis. You can pick up the paddle wheeler at the St. Louis dock and join Sarah there."

Kim excitedly related the idea to Sarah. They checked the boat schedule and the airline schedule, and everything fell neatly into place. It was a done deal.

Kim was very anxious to meet Sarah's grandma. It boggled her mind how Grandma knew about Kim when Sarah hadn't told her anything. Then there was the story about the Lord shuffling the deck and the schedule falling into place. Grandma must be quite a lady!

Kim and Sarah had been gradually packing their clothes over the last few days, preparing to depart the dorm. With their new schedule, all Sarah had to do was wait for her parents and Grandma to show up in the rental car. Kim and Red said good-bye and rode away in the little red Mini Cooper. That night was so very quiet in the dorm; most of the students had already left. Sarah opened up her Bible at random and began to read about Nebuchadnezzar's dream.

The morning brought a joyous reunion with Mom and Dad and Grandma Sarah. In a short while, they were on the Interstate and headed toward Hannibal. Upon arrival, some of Sarah's grade school memories of when she first read Tom Sawyer came flooding back. Sarah really identified with Tom's girlfriend, Becky. She hoped that she could be like Becky. Her psychology class had even discussed Tom's strategy for getting the fence white washed as a way to motivate certain types of students. They visited Injun Joe's cave and also the docks where the Big Missouri steamer picked up passengers in the Mark Twains' olden days. The next morning, they boarded The Girardeau Eagle for St. Louis and a half day of sightseeing. They visited the old courthouse museum down next to the arch and then took in President Grant's Farm. Sarah was relieved to receive Kim's call on her cell phone. Kim had arrived at Lambert Field and was now in a limousine headed toward the river front. She would be waiting for them when they returned from sight-seeing.

Kim was quite excited about meeting Grandma Sarah. Would she be like one of the matriarchs of old? Kim wandered along the old docks and the cobblestoned area between the arch and the river. The ornate iron work of the old Eads bridge stretched across the mighty Mississippi. Finally, a tour bus pulled up, and Kim saw a friendly wave and Sarah's smiling face in the bus window. It was time to meet Grandma.

"Grandma, I would like for you to meet my roommate, Kim."

Grandma gave Kim a big hug and said, "I've really been looking forward to meeting you. Any friend of Sarah's is a very special friend of mine."

Kim thought that Grandma looked much like her expectations, except she was spryer and better dressed than she would expect from a woman that had retired to the farm. Her two piece, burgundy dress was very tastefully done, and she had a twinkle in her eye. And yet, there was something else, for some reason she thought she was part of grandma's family, even though she was sure her natural family and grandma's family were not closely if at all related. An odd feeling.

After the greetings were completed, they boarded The Girardeau Eagle. Kim and Sarah shared a lower port side cabin with Grandma, and Sarah's parents had their own luxury cabin on the upper starboard level of the paddle wheeler. After getting settled, they walked around the deck for a while marveling at the rebuilt paddlewheeler in the style of yesteryear. Old drawings found in the files of the Eagle Packet Company were used for the rebuilding. The dock lines were loosened, and they were underway.

During the sightseeing tour of St. Louis, Sarah's parents had ridden in the Grant's Farm tour bus next to Jake, who was also taking the river boat trip. They were intrigued because Jake had been involved in the $53 million international project that had mapped the genome of cattle. The research was carried out at the Baylor College of Medicine in Houston, which was also involved in mapping the human DNA genome. Sarah's parents made sure to introduce Jake to Kim, who eventually wanted to get a masters or doctorate at Baylor. Jake told her about an upcoming seminar including genetics and biophysics being held in the St. Louis area in early August. Kim was glad to receive a brochure from Jake giving all the details of the seminar.

The tour guide kept them entertained with river tales as the paddle wheeler coasted down the river without much effort from the paddle wheels. Sarah was intrigued by the passage called Grand Tower and the devil's backbone. On one side of the passage was a high ridge like a dinosaur's hump called devil's backbone and on the other side was a tower like island with a very swift current flowing around it. The whirlpool next to the tower had carved out a pool over 200 feet deep, which had sucked in many a boat. The Army Corp of Engineers finally did some blasting until the depth was reduced to less than 100 feet.

And later on, there were the tales of the New Madrid earthquakes starting in 1811. In about a three month period, there were three separate and huge earthquakes estimated to be about ten times the intensity of the 1906 San Francisco earthquake. In one case, the Indians thought that a paddle wheeler had caused the earthquake and vigorously pursued it in their canoes with arrows flying at the belching monster. The crew was lucky to escape with their lives. The fault line of the earthquake crossed the Mississippi River in three places, and the uplifted rifts resulted in dams in the river. Sarah tried hard but could not picture a dam suddenly arising across such a broad river and causing the water to flow backwards to find a new channel on its way to the sea.

That evening, Kim had her very much desired chance to chat with Grandma Sarah.

"How did you know about me before you ever met me?" asked Kim.

"Let's just say I've known for a long time Sarah and some of her friends have a very special calling upon their life," replied Grandma as she opened up her Bible, laid it open in front of Kim and Sarah, and pointed to some verses.

DANIEL *1:3-5 And the king spake unto Ashpenaz the master of his eunuchs, that he should bring* **certain of the children of Israel, and of the king's seed**, *and of the princes; Children in whom was no blemish, but well favoured, and skilful in all wisdom, and cunning in knowledge,* **and understanding science**, *and* **such as had ability in them to stand in the king's palace**, *and whom they might teach the learning and the tongue of the Chaldeans. And the king appointed them a daily provision of the king's meat, and of the wine which he drank: so nourishing them three years,* **that at the end thereof they might stand before the king.**

"When my dear husband, Alberto, passed on, I thought it would not be too long before I followed him. But it seems God has kept me here for a purpose, and I've known my granddaughter namesake, Sarah, is part of that purpose. Kim, you've wondered about studying science and whether it has anything at all to do with your spiritual beliefs. Don't worry, you, like young Daniel, are being groomed for God's special purposes. It will unfold in due time. You will help Sarah, and Sarah will help you."

"Grandma Sarah, if I may call you that," said Kim, "even though I've just met you today, I feel like I've known you for a very long time," said Kim. "Why is it I just can't shake the feeling that you're somehow related to me?"

Grandma smiled at Kim and flipped the pages of the Bible to the third chapter of Ephesians and pointed at verses fourteen and fifteen.

For this cause I bow my knees unto the Father of our Lord Jesus Christ, Of whom **the whole family in heaven and earth is named***,*

"Kim, don't try to figure it out now. We are indeed part of a family. It's a mystery, and it will be revealed at a suitable time."

"OK, Grandma Sarah," replied Kim. "I will put it away on my shelf, but my shelf is getting awfully crowded. Maybe you can help me with some of my other questions."

Being intriged, Kim and Sarah's grandma chatted long into the night. Sarah stayed with them for several hours and then fell asleep.

Next day, the paddle wheeler made a left turn on to the Ohio River and traveled past Paducah. Grandma told Sarah and Kim about listening to the Duke of Paducah's radio tales when she was in her younger years. Sarah had been to Kentucky Dam quite a few times but had never had the experience of riding a boat through the locks. And then they transversed the scenic land between the lakes.

As they traveled the river through Tennessee and down into Alabama, Sarah, Kim, and her grandma had a chance to talk about God and family. They strolled around the deck of the boat, sharing experiences about relatives back in the third or fourth generation of their families who had prayed for their children to be blessed by God. Kim marveled that Grandma was old in body but her spirit was so vibrant and refreshing. She took minimal prescription drugs and was very light on her feet for her age. Sarah and Kim had both been surprised when they had stopped earlier in the trip at the RiverRoc University port of call to pick up Sarah's belongings at the dorm. Granny wanted to walk right along with them to the dorm. Grandma even insisted Kim and Sarah give her a walking tour of the campus and their classrooms. Sarah suspected Grandma was silently praying, blessing, or doing something as they briskly walked along.

After dinner, Sarah's noticed parents seemed to have regained the glow of their youth. Sarah could not help but notice the look in their eyes as they danced in the boat's ballroom to the strains of the Tennessee Waltz."

Sarah's father started out as a high school teacher and gradually amassed enough credits to become a science and math professor at the local community college. Sarah's mother had worked to support her husband in college and then later on graduated with a degree in education and was currently a principal in the local high school. How did they meet? Sarah's dad, Josh, met Mary Anne when he tried to deliver a heifer, purchased by a farmer at an auction, to the wrong farm. Mary Anne told him she was going into town. If he would just follow her, she would take him right by farmer Henry's house. Josh had been following her—or vice versa—ever since. Sarah always loved the summers because she and her family could do fun things without them worrying about their jobs.

Sarah had asked Grandma about her father and also Aunt Myra when they were in their childhood. Granny told her about an incident which occurred about two years after she and her husband had been married and before they had children. She had been weakened by uterine hemorhaging to the point her life was in jeopardy, and she would require a DNC to control the bleeding. Her hemoglobin was extremely low. A lady minister visiting at her church, her regular pastor, and several of the elders came to the hospital to pray for her. At one point, the visiting minister leaned over and whispered in her ear, "This sickness is not unto death, God has plans for you and your seed. Read Isaiah chapter 61 and particularly verse 9."

Curious, Sarah opened her pocket size Bible to Isaiah and read the following:

ISAIAH 61:9 *And their seed shall be known among the Gentiles, and their offspring among the people: all that see them shall acknowledge them, that they are the seed which the LORD hath blessed.*

Grandma smiled at Kim and Sarah and said, "Did you know that the children you will have are with you now?"

Both Kim and Sarah were puzzled by the question.

"Kim, you're majoring in biology and science," continued Grandma. "Somewhere in your books you will find the 'eggs' a woman has are with her from her very birth."

Kim replied, "Oh, that's right. I just never thought of it that way. So, in a way, I already have my children with me."

"That's right," said Grandma. "And we can pray for you and Sarah's seed to be blessed right now."

"How do we that?" asked Kim.

"Prayer is simply an everyday conversation with God. If you like, you and Sarah can put your right hand on your tummies and join your left hands with my hands, and we will just ask God to bless your seed."

"Let's do it," said Kim.

She and Sarah joined hands with Grandma, and then Grandma prayed. Both she and Sarah had goose bumps and a strange warmth for they knew something very profound was taking place within their very being. Sarah thought of the Bible scene where Father Abraham had his servant put his hand under his thigh before he sent the servant out to find a Rebecca for his son Isaac to marry.

Grandma asked them to be mindful of one more thing. They, being college girls, were quite aware of monthly periods and knew that only a select number of the eggs they had carried from birth would actually become children. They should think of these select eggs as having a birthright and a future father in the plan of God. Esau sold his birthright for a pot of beans. They should ask God to give them wisdom and strength in their choice of a mate.

"You mean I should pray for God's help in finding my dove?" asked Kim.

"Oh, you already know about doves?" questioned Grandma. "Well, this conversation is going deeper than I expected. What questions do you have?"

With that, Kim had her long awaited opportunity to ask Grandma directly about doves and what she knew about Andy and Myra. The conversation continued the rest of the morning until the ships steward announced that lunch was served. They enjoyed eating out on a deck table and taking in the mountains of Tennessee and Alabama. Then they began discussing medical and scientific considerations. Sarah and Kim could see that Grandma, being a nurse, had tutored her children well in medicine and science.

"Have you ever heard of the 'doomsday vault'?" asked Grandma.

Sarah and Kim shook their heads no, so Grandma told them the leaders of about five Scandinavian countries had gotten together and built a seed bank deep within a frigid Arctic island. The idea was that if some catastrophe like a comet, nuclear disaster, global warming, ice age, pestilence, or whatever wiped out the seeds on the earth, there would be a cache of seeds to renew life on this planet. Then she queried them about why seeds are so very important.

"I think that is very obvious," said Kim. "Seeds contain the very essence of life as we know it. Without seeds, this planet would be just a dead, inanimate, lifeless landscape."

Grandma heartily agreed with Kim. She said that man has been able to create a lot of things, but he has not been able to create life. He can take living things and even splice their DNA together to a degree, but pondered if man has ever been able to create even a single celled amoeba. Grandma went on to describe the meanings of the words "respiration" and "inspire." When a person breathes, he has respiration, and when inspiration is given, the spirit breath enters the living thing (in-spirit). She quoted the psalmist's description of expiration and inspiration in living things and said that only God could give the living component to DNA. She thought it was only when man began to overcome his carnality in the dawning of the millennium God would begin to share the secrets of life.

PSALMS 104:29-30 *Thou hidest thy face, they are troubled:* **thou takest away their breath**, *they die, and return to their dust.* **Thou sendest forth thy spirit, they are created**: *and thou renewest the face of the earth.*

"Well, there have been a lot of experiments with electricity or lightning striking in a soup solution thought to simulate some primordial broth," replied Kim. "But come to think of it, I don't think these experiments have produced even one single-celled life form. Maybe life *is* only something that comes from God. Could be that life really does have its roots in the spirit world and not in the natural world."

Grandma thought Kim made an astute observation. "For the most part man is *blind* to the spiritual world. But the natural world is only a *shadow* of the spiritual world. Man can look all he wants in the natural world and he will not find the secret of life," Grandma said. She then opened up her Bible and read these scriptures.

REVELATION 3:17 *Because thou sayest, I am rich, and increased with goods, and have need of nothing; and knowest not that thou art wretched, and miserable, and poor, and* **blind**, *and naked:*
HEBREWS 8:5 *Who serve unto the example and* **shadow** *of heavenly things ...*
ACTS 17:28 *for in Him we live, and move ...*

"The scripture mentioning the 'shadow' is so interesting," said Kim. "Some of the scientists think the world we live in is but a four dimensional, holographic shadow of a hidden world of seven dimensions. Maybe true reality is found in the Seven Spirits of God and all we see is width, length, height, and time."

Grandma agreed and related some of her nursing experiences involing science. Having worked in surgery, she was very conscious of the need for thorough hand washing and the sterilization of surgical instruments. There were accounts in her medical books about the history of surgery and particularly about the contributions of Pasteur. Louie Pasteur was a godly man, and he was also a scientist. He came up with this strange idea about germs and the need for a clean and sterile operating room. He entered a contest and conducted a winning experiment that proved that infections were carried by germs from outside contamination and not by spontaneous generation. The theory of spontaneous generation was disproved as the source of the infectious microorganisms. Pasteur was severely persecuted by some of the scientists in his time, but his techniques now form the basis of modern surgical practice. Strange how things change, and yet in some areas they don't. The theory of spontaneous generation of life lives on in the scientific community of today.

Taking a cue from Grandma, Sarah decided to check out spontaneous generation on her laptop. Since they were passing through Huntsville, Alabama, she was able to get an ISP signal to log on. One of the more fascinating descriptions was on a web site provided by The National Health Museum.

> From the time of the ancient Romans, through the Middle Ages, and until the late nineteenth century, it was generally accepted that some life forms arose spontaneously from nonliving matter. Such "spontaneous generation" appeared to occur primarily in decaying matter. For example, a seventeenth century recipe for the spontaneous production of mice required placing sweaty underwear and husks of wheat in an open-mouthed jar, then waiting for about 21 days, during which time it was alleged that the sweat from the underwear would penetrate the husks of wheat, changing them into mice. Although such a concept may seem laughable today, it is consistent with the other widely held cultural and religious beliefs of the time.

Everybody got a big laugh about getting an evolution from sweaty underwear and husks of wheat into mice in a twenty-one day period. Didn't the scientists know it would take much longer than that?

"Twenty-one days! That just can't be!" exclaimed Kim. "But if you will only give me primordial underwear and husks, then twenty one million years might just do it. The chances are one in twenty one million that it could happen."

"Are you sure you calculated that right?" Sarah laughed. Maybe it's like one in twenty-one billion?"

Kim thought Sarah was using TFO. When asked about what TFO was, she said it was Telescopic Fuzz Out. She defined it as intentionally putting something so far away in time and distance the images became fuzzy, and one could concoct any theory they wanted. Because they thought of it, it must exist so there is a mathematical probability it really happened that way, given enough time.

"The scientists back in the Middle Ages were really stupid!" said Sarah. "If they only knew what we know now—we really came from a rock which dissolved in water—the result being a life giving broth."

Over at the next table sat a very well dressed couple who were in earshot of the conversation taking place. The lady, who wore a seal brown turtleneck sweater complete with expensive accessories and jewelry, introduced herself and her fiancé to the group and complimented the girls on their deep understanding of science. She said she was glad to see girls getting involved in scientific discussions. It turned out she was a tenured professor of biology at Ivy Lee women's college. She told the girls she hoped they agreed with evolution because it was the true backbone for understanding living things, all the way from single-celled sea creatures to man.

"Oh, we believe in evolution," replied Kim.

"Well, it didn't sound like it. I thought you were making fun of it," replied the professor.

Kim explained that actually they believed evolution has its place. Within the species of dogs, cats, bears, etc., there is an evolution of different kinds of dogs, cats and so, on. The polar bear is white and the other bears that are colored demonstrate survival of the fittest.

Kim continued, "We would call this microevolution within a species. What we disagree with is you would get a cat-dog, a bear-cow, or a monkey-human. Besides, the human is the only animal that has a third brain—a cerebrum. Henry Ford's company made a Model T, a Ford truck, and even a Ford trimotor plane. But the designer was Ford and his engineers. The Model T did not morph into the truck and then morph into a plane. Every species comes forth after its own kind, with its own variations, but you do not have crossing of species. The species do not morph into each other, but they do have the same designer—using some of the same design building blocks such as an engine, wheels, brakes, and windshield.

"It just makes more sense that life unfolded in evolutionary steps," asserted the professor. "That's the beauty of evolution."

"Not a problem. We would not argue that point at all. Isn't it logical that life began with vegetation, then water creatures to feed on vegetation, then birds, water mammals, land mammals, and then man?" asked Kim.

"That seems logical enough to me," said the professor. "I suppose you actually did learn some things out of your biology books after all."

Sarah smiled and pulled a small Bible out of her purse. "Yes, we did learn that sequence, it's written in this biology book."

The professor was non-plussed at first and then recovered, saying, "Aha, I knew it. You're back to God creating life. I believe that life just evolved from lower life forms to higher life forms on its own!"

Grandma asked the professor if she would answer a question for her, and the professor agreed. She asked her if she believed Jesus Christ rose from the dead.

"No, that is impossible, nobody rises from the dead. I think that is just a Christian myth," replied the lady."

Grandma continued questioning, "Why do you think that is impossible? Look, in His tomb were all the material ingredients to make a full life human. All they had to do was just come together and be a Jesus. Actually, all the ingredients of humans can be found in various cemeteries. Why don't they just morph together and become humans?"

"I don't think that is very probable. It requires a giant leap of faith to believe Jesus could reassemble himself once He was dead. I just don't believe in the resurrection of Jesus Christ," replied the professor.

"Then, doesn't it require an even greater leap of faith to believe we came from some rock that was dissolved in a primordial ocean broth and suddenly sprung to life?" asked Grandma.

"Well, renowned scientists say—"

Grandma interjected, "I'm more interested in what you say."

The conversation reached an awkward impasse. Then the professor launched into a dissertation about life forms taking millions of years to develop and challenged the group to debate with her. Sarah laughed and explained she already had a debate challenge from a fellow student at college and the professor would have to take a number and wait her turn to debate her. They exchanged email addresses and phone numbers and agreed to take up the discussion after the college debate was completed. Professor Deborah Ann Murraye was surprised to learn Sarah's Aunt, Dr. Myra Lee Andreas, was the author of one of her favorite neurology books. They parted on friendly terms and agreed to keep in touch.

Sarah observed Grandma's question to Professor Murraye about Jesus' resurrection was an insightful one. Grandma then explained that one of the techniques Jesus used in dealing with the Pharisees was to answer their question by posing another question they did not want to answer. She cited Jesus deferring the Pharisees' questioning of His authority by asking them a question about the baptism of John that they finally decided to decline to answer. Jesus asked: *The baptism of John, whence was it? from heaven, or of men? And they reasoned with themselves, saying,* **If we shall say, From heaven; he will say unto us,** *Why did ye not then believe him?* **But if we shall say, Of men***; we fear the people; for all hold John as a prophet.*

Sarah and Kim were impressed and filed this tactic away for future use.

Grandma went on to discuss the relationship between the unseen spirit world and the world as we know it today. She told of some instances where she had been allowed to see into the spirit world and even see the presence of ministering angels. She hinted that some could even be present with them on this boat trip. However, Grandma said she found it to be wise to say very little about the spirit world because many people don't think it exists, and they would be spooked.

Kim was very pleased to converse with Grandma first hand about the unseen world such as spirits, and Sarah was pleased to have Grandma there to help with Kim's questions.

Kim asked, "Why do some people say that humans have *two* parts—a soul and body—and others say that humans have *three* parts—spirit, soul, and body? Are the soul and spirit one entity or two?" asked Kim.

"Well, it can be one entity, or it can be two," smiled Grandma.

"Oh, no!" exclaimed Kim, "now I know where Sarah gets her teaching methods. She must have learned them from you!"

"Could be," laughed Grandma. "There are those who say that the human is a trichotomy of spirit, soul, and body; and others say we are a dichotomy of soul and body. So, how can this be explained? Let's look at these scriptures:"

GENESIS 2:7 *And the LORD God formed* **man of the dust of the ground**, *and breathed into his nostrils the* **breath of life; and man became a living soul**.

HEBREWS 4:12 *For the word of God is quick, and powerful, and sharper than any twoedged sword,* **piercing even to the dividing asunder of soul and spirit**, *and of the joints and marrow, and is a discerner of the thoughts and intents of the heart.*

Grandma continued, "God permitted a choice to be made in the garden. An allegory of this choice is Eve being taken out of Adam as it were by surgery. Remember, in the New Testament, it says *The first man Adam was made* **a living soul***; the last Adam was made* **a quickening spirit** ... The *twoedged sword* divided *asunder* between the spirit and soul so that choices could be made.

"I've heard preachers try to explain this scripture by saying the *last Adam* is Christ," said Sarah. "But now I'm beginning to wonder if this scripture is really saying that the spirit & soul entity of the *first Adam* was severed by the *quick and powerful* sword of the Lord into a spirit **and** a soul so the *last Adam* was an Adam that could make a choice."

"That is something worth pondering," said Grandma. "But let us continue to look at the results of the process. The soul became a lover with two choices. She could marry the husband spirit, or she could be seduced by another spirit. Paul said this:

2 CORINTHIANS 11:4 *For if he that cometh preacheth another Jesus, whom we have not preached,* **or if ye receive another spirit**, *which ye have not received, or another gospel, which ye have not accepted, ye might well bear with him.*

"So, at the beginning of our journey, we have a virgin soul that can make choices. Will that soul choose Jesus as a lover and then a husband, or will that soul receive another spirit—a false Jesus—and go the ways of the world?"

"You're saying, at this point, before we have made choices, we are a three-part being having a spirit, a virgin soul, and a body?" asked Kim.

"That's right," agreed Grandma. "Paul hoped we would be able to present a chaste soul to our husband spirit. *But even if our soul is stained by intimacy with another spirit of a dark nature, it can still be cleansed and presented as a chaste virgin by the blood of Jesus Christ.* Look at what Paul said:

2 CORINTHIANS 11:2-3 *For I am jealous over you with godly jealousy:* **for I have espoused you to one husband, that I may present you as a chaste virgin to Christ**. *But I fear, lest by any means,* **as the serpent beguiled Eve through his subtilty, so your minds should be corrupted from the simplicity that is in Christ.**

"Oh, I see what you mean," said Kim. "Paul puts the comparison side by side. Are you saying when our spirit and soul are separated, we are a three-part being of spirit, soul, and body? Then, what happens after our soul has made a choice of either Jesus or another spirit of a dark nature, as you say?"

"OK, young lady," said grandma, "what would be your next logical step once you have found a boyfriend, fallen in love with him, and become engaged?"

"Have cold feet," laughed Kim. "No, OK, we would get married."

"Good answer," acknowledged Grandma. "Now let's look at what Paul says happened when we become the bride of Christ."

EPHESIAN 5:30-31 *For we are members of his body, of his flesh, and of his bones. For this cause shall a man leave his father and mother, and shall be joined unto his wife, and* **they two shall be one flesh**. *32* **This is a great mystery: but I speak concerning Christ and the church**.

REVELATION 19:9 *And he saith unto me, Write,* **Blessed are they which are called unto the marriage supper of the Lamb.** *And he saith unto me, These are the true sayings of God.*

"Kim, you have just solved a great mystery. *When the spirit and soul become one, then the trichotomy becomes a dichotomy.* This is the *marriage supper of the Lamb.*"

"Wow!" exclaimed Kim. "It is so clear when you explain it in this manner. But what about those who would choose the dark side?"

Grandma explained that the same principles apply for the dark side. The soul marries with the evil side and the two become one. The intellect becomes deceived into thinking it is the boss when, in reality, it has been deceived. The soulish religions celebrate the "Great Soul" or some variation of adjectives glorifying the soul or self. The soul or psyche is the vehicle used by psychics and can be honed to give answers which sometimes give some remarkable results. The only problem is psychic predictions are like walking on a frozen over lake. One gains confidence that the predictions are solid, and then the ice cracks and one drowns in the dark, murky waters of Ego Lake and sinks into the soulish sediment."

"But I have a soul—doesn't God want me to use it?" asked Kim.

"By all means, use your soul," replied Grandma. "The soul was created by God, and it has its beauty. But remember that the soul's beauty blossoms when it is led by its husband human spirit. When it is led by something else, the beauty turns to ugliness. Paul said the *spirit* of the prophets must be subject to the prophets. In other words, those who evaluate predictions should be sure they came out of the divine spark that God has placed in every person—the human spirit. *The Holy Spirit speaks through the husband human spirit.*"

Grandma hoped that now Kim understood why she had given what appeared to be an evasive answer to her question. Kim said that she now understood how the spirit and soul could be one.

"In a way, the account of Adam and Eve is an allegory of how the soul and spirit were separated. Which is more important—the lessons of the allegory or the actual events themselves?" asked Grandma.

"Well, since Sarah was used as an allegory describing the New Jerusalem by Paul, I think that I will stick with my namesake as being more important," laughed Sarah, "OK, maybe not. I do believe Adam and Eve were actual people in the garden, but God used their story as an allegory. However, if we try to read too much into the types and shadows of the physical world, we will miss the true reality of the spiritual world. Only so much can be learned from the limited dimensions and lack of depth of a shadow."

Kim said, "I have other questions about the spirit realm and science."

"Nap time," said grandma. "And then it will be time for dinner. Suppose we wait till tomorrow? In the meantime I will give you a scripture to ponder on overnight. Maybe God plans to give you a dream or an inspiration concerning the scripture."

"I'm ready," said Kim. "Show me the scripture."

Grandma opened her Bible and pointed to Luke 12:27: *But even the very hairs of your head are all* **numbered**. *Fear not therefore: ye are of more value than many sparrows.*

"I suppose numbering the hairs on the head of my husband Al would have been quite a challenge." Grandma laughed. "His hairs kept falling out until he finally looked like a monk with a large bald spot on the top of his head. I could always pick out his shining head in a crowd. Of course, it helped that he was always a head taller than most everyone else."

"This is a strange scripture to give to me," said Kim. "I'll sleep on it."

Next day, Kim could hardly wait to tell Grandma about her dream as they took an early morning stroll around the Girardeau Eagle. Her dream was about how the hairs on one's head were numbered.

"Tell me," encouraged Grandma.

"The hairs on your head are numbered, but not in the way you might think," said Kim. "They are truly numbered in your DNA code. Take identical twins, they have exactly the same number of hairs because it is written in their DNA."

"This is exciting," replied Grandma. "When I was born, no one would have understood what you're talking about other than maybe God and Jesus. And now, they have mapped the human genome."

Kim elaborated on the human genome: "There are about three billion nucleotides in the genome, and it has taken scientists years just to decode it. When you consider that each cell in our body has this genome library in it and there are about 100 trillion cells in the human body, each containing this enormous library of information, it is mind boggling! Imagine in your car, if the steering wheel, gas tank, pistons, radiator, and tires each had the entire blueprint of the car contained within it. Then, also add this library to the inside of every nut, bolt, washer, and particle of paint. The car would probably weigh a million pounds, just from the file cabinets of engineer's blueprints tucked in each part—well, maybe less if they stored the plans on a CD. But each part would have to have a computer to read the CD."

"Kim, how did you get this revelation about the hairs being DNA numbered in the dream?" asked Grandma.

"I remembered some scriptures that Sarah had shown me, and we thought it might relate to DNA. I looked it up at 3:30 A. M. this morning just after I had a dream about cattle at a watering trough. Let me borrow your Bible and I will show you. Amazingly, in describing DNA components, scientists refer to genome rods."

GENESIS 30:37-39 *And Jacob took him rods of green poplar, and of the hazel and chesnut tree; and pilled white strakes in them, and made the white appear which was in the rods. And he set* **the rods which he had pilled before the flocks in the gutters in the watering troughs when the flocks came to drink, that they should conceive when they came to drink**. *And the flocks conceived before the rods, and brought forth* **cattle ringstraked, speckled, and spotted**.

"Who knows," smiled Grandma, "maybe God, Jesus, and Jacob knew about DNA."

Later, at breakfast that morning, Kim told Grandma that scientists were even having to acknowledge the existence of an 'other' world.

She said, "Not only were they finding matter, but they were finding 'antimatter.' She said that Einstein's equation $E = mc^2$ was having to be modified to account for this 'imaginary' world. For example, when one took the square root of four, normally it would be 2. But actually the square root of four more correctly would be plus 2 or minus 2. Therefore, Einstein's famous equation was being modified to $E = [+/-]\ mc^2$. Apparently, the math genius had 'slipped up' in his derivation and forgot that a square root could be minus as well as plus! Does minus matter result in minus energy?"

Sarah spoke of her reservations about the probable upcoming debate with Floyd on the creation sequence. She said, "I know how I let myself be painted into a corn—"

Grandma suddenly stopped her and emphatically told her not to worry about the upcoming debate! She motioned Kim and Sarah to come closer and join hands with her for prayer. She prayed that the mantle of Daniel would be upon them and they would be 'Danielles' and should not be worried about any lion's den. The prayer contained other words of encouragement. When Grandma finished praying, she opened her Bible and pointed to the following verses:

LUKE 12:11-12 *And when they bring you unto the synagogues, and unto magistrates, and powers, take ye no thought how or what thing ye shall answer, or what ye shall say: For* **the Holy Spirit shall teach you** *in the same hour what ye ought to say.*

Grandma went on to say, "That doesn't mean you shouldn't prepare for the debate; it means you shouldn't worry about it. The Holy Spirit will be your teacher and will make provision for you. And don't fret if you make a mistake, the Holy Spirit will help you to correct it."

Again, Sarah and Kim felt goose bumps. Grandma prayed some very powerful prayers.

"One thing concerns me," said Kim. "How do I go about being sure the Holy Spirit is guiding my spirit and those thoughts are being received by my soul? It seems so difficult."

"Let me put it this way," replied Grandma. "When you first began to type, did you find it difficult? When you first began to ride a bicycle, did you find it difficult? Yes? How did you overcome the difficulty?"

"By continuing to practice until I mastered it," replied Kim.

"Practice, practice, practice!" said Grandma. "Paul wrote to the Hebrews that the mature Christians are *those who by reason of* **use** *have their senses* **exercised** *to discern both good and evil."*

"It's not the easy answer I was looking for, but you made your point," said Kim.

"Look!" exclaimed Grandma. "There's Lookout Mountain."

Sarah and Kim marvelled at the majestic mountain that extended from Chattanooga like the flat deck of an aircraft carrier many miles southward into Alabama and Georgia.

When they got within range of Chattanooga, Kim borrowed Sarah's laptop and made reservations for the August genetics and physics seminar in the St. Louis area that Jake had told her about. She was pleased that the registration fee for students was only $50. She decided to find Jake to tell him that she was signed up but did not see him either on deck or at lunch. She asked Sarah's parents if they knew what cabin he was staying in. They said he came out of cabin 37. However, when Kim knocked on the door, there was no answer. She went to the ship's purser and asked about Jake in cabin 37. She was told that no one on board was named Jake and cabin 37 had been unoccupied since the beginning of the trip. "Oh well," she thought. "Maybe Jake was his nickname. Hopefully, I'll run into him when we debark in Chattanooga."

The paddle wheeler made its way around the winding Moccasin Bend at the foot of Lookout Mountain and docked in Chattanooga. Sarah's father called a cab, and they all rode to the incline railway and took it to the top of Lookout Mountain and enjoyed a breathtaking view of the city and the mountains to the north and east.

Sarah walked the three blocks to Grand Aunt Thelma's place so they could get her to bring her car back to the incline for their luggage. After getting settled, they all walked down to Point Park to look at the old civil war cannons that overlooked the city. Sarah read about the "Battle Above the Clouds" where the Union forces came in just under the muzzles of the Confederate cannon one very foggy morning and hooked up with the Union forces that had been trapped in Chattanooga.

Grandma had wanted to spend some time visiting with her sister Thelma. The next day Sarah, Kim, and her parents drove up into the Tennessee mountains in the car borrowed from Thelma and spent a wonderful day tubing down past the scenic cliffs of the Hiwassee River. As Sarah tubed down the particularly difficult rapids with a sudden turn called 'devil's elbow,' she gave him a symbolic kick on the funny bone. Then, it was on up into the Smokeys and a visit to the Cherokee Indian village. Sarah was much intrigued by the seven-sided meeting house and the Cherokee's knowledge of the Great Spirit. She wondered how they knew about the Seven Spirits of God before the white man brought the Bible to them.

And then, it was back to Chattanooga to Thelma's house. Thelma had planned to visit at Granny's so she dropped off Kim, Sarah, and her parents at their homes. It had been a very relaxing trip for Sarah. She now had a great appreciation of the spiritual dimensions of her grandmother and had enjoyed the stimulating discussions with her and Kim. And the trip had done wonders for Sarah's parents—they had that honeymoon glow.

Editor's Note: See http://www.TheAncientChest.com/origins

Post your thoughts about the origin of life: __________

Chapter 11

Exploring the House of Treasures

After spending three days visiting with her parents and getting settled in at home, Sarah contacted Kim to get together for their plans for the summer. Kim had told Sarah that her ride back to her home with Red was interesting but did not volunteer any more than that cryptic description. Kim had found a summer job three nights a week at the local pharmacy, but her days were free for the most part. She really wanted to go to the empty house left by Sarah's uncle and aunt and see what treasures she and Sarah might find. Sarah had considered taking a summer job at the library but decided that Mike and Marie's (her uncle and aunt's children) offer to pay her for cataloging the possessions in their parents vacant house was more rewarding and perhaps she might find more treasures.

Since Kim had volunteered to help they worked out a system where both of them spent a portion of their time doing clerical type cataloging and the rest of the time, they pored over the letters, books, and emails that had been left in the house. Sarah and Kim began a process of photographing the significant furniture and smaller items in the house and sent it via email overseas to Mike and Marie, They then checked off what they wanted to keep and sent the remaining list to other family members. The keepsake items were to be stored and locked in the library and den rooms. Sarah then planned to work with a local antique dealer and auctioneer to have a red tag sale. Then, any unsold items would be taken to the auction barn. There was an amazing amount of stuff in the house, and sorting it out was no small task. The summer heat was becoming oppressive so they were thankful that the air conditioner still worked.

Sarah showed Kim her Aunt Myra's studies on the parallels between the construction of the tabernacle and the human tabernacle or body. Kim was particularly astounded by the secrets hidden in Solomon's temple [Editor's Note: See Appendix E for details]. She would plop out her *Grey's Anatomy* book and spend hours on the dining room table making comparisons and taking notes. She also checked out additional medical books from the community college and continued her comparisons.

"It is hard to believe that those writing the Bible could know so much about the construction of the human body," remarked Kim. "This was back in the days before they had x-rays and PET Scans."

"The writers probably didn't know all the details," replied Sarah. "They were just writing under the inspiration of the Holy Spirit. And the Holy Spirit knows exactly what is written in the manufacturer's handbook for the human body."

Kim told Sarah about the interesting dialog that she had with Red on the way back from the RiverRoc. They had discussed the origins of life. Their biology books and professors had drilled them in the scheme of life evolving from simple-celled creatures formed in the primordial soup through the fishes, reptiles and birds, animal vertebrates, on up to man. They discussed whether this progression was evidence of an evolutionary process or evidence there was one designer who had used similar building blocks in the different species.

"And what was Red's viewpoint?" asked Sarah.

"Well, he's still searching. He said that his parents taught him that God created it all. And then, to some extent, in high school and much more in college, he was taught the evolutionary process. He more or less reconciled it in his own mind that maybe God used the evolutionary process for creation. He said he brought up God using this process one time in Biology and was immediately quashed and ridiculed by the professor. We both agreed that our biology professors had force fed us like geese to produce foie gras.

"I hope that you don't end up with your livers cut out. The liver purifies the body, you know."

"Sarah, it does wonders for my faith to see that the Bible has all this information about the human body encoded in it. And Job's description of the earth hanging on nothing would do credit to a NASA scientist."

"Where do you think Red is spiritually?" asked Sarah.

Kim thought it was hard to tell. She reported Red was given a basic Christian upbringing. But now he has sailed the seas and then come back to college, he's been sort of drifting. Regarding having the liver cut out, she told about pulling out her little pocket New Testament and reading some verses to Red about those who professed to be wise but who worshipped the creation rather than the Creator. She wondered if what is wrong with them is that they have lost their livers.

"Oh, and what verses did you read to him?"

"Here, I'll show you," replied Kim as she opened her Bible to the book of Romans.

ROMAN 1:20-28 **For the invisible things of him from the creation of the world are clearly seen, being understood by the things that are made**, *even his eternal power and Godhead; so that they are without excuse: Because that, when they knew God, they glorified him not as God, neither were thankful; but became vain in their imaginations, and their foolish heart was darkened. Professing themselves to be wise, they became fools, And changed the glory of the uncorruptible God into* **an image made like to corruptible man, and to birds, and fourfooted beasts, and creeping things**. *Wherefore God also gave them up to uncleanness through the lusts of their own hearts, to dishonour their own bodies between themselves: Who changed the truth of God into a lie, and worshipped and* **served the creature more than the Creator,** *who is blessed for ever. Amen. For this cause God gave them up unto vile affections: for even their women did change the natural use into that which is against nature: And likewise also the men, leaving the natural use of the woman, burned in their lust one toward another; men with men working that which is unseemly, and receiving in themselves that recompence of their error which was meet. And even as they did not like to retain God in their knowledge, God gave them over to a reprobate mind, to do those things which are not convenient;*

"I told Red that the credit for creation had been changed into portraying our Creator as some random chance progression of *an image made like to corruptible man, and to birds, and fourfooted beasts, and creeping things* as Paul wrote in Romans.'

"And how did Red respond to this?" asked Sarah.

"I don't really know because then we came to the turnoff from the Interstate, and I was busy from that point in giving directions to my house," replied Kim.

Week by week Kim and Sarah made progress in the cataloging of the household goods. They got some help from their parents in moving the heavy furniture who was to be retained in the den and library. The antique-auctioneer dealer went through the house with them and red tagged the "for sale" items at a price at which he thought about 80% of the items would be sold. The sale took place on the weekend, and Sarah was somewhat sad to see people picking over her aunt and uncle's belongings but glad to get the job completed. The dealer picked up the unsold items and removed them to his auction barn. Then, the keepsake items were moved from the den and library into some of the empty rooms.

The following Monday, Sarah came to the almost empty house and wondered aimlessly through it, letting various memories flow through her mind. She sat down on the old loveseat and randomly opened her Bible to the first chapter of Genesis and started reading about the days of creation.

The thoughts of Floyd's debate challenge came rushing back to her. Was it Floyd and Professor Harper that set this up, or was it God? "Well, God, if it's You, You had better show me what to say," she thought and then decided to enter the thought as a prayer request to God in the name of Jesus. Tired from the weekend's activities, Sarah decided to take a short nap.

Her cell phone rang, and it was Kim. She said Red had called and asked for a date. Did she want to double date with them? Sarah's high school sweetheart had been out of town on a construction job in New Orleans but was home for a visit for about three weeks. He had been asking her to go out, but she had put him off because of the red tag sale. She called Gary and asked him if his invitation was still open. It was, so Sarah called Kim back and the details for the double date were arranged.

Sarah settled back down comfortably in the love seat, and as she was about to close her eyelids, she gazed at Uncle Andy's bookcase of Christian writers throughout the centuries. On the end was a book by Thomas Aquinas. Curious, she got up and pulled the book off the shelf. She began glancing through the index and saw an entry concerning the days of creation. "Hmm, I wonder what this guy thought? He lived about three centuries before Galileo, and the preface says he studied at Universities in Paris and Naples." She began scanning the account about the third and fourth day of creation and started reading.

Reply Obj. 3 Basil says that day and night were then caused by sending out and contraction of light, rather than by movement. But Augustine objects to this that there was no reason for this alternation of emission and contraction since there were neither men nor animals on the earth at that time, for whose service this was required. Nor does the nature of a luminous body seem to admit of the withdrawal of light, so long as the body is actually present; though this might be effected miracle. As to this, however, Augustine remarks that in the first founding of the order of nature, we must not look for miracles, but for what is in accordance with nature.

We hold, then that the movement of the heavens is twofold. Of these movements, one is of day and night. This, as it seems, had its beginning on the first day. The other varies in proportion as it affects various bodies, and by its variations is the cause of the succession of days, months, and years. Thus it is that in the account of the first day the distinction day and night alone is mentioned, this distinction being brought about by the common movement of the heavens. The further distinction into successive days, seasons, and years recorded as begun on the fourth day, in the words, *let them be for seasons, and for days, and years* is due to proper movements."

"I know! I know what the key is to this," exclaimed Sarah within herself. From that moment on, she stopped dreading a debate with Floyd and started planning her strategy. "The nerve of Floyd saying the Bible is full of errors!"

Red and Gary conferred by phone and decided to invite the girls to both dinner and a movie. Belliguries was the first stop, and they sampled ravioli and laughed at each other eating the long strings of spaghetti along with the meatballs. The garlic bread was great and hopefully when it came time for a good night kiss, both of the kissers would have partaken of the bread so that the effect was neutralized. The movie was kind of a fun one and not too heavy. When the movie was over, they went out for shakes at the Ice Cream Parlor. Then it was time for the girls to return home and Sarah and Gary resumed their good night kiss routine, established in their senior year of high school. Kim had never been kissed by Red before, so she wondered if bells would ring or if she would feel like swooning. How silly to think such thoughts, she reasoned, the anticipation will probably be much greater than the reality. Maybe he will be too shy to ask for a kiss, or maybe not—he was in the Navy.

They had one more double date the next weekend, and then Red left with his Navy buddies to go camping and rafting on the Nantahala River. With the hard work of cataloging and selling the household items out of the way, Sarah and Kim spent their free time digging through the old chest, looking at the emails and discussing a wide range of spiritual subjects.

"I've been thinking," said Kim.

"That's always dangerous," interrupted Sarah with a laugh. "And what have you been thinking?"

"The Dove Scrolls are fine for young single people. They are eligible candidates for marriage and can look forward to courtship and marriage. But what about the case where someone is married and meets another person outside of their marriage that they think is the dove they should have married?"

"And what is your thinking on this?" asked Sarah.

"I just don't know. I realize that in death and the resurrection the question of *whose wife shall she be of them* is no longer a question because the marriages are dissolved. But in the here and now, what if someone married the wrong person?"

"I really wish you hadn't asked that because The Dove Scrolls are great where each person is eligible for marriage. However, Uncle Andy and Aunt Myra agonized over this when they saw the concepts being abused by those that were already married and decided to look for greener pastures."

"Did they write about this?" asked Kim.

"They did. Let me find it ... Uncle Andy put it this way. See?"

If a marriage partner thinks that he or she has made a mistake in their choice of a spouse, they can take matters into their own hands, or they can let the Holy Spirit work things out. Eventually, one will get to the same place, the question is which route will they take?

If you have a choice of routes to take to a destination, would you rather take the high road with its soft gentle breezes or would you rather cut through the swamp; be covered with slimy mud; swat mosquitos, horse flies, and gnats; get cut by saw grass and briars; become inflamed with poison ivy, be bitten by water moccasins; and snapped at by crocodiles? One way is to be led of the Spirit, and the other way involves a lot of heartache. Those who have tried it look back and say that they wish they had handled it differently.

"Do you think that in some cases, in the volume of the book of their lives they didn't marry their dove because God had lessons for them to learn first?" asked Kim.

"It could be," replied Sarah. "Let's see, let me show you two methods of finding a wife which was employed by Bible patriarchs. Here's one ... let me find the other."

GENESIS 24:2-4 **And Abraham said unto his eldest servant of his house**, *that ruled over all that he had, Put, I pray thee, thy hand under my thigh: And I will make thee swear by the LORD, the God of heaven, and the God of the earth, that thou shalt not take a wife unto my son of the daughters of the Canaanites, among whom I dwell:* **But thou shalt go unto my country, and to my kindred, and take a wife unto my son Isaac.**

GENESIS 28:1-2 *And Isaac called Jacob, and blessed him, and charged him, and said unto him, Thou shalt not take a wife of the daughters of Canaan.* **Arise, go to Padanaram**, *to the house of Bethuel thy mother's father; and take thee a wife from thence of the daughters of Laban thy mother's brother.*

Sarah explained the Holy Spirit is our servant and guide, and Abraham was a much wiser father than Isaac. Abraham sent his servant out to find and wife. Isaac sent Jacob out on his own. Once we go out on our own without the help of the Holy Spirit to guide us, we are quite vulnerable to whatever tricks that might be played upon us, like the switching of our dove for the one her father wanted to marry off.

"I understand," responded Kim. "Isaac's path to finding a wife was very straightforward because Abraham sent his servant out to find one for him. On the other hand, Laban tricked Jacob into marrying Leah first, and he had to wait another seven years before he could marry his true love, Rachel. And then he ended up with four wives altogether. However, the bloodline of Jesus did come through Leah, Judah, David, etc. Maybe this was in God's plan after all so that Jacob's family serves as an allegory. The Bible uses Sarah as an allegory for the New Jerusalem. It has four sides and twelve gates."

"Then what you're saying is we should ask the help of God's Holy Spirit to go out as a servant for us to find our true love?" asked Kim.

"Exactly," replied Sarah. "Take my situation with Gary. You remember how much in love we were during high school. Yet he seems different now that he's come back from New Orleans. Maybe it's part of the life of some of those that are on contract for cleaning up the debris."

Kim queried, "How does one pray to have the Holy Spirit find one's dove?"

Sarah summarized an Aunt Myra email discussion about how she and Uncle Andy explained it to their daughter Marie. Aunt Myra had told Marie that even though she didn't know who her dove was, she should be praying for him. Perhaps, a more generic way of putting it for those who do not understand doves is that one should pray for their future marriage partner. Marie gave her own interpretation to her mother's instructions and prayed what she called the "Herman" prayer. When Marie shared with her roommates in med school she was praying the Herman prayer, they asked her what that was. She explained that even though she didn't know who her future husband would be, she was praying for her~man. It turned out that not long afterwards she met and married her future husband. Boy, were her roommates impressed. They started their own Herman prayers. However, Sarah cautioned that God will unfold marriages in his own timing.

"I think it's a wonderful concept," said Kim. "Even if we don't know who our dove is, we can still be praying for him in a generic sort of way. After all, he is going through trials and tribulations just like we are and needs God's help."

"It really is an exciting concept," said Sarah. "I don't know who my dove is, but I pray for him because I feel that he is part of me—even if I don't know who 'Herman' is. And who knows what is written in the volume of one's book; one's dove may not even show up until late in their life."

"What about Jacob?" asked Kim, "He was the pillar of Israel with his twelve sons and one daughter as offspring. Do you think his life as it unfolded was written in the volume of his book?"

"Probably so. He may have taken some detours here and there, however. Didn't Paul write that these things were our examples and we should learn from them?" said Sarah.

"Suppose a woman or man marries someone who is an unbeliever. What should happen then?"

"One of the scriptures directly addresses this. Let me find it," said Sarah.

1CORINTHIANS 7:12-13 *But to the rest speak I, not the Lord: If any brother hath a wife that believeth not, and* **she be pleased to dwell with him, let him not put her away**. *And the woman which hath an husband that believeth not, and* **if he be pleased to dwell with her, let her not leave him.**

Sarah reiterated that the answer is to ask for the guidance of the Holy Spirit. Not every situation is the same, and the Holy Spirit knows the thoughts and intents of the heart.

JOHN 14:16-17 *And I will pray the Father, and* **he shall give you another Comforter**, *that he may abide with you for ever; Even the Spirit of truth; whom the world cannot receive, because it seeth him not, neither knoweth him: but ye know him; for he dwelleth with you, and shall be in you.*

"You're right. I think I will just quit turning over the question of who I should marry in my mind and ask the Holy Spirit to go out and find my true love, my dove," said Kim.

"I think the angels are joyous about your decision," said Sarah.

"I still would like to look at another one of the emails about doves and the problems that can arise," said Kim, "What else do you have?"

"Well, there is another one," replied Sarah, "It could be quite controversial, even among Christians. Are you sure you want to go there?"

"Why is it so controversial?"

"It is the old question of the heredity versus environment. Did the daughter go wrong because of a hereditary predisposition or was it because she was unsuspectingly seduced by a boyfriend she trusted? Or, turn the question around for the boy going wrong?"

"In my opinion, problems can arise from both heredity and environment," said Kim. "But why are you trying to withhold this from me? You know that once you mention a subject to me, you will eventually tell me about it."

"OK, you asked for it," said Sarah. "I still ponder it myself. Here it is."

As my spirit was stirred in the early morning season I realized that I was experiencing a moment in the foretelling of the doves that changed their destiny.

I came upon a man, this man was nameless and faceless, yet I know ...I knew him well.

The man was switching the dove eggs from nest to nest and laughing a very sinister laugh.

He did not give the switching of dove eggs a second thought. In fact one egg could be moved several times, which resulted in there being no way to identify where the egg originated.

When I realized what this man was doing, I became extremely upset. I tried to stop him. The more I protested, the louder he laughed and the more he mixed up the dove eggs.

In my desperation, I attempted to explain the nature of the doves, "You do not know if you are placing two male eggs or two female eggs together." I tried to explain that even the male and female eggs had to be the right pair together because they were created to be together. A perfect match. Just any male and female egg placed together would not be the same.

The more I spoke, the worse the situation became. The experience ended with me desperately pleading with the Lord to stop this atrocity.

"I see what you mean," said Kim. "It does make you think. Even in the case of Laban tricking Jacob by switching Leah for Jacob's dove Rachel in the marriage chamber, it is difficult to decide if it were predetermined or the result of environment? Was this message something your Uncle Andy or Aunt Myra dreamed or was it from another source?"

"I'm not sure," replied Sarah. "It's too late to ask them now. However, I do think there is a set of scriptures that we can use to deal with problems of heredity."

"And those are?"

EZEKIEL 18:1-3 *The word of the LORD came unto me again, saying, What mean ye, that ye use this proverb concerning the land of Israel, saying, The fathers have eaten sour grapes, and the children's teeth are set on edge? As I live, saith the Lord GOD,* **ye shall not have occasion any more to use this proverb in Israel.**

Sarah surmised that the LORD was saying He does not want the sins of the fathers being passed on to the children. He wants each person to be judged on their own merits. So, if God is telling one *not* to use the proverb about the children's teeth being set on edge any more, one shouldn't use it. She believed the ministry of Jesus and the Holy Spirit gives the dove eggs the hope of restoration to their rightful relationship. The first step is a request for help.

"My oh my, I will have to think about this one," said Kim.

"One other thing," said Sarah, "there is a big difference between us making poor decisions that lead us into the immoral swamps of life— compared to walking out a Christian life where we may be persecuted and encounter fiery trials. Take Job for example, he lived a righteous life and yet he went through much suffering. Job's comforters assumed that Job must have done something terrible and made God mad at him, else he would not have been in such a sorry state."

"Job's trials still puzzle me," said Kim. "I always thought that when we walked in righteousness, we would be totally blessed by God. Everything would go perfectly when we are led by the Spirit."

Sarah agreed that's true, everything will ultimately work out when one is led by the Spirit. She noted with new Christians, God blesses their every need in much the same way that a mother takes care of a new baby. However, as they grow up, they find that God is not a vending machine of blessings where you are automatically blessed every time you put in a quarter. Sometimes He requires walking through fiery trials, and the belief in God's love gives faith that everything will work out in the end. Otherwise, His children would never grow up and mature.

"What do you think the need is for our trials?" asked Kim.

"Let me put it this way," said Sarah. "Fiery trials are those experiences that God allows to move us towards perfection. It is easy to say the enemy is causing our burdens and trials, but the fire of God is no cake walk, it hurts! Let me pull up a scripture about the fiery trials."

1PETER 4:12-13 *Beloved,* **think it not strange concerning the fiery trial** *which is to try you, as though some strange thing happened unto you: But rejoice, inasmuch as* **ye are partakers of Christ's sufferings***; that, when his glory shall be revealed, ye may be glad also with exceeding joy.*

"God did not say we could avoid going through His fire, but He did say that He would walk through it with us, much as he did with Shadrach, Meshach, and Abednego when they were thrown into the fiery furnace."

ISAIAH 43:2 *When thou passest through the waters,* **I will be with thee***; and through the rivers, they shall not overflow thee: when thou walkest through the fire, thou shalt not be burned; neither shall the flame kindle upon thee.*

"Oh, joy!" groaned Kim. "For the joy we get when we complete the fiery trials God puts us through."

That evening the phone rang, and Sarah's mother yelled upstairs, "Sarah, pick up the phone, it's Gary."

Gary had received word that the government had renewed his company's debris clean up contract, and he was to head back to New Orleans tomorrow. He wanted to take Sarah out on a special date before he left. Would she like to have dinner at the Lakewood Club Stage Festival? It was a high end dinner club with a stage show thrown in. Sarah accepted the invitation.

That evening Gary, dressed much classier than usual, picked up Sarah, and they were off on their special date. Sarah and Gary ordered a rack of lamb, garlic roasted potatoes, and asparagus dribbled with hollandaise sauce. For desert, they had flaming cherries jubilee. And then the stage show had a 1920s setting in a Victorian house in New York. Sarah really enjoyed the play and told Gary so.

As they were leaving Lakewood Club, Sarah was pondering her four dates with Gary during the summer. How did Gary fit in with her idea of a three-fold cord marriage? Well, on the physical level, she definitely was attracted to him. He was strong and muscular, and she knew he would definitely stir up her desires. On the soul level, she had definitely thought she and Gary were soul mates in high school. But this summer she noticed that their animated conversations were usually about recalling something from high school. Other than a few horror tales about Katrina damage, they seemed to have little to discuss about what was going on now. Give him a 50% grade on being a soul mate. The spirit-to-spirit cord was more troubling to Sarah. She thought he had gone backwards since high school. She was a little confused about Gary's place in her life at the start of the summer, but now she knew her inner feelings. In a way she was glad Gary was being called back to New Orleans. This would be a polite way to end their dating relationship because distance would make the attraction grow weaker.

As they traveled along the lake road, Gary said, "Hey Sarah, scoot over here and sit close to me." Sarah was uncomfortable with the request, but she decided it couldn't hurt anything and scooted over next to Gary. As they continued to drive, Gary told Sarah how much she really meant to him, and he hated having to leave for New Orleans. He would miss her very much. Then, without warning, Gary suddenly turned into a lane with an overlook over the lake. The moon was full and shone directly in through the front windshield. Sarah was uneasy about this unexpected change in the evening; she wasn't sure what Gary had in mind.

"Look at that beautiful moon and its reflection in the lake," said Gary as he put his hand on Sarah's shoulder. "This is really a night for romance."

Sarah stiffened slightly, wondering what Gary would do next. Now she wished she was hugging the right side door with her legs crossed. Something about the parking place Gary had picked troubled her. Instead of feeling romantic, she had the impression that invisible eyes lurking in the bushes at this secluded spot were watching them. Was this the place of previous seductions—or worse—like she had read about in the Herald? She pushed the thought out of her mind.

"Sarah, you mean so much to me," repeated Gary as he placed his left hand just on the inside of Sarah's knee at the skirt line.

Sarah's mind raced as his hand touched her knee. In the next few split seconds she needed to decide how to handle this. Gary's intentions had become clear. What should she do? Sarah was a different person than in high school. She was now more mature and knew that romance is not comprised of just a 'good ol' necking' session. Allowing Gary to advance to second base, third base, or home plate was out of the question! Home plate is for when one is ready to make a home. Even birds know to build a nest before laying eggs.

Does Gary think he has the right of passage because he took me to a nice dinner and show? He seems to be still in high school where relationships depend on puppy love. Now what do I do? We have been friends for a long time but that does not give him any special rights either. No means No! these days. How do I tell him that nicely?

As Sarah mind was racing, Gary was sweet talking her. He told her how beautiful she was in the moonlight, that her eyes glistened and her hair shined. He also said that he was still in love with her and could not forget her since high school. His hands continued to rove.

Sarah thought, "He is in love with the idea of being in love with me. That was puppy love when we were just pups ourselves. Now I have matured beyond the puppy love stage and apparently he has not."

As Gary talked, he inched closer to Sarah and extended his arm around her shoulder. It seemed he was pressing against her everywhere. This made Sarah extremely uncomfortable so she coughed loudly and used the opportunity to push him away. Gary was persistent and moved with her like a shadow moves with a body.

"Well, that didn't work," thought Sarah. "I'm not a prude, but Gary has selected this secluded place, and I have a bad feeling about what his intentions might be."

Gary took his left hand from her knee and played with the collar around her neck and then found her top blouse button. Her blouse had a slightly curved collar line. Sarah did not wear low cut blouses because of her long neck. Gary started to kiss her on her neck and said, "I love your beautiful neck; it is so irresistible." He then ran his finger down the side of her neck toward her shoulder.

Sarah was disgusted with Gary at this moment. "STOP!" she exclaimed. Gary was shocked and pulled back quickly.

"What is wrong?" he asked.

Sarah was in a pickle. She did not want to hurt Gary's feelings but was not going to allow this to continue any further. What to say? "Nothing really" replied Sarah as she searched with her mind in overdrive for a way out of this situation, then she remembered her cell phone.

"Oh, there it is. Gary, I have left my cellphone on vibrate," said Sarah as she put her hand in her left inside coat pocket. Sarah had to move over to the window in order to get her hand into her inside pocket. As she moved she put her purse on the seat between them, she then dexterously depressed the speed dial for home as she held it in her right hand. Her mother answered.

"Hi Mom. What's going on?" asked Sarah. " Oh, Aunt Rose wants me to call her as soon as I get home? Is everything all right? OK, Gary and I are just a few miles south of town on the road from the lake to Highway 41. I'll be home shortly. Love you. Bye."

Sarah turned to Gary. "I need to get on home. I have some matters to attend to."

Irritated, Gary reluctantly switched on the engine, and they traveled to Sarah's house.

Sarah rejoiced to see the friendly outline of her home safe home. As Sarah got out of the car, Gary masked his true feelings and asked, "When can we see each other again?"

Sarah replied as she ran towards the front door, "I don't know, call me." She shut the front door behind her and gave a big sigh. She was so relieved to be home and safe! Sarah's Mom was standing a few feet away and asked Sarah what was wrong. Sarah wanted to talk to her Mom, and yet at the same time she did not. She replied, "Nothing, Mom" and ran upstairs to her room.

Sarah's Mom was a very intuitive lady, and she knew the look and sigh. Before she met Sarah's father there was an old flame in her life who thought he owned her. She broke up with him several times, but he simply would not listen. Besides, Sarah's quick phone call that didn't make sense bothered her.

Her old flame, Bill Walters, was a handsome young man with dark hair and eyes. Naturally, he was the quarterback and captain of the football team. She remembered that he was on the student council and tutored students in math. He had a wonderful singing voice and sang in glee club. He also sang in the choir, which is how they met. Bill was very nice at first, but it did not take long for his ego to start to show. He wanted to go from first base to a home run in one night. When she resisted he said that he could have any girl he wanted so she had better shape up. She shoved him away and asked him to take me home. He argued at first and told her she was a fool and if he took her home, she would never have another boy friend. He would see to it!

I repeated, *Please take me home!* and with that he started the car, slammed it into reverse, and spun out to take me home. Home was only a few blocks away for which I was very glad. Bill yelled and called me names all the way. When he stopped in front of my house, I jumped out of the car and ran inside my home. I shut the door behind me and sighed just like Sarah did. I also ran to my room without speaking to my parents.

My mom noticed my distress. She came to my room and we talked. Mom understood and said I did the right thing. Bill was not worth the heartache or the trouble. She told me not to worry, there were plenty of boys that would not listen to his lies. I was a lot like my mom. She raised me and I in turn raised Sarah to keep her standards and not to sell them out for anyone or anything.

After a couple of hours there was a knock on Sarah's door. "Who is it" Sarah asked.

"It's Mom. May I come in?"

"Yes," replied Sarah.

Sarah's mom entered the room and found her daughter wiping away tears. "Sarah, did Gary try to take advantage of you tonight?" she asked.

"Well, yyyyyess," Sarah replied as she wiped her nose. "How did you know?"

"This is nothing new, dear," replied her mom. "Boys have been pulling this old line since the first days. Girls have never understood why boys think a dinner, show, going steady, or showing special attention give them special rights," Mom continued. "Although, I know you are hurting badly now, soon the hurt will turn to anger. You will deal with the anger, and then finally you will be proud of yourself for handling Gary in such a mature manner."

"Do you really think so, Mom?" asked Sarah as she tried to smile at her mother.

"And if there's anything else to this, please tell me, and I will help and support you," said her mom.

"Thanks for understanding and supporting me, Mom. I'm OK, now—really, I'm Ok." said Sarah as she hugged her mom.

The next morning Sarah wondered how she was going to handle Gary. She was glad he was going to New Orleans, but she wanted to part on as friendly terms as possible. If he called, what would she say? She was going to have to give this some deep thought in order to terminate their dating relationship and still remain friends.

She found it reassuring to learn from her parents at breakfast that there had been concern about the strange phone call about Aunt Rose. Aunt Rose lived in Australia. Sarah's father had taken the car down Highway 41 toward the location she had given on the cell phone. When he recognized Gary's car coming into the outskirts of town, he darted into a side street, turned around, and then followed at a discreet distance. Sarah was a big girl, but even 'big' girls appreciate the love and support of their parents. They suggested that "Aunt Rose" be a cell phone code word if Sarah ever needed help again in a difficult situation.

Gary was very upset that the dream he had for his last night with Sarah before going back to New Orleans had a very dismal third act. "That Sarah—ever since she went to college, she has changed. We used to smooch on her parent's porch at the end of a date when we were in high school. What's her big deal, now? Maybe I moved too fast? With ten minutes more of light kissing and maybe some hand holding, she might have come around. She would have to get that silly phone call just when I was ready to make my move!

What could I do? She told her folks where she was and that she would be home in a few minutes. Should I have called her before I left this morning? No! Maybe, college girl Sarah thinks she's too good for this ol' working boy. We had such a great evening until.... Well, I'll show her. Wait till I get my own demolition contract and make money hand over fist. She won't be able to ignore me then when I show up in my new Porsche Cayman S. That is, if I'm still interested in her. As the guys said, with a car like that, by the third date...." thought Gary as he pounded the steering wheel of the Taurus so hard that it rattled. He floored the accelerator in a surge of emotion and raced south on Highway 41.

When Gary pounded the steering column, he pounded it with authority! He was just under six feet tall, solidly built, leaning toward husky. In his junior high school year, he had won the district wrestling championship and gone on to state where he won a third place medal.

Sarah did not want to give any publicity to her episode with Gary, so when she talked to Kim that day, she told her Gary had gone back to New Orleans and that she thought Gary was not her dove. Sarah was quite happy Gary did not call before leaving, at least she hoped he had left that morning. Sarah thought it ironic that she had warned Kim repeatedly about rushing headlong into finding a dove. Kim seemed to have heeded her advice, but it was now Sarah who was struggling with a romantic relationship.. Kim said that her dates with Red had been friendly but not passionate. She had reservations about giving an ex-Navy guy any undue encouragement.

Sarah wondered if she had given any undue come-ons to Gary. She thought, "He seemed so different than when we dated in high school." As she thought about it, she wondered whether Gary had fallen in with bad company in his particular demolition crew and taken advantage of easy girls or even visited a brothel. "Oh well, I'll learn from the past but not dwell on it. It's time to think about returning to college."

Kim and Sarah made one last sweep through their house of treasures and gathered up the documents that they wanted to take back to the dorm with them. They started up the old, outdated Windows 98 system computer once more and checked for anything they might have missed in the email archives. Sarah's curiosity was tweaked by an email file named "The Beetlejuice Beetle." When she pulled it down and read it, she found that Beetlejuice was the joking result of a static filled phone conversation misunderstanding between Myra in Brazil and Andy in the States. Actually, Beetlejuice was the star Betelgeuse (correctly pronounced as BET' l jooz) in the right shoulder of the constellation Orion. (The diameter of Betelguese at its fullest expansion is about 100,000 times the diameter of the earth.) It took some deciphering to discover that the Betelgeuse Beetle was actually a VW beetle being used for a time space experiment.

Kim looked over the email and finally figured out the gist of the experiment. Sarah's Uncle Andy was describing an experiment where a VW beetle was to be driven from Los Angeles to New York. Since the speed of the governor on the VW was set by the Master Mechanic at exactly 65 miles per hour, it should be possible to determine the distance by measuring the time in transit. So, the beetle driver, Photon Phil, set out from Los Angeles to New York and 43 hours later phoned back to Los Angeles to say he had arrived in New York. Then, it was calculated that 65 miles per hour times 43 hours gave a distance of 2795 miles.

Photon Phil wanted to double check the experiment by driving back to LA from New York so he phoned the Master Mechanic in LA he would be leaving New York in exactly 10 minutes and wanted the Master Mechanic to have his timekeeper wait for him to arrive and determine the time down to the very second. The experiment was set up.

Just after Phil had called, the Father of the Master Mechanic quoted a verse from an ancient writing that read: *Thus saith the LORD, thy redeemer, and he that formed thee from the womb, I am the LORD that maketh all things;* **that stretcheth forth the heavens** *alone; that* **spreadeth abroad the earth** *by myself* (ISAIAH 44:24). So, the Father of the Master Mechanic decided to stretch out the earth to have a diameter just about 100,000 times larger than its present diameter, and he did it instantaneously by the speed of thought otherwise known as the speed of *LetThereBe*.

At the same instant, (January 1, 2000) Photon Phil had started back from New York to LA oblivious to any change because Photon Phil traveled at the same speed no matter what the frame of reference. The Master Mechanic's timekeeper in LA was ready with his stop watch to time it down to the very second when

42 hours had expired and Phil would likely show up in the next hour. The next hour came and went—no Phil. The wait continued into the next day and then into the following day and finally into the next year. The timekeeper waited patiently for a century and still Phil had not arrived in LA. However, the timekeeper had the gift of patience and was willing to wait for Phil, no matter how long it took.

The scientists realized that the time span was really stretching out—so they came up with a measure of distance called a "Beetleyear." At 65 miles per hour, a Beetle could travel 1560 miles per day. Then by multiplying 1560 miles per day times 365.24 days per year they were able to come up with the distance a VW Beetle would travel in one year: 570,000 miles. When the year 3000 AD arrived, they were well prepared to use their new measurement of distance, if only the darn Beetle would show up in LA. Photon Phil, where art thou?

Finally, in the year 3377 AD, Photon Phil arrived in LA. There was great excitement among the scientists because they could now measure the distance between New York and LA since they knew that Photon Phil traveled at 65 miles per hour. Phil's transit time was 1377 years and the distance in a Beetleyear was 570,000 miles. Therefore a simple multiplication gave a New York to LA distance of 785 million miles—close to a billion miles! Then, the scientists in LA got into an argument with the scientists in New York about whether the earth was 1377 years older or just 43 hours older.

Kim and Sarah got a big laugh about Photon Phil traveling in his Betelgeuse Beetle. Kim supposed that the 65 miles per hour in the example was symbolic of the speed of light in everyday terms we could understand. Both Kim and Sarah had not realized there was a verse in the Bible that the Lord "stretcheth forth" the heavens and "spreadeth abroad" the earth.

But that was not the end of their mirth. In the same file directory, Sarah found other emails on the same subject. One was from CowboyBobr with the title: "Jesus is bigger in Texas than anywhere else." It seems that Myra had met a colleague at a medical conference at M. D. Anderson in Houston. Her colleague's husband worked for certain periods of time during the year at the McDonald Observatory in the Davis mountains of West Texas. When Myra received Andy's Betelgeuse Beetle email, she forwarded it to her doctor friend in Texas to run it by her husband.

CowboyBobr replied that Andy and Myra were thinking way too small. They needed to "Texas Size" their thinking. Just because Betelgeuse is so big that if it were placed in the center of our solar system that its surface would go out beyond Jupiter's orbit doesn't mean that it's really, really big. He suggested that instead of Betelgeuse's size of 100,000 times the earth's diameter, why not make it 100,000,000,000 times the diameter of the earth? After all, it's only a stretching out by one hundred billion. Texas probably has that much in oil money without breaking a sweat. Then, the Master Mechanic's timekeeper would only have to wait a mere 1.377 billion years for the Beetle to arrive. He said that maybe they should add one day to that time, because the stretching out might take the Father of the Master Mechanic about one day instead of being almost instantaneous.

And some Texans were petitioning the Master Mechanic to declare Texas a separate universe and to increase the governor setting on the VW Beetle to 100 miles per hour. Sixty-five miles per hour was way too slow if you were driving the plains of West Texas! And besides, all the Master Mechanic had to do was tweak the governor setting slightly and soup up the fuel slightly to get the physical constants for a separate universe. And, adding several more things, a variable speed transmission and some brakes so they could stop occasionally to smell the flowers of the century cactus that bloom only every 100 years would be nice.

"Oh, those Texans," exclaimed Kim. "Oh well, it is a funny story—Oh look, there is a PS on the next page."

CowboyBobr went on to spin a yarn about Methuselah's nephew who decided to sneak his dad's rocket ship out for a spin—thinking his folks wouldn't know because they were away celebrating an anniversary in Paris. Being like most teenage boys, he wanted to see what kind of speed he could get out of the sleek baby and he pulled the control stick back to full warp. Unfortunately, it took him some time to determine how to unwarp the rocket to get back to home base before his dad discovered his escapade. When he got back, he was in total shock to find himself attending his Uncle Methuselah's 969th birthday party!

After getting over his shock, he was told that his mother, Dad and siblings had long, long passed away and only his Uncle Methuselah was still living. Methuselah credited his long life to what his dad Enoch had taught him in his younger years, but, as he aged, his memory of his dad's teachings dimmed.

Who was right? Did a lot of time pass as evidenced by Uncle Methuselah's age or did a short time pass as evidenced by the nephew taking the ship out for a spin and trying to get back before he thought his Mom and Dad would return? CowboyBobr said that every story should have a moral: *One's opinion of whether the **ELAPSED TIME** is long or short depends on which side of hyperexpansion [or hypercontraction] one is considering it. It is all relative you know.*

Kim was intrigued that the email in CowboyBobr's Methuselah example was actually more in line with modern man's view from the earth of classic hypercontraction rather than hyperexpansion. So, she and Sarah decided to put their heads together and come up with a hyperexpansion example.

It seemsthat Methuselah's nephew Fast Eddy wanted to impress his girlfriend by taking her for a spin in his dad's rocket while his parents were away in Paris. As they left metropolitan space into the countryside, his girl friend cuddled up next to him and began giving him amorous kisses. Not wanting to have distractions from his priorities, Fast Eddy put the rocket in **autopilot_time_lapse_hyperexpansion** and proceeded to return his gal's kisses. It was like having a honeymoon on a slow boat to the China galaxy—the longer it lasted—the better. However, after a time, Fast Eddy wanted to get back before his parents returned and his gal's folks missed her. When he tried to reverse the elapsed time hyperexpansion, there was no response, the autopilot relay was stuck in the 'on' position. Many years later, Fast Eddy found the wiring diagram under the dash and devised a bypass. The return home was a shocker to Eddy parent's. They had only been in Paris for seven days and when they returned, they found they had a new daughter-in-law and were grandparents, great grandparents, and great, great grandparents as all 64 members of Eddy's family returned to greet them. Eddy had a lot explaining to do.

After laughing at their example, Sarah and Kim found some earlier files along the same vein with a discussion something about grapes, apples and oranges, and an ant. Since they were running out of time, they decided to copy them on a CD and review them later.

Kim had signed up for a symposium at University City just west of St. Louis to hear one of the genetics professors at Baylor speak. She managed to get permission to take Sarah with her since the seminar organizers went out of their way to encourage students to attend.

The plan was that they would go to the symposium, then come back home to spend a few days with their parents before school started.

Kim attended the sessions by the Baylor genetics professor; she had read all the books and took advantage of the opportunity to ask face to face questions. In the meantime, Sarah had wandered around the meeting complex and saw that there were simultaneous meetings dealing with everything from nano-technology computers and supercritical thermodynamics to astrophysics. Astrophysics—hey, she thought that might be interesting!

After Kim finished her sessions with her hero professor, Sarah told her about the astrophysics symposium and there were four speakers yet to make their presentations. So, with the impending debate with Floyd, they decided to take in the astrophysics sessions.

Sarah thought that most of the technical jargon went right over her head, but the last session entitled "Hyper expansion of the Universe" really caught their eye. So they sat in on the presentation to find out if it had anything to do with the stretching out of the heavens and spreading out of the earth. It seemed the scientists could not account for how the universe suddenly became as large as it did. But, if in the mathematical treatment of the origins of the universe, a 'hyper expansion function' were added in, then the equations flowed very smoothly. In the physical world, scientists struggled with this as the "Horizon Problem."

Sarah and Kim were not exactly sure what was meant by the "Horizon Problem" but decided to dig into it in more detail when they had the opportunity [See Appendix B]. The speaker gave a history of some of the scientists' struggles with these seeming anomalies. In the early 1900s, the Dutch physicist, Willem de Sitter found an unusual solution to Einstein's equations for a universe that was empty of matter and yet hyper expanded. Sarah and Kim remembered the verses from Hebrews and wondered about a connection between the invisible spirit world and the visible world containing matter. They wondered if the spirit world hyperexpansion come first and then the material world, as we know it, was framed within?

HEBREWS 11:1-3 *Now faith is the substance of things hoped for,* **the evidence of things not seen**. *For by it the elders obtained a good report. Through faith we understand that* **the worlds were framed** *by the word of God, so that* **things which are seen were not made of things which do appear.**

Then, the seminar speaker went on to discuss the work of MIT physicist Alan Guth. Guth came up with the "Inflationary Universe" idea. He proposed two parts to the expansion. The first was a quick and exponential expansion in the beginning. After that, the expansion slows down to resemble the expansion being observed by the telescopes of today. Sarah and Kim were quite excited, because if they had not realized that the "stretching out" or expansion concept was in the Bible, it just might be true that most scientists had not yet realized it either.

Both Kim and Sarah found the discussion of "sparticles" fascinating. Apparently, sparticle was a name given to super particles. There were *selectrons, sneutrons, sneutrinos,* etc. Kim had told Sarah that a Columbia University lecturer had called neutrinos "ghostly particles ... that can pass through trillions of miles of lead as easily as we pass through air." Sarah thought maybe the 's' should stand for 'spirit particle' rather than super particle. Or, were spirit particles just small particles or even anti-matter particles? The scientists were pretty certain that these sparticles existed, if only they had a machine that could summon up enough energy to produce them. Paul wrote about removing the vail between the spirit world and the natural world in 2 Corinthians chapter three. Sarah wondered if we, with open face, would behold in the glassy mirror a change from a lower glory to a higher frequency of glory as the Holy Spirt and Jesus provide an open door. Would it be possible to step through that door or to have the spirit world freely come through the door to us?

Then, there was a discussion of possible cycles of expansion and contraction. Sarah was somewhat befuddled by something called membrane technology. She wondered if the universe were like some gigantic etch-a-sketch. When it was time for a new earth and heavens, would the etch-a-sketch be shaken up and something new written on it? She wondered about the old earth and old heavens. She pondered the translation controversy about whether the first verse of Genesis should be read, "In *the* beginning ..." or "In *a* beginning ..." as the more literal translation. She pondered if Genesis chapter 1 was a spirit creation and if Genesis 2:5 described the creation, *before it was in the earth,* as being changed into matter. When black holes were discussed, she wondered if there were any relationship between these and the bottomless pit of Revelation. The speaker said that black holes were only discovered in the last century.

And the last speaker of the session, an Asian man from Oxenbridge University delved into string theory, membrane theory, and hyperexpansion of membranes. He explained that the theory of atoms, protons, and neutrons worked very well until one got down into the really small particles. Then, the atom smashers produced such a plethora of particles that scientists suspected that these particles were not really new particles at all. Instead, they were vibrating nodes on strings, kind of like the different sizes and tensions of wires in a piano that could play many different songs. Then, the speaker proposed that beyond string theory was membrane theory where the universe was like a giant membrane that was being stretched, and somehow it was stretched faster than the speed of light just after the Big Bang.

He then gave an example of a track meet where the stadium cinder track had been replaced by a rubber membrane to keep the athletes from skinning their arms and legs when they fell. Lined up for the 100 yard dash were seven runners in red, orange, yellow, green, blue, purple, and white tee shirts, respectively. Just as the starting gun sounded, the membrane suddenly was stretched out so the finish line was actually twice as far from the starting line as it had been previously. He then asked if it were true that after the distance was stretched double, would the time required to cover that distance seem to be doubled? He asked if the red, orange, yellow, green, blue, purple, and white light runners would still run at the same speed as they did in previous meets, or would they run at a different speed? Would the runners stay in the same octave of light? Further, if the different colors of light always traveled at identical speeds, what was the point of even having a race?

Kim wanted to ask questions: What would happen if the stride of the runner was also stretched out from say three feet to six feet, wouldn't the runner get there faster? Or, would his steps be longer but the frequency of his steps be less because time was affected by the stretching? Or, would the runner's speed of light be changed at all? If the runners were precisely at the starting line and the starting line suddenly stretched forward 100 yards, would they have gone faster than light? Dare she, a mere student, ask questions of such a distinguished professor and his collegeages? When the questioning period arrived, Kim was about to raise her hand when the fire alarm bell sounded. Everyone was herded out into the street and fire engines arrived. A report was given that a large pot of cooking oil used for French fries had ignited in the hotel kitchen. The alarm was resolved, and they returned to the hotel. Since, the alarm was at the very end of the last session, the seminar leaders said it would be impractical to have everyone reassemble for just a few minutes. The seminar was over. Kim wondered if the Guinness racing records people were saved by the bell. In her mind she wondered how they would record the distances, times, and velocities of the world's most bizarre race. Would runner speed and time averages mean anything at all in a time and space-warped race?

Feeling the pangs of hunger, Kim and Sarah decided to go to McDonald's to get a bite to eat. Inspired by the words spoken in the seminars, Sarah dug out Aunt Myra and Uncle Andy's email file and found the email on peas, grapes, apples, oranges, grapefruits and the travels of the ant.

She wondered, "Wasn't there a proverb which directed us to the ant with the admonishment 'consider her ways'?" She and Kim dug into Aunt Myra's ant story in earnest.

Sarah had been somewhat surprised to learn in the seminar that the geniuses Albert Einstein and Niels Bohr had once spent days in an OK Corral type verbal shoot-out—debating about whether one could tell if a cat in a closed box was alive or dead. Maybe considering the travels of an ant was not so silly after all.

Myra had apparently started the whole space time discussion with Andy while eating breakfast on her patio in Belém—when she watched an ant crawl up the side of a grapefruit. When Sarah and Kim finally realized what was being proposed, they had such a huge laugh to the extent that people in the restaurant were looking at them. Then they wrote some poetry about the ant. They discovered that the ant experiment was kind of the opposite of the Beetle experience. What would happen if just when the ant left New York, the world suddenly shrunk by a factor of 100,000? New York to LA distance would be shrunk down to less than 150 foot. Was the ant a normal-sized ant, a Brazil-sized ant, or even a Texas-sized ant and how long would it take it to make the trip? What a controversy this would generate! The New York scientists would have predicted that it should have taken a long time for a little ant to crawl that far, but the L.A. scientists didn't agree. They thought the ant got to L.A. so very quick.

Kim and Sarah decided—enough of the brain teasers, they needed to get back home. The plan was to visit several more days with their parents, get packed up, and head back to school.

Chapter 12

Mary Magdalene in the Eyes of Hollywood

As they arrived on campus, the football team was sweating through a practice. The Burrs had a 4-8 record last season, but with a new coach, hope springs eternal. They were considered an underdog in their on the road opener with the University of Central Missouri at Warrensburg. Burrhead, the big headed cuckle burr mascot, was doing some high fives with a group of grade school children that had come to watch their favorite college team scrimmage, and the cheerleaders practice their cheers. The canus major dog days of August had everyone fleeing from the heat. Kim made a beeline for the thermostat when entering the dorm room. The old stone building was usually cool in the summer, but the heat wave had infiltrated almost every place of refuge.

During the beginning days of classes, they had an opportunity to visit with their classmates and catch up on the summer activities. Fred and Katie had gotten married and seemed very happy. Nancy proudly showed them through the old courthouse the Criminal Justice Department had revamped during the summer. There was one quite large courtroom with its ancient furniture that had seen many courtroom dramas even from the 1800s. A smaller courtroom was set up for what might have been misdemeanors offences. One could only imagine the land tax sales that occurred on the courthouse steps, the conditions in the dungeon which had housed civil war prisoners, or the civil and criminal trials that had played out over the years. Nancy said the offer of using the facilities for the debate was still open, but it would be a while before everything was organized and running smoothly. They had run into Floyd in the cafeteria, and he had pleasantly greeted them, asked them about their summer, and made no mention of a debate on the sequence of the sun and planet creation days in the Bible.

Floyd's appearance had changed somewhat over the summer. His hippie-like hair had been trimmed; he no longer had a beard but had retained a mustache. Even it was neatly trimmed. He was short, but wiry and energetic. Floyd's major was in physics with a minor in patent law; he was also a member of the University debate team. Sarah surmised that Nancy had worked Floyd over just a bit about presenting a more professional appearance for his patent law class debates.

Early Friday evening, there was a knock on the dorm door. It was Tiffany. She was quite excited about having been with her mother to the matinee to see the just released movie, *The Towers of Magdala.* Kim and Sarah had been so preoccupied with Sarah's uncle and aunt's house, they did not realize the movie had been released. Apparently there had been a whole tangle of issues other than foreign rights that had to be worked out, and the parties involved finally decided they would go forward with the release of the movie and settle their differences through binding arbitration. Not releasing the movie was costing both sides too much money. Tiffany invited Sarah and Kim over to her mother's house so they could hear the reactions of both Tiffany and her mother. She did not say whether she liked or disliked the movie but was clearly excited about it.

Tiffany and her mother lived in a restored townhouse type building a few blocks from the river. It was nicely furnished and the old painted brick walls added an antique ambience to the living and dining room.

"OK, we're here. Tell us what happened. Did our Christ Scene Investigation Jerusalem come close to the plot?"

"Much more than you might have thought," said Velda, Tiffany's mother. "You've heard the phrase 'Can anything good come out of Hollywood?' Actually, this was a very good movie. I would have changed a few things, but of course the producers have their artistic license in filling between what the scriptures say."

Tiffany unfolded the story. She said, "It started out with Jesus and his father, Joseph, taking a trip to what is now Tiberias on the sea of Galilee to get carpenter supplies. Jesus appeared to be in the eight- to ten-year-old range, and his father wanted to give him the experience of riding on a sailboat.

They arranged passage by sea to Magdala and then put ashore to begin the trip back to Nazareth. Jesus was sent down to the well to fill the water bag while Joseph purchased some bread and other food for the journey. As Jesus was drawing water from the well, he noticed a young girl about his age that had come to the well for water, also. Jesus offered the water he had just drawn to her before filling his own water skin. There was a moment when their eyes met and yet the glance seemed like looking into the pools of eternity."

"Maybe they recognized each other in spirit," offered Kim.

"Could be. From there the movie was narrated from point to point through the eyes of Joanna and Susanna. The movie showed the passage from Luke about the women who followed Jesus," said Velda. Opening her Bible, she pointed to the verses:

LUKE 7:49-8:3 *And they that sat at meat with him began to say within themselves, Who is this that forgiveth sins also? And he said to the woman, Thy faith hath saved thee; go in peace.*

And it came to pass afterward, that he went throughout every city and village, preaching and shewing the glad tidings of the kingdom of God: and the twelve were with him, And **certain women,** *which had been healed of evil spirits and infirmities,* **Mary called Magdalene**, *out of whom went seven devils,* **And Joanna the wife of Chuza Herod's steward, and Susanna, and many others, which ministered unto him of their substance.**

Velda thought Joanna and Susanna were good choices for narrating the story. Joanna, mentioned in verse 3, could relate what was going on with the Pharisees and the government because her husband had an inside view from King Herod's palace. The movie treated Susanna more like a successful business woman that could leave her household with trusted servants and follow Jesus as He went from city to city.

"How did the movie portray the woman sinner who broke the alabaster box at Nain and wiped Jesus' feet with her hair. Was she portrayed as being Mary Magdalene?" asked Sarah.

Velda thought it was difficult to tell. The narrative part started with Jesus walking along the sea of Galilee, and many women came to hear Him and He ministered to their needs. This scene included his ministry to Mary Magdalene and showed the seven devils departing as kind of dark, cloudy like figures receding into the distance. However, there were many other women there with about the same hair color and style as Mary Magdalene."

"Why are you mentioning hair color and style?" asked Kim.

"Well, after the scene where Jesus ministered to the women, there was a confrontation with the Pharisees about Jesus slumming with the publicans in the taverns, and as we would say, visiting on the wrong side of the tracks. When Simon the Pharisee invited Jesus to his house, the camera was set up so that we only saw the back of the woman and not her face. It could have been Mary Magdalene, but it just as well might have been some of the other women He had ministered to in the earlier scene."

"So, the movie did not solve this mystery for us?" asked Sarah.

"No," replied Velda. "And actually, I think I liked this treatment of the woman sinner. It was only after I had asked forgiveness for my sins along the ship channel, and they were covered by the blood of Jesus that I could be free of the guilt from them. Oh yes, there were a few Pharisees in my church that still looked down their long pious noses at me, but I knew that God had covered my sins, and I was washed white as snow. And, eventually, they accepted me.

"I liked the way the movie handled it, if Jesus and God had forgiven this woman's sins and had even purged them from their remembrance, why should we insist on attaching this woman's name to the sins of her past? And if the sinful woman wasn't one and same as Mary Magdalene, then so be it." "

"Very good observation," agreed Sarah. "Where did it go from there?"

"The story took various twists and turns as these women followed Jesus from city to city in His ministry.

Did the movie portray Mary Magdalene and Mary of Bethany as being one and the same person?" asked Sarah.

"Yes and no," replied Tiffany.

"Oh No! No!" protested Kim, "You are getting just like Sarah with her yes and no answers. Explain please."

"You would have to see the movie to understand." replied Tiffany. "The actress Miriam Marseille played the role of Mary Magdalene. Her fraternal twin, Marina, played the role of Mary of Bethany. In the movie, Jesus, Martha, Lazarus, and the other characters only used the first name of 'Mary' in the almost all of the conversations. In none of the scenes did Miriam and Marina appear simultaneously. Neither did they wear an identical wardrobe in any of the scenes. Were there two Marys—or only one? Were they one person—or only sisters in the Lord with a similar appearance? After watching the movie, I'm still not sure—Miriam and Marina looked so very much alike."

"OK," said Kim, "I'll watch the movie and judge for myself. Please go on with your narrative, Tiffany."

"The scene of Lazurus' resurrection is a very moving one because the movie shows how close Mary, Martha, and Lazurus were as a family and how Jesus loved to visit them. Their house was just outside of Jerusalem, and He could escape there to rest from the turmoil and confrontations in Jerusalem. The Bible says that Jesus feels our infirmities and knows about our trials, and when Jesus wept over Lazarus' death, I wept too."

Velda told about the well-known scene where Mary sat at the feet of Jesus while her sister Martha was doing the housework. She said that sometimes she wanted to scold Tiffany for sitting around reading when she needed help with housework. But, when she saw it was the Bible Tiffany was reading, she would hold her tongue. But a magazine was a different story.

Tiffany thanked her mom for her understanding but said her mom didn't allow her to get by with much. She was somewhat surprised to see how the movie portrayed Mary Magdalene as just like one of the disciples—a very prominent one at that. There were scenes where Peter expressed a deep seated jealousy about a woman discussing doctrine with Jesus. Mary Magdalene was considered an *Apostle to the Apostles* because she had brought the news of the resurrection to the Apostles. And there were interesting dialogs where Jesus and Mary sat on a rock ledge—overlooking the garden of Gethsemane—and discussed many spiritual subjects. It gave Mary the opportunity to ask questions that were deep within her heart. Later on, the plot of the movie picked up some of the themes from the Song of Solomon. For example, Jesus points out to Mary the secret place of the stairs in the cleft of the rock.

"Really?" remarked Kim, as she glanced at Sarah. "It is surprising that movie script writers would be aware of the Song of Solomon, much less incorporate the themes into the movie."

Tiffany reported that the scenes were so touching. Jesus had told Mary about the script that he must walk out as a sacrificial lamb. Mary was shown the old testament prophecies and she knew. She knew. She knew! Mary hugged Jesus and wept with heart breaking sobs. Later, there was the scene where the alabaster box was broken and the expensive ointment was poured on the head of Jesus—for his burial. Judas complained about the waste of expensive ointment, but Jesus strongly defended the anointing and said that this would be a memorial wherever the gospel is preached.

Velda thought the choice of Joanna as a narrator was a good one. Her husband, Chuza (Herod's steward), would confer with her in the evenings about the strategies taking place in Herod's palace and with Pilate around the time of the crucifixion. Additionally, Chuza gave a first-hand account of the events leading up to the beheading of John the Baptist, and this was given as a flashback in the movie.

"How did the movie handle the crucifixion?" asked Kim.

"It handled it more from the standpoint of the women standing from afar," said Velda. "I've marked the scripture, actually I have been busy looking up a multitude of scriptures since we got home from the movie."

MATTHEW 27:54-56 *Now when the centurion, and they that were with him, watching Jesus, saw the earthquake, and those things that were done, they feared greatly, saying, Truly this was the Son of God.* **And many women were there beholding afar off, which followed Jesus from Galilee, ministering unto him:** *Among which was Mary Magdalene, and Mary the mother of James and Joses, and the mother of Zebedee's children.*

"The scenes of the brutality to Jesus and the crucifixion were there, but they were shown from afar off from the vantage point of the women. It was done in such a way that graphic, close-up scenes of blood and gore were not shown."

"I think that is a good thing," said Sarah. "I know that Jesus suffered terribly when He was whipped and nailed to the cross. But while I appreciate His suffering for us, it bothers me when I see the blood and gore that goes with it. In some of the past movies about the crucifixion, I have had to put my hand over my eyes in order to stay in the theatre. Kim does all kinds of biology experiments, and it doesn't seem to bother her, but it bothers me."

"I understand," responded Velda. "It bothers me too. The movie showed the tears that the women cried when Jesus was crucified and how they cried over Him when Joseph of Arithmathea had begged Pilate for the body. The women came to the tomb and sadly watched as Jesus was entombed and a guard placed over the tomb so no one could steal his body. Can you imagine the sadness as these women departed to their homes? I cried again—maybe Tiffany and I are just a bunch of cry babies."

"It may be that women feel these things more deeply, and this movie was made from the viewpoint of the women around Jesus," said Sarah.

Tiffany agreed with her mother. She was deeply touched when Mary Magdalene came to the tomb on the first day of the week. One could still feel her sadness and then the puzzlement when the tomb was found to be opened and the body was missing. There was a flashback to the scene where Jesus had told her He would be the sacrificial lamb for the Passover and would rise again. She struggled within herself and then ran to tell the disciples that Jesus' body was missing.

Velda said, "I loved the scene where, after Peter and John leave after inspecting the empty tomb, Mary finds herself talking to the one she supposes to be the gardener. I'll never forget this.

JOHN 20:10-18 *Then the disciples went away again unto their own home. But Mary stood without at the sepulchre weeping: and as she wept, she stooped down, and looked into the sepulchre, And seeth two angels in white sitting, the one at the head, and the other at the feet, where the body of Jesus had lain. And they say unto her, Woman, why weepest thou? She saith unto them, Because they have taken away my Lord, and I know not where they have laid him.* **And when she had thus said, she turned herself back, and saw Jesus standing, and knew not that it was Jesus.**

Jesus saith unto her, Woman, why weepest thou? whom seekest thou? She, supposing him to be the gardener, saith unto him, Sir, if thou have borne him hence, tell me where thou hast laid him, and I will take him away. Jesus saith unto her, Mary. She turned herself, and saith unto him, Rabboni; which is to say, Master. Jesus saith unto her, **Touch me not; for I am not yet ascended to my Father***: but go to my brethren, and say unto them, I ascend unto my Father, and your Father; and to my God, and your God.* **Mary Magdalene came and told the disciples that she had seen the Lord***, and that he had spoken these things unto her.*

I remember the joy that I felt when I truly began to walk with Jesus," said Velda. "And I can only imagine that deep inner joy that Mary Magdalene felt when she realized everything Jesus had told her was true; even the hard-to-believe part about Him rising from the dead. How she managed to avoid running to Him and embracing Him, I just don't know."

Tiffany told them the latter part of the movie showed Mary Magdalene as one of the disciples and she had a place of honor among the disciples because of the many secret things Jesus had told her. She would reveal these from time to time as she was led to do so by the Holy Spirit. However, the movie did have a surprising interlude that occurred after Mary was told not to touch Jesus until He had ascended to *my Father, and your Father* and before Jesus walked through the walls and appeared to His disciples in a closed room."

"Oh?" questioned Kim, "And what was that interlude?"

"At first, it seemed like a flashback to the beginning of the movie, when Jesus drew the water from the well for the young girl; then it went forward to Magdala when Jesus encountered Mary Magdalene. These verses were read from the Song of Solomon by the narrator:

SONGS 1:5-7 *I am black, but comely, O ye daughters of Jerusalem, as the tents of Kedar, as the curtains of Solomon. Look not upon me, because I am black, because the sun hath looked upon me: my mother's children were angry with me; they made me the keeper of the vineyards; but mine own vineyard have I not kept. Tell me, O thou whom my soul loveth, where thou feedest, where thou makest thy flock to rest at noon: for why should I be as one that turneth aside by the flocks of thy companions?*

"Mary was smudged by some set of circumstances—what we do not know. Then, as the dark figures of the seven devils recede into the distance, her countenance brightens and the narrator reads these verses:"

SONGS 2:9-14 *My beloved is like a roe or a young hart: behold, he standeth behind our wall,* **he looketh forth at the windows, shewing himself through the lattice**. *My beloved spake, and said unto me, Rise up, my love, my fair one, and come away. For, lo, the winter is past, the rain is over and gone; The flowers appear on the earth; the time of the singing of birds is come, and the voice of the turtle is heard in our land; The fig tree putteth forth her green figs, and the vines with the tender grape give a good smell. Arise, my love, my fair one, and come away.* **O my dove, that art in the clefts of the rock, in the secret places of the stairs**, *let me see thy countenance, let me hear thy voice; for sweet is thy voice, and thy countenance is comely.*

Kim and Sarah looked at each other, somewhat in shock, thinking, "Could this be coming out of the Hollywood that we know?"

Velda continued, "In these scenes from the movie, it seems Jesus appeared once again to Mary Magdalene, much as He did after the crucifixion. But this time, Mary Magdalene flew into His arms and hugged Him for joy. She was told the bride of Christ was His church and she was part of the church of the firstborn. I couldn't remember that being in scripture, but when we got home this evening, I looked it up and sure enough, it was there:

HEBREWS 12:22-23 *But ye are come unto mount Sion, and unto the city of the living God, the heavenly Jerusalem, and to an innumerable company of angels,* **To the general assembly and church of the firstborn, which are written in heaven, and to God the Judge of all, and to the spirits of just men made perfect,**

"It is curious," said Kim, "that Jesus asked Mary Magdalene not to touch Him until He had ascended to the Father. Yet, over a week later, He invited Thomas to put his hand into the wound in His side. It makes me wonder if there was a secret ascension to the Father in the intervening time."

"Never gave that any thought," said Velda. "But it could be—it fits in with the movie."

Tiffany thought it could be poetic license, but the next scene in the movie showed a change occurring in Mary Magdalene's body as she flew into the arms of Jesus. Her earthly clothes lay at her feet, but she was not naked or ashamed for her body was a body of light, and it was clothed with light. It was the same sort of transformation Jesus experienced on the mount of transfiguration with Peter, James, and John.

Velda pointed to her butterfly pin. "It seems," she said, "that the caterpillar had changed into a butterfly. There was such a presence of love and purity about them that it brought tears to my eyes once again. This little Cinderella was given the chance to try on the golden slipper. And the narrator read once more from the Song of Solomon about the ascent up Mount Hermon:"

SONGS 4:8-9 *Come with me from Lebanon, my spouse, with me from Lebanon:* **look from the top of Amana, from the top of Shenir and Hermon**, *from the lions' dens, from the mountains of the leopards.* **Thou hast ravished my heart, my sister, my spouse**; *thou hast ravished my heart with one of thine eyes, with one chain of thy neck.*

Velda related that as they stood on the top of the mountain, Mary could hardly believe the transformation that had occurred to her body. The angels were there, but Jesus' and Mary Magdalene's bodies were more luminous than the angels. There was a flash back to the dialog of Jesus and Martha. Then, Mary Magdalene understood the precious words of Jesus that Martha had received and passed on to be recorded in John's gospel.

JOHN 11:25-26 *Jesus said unto her, I am the resurrection, and the life: he that believeth in me, though he were dead, yet shall he live:* **And whosoever liveth and believeth in me shall never die**. *Believest thou this?*

Like Jesus, Mary Magdalene had accepted Jesus' statement at face value and had overcome death while still living. She had been transfigured.

"This is confusing," responded Kim. "I thought that Mary Magdalene died, and her grave is thought to be somewhere in France—at least this is the popular culture opinion.

Tiffany admonished Kim for jumping ahead—the end of the movie had not yet been reached. It was then that both Jesus and Mary Magdalene were caught up to the third heaven, and Mary learned many secret things, some of which were not to be shared in the earth. One of the scenes in the third heaven is from the Song of Solomon. The narrator read these verses as Mary and Jesus walked to *the house where the Holy Spirit resided.* It was there the arrangements were made for the Holy Spirit to be sent back to earth for Pentecost—ten days after Jesus would make His ascension from the earth. He had already told His disciples that He would go away, but that He would send the Comforter, the Holy Spirit, to be with them.

SONGS 8:1-2 *O that thou wert as my brother, that sucked the breasts of my mother! when I should find thee without, I would kiss thee; yea, I should not be despised.* **I would lead thee, and bring thee into my mother's house, who would instruct me: I would cause thee to drink of spiced wine of the juice of my pomegranate.**

Tiffany went on to answer Kim's question about Mary Magdalene dying and *maybe* being buried somewhere in France. She said, "Mary Magdalene was given the choice of continuing in a transfigured body in the third heaven or returning back to the earth. She was taken to a high hill and was shown a pasture where thousands of sheep were wounded and many were dying. She was told that if she returned to earth these sheep would be saved as a result of the ministry of the Holy Spirit that would flow through her. However, to do this, she would have to lay down her transfigured, celestial body and once more be subject to death as it happens in the earth. Jesus told her that after His transfiguration, He could not have been crucified unless He had willingly laid down His celestial body and allowed His captors to crucify Him."

JOHN 19:10-11 *Then saith Pilate unto him, Speakest thou not unto me? knowest thou not that I have power to crucify thee, and have power to release thee? Jesus answered,* **Thou couldest have no power at all against me, except it were given thee from above**: *therefore he that delivered me unto thee hath the greater sin.*

"Wow!" exclaimed Kim. "What a choice to make. I think I know what her decision was."

"Yes," said Tiffany. "In the next scene, she was back on earth, in her earthly body and clothes, and it seemed her earthly life picked up exactly where it had left off. The movie showed various scenes as Jesus appeared to His disciples and finally the journey from Jerusalem to Bethany where Jesus ascended into the heavens and left these words for his followers:"

LUKE 24:49-51 *And, behold, I send the promise of my Father upon you: but tarry ye in the city of Jerusalem, until ye be endued with power from on high.* **And he led them out as far as to Bethany,** *and he lifted up his hands, and blessed them. And it came to pass, while he blessed them,* **he was parted from them, and carried up into heaven.**

"I love this movie," said Sarah. "And I haven't even seen it. And what happened next, was it the upper room and the Pentecost scene?"

Tiffany confirmed that, yes, Mary Magdalene and the other women were in the upper room and the Holy Spirit fell upon all of them.

Then, as the movie progressed, there were various scenes where Mary Magdalene and the other disciples were forming the core of the Christian church. And there was dialog between Mary and some of the disciples wanting to know some of the secret things Jesus had told her during their walks and talks. Mary Magdalene was shown to be a disciple to the disciples, and also she touched many people in her ministry.

"Did the movie show her death?" asked Kim.

"No," said Velda. "At the end of the movie, she was on a sailboat leaving Israel for lands that were not identified in the movie. The dialog hinted she had already traveled to the eastern part of the Mediterranean Sea with Phillip—hence she is mentioned in the gospel of Phillip. Also, she had a close relationship with Thomas who defended her from time to time when some of male disciples were jealous of her ministry.

"Did the movie say she was married to Jesus?" asked Kim.

"No, not in the earthly sense that we would think of marriage," replied Tiffany. "The only reference to this was Jesus told her she was part of the bride of Christ and was of the church of the firstborn. As such, she was entrusted with a very special and unique ministry. The movie did not try to distinguish between a corporate bride of believers and an individual, personal bride, specifically for Jesus."

"I'm very curious about one thing," said Sarah. "What kind of rating was the movie given—was it an R rating?"

"It was given a PG rating." replied Velda, "The crucifixion scenes were shown from afar and without the blood and gore scenes; the movie did not have to be rated R."

"That truly is a miracle," responded Sarah. "When you mentioned scenes from Song of Solomon, I thought that would be where Hollywood will ruin the movie for sure."

Velda thought it rather strange that the scenes from Song of Solomon reminded her of the story of Cinderella. Remember in the Song of Solomon, the girl is darkened in the vineyard. In the fairy tale, the girl was called Cinderella because she was smudged with the cinders and ashes from keeping the fireplace. She was looked down upon by her sisters. Cinderella's position did not seem much different than the passages the first chapter of the Song of Solomon:

SONGS 1:5-6 *I am black, but comely, O ye daughters of Jerusalem, as the tents of Kedar, as the curtains of Solomon. Look not upon me, because I am black, because the sun hath looked upon me:* **my mother's children were angry with me; they made me the keeper of the vineyards;** *but mine own vineyard have I not kept.*

"The movie was beautifully handled," continued Velda. "As far as taking children to the Towers of Magdala, I really see no difference in rating between it and Cinderella."

"Again, I am astounded," said Sarah. "Maybe something good can come out of Hollywood after all."

"I think I owe you and Kim an explanation about why I cautioned Tiffany so strongly about not going to this movie or at least being prepared for what might be shown," offered Velda. "You see, some years ago I went to a movie about the battles that Jesus supposedly went through in choosing between the flesh and the spirit. When I went to the movie, I was aware of this scripture and thought the movie might portray how Jesus dealt with temptation:"

HEBREWS 4:14-15 *Seeing then that we have a great high priest, that is passed into the heavens, Jesus the Son of God, let us hold fast our profession. For we have not an high priest which cannot be touched with the feeling of our infirmities;* **but was in all points tempted like as we are, yet without sin**.

"Since the Bible says Jesus was tempted in all points with the same temptations we face, I thought I might learn something. The movie was terrible. You guys may not remember the TV show *All in the Family*, but Jesus was portrayed in this movie like the bumbling son-in-law called 'Meathead.' Judas was portrayed as the mentor that kept Jesus on track. Mary Magdalene and Mary of Bethany were two women in the movie Jesus romanced. When it reached this point, I could take it no more and just got up and left. Yes, I do believe Jesus was tempted, even as the birds of the air would like to build their nests in our mind. I think it was part of God's plan that these temptations were intense and very real, but I do not believe that Jesus sinned by letting these birds of thought build nests within his mind. The scripture says He was without sin, and the awful movie did not portray Jesus' life that way."

"I can appreciate your concerns," said Sarah. "At least, I'm glad Hollywood did no more to the Magdala movie than exercise its poetic license in a wholesome way. Whether it happened just like this in the movie, I suppose we will never know until it is revealed to us by Jesus."

"So," said Tiffany, "are you and Kim going to the movie."

"I feel like we've already seen it," said Sarah, "at least through your eyes."

"Oh, we wouldn't miss it," said Kim. "You have whetted our appetite for a good movie."

With that, Sarah and Kim accepted a ride from Tiffany to the dorm. It was a beautiful evening; the star Sirius near the constellation Orion was showing brightly in the night sky as they walked into the dorm.

Kim and Sarah spent the Saturday morning stocking up on necessities, visiting the laundromat, and generally getting organized for the fall semester. Katie called, and Kim answered.

"Sarah, it's Katie, she wants to talk to you."

"I would like to talk to you about how to handle a marriage problem," said Katie.

"Are you and Fred having problems?" asked Sarah.

"No, it's not us; we're doing just great. But it does affect us. It's Fred's sister's marriage, and it has Fred very upset and in a quandary. I suggested to Fred we might call you and maybe you could help us sort it out. It's difficult to talk about this over the phone. I'm wondering if we could get together with you somewhere and talk about it?"

Arrangements were made to meet in one of the conference rooms at the library late in the afternoon. When they arrived, Fred related to Sarah the problems his sister was having in her marriage. On the surface, Deanna's marriage seemed like out of a story book. They were active in the church, they had three children, and her husband, Charlie, had a successful business. Deanna had voiced a few complaints about how controlling her husband was, and it was placing strains on their marriage. When she talked to her parents about it, they told her just to buckle down and be a good wife and submit to her husband. It seemed like the storm had passed. However, as time went by, it was clear something was bothering Deanna—everyone could see the premature aging lines in her face, and it was affecting her health.

Fred asked her about it, and Deanna confided in him that Charlie was the source of the stress but did not say what the problem was. Fred asked if Charlie had a drinking problem or was having an affair or what? Deanna started crying and then struggled to keep it hidden but finally told Fred that she was being both verbally and physically abused.

She said it started on their honeymoon and had gotten worse year by year. She said she felt trapped because she didn't know what to do because their three children had to be considered. Charlie seemed like such a nice, church going guy to Fred. He said he had a such hard time believing this and thought maybe Deanna was just making it up because she didn't want to submit to Charlie. Deanna talked about separation or even divorce, and Fred told her this was not the solution—divorce was out of the question.

Then, in the week before classes resumed, Fred and Katie and Deanna and Charlie had rented a cabin at Big Springs for a vacation. Deanna and Charlie's children were staying with their grandparents. Fred and Katie decided they would drive into Van Buren to get some ice and other supplies, but after having gone about five miles, Fred realized he had left his wallet on the dresser when they had gone swimming that morning and had not picked it up. Katie only had ten dollars with her, so they went back to the cabin to get the wallet. When they opened the door to the cabin, they heard Charlie berating Deanna in the next room and then Deanna screamed. They rushed in and found Charlie beating up on Deanna. Fred stepped in and told Charlie to back off, and if he couldn't refrain from beating his sister, she needed to separate from him. It was ugly from that point, and Fred was having difficulty handling the prospects of his sister separating or even getting a divorce. He was also having problems understanding how Charlie had done this and managed to hide it so many years from the church, their parents and even Fred. And then, just this week, Fred learned from his brother that Deanna had separated from Charlie and had taken the children with her.

After Fred had poured out the sad story, he asked Sarah, "What would you do?"

"Have Charlie and Deanna arranged for counseling, maybe through their church?"

"Deanna was willing to accept counseling, but Charlie said he didn't need it. Deanna was the one having the problems, and she should be the one that should be counseled," said Fred.

"Tell me, Fred," asked Sarah, "in the days before you and Katie were married, didn't you have an apartment where you and your roommate lived and also cooked your meals?"

"Yes, it was the apartment over on Pacific Street."

Sarah posed a hypothetical to Fred about a roommate who was very controlling about what groceries were to be bought, how much money was to be spent, how the food was to be cooked, what TV programs would be watched, and a whole host of picky details such as whether the salt and pepper was in the exact center of the table. She queried him about whether it would bother him, and if so, what would he do about it?

"Well, I would try to work it out with him—after all it's my apartment, too."

"And if when you tried to work it out, your roommate delighted in putting you down, saying that you knew nothing about how to keep an apartment, and that your ideas were dumb, would that bother you?"

"It certainly would," replied Fred. "I think that kind of stress would affect my grades."

"Now," said Sarah, "suppose your roommate is a burly 250 lb. guy, and when you confront him about his actions, he grabs you, twists your arm, and throws you to the floor, well beyond normal horseplay. This is vicious and has happened more than once. What would you do then? And, oh, by the way, you had just paid next month's rent and barely had enough money to pay for food."

"I would move out of there," said Fred. "I wouldn't take that kind of abuse."

"I don't know the specific circumstances between Charlie and Deanna, but it boils down to simply this. If you wouldn't take this kind of abuse, why would you want Deanna to take it?"

"I know you're right," said Fred. "I love my sister. Her well-being is more important to me than worrying about the possibility that she could end up in a divorce."

"Then, I think you did the right thing in advising your sister to separate if Charlie continued beating her up. The next question is: since the separation occurred, what should be done about it?"

Fred related his parents weren't very happy with him. They had believed Charlie's side of the story, he guessed because Charlie was such a good talker. There had been an earlier incident when Deanna had complained to her parents. Her parents had been telling Deanna all along she needed to get over her whining and just be a good wife for her husband.

They told her the wife just needed to submit to her husband and to forget separation or divorce. Fred said he just couldn't understand why he had such inner turmoil about it.

Katie described how it was only after both she and Fred got on the phone and graphically described the beating that Charlie was laying on Deanna that the parents changed their tune. She had pointed out to them there were three witnesses contradicting Charlie's story: Fred, herself, and Deanna. They then changed their attitude completely and took Deanna and the children into their home and became much more supportive of her.

"OK," said Sarah, "I'm glad your parents are seeing the light; they can be of tremendous help to your sister while this is being sorted out. And, for the present, she is out of danger and doesn't have to worry about being beaten up. I would think the next step would be to get both Charlie and Deanna to obtain counseling, individually at first, and jointly when the counselor thinks they are ready."

"I agree," said Fred. "I will suggest that to Deanna and my parents. And Sarah, you've been very helpful to us in understanding this situation. How would you sum up this 'submission' thing?"

"Good question, Fred," replied Sarah. "There is a scripture saying we are under governors and tutors until the time appointed by the Father. So, we should give due honor to those God has placed there for our benefit. I think that you agree with that."

"But what about those situations that don't fit neatly into this box?" asked Katie.

"OK, examples of this would be Deanna's situation. Other examples might be a young girl who is told by her father God wants her to obey his wishes no matter what, even if he molests her. Fred and Katie, I'm going to show you a little picture that I found in a writing that might help in getting down to the root of this discussion. I've been somewhat reluctant to share this previously, but here it is. Look at it, and tell me if something is wrong with this picture." [See next page].

"The drawing does make it rather graphic," responded Fred. "I see the distinction you are making."

Sarah related other examples: A pastor who tells his subjects the Bible says "*Obey them that have the rule over you ...*" and then abuses his authority by saying God wants them to give him their money. A political leader who commits atrocities and then justifies it to the citizens by telling them "*to be subject to principalities and powers, to obey magistrates ...*" and not to question his authority.

Sarah told them that submission to others does not have to be a lot of rules and regulations. It is simply this: *If the Christ spirit is speaking out of another person, we should submit ourselves to what is being said. If the flesh is speaking out of another person, we are not obligated to submit to the flesh. However, we are obligated to respond in a Christ like way.* This is very simple, and it boils down to just two principles based on the first two commandments—loving God enough to ask for His discernment of the thoughts and intents of the heart.. And, then loving our neighbor by giving him the response that is best for him in the long run."

"If the flesh is speaking out of another person, does this mean we simply turn the other cheek and take the punishment?" asked Katie. "Is that what you mean by a Christ-like response?"

"Not necessarily," said Sarah. "You know Jesus is known as the 'Lamb of God.' You also know He is known as the 'Lion of Judah.' When dealing with those that were hurt and oppressed, He was very tender. But if the situation warranted it, He could respond like a lion as when He drove the money changers out of the temple. If we ask, the Holy Spirit will witness within our spirit, and we will know the proper response."

"That helps a lot. I think I understand how to deal with an abuser," observed Katie. "It required lion-like courage for Deanna to consider her own safety and separate herself from Charlie."

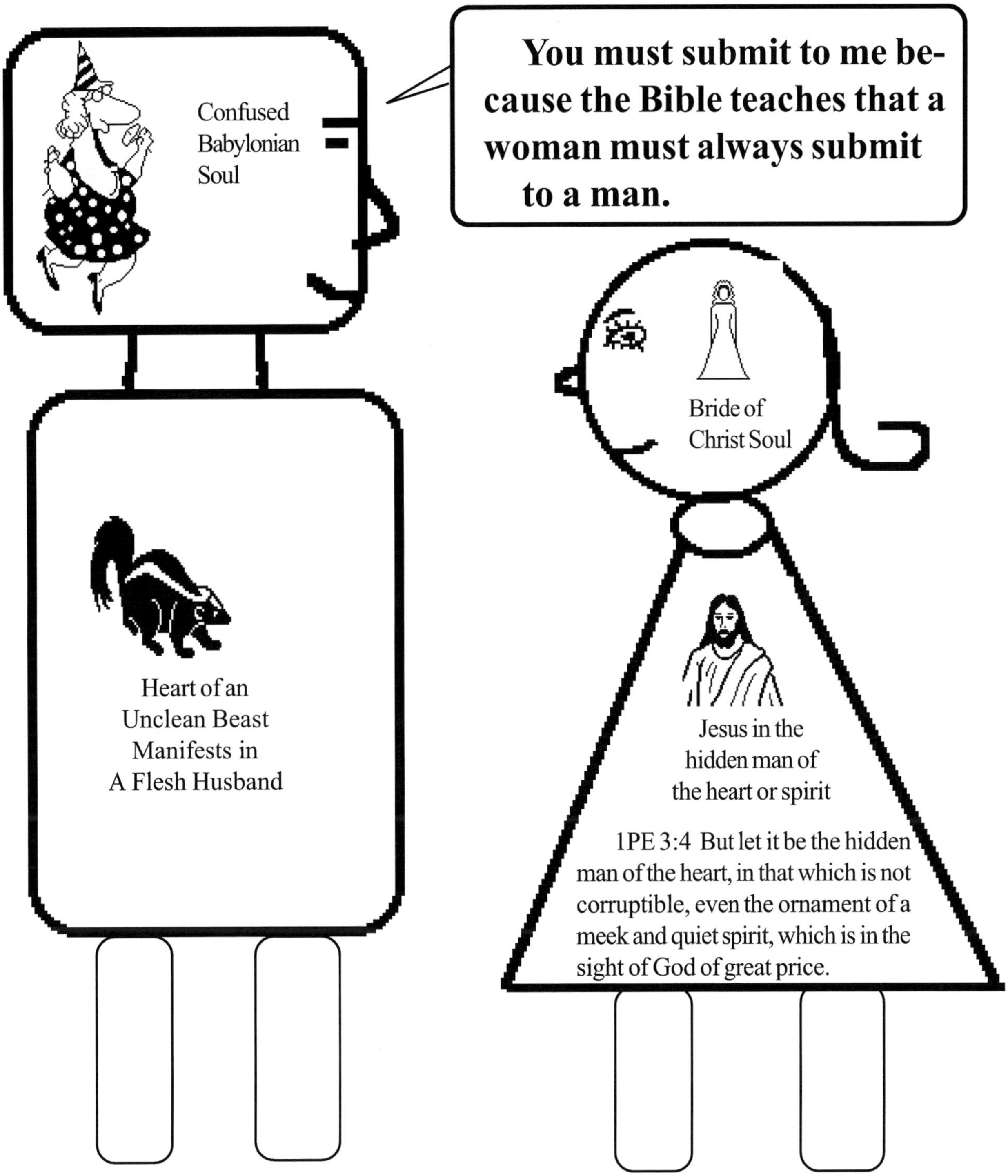
You must submit to me because the Bible teaches that a woman must always submit to a man.
Confused Babylonian Soul
Heart of an Unclean Beast Manifests in A Flesh Husband
Bride of Christ Soul
Jesus in the hidden man of the heart or spirit
1PE 3:4 But let it be the hidden man of the heart, in that which is not corruptible, even the ornament of a meek and quiet spirit, which is in the sight of God of great price.

Is there something wrong with the above picture? If we were like the Pharisees and only saw the whitewash of the outside of the cup (natural gender), we would likely say that everything is fine. But, we can see and discern in the Spirit. And both men and women have spirits and souls. The man above has a confused, Babylonian soul which has mated with the flesh (instead of the spirit) and brings forth the unclean.

But the natural woman above has a chaste, bride of Christ soul, and this soul (woman) is submissive to the hidden man of the heart which is a meek and quiet spirit. For this spirit is the husband of the bride of Christ soul. For each of us must realize that both natural men and women have souls. Therefore, a natural man with a carnal soul woman may violate Paul's admonition not to let the woman (the soulish voice) to speak in church.

"That's right," Sarah said. "Don't be surprised if, because of the separation, the abuser suddenly becomes apologetic and says that it will never happen again. That is a good first step, but it needs to be a *sincere and repentant first step rather than just mouthing the words that the abuser has found will cause his spouse to return.*"

"That's a good point. Deanna said that the pattern would be abuse, and then Charlie would promise never to do it again but that turned out to be only until the next time he did it again," observed Fred. "Anyway, I've been thinking over some of the things we discussed at Council Rocks before Katie and I got married. Maybe we could discuss them further some time?"

"That would be good," replied Sarah. "However, I think this situation with your sister is too raw in your mind right, now. Let's let things settle down. We can discuss this later when things are more relaxed."

Fred and Katie thanked Sarah, and they both hugged her. Katie gave Sarah's hand a warm squeeze as they were departing.

When Sarah returned to the dorm, she found Kim smiling, "I have a date with Red tomorrow afternoon. He has asked me to go to the movies with him and guess what movie I picked."

"The Towers of Magdala? Are you sure it's the type of movie you want to see?" teased Sarah.

"I'll take my chances," said Kim. "And guess what—you're invited to go with us."

"I don't even have a date," replied Sarah. "I would be like a fifth wheel or something like that."

"No problem," said Kim. "Red asked if you would like to go with us, and I said I thought you would. And besides, we will bring you back to the dorm after the movie, deposit you there, and continue our date."

"You've got a deal," said Sarah. "But I'm not sure if I've ever been deposited before."

The next afternoon, Red picked up Kim and Sarah, and they headed to the movies. Some parts of the movie had been done on location in Israel where political conditions permitted, and the scenery was breath-taking.

Having done so much background study on Mary Magdalene, both Sarah and Kim were impressed with the integrity of the movie, particularly since it viewed the ministry of Jesus through the eyes of women. There were many scenes where Jesus taught and interacted with the children, and that appealed to Sarah's mothering and teaching instincts. Red seemed moved by the movie and told Kim it was one of the better movies he had ever seen.

As was promised, Sarah was dropped off at the dorm, and Red and Kim continued their date. Sarah decided to drop by the church about three blocks from the campus where they were having a city-wide youth rally. The music was anointed, and prayers were said for the city, the university, the state, and the nation. Kim was back when Sarah returned to the dorm. She and Red had been invited out to dinner by Red's brother who was driving through on his way to Springfield. They had dinner at Houston House, and Kim had learned more about Red's family. His brother was redheaded but was not as tall as Red.

"Is this serious?" asked Sarah.

"Just a date," responded Kim. "But I really did enjoy myself, and it was great that you could go to the movie with us."

"What impressed you about the movie?" asked Kim.

"There were several things that really surprised me," said Sarah. "One was the scene where Mary Magdalene flew into the arms of Jesus and her body was transformed. I was just looking at a passage from the book of Thomas on the computer:"

THOMAS 37 His disciples said, "When will you appear to us, and when will we see you?"

Jesus said, "**When you strip without being ashamed**, and you take your clothes and put them under your feet like little children and trample then, then [you] will see the son of the living one and you will not be afraid."

"I think that's why the reunion scene was so touching," said Kim. "The spirit of love and purity was present in the embrace. And what was the other scene that impressed you?"

"It was when Mary Magdalene and Jesus were going to the mother's house. Have you ever thought why it was necessary to go back to the Father and request that the Comforter, the Holy Spirit, be sent to the earth?"

"I've wondered about it." said Kim.

"The book of Jude says that Enoch was a prophet, and there are some passages in the book of Enoch that tell about the reason Wisdom had left the earth."

JUDE 1:14 **And Enoch also, the seventh from Adam, prophesied of these***, saying, Behold, the Lord cometh with ten thousands of his saints,*

Sarah described how in the early church, the first book of Enoch and the book of Revelation were both freely used as sources and pretty much equally esteemed, but only the book of Revelation was included in the Bible.

ENOCH 42:1-2 **Wisdom found not a place on earth where she could inhabit***; her dwelling is therefore in heaven. Wisdom went forth to dwell among the sons of men, but she obtained not an habitation.* **Wisdom returned to her places and seated herself in the midst of the angels.**

She thought early mankind simply became so wicked that the feminine part of God, Wisdom, left the earth and was only invited back when Jesus asked the Father if she might return—and she then returned on the day of Pentecost. That's why she found it so touching, in the movie, that Jesus and Mary Magdalene returned to the mother's house. Perhaps they were sent by the Father to invite Wisdom to return to the earth.

"I remember," said Kim, "we talked about this when we discussed the Godhead and said El Shaddai or Wisdom was the feminine nature of God. When the Holy Spirit left the earth, what kind of shape was mankind left in? Didn't it leave a void or split?"

"There was a residue of the Spirit left on the earth. And the residue was much stronger on some of the patriarchs and prophets, such as Samuel, David, and the major prophets. Malachi put it this way:"

MALACHI 2:15 *And did not he make one?* **Yet had he the residue of the spirit***. And wherefore one? That he might seek a godly seed. Therefore take heed to your spirit, and let none deal treacherously against the wife of his youth.*

"Sarah, I have a question. This scripture talks about *the wife of his youth.* We've said Jesus and Mary Magdalene may have been doves and in the movie Jesus reminds her that she is part of *the church of the firstborn.* Let's assume that when Jesus and Mary Magdalene went back to Mother Wisdom's house, they were both endued with celestial bodies. At that point, could they have produced celestial children—or maybe I should say the spirits of celestial children?"

Sarah's jaw dropped, "Kim, how do you manage to come up with such questions? Don't you think we should finish the foundation of the house before tackling such hypotheticals?"

"OK, Ok, maybe you're right." replied Kim. "But I wondered about this in the movie, when Jesus told his disciples he would do the same things that his Father does. Now, we know his Father is *the Father of spirits.* Let me borrow your computer to find the scripture recording Jesus' words."

JOHN 5:19 *Then answered Jesus and said unto them, Verily, verily, I say unto you, The Son can do nothing of himself,* **but what he seeth the Father do***: for what things soever he doeth,* **these also doeth the Son likewise.**

"Interesting observation." replied Sarah, "But, lets leave it as a hypothetical, and not stretch ourselves out spiritually into very unknown areas—at least for now."

"OK, I can take a broad hint, you want to change the subject. What other thoughts did you have about the movie?"

"There is one thing that just struck me as being so funny. It was when the women came back to report to the apostles after the resurrection."

"What is it?" asked Kim.

"Let me find it on my computer. Here it is."

LUKE 24:7-11 *Saying, The Son of man must be delivered into the hands of sinful men, and be crucified, and the third day rise again. And they remembered his words, And returned from the sepulchre, and told all these things unto the eleven, and to all the rest. It was* **Mary Magdalene and Joanna, and Mary the mother of James, and other women** *that were with them, which told these things unto the apostles.* **And their words seemed to them as idle tales, and they believed them not.**

Sarah thought it was so, so funny in retrospect. Mary Magdalene, Joanna, and Mary the mother of James, and other women told the eleven that Jesus had risen, but these men castigated them for telling idle tales. Well, finally these women have a movie that shows what happened through their very own eyes, and it is no longer just the idle tales of women. Kim agreed with her and referred to the proverb about laughter being a good medicine.

"One thing still bugs me about our Bible study on Mary Magdalene and even in the movie," said Kim. "They show a scene where Mary Magdalene and Jesus are both caught up to the third heaven, and they go to the Mother Wisdom's house to request that the Holy Spirit, or the Comforter, be returned in greater measure to the earth. This seems to occur sometime after Mary Magdalene was told she couldn't touch Jesus, but before Thomas was told he could thrust his hand into Jesus' side. I just don't understand the timing."

"You're right," replied Sarah, "I think for sure that Jesus was caught up, and the Holy Spirit was given to the 120 at Pentecost. However, what you say is a puzzle. Wait a minute, I think I remember something that happened with the Holy Spirit before Pentecost. That could be it! Let me look for it."

"Let's see key words 'receive,' 'breathed,' here it is—it's the same as the idle tales scenario."

JOHN 20:17-22 *Jesus saith unto her,* **Touch me not; for I am not yet ascended to my Father:** *but go to my brethren, and say unto them, I ascend unto my Father, and your Father; and to my God, and your God. Mary Magdalene came and told the disciples that she had seen the Lord, and that he had spoken these things unto her.* **Then the same day at evening,** *being the first day of the week, when the doors were shut where the disciples were assembled for fear of the Jews, came Jesus and stood in the midst, and saith unto them, Peace be unto you.* **And when he had so said, he shewed unto them his hands and his side.** *Then were the disciples glad, when they saw the Lord. Then said Jesus to them again, Peace be unto you: as my Father hath sent me, even so send I you.* **And when he had said this, he breathed on them, and saith unto them, Receive ye the Holy Spirit:**

"Look, you're right," said Kim. "There was a period of time between the morning when the women received the idle tales rebuke and the evening when Jesus breathed on the disciples to receive the Holy Spirit."

"I know most people don't think of the disciples having been given a preview of what would happen to the believers generally on the day of Pentecost," said Sarah, "but there it is. Jesus said *receive ye the Holy Spirit.* Also, look at the verses 24 and 25 about Thomas."

JOHN 20:23-25 *Whose soever sins ye remit, they are remitted unto them; and whose soever sins ye retain, they are retained.* [24]**But Thomas, one of the twelve, called Didymus, was not with them when Jesus came**. [25]*The other disciples therefore said unto him, We have seen the Lord. But he said unto them,* **Except I shall see in his hands the print of the nails, and put my finger into the print of the nails, and thrust my hand into his side, I will not believe.**

Kim thought that there was one other thing about the movie Sarah hadn't said anything about, but she knew it had surprised her and Sarah had surely been thinking about it. So Kim asked Sarah about surprises.

"You're right and very perceptive," responded Sarah. "You're referring to the scene toward the end of the movie where Mary Magdalene is leaving on the ship with a young girl named Sarah at her side?"

"Yes, and Velda and Tiffany didn't bring it up either. They didn't want to spoil the surprise for you, but they told me about it ahead of time."

"Scheming as usual," said Sarah. "OK, it was difficult for me to understand at first until the flashback was shown. I think I would have done the same thing as Mary Magdalene did as she came over the hill near Joppa. I was shocked by the incident and the screams of the little Sarah as she came running toward Mary."

"I think that the way the Pharisees handled it was extremely cruel," said Kim. "Surely, the little girl could have been shielded from seeing her mother stoned."

"I doubt think she even knew what adultery was," said Sarah. "Apparently, the little girl had lost her father in a drowning incident at sea and her lonely mother had an affair with a married soldier. The loss of two parents in a year would shell shock any of us."

"Maybe the young Sarah was one of the wounded sheep that Mary came back to comfort," said Sarah. "I think the movie wonderfully portrayed God's love through Mary Magdalene. I was extremely touched when she took the little girl in her arms, dried her tears, and comforted her as the little one related the trauma of losing her parents. It was wonderful to see how Mary introduced this little girl to other children on the ship and little Sarah's tears were dried.

"I suppose that every movie should have a happy ending," said Kim. "I had tears at the end when Mary Magdalene and her adopted little Sarah sailed away on the ship, but they were tears of joy."

"I know," responded Sarah. "The wonderful, beaming little smile on young Sarah's face was priceless."

"Sarah, do you think the movie in general and particularly those last scenes—adopting the little girl and sailing off in a ship—portray what really happened with Mary Magdalene? I know she is called Mary of the town Magdala, but I wonder what is her actual family name? We haven't seriously evaluated some of the old gospels yet, such as the Gospel of Phillip, The Gospel According to Mary Magdalene, and others. The closer we can get to the orignal text, the better—sometimes translators change the meaning or interpret a word incorrectly."

"Well, it was a great and touching story. I suppose we will never know exactly what happened until perhaps someday we will be able to talk face to face with Mary Magdalene and Jesus. In the meantime, maybe we should just consider it as the poetic license of Hollywood."

"I think you're right—I can't wait until that face to face day comes." replied Kim, "In the meantime, I believe I will take the Bible's descriptions at face value. I will let the *woman in the city, who was a sinner* be the sinful woman, *Mary Magdalene* be Mary Magdalene, and *Mary* of Bethany be Mary of Bethany. Maybe its just my scientific training kicking in, but I would need more information before drawing definite conclusions about who is who."

"After all of our discussions about Mary Magdalene, I can't agree more. However, in my role as moderator for the discussions with Tiffany and her mom, I have tried to be relatively neutral. It was a wonderful movie. It's late, Kim ... sweet dreams."

"Sweet dreams."

Editors Note:
See http://www.TheAncientChest.com/Women

Post your thoughts about the script of the movie:
The Towers of Magdala: ________________

Post your thoughts about how the Deanna's parents should have counseled their daughter when she divulged Charlie's physical abuse: ______________________________

Post your thoughts about submission: ______________

Chapter 13

Preparing for the Lion's Den

Labor day weekend was quiet for Sarah. She had stayed on campus, and Kim and Red had gone out of town to Kim's parents for the labor day weekend. Before Kim left, she said Dr. Harper had asked her how Sarah's debate with Floyd was coming along. Dr. Harper said Floyd had been preparing for it. So, Sarah knew this topic had not been dropped at all but was still on the radar screen. But she didn't dread it anymore, she had a plan and decided to spend the weekend developing that plan.

GENESIS 1:1-4 **In the beginning God created the heaven and the earth**. *And the earth was without form, and void; and darkness was upon the face of the deep. And the Spirit of God moved upon the face of the waters.* **And God said, Let there be light: and there was light.** *And God saw the light, that it was good: and God divided the light from the darkness.*

Floyd's main point of contention seemed to be the sun mentioned on the fourth day would more logically have been created in the beginning rather than on the fourth day.

GENESIS 1:13-19 *And the evening and the morning were the third day. And God said, Let there be lights in the firmament of the heaven to divide the day from the night; and let them be for signs, and for seasons, and for days, and years: And let them be for lights in the firmament of the heaven to give light upon the earth: and it was so.* **And God made two great lights; the greater light to rule the day, and the lesser light to rule the night: he made the stars also.** *And God set them in the firmament of the heaven to give light upon the earth,* **And to rule over the day and over the night, and to divide the light from the darkness: and God saw that it was good.** *And the evening and the morning were the fourth day.*

Sarah spent time looking at various theories of planetary formation she found on Google. Most of the discussions involved having a central star around which disks of gas and other matter were swirling. Astronomers noted these disks of gas are seen around young stars and are the precursors to formation of planets. Typical of the theories on the leading edge was this discussion about computer simulation of the formations of planets.

Watching his simulations run on a computer monitor, it's easy to imagine looking down from a vantage point in interstellar space and watching the process actually happen.

A green disk of gas swirls around a central star. Eventually, spiral arms of yellow begin to appear within the disk, indicating regions where the gas is becoming denser. Then a few blobs of red appear, at first just hints but then gradually more stable. These red regions are even denser, showing where masses of gas are accumulating that might later become planets.

Sarah knew it was quite important how the challenge for the debate would be stated. This was meticulously planned as she kept in mind the scripture:

MAT 10:16 *Behold, I send you forth as sheep in the midst of wolves:* **be ye therefore wise as serpents, and harmless as doves.**

Sarah needed a very special globe of the earth for use in the debate. She found one on the internet but its cost was in the $500 range, and Sarah did not have that kind of money to spare. She was on a very good scholarship; she had accumulated some money from her summer jobs and received help from time to time from her parents. But this was a budget buster. She remembered meeting David at the city-wide youth rally and hearing his presentation about raising funds for the science club for Christians. She found his name in the campus phone book and thought he might be in town over the Labor Day weekend since he was involved with local city activities. The response to the phone call was positive—David remembered her since they had talked after the rally. He would meet her at Chicken and Egg for breakfast on Monday morning, and they could discuss her request. Sarah did not want to reveal her strategy for the debate prematurely to anyone, but she did tell David the special globe would be used to illustrate Job's astronaut-like description of the earth. This would be used as a counter to the Galileo versus the church "flat earth" example that most certainly would be brought up by the opposition.

JOB 26:7-10 **He stretcheth out the north over the empty place, and hangeth the earth upon nothing.** *He bindeth up the waters in his thick clouds; and the cloud is not rent under them He holdeth back the face of his throne, and spreadeth his cloud upon it.* **He hath compassed the waters with bounds, until the day and night come to an end.**

The breakfast meeting went very well. David was quite interested in the challenge that lay ahead of Sarah and agreed to try to get full or at least partial funding for the globe. As they were leaving, David asked Sarah for a date for the following Saturday night, and she accepted.

Sarah then walked down to the old court house, which was open for historic tours during the Labor Day weekend. When the tour was completed, Sarah lingered behind in the ancient courtroom and sat down at the barrister's table. She bowed her head and asked for the guidance of the Holy Spirit in what might take place in this courtroom. At the front of the court room was a Bible laying open. Curious about where it had been opened, she went forward to read it. It was opened to Genesis chapter one.

That evening Kim was back and told Sarah about the weekend, Red meeting her family, and the big barbeque at the lake.

"I suppose your weekend was dull," said Kim. "What was there to do around a deserted campus?"

"I went to a youth rally," replied Sarah. "And guess what, I have a date with Dave for next Saturday night."

"Gee, maybe the Holy Spirit has gone out and found your dove," surmised Kim. "What do you think?"

Sarah thought this fell more into the "wait and see" category. She had been learning not everything which pops up in front of you is due to the Holy Spirit wanting you to act on it. For young Christians, the Holy Spirit is like a mother who brings good things to the young much like a child would be lifted up to pick a cherry from a cherry tree. It seems to the young one that coincidence after coincidence of good things are being provided. The life of being led by the Spirit is wonderful. Then comes the maturing process, and the young one matures to the point of knowing not everything coming across their path by coincidence is good for them.

"Then, are you saying my meeting and dating Red and your date with Dave may or possibly may not be the work of the Holy Spirit in bringing our future spouse to us?" asked Kim.

"That's true," said Sarah. "God wants us to grow up from being baby Christians on the milk of the word to more mature Christians who can chew the meat of the word. We must learn to discern between good and evil. It's in the Bible."

HEBREWS 5:13-14 **For every one that useth milk is unskilful** *in the word of righteousness: for he is a babe.* **But strong meat belongeth to them that are of full age**, *even those* **who by reason of use have their senses exercised** to discern both good and evil.

"Uncle Andy and Aunt Myra agonized over the situations where Christians, who should have known better, would read The Dove Scrolls and then run out and jump into a relationship which proved out in the end not to be with their dove. When the saints go marching in, who will be at my side? God reveals these mysteries in his time—not ours. I hope we don't have to wait until the age of ages to know." mused Sarah.

"Hmmm," responded Kim, "I had hoped that I could just ask the Holy Spirit to send my dove to me, and poof!—just like the waving of a magic wand, he would appear."

"Unfortunately, the enemy of your soul can call on his resources too and what seems so attractive, so wonderful, and so spiritual on the surface may not be that at all," said Sarah.

"You mean I have to mature so I can discern between good and evil?"

Sarah confirmed Kim's observation. Her Uncle Andy had said not to worry if you make mistakes because it would be part of your learning experience and maturation. After all, the senses have to be *exercised* to discern both good and evil. Someone once said that good judgment is the result of experience. And experience results to some degree from bad judgments in the past.

The next few days of classes passed routinely, and there was no contact from Floyd or Dr. Harper about the debate. Then, on Thursday morning, Nancy called and asked Sarah if she would like to watch a mock trial down at the old courthouse that afternoon. Floyd had asked to see it, and Nancy had suggested they both come at the same time to watch the proceedings. Floyd and Nancy picked up Sarah, and they headed for the ancient court house.

"Well, Sarah, have you changed your mind about this? I had hoped over the summer you would look at the scientific data and agree with me that the part about the sun, moon, and stars being made on the fourth day was somehow out of sequence." said Floyd.

"I disagree with your statement that the scripture is in error," said Sarah.

"OK, I just can't see how you can reasonably conclude that with all the data which leads to the opposite conclusion," replied Floyd. "I suppose this debate is still on, or do you plan to back down?"

"The debate is on if you want it to be on," said Sarah.

"Then it's on," said Floyd. "I just want to look at this courtroom atmosphere and see if I feel comfortable there."

The mock trial courtroom was in session. Nancy, Sarah, and Floyd slipped in and sat down on the back row. The jury was made up mostly of senior citizens. The elderly judge was balding, with white hair and a neatly trimmed white beard. He resembled the Sage of the Ages as he would wield his gavel and assert his authority over the direction of the proceedings. The lawyers were young prelaw students, and the defendant was an off-duty fireman posing as an accused arsonist. Most of the audience were students that were there to critique the trial, and some were just people from off the street who had heard about the trial.

"Judge Emerson is a retired federal judge, and he seems to be enjoying himself," whispered Nancy. "He brings a lot of realism to the trial because he has pretty much seen it all. And he doesn't let the young lawyers get away with anything."

After watching for a while, Nancy, Sarah, and Floyd slipped out of the courtroom and went into the reception room to what appeared to be the judges chambers. Nancy told them she had talked to the chairman of the department about the possibility of having a debate with a judge and jury. The chairman was interested and said he would work with the debating parties if they wanted to proceed.

"So folks, what do you want to do?" asked Nancy.

"I had some reservations about doing this in a courtroom," said Floyd, "But the courtroom isn't all that big, and I think a jury will see the logic of my presentation, so I'm game."

"If you're game, I'm game," replied Sarah.

Nancy then invited them in to see the chairman, and he explained the rules for the use of the courtroom and referred them to an oversight committee for the trial that would be contacting them. This committee would have a member assigned to Sarah and one to Floyd to help them prepare to present their case. The debate scheduling would have a lesser priority than the regular cases, but the chairman thought it could be fitted in the docket sometime during the semester.

Then, everyone shook hands, and Floyd dropped Sarah off back at the dorm. Sarah felt relieved the debate was no longer up in the air and the conditions had been resolved. As she set her face to the course she would take, she remembered the Bible verse:

ISAIAH 50:7 *For the Lord GOD will help me; therefore shall I not be confounded:* **therefore have I set my face like a flint,** *and I know that I shall not be ashamed.*

Dave picked her up on Saturday night and they went to the sing-a-long River Fest that had folk music, street dancing, and a barbeque cook-off contest. Sarah and Dave sang, folk danced, and ate too much of many offerings from the barbeque cook-off. Sarah updated Dave that the debate was definitely on. At the end of the evening, Sarah thanked Dave for the wonderful time she had.

"Well," said Kim, "Dave is a handsome guy, he's certainly a Christian, what do you think?"

"He is all of that," replied Sarah. "Time will tell."

The next afternoon Sarah set her mind to how the debate challenge should be worded. She decided that Floyd would state the negative of what she wanted to prove, so she came up with the following statement.

Resolved: The sun was formed before the planets (including the earth) were formed. Therefore, the sequence that God made the sun after the formation of the earth as given in Genesis chapter 1, verses 1 through 18 is incorrect.

Next, she began reading a book she had checked out from the library on court trials and the order of events that would take place. It was difficult for her to know just how the debate would be couched—whether it would be like a civil trial where only a majority is required or like a criminal trial where only reasonable doubt must be established. Then she turned her mind to Voir dire. Looking up the meaning of this as related to jury selection she found that "voir" is French for "to see" and "dire" is French for "to speak."

She then looked at this in the jury context and found a legal definition: [*Old French, To speak the truth.*] The preliminary examination of prospective jurors to determine their qualifications and suitability to serve on a jury, in order to ensure the selection of fair and impartial jury. Voir dire consists of oral questions asked of prospective jurors by the judge, the parties, or the attorneys, or some combination thereof. This oral questioning, often supplemented by a prior written questionnaire, is used to determine whether a potential juror is biased, knows any of the parties, counsel, or witnesses, or should otherwise be excluded from jury duty. The judge asks the jurors to "tell what you see" and speak the truth since "eyes don't lie."

Next, Sarah turned her attention to getting more details on the special globe of the world that she wanted. Uncle Andy had mentioned this kind of globe in one of his emails to Myra. One could order directly from the web site, but Sarah wanted to discuss the details with the vendor. So she sent an email, asking some questions and gave her phone number. The following afternoon, when Sarah had returned to the dorm from her morning classes, she received a phone call from the vendor. After going over the details of the various models available, the vendor asked her about the intended use. She told him that she was having a debate and wanted it to illustrate Job's writings. She said that she didn't have the funds yet, but that perhaps, in a few weeks, she would be ready to buy it. It turned out that the vendor was a retired aerospace engineer who lived in Newmarket, Canada. He also happened to be a Christian. After chatting for a while about spiritual topics, the vendor made an offer to Sarah.

The vendor very much liked what Sarah was doing. He proposed shipping her his very best and most expensive model on loan for use in her debate. This one had just come out for offering to the public. And there was no hurry, she could keep it until the debate is over and then ship it back."

Sarah jumped at the offer and thanked him profusely. They arranged the shipping details; one more item of preparation had been completed. She called Dave and told him the good news. The special funding would not be needed after all. When Sarah told Dave the details, he became very excited about what was being shipped. He wanted to be there when it was unpacked and set up.

Later in the week, Floyd and Sarah met with the steering committee to set up the ground rules for the debate. If Judge Emerson were available, he would preside. A full jury panel of twelve would be set up for the debate and they talked about the jury pool and Voir dire procedures. Floyd objected to the idea of them all being senior citizens.

"A lot of these old heads are probably Bible thumpers," he said. "We need to have some college students on the jury so that the scientific presentations are properly appreciated."

"It makes no difference to me," said Sarah. "Set up the jury pool so that it is all college student volunteers if you like. The only requirement should be that jury members agree to be fair in their verdict and are not personal friends of any of the litigators."

Floyd was shocked by Sarah's statement and wondered why she might give away what he considered an advantage for her side. "Uh, uh, well, that's not necessary, let's set up the jury pool so that it is half senior citizens and half college students. Would that be fair?"

"Fair enough," replied Sarah.

Then the requirement for a verdict was discussed. Floyd vacillated back and forth, trying to decide if the verdict would be based on a majority or require a unanimous consent by the jury. He was afraid that one of the old head Bible thumpers would vote Sarah's way no matter what, but on the other hand, his case was so convincing, the victory would be much sweeter if it were a unanimous verdict.

Again, Sarah shocked Floyd by saying that either way was acceptable to her. He could decide.

Then, the subject of witnesses was discussed. Floyd said that Sarah could call any witnesses she liked. He added he had consulted on his case with Dr. Harper, but Dr. Harper thought that him being called as a witness might be unfair to Sarah.

"No problem," said Sarah. "Please do use Dr. Harper as a witness or any other professor, philosopher, theologian, or anyone else you think might be useful to your case."

Sarah's generous cooperation began to worry Floyd. Floyd wondered, "What does she know that I don't know? Maybe she's just going through the motions and will just roll over and give up? But Sarah doesn't seem to be the type that would surrender. Is she doing this just to grind on me?"

Then the steering committee assigned court protocol advisers to both Floyd and Sarah. These advisors would not enter into the debate but would advise the litigators on court procedures.

They then discussed the wording of the case as it would appear on the court docket. Sarah was asked first for her proposal. She declined and asked that Floyd present his idea of how the case should be presented. Floyd rambled on for a while about the Bible being full of errors and Christianity was just a bunch of myths. Then the steering committee chairman asked him to be more specific about what would actually be debated—the statement of the case had to be very focused or the proceedings would never end. Floyd then wrote down a statement about the order of formation about the sun and the earth, and Sarah was asked to respond to it. After additional discussion, the statement of the case was agreed upon as follows:

Resolved: The sun was formed before the planets (including the earth) were formed. Therefore, the sequence that God made the sun after the formation of the earth as given in Genesis chapter 1, verses 1 through 18 is incorrect.

Sarah would be the defendant of the Bible's statements, and Floyd would be the plaintiff that would bring the accusation that they were incorrect. Was it a debate or a trial? The litigants agreed the use of either term was considered acceptable. Then there was the scheduling of the debate. The steering committee chairman pulled up the court docket schedule and said, "We will put you down for the first week in November—will this work? Do either of you need more time to prepare than that?"

Floyd and Sarah were agreeable to the schedule. Then Sarah was given the name of her court protocol advisor and told that the advisor would contact her. The same was done for Floyd. The planning was all wrapped up and Floyd and Sarah shook hands as friendly adversaries in the upcoming case.

On Friday, Sarah received a phone call from Virginia, who had been assigned as her court protocol advisor. They agreed to meet in the library conference room on Thursday of the following week. During the weekend, Sarah caught up on her studies; her first tests were scheduled for the coming week. When she discussed the upcoming debate with her communications professor, she was pleasantly surprised that she could use the account of the debate as a term paper, no matter which way it turned out. He said that he might even send some of his students to the debate to cover it and gain some journalism experience.

Each day, Sarah anxiously checked the dorm mail receiving room to see if her package from Canada had arrived. Wednesday was the big day; a large box had been delivered that afternoon. She took it up to her room was excited as a small child opening a Christmas present. Then she paused, remembering she had agreed to call Dave to help set it up. Dave agreed to come within the hour. In the meantime, Sarah found the directions and began reading. The assembly directions were not very complicated, but Sarah was impressed with its capabilities as she read about the controls of this globe of the earth. She remembered her Uncle Andy's advice to always consult the manufacturer's handbook before you try to fix or assemble something.

PSALMS 139:13-16 *For thou hast possessed my reins: thou hast covered me in my mother's womb.* **I will praise thee; for I am fearfully and wonderfully made:** *marvellous are thy works; and that my soul knoweth right well. My substance was not hid from thee, when I was made in secret, and curiously wrought in the lowest parts of the earth. Thine eyes did see my substance, yet being unperfect;* **and in thy book all my members were written, which in continuance were fashioned, when as yet there was none of them.**

When Dave arrived, they began setting up the globe. The globe itself was about 18 inches in diameter and was very light. Sarah had read the interior of the globe had been filled with helium to counteract the weight of the internal magnets. It rested on a device that looked somewhat like a small, slightly dished, hot plate with a cord attached to one side. The device had small lights around the periphery of the hot plate looking device, and there also was the face of a clock embedded in it. The globe and the hot plate were designed to set on a table. Also, included was a separate, floodlight-like "sun" to be mounted at a specific distance away from the globe. Then, there was a dark panel that had twinkly little lights embedded in it that would be mounted on the opposite side of the sun in the earth's shadow. The amazing part of the device was the remote which was programmed to put the globe through its paces.

When all was assembled and in place, and the hot plate and sun were plugged in, Sarah picked up the remote and programmed in the local time and date as exacting as she could get it by calling time on her cell phone. Then she and Dave held their breath as Sarah pushed the Normal Rotation key. Silently but surely the globe gradually lifted off the hot plate until it was about 12 inches above it and hovered there in perfect suspension. The clock face was exposed and the little lights flashed around the periphery in three concentric circles to show hours, minutes, and seconds. The dark panel twinkled; amazingly, the precession of the constellations was programmed into it as the globe ever so slowly turned.

Sarah then pushed the home key, and the globe very slowly settled back down on the dish. Dave and Sarah were totally amazed at what they had just witnessed. They tried it again, and this time Dave and Sarah did the "blow out the birthday candles" routine to see if the globe would deviate from its position. It did not; it seemed as if some invisible hand were holding it in place. However, the instructions said not to worry if there was a power failure, the very light globe could easily withstand a fall to the floor.

Then Sarah pushed the 24/1 key so what normally took place in 24 hours was done in one hour. They were amazed to see the image of the moon beginning to appear on the dark plate. Dave wanted to try his hand at it so they happily tried out the various routines suggested and put the device through its paces. They heard the dorm door open.

"It's Kim," whispered Sarah. "Sit it back down on the hot plate, and we will show her the new globe that we bought, and then, without her knowing, we'll press the remote. It will freak her out!"

Dave chuckled. "Good plan. Should be fun. Let's go for it."

Sarah and Dave proceeded to tell Kim the globe they had been waiting for had come in, and they had it set up in the study. They explained that the sun lamp could be turned on and the dark plate represented the night sky. Kim remarked it was certainly realistic. They all sat down near the study table. Dave and Sarah had arranged the chairs to insure that Kim was sitting in front of them and facing toward the globe.

"Have you tried out the sun lamp on it yet?" asked Kim.

"Oh yes," said Sarah as she pushed the remote key. "It shines on the earth just like the real sun."

The sun lamp came on, the globe began to slowly rise, and the stars began twinkling. Kim's mouth dropped open.

"What … what is happening?" she exclaimed. "Do you guys have a wire suspending that globe?"

"See for yourself," replied Sarah.

Kim went over to the globe and swiped her hand above it. "There's nothing there; how does this thing work?" she asked in astonishment.

Sarah and Dave were laughing themselves silly. After they regained their composure, they explained how the globe was set up and what it could do. They handed the remote to Kim, and she took it through numerous ascensions and descents and tried the recommended routines.

"This thing is fantastic," said Kim. "How did you manage to get it?"

Sarah then told her the story of how the Canadian aerospace engineer had loaned it to them.

Sarah asked Dave and Kim to keep what they had seen under wraps until it was unveiled at the debate. The globe would be left in the study, but to anyone looking at it, it would just appear to be a large, very well done globe of the earth. The sun lamp and the night sky devices were to be put away in Sarah's closet. Sarah was very pleased; the globe was just what she needed to illustrate her points. She set it up on normal rotation and every hour or so, she or Kim would drop in to see how much it had moved. It was their new toy.

Kim reported Dr. Harper chatted with her again after class. He seemed very interested in the upcoming debate, and she thought he was just fishing for information on what Sarah's strategy could possibly be.

"Did he say anything about appearing as a witness or giving expert testimony at the trial?" asked Sarah.

"Oh, yeah," replied Kim. "He said that he was surprised that you would allow University professors to testify, but since you didn't mind, he would help out Floyd as needed."

"Good, I hope he does," responded Sarah.

"Speaking of the debate," said Kim, "it does bother me. It looks to me like you're walking right into a trap. I think I would have left it that I have faith in what the Bible says and eventually man will have enough understanding to know the scriptures are right. It seems to me Dr. Harper is licking his chops, just waiting to gobble up one Sarah Fidellus."

"Good," said Sarah, "he's coming along nicely."

"I just can't figure out your strategy," said Kim. "I know you have one."

Sarah told Kim the story that her father had shared with her about the snapping turtle. It seems that Josh and Myra were walking along a wet spring ditch and Myra came too close to a snapping turtle which nicked her just above the heel. They ran to their father who cleansed and bandaged the wound and then they went looking for Mr. snapping turtle. He was a big turtle and had a very ugly and vicious disposition. He would lie in wait under his shell and then make a thrust at his target with his snapping jaws. Dad's father put a stick out in front of him, and the turtle latched on to it and wouldn't let go. With one swift swing of the meat cleaver, mister snapping turtle lost his head and ended up in turtle soup that evening. The strategy was to bait the the turtle with a stick. Her grandparent's family considered turtle soup a delicacy.

"Yuck! Your parents can have the turtle soup!" exclaimed Kim. "Anyway, know that I pray for your success. This may turn out to be a battle with a crocodile, rather than a snapping turtle."

"No doubt, I do not underestimate the resources which will be thrown at us."

Sarah and Kim met with her court protocol advisor, and it went very well. Virginia was not only very knowledgable, but she was a dedicated Christian as well. She really wanted Sarah to succeed and told her she would be praying for Sarah's success in the debate. Kim thought the word "pert" described Virginia very well.

She had dark brown hair, blue eyes, and a light complexion. Virginia was attractive, slender and modest in her manners and appearance. She was a smart dresser and looked very professional in her navy blue suit. Sarah really liked her because she listened and maintained eye contact when in a conversation. Virginia, Kim, and Sarah went over the probable court activities, and Sarah was quite thankful for Virginia's efficient and professional input.

In the next month, Sarah and Kim double dated several times with Dave and Red. They heard from Katie about Fred's sister and her husband, with reluctance, had started in counseling. The controversy over *The Towers of Magdala* movie heated up in the newspapers, magazines, and documentary shows. The *History Channel* presented a series on the themes of the movie and how it related to known information. All kinds of opinions from respected scholars contradicting each other came out of the woodwork. However, the controversy only sparked more interest in the movie, and it was breaking records at the box office.

When Dr. Harper continued to fish for information on Sarah's strategy, Kim told him the story she had read about the scientists ascending the mountain of discovery. There was excitement about being able to look over the top of the mountain to see what was on the other side. When they reached the top of the mountain, they found a group of theologians sitting on some rocks on the other side. The theologians looked up at the scientists and asked, "What took you so long to get here?" Kim told Sarah that the story seemed to unsettle Dr. Harper. He had told Kim the argument that *science was one thing and faith was another*— wouldn't get Sarah very far in the debate.

Sarah and Kim had worked out a plan for sharing the defense duties at the trial. Kim would handle the voir dire, and Sarah would make the opening statement after the plaintiffs made their statement. Sarah had confided the defense strategy to Kim and cautioned her to keep it completely under wraps. The element of surprise was critical, not so much to the truth, but as to how the trial would unfold. Kim and Sarah would work together to spring the "hanging on nothing" globe into the evidence of the trial, but choosing the right moment would add to the drama. Initially, Kim had been very worried Sarah was walking into a trap sprung by Floyd and Dr. Harper. But when she learned Sarah's strategy, her outlook about the debate brightened considerably. One of the scriptures which Sarah planned to use came as a surprise to Kim. She had overlooked it when she read the book of Proverbs in her earlier years. The verses were about Wisdom, Yahweh's delightful companion in the Godhead.

PROVERBS 8:22-31 **The LORD [Yahweh] possessed me in the beginning of his way, before his works of old. I was set up from everlasting, from the beginning, or ever the earth was.** *When there were no depths, I was brought forth; when there were no fountains abounding with water. Before the mountains were settled, before the hills was I brought forth:* [26]**While as yet he had not made the earth, nor the fields, nor the highest part of the dust of the world. When he prepared the heavens, I was there: when he set a compass upon the face of the depth:** *When he established the clouds above: when he strengthened the fountains of the deep: When he gave to the sea his decree, that the waters should not pass his commandment: when he appointed the foundations of the earth:***Then I was by him, as one brought up with him: and I was daily his delight,***rejoicing always before him;*
[31]**Rejoicing in the habitable part of his earth; and my delights were with the sons of men.**

Sarah had pointed out to her verse 26 about the "highest part of the dust of the world." She also pointed out verse 31 and reminded Kim of what they had read from the book of Enoch about Wisdom eventually leaving the earth because the sons of men became so wicked she could find no habitation there.

Word of the debate had spread around campus. The comparative religions class expressed an interest in attending the debate. Nancy called Sarah to tell her interest had intensified to the point they would have to draw numbers to allocate the remaining seating in the courtroom. And then, there was an article in the campus newspaper that showcased how well the old court house was being utilized by the Criminal Justice Department and the Prelaw Department. It mentioned the upcoming debate, the topic of the debate and said its reporters would cover it for the newspaper.

"It looks like your initial idea of you and Floyd having a quiet little debate in the dormroom has completely flown out the window," said Kim.

"I know," said Sarah. "This has grown all out of proportion. At least if God wants to make fools out of us, we will be God's fools. There's no turning back now."

1 CORINTHIANS 3:18 *Let no man deceive himself. If any man among you seemeth to be wise in this world,* **let him become a fool, that he may be wise.**

Nancy called once again and said Floyd had asked for a delay in the debate. One of his key witnesses who was flying in for the debate had a conflict. The steering committee had looked over the schedule and decided it was possible to do some switching and reschedule the debate for the second week in November if Sarah was agreeable. Sarah said it made no difference to her so they were free to go ahead and make the change. Then later in the day, when Kim returned from classes, she told Sarah they were going to have a guest lecturer for some of the advanced physics classes in mid November. Kim and Sarah put two and two together and speculated that the renowned astrophysicist and astronomer, Dr. Bertrand Eisenhoff from prestigious UNBA would most likely be Floyd's key witness. They had little doubt they would hear from the plaintiffs how the church had stifled debate and misled scientists in the Copernicus and Galileo era when arguments erupted about the earth or the sun being in a central position.

"You know," mused Kim, "this debate happened centuries before Einstein's theory of relativity was proposed. Is the train going by the ground or is the ground going by the train or is the train track a treadmill? It's all relative. Only the relative motion between the earth and the sun really matters."

"I'm not sure where the earth centered idea really came from, anyway—probably man's idea," said Sarah. "Both the Psalms and Isaiah refer to the heavenly throne as being on the '*sides of the north*.' The scriptures call the patriarchs '*strangers and pilgrims on the earth*.' The spiritual center is not always in the geographical center. Trying to make everything revolve around the earth makes my head spin."

"A lot of people would find it confusing, too," replied Kim. "Oh, we could use spherical supersymmetry to correct your dizziness problem; we can say the earth is essentially spherical and 'freeze frame' on the axis spin, but doing all this would probably lead to more courtroom confusion rather than enlightenment. It's a good point to make, but not worth the effort."

"I agree," said a relieved Sarah. "I'm feeling less dizzy already."

Kim and Sarah welcomed the extra week of preparation time because the upcoming debate was becoming a distraction from their regular studies. Finally, they reached the point of saying when they're ready, we are ready. The plans were complete.

Kim had received a list of the jury pool and was going over the names. She had collaborated with Floyd to have a short questionnaire prepared that the potential jurors would fill out when they reported for duty. She had been told by Virginia that normally each side might exercise three or four strikes but not to get too carried away because since this was a mock trial. They didn't want to have to deal with a whole host of jurors.

"Sarah," asked Kim, "what do you think? Should we just accept every juror and not exercise our strikes? I think Floyd will certainly exercise his in order to get the advantage."

"Kim, just go with your gut feel—deep down in your spirit. Don't try to reason it out so much with your soul."

"Well, I have a soul for reasoning, but if I don't use it what use is it?"

"Kim, the soul is beautiful, it's only when the soul gets out of step with the spirit that it gets in trouble. A soul without input from the spirit is like a garden without water. Look at these scriptures."

ISAIAH 58:10-11 *And if thou draw out thy soul to the hungry, and satisfy the afflicted soul; then shall thy light rise in obscurity, and thy darkness be as the noon day:* **And the LORD shall guide thee continually, and satisfy thy soul in drought,** *and make fat thy bones: and* **thou shalt be like a watered garden,** *and like a spring of water, whose waters fail not.*

"Your spirit knows the thoughts and intents of the heart. Your soul reasons things out from what it can see on the outside. Use your spirit and let it lead your soul, and then your soul will flourish like a beautiful, watered garden—a thing of beauty."

"I understand," said Kim. "I will use my soul to do due diligence in looking over the potential jurors, but in the final analysis, I will go with my gut feel."

"Diligence is a good way to describe it," said Sarah. "Your soul should be diligent like the virtuous woman of Proverbs 31."

"I still have trouble when I am listening to someone speak about religious topics," said Kim. "It's so hard to tell whether the message is coming through their spirit or their soul."

Sarah described the soul without input from the spirit as being prideful and egotistic. Eventually, in someone's speech or in their writings, pride will creep out; they will begin to extol the great capabilities of the soul or refer to the self or Great Soul. Just be patient, and the speaker or writer will eventually reveal the source of their message.

Perhaps, its an unwritten law that they *must* reveal their source as originating in the soul or in self. Or, maybe pride just cannot resist drawing attention to itself.

"I'm beginning to understand," said Kim. "It is shocking once you realize that some people who seem so spiritual and so religious are actually speaking out of a prideful soul. I suppose as the old saying goes, not everything that glitters is gold. Maybe that is why Jesus is a refiner of silver and gold."

Kim and Sarah felt a huge relief because their preparations were relatively complete and decided to celebrate by riding their bicycles down to The River Dog Cafe—located on the cobble stone street adjacent to the river. They enjoyed their Mark Twain Steamer Reubens as they watched The Delta Queen casting off for an upstream journey. Then, they rode their bicycles up to the old courthouse and climbed the stairs to the courtroom that overlooked the river. On the wall was a framed copy of the bill of rights beginning with the first amendment regarding religion.

Sarah told Kim that in the old, old days of the courthouse, she had read the ministerial alliance of Christian churches in the city had held 'Union' services on the lawn of the old courthouse.

"Too bad," mused Kim, "we can't have similar services today. I suppose a Christian service on any type of government property would be swooped on by various legal organizations like ducks on a June bug. You remember my friend PK? He said that the courts and certain legal organizations were becoming the *vacuum uncleaners*."

"What did he mean by that?"

Kim related PK's rationale. He thought the original intent of the framers of the constitution was to avoid having a state religion—but not to hinder the worship of God. God is a universal concept even among those who say there is no God—and in the process make themselves their own god. The founding fathers were concerned about sects, denominations, and religious movements **that were so insecure** they sought to recruit 'converts' by force—rather than drawing them by God's love. Kim pointed to the first amendment on the wall: *Congress shall make no law respecting an establishment of religion, or prohibiting the free exercise thereof; or abridging the freedom of speech, or of the press; or the right of the people peaceably to assemble, and to petition the Government for a redress of grievances.* While Congress, for the most part has largely respected this, the courts and certain legal organizations have generally vacuumed any mention of God and moral compass concepts out of the government and government funded schools. The vacuum **uncleaner** has left filth, pornography, and greed in our government and its schools and the results have been disastrous. Honesty, virtue, and chastity have been vacuumed out to a significant degree.

"Wasn't PK in some of your physical science classes?" asked Sarah.

"Oh, yes. And he and Floyd often butted heads and sometimes it erupted in the class discussions. However, physical science was only PK's minor. Actually, he was somewhat of a lightweight in the physical science classes. His major was political science and I think that is where his talent really lies. He is an excellent debater and will probably end up serving as an elected official—possibly a high office."

Chapter 14

In the Court of the Ancients

Sarah's communications professor asked her to drop by his office after class. He told her he had received a request from Floyd and Dr. Harper to videotape the debate. He wanted to explore her feelings on this. He then made Sarah an enticing offer—if the debate were videotaped, this would serve as Sarah's visual presentations project. Sarah had very mixed feelings and wanted to talk it over with Kim before reaching a decision. Kim thought if Sarah were going to do the debate anyway, she might as well get credit for it.

"This is a two-edged sword," said Sarah. "If the debate goes for us, it will be great. If it goes against us, we could end up with egg on our face."

"The same goes for Floyd and Dr. Harper," said Kim. "But the idea of your not having to do a separate project is very appealing, even if we do get egg on our face."

After a while, the decision was made to go with the videotaping. As Kim put it, if they didn't, Floyd and Dr. Harper would play the 'Chicken!' card.

The schedules were set for the court coming together on Thursday afternoon and introductory statements to be made by the litigants. Then the court would go through the procedure to empanel the jury and adjourn until the following Monday afternoon to actually begin the presentations. Tuesday and Wednesday afternoons would be available if needed for completion of the case. Floyd had requested the verdict from the jury be unanimous and Sarah had agreed. However, this meant that Kim's task of handling jury selection was very important because one recalcitrant juror could derail the whole thing.

Virginia, Kim, and Sarah huddled together in one of conference rooms provided for the litigants and rehearsed how events would likely unfold and set up contingency plans if needed. Sure enough on the list of witnesses for the plaintiff was Dr. Floyd Harper and Dr. Bertrand Eisenhoff. When they walked into the courtroom, Floyd, Dr. Harper, and his court protocol advisor, Harry Jamieson were there. Virginia had told Sarah beforehand that Jamieson was a brilliant prelaw student and had landed a full scholarship to Yale to complete his legal training. The teams shook hands with each other and settled down to wait for the time the trial would begin. The courtroom was already 80% full, and the video camera had been set up in the back corner of the room on a little platform with a stationary, wide-angled camera placed on the wall at the front. Microphones had been strategically placed, and the crew was doing some audio checks to be sure they were functioning properly.

Then the bailiff led the potential jurors into the courtroom and seated them in the reserved seats in front. "All Rise!" intoned the bailiff, "The RiverRoc State University Pseudo Court is now in session with the Honorable Judge Marvin Emerson presiding."

The judge took his seat, gaveled the court to order, and told the occupants of the courtroom to be seated. He then began to introduce the case and explained the procedures to the court and the potential jurors. It was time for introductory statements, and Floyd was up first.

Floyd read the resolved statement to the potential jurors and said, " Your Honor, Ladies and Gentlemen, we have no quarrel with religion or even the Bible as used in religion. However, it is important that religion not be used to contradict and stifle the discoveries of science and the use of the scientific method."

Floyd continued, "An example of the stifling of scientific discovery was the controversy centuries ago between Galileo and the church. Eventually, science and Galileo prevailed, and everyone knows today that the antiquated church views of a 'flat earth' have been proven incorrect.

We would be asking you as jurors to simply use your God-given common sense and return a verdict that we have proven our point of the sun being formed before the earth. If you can agree to simply use common sense in deciding this case, we want you to be on the jury."

Sarah had been somewhat nervous when she had entered the courtroom and had butterflies as the trial began. However, when Floyd made his introductory statement, her adrenaline took over, and she was ready to debate when the judge called upon her.

"Thank you, your Honor. Ladies and Gentlemen of the jury pool, we thank you for your willingness to sit as jurors for this trial. We believe true science and the Bible are consistent with each other. However, the focus of this trial is much narrower than that. The plaintiffs have alleged the order of formation of the sun and earth, as shown in the first eighteen verses of Genesis in this Bible laying open in front of you, is in error. We will prove to you beyond a reasonable doubt that these scriptures are not in error.

What the plaintiff did not tell you about Galileo is many scientists of Galileo's time also thought that the earth was flat and they had to swallow their theories. During this trial, we will respond to the 'flat earth' account as given by the plaintiff. Furthermore, it is not unusual for a scientist making a breakthrough discovery to be persecuted by other scientists. Take the example of Louis Pasteur, a dedicated Christian, who made the proposal that germs were responsible for infections. He was ridiculed and persecuted by fellow scientists. They said the germs were due to 'spontaneous generation.' How many of you today would like to have an appendectomy performed with surgical instruments that were not sterilized? So science makes its share of mistakes and undergoes change as advances occur.

I appreciate the plaintiff's acknowledgment that common sense is God given. We are not asking you to set aside either your God-given common sense or your faith in God to make a decision. We think that we will have proven, by the end of this trial, that faith and common sense are consistent with each other. We look forward to presenting our case."

Virginia squeezed Sarah's hand after she was seated and whispered, "Good job. Keep it up."

Next the judge gave further instructions to the jury pool and turned it over to the litigants to question the prospective jurors. Kim conducted the jury selection process for the defendants, asking pertinent but diplomatic questions. The first prospective juror was an elderly woman, and she was accepted by both sides. The next one was a college student, and both sides accepted without a strike. The third one was an elderly man, and Floyd exercised his first strike. And so it continued, with Floyd striking on every senior citizen and accepting the college students. The eleventh prospective juror was a senior citizen and one that Floyd thought would be accepted by the defense. To his surprise, Kim struck on this juror and accepted the next one, which was a college student in his mid-twenties. The jury was finally empaneled; the judge gave instructions to the jury not to discuss the case among themselves and to return to the courtroom at 1:30 on the following Monday. Session 1 of the trial was completed. Sarah and Kim were both relieved to have this part done and to have the weekend to decompress.

Sarah asked Kim about her decision to strike on the senior citizen.

"It was just like you said," replied Kim. "There was something about this guy that bothered me. Also, did you notice, he wouldn't look me in the eye."

"We may never know what might have been with this fellow, but I think you did the right thing. He seemed a little on the evasive side to me, too" replied Sarah.

With that, Sarah, Kim, and Virginia headed down to the River Dog Cafe to get a bite to eat.

"You were looking for an opening to reply to the Galileo story which is always brought up," observed Kim, "You didn't have to wait long; Floyd seized upon it in his introductory statement."

"How very considerate of him," smiled Sarah. "Since he brought it up first, I can work in my response at any time I want. Right, Virginia?"

"You certainly can. Probably your best time would be when the plaintiff rests."

The next day Sarah received a call from her communications professor. Floyd and Dr. Harper would like her permission to release some clips of the introductory statements to the local television station and the newspaper. He wondered if she had any objections.

"They certainly do want the publicity," Sarah remarked. "Go ahead, our class is a communications class, and TV and newspapers are part of communications."

Sarah and Kim watched the local news on Friday evening, but there was no mention of the trial. However, in the morning newspaper, an article appeared on the third page. Then on the Saturday evening local news, there was a short interview with Floyd and Dr. Harper, and then the introductory statements video clip was played.

"I think I would have been more nervous if I had known this would be picked up by the local TV station," said Sarah. Kim teasingly asked her for her autograph.

On Sunday, Dr. Stansel, the retired Campus Christian Center Sponsor, invited the girls to his Sunday School class where they all prayed for wisdom and guidance for the coming trial. Monday afternoon rolled around soon enough. Sarah and Kim went into the courtroom early to set up the globe on a table they had already picked out near the front of the room. The sun lamp and the dark panel were tucked away out of sight but in readiness for use. The globe seemed at home in the courtroom as just another part of the decor.

Virginia arrived early and said, "Guess what, there are reporters here from Nashville, Memphis, Little Rock, Springfield, Kansas City and St. Louis newspapers. They have requested reserved seats for the trial."

"I suppose Floyd and Dr. Harper want to be sure my demise is documented," commented Sarah.

The court room was packed. Sarah noticed a very distinguished looking gentleman in a three piece, pinstriped suit talking to Dr. Harper and surmised he was Dr. Bertrand Eisenhoff, the giant of astrophysics and astronomy. Her surmise was proven correct when Floyd brought the renowned doctor over and introduced him to the defense team. Dr. Harper was smiling in the background.

The jurors came into the courtroom and took their places in the jury box. "All rise!" cried the bailiff. "The RiverRock State University Pseudo Court is now in session with the Honorable Judge Marvin Emerson presiding."

The judge greeted the jurors, asked about their weekend, and if they had any questions. Satisfied all was in place, he asked the plaintiffs if they were ready to present their case."

"We are, your honor." replied Floyd.

The judge then directed the jury's attention to the paper which had been handed to them by the bailiff.

Resolved: The sun was formed before the planets (including the earth) were formed. Therefore, the sequence that God made the sun after the formation of the earth as given in Genesis chapter 1, verses 1 through 18 is incorrect.

Ladies and gentlemen of the jury, the document which you have just been handed is a statement of the case to be debated and then decided by you, the jury. The plaintiff will present evidence to prove the statement as written, and the defendant will present evidence to disprove the statement.

"Is the plaintiff ready to begin the opening statement?" asked Judge Emerson.

"We are, Your Honor," replied Floyd.

"Then proceed."

"Your Honor, ladies and gentlemen of the jury: We will present conclusive evidence that the planetary system, which includes the earth, was formed after the sun was formed. This evidence will show how the planets formed from interstellar gas which circulated in a disk-shaped pattern around the sun. Further, we will show pictures of various star systems where you will see interstellar gas and also planets in various stages of formation. We are pleased to have present with us two expert witnesses to discuss how planets are formed.

Unfortunately, the sequence of formation given in the Bible is in error or for some reason has been mistranslated. We, of the plaintiffs, are not out to prove the Bible wrong, but we just want to be sure scientific exploration is not stifled by incorrect information. Again, I must refer to the persecution of Galileo by the church when Galileo proposed the sun and planetary system that we generally accept today. So all we ask of you is to use your common sense in this matter. We look forward to presenting our case. Thank you."

"The defense may now make its opening statement," said Judge Emerson.

"Your Honor, ladies and gentlemen of the jury, we welcome the opportunity to present our case in defense of the Bible scriptures as outlined in the debate statement. The plaintiff says the sequence of formation of the sun and earth in these scriptures is incorrect. We will prove instead that the conclusions the plaintiff has drawn from these scriptures is itself in error. I must repeat. We will prove instead that the conclusions the plaintiff has drawn from these scriptures is itself in error. May I ask the court recorder to please read back my last statement?"

"Yes, your last statement was: '*We will prove instead that the conclusions the plaintiff has drawn from these scriptures is itself in error.*'" reported the court recorder.

Sarah continued. "Thank you. Then, if you agree that the conclusions the plaintiff has drawn from these scriptures is in error, you must cast your vote with the defense. All we ask is that you use your God-given common sense. You may have noticed the plaintiff has now dropped the words God-given in front of the words common sense when he asked you to use your common sense. So, we are left to wonder what the source is of the common sense to which he refers."

"As to the case of Galileo, which has been brought up a second time by the plaintiff. We will address that in due time, and you will be surprised by what the scriptures say. Ladies and gentlemen of the jury, we look forward to presenting the details of our case to you for your consideration. Thank you."

"The plaintiff may now begin presentation of its case," said Judge Emerson.

"Ladies and gentlemen of the jury," began Floyd, "We will present to you convincing evidence the sun was formed before the earth was formed. We are pleased to have two eminent scientists with us today. They will show you how not only the sun's solar system was formed but also give pictures of the formation of other solar systems in various stages of development. It will become clear to you the central sun is first formed and then planets are formed as clouds of orbiting matter which densify into planets. Our first witness is the distinguished professor of Biophysics at RiverRoc State University, Dr. Gordon Harper. Dr. Harper will give an overview of how planets are formed from stars such as our sun. Dr. Harper, will you please take the stand?"

"How about this?" whispered Kim to Sarah, "Floyd isn't even going to do the presentation himself. They've brought in their big guns."

The swearing in of the witness was somewhat abbreviated, since it was a mock trial, but the witness was simply asked to tell the truth, and Dr. Harper agreed. Floyd then went through the routine procedures of qualifying the witness by giving name, profession, and educational pedigree. Dr. Harper's qualifications were impressive even to Kim and Sarah.

"Dr. Harper, will you please present an overview of how planets are formed for the jury?" requested Floyd.

Then, Dr. Harper proceeded to outline the various stages of planetary formation. Three large, professionally done charts were brought into the courtroom by assistants to the plaintiff. The pictures on the chart were beautiful and of full photographic quality.

"The earth was formed some 4 to 5 billion years ago, and its source was a nova or supernova system which ultimately was the seed material for the formation of the planets. The days of the creation account in the Bible is simplistic and doesn't at all correspond with the time periods scientists now know were required for the formation to take place. These processes required millions and billions of years—not days or even possibly thousands of years as the Bible seems to—"

Judge Emerson sternly rapped his gavel and addressed the witness. "The debate question before us is not to determine the age of the universe or of the earth. While this might be material for another debate at another time, the witness will confine his arguments to the case before the court. The court calender will not permit the time required to debate the age of the universe and the age of the earth. Therefore, the witness must show these ages have direct relevance to the formations of the sun and earth or move on to another topic."

Floyd whispered something to his court protocol advisor, Harry Jamieson. Harry whispered back, and Floyd said, "Thank you, Your Honor. We will keep it in mind. Now, Dr. Harper, please describe how planets are formed."

Dr. Harper described the formation process as a swirling disk of gases and dust that rotated around a central sun. He pointed out the planets and the sun itself all rotated in the same direction. Then he said small dust grains of condensed material and gas began the condensation of the gas cloud into larger bodies such as planets. Gravitational effects result in compression, and the density of a given planet generally is higher for the orbits that are closer to the sun.

When he finished, Floyd asked Dr. Harper a few questions which Sarah noticed he and Dr. Harper had likely pre-planned. Floyd glanced from time to time at a small index card in his hand as he proposed the questions.

"Dr. Harper," questioned Floyd, "in this process of planetary formation, would the sun be in place first and be shedding light on the planets during the period in which they were being formed?"

"Oh, yes, definitely," said Dr. Harper. "The central sun would have been in place first to serve as a core for the rotation of the gas, dust, and ultimately the planets as they would orbit the sun."

"Thank you, Dr. Harper. Your Honor, the presentation of this witness has been completed."

"Does the defense have any questions for this witness?" asked the Judge.

"Not at this time, your Honor, however, we do reserve the right to recall the witness at a later time," replied Sarah.

"So noted. You may step down, Dr. Harper. Next witness," said the judge.

Dr. Eisenhoff was a short man in stature but a giant in intellect. He confidently strode to the witness chair, and the bailiff proceeded to swear him in and the essential details of name and profession were entered into the court record by the young lady court stenography student who was getting real time training. Kim had seen Dr. Eisenhoff previously on a Discovery Channel science program. She told Sarah when she had asked about him earlier in the week that he was "whizzy wig."

When Sarah looked blank, Kim said that it was an acronym, WYSIWYG, meaning what you see is what you get. Kim thought he was a very dedicated and straight forward scientist. Perhaps his attitude of letting the chips fall where they may was the key to his success in unraveling scientific mysteries. He had a European accent, but Sarah could not distinguish which country he was from. She thought him to be like an Italian opera singer His black hair was parted down the middle; his features were coarse but still handsome.

"Your Honor, the plaintiffs would like to enter into the court record, Exhibit 'A,' which is a resume of Dr. Eisenhoff's qualifications. Also, we have made copies of this resume to give to the jury and to the defense team with permission of the defense and your permission," requested Floyd.

"Any objection from the defense?" queried the judge.

"No objection, Your Honor," replied Sarah.

"Then, it is so ordered," said the judge. "Proceed with the questioning of your witness."

"Look at this thing," Kim whispered to Sarah. "This guy has enough credentials to choke a horse. He has even served as science advisor to the president and to NASA. He was a guest professor in a Tokyo University for two years, has a master's degree from a Swiss University—he has done it all."

Floyd proceeded to ask Dr. Eisenhoff about his credentials until he was certain that the jury had been sufficiently impressed with the stature of this man. This doctor had made time in his important schedule to visit this little courtroom. Floyd asked Dr. Eisenhoff to explain how planets were formed and to particularly give information on what astronomers observed as young suns developing an array of planets. To facilitate the explanation, Dr. Eisenhoff requested that two 42 inch TV screens be brought in and strategically placed so that both the jury and the courtroom audience could see the presentation. These were brought in and set up by a crew from the local appliance rental firm.

[Excerpts from Dr. Bertrand Eisenhoff's Presentation]

YOUNG STARS AND STELLAR DISKS

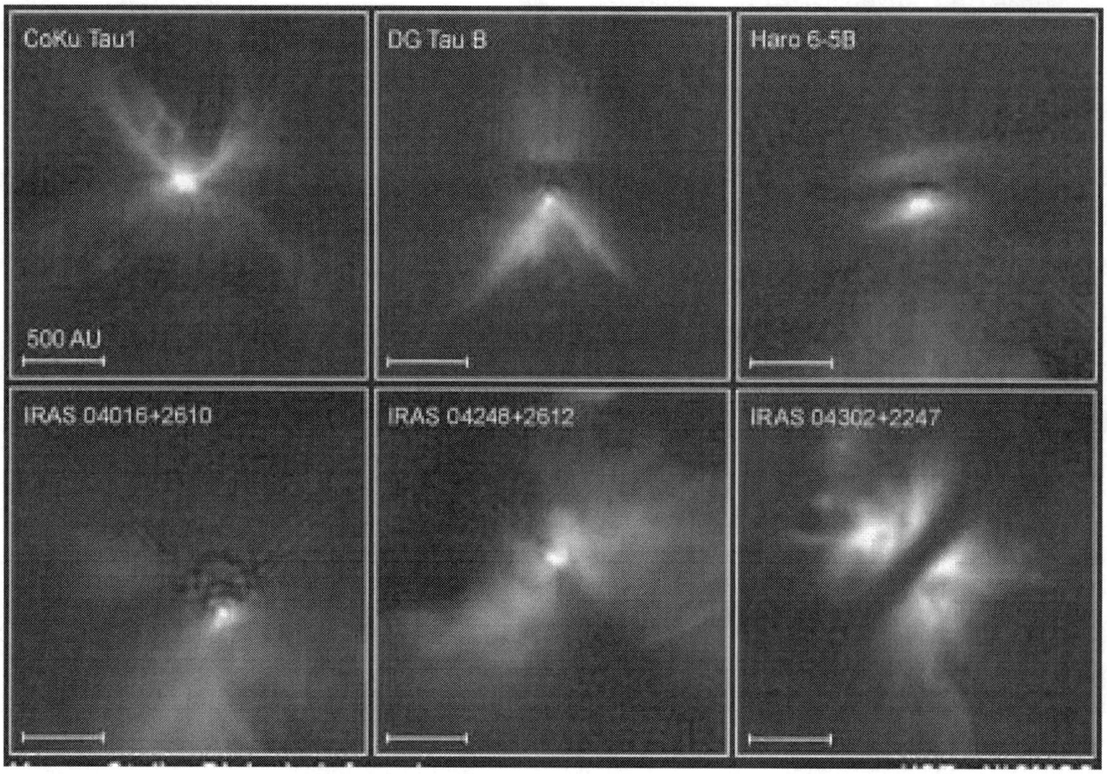

Photo Credit: D. Padgett (IPAC/Caltech), W. Brandner (IPAC), K. Stapelfeldt (JPL) and NASA
PRC99-05a.STScI OPO HST NI.MOS

Dr. Eisenhoff brought up his Windows control program and clicked on the Planet Debate icon and proceeded to give an extremely well done presentation of beautiful galaxies, suns, and planets. Some of the pictures were taken from the Hubble telescope. When the presentation was over, the good doctor got a little bogged down trying to explain Bode's numerical rule of planetary formation distances from the central sun, astronomical units, gravity, and angular momentum to the jury. Finally, Dr. Eisenhoff was finished, and the judge asked if the defense had any questions of the witness.

"Yes, we do, your Honor," replied Kim.

Sarah, Kim, and Virginia had conferred on strategy, and it was decided that Kim would tackle this highly technical witness.

"Proceed," said the judge.

"Dr. Eisenhoff, thank you for showing us such a beautiful and well done presentation on the stars and the formation of the planets."

"You're welcome," brightened Dr. Eisenhoff. "It was my pleasure."

"I have a few questions for you," said Kim. "The first is that after watching the supreme beauty of galaxies and the universe as shown in your videos, how can you not believe there is a God?"

Harry Jamieson, the court protocol advisor, gave Floyd a sharp nudge in the ribs.

"Objection, Your Honor! The witness' belief or lack of belief in God is not on trial here," protested Floyd.

"Objection granted," said the judge.

"Dr. Eisenhoff, what are your views about the Bible?" asked Kim.

"Objection! Your Honor, " cried Floyd. "Dr. Eisenhoff is here as a scientific witness and not here to give his personal views about the Bible."

Dr. Eisenhoff looked at Floyd and then the judge and said, "Your Honor, I would be happy to answer the question and give my views about the Bible."

The Judge looked at Floyd who nodded OK. "I'll allow it. You may proceed to give your answer, Dr. Eisenhoff."

Dr. Eisenhoff began, "I would treat the Bible just like any other history book. History books have errors in them and so does the Bible. In my opinion, some of the stories in the Bible are clearly myths that were made up in the imaginations of the writers. Some of the so-called miracles are not scientifically plausible."

Dr. Eisenhoff continued, "Yes, the teachings of Moses and Jesus are good moral standards to live by, but you find most of these same moral standards in other religions. I respect the Bible as a source of history, literature, and moral values, but I do not believe it to be sacred. And I certainly believe that passages in the Bible should not be used to inhibit the advancement of scientific knowledge."

"Thank you for graciously answering the question, Dr. Eisenhoff. I think it was important for the jury to understand your personal viewpoint of the Bible and the effect, if any, your viewpoint might have on your scientific conclusions," said Kim.

"You're welcome," smiled Dr. Eisenhoff, thinking that it was fortuitous that he was allowed to say the things he knew should be said about the Bible.

"I have several other questions for you," continued Kim. "Given the billions and billions of stars in the universe, do you think there might be other planets where life forms comparable to earth exist?"

"Yes, when you do mathematical probability analyses, given the tremendous number of stars in the universe, it does appear life forms may exist elsewhere because they exist here on earth."

"Are you familiar with the classes of civilizations some of your colleagues have proposed that may exist at various places in the universe?" asked Kim.

"I certainly am," responded Dr. Eisenhoff. "I participated in setting up these models."

Sarah noticed that Harry Jamieson was conferring in a nervous whisper with Floyd. She hoped Kim would be able to continue her dialog just a little longer before the line of questioning received an objection from the plaintiff. However, Dr. Eisenhoff seemed to be enjoying showing off his vast knowledge.

"Would you tell us what these classes of civilization are?" asked Kim.

"They are numbered one through four, with four being the highest level of civilization. The earth is approaching a level one civilization, and when we can control weather and develop certain other technologies, we will have reached level one.

"What about level four?" asked Kim, "What are its characteristics?"

"Oh, level four is the very highest technology," replied Dr. Eisenhoff. "Travel through the universe will be routine. Problems with food, weather, and environment will completely be problems of the past. It will be a utopia for mankind."

Kim asked, "Dr. Eisenhoff, have you ever considered the possibility the level four civilization might be God and His holy angels?"

A stunned look spread over Dr. Eisenhoff's face. "Uh, no, I never really gave that any thought."

There was a ripple through out the courtroom. Floyd jumped to his feet and roared, "Your Honor, Your Honor, I move the last question and the answer given be stricken from the court record! The counselor is leading the witness!"

"Motion granted," ordered Judge Emerson. "The last question and its answer are to be stricken from the court record. The jury is instructed to disregard the question and its answer. The counselor is instructed to refrain from leading the witness."

The court stenographer busily deleted the exchange. She thought, "This is great training, just like in a real courtroom."

"Do you have any more questions for this witness?" asked the judge.

"No, Your Honor, but we request the right to recall this witness at a later time," replied Kim."

"Plaintiff, do you have any more witnesses that you wish to call at this time?" asked the judge.

Harry and Floyd conferred and said, "No, Your Honor. We plan to summarize our case and then rest."

"Very good," said the judge. "We will have a 30-minute recess and resume on the hour. Again the jury is admonished not to discuss this case among themselves or with outsiders."

Sarah congratulated Kim on a job well done. Virginia told her not to worry about the question and answer being stricken from the court record. It may no longer be on paper, but you can bet the jurors are thinking it over. If scientists think there is a probability of more advanced civilizations somewhere out in the stars, it just could be the civilization of God and His holy angels.

Sarah noted Floyd, Harry, and Dr. Harper had gathered around Dr. Eisenhoff and were having an earnest discussion. She thought Dr. Eisenhoff might be getting some advice about only answering the questions that were asked by the defense and to avoid volunteering information. She wanted to escape to the court restrooms but on the way was apprehended by a newspaper reporter and a TV reporter. She responded to several questions about who she was and how she thought the trial was going. She then excused herself saying that she had to prepare for the next session. When she returned to the courtroom, she saw Nancy chatting with the newspaper reporters about how the university had taken over the old courthouse for historical preservation and, at the same time, had integrated it into its Criminal Justice and Prelaw programs.

Sarah, Kim, and Virginia huddled on strategy. Virginia advised Sarah on how to handle the likely objections if they were made by the plaintiffs. Kim and Virginia set up the globe, and Sarah bumped the remote button just enough to be sure the system was powered up and ready to go. Promptly, on the hour, Judge Marvin Emerson gaveled the court back into session and asked the plaintiffs to continue presenting their case. Floyd summed up for the plaintiffs. The defense was then asked to present their case.

"Your Honor, members of the jury, ladies and gentlemen, we are pleased to begin our defense," began Sarah. "We will prove to you beyond reasonable doubt the Plaintiff's interpretation of the scriptures is in error. However, before we begin that proof, we would like to address comments made by the plaintiffs concerning the flat earth debate between Galileo and the church. The plaintiff has portrayed Christians as being ignorant of scientific principles and persecuting Galileo. We admit some in the church were wrong in this matter. However, there were scientists at the time who also disputed Galileo's proposition. We would like to present to you what the scriptures really say about the shape of the earth."

Floyd jumped to his feet, "Objection, Your Honor! The defense is deviating from the debate statement. If we were not permitted to discuss in detail the age of the universe, then the defense should not be permitted to discuss matters not relevant to the debate."

"Your Honor," replied Sarah, "the plaintiff has used the Galileo issue twice, once in the introductory statement and once in the opening statement. We should be permitted to respond to the allegations made which were designed to discredit Christianity and the Bible in the eyes of the jury."

"Objection overruled," the judge ordered. "The plaintiffs have opened the gate for this discussion by bringing it up in their opening statements. Therefore, I am allowing the defense to respond to it. Please proceed."

"Thank you, Your Honor," said Sarah. "We will show you that the Bible scriptures, written long before Galileo was born, give a beautiful description of the earth. Furthermore, this description could have just as well have been written by any NASA astronaut observing the earth from the moon or somewhere in space."

"Your Honor, the defense would like to enter into evidence a NASA picture of the earth taken from space and the words written by the Bible patriarch Job as recorded in the Bible in the book of Job. We have also made identical copies which might be made available for the jury."

Sarah handed a copy of the proposed exhibit to the judge and one to the plaintiffs. Floyd and Harry Jamieson whispered to each other. They decided if they objected, the jury would think that they were hiding something.

"The plaintiff has no objection, Your Honor," responded Floyd.

DEFENSE EXHIBIT A

THE EARTH HANGS ON 'NOTHING' AND DAY AND NIGHT COME TO AN END

Courtesy: NASA/Graphics/Apollo 11_earth

JOB 26:7 **He stretcheth out the north over the empty place,** *and* **hangeth the earth upon nothing**.
8 He bindeth up the waters in his thick clouds; and the cloud is not rent under them.
9 He holdeth back the face of his throne, and spreadeth his cloud upon it.
10 He hath **compassed** *the waters with bounds,* **until the day and night come to an end.**

"Fine," said Judge Emerson, "the clerk will please enter this into evidence as defense exhibit 'A.' Please proceed with the defense."

"Thank you, Your Honor," said Sarah. "Ladies and gentlemen of the jury, please direct your attention to exhibit 'A.' Please read this description of the earth penned about 3500 years by the Job, the well known author of the Bible's book of Job. Could this same description have been penned by a NASA astronaut?"

Sarah walked forward to table at the front of courtroom and picked up the Bible. She walked over to the jury box rail and opened the Bible to Job chapter 26 in such a way that the jury could look at the face of the opened Bible, and she then began to read the verses that were given at the bottom of exhibit A.

"Members of the jury, please direct your attention to verse 10. *He hath compassed the waters with bounds, until the day and night come to an end.* A compass makes a circle, does it not? Is not the outline of the earth circular? Do you not see on the lower left hand side of the picture a boundary—where the day and night come to an end? I repeat—this writer lived about 3500 years ago and penned these words—even before the birth of Christ. Do these words describe a flat earth to you?"

Kim and Virginia were carefully watching the jury. They could see Sarah's words were making a deep impact on the jury. Some of the jurors even opened their mouths in surprise.

Sarah then pointed to verse 7 and read, "*He stretcheth out the north over the empty place, and hangeth the earth upon nothing.* Doesn't it look to you like the earth is suspended—and yet it is hanging on nothing? How could it be the earth is **hanging on nothing**?"

Sarah walked back to the barrister's table and picked up the remote. She continued, "On the table next to the window is a globe of the earth. How could Job have written the words that God hangeth the earth on nothing unless he had been inspired by God to write those words?"

Just as she placed the remote in her pocket, she pressed the normal rotation key. The globe slowly lifted off its hot plate stand and remained suspended as if it were *hanging on nothing.*

Everyone, including even the judge, seemed nonplussed, wondering how did that happen?

Dr. Harper stood up and demanded, "What kind of trick is this? Do you have the globe suspended by a wire?"

"See for yourself," said Sarah.

Dr. Harper immediately went to the globe and swiped his hand above, below, and all around it. There was no wire, no support, nothing. He looked dumfounded.

"How ... how did you do this? There's no wire." demanded Dr. Harper.

"If you will tell me how God hung the earth on nothing, I will tell you how I did it," replied Sarah.

"Uh, maybe he ... no ... it ... uh ...." stammered Dr. Harper.

"Then, I won't tell you how I did it," replied Sarah.

By this time Judge Emerson had recovered from his surprise. "Dr. Harper!" he thundered, "You are out of order. Please return to your seat at the counsel's table. The defense counsel may now continue with its presentation."

"Thank you, Your Honor," continued Sarah. "Now I would like to direct your attention to an additional verse from the Bible that not only shows the circular nature of the earth but also gives marvelous insight into the process of how planets are formed. Kim, would you please handle the explanation?"

"Thank you, Sarah," said Kim as she strode to the front of the courtroom. "Your Honor, ladies and gentlemen of the jury, you are most likely acquainted with the story of Galileo and how he used an eight power telescope invented in the early 1600s by a Flemish spectacle maker. The telescope gave Galileo marvelous insights into the heavens, which he recorded in his writing *Starry Messenger*. But what about the time periods previous to the invention of the telescope? The ancients were more or less limited in their observations to the naked eye. Did our good friend Job have the benefit of observations through a telescope when he wrote these words about 3500 years ago?" questioned Kim as she displayed this scripture:

JOB 38:9 When I made the cloud the garment thereof, and thick darkness a swaddlingband for it,

Kim continued, "Is not a band circular? Is it not true that swirling bands do exist on Jupiter's surface? Does not Saturn have its rings? And what about Venus? Does it not have thick, chaotic clouds covering its surface which hide the surface from our view? It was only in the 1990s the Magellan satellite was able to peer within the dark clouds of Venus to map its topography. The scientists of today get a sheepskin as a diploma citing their educational degrees. But it seems this lowly sheepherder of antiquity named Job was able to make some fantastic observations long before the telescope was invented."

Dr. Harper's face became agitated as if he felt he had been insulted, and he started to rise to his feet once again. Judge Emerson, noting the impending outburst, wielded his gavel and said, "Ladies and gentlemen, the hour is getting late. We will recess for the day. I would remind the jurors not to discuss the case among themselves or with outsiders. We will resume tomorrow at 1:30. Court is adjourned for the day."

A small crowd gathered around Sarah and asked her to demonstrate what happened with the globe once again. Sarah declined, noting jurors were present, and she did not want to influence them outside of the trial. Then, she put her hand in her pocket and pressed the Home key. To everyone's amazement the globe slowly settled back down on its base. Kim and Virginia brought a box and put the globe in it and packed it away for safekeeping until tomorrow's court session.

Reporters hustled their way through the onlookers and began asking Sarah questions about who she was and where she was from and how she thought the trial was going. Virginia popped in front of the group and told them to come out to the bandstand shelter beside the court house, and Sarah and Kim would try to answer their questions.

It was a beautiful November afternoon with some of the red and golden leaves still floating to the ground. A river grain barge cruised downstream toward the distant bridge, most likely heading for the gulf coast. Dr. Stansel, Red, Dave, and Tiffany all gathered around the periphery of the pavilion waiting for the questions to subside. When the last interview was done, they all gathered around Sarah, Kim, and Virginia and excitedly rehashed the afternoon's events.

Dave and Dr. Stansel had a proposal for Sarah, Kim and Virginia. It was thought that trial itself might wind up on the following evening and the judge would give the charge to the jury at the end of the afternoon. In order to show Christian graciousness, they proposed inviting the plaintiff team to dinner with them at Houston House on Tuesday evening, whether a verdict was in by that time or not. Houston House had a lot of memorabilia, not so much of the Texas years but of Sam Houston's efforts to help the Indians—particularly the Cherokees—during his years as a congressman. Dr. Stansel, who looked like Abraham himself with his shock of white hair, said it would be his pleasure to pay the bill for the group. They then went to Wimp's to get a bite to eat and continue their discussions.

In the meantime, after completing some interviews, Floyd, Dr. Harper, and Dr. Eisenhoff retired to one of the attorney's counsel rooms in the courthouse to discuss how things went and to plan strategy.

Dr. Harper was quite frustrated and vented, "These little undergraduate girls are kicking our collective butts! We can't let them get away with it! We men need to charge and charge hard!"

"Well, I'm an undergraduate too," said Harry Jamieson. "And, for your own sake, Dr. Harper, please keep gender out of this, or we will have a bigger problem. I know Virginia, on the defense team, very well. She is only a semester behind me. I have faced her before in mock trials. She is an excellent strategist, and she has ambushed me several times. I think Vanderbilt University is planning to give her a full scholarship."

"Harry, what is your take on the trial?" asked the more contemplative Dr. Eisenhoff.

"We are getting beat-up on the side issues. Apparently, their strategy is to dent our fenders enough with peripheral issues, so that our main argument looks like a wreck when we get to the finish line. All of you seem confident you have the evidence to convincingly win the main argument. We need to stick to it and not let them damage us with side issues."

"Wait a minute!" exclaimed Dr. Harper. "If they can use peripheral issues against us, we can use peripheral issues against them. For example, the issue of the true scientific age of the earth compared to the Bible description."

"You have a problem there," replied Floyd. "The defense didn't even object to this, but the judge cut you off because he thought either it wasn't relevant to the main part of the trial and/or he didn't want to have a prolonged trial."

"I would not advise bringing this up again and being corrected by the judge," warned Harry.

"You know, it's strange," reflected Floyd, "Sarah and Kim both have been very cooperative on the setup for whole trial. They didn't object to us having part college students on the jury. They didn't object to letting you doctors testify as expert witnesses. It bothers me they seem so confident. But what I'm leading to is—I think I know Kim and Sarah well enough—I could ask them to permit us to put in our views on the age of the earth. I don't think they would object, and if both parties request it of the judge, he just might go along with it. I can appeal to their sense of fairness."

"I think it's worth a try," said Dr. Harper. "I say let Floyd go for it; all they can do is say no."

"Harry's warning about side issues is probably right," observed Dr. Eisenhoff. "But I would love to get on the stand and point out that the Triangulum Galaxy (M33) is about 3.14 million light years away. This would put the defense into a tizzy, particularly if they are of the religious group which believes the earth is only about 6000 years or so old. How could they explain it took the light 3.14 million years to get here? By the way, these girls seem pretty smart. I wonder how they are getting their information? Kim is in your class—right Dr. Harper?"

"Maybe I've taught her too well," said Dr. Harper. "She is a very sharp girl. She's really only a sophomore, but she placed out of most of her freshman science courses, and the bulk of courses she's taking now are at junior level and even one at senior level. I'd say, for a girl, she's doing pretty well."

"Dr. Harper! Consider the women on the jury! Don't show your prejudice in court," admonished Harry.

"OK, OK," responded Dr. Harper. "But I say, let us have Floyd make the request. Again, all they can do is say no. We owe it to science to be sure the truth comes out."

"You can try," said Harry. "But in my opinion, you have already made a good case for the sun being created before the earth. The age of the universe question might help you, but it might just muck things up if you get into an indecisive debate."

"I'm still a little leery of this," reflected Dr. Eisenhoff. "I can't quite figure where these girls are getting their information and their props. I was shocked when I saw the globe lift off, and then I realized it was getting an ample source of power from the plug in on its nearby base. It may not be ion pulse technology after all. In some of the top secret labs, I've seen things overcome gravity with a light internal power source—they have no wings nor can you hear any noise of an engine. We can have Floyd make the request about debating the age of the universe, but if they grant it and the judge accepts it, we still need to be very, very careful. These girls seem to be masters at laying traps."

"One other thing, Floyd," asked Harry, "the defense hasn't given us any names for their witness list. Did they say anything about last minute witnesses to you?"

"No, not a word," said Floyd.

"I find this somewhat troubling. It makes me really wonder about their strategy," said Harry.

"They were very lenient in letting us bring in Dr. Eisenhoff. Do you think they might try to spring someone like a Billy Graham who has a reputation in theology like Dr. Eisenhoff has in science at some point in the trial?

"They then could request a similar leniency for witnesses for the defense, since we were allowed to bring in Dr. Eisenhoff," worried Harry.

"I don't think so," said Floyd. "They haven't mentioned any witnesses. Knowing what I know about the debate style of Sarah, I would say she will make a frontal attack using her own resources."

"If the defense has no witnesses," said Harry, "we will not be able to trip up witnesses in cross examination. We will just have to shred their main argument."

"I don't think it's a problem," said Dr. Harper. "Our position is so strong—we have them boxed in."

"OK, back to the age of the universe discussion," said Floyd. "I'll call Sarah tonight and see if she will support making a joint request to the judge to let us discuss time spans."

Chapter 15

Comparing Apples, Oranges, Peas, Grapes and Grapefruit

1CORINTHIANS 1:27 *... and God hath chosen the weak things of the world to confound the things which are mighty;*

Sarah and Kim returned to the dorm after the get together with Dr. Stansel and Virginia at Wimp's. The phone was ringing as they came in the door. It was a producer from one of the cable news networks wanting to set up an interview. Sarah declined the interview saying she needed time to prepare for the rest of the trial, but suggested that the producer get in touch with the communications department at the college for video tape footage which had already been taken at the trial.

No sooner had she hung up the phone, than it rang again. This time it was Floyd. Sarah listened carefully as he outlined his request, and at the end, made a request for fairness in presenting information on ages of time in the trial. Sarah asked a few questions, told Floyd to hold while she talked to Kim, and then got back to Floyd. She thought this was too complicated to try to settle over the phone. Instead, she suggested meeting at the Chicken and Egg at 7:00 in the morning. Also, she wanted Virginia to be present. Floyd readily agreed and offered to pay for the breakfasts since he was the requestor of the meeting.

"That reminds me," responded Sarah, "Dr. Stansel, the retired CCC sponsor has invited all of us, including the plaintiff's team to go to dinner with him at the Houston House tomorrow evening at 7:00. The way he put it was—win or lose—we can still be gracious to each other. He said he wants to foot the bill."

"That's very generous of him. I may not agree with him on some things, but he certainly is a kindly man. I'll pass on the information to my team," replied Floyd.

Sarah contacted Virginia, updated her on Floyd's request, then worked with Kim to pull together some notes and a few books for the meeting with Floyd the next morning. In the morning they met for breakfast, and Floyd was in a friendly mode, wanting to get his request granted. After listening for a while, Sarah, Kim, and Virginia stepped out into the hall to confer and then returned. The waitress brought orange juice and said the rest of the orders would be there shortly.

"Floyd, we would be willing to support your request to the judge, if that's what you want," outlined Sarah. "However, since you are a friend, I would advise you not to make the request."

"Why?" asked Floyd. "Do you think the Judge Emerson would knock it down, even if both sides requested it?"

"Maybe, but no, that's not it," responded Sarah. "I just think you would come out on the short end of the debate."

"I can't see how," said Floyd. "There's the geologic column and fossil records. There is the millions of light years that it took for light to get here from distance stars so the universe has to be at least that old. I just don't see how you can come up with the conclusion that we would come out on the short end of the debate. Tell me why you can't see what is so obvious to me?"

"Thank you for asking," said Sarah. "If you really want me to tell you, I will."

"At the risk of showing us your defense strategy?" asked Floyd.

"At the risk of showing you our defense strategy," replied Sarah.

"I couldn't ask for more. Tell me why I might lose the debate about the ages," requested Floyd.

"OK, Floyd, here goes," said Sarah. "I will start by asking you a question."

"I'm ready."

"Why is it," asked Sarah, "that you almost never see Einstein clocks being used by the geologists? The rocket scientists and others of that type talk about approaching the speed of light and the contraction of time and space, but why do the geologists not talk about it?"

"Gee, well I suppose it's because they are looking at events that have already happened, like fossils, etc. and not future events," replied Floyd.

"Look here," said Sarah, "in our physics reading club book of the month, it describes Einstein clocks on the earth, on the moon, on Jupiter, on the sun, on space ships, in the galaxies, all beating at different rates. And in another book, it even mentions the military uses the Einstein time-space equations in order to refine the satellite global positioning device output to be more accurate. Now, why wouldn't geologists, archeologists, and paleontologists avail themselves of this same information?"

"I told you, these disciplines are more concerned with the past," replied Floyd.

"Oh, then are you saying things that could happen now, or in the future, could not have happened in the past?" asked Sarah.

"No, I see your point, but I still say that these disciplines are more focused on the past," responded Floyd.

Kim decided to spell Sarah and asked, "Floyd, what if you put an atomic clock on a spaceship and approached 90% of the speed of light? Would it still beat at the same time as an atomic clock here on earth?"

"I don't think so," replied Floyd. "I think the clock would beat slower, and the occupants of the space ship would age slower."

"Good, then you agree they would be younger than we here on earth would think they would be," said Kim. "Floyd, do you like poetry?"

"Yes, but what has this to do with the ages?"

"Come on, now, Floyd," admonished Kim. "You remember this poem from physics 435?"

There was a young lady named Bright,
Whose speed was much faster than light,
She set off one day in a relative way,
and returned the previous night.

"Now, what if God was light and light travels very fast—would it take him millions of years to make a mere earth?" asked Kim.

"Don't be silly," replied Floyd, "How could God be light?"

"I can't tell you, but in the book of 1 John, the statement is made *God is light*—it just doesn't say what octave of light it is. And further, he is called *the Father of the lights.* [lights = spirits?]"

"All right, don't pull that Bible stuff on me. Stick to science!" complained Floyd.

"OK, here's another poem for you from physics 435. You remember the Lorentz-Fitzgerald contraction equation. You know, the one about where as you approach the speed of light, time would slow down and distances would contract?" asked Kim.

"Yeah, I remember it," said Floyd. "We had to determine the contraction of both time and space for a space ship at 75% of the speed of light on Dr. Winget's test last month."

"Good," said Kim, "and would you agree it's sort of like an accordion when it is compressed—the time increment and space distance continuum becomes smaller?"

"I remember," replied Floyd. "But how's this related to a poem?"

"I just happen to have it with me," grinned Kim. "Would you like to read it?"

"Oh, I'm so, so surprised that you have it with you. Please do let me read it," satirized Floyd.

There was a young fellow named Fisk
Whose fencing was exceedingly brisk.
So fast was his action,
The Fitzgerald contraction
Reduced his rapier to a disk.

"Now, if time passage is reduced when you speed up, would you agree time passage increases when the environment in question slows down?" asked Kim.

"That's the way the equations work," replied Floyd.

"Then after the universe was stretched out, the *supposed* time to have traveled that distance increased?"

"Right."

"So if you were in an environment that had been recently stretched out, and you assumed that the long time to travel that distance had always been that way, is it possible you could draw the wrong conclusions about how long ago it was when it had been stretched out?" asked Kim.

"I guess it's possible, but I don't think it's probable," responded Floyd.

"Oh, come on now, Floyd, remember in physics 435, we discussed inflation, hyperinflation, and the resulting flatness of the universe problems. Some people didn't like these concepts, but strangely enough the mathematical equations work beautifully when inflation factors were added. You remember those guys who worked on it—DeSitter, Guth, and others?" asked Kim.

"OK, I remember, but now I suppose you're going to tell me God created the universe by inflation?"

"Floyd, you're a perfect straight man. I couldn't have said it better myself. Matter of fact, we told you yesterday that inflation occurred during creation. You just didn't catch it," noted Kim.

"If you said anything about inflation yesterday, I certainly don't remember it."

"Floyd, inflation = stretched out—remember? Let me borrow your laptop, Sarah. Ah, here it is."

JOB 26:7 **He stretcheth out** *the north over the empty place, and hangeth the earth upon nothing.*

"Oh, come on, girls," said Floyd. "With all the stuff in the Bible, you pick out some little something here and there and say it's proof. Well, in my teen years, I studied the Bible too, and I know it says that everything must be proven from the mouths of two or three witnesses. So, one little skimpy verse that only half says what your trying to say kind of stretches, or should I say inflates, the truth."

"OK, you want more proof. Let me do a search on stretching and heavens," said Kim. "How about these?"

PSALMS 104:1-2 *Bless the LORD, O my soul. O LORD my God, thou art very great; thou art clothed with honour and majesty. Who coverest thyself with light as with a garment:* **who stretchest out the heavens like a curtain:**

"Or, how about this one?" asked Kim.

ISAIAH 40:21-22 *Have ye not known? have ye not heard? hath it not been told you from the beginning? have ye not understood from the foundations of the earth? It is he that sitteth upon the* **circle of the earth**, *and the inhabitants thereof are as grasshoppers;* **that stretcheth out the heavens as a curtain, and spreadeth them out as a tent to dwell in.**

"These two references speak of stretching out the heavens like a curtain. Doesn't this resemble the membrane theory we studied in our advanced physics class. Membranes can stretch, you know. I remember it because Lisa Randall, a mere woman, worked on its development. I heard her speak one time at a symposium," said Kim. "And you talk about Galileo and the flat earth—how about verse 22, where God is sitting on the circle, note it says *circle of the earth*? And here's more scriptures about stretching out the heavens. I'll keep going until you get off your '*picking out one verse to prove something*' high horse.'"

ISAIAH 42:5 *Thus saith God the LORD, he that created the heavens,* **and stretched them out; he that spread forth the earth***, and that which cometh out of it; he that giveth breath unto the people upon it, and spirit to them that walk therein:*

ISAIAH 44:24 Thus saith the LORD, thy redeemer, and he that formed thee from the womb, I am the LORD that maketh all things; **that stretcheth forth the heavens alone; that spreadeth abroad the earth** *by myself;*

ISAIAH 45:12 I have made the earth, and created man upon it: I, even my hands, **have stretched out the heavens***, and all their host have I commanded.*

ISAIAH 51:12 I, even I, am he that comforteth you: who art thou, that thou shouldest be afraid of a man that shall die, and of the son of man which shall be made as grass;
13 And forgettest the LORD thy maker, **that hath stretched forth the heavens***, and laid the foundations of the earth; and hast feared continually every day because of the fury of the oppressor, as if he were ready to destroy? and where is the fury of the oppressor?*

JEREMIAH 10:12 He hath made the earth by his power, he hath established the world by his wisdom, **and hath stretched out the heavens** *by his discretion.*

JEREMIAH 51:15 He hath made the earth by his power, he hath established the world by his wisdom, **and hath stretched out the heaven** *by his understanding.*

ZEC 12:1 The burden of the word of the LORD for Israel, saith the LORD, **which stretcheth forth the heavens***, and layeth the foundation of the earth, and formeth the spirit of man within him.*

"Now, let's see, we have verses from Job, David the writer of Psalms, Isaiah, Jeremiah, and Zechariah—five witnesses—is that enough for you?" asked Kim.

"Kim, you can quote all the scriptures you like, but the creation sequence just doesn't agree with our scientific theories."

"Well, Floyd, maybe your 'scientific theories' have a little catching up to do before you begin to fathom how God created the universe." replied Kim. "Case in point—in the first part of the twentieth century, most scientists thought the universe existed in a *steady state*. Einstein even added a cosmological constant as a 'fudge factor' to keep the universe from *neither expanding or contracting*. According to Hoyle—the Fred Hoyle who was a confirmed atheist until his famous discovery about how elements were formed—the universe exists in a steady state which was his belief until his dying day in 2001. Yet, we have these scriptures in the Bible about an expanding universe written in antiquity. Hoyle eventually came to believe in God being the creator when he understood the complexity of the carbon element formation process—the carbon element being a prime constituent in the human body. Maybe scientists don't know everything just yet—and more 'discoveries' are needed before they understand how God created the world.."

"OK, OK," said Floyd. "I agree that the Bible talks about stretching out the heavens. Yes, it's possible God did it, but I still don't think it's probable that the universe was formed by God. You've still got the problem of the geologic strata columns and the fossils which are millions and millions of years old."

"Floyd, have you ever heard of *circulus in probando*?" asked Virginia.

"Oh Lord," responded Floyd, "Now I have a lawyer springing legal phrases on me. Virginia, you're supposed to be a legal protocol advisor to Sarah and Kim in court—you're not supposed to be directly attacking me."

"Oh, no problem, we're not in court. You're fair game outside of the courtroom. And by the way, I appreciate you saying 'Oh Lord.' At least you're beginning to give God His proper respect," responded

Virginia. "Now, Floyd, do you know what *circulus in probando* means? Answer the question yes or no please."

"No."

"OK, I'll tell you. It is Latin for a *circle in a proof.* It deals with the line of reasoning which says that *this is used to prove that, and that is used to prove this.* It is called reasoning in a circle," said Virginia.

"Aha, now I know where you guys are coming from. It's the old argument that creationists use against the mainstream of geology. You say we use fossils to date rocks, and we use rocks to date fossils. You can't trap me on that one; I've heard the arguments and scientists have proven that both the rocks and fossils are millions of years old."

"Really." said Sarah. "Actually, the *circulus in probando* is hanging like an albatross around the neck of some die hard scientists to the point it's beginning to stink. It's a Galileo in reverse situation that is becoming undefendable. You can go on Google with *fossils, rocks, dating, circular reasoning,* and look at all the problems these guys have in defending it. How can you say the fossils are millions of years old because they are in rocks which are millions of years old and then turn right around and say the rocks are millions of years old because the fossils in the rocks are millions of years old? Some scientists have said that that petrified trees growing through layers of sediment date back millions of years. How is it 'some of the trees' trapped in the volcanic lakes after the 1980 Mt. St. Helen's eruption are already in the process of petrifying?""

Floyd replied, "Like I said, I've been through these arguments before. The answer is it is not even necessary to date rocks by fossils, or vice versa as you say. We know the ages from radiometric dating and also from isotope ratios. We know the rate of decay and can therefore date the fossils and rock independently. We do not even have to defend what you call an undefendable argument."

"Floyd, I have a question for you," said Kim.

"Yes."

"Didn't you agree atomic clocks in different environments would beat at different rates?"

"Yes."

"Then how do you know the atomic decay rate that you are measuring now is the same decay rate existed before the heavens and the earth were stretched out?" asked Kim.

"Wait a minute. This stretching out is a Bible term that you are using. I can't agree to Bible terms."

"OK," said Kim. "How about inflation, hyperinflation, and membrane technology that you find discussed in the physics books. Wouldn't that affect the rate of atomic decay?"

"I don't know," replied Floyd.

"Do you really mean you don't know, or are you like some of your other colleagues who would do most anything to avoid acknowledging God might be the creator of the universe?" asked Virginia.

"That's an unfair question! I, uh ..." exclaimed Floyd.

"Question withdrawn," interjected Virginia in true courtroom style.

"Floyd, if you want to pursue the dating issue in the court, we will even go to the judge and make a joint request with you," said Sarah. "Don't be surprised if the judge doesn't agree. He has a courtroom docket to keep on schedule. However, if the judge does grant the extra time, we will expect to be given a full opportunity to rebut your arguments."

"Let me think about it," said Floyd. "I'll have to talk it over with Dr. Harper, Dr. Eisenhoff, and Harry. By the way, how come you guys developed all these counter arguments on the age of the universe?"

"We expected to have to defend against your age arguments in court, but the judge didn't let us."

"Sarah, let me ask you a question, and give me a straight non-court room answer. Do really think the creation is only six or seven thousand years old?" asked Floyd.

"Well, some scientists say the universe is somewhere between four and twenty billion years old, depending our the latest refinement of their numbers. I say it's much older than that," replied Sarah.

Floyd's jaw dropped, "What—how can you say that? Explain yourself."

"Let me show you some scriptures," said Sarah.

REVELATION 1:8 *I am Alpha and Omega, the beginning and the ending, saith the Lord,* **which is, and which was, and which is to come**, *the Almighty.*

HEBREWS 11:1-3 *Now faith is the substance of things hoped for, the evidence of things not seen. For by it the elders obtained a good report. Through faith we understand that the worlds were framed by the word of God,* **so that things which are seen were not made of things which do appear.**

"Floyd, what was God before He 'was'?"

"I don't understand your question," said Floyd. "How can God be before He 'was'?"

"Exactly, the point," replied Sarah. "God is not 4 billion years old; He's not 20 billion years old; He is infinitely old. He was before he was—He's always been there."

"OK, granted, God may be infinitely old in that time has gone in a circle. But how old is the universe as we know it?"

"The invisible universe is older than the visible universe because God framed the visible world from things which do not appear. When you look at the visible electromagnetic and light spectrum, you realize the visible things we see are but a small portion of the invisible things in the universe. I personally believe the invisible things are more real and even older than the visible. The visible things that we see are just the mere shadows of the invisible things God has created. Look at this scripture," said Sarah.

ECCLESSIASTES 1:9-10 *The thing that hath been, it is that which shall be; and that which is done is that which shall be done: and there is no new thing under the sun. Is there any thing whereof it may be said, See,* **this is new? it hath been already of old time**, *which was before us.*

Sarah continued, "My answer to you would be God created the heaven and earth as we know it in a six-day period and on the seventh day He rested. Whether that seven-day period was before, during, or after He stretched out the heavens, I do not know. I believe what God said, and it is apparent to me true science will eventually appreciate the truths written in the Bible."

"Really, really, now, you can't be thinking these were 24 hour days as we know them? You know some say that a day is as a thousand years," questioned Floyd.

"Let's look at that scripture," said Sarah as she pulled it up on the computer.

2PETER 3:8-9 *But, beloved, be not ignorant of this one thing,* **that one day is with the Lord as a thousand years, and a thousand years as one day**. *The Lord is not slack concerning his promise, as some men count slackness; but is longsuffering to us-ward, not willing that any should perish, but that all should come to repentance.*

"And yes, yes, I know," said Sarah, "you will probably bring up the other scripture about Adam and Eve not dying the same day they ate of the forbidden fruit. So let's pull up that information, too."

GENESIS 2:17 *But of the tree of the knowledge of good and evil, thou shalt not eat of it:* for in the day that thou eatest thereof thou shalt surely die.

GENESIS 5:5 *And all the days that Adam lived were nine hundred and thirty years: and he died.*

"OK, I agree Adam died within the one thousand years, if one day is as a thousand years," said Floyd. "But I still think the Bible is really antiquated when it comes to timing."

"Antiquity is probably a good word," observed Sarah. "The antiquity of the Bible shines light on an ancient period that we as humans know very little about. It goes back to 'Let there be light.' Look."

Comparing Apples, Oranges, Peas, Grapes and Grapefruit

GENESIS 1:1-5 *In the beginning God created the heaven and the earth. And the earth was without form, and void; and darkness was upon the face of the deep. And the Spirit of God moved upon the face of the waters. And God said,* **Let there be light: and there was light**. *And God saw the light, that it was good: and God divided the light from the darkness. And God called the light Day, and the darkness he called Night. And the evening and the morning were the first day.*

"I think even you would agree," said Sarah, "the description here is not that much different than what you read in your science books, Floyd. Out of the darkness and the deep comes light. And the interface of darkness and light began a period of time, whatever you might argue that period of time to be."

"I suppose the deep could be considered a black hole or an abyss," said Floyd.

"And actually, in the beginning," interjected Kim, "when things were formless and chaotic, what is the meaning of time? How would we measure time if the sun, moon, and stars are formless and not yet in their orbits? We could use our luminous watches for a while, but once the batteries went dead, we would be without concept of what time really is."

"Well, maybe we could determine time by the speed of light at the interface between darkness and light," said Floyd.

"Yeah, Floyd, but remember," said Kim, "the space time continuum is like an accordion. As God began to play the music of creation, was the accordion compressed? Then as the accordion was expanded, the period of a day, whatever that interface of light-darkness was, had a certain relationship to the expansion of space. You know, the old joke about what is the speed of darkness?"

"No, tell me," responded Floyd.

"Well, the speed of darkness is just ever so slightly greater than the speed of light because darkness has to flee from the light."

"Ha, ha, very funny." Floyd chuckled. "But let's get serious here. Let's get back to measuring time—it just came back to me. Kim, remember the class where we talked about the pennies on the balloon—how the universe would stretch, but the pennies attached to sides of balloon would stay the same?"

"Yes."

"Well, our example said the balloon would stretch, but the atomic clocks in the pennies would stay the same. So there! That's how we know how old the universe is," stated Floyd.

"Really, and in the same example, you pulled the balloon universe as we 'know' it out of a speck as small as a period at the end of a sentence. Well, maybe you need to have God as a banker to hold the pennies while you blow up the balloon to a big enough size to stick the pennies on the side of it. Floyd, please be thrifty and make your pennies stretch. Did everything come out of a dot as small as a period?"

"Well, we don't know if the universe expanded like a balloon, saddle, or a very flat membrane."

"Glad to hear you say *we don't know ...*" replied Kim, "but why did you pick the balloon, saddle, and flat membrane examples so very carefully? Or did you do it so you could claim symmetrical stretching in all directions? What if it wasn't one of these three, and there was an asymmetrical stretching time warp—maybe like stretching out a scroll or unfolding a tent or expanding a curtain? Or maybe the time warp is due to a localized gravity or black hole stretching of the cosmic fabric?"

"I suppose you are going to tell me that the universe is like a scroll or a curtain and a tent?" chided Floyd. "And I suppose it is in the Bible?"

Kim replied, "The prophet Isaiah and the Apostle John both spoke of the heaven being rolled up like a scroll, so I suppose it could be unrolled like a scroll also. You know, the expansion-contraction thing the physicists like to debate. And you've got to admit, a scroll does fit in very well with the R and 1/R winding energies on a minuscule and macro scale that we have studied [Editor's note: R represents the radius of the winding]. And scientists seem to think they have 'invented' all these concepts—including parallel universes. Strangely enough the Bible has been discussing these parallel realms all the way from the *lowest hell* to the *third heaven*—and probably there are heavens even beyond that! And now scientists have expanded their vocabulary from *cosmic fabric* to a *stretchable **membrane*** to ***multi-branes***. Don't you think it fascinating this was all written in the Bible from antiquity? Is God patiently waiting for man to make new 'discoveries'?

Even wormholes and time tunnels go from the bizarre to almost logical when you consider adjacent fabric in a scroll configuration. I've already shown you the tent and curtain scripture in Isaiah chapter 40, maybe you forgot. Then there are scriptures in Hebrews 1:10-12 that speak of the old earth being folded up like a cloth. Do you want me to find the scroll scriptures for you?"

"No, no, that won't be necessary. I'll trust you that the scroll scriptures are in the Bible," replied Floyd.

"Oh, heck," laughed Kim, "I wanted to show them to you. Please, pretty please let me show them to you."

"Let's get away from scrolls, tents, and cloths and go back to the atomic clock question again," said Floyd. "Kim, you know that even though there may be localized time warps, as in a galaxy, scientists think, *on the average,* the atomic clocks are all beating at about the same rate. So this is how they calculate the age of the universe."

"Floyd, can you swim?" questioned Kim.

"No, I can't swim. Why do you ask?" replied Floyd.

"Well, suppose that I told you a river only *averaged* 18 inches deep. I'm sure you would have no qualms about crossing it, even if you didn't know how to swim?"

"OK, OK, but most of the time, averages can be trusted," replied Floyd.

"Hey Floyd, try this example," said Sarah. "There was a guy who had one foot in a bucket of ice water and the other foot in a bucket of boiling water, but *on the average*, he felt very comfortable."

"Oh, come on guys, leave off your examples," complained Floyd.

"Now, Floyd, you know we have your best interests at heart," said a very concerned Sarah. "We love you so much that we wouldn't want you to get drowned, frostbitten, or scalded. After all, you're not just an *average* person."

"Thanks for your loving concern for me. But how do you explain this?" asked Floyd. "We know that light travels in a straight line. So, if we are measuring light coming out from the Big Bang, why isn't it a good measure of the beginning of the universe?"

"Floyd, when light began traveling out from the Big Bang, was it *hyperexpanded* so it traveled *faster* than the speed of light before it began traveling at the speed that we measure today?" asked Kim. "Yes? No? You don't know? How would you calculate its *average* speed and time if you didn't know? No answer? OK, then, let's look at your statement that light travels in a straight line. How do you know it's a straight line?"

"Well, everybody knows its a straight line!" exclaimed Floyd.

"Really?" questioned Kim. "How about the 1919 sun eclipse experiment which made Einstein famous? Didn't it prove that light rays were bent because of the warping presence of the sun?"

"Well, yeah, but you can't use—"

"Oh, yes I can," interjected Kim. "How do you know that light doesn't travel parallel with the fabric of the cosmos? Could it be like a photon car traveling over the surface of a road from Kansas City to Los Angeles? The road has hills, valleys, and even mountains. Every now and then we might even throw in a tunnel through a mountain and have a time warp. By the way, do you think light always goes straight into a black hole, or is it pulled into it much like a piece of driftwood circulating around a whirlpool? Does light bend around a black hole? Floyd, wake up! Why is it you want to relegate God's scientific knowledge to 'stone age' science—then you turn right around and toss terms like time warps, worm holes, and parallel universes around as though they have only existed since modern man 'discovered' them? Why does man's science more or less admit that at one time water covered the earth, but if any scientist dares to mention the flood account in the Bible, it would bring a stinging censure by their peers and be toxic to their careers?

Or why does 'science' want to concentrate on the materialistic world and ignore the near death experiences reported of being transported through 'wormhole' like tunnels of light into another realm? Why would a linguistics science professor be reluctant to mention the tower of Babel to explain the thousands of dialects? Would it be because they would be censured? The academic hierarchy and their without a clue legal friends would be all over them like fire ants picnicking on your Mom's apple pie. Floyd, the coffee is brewing—wake up and smell the coffee!"

"OK, OK," replied Floyd, you made your point. What else do you have in your plan to throw at us?"

Just then Kim's cell phone rang, and she answered. "Hi Percy ... The debate is in your local paper? ... Yes, we're doing just fine. As a matter of fact Sarah and I are having a conference with Floyd just now ... Floyd, Percy says 'Hi.' ... May I call you back later? ... OK, bye."

Floyd responded: "So, Percy of PK fame. I suppose you plan to use his off-the-wall examples about the lemonade ice cube meltdown and the infamous basketball pizza experiment?"

"Well, we could, but I'm not saying we would. Would it bother you if we did?" questioned Kim.

"You all are tough debaters." Floyd nervously laughed. "However, we will see you in court this afternoon. I don't think you have a ghost of a chance in proving the sun was created after the earth."

"Don't forget to ask your friends about going to Houston House tonight," reminded Sarah.

"Oh, I almost forgot—give me the bill for breakfast. Yes, I have already asked them. Dr. Eisenhoff and Harry can go. Dr. Harper says he has a previous commitment. By the way, would it be OK if I bring Nancy? She was the one who arranged for the court house."

"By all means, we forgot about Nancy because she wasn't listed on the plaintiff's team," replied Sarah.

"See you in court," said Floyd as he departed toward the cashier.

"See you in court," chimed in the girls.

"Well, what do you think?" said Kim. "Do you think we will have the same debate in court about creation time spans that we had here this morning?"

Virginia surmised it was good to be prepared for it. However, after watching Floyd's body language, she thought he didn't want any part of it—and he left rather suddenly. What really got to him was that Kim answered his every point with a counter point, so he got a very unsettling preview of what might happen if time spans were debated. Virginia didn't have Kim's technical training, but she could follow enough of the argument to know Floyd was wanting to retreat to the original debate statement. In his mind, the original debate statement was still a slam dunk. He could get overruled by the rest of his team that wasn't here. It was unlikely that Judge Emerson would permit the request. He's a stickler for the rules, and his ruling would probably be the parties could have a separate debate on the age of the universe.

Kim was disappointed Floyd left before they had a chance to discuss Noah's flood and the Stoke's law application of how particles settle in liquids. Those hydraulic experiments were so much fun. They had stirred up mixtures of various things like algae, gravel, sand, silt, mussel shells, fish bones, leaves, sticks, you name it, in a big glass column, agitated it with air, and then let it settle. It was interesting to observe the layers as they formed from settling day after day, like layers in a rock.

"Oh, were those the experiments where you went to the block house?" asked Sarah.

"That was it. In one experiment, we wanted to accelerate the agglomeration process and simulate the huge pressures on the various layers. So we used a tube with explosives in one end to do it. It was kind of like making artificial diamonds with explosives. Dr. Winget was so nervous about this—he had us go through a five-page detailed check list to be sure we didn't blow ourselves up."

Kim elaborated, "Many people do not realize the hugeness of the disruptive process which resulted from Noah's flood. Take the tsunami, Mount St. Helens eruption and its mud lakes, Katrina, the Profitt Mountain reservoir collapse, the 1993 Mississippi River flood, and California mud slides, and roll them all into one—they are only an extremely small fraction of the power of Noah's flood. The reservoir that collapsed on Profitt Mountain dumped about a billion gallons of water in a huge deluge down the mountain and flattened the forests. If there had been silt piled in high layers on top of the forest layer for a long period of time, a small bed of coal might have eventually formed there. It's hard to imagine the effect of having water 15 cubits over the top of the highest mountain sitting on the earth for 150 days. And then, as the water began to recede for an additional 150 days, there were the various layers of silt, sand, rocks, and fossils beginning to appear on the drying land. But Noah had to stay in the ark for a number of months more waiting for the muck to dry up. If one has ever had their house flooded, they know what a mess the muck can be."

"Kim, I must say," Virginia observed, "you guys are very well prepared. In a way I almost hope the plaintiffs ask us to make a joint request to the judge to debate the ages of the earth."

"Well, at least, we don't have to use the banana peel, pea, grape, apple, orange, grapefruit, and ant example." Kim laughed. "If we were to use it, they would probably laugh us out of court."

"I agree," said Sarah. "But wouldn't it be fun to watch the expressions on their faces?"

"What example is it?" asked Virginia.

"You don't want to know," replied Kim.

"Oh, come on, guys, if it's funny, I like funny stories." begged Virginia.

"OK, you asked for it," said Sarah. "Last summer, our cousins overseas in the military had asked us to go through the remaining belongings and correspondences of my late uncle and aunt. My uncle and aunt had sent forth a great number of emails between the US where my uncle was and Brazil where my aunt was working on a medical evaluation. Kim and I printed out about two file folders of these emails to read. Kim had planned to go to a summer symposium at University City where a Baylor professor was speaking on genetics. I was able to go as her guest. I started reading the emails to Kim on the way there and later on in the week, we went to a McDonalds to get some lunch. One of the set of emails was so funny, the other customers there probably wondered what we two giggly girls were on. They didn't know we were discussing how the earth might have been created, which was the subject of the emails."

"Uh oh," said Sarah. "I've got to run. I don't want to be late for class. Kim, will you finish the story for Virginia?"

"OK," agreed Kim. "Anyway, Sarah's Aunt Myra was responding to an email from her husband, Andy, which pondered the time spans of creation. She told of sitting on the patio with a bowl of fruit on the table beside her. She peeled a banana and laid the peel on a plate as she watched an ant climb up the side of the bowl and begin crawling over the top of the grapefruit. Then, out of the blue, came this idea about the stretching out of the heavens, like the unfolding of a tent as the Bible says."

"Gee, maybe this was her Newton's apple falling from a tree," said Virginia.

"Then Myra went into her landlord's garden and got a pea pod and a bunch of grapes and returned to the patio. She went inside to get some stretchy type ladies hose, some stick pins, and a yellow wooden pencil.

"OK, I'm with you. What a cast of characters, we have here." Virginia laughed. "Will a monkey enter the plot, too?"

"Not in this scene," replied Kim. "Anyway, she turned over the disposable coffee cup and embedded a pencil straight down in the middle of it. Then she hung the banana peel over the pencil eraser and spread it out over the upside down cup. Then she spread the lycra hose loosely over the banana peel."

"Is this membrane theory?" laughed Virginia.

"Well, actually, there was a speaker on membrane theory at the symposium we were attending." said Kim, "But on with the story, she then took a pea and pinned it carefully near the apex of the tent. Then she took a grape and pinned it further down so it just fitted in between the spread banana peels, then further out from the apex, she placed the apple, the orange, and the grapefruit in sort of a line that would be between the banana peels if they could be stretched out for some distance. This, she said represented the size of the earth at various times as the heavens were being stretched out. Then she went looking for the ant."

"Oh, my God," exclaimed Virginia, "what a story!"

Kim related that they were just coming to the good part. Myra found the ant and put him in an empty juice glass for safekeeping while she made little dots on the pea, grape, apple, orange and grapefruit where she judged New York and Los Angeles would be on a globe. Then she was ready for the great experiment: how many seconds would it take the ant to get from New York to Los Angeles?

"This is wild." Virginia laughed. "Please continue."

"Well, she put the ant on the grapefruit, and after giving him a few hints on which direction to go, he made it in about ten seconds. She said her very fortuitous guess was that the grapefruit city New York and grapefruit city Los Angeles were exactly 1.86 inches apart, so the speed of the ant would have been 0.186 inches per second. Then she tried the ant on the lesser sized fruits with varying results. Then, it came to the pea. We about cracked up when Myra wrote that the butt of the ant was in the Atlantic Ocean and his head was in the Pacific Ocean—he got there before he started!"

ISAIAH 44:24 Thus saith the LORD, thy redeemer, and he that formed thee from the womb, ***I am the LORD*** *that maketh all things;* that stretcheth forth the heavens alone;

that spreadeth abroad the earth by myself;

Model Building Props:

Grapefruit, orange, apple, grape, pea, banana peel, pencil, disposable cup, lycra hose, pins, and one energetic ant..

Virginia laughed, "Sometimes, the simplest things are the most revealing. This is a real takeoff on the old saw of 'you are comparing apples and oranges.'"

"So we have the classic Einstein comparison of an observer with a clock and a yard stick on a fast moving train and an observer with a clock and yard stick on the ground. Since it is relative, is the train sitting still and the ground going by or vice versa?" questioned Kim.

"Wow! It really is apple clocks and apple yardsticks versus orange clocks and orange yardsticks."

Kim agreed that in the time-space continuums, your yard stick and clock in the grapefruit environment are going to be much different that in the pea environment. Otherwise, one truly is comparing grapefruit and peas. She thought much of the today's controversy is due to trying to use the clocks and yard sticks in different environments.

"So man looks at a stretched out universe and says the distant Captain Kirk star is four billion light years away, so the earth must be about four billion years old?" asked Virginia.

"It's somewhat more complicated, but that is a simplified way of putting it," replied Kim. "But here is the funniest thing. Sarah and I wrote a poem about it. We wrote it on the back of a napkin while we were in McDonalds, and we cracked up laughing at it. Let's see ... I think it goes like this."

There was a young ant named Mac
Who went out for a snack.
Before he went out,
and moved about,
He said, "I'm back."

"I can see why you were almost ROFL,*" said Virginia as she held her sides. "Maybe this wouldn't be a real good example to use in the courtroom after all."

"Well, we are trying to avoid using it," chuckled Kim.

"While you and Sarah were talking to Floyd earlier," said Virginia, "a thought came to my mind. It was like I saw God carrying a briefcase. He retrieved a zip file for the universe and began unzipping it. The amazing part was how such a big universe could be compacted together in one little zip file. Oh well, I'm probably just day dreaming."

"That's what they said about Joseph, but sometimes dreams come true," said Kim. "You may be very close to the truth on the compaction idea, as we discussed, the Bible speaks about a new heaven being unfolded like a tent and also speaks of an old heaven being rolled up like a scroll. Some scientists today are even proposing a 'new' idea of a membrane being rolled up like a scroll. So I suppose if you were uploading, the tent would be folded first, and then the fabric would be rolled up tightly like a scroll into a zip file.

"Can't you just see Father God and his companion Mother Wisdom, that you guys talk about, deciding to go on a trip for a week where our universe is now," mused Virginia. "For six days, they work very hard in downloading and expanding zip files into billions and billions of files containing the DNA of creation. Then they rest for a day and go back to wherever heaven's palace is. And these creation files unzip son and daughter files of their own. And here comes along man, and he looks at these billions and billions of files and tries to calculate how long it took the Godhead to download them."

Kim laughed. "Yeah, and then comes man with his dial-up connection and tries to calculate how long it took God to download the universe. Oh, it took over 200 billion years. Whoops, we've invented broadband now, it really only took ten to twenty billion years. And God laughs because man does not know He used thoughtband. I think David tells God in the Psalms that *thou understandest my thought afar off.* I feel at a loss for words to describe how creation could have taken place. But deep down, it seems like God fashioned the design of the world in the spirit world, which is not even subject to time and space as we know it. Then when all was prepared, our world quickly materialized out of the spirit world, like as you say, expanding a highly condensed computer zip file."

"Well, probably God doesn't use computers at all in His creative work. You know some Christians think the computer is the beast spoken of in the book of Revelation," said Virginia.

* Rolling on the Floor Laughing

"I've heard discussions along that line," replied Kim. "Actually clay is primarily silicon and the book of Daniel, chapter 2, speaks of an image with feet of clay. The clay coexists with the metal but is not mixed with it. Kinda sounds like a computer chip to me. But anyway, God created the elements, and we use gold, silver, brass, and iron which are also parts of the image Daniel saw. I don't think silicon will do us harm unless we are forced to make a choice between its application in a computer and allegiance to God. However, it would be naive not to be prepared for such an eventuallity. Bowing to an evil computer system would be like worshipping an idol."

Virginia observed how Daniel wrote that God has a stone cut out of a mountain that crushes the feet of the image. She wondered what that stone could be. Kim told her about the Bible describing *upon one stone shall be seven eyes.* Kim shared the seven eyes of the stone represents the Seven Spirits of God. When this halo-like stone becomes *marvellous in our eyes,* we will be able to communicate directly via the Seven Spirits of God. Then the computers and internet, as we know it, will become obsolete. The internet and computers will be a mere archaic blip on the radar screen of history like chaff and dust blown away with the wind. Virginia liked the example because it teaches Christians not to be fearful. But she had thoughts about how much Sarah liked to use her computer to find scriptures.

"Oh yeah," said Kim. "Sarah loves the Bible software on her computer, and her aunt and uncle used it extensively to communicate. I think it is like in the New Testament days—while they weren't forbidden to eat meat, they were concerned about eating meat which had been offered to idols. The computer is just a tool—like the phone, it can be used for good or for evil.

"Well, maybe this is the case." observed Virginia, "But, somehow, I feel that this computer thing is much deeper than the chunk of metal and silcon which sits on our desk. Its just intuition, I guess."

"Well, if you really want to go off the deep end on this, read Revelation 17:8." replied Kim. "If you consider that the clay might actually be a human 'vessel of clay', then you might infer the beast from the bottomless pit hybridizes some sort of 'biocomputer' that Daniel describes as being mingled *with the seed of men.* And the curious thing is what is coming out of the bottomless pit will not be at all recognized **except by those saints who were present at the very foundation of the world**. But, speaking of bottomless pits, this is getting too deep—lets go on to something else."

"Since Floyd is gone, I can bring this up without giving him ammunition," said Virginia, "What about the scripture in Revelation about four corners of the earth? I have often wondered if it means a flat earth."

"Some have interpreted it that way," replied Kim. "Sarah and I have talked about it in case it came up in the trial. Actually, the translation in the original refers to the four angles or the 'knees' of the earth. If you take an apple and cut it twice into four equal pieces, you will have four quadrants or four equal angles of an apple. So, our plan was to refer our court adversary back to basic spherical geometry, where out of a 360 degree circumference there are four 90 degree quadrants. Sarah found the answer in one of her Uncle Andy's emails."

"I see what you mean. By the way, what was Sarah's Aunt Myra doing in Brazil?" asked Virginia. "Sarah said she was doing a medical evaluation."

"Its never been very clear to me." responded Kim, "Myra was a very well known and respected neurologist. She was doing medical evaluations for nerve damage including tests for hyper-creatine phosphokinase levels and THNA parasites—that is Trojan Horse Neuro-Assimulations. Let me explain—some years ago, there were incidents that happened to some of the natives.

Some say it was due to bat bites, others say it was only communist guerillas in the area using scare tactics. Others say it was piezoelectric light effects of the kind that sometimes precede earthquakes, and then there were even those that attributed it to other-worldly visitors. You know, abductions, harvesting human eggs and sperm —the Roswell scene sort of thing for Brazil. Myra and her husband even had some discussions about the *strange god* and *God of forces* described in the last part of Daniel Chapter 11. They discussed counter-measures for Christians including the sealing of the forehead mentioned in Revelation Chapter 6.

Anyway, COMAR—an acronym for an air force group—and the Brazilian government itself was very concerned about its people. Brazil contracted with her to do a follow-up neurophysiologic evaluation for those natives who were affected thirty some years before."

"Interesting story," said Virginia, "I still have to chuckle when I visualize Myra getting the revelation about the ant. It has such simplicity."

Kim agreed with Virginia's simplicity observation—indicating a fallacy many fall into—is taking the measurements from one frame of reference into another. The ant may have taken millions or billions of years in our stretched out frame of reference, but maybe only one day in the heaven and earth creation frame of reference. Virginia observed the ant probably didn't really get there before it left—but its still so funny you know. She had been taking a legal class on weights, measures, and standards—she questioned if the standard meter bar the French have in Paris is getting longer as the earth and the universe expands?

Kim shared that scientists tell us that the universe is still expanding. Who knows whether the expansion rate curve is linear or has an exponential increase or decay? However, if the universe is getting bigger, one wonders if the earth is also increasing in size, but we don't notice it because it is all relative.

"Interesting insight," said Virginia. "Our prof also said that they now use radiation waves from Superman's krypton element traveling through vacuum as so many wavelengths per second. This is said to be a more accurate length measurement than the meter bar. Doesn't it get around the length expansion problem?"

"It does, and it doesn't." said Kim. "Remember we have a space *time* continuum and *the value of time elapse is subject to change* as length increases. It could be the radiation wave gets redshifted."

"I just wish we could get some additional details about the creation account in Genesis," mused Virginia. "We could fill in a lot of the missing blanks."

"There are a lot of additional details about creation in Job chapter 38," noted Kim. "Apparently creation was a fragile process, and God 'babied' the creation of the earth so that it would turn out exactly like He wanted. It would appear that thick, dark clouds covered the atmosphere of the earth like a swaddling blanket. Look at these verses from Job."

JOB 38:8 *Or who shut up the sea with doors, when it brake forth, as if it had issued out of the womb?* 9 *When I made the* **cloud the garment thereof, and thick darkness a swaddlingband for it**,

"I see what you mean." said Virginia. "Hey, time has flown by, I need to get going for my constitutional law class."

"See you this afternoon," said Kim.

In the meantime, Floyd had gotten back together with Dr. Harper, Dr. Eisenhoff, and Harry Jamieson to discuss strategy on the case. He reported to them that the defense would support the request to the Judge Emerson to expand the debate to include time spans and ages. He told them this was the good news. The bad news was the defense had expected to debate this anyway, and they were totally prepared to do so. Dr. Harper wanted to charge ahead with the request to the judge, but Harry and Dr. Eisenhoff were somewhat more cautious.

"My God!" Dr. Harper exploded, "We have the world's expert on Astrophysics on our team and serving as an expert witness no less. Are we going to let these mere upstarts push us around like some timid little mice running from puddy cats? Let's go for the jugular!"

Dr. Eisenhoff shushed Dr. Harper with his hands to settle down. He cautioned, "If I really believed the bios some people have written about me, I would completely lose my scientific objectivity. I am just a humble man who has learned pride can lead to wrong conclusions—I know that from my personal experience! It seems to me that this is just as much a matter of presentation and legal maneuvering as it is science. Harry has a better feel for the courtroom than we do. Let's hear him out."

"Floyd, what were some of the details of your session with the defense?" asked Harry.

"Well, actually they volunteered to share some of their defense strategy if we were to debate the time issue."

"And what did they share as a defense strategy?" asked Harry.

Floyd characterized the defense strategy as elapsed time/space interactions due to hyperexpansion.. He said they would say science's hyperexpansion as confirmation of the heavens and earth being "stretched out" in the Bible. He then said that without a doubt, in the cross-examination, Dr. Eisenhoff would be asked to calculate how much of the expansion after the Big Bang was almost instantaneous hyperexpansion and how much was at today's observed expansion rate. They really grilled me when I tried to use averaging calcs."

"They do seem to have a knack for finding the Achilles' heel of what we don't know. It is obvious they are trying to negate our computations on the age of the universe where we use the velocity of light and the distance light has traveled," complained Dr. Eisenhoff. "But thanks for the notice, I think I can handle this in cross examination."

"Very good, I trust that you will. What else did they share?" asked Harry.

"I think time space expansion interaction is their main argument, but the PK arguments came up ...."

"Oh, that kid!" exclaimed Dr. Harper. "I hope they do use his silly fables. PK was just a misdirected zealot who took up the class's time with nonsense examples. He's long gone now, graduated last spring thank goodness. Not to worry about the PK arguments, I quashed him in class and I can do it again on the stand if they even dare to bring it up."

"Who is PK?" asked Harry. "I feel like I have come in on the third act of a play."

Floyd described PK as Percival Kervine, the overzealous son of a Presbyterian minister. They called him PK—both after his initials and for being a "Preacher's Kid." He didn't think the PK arguments really posed any major threat in the courtroom, just a distraction.

"Maybe you don't think the PK arguments pose a threat, but let me play the devil's advocate and suppose that they do," admonished Harry. "Er ... this is sort of confusing. I'm not sure whether I'm playing the devil's advocate or God's advocate, so I will just play the defense's advocate. What are the PK arguments and what would the defense likely bring up in the courtroom. Floyd, role play a defense strategy with **bias**, please."

Floyd reported PK had two examples: the lemonade ice cube meltdown and the basketball pizza example. Harry thought that the names were creative and asked Floyd to elaborate.

Floyd reported the ice cube lemonade case as describing a tourist sitting on a mountain in Hawaii drinking lemonade. Adjacent to the mountain was a valley with hot lava flowing through it from a volcano erupting from the next mountain. The tourist wants to know how long it takes for an ice cube to melt. So he takes two identical ice cubes and at the same time as a friend puts cube one in the lemonade, he uses his slingshot to send cube two into the valley. The tourist doesn't want to go down into hot magma in the valley to do a time measurement, so he measures the time for the ice cube to melt in the lemonade at say 44000 seconds. He then concludes every ice cube takes 44000 seconds to melt. Apparently, what PK was trying to do was undermine our radioactive uranium to lead decay dating process which gives the billions of years times.

"This ice cube meltdown experiment is just a crock," interjected Dr. Harper. "I countered it by saying I agreed while magma temperatures in 2000 to 10,000 deg. F. range would greatly accelerate chemical reactions, they would have little effect on the rate of tightly bound nuclear decay reactions."

"Dr. Harper, I realize you are quite passionate about this, but I'm going to again ask Floyd to role play what PK's response was or what the defense's rebuttal might be," requested Harry.

Floyd related it got quite heated in the class. PK said the earth, unlike a dead planet, still had a radioactive furnace deep within, and Dr. Harper had not yet made a trip to the center of the earth to observe the internal temperature and pressure conditions in the earth. He proposed that uranium, being a heavy element, could have enough density stratification to have reached critical mass concentration.

Then he and Dr. Harper got into a debate about whether convection currents and volcanic eruptions let us really know conditions within the earth.

"PK said convection currents could even now be carrying decay products to the surface in magma from volcanos, which would distort the dating process. Finally, PK quieted down after telling Dr. Harper to come back and tell him about the deep core layers of the earth when he had 'moholed' enough to have 'been there' and 'done that' in the way of making measurements."

"I am confident that I can handle this one on cross examination," said Dr. Harper. Let's not waste any more time on it. Let's go on to PK's silly basketball-pizza lab experiment and get this over with."

Floyd summarized that PK tried to undermine geology's contention that the erosion in the Grand Canyon had occurred over millions of years. PK placed a partlly deflated basketball in the lab sink and then put a Big Daddy's "The Works" pizza over the top of it. He said the Grand Canyon and its surroundings had raised up from the sea floor to about 8000 feet and had trapped a great quantity of sea water upstream.

He then pumped up the basketball and the topping cracked in several places down to what he called the volcanic rock dough crust. Then he turned on the sink faucet full blast and eroded a big gully in the sea floor sediment topping all the way to the volcanic rock crust. PK then said the now puny flow rate of the Colorado River was nothing like the amount of water that initially flowed through the canyon. He used the example of trapped seas like the Great Lakes suddenly roaring through a Niagra Falls type canyon. He said that the Utah great salt lake may be a residual of trapped great lakes. PK said this canyon may have even preexisted as an ocean floor rift. PK even referred to a similar wild theory about rushing glacial ice and water suddenly carving out the English Channel. The group laughed at this example and decided if this came up, they would simply request Dr. Hughes of the Geology Department to come to the stand and summarily quash it.

Dr. Eisenhoff turned the group's discussion back to what Floyd thought would be the defense's main argument: Hyperexpansion's interaction with space and elapsed time parameters. He asked if, during Floyd's discussion, the defense had mentioned the "gap theory." Floyd reported that while they discussed God as being infinitely old and a day with God being like 1000 years, there was no mention of the gap theory by the defense. He then asked the purpose of Dr. Eisenhoff's question. Dr. Eisenhoff said he had been on a panel with a group of scientists debating a creationist. When confronted with the ancient age of the earth, the gap creationist said between the events of creation of the heavens and earth in verse 1 of Genesis and the chaos and darkness of verse 2 there was a major gap of time, perhaps involving thousands or even millions of years. The creationist said the earth was initially created perfect in verse 1, and then it fell into chaos and darkness due to some (Yucatan asteroid /Indonesian Toba volcano/ or whatever type) disaster described in verse 2. I think he said Psalm 82 gives a flashback of the disaster in that time gap. Then God began restoring the earth in Genesis 1:3. This guy was sort of a cross between Indiana Jones, a Navy Seal and a submariner—David Jonah was his name. He said the earth had been subject to two major floods—one in Noah's time and a previous one which is described in the watery chaos of Genesis 1:2. He even said some of the Greek mythology was partly true and tied it in with the *giants in the earth* and the *mighty men which were of old, men of renown*—that the scriptures have described just before Noah's flood. He said these were the fallen sons of God. He said eventually man would understand scriptures about submerged *channels of the sea* appearing and the *foundations of the world* being discovered.

Dr. Eisenhoff reported he and his fellow scientists had trouble pinning down Jonah because he more or less said 'So what if you think the earth is millions or billions of years old.' He kept referring to a time gap of undetermined length between the creation in Genesis 1:1 and the subsequent chaos in verse two. Then Dr. Eisenhoff triumphantly said "We finally **nailed** this guy so he couldn't provide an explanation for an obvious gross error in the Bible's creation account".

"I heard nothing at all about this two flood theory from Sarah and Kim. Maybe they are 'young earth' enthusiasts." said Floyd, "How did you manage to pin Indiana Jonah down?." he asked.

"It's just like this debate we are having," said Dr. Eisenhoff. "We showed him all the information about suns and even pictures showing planets being formed. He was completely bumfuzzled when he tried to explain how the sun, moon, and stars were created on the fourth day. We had him cornered, and he couldn't get away. This is the very reason I agreed to be a participant in this debate.

The Achilles' heel of the defense is the creation of the sun, moon, and stars on the fourth day. I just want to get this faulty thinking cleared away. It is critically important we win this debate because it undercuts the rest of the creationist arguments. I can't tell from Floyd's description if the defense girls are 'young earth' creationists or 'gap theory' creationists, but since they didn't mention it, I suppose they believe God created the earth in literal 24 hour days. But it doesn't make any difference, we just need to win this debate."

After some more deliberation, Harry said, "Look, you guys seem to have a strong case on the sun being formed before the earth. Stick to your strong points. They are probably more prepared than we are on short notice to discuss time spans. If we get mouse-trapped once again on these side issues, we will be in deep doo doo, and it will only weaken what should be an easy case to win."

Dr. Harper reluctantly went along with the decision of the group.

"OK," said Floyd, "I will let Sarah know before the trial starts—we will not pursue the request."

Chapter 16

The Verdict

Virginia picked up Sarah and Kim from the dorm, and they headed for the courthouse.

"Oh, no! Look!" cried Sarah. "There's a satellite TV truck in the parking lot. I see Dr. Harper and Floyd being interviewed."

"We can drive around the block and come in the back way if you like," volunteered Virginia.

"Good plan," said Kim. "We need to concentrate on the trial right now and not be distracted by interviews."

They made their way into their assigned counsel room. Virginia ran interference for them and asked a couple of reporters who had spotted them to wait until the afternoon court session was completed before doing their interviews. Sarah was particularly concerned the judge and the plaintiffs might react negatively to a critical part of her case strategy. Virginia reassured her and told her how to handle any impasses or objections. Virginia got Dave and Red to help set up and test the globe in advance so that Sarah and Kim could enter the courtroom just a few minutes before the trial resumed. Floyd spotted Virginia and told her that the plaintiffs had decided against approaching the judge on expanding the debate to ages and time spans. Sarah and Kim were somewhat relieved to hear this because it meant they could concentrate on the main case at hand without dealing with side distractions.

The courtroom was packed, and people were standing in the lower hall watching video feeds to the two 42" TV's that had reappeared. It was said one of the national cable channels would pick up parts of the trial live from time to time.

"All rise," intoned the bailiff, "The RiverRoc State University Pseudo Court is in session with the Honorable Judge Marvin Emerson presiding."

The judge went through the normal routine of making sure everyone and everything was in place and then called upon the defense to resume presenting their case.

"Your Honor, ladies and gentlemen of the jury, we look forward to continuing presentation of our case to you," Sarah began. "Before we do that, I would like to revisit the issue before us and tell you exactly what we will prove." Sarah pointed to a flip chart which had been positioned near the jury box and turned the first blank page over to reveal the full statement of the debate issue and read it slowly to the jury.

Resolved: The sun was formed before the planets (including the earth) were formed. Therefore, the sequence that God made the sun after the formation of the earth as given in Genesis chapter 1, verses 1 through 18 is incorrect.

"The full burden of proof of the debate statements rests with the plaintiffs. If the plaintiff fails to prove any part of the debate statements, then you must find for the defense. When we have completed presenting our case, I think you will agree that the preponderance of the evidence supports the defense. Now, the defense would like to recall Dr. Bertrand Eisenhoff to the stand."

Judge Emerson summoned Dr. Eisenhoff to take the stand and reminded him he was still under agreement to tell the truth.

"Dr. Eisenhoff, thank you once again for consenting to share your expertise in astronomy and astrophysics with us," said Sarah. "I would like to go over the debate statements with you one by one."

The sun was formed before the planets (including the earth) were formed.

"Dr. Eisenhoff, you have presented information and pictures about the formation of planets as a spin off from the dust clouds around stars. Are you just relatively certain this is how planets are formed, or are you absolutely certain this is how planets are formed?" queried Sarah.

"I am relatively certain," replied Dr. Eisenhoff.

"Dr. Eisenhoff, there is a principle used in quantum mechanics called the Heisenberg Uncertainty Principle. Are you familiar with it?"

"Yes."

"Good," said Sarah with a slight smile. "But don't worry about it. I won't try to use it on you. It is a two-edged sword and can cut both ways."

"Thank you for your shrewd observation," replied Dr. Eisenhoff.

Sarah turned to the next page of the flip chart, which displayed the following information.

GENESIS 1:1 In the beginning God created the heaven and the earth.
2 And the earth was without form, and void; and darkness was upon the face of the deep. And the Spirit of God moved upon the face of the waters.
3 And God said, Let there be light: and there was light.
4 And God saw the light, that it was good: and God divided the light from the darkness.

"Now, Dr. Eisenhoff," continued Sarah, "Verse 1 says 'In the beginning God created the heaven and the earth.' Since it says He created the heaven and the earth, would it be possible the heaven and the earth were made in that order?"

"Yes, I think it is possible, if you include the sun and stars as being in the heaven, but you are only proving the points we have already made, not by any means disproving our evidence."

"OK, Dr. Eisenhoff," said Sarah as she turned the flip chart, "please look at this scripture and tell me your reaction to it."

PROVERBS 8:22 The LORD possessed me in the beginning of his way, before his works of old.
23 I was set up from everlasting, from the beginning, or ever the earth was.
24 When there were no depths, I was brought forth; when there were no fountains abounding with water.
25 Before the mountains were settled, before the hills was I brought forth:
26 While as yet he had not made the earth, nor the fields, nor the highest part of the dust of the world.
27 When he prepared the heavens, I was there: when he set a compass upon the face of the depth:

"Dr. Eisenhoff, the context of these particular verses is a description of the wisdom of God," continued Sarah. "Please turn your attention to verse 26 where it speaks about 'highest part of the dust of the world.' Would this be an apt description of the gas and dust clouds you referenced in your description of star formation and planet formation?"

"It is similar," replied Dr. Eisenhoff, "however, when you speak about gas clouds and dust coalescing into a star, you are only proving the points we have already made. I didn't realize this scripture was in the Bible, but I thank you for using it—it only helps our case."

Harry whispered to Floyd and Dr. Harper at the plaintiff's table. "What is she doing, she's wrecking her own case. She's either crazy or is crazy like a fox and baiting a trap!"

"Now, Dr. Eisenhoff," said Sarah, "I want to return to the first verses in the book of Genesis."

GENESIS 1:1 In the beginning God created the heaven and the earth.
2 And the earth was without form, and void; and darkness was upon the face of the deep. And the Spirit of God moved upon the face of the waters.
3 And God said, Let there be light: and there was light.
4 And God saw the light, that it was good: and God divided the light from the darkness.

"In verse 3, note the well known phrase, 'Let there be light.' Could this light be from the gases and dust coalescing into a star and then igniting? The star began to give off light which we call the light of the sun?"

"That's a wonderful description!" replied Dr. Eisenhoff. "I couldn't have said it better myself. I very much appreciate your help in making our case. It looks to me like you are using the Bible to contradict itself and prove it is in error."

"An interesting comment. Why do you say that, Dr. Eisenhoff?" asked Sarah.

"Well, isn't that the subject of this whole debate? The Bible says the sun was created some days later. So how can you have it both ways?"

"You've made a very good point," said Sarah as she turned the flip chart. "Let's look at those verses and see if we can come up with an answer."

"I don't like this at all," whispered Harry. "Even the jury is trying to figure out why Sarah is destroying her own case. They're hanging on every word. Why is she doing this?"

GEN 1:13 And the evening and the morning were the third day.
14 And God said, Let there be lights in the firmament of the heaven to divide the day from the night; and let them be for signs, and for seasons, and for days, and years:
15 And let them be for lights in the firmament of the heaven to give light upon the earth: and it was so.
16 And God made two great lights; the greater light to rule the day, and the lesser light to rule the night: he made the stars also.
17 And God set them in the firmament of the heaven to give light upon the earth,
18 And to rule over the day and over the night, and to divide the light from the darkness: and God saw that it was good.
19 And the evening and the morning were the fourth day.

"Now, Dr. Eisenhoff, we are looking at the verses in question. What is it you find inconsistent about these verses as compared to the verses in Genesis verse 1 through 4 which we have already discussed?'

"It's certainly very obvious," said Dr. Eisenhoff. "If the sun was made when He said, 'Let there be light," how could it have been made on a later day when verse 16 says 'God made two great lights,' and it is obvious one of them is the sun. It rules the day on the earth."

"Another very good point, Dr. Eisenhoff," said Sarah. "So you're saying that one of the great lights that the scriptures say God made is the sun. And you draw that conclusion because it rules the day?"

"Yes,"

Sarah abruptly said, "Your Honor, at this time I have no further questions of this witness."

There was a titter in the courtroom and the plaintiff team was very surprised Sarah had not tried to cross up Dr. Eisenhoff, but seemed to be making points for the plaintiffs. In fact she seemed to be helping him make his points.

"Order in the courtroom," gaveled Judge Emerson. "Does the plaintiff have any redirect for this witness?"

Floyd quickly conferred and said, "No, Your Honor, we do not have a redirect."

The judge told Dr. Eisenhoff he could step down and thanked him for being a witness. He called a fifteen minute recess. The jurors were once again cautioned not to discuss this case among themselves or with others outside the jury. Virginia ran interference for Sarah and Kim as they hustled off to their assigned conference room.

"So far, everything is working as we planned," whispered Virginia. "I think we are about to drive the plaintiffs up the wall. They can't figure out why we're being so agreeable."

"Yeah, if this weren't such a serious case, it would almost be fun," agreed Sarah. "But the touchy part still lies ahead."

"Don't worry about it," said Virginia. "You've done great so far, and you can finish the task. Remember the scripture that Jesus is the author and finisher of our faith?"

"Yeah, but what a script!"

In the other conference room, the plaintiff team was busy trying to figure out the defense's strategy.

"I don't think they are just going to lay down and roll over. There is something we're missing," said Harry.

The court resumed exactly fifteen minutes later, and Judge Emerson asked the defense to proceed.

"Your Honor, at this time we would like to recall Dr. Gordon Harper to the stand," said Kim.

"Dr. Harper, please take the stand. Remember you are still under agreement to tell the truth."

Kim looked Dr. Harper in the eye and thought, "I hope if we win this case Dr. Harper won't retaliate by giving me a low grade in his class. Oh well, that's in God's hands and not mine."

"Thank you, Doctor Harper, for agreeing to be a witness," said Kim. "You have heard the testimony of Dr. Eisenhoff about the sequence of formation of a solar system. Are you in agreement with that testimony?"

"Yes, Dr. Eisenhoff is a world renowned astronomer and astrophysicist. I certainly do agree with his testimony."

"Do you believe there is a contradiction between the first four verses of the Bible as shown on this chart [flips to Genesis 1:1-4 chart] and the verses shown on this chart?" asked Kim.

GEN 1:13 And the evening and the morning were the third day.
14 And God said, Let there be lights in the firmament of the heaven to divide the day from the night; and let them be for signs, and for seasons, and for days, and years:
15 And let them be for lights in the firmament of the heaven to give light upon the earth: and it was so.
16 And God made two great lights; the greater light to rule the day, and the lesser light to rule the night: he made the stars also.
17 And God set them in the firmament of the heaven to give light upon the earth,
18 And to rule over the day and over the night, and to divide the light from the darkness: and God saw that it was good.
19 And the evening and the morning were the fourth day.

"Yes, I do," replied Dr. Harper.

"And what might that contradiction be?" asked Kim.

"It just like Dr. Eisenhoff said, you can't have the sun created the first day and then also have it created here. As the old saying goes, you can't have your cake and eat it too."

"A very good point, Dr. Harper. Do you believe the Bible is in error on the sequence of creation of the sun and earth?"

"That's what this debate is about, isn't it?" answered Dr. Harper.

"The witness will answer the question," admonished Judge Emerson.

"Yes, I believe the Bible is in error on the creation sequence regarding the sun and earth."

"Then, if we can prove the Bible is not in error on this sequence, and the jury concurs, would you personally concede we have won the debate?" asked Kim.

"I will definitely respect the decision of these distinguished jurors," replied Dr. Harper, "but if you can *prove to me* that the Bible has not made an error on this creation sequence, I would concede you had won the debate."

"Now, Dr. Harper, please look at the set of scriptures once again and tell me if you think verse 16 is referring to the sun and moon as the two great lights.

GEN 1:13 And the evening and the morning were the third day.
14 And God said, Let there be lights in the firmament of the heaven to divide the day from the night; and let them be for signs, and for seasons, and for days, and years:
15 And let them be for lights in the firmament of the heaven to give light upon the earth: and it was so.
16 And God made two great lights; the greater light to rule the day, and the lesser light to rule the night: he made the stars also.
17 And God set them in the firmament of the heaven to give light upon the earth,
18 And to rule over the day and over the night, and to divide the light from the darkness: and God saw that it was good.
19 And the evening and the morning were the fourth day.

"Yes, I think the two great lights do refer to the sun and moon."

"And why is that, Dr. Harper?" asked Kim.

"I think it is very obvious the sun rules the day, and moon and stars rule the night," replied Dr. Harper.

Kim abruptly said, "Your Honor, at this time we have no further questions of this witness."

"Does the plaintiff have any redirect for this witness?" asked Judge Emerson.

A puzzled Floyd answered, "No, we have no redirect, Your Honor."

"You may step down, Dr. Harper, the court thanks you for being a witness," said Judge Emerson. "The defense may continue with presenting its case."

"Thank you, Your Honor," said Sarah. "Ladies and gentlemen of the jury, you no doubt have been impressed by the testimony of these two brilliant scientists, Dr. Eisenhoff and Dr. Harper. They have presented to you a very plausible explanation of how stars are formed and how the solar system planets are formed. They have even shown you pictures of solar systems in various stages of formation. After listening to their testimony and explanations, we of the defense team are also very impressed with their description of the formation process. In fact, **we agree with it and support it!**"

A hush fell over the courtroom as jaws dropped and then they was a rustling wind of whispers.

Floyd jumped up. "Your Honor, we object to the antics of the defense!"

Judge Emerson gaveled for order and then sternly said, "The plaintiff cannot object to a statement that supports the plaintiff's case. What is the basis for your objection?"

Harry Jamieson leaned over and whispered to Floyd.

"Your Honor," said Floyd, "May both teams approach the bench?"

"Both teams will approach the bench," granted the Judge. "The jury will return to the jury room until summoned."

Floyd then proceeded to say this whole debate was a travesty. He was pleased that the defense was conceding the case, but why even have a debate if the defense had no intention of defending their case?

"What makes you think we have conceded the case?" interjected Sarah. "*We have not conceded the case at all. In fact, we intend to win this case.*"

"How can you do that?" asked Floyd. "You've already agreed the sequence of formation that we presented is correct. After doing that, you don't have a case!"

"Oh, we have agreed the sequence of formation that you presented is correct," replied Sarah, "What we have not agreed to is your contention that the Bible scriptures concerning this are in error."

"I don't see how that's possible." said Floyd.

"Then, I suppose you will just have to listen to us present our case and see," responded Sarah.

Harry whispered something to Floyd.

"Your Honor," requested Floyd, "May the plaintiff have a short recess to consider this development in the trial?"

"Recess granted," said Judge Emerson. "Be back on the hour."

Promptly, on the hour, the jury had returned to their seats, and the judge gaveled the trial back into session. "The defense may resume presenting their case."

"Thank you, Your Honor, ladies and gentlemen of the jury, we want to take another look at the debate statement, and we will tell you what we agree with and what we disagree with," said Sarah.

Resolved: The sun was formed before the planets (including the earth) were formed. Therefore, the sequence that God made the sun after the formation of the earth as given in Genesis chapter 1, verses 1 through 18 is incorrect.

"There are two sentences in the debate statement. The first statement about the sun being formed before the planets, we have already told you we agree with. Dr. Harper and Dr. Eisenhoff have made a superb presentation to you using various available evidence. However, the debate statement is only a half-truth. We intensely disagree with the second statement that the Bible's description is incorrect. At first, this may seem to be a paradox to you, but when we finish our explanation, I am confident you will agree with us that the Bible is correct in this matter."

The jury, the plaintiffs, the courtroom audience listened intently to Sarah. The question going through everyone's mind was, "How is she going to get out of this deep, deep hole she has just dug?"

Sarah continued, "How can this be? Let me give you an example, and you will see how it can be. Ladies and gentlemen of the jury, I have a question for you to consider. When was this jury made to rule? Supposedly, you will get the case later this afternoon or maybe tomorrow, and you will arrive at a ruling on the case. Then we can say that the jury and the court has ruled. But when were the preparations made for the jury to rule? Was it when you were empaneled as a jury last Thursday? Or did it start when this courthouse was built in the early 1800s? Or did the preparation for ruling start when you were born?"

"Objection, Your Honor," cried Floyd. "The defense is presenting information not relevant to the case."

"Objection granted," ruled the judge. "The defense will confine its presentation to matters relevant to the case at hand."

Sarah glanced at Virginia, and Virginia nodded. It was time to activate the contingency plan.

"Your Honor, may we approach the bench?" asked Sarah.

"The defense and plaintiff teams may approach the bench," said Judge Emerson.

"Your Honor," said Sarah, "the completion of the explanation of this example will elucidate our case and besides, I only need a few minutes more to complete the example."

"I'll allow it," said the judge, "but if you do not quickly establish the relevance to this case, I will cut you off."

"Thank you, Your Honor," said Sarah.

Sarah continued, "Ladies and gentlemen of the jury, I think you can see that the preparations for the jury to rule on this case have been going on for a long time. We can start with the building of the courthouse, we can see the preparations in the way of the births and educations of the members of the jury, of the litigants, even of the judge. Then, there was the empaneling of this jury. So, yes, this jury will rule, but many preparations have already preceded that ruling. Now what does this have to do with this case? What is the relevancy the plaintiff has requested? I'll tell you. It concerns the words 'made' and 'to rule' in verse 16 of these scriptures on the chart."

GEN 1:1 In the beginning God *CREATED* [*bara'*] the heaven and the earth.

GEN 1:13 And the evening and the morning were the third day.
14 And God said, Let there be lights in the firmament of the heaven to divide the day from the night; and let them be for signs, and for seasons, and for days, and years:
15 And let them be for lights in the firmament of the heaven to give light upon the earth: and it was so.
16 And God *MADE* [*'asah*] two great lights; the greater light *TO RULE* the day, and the lesser light *TO RULE* the night: he made the stars also.
17 And God set them in the firmament of the heaven to give light upon the earth,
18 And *TO RULE* over the day and over the night, and to divide the light from the darkness: and God saw that it was good.
19 And the evening and the morning were the fourth day.

"Now, I ask you," questioned Sarah, "Does it say God ***created*** the two great lights in verse 16? No, it says He ***made*** the two great lights? What did He **make** them do? He ***made*** the greater light ***to rule*** the day and He ***made*** the lesser light along with the stars ***to rule*** the night."

Sarah paused to look around the courtroom. The jury and the audience seemed to be following her. The plaintiff team was frowning. Harry was whispering to Floyd.

"Now, let me point out that in Genesis 1:1 at the top of the chart, it says that God ***created*** the heaven and the earth. It doesn't say He *made* the heaven and the earth to do some action, for example *to rule*. And lest our good friends on the plaintiff's team object, I have put in [ ] the original language Hebrew words so that you can see 'create' is translated from a different Hebrew word than 'made.'"

"Ladies and gentlemen of the jury," Sarah continued, "What is happening here? If the sun, moon, and stars, along with the earth were already created, and it does say that the heaven was created in verse one, what is God making to rule? What action could He be taking to bring about **signs, seasons, days, and years** as it says in verse 14?"

"Kim, will you please answer those questions for the jury?"

"Thank you, Sarah," began Kim. "Your Honor, ladies and gentlemen of the jury, it is only logical to ask the question, 'What did God do to bring about **signs, seasons, days, and years?'** I think most students that have studied astronomy would tell you signs and years result from the earth's orbit around the sun. Further, they would tell you a day results from the earth's rotation every 24 hours and that the seasons result from the gradual tilt to and fro of the earth's axis as it orbits around the sun."

"Your Honor, with your permission, I would like to demonstrate with the globe over on the table, the process of how God made the sun and stars to rule the days and seasons."

"Permission granted," said Judge Emerson. "Actually, I would like to see that globe go through its paces again, myself."

"Thank you, Your Honor. Now, if I might have the courtroom darkened just a bit by pulling the blinds on the windows near the globe, I will demonstrate how the days and seasons are ruled. While we are waiting for that to happen, I would like to acknowledge the generosity of New Earth Globes of Newmarket, Canada, for loaning the globe to us for this trial."

Sarah handed the remote to Kim. There was an expectancy in the courtroom as Kim pushed the normal rotation key. The globe slowly lifted off of its base and appeared to be hanging on nothing. There was a hush in the courtroom.

"I remind you of the scripture that we quoted from the book of Job yesterday," said Kim. "*He stretcheth out the north over the empty place, and* **hangeth the earth upon nothing**."

Then Kim pushed the sun key and the stars key. The part of the globe facing the sun lamp lit up and the darkened area in the shadow of the earth displayed the appropriate constellations. Another hush settled over the courtroom.

"Yesterday, we quoted a scripture from Job about compassing the earth until the day and night come to an end," said Kim. She then went to the front of the courtroom, opened the ancient swearing in Bible, and read, *"He hath compassed the waters with bounds, until the day and night come to an end."*

"Some of you may be saying, 'The earth is hardly moving; it almost seems to be standing still," and you would be correct. The globe is programmed to rotate only once every 24 hours, so if you came back twelve hours from now, the day side would be night and vise versa. That's a long time to wait, so we will speed up the rotation so the globe rotates once every hour instead of once every 24 hours."

Kim pushed the 24/1 key, and the audience was surprised to see the image of the moon begin to come across the dark side screen along with the stellar constellations.

Kim continued, "We would be here quite a while if we wanted to observe the tilting of the earth on its axis that brings about the seasons. So, in order to illustrate this within the time limits that we have, I will cause the earth globe to rotate 365.24 times faster than it rotates in one day. So, in approximately the next four minutes, you will see what the earth goes through in one year. Watch the axis of the earth as the angle changes between it and the sun."

The globe began spinning at just under 100 rounds per minute. The moon and stars on the dark side became just a blur of light as they rapidly traversed the dark side screen. The audience watched with fascination as the axis of the earth tilted to bring summer to the northern hemisphere and then tilted back to bring winter. Floyd leaned over to Harry and whispered a question about objecting to the defense taking up the court's time. Harry advised him against it, saying—everybody including the judge and jury—wanted to see it. He told him if he objected, he would come off as a spoilsport.

After going through a complete cycle of seasons, Kim slowed down the globe to a 24/1 rotation so that the jury could better observe the day and night cycles, the star constellations, and the phases of the moon waxing and waning.

Kim continued, "The creation process seems to have unfolded in phases. First God created the heaven and the earth. Once these were made, He fine tuned the orbit, rotation, and tilt of the earth to make a place habitable for man. Look at the verses on the chart again. Everything I've shown you using the globe system is right there in scripture."

GEN 1:1 In the beginning God *CREATED* [*bara'*] the heaven and the earth.

GEN 1:13 And the evening and the morning were the third day.
14 And God said, Let there be lights in the firmament of the heaven to divide the day from the night; and let them be for signs, and for seasons, and for days, and years:
15 And let them be for lights in the firmament of the heaven to give light upon the earth: and it was so.
16 And God *MADE* [*'asah*] two great lights; the greater light *TO RULE* the day, and the lesser light *TO RULE* the night: he made the stars also.
17 And God set them in the firmament of the heaven to give light upon the earth,
18 And *TO RULE* over the day and over the night, and to divide the light from the darkness: and God saw that it was good.
19 And the evening and the morning were the fourth day.

"It is abundantly clear," Kim said, " that we have shown how God **made** the sun **to rule** the day, and the moon and stars **to rule** the night. The seasonal tilting of the axis of the earth in its orbit determines the setting of the stars observed in the heavens at any given location on earth. We have even shown how in verse 18 the light is divided from the darkness.

I am confident when you consider the evidence we have presented, you will conclude that the Bible is not in error on this matter. Instead, the plaintiffs are the ones in error.

"Now, some of you on the jury may have one more question about the sun, moon, and stars being made to rule because the earth was made to rotate on its axis," continued Kim as she made eye contact with the jurors. "We know some heavenly bodies rotate on their axis, and some do not. For example the moon does not rotate on its axis. I suppose if a comet or stellar wind whizzed by, the moon could begin rotating. So a reasonable question is: When did the earth begin rotating? If it was already rotating on the first day of creation, why weren't the sun, moon, and stars ruling the day and night then?"

Some of the jurors nodded, so Kim knew this question was on their mind.

"I do not know when the earth began to rotate so that we have our present 24 hour day," said Kim, "and I do not pretend to know. But I will show you something out of the creation sequence described in Job chapter 38 so you can consider this for yourselves. Look at these scriptures."

JOB 38:8 Or who shut up the sea with doors, when it brake forth, as if it had issued out of the womb?
9 **When I made the cloud the garment thereof, and thick darkness a swaddlingband for it,**

"Now, it would seem that when God first made the earth, He treated it like a newborn baby. A baby is given a swaddling blanket to keep it covered in its crib. I have brought a swaddling blanket with me to help each of us consider this allegory of swaddling a newborn baby. Or, maybe it's like babying little seedlings in a greenhouse. However, in actuality, thick dark clouds must have blanketed the earth in the beginning of its formation. Even today, we see thick dark clouds blanketing Venus. We cannot see the surface of Venus, and if we were on its surface, we would not be able to make out the features of the sun through the dark clouds," continued Kim. She watched the jurors—they were nodding. Virginia had taught her well to watch the juror's response.

Kim continued, "Let's suppose the earth began rotating on the very first day rather than on the fourth day. Would that make any difference from the viewpoint of one standing on the earth and looking up at the sky? From your own experience, do you see the sun, moon, or stars on a very dark cloudy day? Well, you might see a slight filtering of light through the clouds, but you would not be able to make out the features of the heavenly bodies.

"It is said a picture is worth a thousand words," said Kim, "so maybe a live demonstration is worth more than a thousand words. We are going to use the swaddling blanket to represent thick, dark clouds. Now, please move the table with the globe around, so the jury can see exactly what happens when the earth is swaddled. Now, please dim the overhead lights."

The lights were dimmed, and Kim started the New Earth globe into its rotation. The jury could see the effect of the sun shining on its side of the earth. They could see the moon and constellations displayed on the shadow side of the earth on the dark sky plate.

"Your Honor, ladies and gentlemen of the jury, you can see the sun ruling the day, and the moon and stars ruling the night. Now, if you were standing on the earth, and someone put a thick blanket of clouds around the entire earth, what would you see?" asked Kim, as she motioned Red to come forward and drape the blanket around the earth so that the ability to see the sun, moon and stars was blocked.

The jury peered intently. They could see a few tiny beams from the sun lamp filtering through the threads of the swaddling blanket, but that was it. The blanket was like a protective greenhouse for the earth. The shape of the sun, moon, and stars was not distinguishable through the baby blanket. Sarah motioned for Red to pull the blanket away. Sharp divisions for day and night returned to the globe.

"As far as the sun ruling the day, and the moon and stars ruling the night, would it have made any difference if the earth was already rotating on the first day? You have seen the demonstration—maybe that was the way God did it. We have presented a logical and straightforward scenario for the creation of the earth, and it is in harmony with the scriptures. Now, let me use this chart to emphasize our key points.

KEY POINTS

- **We agree God created the heaven (including the sun) and the earth in the beginning**

- **The RULE *(not the creation)* of the sun, moon, and stars became visible from the earth on the fourth day**

- **THEREFORE, the plaintiffs have NOT PROVEN that the creation sequence given in Genesis chapter 1, verses 1 to 18 is incorrect.**

"We have given a logical and plausible description of what happened in the first verses of Genesis. We strongly disagree that the scriptures are in error, and we ask you to return a verdict in our favor of the defense," continued Kim.

Kim paused to gauge the effect of her presentation on the jury. Satisfied and receiving OK signs from Sarah and Virginia, she said, "Your Honor, the defense rests its case."

"Thank you," responded Judge Emerson. "We will have a one-hour recess and then return to have the summations. Again the jury is admonished not to discuss this trial among themselves or any persons outside of the jury."

Sarah, Kim, and Virginia fled through a couple of reporters to the assigned counsel room. Red and Dave stood on guard by the New Earth globe and put it through its paces for the curious that had gathered around in the courtroom, including those operating the video feed.

"Virginia, what do you think?" asked Kim. "Did we make our points?"

"I think you and Sarah did a bang-up job," replied Virginia. "I would not like to be in Floyd's shoes. I don't think Floyd's heart is in it any more. I'm sure he planned major, major emphasis in his summation to proving that the sun was created before the earth. Now, we have thrown his plans into disarray, and he has only one hour to redo his summation. Maybe Floyd is beginning to doubt his doubts about the integrity of the Bible. We just need to see this through and make a good summation ourselves, just as we planned in our strategy sessions. Keep your confidence up, you've already come through the hardest part."

Judge Emerson gaveled the court to order right on time and asked if the plaintiffs were ready to present their summation. Floyd indicated he was ready to proceed.

"Your Honor, ladies and gentlemen of the jury, we have been very pleased to learn the defense has come around to our way of thinking. They have essentially agreed with us that our presentation on the formation sequence of the sun and the earth is correct. We, in science, have often been persecuted by religious groups who have asked us to put our common sense aside and blindly accept concepts which we know to be wrong. I would direct your attention to the first part of the debate statement."

Resolved: The sun was formed before the planets (including the earth) were formed.

"I am confident you will agree with me that we have proven this statement beyond a reasonable doubt. Further, the preponderance of the evidence proves this statement to the extent that even the defense has conceded it to be true. Therefore, you must cast your vote with the plaintiffs.

"Now, let us look at the second statement," continued Floyd.

Therefore, the sequence that God made the sun after the formation of the earth as given in Genesis chapter 1, verses 1 through 18 is incorrect.

"Almost all of the religious community has read those verses to mean that God made the sun, moon, and stars after the earth was created. Here, we have a group of three who would place an unwieldy interpretation on it which is outside of the mainstream of Christian religion. Not only are they outside the mainstream, but they have brought this smoke and mirrors globe gadget into the courtroom to try and confuse you by putting it through its gyrations. We ask you to use your common sense to reject this travesty on the English language and even the Hebrew language. To sum up, we have undoubtedly won the first statement, even the defense agrees with us. We only ask you to use your common sense to reject the spurious, off-the-wall arguments of the defense and agree with us that we have proven our points in this debate. Your Honor, that completes our summation."

"Thank you," said Judge Emerson. "Is the defense ready to present its summation?"

"We are, Your Honor," responded Sarah.

"Proceed."

"Your Honor, ladies and gentlemen of the jury, we have been pleased to have your attention as we have presented the case for the defense. As the plaintiff has repeatedly noted, we do not contest the sequence of creation of the sun and the earth. In fact, we would congratulate Dr. Harper and Dr. Eisenhoff on making a splendid presentation concerning this. We did not tell you at any point in this case, even from the first day, that we disagreed with the first statement. We simply told you we would prove to you that the Bible was not in error concerning the sequence of formation.

"Do you not find it humorous that the plaintiffs tell you the evidence we have presented is outside of the mainstream of Christian religion? I wonder why the plaintiffs did not tell you at the same time the mainstream of Christian religion believes the Bible, as written, to be true and not in error? I believe the record will show that one of the plaintiff's witnesses said, 'You can't have your cake and eat it too.'

"Now, what the plaintiffs did not tell you in their summation was they prepared and argued their case on the basis of what they thought the defense's arguments would be. They were in total shock when we agreed to the first part of the debate statement without contesting it. They even objected to us supporting their argument about the sun being formed before the earth. Then, when cold hard scientific facts were used against them, it was called 'smoke and mirrors.' Ladies and gentlemen of the jury, I am sure all of you, at one time or another, have studied the basics of astronomy. I don't think any of you have any difficulty understanding how the earth orbits around the sun in one year, how the earth rotates every 24 hours so we have day and night, and that there are different seasons depending on the tilt of the axis of the earth toward the sun. The Indians, before the white man ever landed on these shores, had a thorough knowledge of the constellations in the night sky. And yet, the plaintiff calls it 'smoke and mirrors.'

It is clear when God had created the heaven and the earth, the two great lights were fine tuned so the sun would rule the day, and the moon and stars would rule the night. At some point, when the earth rotated on its axis, day and night resulted in the surface of the clouds incubating the newborn earth. Then, by the end of the fourth day, the rule of the sun moon, and stars became visible on the earth. I think most of us would agree God has powers far above and beyond the powers understood by man. There were even instances in the book of Joshua and the book of Isaiah where God temporarily suspended or altered the rotation of the earth for specific purposes. So, this fine tuning is not without precedent in the Bible scriptures.

Dr. Harper, who had nervously been rubbing his thumb against his forefingers, could finally stand it no more. He jumped up and said, "I know about those passages in the Bible! That's a bunch of hooey! If the earth stood still or even reversed itself for even a second, the change in angular momentum would cause chaos."

"Dr. Harper!" thundered the judge, "You are completely out of order! One more outburst like this, and I will have the bailiff remove you from the courtroom!"

After things settled down a bit, the judge asked Sarah to continue the summation.

"I do not mind answering Dr. Harper's concerns, in fact I welcome them," said Sarah. "Some have criticized the Bible for saying the sun hasted not to go down for a period of time. But, I ask you, when twilight comes, do we say the earth came up? No, we say the sun is going down. I wonder if there is any one on the jury who gets up in the morning and says 'the earth went down.' I very seriously doubt it.

Now, to deal with the question about the change in angular momentum causing chaos. The New Earth globe is currently turning at one rotation per day. Watching it turn is like watching paint dry. The hour hand on a regular clock turns twice as fast as the earth turns, rotating every twelve hours. Is there any one here that can see the globe actually moving at this very slow rotation? I wonder if Dr. Harper would like to press the stop rotation button? Well, no response, so I will stop the rotation of the globe."

The globe stopped turning and remained perfectly suspended in mid air. It did not fall apart. Dr. Harper stared sullenly straight ahead, ignoring the intact globe. Then, Sarah told the court she would press the 'reverse' spin button and let the earth rotate backward for the next fifteen minutes. Again, the motion was so slow it was almost imperceptible.

Sarah gave the example of the space shuttle Discovery orbiting the earth and turning lazily on its own axis every 24 hours. Then, a little vernier rocket controlled by a gyro gives a few small bursts to stop the rotation. She asked if an astronaut tossing a piece of bread from his hand to his mouth hardly notices the slight reduction in rotation? She wondered what would happen if NASA mathematically regressed the earth's rotation to Old Testament times. Would they find a discontinuity of about 24 hours?

Sarah continued, "I think all of us have a lot to learn when it comes to understanding the awesome power of God. Maybe he has an electromagnetic brake and accelerator. Was the braking done gradually and the re-acceleration to normal spin done gradually—like one drives a car? We don't understand how it was done. Even today, some scientists will admit that while they know about effects of electromagnetism and gravity, they really don't understand their inter-workings. If God can hang the earth on nothing, he certainly can fine tune how the earth rotates.

On the other hand, consider the perspective of the little ants happily eating away in the picnic basket. Suddenly, some powerful, unrecognized force picks up the basket and takes it back to the car and not even one dish is broken. There may be those who insist on retaining the limitations of the ant's world and say such a thing could not happen—what can we do to enlarge their perspective and enlighten them? Oh, by the way, one of the ants named Occam insisted that the simplest explanation was the most likely. He tried to persuade the other ants the earth didn't really stop rotating on its axis—instead it was simply a reset time warp. You know—like the somewhat numerous reports by sailors and aviators of incidents where the hands on their watches began turning backwards and their electronic instruments were going berserk. But the other ants scoffed, and said these were just a bunch of myths fomented by sailors who had too much to drink and aviators dreaming while on autopilot. Oh well, what do ants know?

Now, Ladies and Gentlemen of the jury, please turn your attention to the debate statement."

Resolved: The sun was formed before the planets (including the earth) were formed. Therefore, the sequence that God made the sun after the formation of the earth as given in Genesis chapter 1, verses 1 through 18 is incorrect.

The defense has consistently told you from the beginning of this trial that we would prove that the plaintiff's assertion that the Bible is incorrect is an error on their part. We have sufficiently demonstrated the Bible is not in error in this matter by using cold, hard scientific facts. The explanation that we have given is scientifically consistent and one a reasonable person would accept.

"Now I ask you to carefully review the debate statement. I think you will agree with me that it is a half-truth. I believe that those on the plaintiff's team are honest and sincere in holding their beliefs, but the problem is they have believed a half-truth. As you well know, mixing in some truth into a deception is a way of making a deception more believable, but it is still a deception."

Sarah walked over to the table where the old Bible lay. She picked it up and said, "This old Bible, part of the history of this courtroom, has been used to swear in many witnesses over the centuries. The witnesses agreed to tell the truth, the whole truth, and nothing but the truth. Let me read you a scripture from this Bible.

And ye shall know the truth, and the truth shall make you free

.

"Ladies and gentlemen of the jury, if you are satisfied with the half-truth which has been presented to you by the plaintiffs, then you may find for the plaintiffs. But if you are one who desires the whole truth, then we ask you to find for the defense. We thank you for your kind attention. Your Honor, the defense rests."

"Thank you," said Judge Emerson. "I will now give the charge to the jury. The document the clerk is giving to each one of you will be your basis for arriving at a decision in this case. I will carefully go over it with you." Then the judge proceeded to elaborate on the charge to the jury.

****

CASE 200611B

RIVEROC STATE UNIVERSITY PSEUDO COURT

Resolved: The sun was formed before the planets (including the earth) were formed. Therefore, the sequence that God made the sun after the formation of the earth as given in Genesis chapter 1, verses 1 through 18 is incorrect.

CRITERIA FOR MAKING A FINDING:

If you find that the plaintiffs have proved their case beyond the doubt that a reasonable man would have *and* the preponderance of the evidence supports the plaintiff's case, you must find for the plaintiff.

If you find that the plaintiffs have not proved their case beyond the doubt a reasonable man would have *and* the preponderance of the evidence does not support the plaintiff's case, you must find for the defense.

The jury should deliberate until a unanimous opinion is reached. If it fails to reach a unanimous opinion, the jury should report back to the court for further instructions.

****

"Are there any questions?" asked Judge Emerson. "If not, the jury will retire to the deliberation room. If a verdict is not reached before 5:00 today, the jury will resume deliberation at 1:30 on Wednesday. The jury is cautioned not to discuss this case with outsiders or to be influenced by news reports of any kind. Thank you, ladies and gentlemen, the court will adjourn until we have further communication from the jury." Then the judge gaveled the session to a close.

The courtroom exploded with a gaggle of voices. Sarah had slumped down on the defense table's chair, just glad it was over. When reporters pushed around asking questions, Virginia ran interference and asked them to come to the pavilion outside the courthouse so the questions could be asked in a more orderly environment. The interviews were like a blur to the girls. They were on their game in responding to the questions, but very glad when the cameras and reporters left.

Red, Dave, and Dr. Stansel hugged them and congratulated them on the trial. They were given a ride back to the dorm. It was time to get a little rest and prepare to go to the dinner at Houston House that evening. Sarah took the phone off the hook to avoid the constant interruptions. She saw on her cell phone her parents had called and she called them back. They were excited because they had seen parts of the trial on cable news and also on local TV news. She noticed on her laptop there was a message from the owner of New Earth Globes. He said the trial had already generated 500 hits on his web site, and he had about 30 orders so far for the globes. He said Sarah should keep the globe; it was no longer a loan.

That evening Dr. Stansel, Dave, and Red picked up Sarah, Kim, and Virginia from the dorm and they headed to Houston House for dinner. Shortly after arriving, they saw Floyd, Nancy, Harry, and Dr. Eisenhoff coming in the door. The parties warmly greeted each other and congratulated each other as being worthy adversaries. Then they humorously wished each other the worst of luck concerning the trial verdict. The Frontier Room was wonderfully done with its wooden plank tables, rustic chairs, and log walls. The food was served on pewter plates and Sarah ordered a house specialty, prime rib. Dr. Stansel returned thanks for the meal and everyone settled down to a frontier gourmet's delight.

The conversation turned from the more mundane topics to the earth, the universe, science and the Bible. The Houston House waiter was asked to get some blank sheets of paper from their copying machine and before long Floyd, Sarah, Kim, Red, and Dr. Eisenhoff were drawing diagrams and explaining concepts to each other. These college students were thrilled to have a one on one—so to speak—opportunity to discuss science with someone with the credentials of Dr. Eisenhoff. And Dr. Eisenhoff had some questions for them.

Virginia, Harry, Nancy, Dave and Dr. Stansel were on the periphery of the conversations. The discussions were animated and words and phrases like darkness on the face of the deep, recently discovered dark energy and dark matter, black holes, chaos, quantum jitters, firmament, membrane, brooding over waters, order, rod of Melchisedek, bringing light out of darkness, coding in the candle stick, and genetics were flying back and forth. When the lights began dimming at Houston House signaling it was closing time, it was decided that Floyd, Sarah, Kim, Red and Dr. Eisenhoff would go to the all nighter Chicken and Egg to continue their conversations. The rest of the group decided to call it quits for the evening.

Dr. Stansel whispered to Dave and Virginia on the way out of Houston House, "I think the Holy Spirit is doing some bonding here."

Sarah and Kim were tired the next morning. They had gotten to bed at 1:00 am, but after brisk showers and having their bowls of cereal, they were ready to go for the day. Would this be the day of the verdict?

That afternoon, the litigants met back at the courthouse where Judge Emerson had assembled the jury once more. They had not arrived at a verdict but did have some requests for the judge. They wanted a Bible, a Hebrew-English concordance, and an English dictionary. The judge didn't want to give up the historical Bible from the courtroom. A dictionary was found in one of the offices. Dave quickly walked down to a nearby church and borrowed a standard King James Bible and a Strong's Concordance from the pastor. The litigants looked over the books with the judge and agreed they were suitable to give to the jury. The jury departed to the deliberation room, and the clerk took the cell phone numbers of the litigants so they could be notified when a verdict was returned. The wait was on.

The Verdict

There was still a number of reporters and TV crews hanging around the court house waiting for the verdict. Sarah, Kim, and Virginia went down to the River Dog to get some soft drinks and wait for the verdict. After about an hour, Floyd and Dr. Eisenhoff showed up, and they were invited to join them. Before long, the sheets of paper were back on the table, and the group was busily discussing the secrets of the universe such as the firmament, glassy sea, terrible crystal, membrane stretching, etc.

Floyd's cell phone rang. It was the clerk. "The jury has a verdict!" exclaimed Floyd.

Shortly, thereafter, the other cell phones began ringing. Everyone headed back to the courthouse. The TV satellite truck was back, the reporters were there with their notebooks, tape recorders, and cameras. The courtroom was packed, and there was a buzz of anticipation.

The distinguished Judge Marvin Emerson called the court session to order. "Has the jury reached a verdict?"

"We have Your Honor," replied the foreman.

The foreman of the jury was a college student, but was somewhat older than the other students. He was married, had two children, and was attending the university on a grant from his employer. Kim remembered him as one of the last jurists to be selected. The judge asked the clerk to bring the verdict to the bench. The suspense in the courtroom was building to a crescendo.

Judge Emerson opened the verdict document and looked it over. He then took off his reading glasses and very carefully cleaned each lens. A thousand trumpets of silence sounded in the courtroom and permeated through the ancient walls even to the bystanders outside. He then put his glasses back on and continued reading the document as a frown slowly spread across his face. He looked up at the courtroom and then directly at the jury.

"Ladies and gentlemen of the jury, I thank you for your deliberation efforts. However, in this case, it is not appropriate to return a verdict with a footnote added to it," admonished Judge Emerson. "You must either find for the plaintiffs or for the defense without adding qualifications of your own. Therefore, please return to the jury room and continue your deliberations until you reach a proper verdict."

END OF VOLUME I

To be continued, God willing ...

JAMES 4:13-15 *Go to now, ye that say, To day or to morrow we will go into such a city, and continue there a year, and buy and sell, and get gain: Whereas ye know not what shall be on the morrow. For what is your life? It is even a vapour, that appeareth for a little time, and then vanisheth away. For that ye ought to say, If the Lord will, we shall live, and do this, or that.*

Editor's Note: See http://www.TheAncientChest.com/Verdict
Express your opinions by choosing one or more of the following:

The plaintiff (Floyd and company) could have better presented their case by: ____

The defense (Sarah and company) could have better presented their case by: ____

If I were on the jury, I would find for:

- ☐ a. The plaintiff
- ☐ b. The defense
- ☐ c. Undecided
- ☐ d. None of above - Explain Why

APPENDICES

A through E

What Must I Do to Be Saved?

Paul and Silas Preach at the Prison

ACTS 16:30 And brought them out, and said, Sirs, what must I do
to be saved?
31 And they said, Believe on the Lord Jesus Christ, and thou shalt
be saved, and thy house.
32 And they spake unto him the word of the Lord, and to all that
were in his house.
33 And he took them the same hour of the night, and washed their
stripes; and was baptized, he and all his, straightway.

If you would like to share the concepts about science and related scriptures outlined in the Appendices with your friends, you will find an online file at:
http://www.TheAncientChest.com/destiny

APPENDIX A - Andy's Email to Myra - The Candlestick Dimensions

Subject: Candlestick
Date: April 9, 2001, 8:00:08 PM Central Daylight Time
From: Andy_Andreas@aol.com
To: Myra_Andreas@aol.com
Sent from the Internet (Details)

Hi Honey,

Have been looking at the poem you sent about the candlestick from your Kansas friend, Irene. This has a higher octave of colors/frequencies than what we see in the natural rainbow. The candlestick appears to have its symbolic roots in the Seven Spirits listed in Isaiah 11 (Shown in italics). The six branches are enfolded into a total envelope of white light which would be the Spirit of the Lord.

ISA 11:1-2 And there shall come forth a rod out of the stem of Jesse, and a Branch shall grow out of his roots: And the *spirit of the LORD* shall rest upon him, the spirit of *wisdom* and *understanding*, the spirit of *counsel* and *might*, the spirit of *knowledge* and of *the fear of the LORD*;

The curious thing is that this seems to come out of the almond rod which traces back to the priesthood of Levi who had the almond rod that budded (Numbers 17:8). Moses used the rod to part the sea.

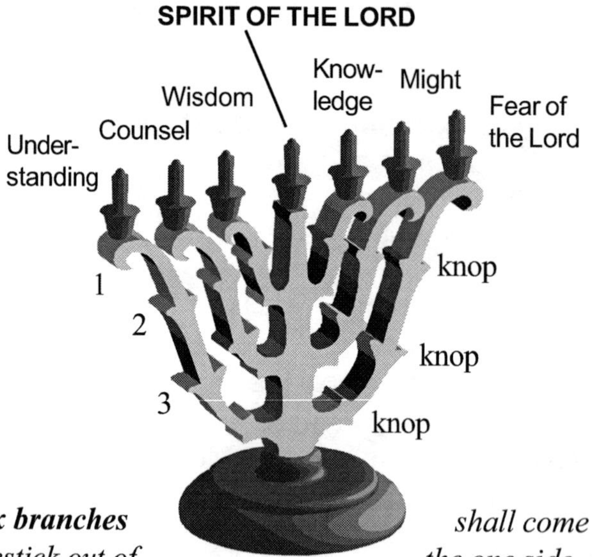

EXODUS 25:32-34 *And* ***six branches*** *shall come out of the sides of it; three branches of the candlestick out of the one side, and three branches of the candlestick out of the other side:* ***Three bowls*** *made like unto almonds, with a knop and a flower in one branch; and three bowls made like almonds in the other branch, with a knop and a flower: so in the six branches that come out of the candlestick. And in the candlestick shall be* ***four bowls*** *made like unto almonds, with their knops and their flowers.*

I counted up the almond knops and found six branches with a total of three knops in each branch which gave me eighteen knops. Then, I added the four knops in the main branch to get a total of 22 knops. Then, it dawned on me, the 22 knops represent the 22 letters of the Hebrew alphabet. It looks like the candle-stick represents the invisible building blocks of creation emblazoned in "*Let there be light.*" Fortunately, the 22 letters of the Hebrew alphabet are given in an acrostic in Psalm 119. Look at the arrangement.

APPENDIX A CONTINUED

ALEPH

PSALMS 119:1 Blessed are the undefiled in the way, who walk in the law of the LORD.
2 Blessed are they that keep his testimonies, and that seek him with the whole heart.
3 They also do no iniquity: they walk in his ways.
4 Thou hast commanded us to keep thy precepts diligently.
5 O that my ways were directed to keep thy statutes!
6 Then shall I not be ashamed, when I have respect unto all thy commandments.
7 I will praise thee with uprightness of heart, when I shall have learned thy righteous judgments.
8 I will keep thy statutes: O forsake me not utterly.

BETH

9 Wherewithal shall a young man cleanse his way? by taking heed thereto according to thy word.

AND SO ON THROUGH THE REST OF THE LETTERS . . .

GIMEL DALETH HE VAU ZAIN CHETH TETH JOD CAPH LAMED MEM NUN SAMECH AIN PE TZADDI KOPH RESH SCHIN . . .

TAU

PSA 119:169 Let my cry come near before thee, O LORD: give me understanding according to thy word.

The first letter of the first eight verses starts with the letter Aleph, the first letter of the next eight verses start with the letter Beth, and then so on until you reach the final eight verses (169 - 176) in Psalm 119 that start with the letter Tau.

Do you think there is some sort of code embedded in Psalm 119? The physicists have been looking for a long time for the six, invisible, curled up dimensions that seems to fit their mathematics. They even think there may be a seventh invisible dimension. The candlestick seems to be a symbol of the invisible realm from which the worlds were created. Is it time for rod of the priesthood of Melchizedec to be revealed in fuller measure?

PSA 110:2 *The LORD shall send the rod of thy strength out of Zion: rule thou in the midst of thine enemies.* [3] *Thy people shall be willing in the day of thy power, in the beauties of holiness from the womb of the morning: thou hast the dew of thy youth.* [4] *The LORD hath sworn, and will not repent, Thou art a priest for ever after the order of Melchizedek.*

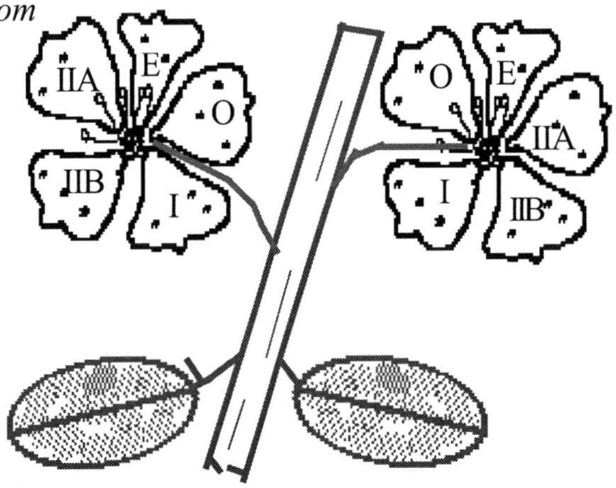

The flower of the almond is unique in its appearance in that it has five petals which are connected in the center. Seems to be some type of a code in the flower arrangement. What do you think?
Love,
Andy

APPENDIX A CONTINUED

Subject: Reply to Candlestick Email
Date: April 12, 2001, 12:12:07 PM
From: Myra_Andreas@aol.com
To: Andy_Andreas@aol.com
Sent from the Internet (Details)

Hi Sweetheart, 23 female chromosomes 1 1 male chromosomes 23
^{xx}FFFFFFFFFFFFFFFFFFFFFF---- MMMMMMMMMMMMMMMMMMMMMM^{XY}

Your last email about the candlestick opens up a lot of vistas. There probably is some kind of code embedded in Psalm 119. I wonder if it could be a genetic code. In human reproduction, we get 23 chromosomes from the father and 23 chromosomes from the mother, giving us a total of 46 chromosomes. However, the final twenty-third chromosome from the parents determines the sex of the child. I wonder if Adam only had 44 chromosomes before Eve was taken out of Adam? (2 X 22 Hebrew letters = 44 Hebrew letters). You do have an eight verse setup in Psalm 119 which could fit in with the G, C,T, A genetic building blocks. I checked the internet and found this representation of the letters in a biblicalhebrew.com site. It is so fascinating to contemplate the shapes of the letters, their sounds, and symbolic references. As I gaze at them, I sense a moving, swimming alphabet of God's creative life force. Perhaps, someday, the eyes of our understanding will be enlightened to know what these really represent.

THE CHARACTERS AND THEIR PICTURE-IMAGES

Character		Name	Original Picture Symbolism
א		*'Aleph*	ox head, yoke, learn
ב		*Beth*	house, tent
ג		*Gimel*	camel's neck, soul
ד		*Dâleth*	door, curtain to tent
ה		*Hê*	window, lattice
ו		*Wâw or vâv*	hook, nail, peg
ז		*Zayin*	weapon
ח		*Cheth*	hedge, fence, surround, gird
ט		*Teth*	serpent, snake, roll, curve
י		*Yodh*	hand (bent)
כ	ך	*Kaph*	wing, palm (hollow of the hand)
ל		*Lâmedh*	ox goad, correction, learning
מ	ם	*Mem*	waves, water
נ	ן	*Nun*	fish (tadpole?), snake
ס		*Sâmekh*	prop, support
ע		*'Ayin*	eye
פ	ף	*Pê*	mouth
צ	ץ	*Tsâdhe*	fish hook? tool for cutting down?
ק		*Qoph*	axe, monkey, back of the head
ר		*Resh*	head
שׂ שׁ		*Sin, Shin*	tooth
ת		*Tâw*	sign, branded cross, mark, 'T'

I had a strange dream in which it seemed the Most High was speaking to me about creation. I found it fascinating and yet somewhat unsettling to have the revelation that our very being is based on numbers and their arrangements. Can love be a number or a matrix and a patrix of numbers? Perhaps in the spirit world, numbers and their arrangement can and do constitute light and love.

Since we have talked about the candlestick, I have found a drawing in my files I put away about thirty years ago, with a note saying it was to be revisited only after the beginning of the third day. Jesus said in *the third day I shall be perfected.* If a day is a thousand years, it has been two thousand years since he was born and we are in the dawning of the third millennium. I'm not sure why the drawing was to be kept secret for this time, but, perhaps it is time to revisit it. I have this overpowering feeling a mystery is about to be revealed - and as we understand more about God, we will see his face. Paul said *For now we see through a glass darkly; but then face to face.* See the scan below.

As Always, Love, Myra

REVELATION 10:7

But in the days of the voice of the seventh angel, when he shall begin to sound, the mystery of God should be finished, as he hath declared to his servants the prophets.

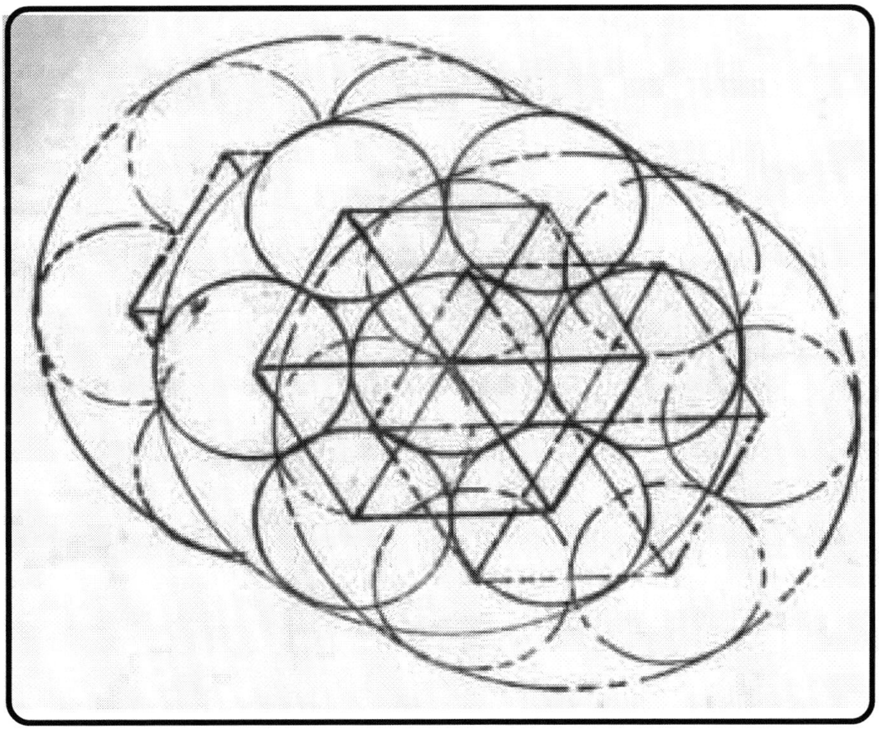

PS: I suppose that when we begin to understand the geometry of God, we will start to see his face. Peter was made a 'fisher of men'. Do we live and move in an ocean of the pure poetry of God's Divine Spirit?

ACTS 17:26 And hath made of one blood all nations of men for to dwell on all the face of the earth, and hath determined the times before appointed, and the bounds of their habitation; [27] That they should seek the Lord, if haply they might feel after him, and find him, **though he be not far from every one of us**:
[28] **For in him we live, and move, and have our being**; as certain also of **your own poets have said**, For we are also his offspring.

APPENDIX B - Andy's Email to Myra - The Horizon Problem

Subject: Heaven, A Scroll and the Horizon Problem
Date: September 23, 2002, 3:05:08 PM Central Daylight Time
From: Andy_Andreas@aol.com
To: Myra_Andreas@aol.com
Sent from the Internet (Details)

Hi Honey,

In your last email you were saying scientists were mulling over what they call the "horizon" problem - the horizon being the perimeter of the light sources viewable from the earth. You said the puzzle was that parts of the universe separated by vast distances have the same temperatures These temperatures are so identical that the universe is like two identical twins separated at birth and expanded to a huge distance one apart from the other. How could these two identical twins communicate with each other in messages faster than the speed of light in order that the same temperature is maintained? Some scientists have used a term called inflation or even hyperinflation to explain it. It appears without a generous helping of fudge factor and some serious tweaking, the big bang theory fizzles when it comes to explaining the horizon problem.

I took your hint about looking at creation as being a scroll unrolled and dissolution as being a scroll rolled up and I found these verses.

ISAIAH 34:4 *And all the host of heaven shall be dissolved, and the heavens shall be rolled together as a scroll: and all their host shall fall down, as the leaf falleth off from the vine, and as a falling fig from the fig tree.*

2PETER 3:10 *But the day of the Lord will come as a thief in the night; in the which the heavens shall pass away with a great noise, and the elements shall melt with fervent heat, the earth also and the works that are therein shall be burned up.*

2PETER 3:13 *Nevertheless we, according to his promise, look for new heavens and a new earth, wherein dwelleth righteousness.*

REVELATION 6:13 *And the stars of heaven fell unto the earth, even as a fig tree casteth her untimely figs, when she is shaken of a mighty wind.*
14 And the heaven departed as a scroll when it is rolled together; and every mountain and island were moved out of their places.

I found a depiction of a Torah scroll on a Hebrew site on the internet. If the old heaven departs like a scroll, maybe a new heaven unrolls like a scroll. The right and left hand scrolls would be a mirror image of each other and would act like identical twins. It would take a tremendous energy of unwinding to pull apart the rolls. Maybe the left and right rolls are like two spring loaded window shades. Two window shade rolls suddenly let go to their center would make a 'great noise'. (A big splat? However, if they overwind, there is a recoil.) A new heaven would be unrolled like a Torah scroll, and the identical twins, once together, would be separated.

The Apostle Peter wrote this: "*Looking for and hasting unto the coming of the day of God, wherein the heavens being on fire shall be dissolved, and the elements* [stoicheions] *shall melt with fervent heat?*" The Greek word for elements, *stoicheions*, seems to be referring to principles or something on the atomic or subatomic scale being reconstituted. Could it be both the cosmic scale and atomic scale is affected by the scroll winding and unwinding? A literal interpretation of Genesis 1:1 is "*In **a** beginning ...*" rather than *In **the** beginning ...*" It may be the scroll is eternal but the particular version of heaven and earth is temporal. The Apostle John wrote: "*And I saw a new heaven and a new earth: for the first heaven and the first earth were passed away ...*" Who knows, maybe the connecting fabric of the scroll is the Word of God. The Bible tells that "*through faith we understand that the worlds were framed by the word of God, so that things which are seen were not made of things which do appear.*" What do you think?

Your true love - Andy

APPENDIX C - Parchment Found Folded Up In Old Portugese Bible

(Bible from Serra de Rates, Portugal and bought in Belém, Brazil Flea Market)

See The Songs of the Ancients Section of Book for Song of Melchisedec Music

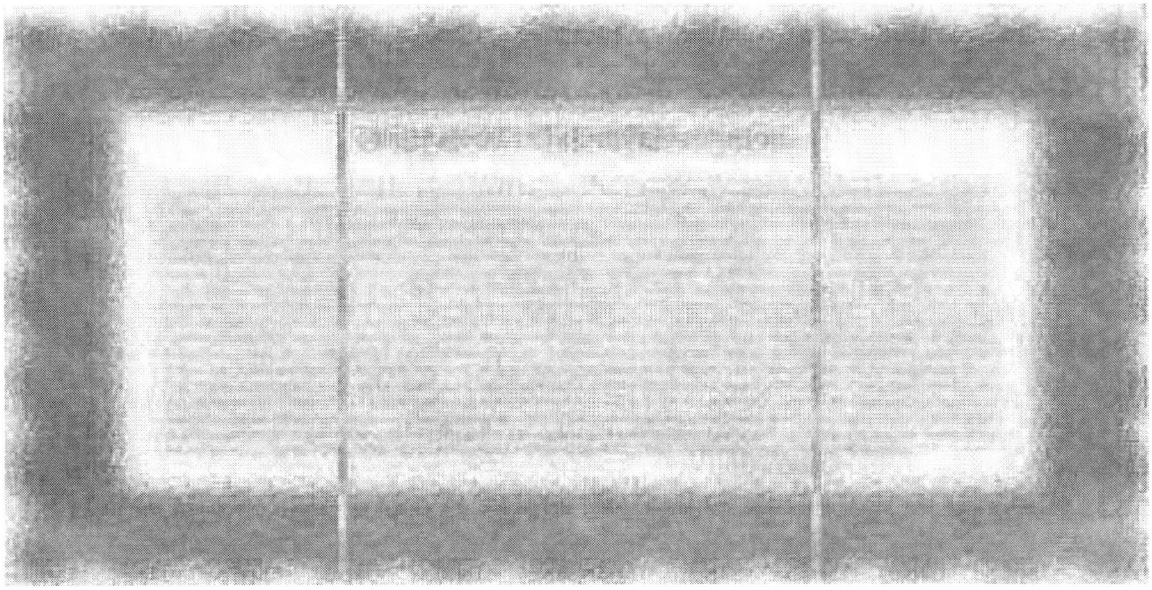

Translation
of
The Song of Melchisedek

The Psalmist sang: Thy people shall be willing in the day of thy power, in the beauties of holiness from the womb of the morning: thou hast the dew of thy youth. The LORD hath sworn, and will not repent, Thou art a priest for ever after the order of Melchizedek. I will declare the decree: the LORD hath said unto me, Thou art my Son; this day have I begotten thee.

We sing in unison: *El Elyon*, I call upon you in the name of the Lord Jesus Christ. As your child, with boldness I enter into your presence, the I AM that I AM, the Holy of Holies, through the torn flesh and blood of Jesus Christ, I decree that you are the Most High God; you are the possessor of heaven and earth and everything in them. You are my *Elohim* creator; My *El Shaddai*, lover, nourisher, and provider; my *Yahweh*, lawgiver, judge, punisher, healer and deliverer. Above all, you are my *Eloah*, Messiah, Christ, Anointing, Life-Giving Creative Force, the Holy Spirit. Within you is complete salvation for my spirit, soul, and body. I decree that Jesus, my *Yeshua*, is the Christ, Jesus is Your Son: Jesus has come in the flesh; Jesus is Lord; and You are full of love and mercy. I will decree these things among the Gentiles, confide my faults to another, and my sins to you. I acknowledge the Holy Spirit as my source of power, teacher, counselor, and personal friend. In the name of the Lord Jesus Christ, through His blood, fire, water, and Spirit, I receive glory, honor, and immortality by imparting His life blood, liquid streams of living light into my blood. My whole spirit by faith, soul by works, body by hope is now being preserved blameless until the coming of the Lord. When I decree a thing, it is established unto me; and Your light shines upon my ways.

I decree that the full manifestation of the Kingdom of God from within me now come forth. I decree that every atom within my earthly physical body bring forth health, light, life, and immortality. My light is now coming forth as the morning, and my health is springing forth speedily, and His righteousness goes before me. Your glory is my rear guard. For I am made in the image of Elohim, after Elohim's likeness. I have dominion over the fish of the sea, and over the fowl of the air, and over the cattle, and over all the earth, and over every creeping that creepeth upon the earth. I am helping to bring about the revelation and restoration of all things which you have spoken by the mouth of all your holy prophets since the world began.

THE BRANCHES ABIDING IN THE VINE

APPENDIX D - Andy's Email to Myra - The Daughters of Zelophehad

Subject: Joseph's daughters climbing over the walls of tradition
Date: March 4, 2001, 7:15:28 PM Central Standard Time
From: Andy_Andreas@aol.com
To: Myra_Andreasl@aol.com
Sent from the Internet (Details)

Hi Honey,

OK, OK, you were right. I researched it, and it probably explains why you are like you are. Your anointing seems to be from the tribe of Joseph. Joseph's blessing given to him by Jacob was as follows:

GENESIS 49:22 Joseph is a fruitful bough, even a fruitful bough by a well; whose branches run over the wall (King James Translation).

GENESIS 49:22 Joseph {is} a fruitful son; A fruitful son by a fountain, Daughters step over the wall (Young's Literal Translation).

The more literal translation indicates the daughters of Joseph were bold and stepped over the wall. And yes, I did research it and the daughters of Zelophehad were direct descendents of Joseph. (Joseph /Manasseh/Machir/Gilead/ Hepher who begat Zelophehad who begat five daughters and no sons) So, it seems these great, great, great, great granddaughters of Joseph wanted their inheritance in Israel just like the sons of their uncles received. When the matter came to Moses, he was pretty nonplussed about these upstart daughters wanting an inheritance, just like a son would receive. I guess Moses thought they stepped over the line, because he ultimately had to take the case to the Supreme Court—God. So Dear, I stand corrected; you were right. By the way, I copied Moses' reaction and the disposition of the case below. I suppose he was shocked when the LORD agreed with Zelophehad's daughters.

Perhaps, as I begin to understand and appreciate the role of you as a daughter of God, you and I will begin to ascend in our comprehension through the glassy sea—or glassy ceiling, if you like—that Ezekiel described as being over the head of the cherubim in the most holy place. Is this what is required to repair the breach that has existed from ancient time between man and woman? May the sons accept the daughters and the daughters accept the sons so that we may truly transcend together.

Love - Andy

NUM 27:1 Then came the daughters of Zelophehad, the son of Hepher, the son of Gilead, the son of Machir, the son of Manasseh, of the families of Manasseh the son of Joseph: and these are the names of his daughters; Mahlah, Noah, and Hoglah, and Milcah, and Tirzah.
2 And they stood before Moses, and before Eleazar the priest, and before the princes and all the congregation, by the door of the tabernacle of the congregation, saying,
3 Our father died in the wilderness, and he was not in the company of them that gathered themselves together against the LORD in the company of Korah; but died in his own sin, and had no sons.
4 Why should the name of our father be done away from among his family, because he hath no son? Give unto us therefore a possession among the brethren of our father.
5 And Moses brought their cause before the LORD.
6 And the LORD spake unto Moses, saying,
7 The daughters of Zelophehad speak right: thou shalt surely give them a possession of an inheritance among their father's brethren; and thou shalt cause the inheritance of their father to pass unto them.

APPENDIX E - Myra's Anatomy Email to CowgirlGretr

Subject: Human Anatomy in Temple and in Scriptures
Date: July 2, 1998, 7:47:07 PM Central Daylight Time
From: Myra_Andreas@aol.com
To: CowgirlGretr@rrr.com
Sent from the Internet (Details)

Hi Greta,

It was great to meet you and Bob at the medical conference in Houston. You asked me to send you a short summary of our discussion about the bridge between modern neurophysics and the temple. It is amazing that nerves are also called nerve trees. John wrote in Revelation about *the tree of life, which bare twelve manner of fruits.* The cranium or head has twelve cranial nerves which directly serve the brain. John also wrote *round about the throne were four and twenty seats: and upon the seats I saw four and twenty elders sitting.* It is so amazing to realize the cranium has twelve paired nerve trees, making twenty-four altogether. When we allow the presence of God to sit on the throne of our mind, these nerves are worshiping God with their inputs. REV 4:4 And round about the throne were four and twenty seats: and upon the seats I saw four and twenty elders sitting,

From internet (neurophys.com site)

1. I - Olfactory
2. II - Optic
3. III - Oculomotor
4. IV - Trochlear
5. V - Trigeminal
6. VI - Abducens
7. VII - Facial
8. VIII - Auditory
9. IX - Glossopharyngeal
10. X - Vagus
11. XI - Accessory
12. XII - Hypoglassal

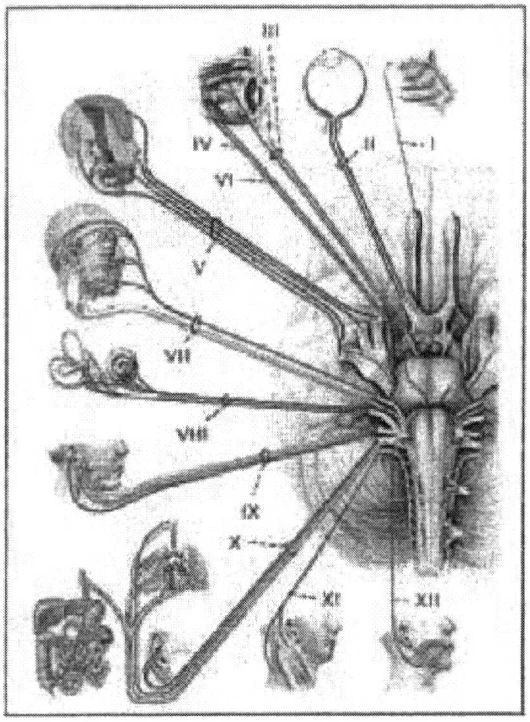

It is also amazing that both the tabernacle in the wilderness and Solomon's temple had three levels of worship. There was an outer court, a mid-court, and a holiest place. Correspondingly, the brain has three levels of functioning. The highest brain, unique to man only, is called the cerebrum, the middle brain is called the animal brain, and the lower brain which enters the skull through the spinal cord is called the reptilian brain. Isaiah called the soul or mind a garden. When one looks at the spinal cord, it appears like a reptile (serpent) is entering the garden.

APPENDIX E

Myra's Anatomy Email to CowgirlGretr Continued

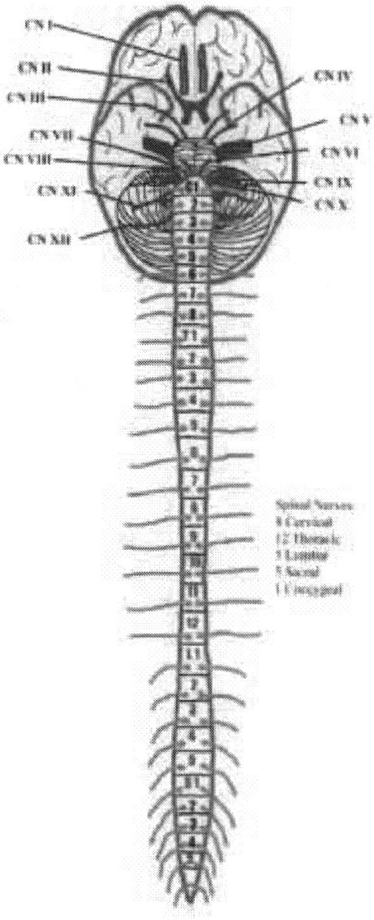

From the internet: Anatomy.med/umich.edu

Paul spoke about *another law in my members, warring against the law of my mind.* It is easy to see the spinal cord serves the nerves in the body and the cranial nerves serve the head. The spinal cord even has the appearance of a serpent as it enters into the garden or the head. Our head is where the battle takes place.

You will also find it amazing that the spinal cord feeds the thirty-one peripheral nerves into the head. What is the significance of thirty-one? Consider that the throne of mind is being contended for between God and Satan. It is the promised land where we must subdue our enemies so we may be at rest from the works of the flesh.

When Joshua went into the promised land, he was told to subdue the kings and take the land. How many kings were there?

And these are the kings of the country which Joshua and the children of Israel smote on this side Jordan ... all the kings thirty and one. (See Joshua chapter 12)

In Solomon's temple, there are thirty chambers around the periphery and one main entry chamber, giving a total of thirty-one chambers. These chambers are arranged in three ascending levels corresponding to the cerebral, animal, and reptilian parts of the brain.

This spinal cord information makes one think twice about trying to raise the energies of spinal cord fire from the bottom up. How much better it is to accept the Holy Spirit and fire from the top of the head down as it happened on the day of Pentecost. The spinal cord will wax old and decay when the celestial body is formed in the place of the terrestrial body. Energizing the spinal cord is like entering a dead end street.

By the way, your associate, Dr. Li, emailed me recently with a spiritual question about karma. I asked her to consider if it might be easier to accept the blood of the Lamb Jesus as a sacrifice for sins rather than trying to work out 'an eye for an eye' and a 'tooth for a tooth'. MATTHEW 5:26 *Verily I say unto thee, Thou shalt by no means come out thence, till thou hast paid the uttermost farthing.* What an impossible task to try, by self effort, to work one's way out of the prison of karma!

Hope this fulfills my promise to you to provide a quick thumbnail sketch of anatomy as shown in the temple and in scriptures. There is so much more, but let's save it for next time.

Andy and I really enjoyed meeting you and Bob. Andy and Bob seem to have really hit it off on their discussions about the universe. Say Hi to Photon Phil.

Your new friend,
Myra

The Ancient Chest

PSALM 91:1,2

He that dwelleth in the secret place of El Elyon shall abide under the shadow of El Shaddai.
I will say of Yahweh, He is my refuge and my fortress: my Elohim; in him will I trust.

See http://www.TheAncient Chest.com for on-line copies
IN FULL COLOR.

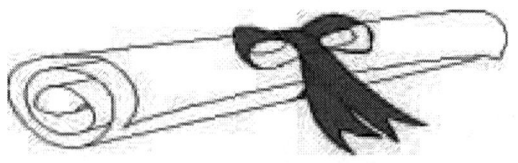

Contents

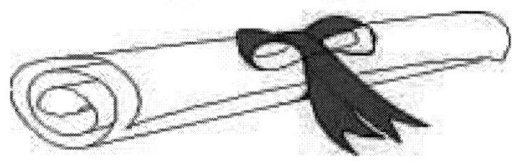

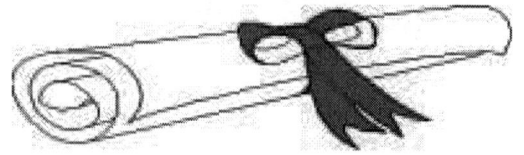

Contents of The Ancient Chest Also Available at
http:// www.TheAncientChest.com
IN FULL COLOR

Dove Marriage Archives

- The Dove Marriage Archive Scrolls
- The Dove Scrolls
- The Dove Marriage Vows
- The Parent's Blessings **[online only]**

Destiny Scrolls

- The Scroll of the Ancients
- Songs of the Ancients

The above documents are free to all online and may be printed out from online for individual use if desired. These documents are not to be sold or packaged with merchandise without first obtaining express, written permission.

Myra's Last Email

Subject: The Old Patterns Foretell the New
Date: September 15, 2002 , 7:47:07 PM Central Daylight Time
From: Myra_Andreas@aol.com
To: Andy_Andreas@aol.com
Sent from the Internet (Details)

Dear Andy,

Thank you for reminding me today is the beginning of the feast of *Sukkot* [or booths]. I'm really looking forward to you joining me soon. We can spend several months catching up. It will be strange to spend both Christmas day and Hanukkah at the beach in Natal instead of walking through the snow.

I think we may have uncovered a pattern in the destiny of the doves. If we are to understand the new, we must be like—as you have said— *every scribe which is instructed unto the kingdom of heaven is like unto a man that is an householder, which bringeth forth out of his treasure things new and old.* Matthew 13:52 I have researched it a little further and I see three patterns emerging involving the uncovering or opening of the ark.

Genesis 8:8 Also he sent forth a dove from him, to see if the waters were abated from off the face of the ground;
9 But the dove found no rest for the sole of her foot, and she returned unto him into the ark, for the waters were on the face of the whole earth: then he put forth his hand, and took her, and pulled her in unto him into the ark. 10 And he stayed yet other seven days; and again he sent forth the dove out of the ark; 11 And the dove came in to him in the evening; and, lo, in her mouth was an olive leaf pluckt off: so Noah knew that the waters were abated from off the earth.
12 And he stayed yet other seven days; and sent forth the dove; which returned not again unto him any more.

The first time the dove left the ark may be compared to Jesus' baptism where he came up out of the water. This was symbolic of the basic salvation given to every Christian—the feast of Passover. *John 1:32 And John bare record, saying, I saw the Spirit descending from heaven like a dove, and it abode upon him. 33 And I knew him not: but he that sent me to baptize with water, the same said unto me, Upon whom thou shalt see the Spirit descending, and remaining on him, the same is he which baptizeth with the Holy Ghost.*

This coming up out of the baptismal waters foretold the next event, for Jesus would return to the Father and ask him to send the dove of the Holy Spirit at the feast of Pentecost. *Acts 2:1 And when the day of Pentecost was fully come, they were all with one accord in one place.2 And suddenly there came a sound from heaven as of a rushing mighty wind, and it filled all the house where they were sitting.3 And there appeared unto them cloven tongues like as of fire, and it sat upon each of them.4 And they were all filled with the Holy Ghost, and began to speak with other tongues, as the Spirit gave them utterance.*

Now, we know the feast of Passover over was fulfilled in the Old Testament when the Hebrews put the blood of the Lamb on their doors in Egypt—and in the New Testament, when Jesus, the sacrificial Lamb was crucified. This is when the feast of Pentecost was fulfilled in the Old Testament in the smoke and fire of Mount Sinai—and afterward in the New Testament upper room [the second story of the ark] on the day of Pentecost. [*When will Isaiah 25:7 covering over the nations finally be lifted?*]

But, as you point out, the third major feast [*known as Sukkot, or Tabernacle, or Ingathering*] has not yet had a New Testament type celebration: *Exodus 23:14* ***Three times*** *thou shalt keep a feast unto me in the year. 15 Thou shalt keep the feast of unleavened bread: (thou shalt eat unleavened bread seven days, as I commanded thee, in the time appointed of the month Abib; for in it thou camest out from Egypt: and none shall appear before me empty:) 16 And the feast of harvest, the firstfruits of thy labours, which thou hast sown in the field: and* ***the feast of ingathering****, which is in the end of the year, when thou hast gathered in thy labours out of the field.*

I wonder what will happen when the dove goes forth for the third time, leaving the top window of the third story of the ark and never returning. Is this when the ark that was symbolically in the tabernacle is fully opened and the face of God is fully revealed? *Isaiah 60:8 Who are these that fly as a cloud, and as the doves to their windows?* Is it possible that when the doves go forth for the third time, they will lift the lid off the ark and reveal the contents of the heavenly ark—signaling the full revelation of Christ to the nations? *Revelation 11:19 And the temple of God was opened in heaven, and there was seen in his temple the* ***ark*** *of his testament: and there were lightnings, and voices, and thunderings, and an earthquake, and great hail.* We may have stumbled on to a revelation—we can discuss it in detail after you arrive.

Love - Myra

PS: When you reach Manaus, give me a call, and I will know when to leave for the Val de Caes Internacional Aeroporto to pick you up. You will get a great view of the Amazon coming into Belém. See you outside customs. Can't wait!

Dove Marriage Archives

Rise up, my love, my fair one, and come away.

________________ & ________________

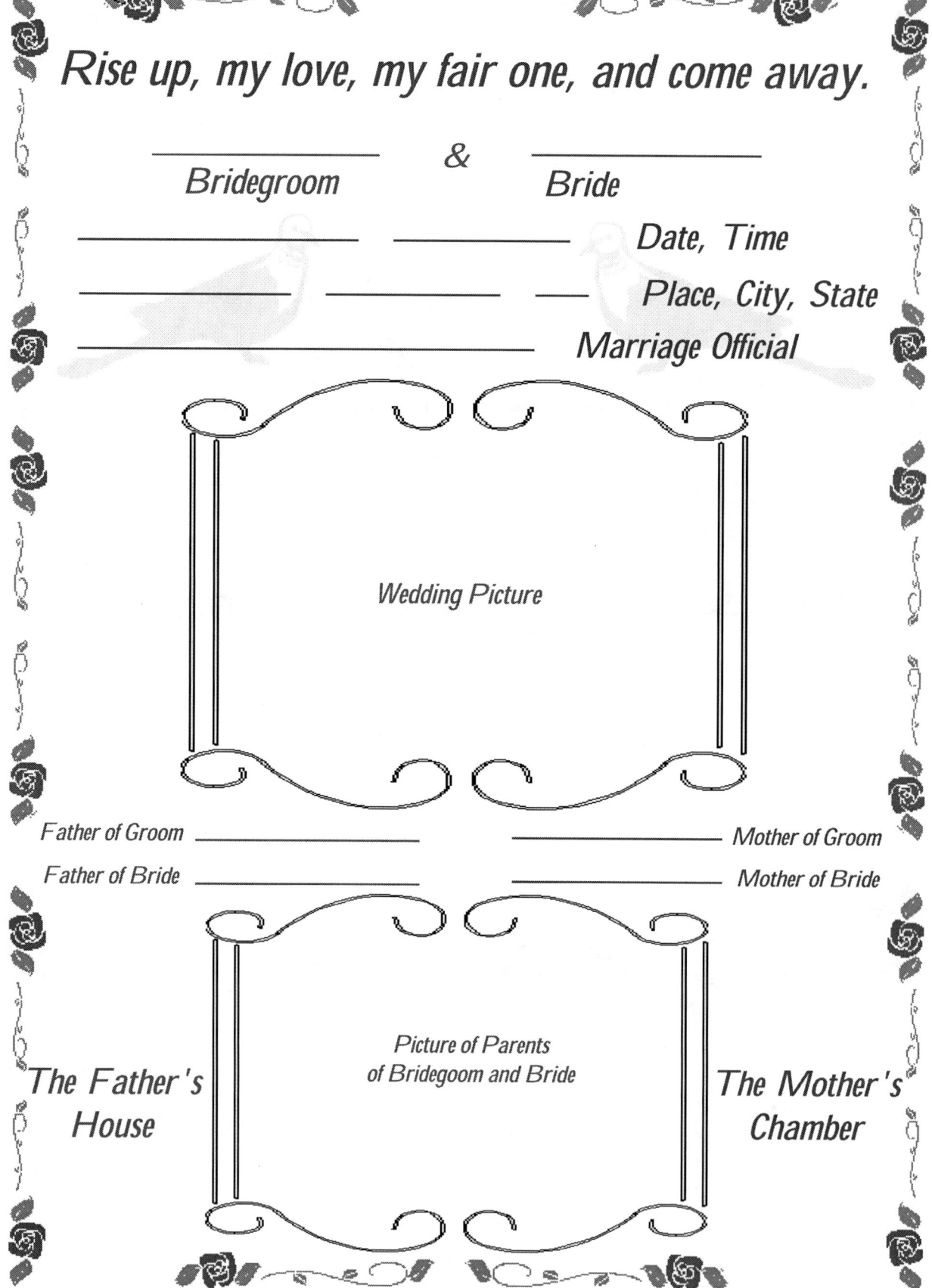

Bridegroom Bride

____________________ ____________ Date, Time

______________ ____________ ___ Place, City, State

________________________________ Marriage Official

Wedding Picture

Father of Groom ________________ ________________ Mother of Groom

Father of Bride ________________ ________________ Mother of Bride

The Father's House

Picture of Parents
of Bridegoom and Bride

The Mother's Chamber

Wedding Party

________________ & ________________

Bridegroom   Bride

____________ ____________ Date, Time

____________ ____________ ____________ Place, City, State

Wedding Party Picture

Bride's Attendants:

____
____
____
____
____
____

Groom's Attendants:

____
____
____
____
____
____

Children of the Doves &

The Father's House ________________ ________________

The Mother's Chamber ________________ ________________

Picture

Picture

Child's Name ________________ ________________
Birthday, Time ________________ ________________
Measurements ________________ ________________
Birth Place ________________ ________________
City, State ________________ ________________

Picture

Picture

Child's Name ________________ ________________
Birthday, Time ________________ ________________
Measurements ________________ ________________
Birth Place ________________ ________________
City, State ________________ ________________

Children of the Doves

The Father's House

&

The Mother's Chamber

______________________ ______________________

______________________ ______________________

Picture

Picture

Child's Name ______________ ______________

Birthday, Time ______________ ______________

Measurements ______________ ______________

Birth Place ______________ ______________

City, State ______________ ______________

Picture

Picture

Child's Name ______________ ______________

Birthday, Time ______________ ______________

Measurements ______________ ______________

Birth Place ______________ ______________

City, State ______________ ______________

Bride # Our Family Tree **Groom**

Paternal Grandparents:

Maternal Grandparents:

Grandparent's Picture

Grandparent's Picture

Father:

Mother:

Mother's Picture

Father's Picture

The Dove Scroll

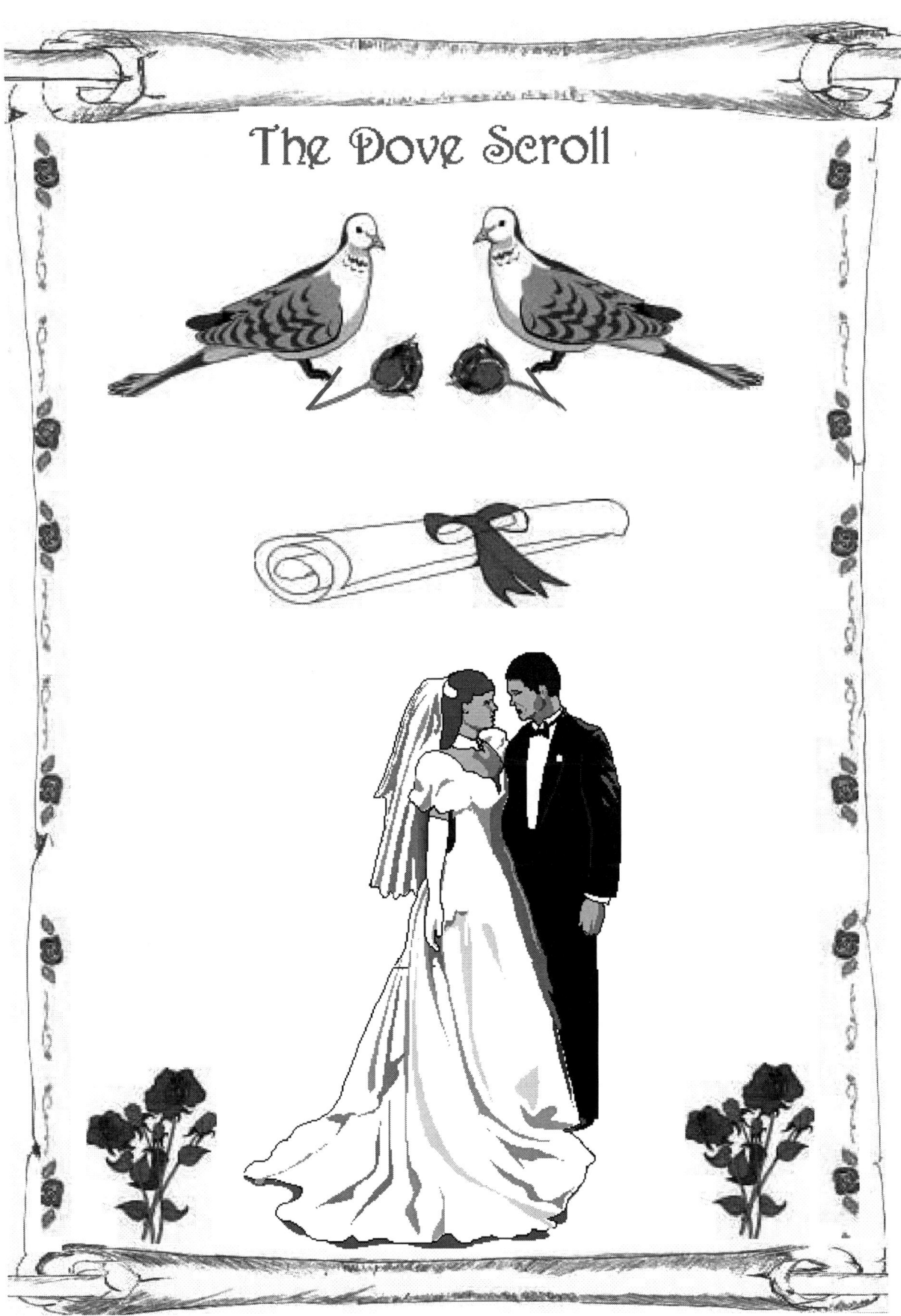

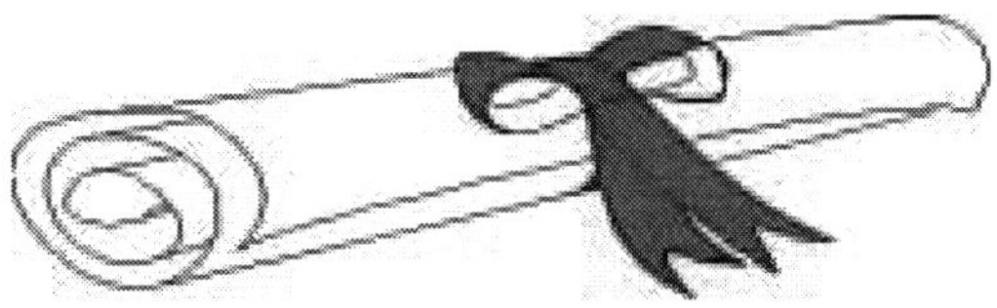

My Love, My Dove

From an ancient people of old, the story of the doves is told. For in the story of the doves is the secret of love's beginning and never ending.

It is a very simple story and yet very profound. Did you know doves are unique and for each other created? You see in the dove's nest, there are always two eggs. One might think in these two eggs might be contained two brothers, or possibly two sisters, or even a brother and sister. But *all* of these combinations do *not* occur. The dove is heaven's symbol of love. And one egg always contains a male dove and the other egg always contains a female dove. For these two doves in the nest were uniquely created for each other from birth. They are destined to be mated with each other from their very creation and birth. And as they mature in the springtime of their birth, there comes a time when the scriptures penned by an ancient king are fulfilled.

> My beloved spake, and said unto me, Rise up, my love, my fair one, and come away.
>
> For, lo, the winter is past, the rain is over and gone;
>
> The flowers appear on the earth; the time of the singing of birds is come, and the voice of the turtle [*dove*] is heard in our land;
>
> The fig tree putteth forth her green figs, and the vines with the tender grape give a good smell. Arise, my love, my fair one, and come away.
>
> O my dove, that art in the clefts of the rock, in the secret places of the stairs, let me see thy countenance, let me hear thy voice; for sweet is thy voice, and thy countenance is comely.

But we know that in this earth those who come into a marriage relationship may not even meet each other until they have matured and are ready for courtship. Others may know each other from childhood and then fall in a more serious love in their later years. But, if we say a marriage is made in heaven, then when does the recognition of that spark of heavenly love come? It is as penned by the prophet that doves come to a window of recognition, and then the doves know they were created for each other.

ISA 60:8 Who are these that fly as a cloud, and as the doves to their windows?

And the ancient king records his description of that wonderful moment when one looks through heaven's window and finds the one that was created for them.

> My beloved is like a roe or a young hart: behold, he standeth behind our wall, he looketh forth at the windows, shewing himself through the lattice.
>
> My beloved spake, and said unto me, Rise up, my love, my fair one, and come away.
>
> For, lo, the winter is past, the rain is over and gone;
>
> The flowers appear on the earth; the time of the singing of birds is come

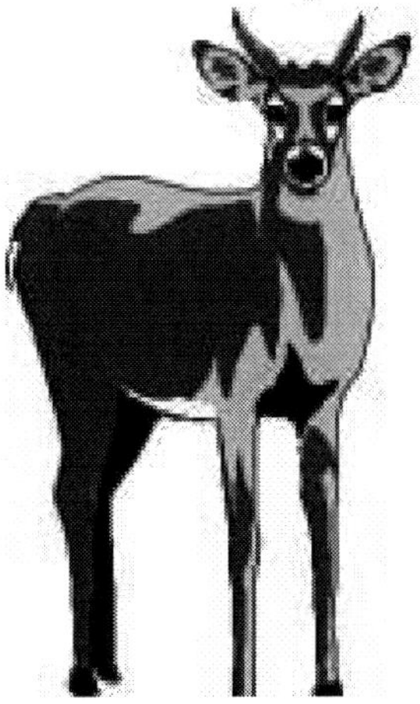

Looking through the window

And the eyes are the window of one's soul. They are the gateway of the beautiful light when one of heaven's spirits first recognizes their dove twin upon the earth. And the ancient king describes his beloved.

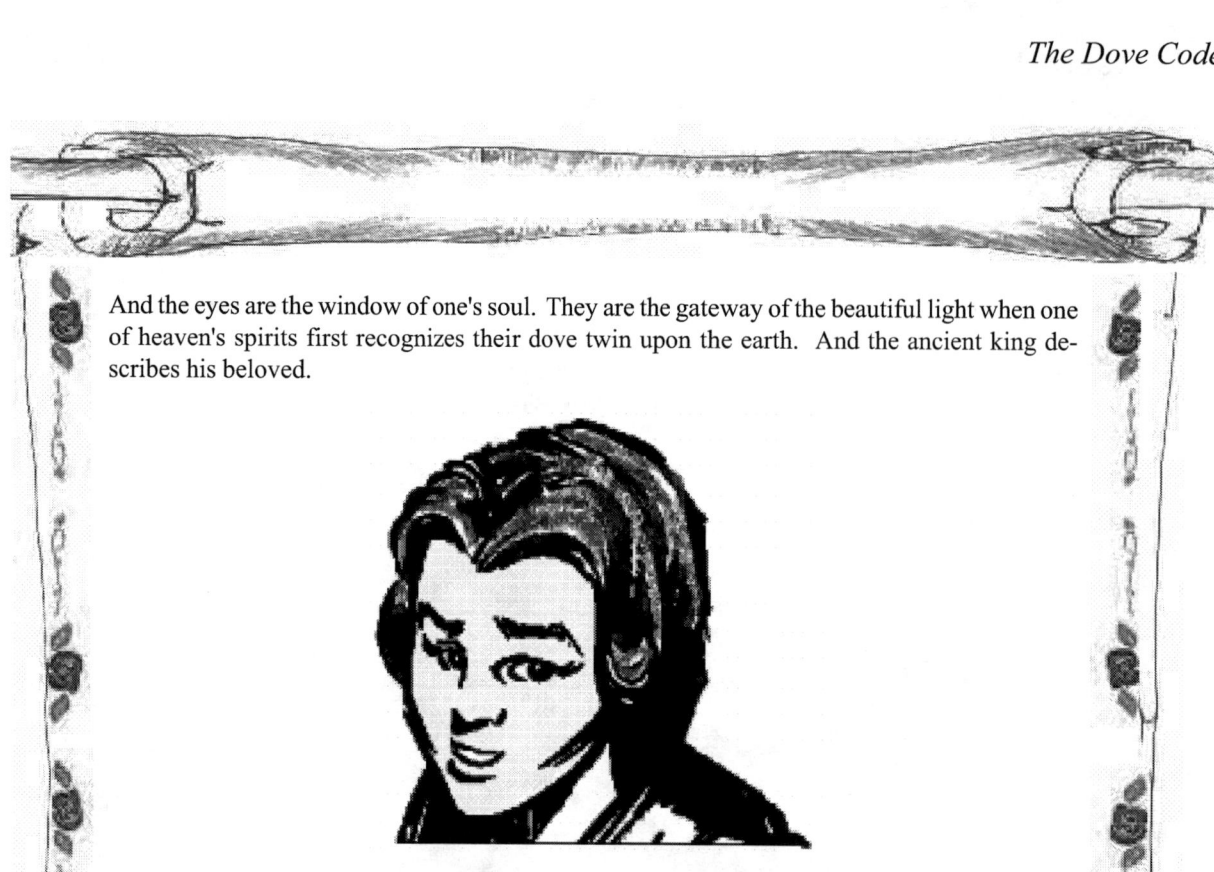

My beloved is unto me as a cluster of camphire in the vineyards of Engedi.

Behold, thou art fair, my love; behold, thou art fair; thou hast doves' eyes.

... behold king Solomon with the crown wherewith his mother crowned him in the day of his espousals, and in the day of the gladness of his heart.

Behold, thou art fair, my love; behold, thou art fair; thou hast doves' eyes within thy locks:

You have encouraged me, O my sister, my bride; you have stolen my heart with a look on one of your eyes, with one necklace of your neck.

And his bride-to-be looks through the window and returns the recognition of the sparkles in the eye seen in the windows of heaven's remembrance.

His eyes are as the eyes of doves by the rivers of waters, washed with milk, and fitly set.

SON 7:4 Thy neck is as a tower of ivory; thine eyes like the fishpools in Heshbon, by the gate of Bathrabbim ...

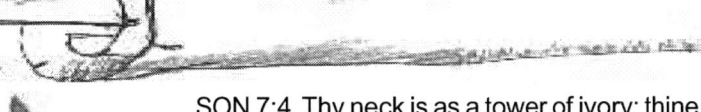

Beautiful is the mystery of the doves meeting one another and looking into the deep pools of each other's eyes. But it is said solving one mystery simply leads to another mystery. And the additional mystery is this: How can it be one can be both a sister and a spouse to her husband at the same time? Not likely that a sister would marry a brother in this earth as we know it today. But is this not what is written by the ancient king and poet?

Thou hast ravished my heart, my sister, my spouse; thou hast ravished my heart with one of thine eyes, with one chain of thy neck.

How fair is thy love, my sister, my spouse! how much better is thy love than wine! and the smell of thine ointments than all spices!

Thy lips, O my spouse, drop as the honeycomb: honey and milk are under thy tongue; and the smell of thy garments is like the smell of Lebanon.

A garden inclosed is my sister, my spouse; a spring shut up, a fountain sealed.

I am come into my garden, my sister, my spouse: I have gathered my myrrh with my spice; I have eaten my honeycomb with my honey; I have drunk my wine with my milk: eat, O friends; drink, yea, drink abundantly, O beloved.

Could it be the twin spirits of the doves were created as sister and brother in the heavens and then at a time and place written upon the pages of destiny, they meet each other in the earth and enter into a spousal relationship? But, to pursue this second mystery, we must look into the very genesis of creation.

GEN 1:26 And God said, Let us make man in our image, after our likeness: and let them have dominion over the fish of the sea, and over the fowl of the air, and over the cattle, and over all the earth, and over every creeping thing that creepeth upon the earth.

GEN 1:27 So God created man in his own image, in the image of God created he him; male and female created he them.

And the second mystery leads to a third mystery. We know God is one God, but who is the "us" that God referred to when He said, "Let us make man in our own image ..."? And if the created being in the image of God were "male and female, would not the creator be the "male and female" that created the created beings in the image of "us"? Could it be God and His companion are in the likeness of doves also? But how could this be? Do we not always think of God in terms of the male gender? But our sense of natural relationships tells us that creation was brought forth in male and female terms when "The Lord by wisdom hath founded the earth ..." Is not Wisdom a "she"? Would a rose by any other name still be a rose? Then if the ancient writings define Wisdom as a "she," then we must consider what is written about her attributes.

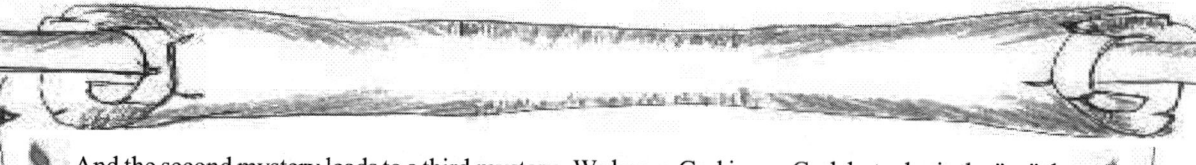

Doth not wisdom cry? and understanding put forth her voice?

She standeth in the top of high places, by the way in the places of the paths.

She is a tree of life to them that lay hold upon her: and happy is every one that retaineth her.

The LORD by wisdom hath founded the earth; by understanding hath he established the heavens.

For do not the ancient proverbs describe the companion of God? "Never!" many would say, but is it not written in the proverbs of the ancient king and poet a description of God's delightful companion called the Wisdom of God?

The LORD possessed me in the beginning of his way, before his works of old.

I was set up from everlasting, from the beginning, or ever the earth was.

Before the mountains were settled, before the hills was I brought forth:

While as yet he had not made the earth, nor the fields, nor the highest part of the dust of the world.

When he prepared the heavens, I was there: when he set a compass upon the face of the depth:

Then I was by him, as one brought up with him: and I was daily his delight, rejoicing always before him;

And there came a day when the Father blessed His beloved Son by sending to Him the Wisdom of God as embodied in His dove of co-creation.

And straightway coming up out of the water, he saw the heavens opened, and the Spirit like a dove descending upon him:

And there came a voice from heaven, saying, Thou art my beloved Son, in whom I am well pleased.

It is only by receiving the Spirit of God's Wisdom that we can begin to fathom the mysteries of the heavens and understand our genesis. So let us now ask for Wisdom from on high to further understand the mysteries of the genesis of the doves. We have spoken of how there are always two dove eggs in one nest. One is always a male dovelet and one is always a female dovelet. These are brother and sister, and yet they are mated as husband dove and wife dove for life. But, in the earth, brothers do not marry sisters—it is forbidden by law.

So, let us examine the creation of these twin spirits in the heavens. Their spirit is later transferred into the flesh and blood of the womb of the earth. We have seen how God is one God and yet has male and female attributes which are passed on to the created image.

So God created man in his own image, in the image of God created he him; male and female created he them.

But what would this image look like? Could it be that the male and female are first together and then separated from each other? "Preposterous!" one might exclaim. But is this not what happened in the creation genesis of man?

And the LORD God caused a deep sleep to fall upon Adam, and he slept: and he took one of his ribs, and closed up the flesh instead thereof;

And the rib, which the LORD God had taken from man, made he a woman, and brought her unto the man.

And Adam said, This is now bone of my bones, and flesh of my flesh: she shall be called Woman, because she was taken out of Man.

Therefore shall a man leave his father and his mother, and shall cleave unto his wife: and they shall be one flesh.

The flesh and bone of Adam was separated out into two parts—one part was called man and one part was called woman.

And how did the created beings look before woman was separated out of man? To attempt to draw this could prove rather difficult. Instead, we will return to our allegorical example of the doves. Those who handle eggs know from time to time there occurs an egg which is slightly larger than usual, and this egg may also have twin yolks inside. God is one God and yet has male and female characteristics. And the beings created were in this same image and were male and female.

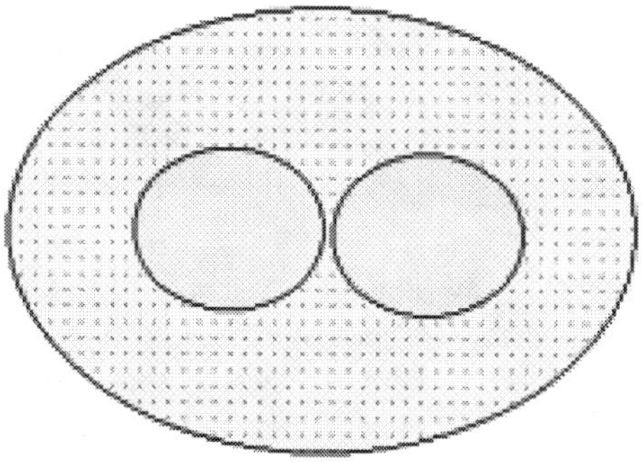

In the heavens, we can think of these two twin spirits created in the image of God as represented by the double yolked dove egg. The ancient king and poet wrote that for those coming into the earth, their spirits would return "unto God who gave it." Therefore, the spirits on earth must have at one time previously been in the heavens.

> Or ever the silver cord be loosed, or the golden bowl be broken, or the pitcher be broken at the fountain, or the wheel broken at the cistern.
>
> Then shall the dust return to the earth as it was: and the spirit shall return unto God who gave it.

Then, could it be these twin dove spirits were separated from each other in the heavens where they were brother and sister—and a veil of forgetfulness was placed over their remembrance of their creation before they were sent into the earth? The ancient poet also wrote:

> All the rivers run into the sea; yet the sea is not full; unto the place from whence the rivers come, thither they return again.
>
> The thing that hath been, it is that which shall be; and that which is done is that which shall be done: and there is no new thing under the sun.
>
> Is there any thing whereof it may be said, See, this is new? it hath been already of old time, which was before us.
>
> There is no remembrance of former things; neither shall there be any remembrance of things that are to come with those that shall come after.

Now, let us trace the path of the twin dove spirits which were created in the heavens in the image of God. We will follow this path of events taking place that results in their being born in the earth and ultimately recognizing each other once again. Let us consider the yolks as representing the twin spirits, and the white of the egg as being the soul or sum total of the mental capabilities of the couple. Then the shell would represent the outer covering or celestial body. And we will say, that similar to Adam and Eve, the surgeon's sword of the Lord separates these twins from one egg into two eggs.

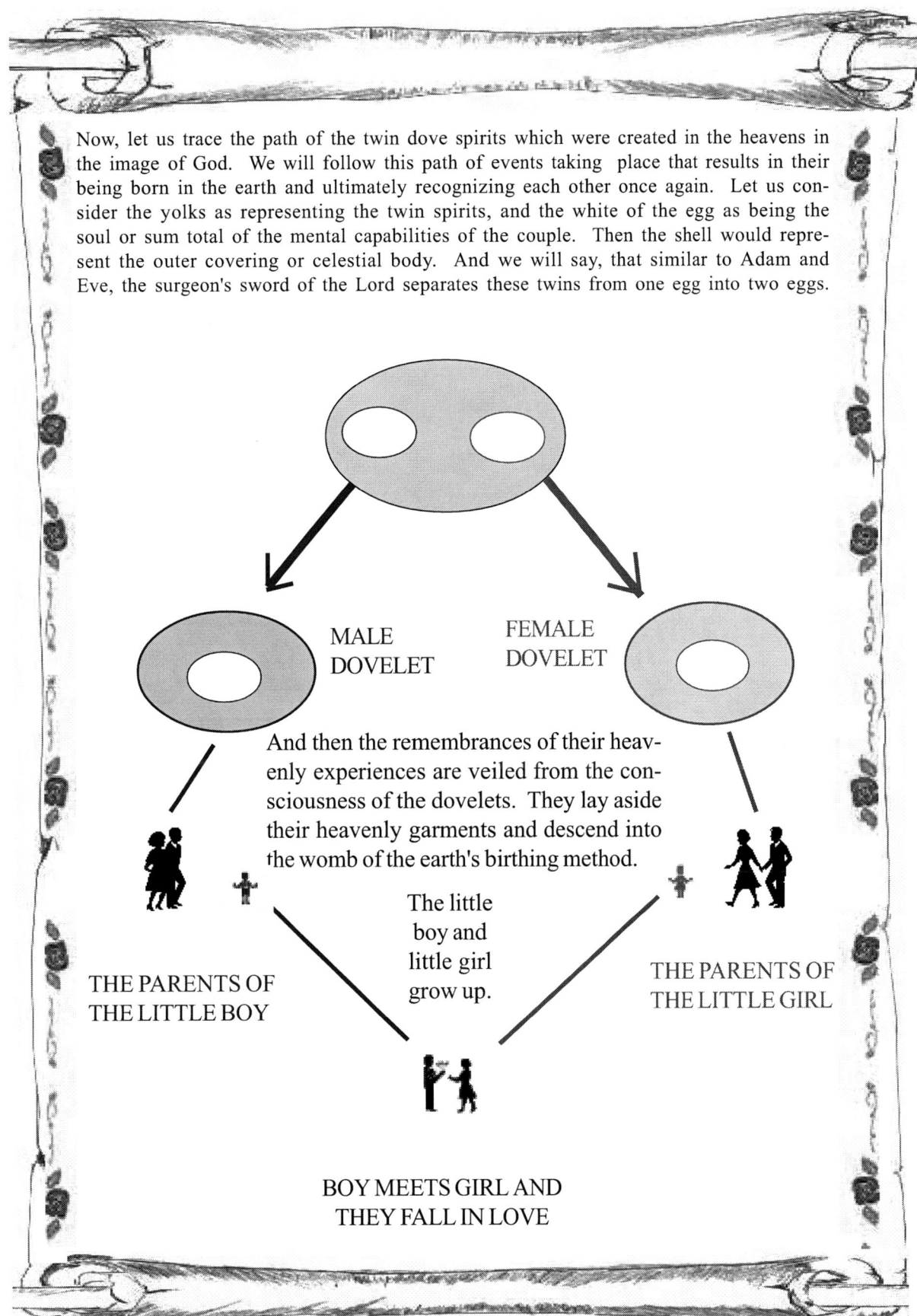

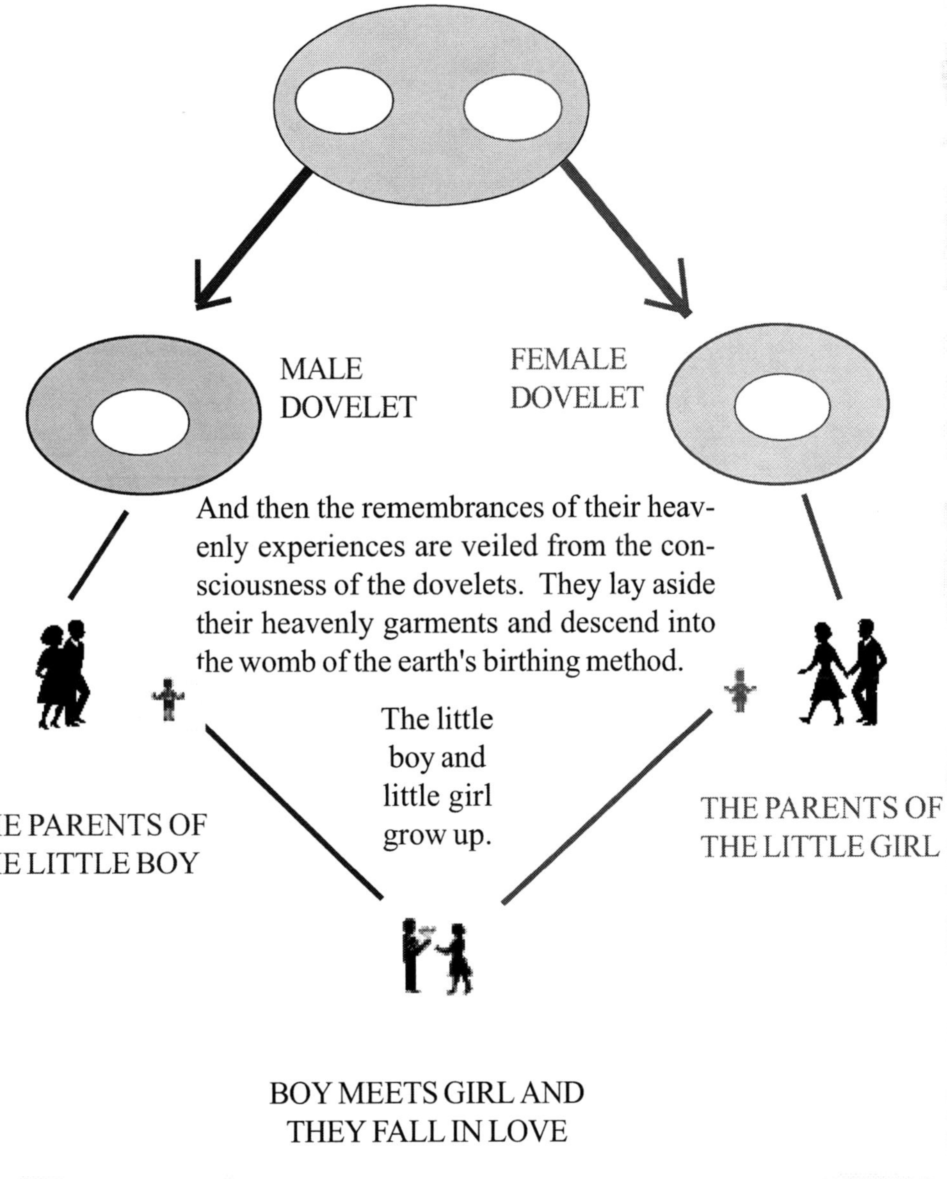
MALE
DOVELET
FEMALE
DOVELET
And then the remembrances of their heavenly experiences are veiled from the consciousness of the dovelets. They lay aside their heavenly garments and descend into the womb of the earth's birthing method.
The little boy and little girl grow up.
THE PARENTS OF THE LITTLE BOY
THE PARENTS OF THE LITTLE GIRL
BOY MEETS GIRL AND THEY FALL IN LOVE

It seems so strange to think of being emptied of the celestial garments of the heavens and to descend into the womb of the earthly birth. But, a heavenly brother of this couple also went through the experience of descending and ascending back into the heavens. And the event is recorded in the scrolls of that time.

... but emptied Himself, taking the form of a bondservant, and being made in the likeness of men.

Touch me not; for I am not yet ascended to my Father: but go to my brethren, and say unto them, I ascend unto my Father, and your Father; and to my God, and your God.

And as we follow the path of the twin dovelets, we find the awakening of the love that these two once knew in the heavens. For it is a time of remembrance and recognition of that which once was. They look through the windows of the each other's eyes and the spark of love is re-ignited.

I charge you, O ye daughters of Jerusalem, by the roes, and by the hinds of the field, that ye stir not up, nor awake my love, till he please.

The voice of my beloved! behold, he cometh leaping upon the mountains, skipping upon the hills.

9 My beloved is like a roe or a young hart: behold, he standeth behind our wall, he looketh forth at the windows, shewing himself through the lattice.

10 My beloved spake, and said unto me, Rise up, my love, my fair one, and come away.

11 For, lo, the winter is past, the rain is over and gone;

Then follows the period of courtship. And recorded in the songs of the wise king are the thoughts of each of the doves toward each other.

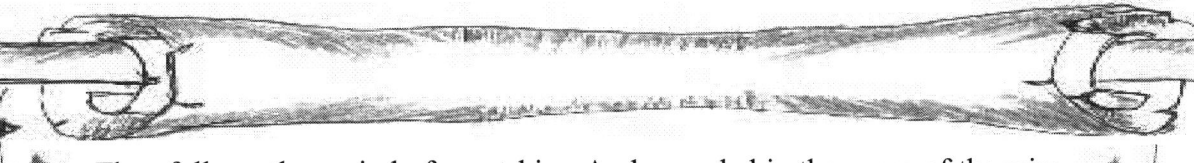

He tells his love the thoughts of his heart ...

Behold, thou art fair, my love; behold, thou art fair; thou hast doves' eyes within thy locks: thy hair is as a flock of goats, that appear from mount Gilead.

Thy teeth are like a flock of sheep that are even shorn, which came up from the washing; whereof every one bear twins, and none is barren among them.

Thy lips are like a thread of scarlet, and thy speech is comely: thy temples are like a piece of a pomegranate within thy locks.

She returns his love with the response from deep within ...

My beloved is white and ruddy, the chiefest among ten thousand.

His head is as the most fine gold, his locks are bushy, and black as a raven.

His eyes are as the eyes of doves by the rivers of waters, washed with milk, and fitly set.

His cheeks are as a bed of spices, as sweet flowers: his lips like lilies, dropping sweet smelling myrrh.

The courtship leads to the making of plans for a very special gathering at a very special place.

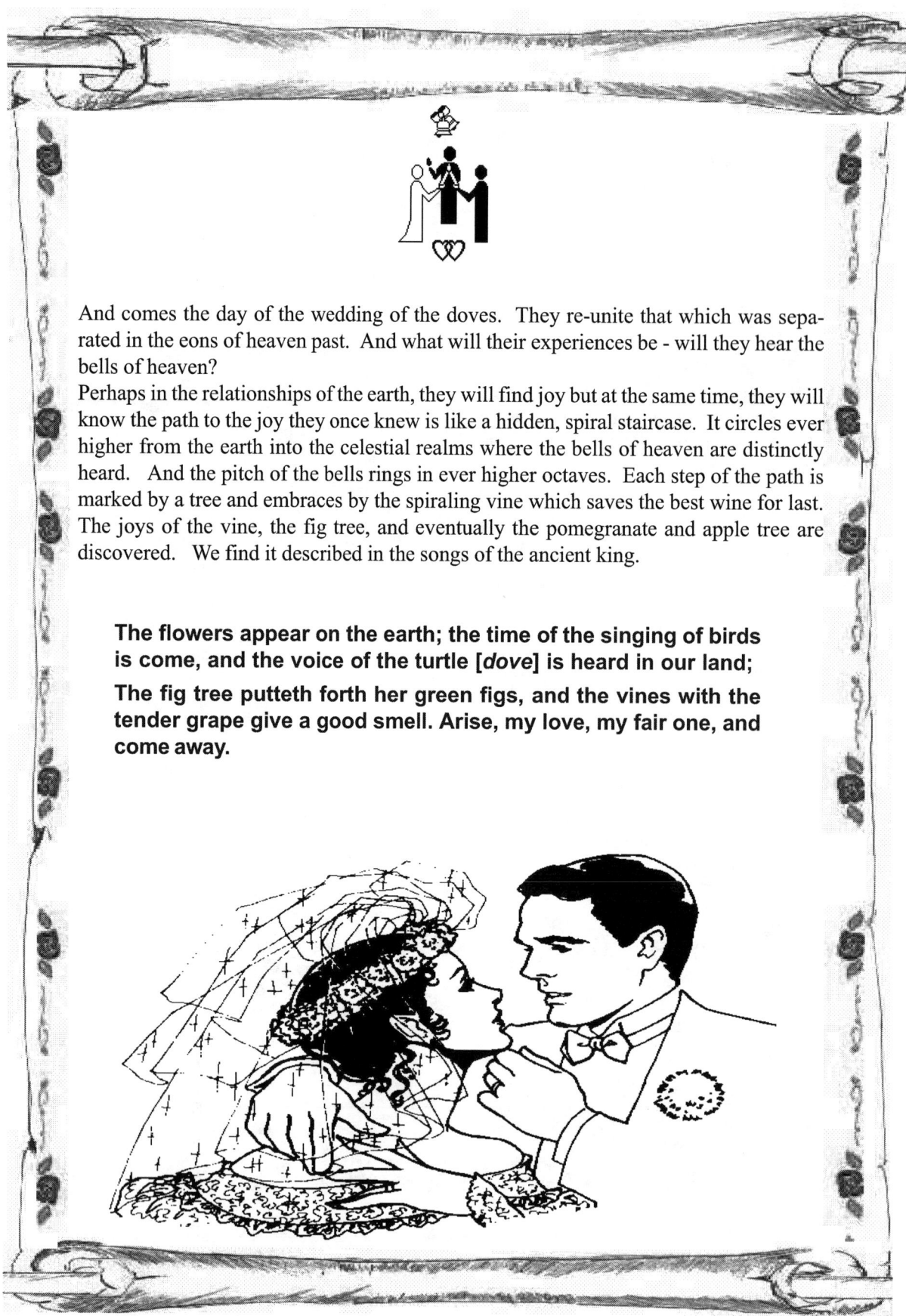

And comes the day of the wedding of the doves. They re-unite that which was separated in the eons of heaven past. And what will their experiences be - will they hear the bells of heaven?

Perhaps in the relationships of the earth, they will find joy but at the same time, they will know the path to the joy they once knew is like a hidden, spiral staircase. It circles ever higher from the earth into the celestial realms where the bells of heaven are distinctly heard. And the pitch of the bells rings in ever higher octaves. Each step of the path is marked by a tree and embraces by the spiraling vine which saves the best wine for last. The joys of the vine, the fig tree, and eventually the pomegranate and apple tree are discovered. We find it described in the songs of the ancient king.

> **The flowers appear on the earth; the time of the singing of birds is come, and the voice of the turtle [*dove*] is heard in our land;**
>
> **The fig tree putteth forth her green figs, and the vines with the tender grape give a good smell. Arise, my love, my fair one, and come away.**

O my dove, that art in the clefts of the rock, in the secret places of the stairs, let me see thy countenance, let me hear thy voice; for sweet is thy voice, and thy countenance is comely.

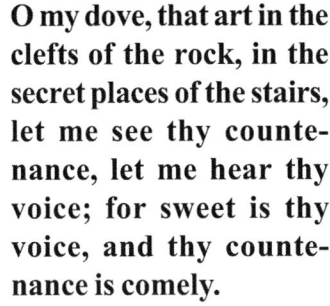

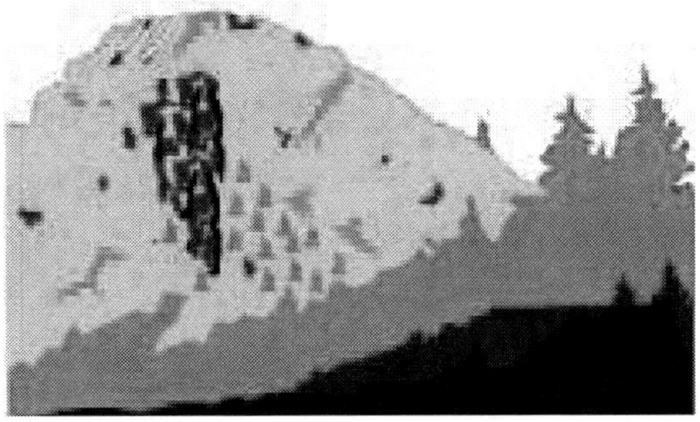

What is this rock which has a cleft in it and contains the "secret places of the stairs"? Is this cleft the window through which the doves fly into the higher realms to hear the bells of heaven? Once upon a time, a patriarch wanted to see the glory of God and he was hidden in the cleft of the rock. He wrote this about the Rock and the tender vegetation planted along the path leading to it.

> Give ear, O ye heavens, and I will speak; and hear, O earth, the words of my mouth.
>
> My doctrine shall drop as the rain, my speech shall distil as the dew, as the small rain upon the tender herb, and as the showers upon the grass:
>
> Because I will publish the name of the LORD: ascribe ye greatness unto our God.
>
> He is the Rock, his work is perfect: for all his ways are judgment: a God of truth and without iniquity, just and right is he.

And the psalmist futher describes the beauty of the ivory palace with the hidden stairs spiraling into the heavens. And the presence of the tender fragrances is found there.

> All thy garments smell of myrrh, and aloes, and cassia, out of the ivory palaces, whereby they have made thee glad.
>
> The king's daughter is all glorious within: her clothing is of wrought gold.
>
> She shall be brought unto the king in raiment of needlework: the virgins her companions that follow her shall be brought unto thee.
>
> With gladness and rejoicing shall they be brought: they shall enter into the king's palace.

Wonderful as the relationships of the earth may be between a bride and bridegroom, the golden harpstrings of the heart long for something more, a remembrance of a love which was higher and greater than can be found on earth.. A remembrance of when the twin spirits were in the youth of their heavenly love under the apple tree of where they were created. This remembrance is recorded in the proverbs and songs of old.

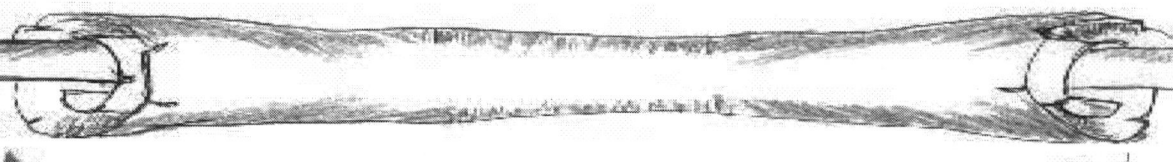

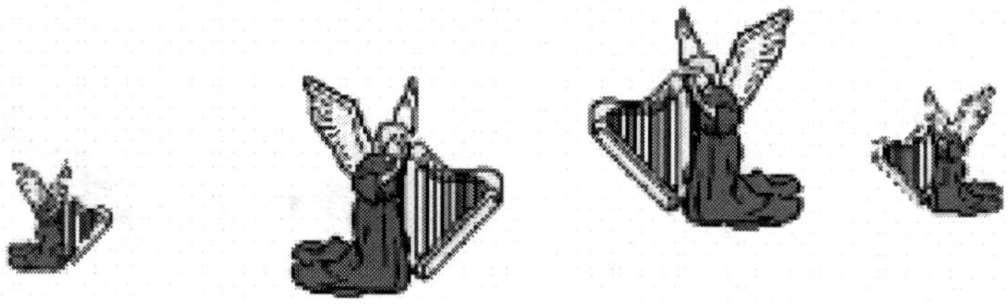

Drink waters out of thine own cistern, and running waters out of thine own well.

Let thy fountains be dispersed abroad, and rivers of waters in the streets.

Let them be only thine own, and not strangers' with thee.

Let thy fountain be blessed: and rejoice with the wife of thy youth.

Let her be as the loving hind and pleasant roe; let her breasts satisfy thee at all times; and be thou ravished always with her love.

As the apple tree among the trees of the wood, so is my beloved among the sons. I sat down under his shadow with great delight, and his fruit was sweet to my taste.

He brought me to the banqueting house, and his banner over me was love.

The wedding ceremony is complete, the honeymoon has been taken and the couple begin the everyday walk of their life together. And life begins to intertwine its various experiences of joy and even sadness into the stream of their lives. And as they follow this stream of life, they realize it is a river whose source they must find. They follow the path along the river and rest from time to time under the trees of experiences. Revelation comes to their understanding.

> And he shewed me a pure river of water of life, clear as crystal, proceeding out of the throne of God and of the Lamb.
>
> In the midst of the street of it, and on either side of the river, was there the tree of life, which bare twelve manner of fruits, and yielded her fruit every month: and the leaves of the tree were for the healing of the nations.

> All the rivers run into the sea; yet the sea is not full; unto the place from whence the rivers come, thither they return again.

For this is a pilgrimage they must make in order to find their source and the completeness of their creation. It is finding the trees of the promised land which grow along the river of life. And as they eat of the fruit of the vine, fig, and pomegranate tree experiences, they come closer to the place of their birthing in the heavens.

> For the LORD thy God bringeth thee into a good land, a land of brooks of water, of fountains and depths that spring out of valleys and hills;
>
> A land of wheat, and barley, and vines, and fig trees, and pomegranates; a land of oil olive, and honey;

And there comes the dawning of blessed day when they discover the path back to mother Wisdom's chamber and the place of the birthing of the their spirits under the apple tree. It is a time of rejoicing for them to return to Father's house. And each twin was given a part of the roadmap of the pathway leading back to the place of their creation. Only by sharing with each other can they piece it together and find their way back. The ancient king and poet describes the dawning of that day when the heavenly sister and heavenly brother return to under the apple tree. And there they will tabernacle together in the eternal realms.

> Come, my beloved, let us go forth into the field; let us lodge in the villages.
>
> Let us get up early to the vineyards; let us see if the vine flourish, whether the tender grape appear, and the pomegranates bud forth: there will I give thee my loves.
>
> The mandrakes give a smell, and at our gates are all manner of pleasant fruits, new and old, which I have laid up for thee, O my beloved.
>
> O that thou wert as my brother, that sucked the breasts of my mother! when I should find thee without, I would kiss thee; yea, I should not be despised.
>
> I would lead thee, and bring thee into my mother's house, who would instruct me: I would cause thee to drink of spiced wine of the juice of my pomegranate.
>
> His left hand should be under my head, and his right hand should embrace me.
>
> I charge you, O daughters of Jerusalem, that ye stir not up, nor awake my love, until he please.
>
> Who is this that cometh up from the wilderness, leaning upon her beloved? I raised thee up under the apple tree: there thy mother brought thee forth: there she brought thee forth that bare thee.

For these two doves have learned the mysteries of the within and the without. She tells her love, "O that thou wert as my brother, that sucked the breasts of my mother! when I should find thee without, I would kiss thee; yea, I should not be despised." Created in the heavens, they knew each other within. Separated from each other and lowered into the realm of the earth, they met each other in the world without. But, in the world without, the happiness that they searched for could only be found in part. Within the harpstrings of their heart, the remembrance begin to return of the days of their youth, and the bride and groom found the window of opening in the cleft of the rock and together ascended the spiraling staircase of love to return to their origins. And the bells of heaven rang out in joy out as one more set of dove twins found their way home. Yes, though they were flesh and blood in pots of clay, they ascend with the wings of a dove as described by the Psalmist.

> Though ye have lien among the pots, yet shall ye be as the wings of a dove covered with silver, and her feathers with yellow gold.

These two doves had found their way home and the ladder of ascension which had only been a dream to them had now become reality. For this was written about by a patriarch of old.

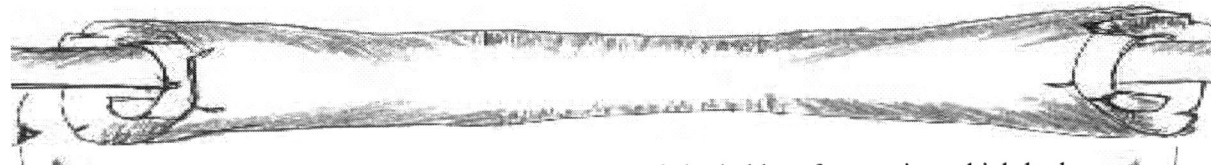

> And he dreamed, and behold a ladder set up on the earth, and the top of it reached to heaven: and behold the angels of God ascending and descending on it.

These doves had heeded the words of One who had taught their spirits before they were sent into the world and now they had returned.

> The kingdom of God cometh not with observation:
>
> Neither shall they say, Lo here! or, lo there! for, behold, the kingdom of God is within you.
>
> This is my commandment, That ye love one another, as I have loved you.

> But these things have I told you, that when the time shall come, ye may remember that I told you of them. And these things I said not unto you at the beginning, because I was with you.
>
> Father, I will that they also, whom thou hast given me, be with me where I am; that they may behold my glory, which thou hast given me: for thou lovedst me before the foundation of the world.

> ... the governor of the feast called the bridegroom,
>
> And saith unto him, Every man at the beginning doth set forth good wine; and when men have well drunk, then that which is worse: but thou hast kept the good wine until now.

> And they came unto the brook of Eshcol, and cut down from thence a branch with one cluster of grapes, and they bare it between two upon a staff; and they brought of the pomegranates, and of the figs.

The best wine of the promised land had been kept for last - for the time of the returning of the doves

* * * * * * *

1

The Scrolls of the Ancients

When we came into the earth the vail placed over our spirits caused us to "forget" our previous experiences of the heavens. And this forgetfulness extended even to forgetting who we were - to the extent that we do not really know our own identity. But, the day will come, and we will know ourselves as we were once known. We will look in the mirror of the Spirit and recognize our own faces.

> 1JO 3:1 Behold, what manner of love the Father hath bestowed upon us, that we should be called the sons of God: **therefore the world knoweth us not, because it knew him not.**
>
> 2 **Beloved, now are we the sons of God, and it doth not yet appear what we shall be: but we know that, when he shall appear, we shall be like him; for we shall see him as he is.**
>
> 3 And every man that hath this hope in him purifieth himself, even as he is pure.

> 2CO 3:16 Nevertheless when it shall turn to the Lord, **the vail shall be taken away**.
>
> 17 Now the Lord is that Spirit: and where the Spirit of the Lord is, there is liberty.
>
> 18 **But we all, with open face beholding as in a glass the glory of the Lord, are changed into the same image** from glory to glory, even as by the Spirit of the Lord.

But is there any record in the scripture of a man remembering the things that he saw in his spirit before he came to this earth? Consider the words of Job that were penned in a day when man truly believed that the earth was flat. Where did Job receive his inspiration?

> JOB 26:7 He stretcheth out the north over the empty place, and **hangeth the earth upon nothing.**
>
> 8 He bindeth up the waters in his thick clouds; and the cloud is not rent under them.
>
> 9 He holdeth back the face of his throne, and spreadeth his cloud upon it.
>
> 10 **He hath compassed the waters with bounds, until the day and night come to an end.**

Look carefully at the description penned by Job. This is something that one would expect an astronaut to write - but not someone like Job whose body was limited to the terra firma of earth. An observer from the moon would view the earth as hanging "upon nothing." The observer would see the bounds where "the day and night come to an end." And he would note how the earth "compassed the waters." In other words, Job - in his spirit - knew the earth was circular long before Galileo.

And yet Job considered himself one of the most miserable of all people - until he encountered the whirlwind. When one is taken up in a whirlwind, they are changed or accelerated from one dimension to another. Enoch was taken up in a whirlwind and so was Elijah. And so it was, when Job had reached the end of himself, the Lord spoke to him out of the whirlwind.

> JOB 38:1 Then **the LORD answered Job out of the whirlwind**, and said,
>
> 2 Who is this that darkeneth counsel by words without knowledge?
>
> 3 Gird up now thy loins like a man; **for I will demand of thee, and answer thou me**.
>
> 4 **Where wast thou when I laid the foundations of the earth**? declare, if thou hast understanding.

JOH 1:1 In the beginning was the Word, and the Word was with God, and the Word was 5
God.
2 The same was in the beginning with God.
3 All things were made by him; and without him was not any thing made that was made.

Thou art not yet fifty
years old, and hast
thou seen Abraham?

JOH 8:56 Your father Abraham rejoiced to see my day: and he saw it, and was glad.
57 Then said the Jews unto him, **Thou art not yet fifty years old, and hast thou seen Abraham**?
58 Jesus said unto them, Verily, verily, I say unto you, **Before Abraham was, I am**.
59 **Then took they up stones to cast at him**: but Jesus hid himself, and went out of the temple, going through the midst of them, and so passed by.

The natural mind has difficulty fathoming the possibility of preexistence of the spirit. The Jews of that day wanted to stone Jesus for even proposing such a possibility. Today, in Christian circles, most will readily accept that Jesus' spirit preexisted and was active before the foundation of the world. But let any propose that their own spirit also preexisted and they will likely be subject to a verbal stoning. But let us examine the scriptures to see if not only Jesus, but a company that was with Him preexisted - even before the foundation of the world.

JOH 14:12 Verily, verily, I say unto you, **He that believeth on me, the works that I do shall he do also; and greater works than these shall he do**; because I go unto my Father.

13 And whatsoever ye shall ask in my name, that will I do, that the Father may be glorified in the Son.

Yes, Yashua's promise to us who believe that even greater works would be done is an amazing promise, but how would we know if our spirits existed before the foundation of the world? Will we bear witness to this in our spirits?

EPH 1:3 Blessed be the God and Father of our Lord Jesus Christ, who hath blessed us with all spiritual blessings in heavenly places in Christ:

4 **According as he hath chosen us in him before the foundation of the world**, that we should be holy and without blame before him in love:

JOH 15:26 But when the Comforter is come, whom I will send unto you from the Father, even the Spirit of truth, which proceedeth from the Father, he shall testify of me:

27 **And ye also shall bear witness, because ye have been with me from the beginning.**

THE CHRIST COMPANY 6

Jesus speaks of a company of believers that are associated with Him from the beginning.

> HEB 2:9 But we see Jesus, who was made a little lower than the angels for the suffering of death, crowned with glory and honour; that he by the grace of God should taste death for every man.
>
> 10 For it became him, for whom are all things, and by whom are all things, **in bringing many sons unto glory**, to make the captain of their salvation perfect through sufferings.
>
> 11 **For both he that sanctifieth and they who are sanctified are all of one: for which cause he is not ashamed to call them brethren**,
>
> 12 Saying, I will declare thy name unto my brethren, **in the midst of the church will I sing praise unto thee**.

If this group of sanctified ones existed with Jesus from the beginning, then what church existed before the church that was formed at Pentecost? Was it a church that existed in the heavens and the firstborn spirits were members?

> HEB 12:22 **But ye are come unto mount Sion, and unto the city of the living God, the heavenly Jerusalem**, and to an innumerable company of angels,
>
> 23 **To the general assembly and church of the firstborn**, which are written in heaven, and to God the Judge of all, and to **the spirits of just men** made perfect,

And was there ever a time that Jesus declared the names of these to the congregation of the church of the firstborn - even at a time before Jesus and they were born in the earth - even in Old Testament times?

> PSA 40:5 Many, O LORD my God, are thy wonderful works which thou hast done, and thy thoughts which are to us-ward: they cannot be reckoned up in order unto thee: **if I would declare and speak of them**, they are more than can be numbered.
>
> PSA 40:6 **Sacrifice and offering thou didst not desire**; mine ears hast thou opened: burnt offering and sin offering hast thou not required.
>
> 7 Then said I, **Lo, I come: in the volume of the book it is written of me**,
>
> 8 I delight to do thy will, O my God: yea, thy law is within my heart.
>
> 9 **I have preached righteousness in the great congregation**: lo, I have not refrained my lips, O LORD, thou knowest.
>
> 10 I have not hid thy righteousness within my heart; I have declared thy faithfulness and thy salvation: **I have not concealed thy lovingkindness and thy truth from the great congregation**.

What great congregation is being referred to in the Psalms? For the above surely prophesies the words of the spirit of Jesus as His spirit was to be lowered into the earth in the form of a newborn babe. These same words are spoken of Him in the New Testament. And what volume of the book are we talking about? In the case of Jesus, all the details of His ministry were written in that book - even the scene from the garden of Gethsemane and the crucifixion. The Old Testament prophets were given glimpses of this book and they prophesied from it.

> HEB 10:5 **Wherefore when he cometh into the world**, he saith, Sacrifice and offering thou wouldest **not, but a body hast thou prepared me**:
>
> 6 In burnt offerings and sacrifices for sin thou hast had no pleasure.
>
> 7 Then said I, **Lo, I come (in the volume of the book it is written of me,) to do thy will**, O God.
>
> 8 Above when he said, Sacrifice and offering and burnt offerings and offering for sin thou wouldest not, neither hadst pleasure therein; which are offered by the law;
>
> 9 Then said he, **Lo, I come to do thy will**, O God. He taketh away the first, that he may establish the second.
>
> 10 By the which will we are sanctified through the offering of the body of Jesus Christ once for all.

THE SPIRIT OF JESUS DESCENDS INTO THE EARTH 7

A Song of the Spirit

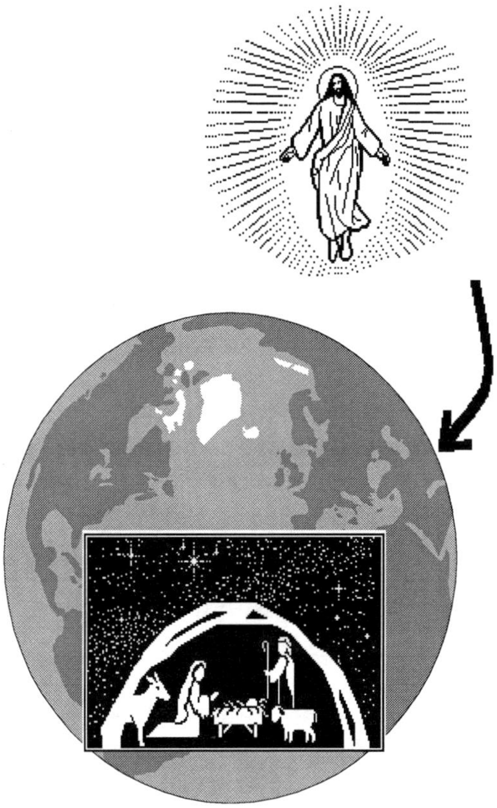

CHORUS

LO, I COME IN THE VOLUME OF THE BOOK

IT IS WRITTEN OF ME TO DO THY WILL, O GOD

LO, I COME, IN THE VOLUME OF THE BOOK

IT IS WRITTEN OF ME TO DO THY WILL, O GOD

LO, I COME TO DO THY WILL, O GOD

LO, I COME TO DO THY WILL, O GOD

LO, I COME TO DO THY WILL, O GOD

LO, I COME IN THE VOLUME OF THE BOOK

IT IS WRITTEN OF ME TO DO THY WILL, O GOD

THE VOLUME OF HIS BOOK

WRITTEN BEFORE THE FOUNDATION OF THE WORLD

REV 13:8 ... the book of life of the Lamb slain from the foundation of the world.

MIC 5:2 But thou, Bethlehem Ephratah, though thou be little among the thousands of Judah, yet out of thee shall he come forth unto me that is to be ruler in Israel; whose goings forth have been from of old, from everlasting.

ISA 9:6 For unto us a child is born, unto us a son is given: and the government shall be upon his shoulder: and his name shall be called Wonderful, Counsellor, The mighty God, The everlasting Father, The Prince of Peace.

ZEC 9:9 Rejoice greatly, O daughter of Zion; shout, O daughter of Jerusalem: behold, thy King cometh unto thee: he is just, and having salvation; lowly, and riding upon an ass, and upon a colt the foal of an ass.

ZEC 11:12 And I said unto them, If ye think good, give me my price; and if not, forbear. So they weighed for my price thirty pieces of silver.

ISA 53:3 He is despised and rejected of men; a man of sorrows, and acquainted with grief: and we hid as it were our faces from him; he was despised, and we esteemed him not.
4 Surely he hath borne our griefs, and carried our sorrows: yet we did esteem him stricken, smitten of God, and afflicted.
5 But he was wounded for our transgressions, he was bruised for our iniquities: the chastisement of our peace was upon him; and with his stripes we are healed.
6 All we like sheep have gone astray; we have turned every one to his own way; and the LORD hath laid on him the iniquity of us all.

A GOOD BOOK HAS A HAPPY ENDING 8

ISA 53:11 He shall see of the travail of his soul, and shall be satisfied: by his knowledge shall my righteous servant justify many; for he shall bear their iniquities.

JOH 20:15 Jesus saith unto her, Woman, why weepest thou? whom seekest thou? She, supposing him to be the gardener, saith unto him, Sir, if thou have borne him hence, tell me where thou hast laid him, and I will take him away.

16 Jesus saith unto her, Mary. She turned herself, and saith unto him, Rabboni; which is to say, Master.

17 Jesus saith unto her, Touch me not; for I am not yet ascended to my Father: but go to my brethren, and say unto them, I ascend unto my Father, and your Father; and to my God, and your God.

REV 21:4 And God shall wipe away all tears from their eyes; and there shall be no more death, neither sorrow, nor crying, neither shall there be any more pain: for the former things are passed away.

5 And he that sat upon the throne said, Behold, I make all things new. And he said unto me, Write: for these words are true and faithful.

6 And he said unto me, It is done. I am Alpha and Omega, the beginning and the end. I will give unto him that is athirst of the fountain of the water of life freely.

And we, as Christians, very well know the story of the volume of the book of Jesus. For before the worlds were created, the Father and the Son discussed the plan and it was written in the volume of His book. Jesus agreed to the plan before His spirit ever came to the earth. It was all there, the role of Herod, Pilate and even Judas. The Old Testament prophets read from a page here and there and they wrote.

ACT 2:25 **For David speaketh concerning him, I foresaw the Lord always before my face**, for he is on my right hand, that I should not be moved:

26 Therefore did my heart rejoice, and my tongue was glad; moreover also my flesh shall rest in hope:

PSA 41:9 Yea, **mine own familiar friend, in whom I trusted**, which did eat of my bread, hath **lifted up his heel against me**.

JOH 13:18 I speak not of you all: I know whom I have chosen: **but that the scripture may be fulfilled**, He that eateth bread with me hath **lifted up his heel against me**.

And we, as Christians, so want to please our Heavenly Father and do the will of God. And what is the will of God concerning us? Would not the **will of God** concerning our lives be written in the volume of the book which is hidden in our hearts to be manifested in our walk upon the earth? **It is our Father's will that we succeed in completing what is written in the volume of our book.**

2CO 3:2 Ye are our epistle written in our hearts, known and read of all men:

3 Forasmuch as **ye are manifestly declared to be the epistle of Christ ministered by us, written not with ink, but with the Spirit of the living God; not in tables of stone, but in fleshy tables of the heart.**

4 And such trust have we through Christ to God-ward:

ROM 8:27 And he that searcheth the hearts knoweth what is the mind of the Spirit, **because he maketh intercession for the saints according to the will of God**.

28 And we know that all things work together for good to them that love God, to them who are the called according to his purpose.

29 **For whom he did foreknow, he also did predestinate to be conformed to the image of his Son**, that he might be **the firstborn** among many brethren.

So the volume of our book need not be a frightening concept. It is an outline of experiences which require choices in order to obtain perfection. And at some appropriate time we will compare what choices we have made in our lives with what is written in the volume of our book. And even the tears - when we realize what opportunities were missed - will be wiped away.

> REV 20:12 And I saw the dead, small and great, stand before God; and **the books were opened**: and another book was opened, which is the book of life: and the dead were judged out of those things which were written in the books, according to their works.
>
> REV 21:4 **And God shall wipe away all tears from their eyes**; and there shall be no more death, neither sorrow, nor crying, neither shall there be any more pain: for the former things are passed away.

It is not difficult for most Christians to accept that there is a plan or a volume of the book for their lives. But what many may find more difficult is the concept that their spirit was with God before they came to earth. And even more mind boggling is the possibility that they, in their spirit, helped plan and even agreed to the words written in the volume of their book before ever being born in the earth. This book is a volume of opportunities presented that will require choices in the earth.

> ECC 12:6 Or ever the silver cord be loosed, or the golden bowl be broken, or the pitcher be broken at the fountain, or the wheel broken at the cistern.
>
> 7 Then shall the dust return to the earth as it was: **and the spirit shall return unto God who gave it.**

In this writing, we will delve into the mysterious subject of what happened in the heavens before our spirits came to earth. Did our spirit say "Lo, I come, in the volume of the book, it is written of me to do thy will." as it departed from the heavens and was lowered into the womb of the earth?

We will approach this subject through the verses of a song entitled, "The Volume of the Book". So, whatever your predisposition of thought is concerning this subject, we would simply ask that you would keep an open mind as we examine this song and accompanying scriptures.

And we will start with the well known **9**
scripture about predestination and foreknowing. Did our spirits really know God and God knew our spirits before we ever came to earth? Was the dwelling place of our spirits with the Lord before we came to earth?

> ROM 8:14 For as **many as are led by the Spirit of God, they are the sons of God**.
>
> 15 For ye have not received the spirit of bondage again to fear; but ye have received the Spirit of adoption, whereby we cry, Abba, Father.
>
> 16 The **Spirit itself beareth witness with our spirit, that we are the children of God**:
>
> 17 And if children, then heirs; heirs of God, **and joint-heirs with Christ**; **if so be that we suffer with him, that we may be also glorified together**.
>
> 18 For I reckon that the sufferings of this present time are not worthy to be compared with the glory which shall be revealed in us.
>
> 19 For the earnest expectation of the creature waiteth for the manifestation of the sons of God.
>
> 20 **For the creature was made subject to vanity, not willingly, but by reason of him who hath subjected the same in hope**,
>
> 21 Because the creature itself also shall be delivered from the bondage of corruption into the glorious liberty of the children of God.
>
> 22 For we know that the whole creation groaneth and travaileth in pain together until now.
>
> 23 And not only they, but ourselves also, which have the firstfruits of the Spirit, even we ourselves groan within ourselves, waiting for the adoption, to wit, the redemption of our body.
>
> 28 **And we know that all things work together for good to them that love God, to them who are the called according to his purpose.**
>
> 29 **For whom he did foreknow, he also did predestinate to be conformed to the image of his Son, that he might be the firstborn among many brethren**.
>
> 30 **Moreover whom he did predestinate, them he also called: and whom he called**, them he also justified: and whom he justified, them he also glorified.
>
> 31 What shall we then say to these things? If God be for us, who can be against us?

Verse One

A LONG TIME AGO WHEN WITH MY SAVIOR FACE TO FACE

I DID AGREE TO THE VOLUME WITH HIS HELP AND GRACE

THE VAILS ARE BEING BROKEN AND I SEE HIS THRONE

THE DAWN BREAKS THROUGH AND I WILL KNOW AS I'M KNOWN

LO, I COME TO DO THY WILL, O GOD

PSA 90:1 **Lord, thou hast been our dwelling place in all generations.**

2 **Before the mountains were brought forth, or ever thou hadst formed the earth and the world**, even from everlasting to everlasting, thou art God.

Can there be any doubt that the spirit of the writer of the above Psalm dwelt with the Lord before the foundation of the earth? For time in the spirit realm is different than time as we know it in the earth realm And when was it that our spirits were chosen in Him for our mission upon this earth?

EPH 1:3 Blessed be the God and Father of our Lord Jesus Christ, who hath blessed us with all spiritual blessings in heavenly places in Christ:

4 **According as he hath chosen us in him before the foundation of the world**, that we should be holy and without blame before him in love:

5 **Having predestinated us unto the adoption of children by Jesus Christ to himself, according to the good pleasure of his will**,

6 To the praise of the glory of his grace, wherein he hath made us accepted in the beloved.

7 In whom we have redemption through his blood, the forgiveness of sins, according to the riches of his grace;

Can there be any doubt that we were chosen in Him **before** the foundation of the world and our predestined adoption was recorded in the volume of our book?

The volume of our book is an outline of the manifest destiny for our lives. So what was predestinated in the heavens would be manifested upon the earth in the fullness of times.

EPH 1:9 **Having made known unto us the mystery of his will**, according to his good pleasure which he hath purposed in himself:

10 **That in the dispensation of the fulness of times** he might gather together in one all things in Christ, both which are in heaven, and which are on earth; even in him:

11 In whom also we have obtained an inheritance, **being predestinated according**

Did we see God face to face when our spirits were with Him? Our remembrance of this was obscured by the vail that was placed over our spirits when we came into the earth. And yet part of the very light of God remained within us, but it was as if we saw through a glass darkly.

1CO 13:12 **For now we see through glass, darkly; but then face to face**: nc I know in part; but then shall **I know even a also I am known**.

JOH 1:2 The same was in the beginning wi God.

4 In him was life; and **the life was the light men**.

5 **And the light shineth in darkness**; and th darkness comprehended it not.

When we came into the earth the vail placed over our spirits caused us to "forget" our previous experiences of the heavens. And this forgetfulness extended even to forgetting who we were - to the extent that we do know really know our own identity. But, the day will come, and we will know ourselves as we were once known. We will look in the mirror of the Spirit and recognize our own faces.

1JO 3:1 Behold, what manner of love the Father hath bestowed upon us, that we should be called the sons of God: **therefore the world knoweth us not, because it knew him not**.

2 **Beloved, now are we the sons of God, and it doth not yet appear what we shall be: but we know that, when he shall appear, we shall be like him; for we shall see him as he is**.

3 And every man that hath this hope in him purifieth himself, even as he is pure.

2CO 3:16 Nevertheless when it shall turn to the Lord, **the vail shall be taken away**.

17 Now the Lord is that Spirit: and where the Spirit of the Lord is, there is liberty.

18 **But we all, with open face beholding as in a glass the glory of the Lord, are changed into the same image** from glory to glory, even as by the Spirit of the Lord.

But is there any record in the scripture of a man remembering the things that he saw in his spirit before he came to this earth? Consider the words of Job that were penned in a day when man truly believed that the earth was flat. Where did Job receive his inspiration?

JOB 26:7 He stretcheth out the north over the empty place, and **hangeth the earth upon nothing.**

8 He bindeth up the waters in his thick clouds; and the cloud is not rent under them.

9 He holdeth back the face of his throne, and spreadeth his cloud upon it.

10 **He hath compassed the waters with bounds, until the day and night come to an end.**

Look carefully at the description penned by Job.[11] This is something that one would expect an astronaut to write - but not someone like Job whose body was limited to the terra firma of earth. An observer from the moon would view the earth as hanging "upon nothing." The observer would see the bounds where "the day and night come to an end." And he would note how the earth "compassed the waters." In other words, Job - in his spirit - knew the earth was circular long before Galileo.

And yet Job considered himself one of the most miserable of all people - until he encountered the whirlwind. When one is taken up in a whirlwind, they are changed or accelerated from one dimension to another. Enoch was taken up in a whirlwind and so was Elijah. And so it was, when Job had reached the end of himself, the Lord spoke to him out of the whirlwind.

JOB 38:1 Then **the LORD answered Job out of the whirlwind**, and said,

2 Who is this that darkeneth counsel by words without knowledge?

3 Gird up now thy loins like a man; **for I will demand of thee, and answer thou me**.

4 **Where wast thou when I laid the foundations of the earth**? declare, if thou hast understanding.

Verse Two

WAS I THERE WHEN PLEIADES AND ORION WERE MADE?

WAS I THERE WHEN THE FOUNDATION OF THE EARTH WAS LAID?

WHEN INTO THE EMPTY PLACE THE EARTH HE HUNG

AND THE SONS OF GOD SHOUTED WHILE THE MORNING STARS SUNG

LO, I COME TO DO THY WILL, O GOD

PRO 8:25 Before the mountains were settled, before the hills was I brought forth:
26 While as yet he had not made the earth, nor the fields, nor the highest part of the dust of the world.

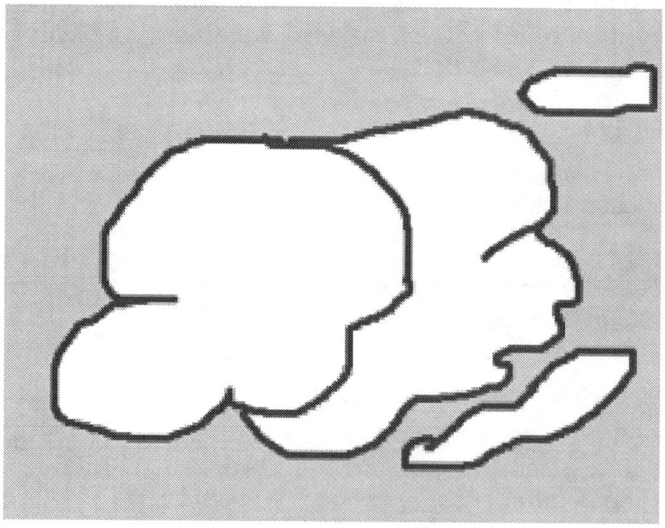

PSA 90:1 Lord, thou hast been our dwelling place in all generations.

2 Before the mountains were brought forth, or ever thou hadst formed the earth and the world, even from everlasting to everlasting, thou art God.

JOB 9:8 Which alone spreadeth out the heavens, and treadeth upon the waves of the sea.

9 Which maketh Arcturus, Orion, and Pleiades, and the chambers of the south.

JOB 38:31 Canst thou bind the sweet influences of Pleiades, or loose the bands of Orion?

32 Canst thou bring forth Mazzaroth in his season? or canst thou guide Arcturus with his sons?

33 Knowest thou the ordinances of heaven? canst thou set the dominion thereof in the earth?

JOB 26:7 He stretcheth out the north over the empty place, and hangeth the earth upon nothing.

10 He hath compassed the waters with bounds, until the day and night come to an end.

13 By his spirit he hath garnished the heavens; his hand hath formed the crooked serpent.

JOB 38:1 Then the LORD answered Job out of the whirlwind, 13
and said,
2 Who is this that darkeneth counsel by words without knowledge?
3 Gird up now thy loins like a man; for I will demand of thee, and
answer thou me.
4 Where wast thou when I laid the foundations of the earth? de-
clare, if thou hast understanding.
5 Who hath laid the measures thereof, if thou knowest? or who hath
stretched the line upon it?
6 Whereupon are the foundations thereof fastened? or who laid the
corner stone thereof;
7 When the morning stars sang together, and all the sons of God
shouted for joy?

The Lord asked Job where he was when the foundations of the earth were laid. And if each of us were asked the same question - how would we reply? Then the Lord put forth the astounding concept that the sons of God and the morning stars watched the earth being formed. Now, in conventional theology, we would say (other than Jesus) that the sons of God came down through the genealogy of Adam - who is referred to as a son of God in Luke 3:38. But Adam, at least in his dust body, did not exist until after the earth was created and the dust was taken to make a body for him (Gen 2:7).

But stand back and look at the above verses from a different perspective. It says that the sons (plural) of God shouted when the foundation of the earth was laid. If the sons of God were not yet created before Adam, then how could they have shouted when the foundation of the earth was laid? The only truly satisfactory explanation is that spirits of the sons of God existed before Adam was ever given a dust body in the earth. Else, how else could anything have existed to shout with the joy of watching creation come forth.

The Lord continued to quiz Job.

JOB 38:18 Hast thou perceived the breadth of the earth? declare if thou knowest it all.

19 Where is the way where light dwelleth? and as for darkness, where is the place thereof,

20 That thou shouldest take it to the bound thereof, and that thou shouldest know the paths to the house thereof?

21 **Knowest thou it, because thou wast then born? or because the number of thy days is great**? (KJV)

JOB 38:21 **You know, for you were born then,** And the number of your days is great! (RSV)

Sometimes a truth is so overwhelming that even the translators have a problem believing it. But after the understanding of Job was elevated in the whirlwind, the Lord, in effect, said to Job that the number of his days was great and that he watched creation take place. How else could Job have penned the words of Job 26:7 - 10 about the earth hanging upon nothing and being encircled by waters?

And who are the morning stars (plural) that sung when the foundation and cornerstone was brought forth in creation's youth? See Psalm 144:12 for a clue.

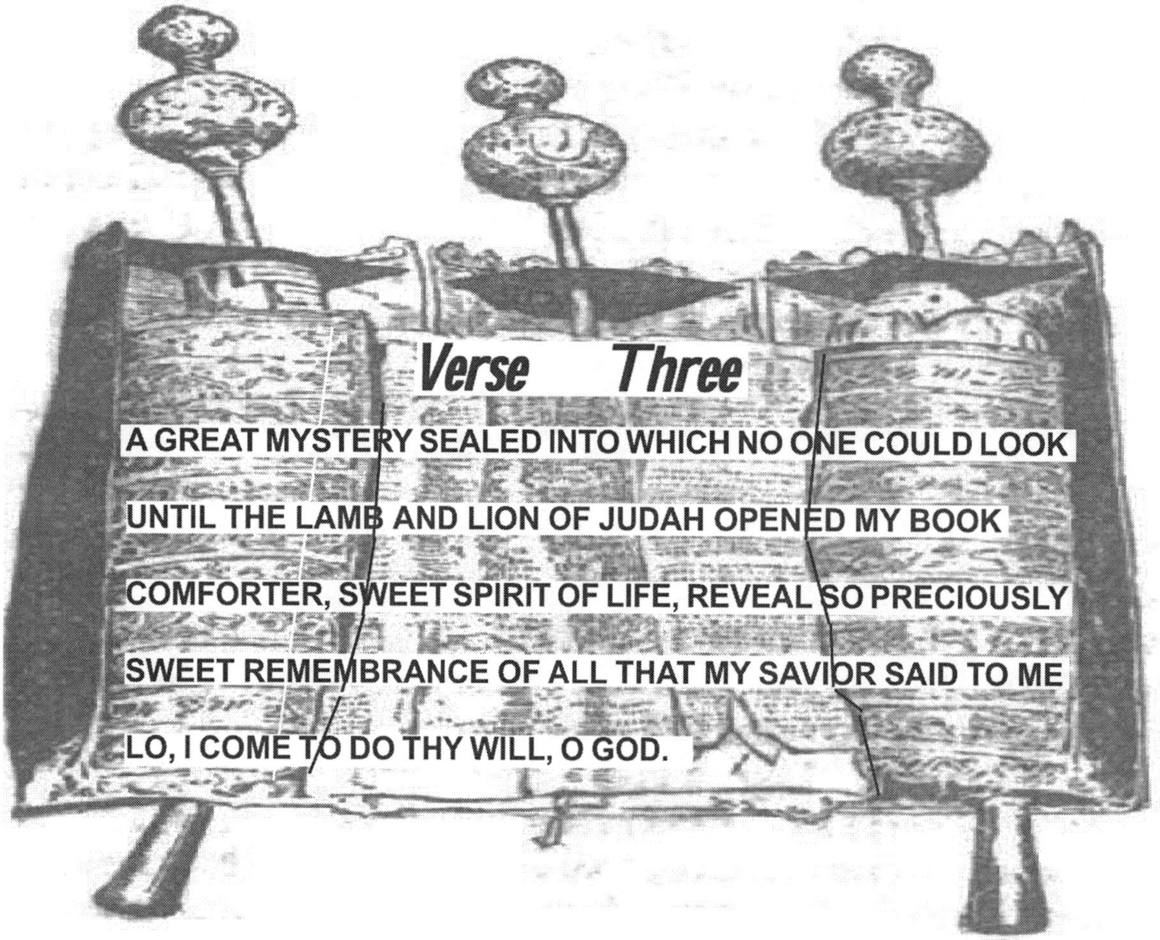
Verse Three
A GREAT MYSTERY SEALED INTO WHICH NO ONE COULD LOOK
UNTIL THE LAMB AND LION OF JUDAH OPENED MY BOOK
COMFORTER, SWEET SPIRIT OF LIFE, REVEAL SO PRECIOUSLY
SWEET REMEMBRANCE OF ALL THAT MY SAVIOR SAID TO ME
LO, I COME TO DO THY WILL, O GOD.

REV 5:1 And I saw in the right hand of him that sat on the throne a book written within and on the backside, sealed with seven seals.
2 And I saw a strong angel proclaiming with a loud voice, Who is worthy to open the book, and to loose the seals thereof?
3 And no man in heaven, nor in earth, neither under the earth, was able to open the book, neither to look thereon.
4 And I wept much, because no man was found worthy to open and to read the book, neither to look thereon.
5 And one of the elders saith unto me, Weep not: behold, the Lion of the tribe of Juda, the Root of David, hath prevailed to open the book, and to loose the seven seals thereof.
6 And I beheld, and, lo, in the midst of the throne and of the four beasts, and in the midst of the elders, stood a Lamb as it had been slain, having seven horns and seven eyes, which are the seven Spirits of God sent forth into all the earth.

Within the book of the Lamb and Lion of Judah is the book of our life. And it is sealed by seven seals. Part of these seals are broken when the Lamb is slain and part are broken by the Seven Spirits of God which are the seven horns and seven eyes of the Lamb - otherwise known as the Holy Spirit. And it is only through the shed blood of Jesus and the ministry of the Spirit of God that the seals will be removed. And once the seals are broken, we will have a remembrance of those events that happened in the beginning. And how is this done?

JOH 14:26 But **the Comforter, which is the Holy Ghost**, whom the Father will send in my name, he **shall teach you all things, and bring all things to your remembrance, whatsoever I have said unto you**.

And yet you might say, when have I been with Jesus? For He walked the earth almost 2000 years ago? But what about remembering what the spirit of Jesus said to your spirit before you descended into the earth? Is this not the ministry of the Holy Spirit to break the seals upon your mind and bring it to you remembrance?

JOH 15:26 But when the Comforter is come, whom I will send unto you from the Father, even **the Spirit of truth, which proceedeth from the Father, he shall testify of me**:
27 **And ye also shall bear witness, because ye have been with me from the beginning**.

If we have been with Him from "the beginning". what beginning are we talking about?

GEN 1:1 **In the beginning God** created the heaven and the earth.

HEB 1:10 And, Thou, Lord, **in the beginning** hast laid the foundation of the earth; and the heavens are the works of thine hands:

ISA 41:4 Who hath wrought and done it, calling the generations from **the beginning**? I the LORD, the first, and with the last; I am he.

There are passages that were written in Jesus' **15**
book from the beginning - even from before the foundation of the world.

JOH 6:64 But there are some of you that believe not. For Jesus knew from **the beginning** who they were that believed not, **and who should betray him**.

REV 13:8 ... written in the book of life of the **Lamb slain from the foundation of the world.**

And have we not known these same things from the beginning?

ISA 40:21 **Have ye not known? have ye not heard? hath it not been told you from the beginning? have ye not understood from the foundations of the earth?**
22 It is he that sitteth upon the circle of the earth, and the inhabitants thereof are as grasshoppers; that stretcheth out the heavens as a curtain, and spreadeth them out as a tent to dwell in:

And it may be that not every one will remember the events of the beginning because there are the "young men" whose spirits were created after the foundation of the earth. But, no matter, because this same information is taught to them by the Holy Spirit and the Father. The young will be given visions of what happened in the beginning and the "old" shall be given remembrance through dreams.

1JO 2:13 **I write unto you, fathers, because ye have known him that is from the beginning**. I write unto you, **young men, because ye have overcome the wicked one.** I write unto you, **little children, because ye have known the Father**.
14 **I have written unto you, fathers, because ye have known him that is from the beginning**. I have written unto you, **young men, because ye are strong, and the word of God abideth in you**, and ye have overcome the wicked one.
ACT 2:17 And it shall come to pass in the last days, saith God, I will pour out of my Spirit upon all flesh: and your **sons and your daughters** shall prophesy, **and your young men shall see visions**, and **your old men shall dream dreams**:

Verse Four

FOR LO, HE DID COMMAND AND SIFT AMONG THE NATIONS

HIS CHILDREN AS GOLDEN GRAIN, THE WINDOWS OF SALVATION

AMONGST EVERY KINDRED, TRIBE, AND PEOPLE THEY WERE GIVEN BIRTH

NOT KNOWING THAT THEY WERE KINGS AND PRIESTS TO REIGN UPON THE EARTH

LO, I COME TO DO THY WILL, O GOD

AMO 9:9 For, lo, I will command, and I will sift the house of Israel among all nations, like as corn is sifted in a sieve, yet shall not the least grain fall upon the earth.
11 In that day will I raise up the tabernacle of David that is fallen, and close up the breaches thereof; and I will raise up his ruins, and I will build it as in the days of old:
13 Behold, the days come, saith the LORD, that the plowman shall overtake the reaper, and the treader of grapes him that soweth seed; and the mountains shall drop sweet wine, and all the hills shall melt.

REV 5:7 And he came and took the book out of the right hand of him that sat upon the throne.
8 And when he had taken the book, the four beasts and four and twenty elders fell down before the Lamb, having every one of them harps, and golden vials full of odours, which are the prayers of saints.
9 And they sung a new song, saying, Thou art worthy to take the book, and to open the seals thereof: for thou wast slain, and hast redeemed us to God by thy blood out of every kindred, and tongue, and people, and nation;
10 And hast made us unto our God kings and priests: and we shall reign on the earth.

The Israel nation of kings and priests in the heavens was sifted as golden grain into the kindreds, tongues, peoples and nations of the earth - so that none would be without representation. And the details of their parents, race, and birth were recorded in the volume of their book. A preview of that last great, endtime harvest was given on the day of Pentecost. And strangely enough, these golden grains were "gathered" together to be at Jerusalem at exactly the right time.

ACT 2:6 Now when this was noised abroad, the multitude came together, and were confounded, **because that every man heard them speak in his own language**.
7 And they were all amazed and marvelled, saying one to another, Behold, are not all these which speak Galilaeans?
8 **And how hear we every man in our own tongue, wherein we were born**?
9 Parthians, and Medes, and Elamites, and the dwellers in Mesopotamia, and in Judaea, and Cappadocia, in Pontus, and Asia,
10 Phrygia, and Pamphylia, in Egypt, and in the parts of Libya about Cyrene, and strangers of Rome, Jews and proselytes,
11 Cretes and Arabians, **we do hear them speak in our tongues the wonderful works of God.**

17
KINGS AND PRIESTS

MAL 3:10 Bring ye all the tithes into the storehouse, that there may be meat in mine house, and prove me now herewith, saith the LORD of hosts, **if I will not open you the windows of heaven**, and pour you out a blessing, that there shall not be room enough to receive it.

The windows of heaven had been opened and these spirits of the king and priest nation of the heavens were dispatched to their destination in the earth. For before the world ever was, in the womb of the morning of creation, an oath was given to the kingly priesthood of Melchisedek. And the promise was made that not the least grain would fall to the ground but those who would go into the sufferings of the earth would return to the throne room of the Father.

PSA 110:1 The LORD said unto my Lord, Sit thou at my right hand, until I make thine enemies thy footstool.
2 The LORD shall send the rod of thy strength out of Zion: rule thou in the midst of thine enemies.
3 Thy people shall be willing in the day of thy power, **in the beauties of holiness from the womb of the morning: thou hast the dew of thy youth.**
4 The LORD hath sworn, and will not repent, **Thou art a priest for ever after the order of Melchizedek.**

Verse Five

IN THE BOOK WERE ALL MY MEMBERS WRITTEN LONG AGO

BEFORE HE FORMED ME IN THE WOMB, HE LOVED ME SO

MY SPIRIT TO EARTH CAME FROM PALACES OF IVORY

HE BREATHED AND LO, THE BREATH OF LIFE ENTERED MY BODY

LO, I COME TO DO THY WILL, O GOD

**PSA 139:13 For thou hast possessed my reins: thou hast cov-
ered me in my mother's womb.
14 I will praise thee; for I am fearfully and wonderfully made:
marvellous are thy works; and that my soul knoweth right well.
15 My substance was not hid from thee, when I was made in
secret, and curiously wrought in the lowest parts of the earth.
16 Thine eyes did see my substance, yet being unperfect; and
in thy book all my members were written, which in continuance
were fashioned, when as yet there was none of them.
17 How precious also are thy thoughts unto me, O God! how
great is the sum of them!**

" ... and in thy book all my members were written, which in continuance were fashioned, when as yet there was none of them." tells us that the volume of the book recorded these details. This means that our birth parents (and / or adoptive parents, and also those that fulfill the role of parents), our physical features, our race, our appearance - all of these details were planned in advance before we were even conceived.

All of us are thrilled to learn of those who overcome physical challenges to lead productive lives. And perhaps even these were recorded in the volume of the book for those who would be known as overcomers. And it would seem that even the DNA in our cells is recorded as part of the volume of our book.

And further, did we agree to accept being born into adversity, whether it be of the physical, mental, or spiritual type? And perhaps those that were born with great beauty or riches have just as much of a cross to bear (vanity) as those who were born into deprived circumstances. Did we discuss the things that we would go through with God before we ever came to this earth? To do this our spirit would have had to have known God and God certainly knew us - as the prophet Jeremiah was told by the Lord, Himself.

JER 1:4 Then the word of the LORD came unto me, saying,
5 **Before I formed thee in the belly I knew thee**; and **before thou camest forth out of the womb I sanctified thee**, and I ordained thee a prophet unto the nations.

There can be little doubt that Jeremiah's spirit accepted his commission in the heavens before he ever came to earth. But perhaps, he did not realize in his spirit form how difficult it would be to walk out his calling in a flesh body.

JER 20:7 O LORD, thou hast deceived me, and I was deceived; **thou art stronger than I**, and hast prevailed: I am in derision daily, every one mocketh me.
8 For since I spake, I cried out, I cried violence and spoil; because the word of the LORD was made a reproach unto me, and a derision, daily.

JER 20:9 Then I said, I will not make mention of him, nor speak any more in his name. **But his word was in mine heart as a burning fire shut up in my bones**, and I was weary with forbearing, and I could not stay.

And what our spirits were very willing to do when we were with God often became an unpleasant choice when we were clothed with the vanity of flesh. Even Jesus found the choices difficult as He labored in the garden of Gethsemane which means "olive press". For the flesh was not a willing partner in overcoming the vanity of the earth.

ROM 8:18 For I reckon that **the sufferings of this present time are not worthy to be compared with the glory which shall be revealed in us**.
19 For the earnest expectation of the creature waiteth for the manifestation of the sons of God.
20 **For the creature was made subject to vanity, not willingly**, but by reason of him who hath subjected the same in hope,
21 Because **the creature itself also shall be delivered** from the bondage of corruption into the glorious liberty of the children of God.

And during the trial of overcoming the flesh and the vanity of the earth, our spirit has a hidden remembrance of the descent into the earth and a yearning to return to its origins in the palace of the heavens above.

GEN 2:7 And the LORD God formed man of the dust of the ground, and **breathed into his nostrils the breath of life; and man became a living soul**.

PSA 45:6 Thy throne, O God, is for ever and ever: the sceptre of thy kingdom is a right sceptre.
7 Thou lovest righteousness, and hatest wickedness: therefore God, thy God, hath anointed thee with the oil of gladness above thy fellows.
8 All thy garments smell of myrrh, and aloes, and cassia, **out of the ivory palaces**, whereby they have made thee glad.

Verse Six

HE PUT MY TEARS IN BOTTLES AT MY GETHSEMANE

WHY DID I AGREE? FOR NOW THY VOWS ARE UPON ME

MY LIFE I HAD PLANNED AND MY RACE I BEGAN TO RUN,

UNTIL, NOT MY WILL BUT THINE BE DONE

LO, I COME TO DO THY WILL, O GOD.

LUK 22:42 Saying, Father, if thou be willing, remove this cup from me: nevertheless not my will, but thine, be done.
43 And there appeared an angel unto him from heaven, strengthening him.
44 And being in an agony he prayed more earnestly: and his sweat was as it were great drops of blood falling down to the ground.
45 And when he rose up from prayer, and was come to his disciples, he found them sleeping for sorrow,

Some of us have lived in the same place virtually all of our lives. Others have moved many times from place to place to place. Have these moves, or lack thereof, been merely chance or quirks of fate - or were they recorded even before we were in our mother's womb?

And for the most part our lives may be free of traumatic events, but each of us have had our share of painful experiences and events which brought tears. Were these experiences also recorded in the volume of our book - or was it merely chance? Let us examine the words of the Psalmist.

> PSA 56:8 **Thou tellest my wanderings: put thou my tears into thy bottle: are they not in thy book?**
> 9 When I cry unto thee, then shall mine enemies turn back: this I know; for God is for me.
> 10 In God will I praise his word: in the LORD will I praise his word.
> 11 In God have I put my trust: I will not be afraid what man can do unto me.

Is it true that our spirit made certain vows to God and God made certain vows to us before we were dispatched into the earth? We continue to read from the lines penned by the psalmist.

> PSA 56:12 **Thy vows are upon me, O God:** I will render praises unto thee.
> 13 For thou hast delivered my soul from death: wilt not thou deliver my feet from falling, that I may walk before God in the light of the living?
> 57:1 Be merciful unto me, O God, be merciful unto me: for my soul trusteth in thee: **yea, in the shadow of thy wings will I make my refuge, until these calamities be overpast.**

And while our life is going very smoothly, we have great confidence in our own talents and abilities. But when the trials and calamities come, we learn that the answer lies in obtaining God's help and protection. And during these periods of great testing and dark nights of the soul, our spirit may yearn, as Job's spirit did, for the days of the youth of his spirit in the heavens above.

> JOB 29:1 Moreover Job continued his parable, and said,
> 2 **Oh that I were** as in months past, as in the days when God preserved me;
> 3 When his candle shined upon my head, and when by his light I walked through darkness;
> 4 **As I was in the days of my youth, when the secret of God was upon my tabernacle**;
> 5 **When the Almighty was yet with me, when my children were about me**;
> 6 When I washed my steps with butter, and the rock poured me out rivers of oil;

Job walked through the valley of weeping called "Baca" and his spirit yearned to return like the swallow to the place of his origins.

> PSA 84:1 How amiable are thy tabernacles, O LORD of hosts!
> 2 **My soul longeth, yea, even fainteth for the courts of the LORD**: my heart and my flesh crieth out for the living God.
> 3 Yea, the sparrow hath found an house, **and the swallow a nest for herself, where she may lay her young, even thine altars, O LORD of hosts**, my King, and my God.
> 4 Blessed are they that dwell in thy house: they will be still praising thee. Selah.
> 5 Blessed is the man whose strength is in thee; in whose heart are the ways of them.
> 6 **Who passing through the valley of Baca** *(weeping)* **make it a well; the rain also filleth the pools.**
> 7 They go from strength to strength, **every one of them in Zion appeareth before God.**

The experiences of the earth are difficult, but necessary in order that we overcome the flesh. Even the enemy has his purpose in this.

> ISA 54:16 Behold, I have created the smith that bloweth the coals in the fire, and that bringeth forth an instrument for his work; and **I have created the waster to destroy.**

So, did we agree to these experiences before our spirit was dispatched from the heavens to the earth? These truths are examined in the heart and we here record on the following page a message of the heart as given to one of His saints.

The Volume of the Book 22

I have a beginning, I have an ending, and I have another beginning, saith the Lord. Yea, you have heard my word even as you have come into this place, saith God. Yea, in this day, I will send you forth now into a new day. For you have sung about it, you have taught it, you have spoken it, you have thought about it, and now it is time to do it, saith the Lord.

Yea, I say unto thee, Sons and Daughters, this is my day. You are my day. You are my love. You are my life. You are my beginning and ending. You are my all, and in all. For I have invested my very life in you, and I trust you - I know you. I've known you from the beginning, and I'll know you to the end, and to the new beginning. And I know what you're capable of, I know what you'll do, I know how you'll handle it, and you will make it saith the Lord.

Yea, for surely I have stripped thee. Did you not hear the word that I created the waster to destroy, saith the Lord? Yea, I hardened that loved one that lives right within the walls of your own home, saith the Lord. I direct thy every move, saith God. Thy every circumstance, saith the Lord, is ordered by my hand. And you knew it, when we agreed upon it before the foundations of the earth. We talked about it, we discussed it, we agreed upon it

I've not lost control. I've not been moved off of my throne by any of your circumstances, any of your trials, nor will I ever be moved by any of your circumstances, by any of your trials - for I sent them! They were right out from me. For I am making you - because I love you. Because I want to show you my love. I do these things for you, not against you.

I do these things because I chose you. You are my beloved. So lift up you heads, Oh ye gates. Even lift them up, ye everlasting doors. For the King of Glory has come in.

Who is this king of Glory? The Lord of Hosts - the Lord of armies. He has come in. Arise, shine, for the glory of the Lord has arisen upon thee, my children. The glory of the Lord has arisen upon thee my children! My glory is upon thee - and the world shall see.

The gross darkness, yea, it will cover the people - but not thee - for my glory is upon thee. It radiates from thy very being.

PSA 24:7 Lift up your heads, O ye gates; and be ye lift up, ye everlasting doors; and the King of glory shall come in.
8 Who is this King of glory? The LORD strong and mighty, the LORD mighty in battle.

ISA 60:1 Arise, shine; for thy light is come, and the glory of the LORD is risen upon thee.
2 For, behold, the darkness shall cover the earth, and gross darkness the people: but the LORD shall arise upon thee, and his glory shall be seen upon thee.

The possibility that many of our trials and tribulations may have been planned in the volume of our book is a difficult concept. But, the Lord knows what combinations of circumstances and choices are needed to bring about our perfection.

ROM 8:18 **For I reckon that the sufferings of this present time are not worthy to be compared with the glory which shall be revealed in us.**
20 For the creature was made subject to vanity, not willingly, but by reason of him who hath subjected the same in hope,
21 **Because the creature itself also shall be delivered from the bondage of corruption into the glorious liberty of the children of God.**

And this poses some rather difficult questions about the volume of the book of pharaoh and also that of Joseph's brothers who betrayed him.

EXO 10:1 And the LORD said unto Moses, Go in unto Pharaoh: **for I have hardened his heart**, and the heart of his servants, that I might shew these my signs before him:

GEN 45:6 For these two years hath the famine been in the land: and yet there are five years, in the which there shall neither be earing nor harvest.
7 **And God sent me before you to preserve you a posterity in the earth, and to save your lives by a great deliverance.**
8 **So now it was not you that sent me hither, but God**: and he hath made me a father to Pharaoh, and lord of all his house, and a ruler throughout all the land of Egypt.

And also, what about the volume of the book of Esau and Jacob. Was God unfair?

ROM 9:11 **(For the children being not yet born, neither having done any good or evil,** that the purpose of God according to election might stand, not of works, but of him that calleth;)
12 It was said unto her, The elder shall serve the younger.

ROM 9:13 **As it is written, Jacob have I loved, but Esau have I hated.**
14 What shall we say then? **Is there unrighteousness with God?** God forbid.

Why was Jacob elected or chosen and Esau rejected? Is it not true that some of these choices were made before the foundation of the world?

EPH 1:4 **According as he hath chosen us in him before the foundation of the world**, that we should be holy and without blame before him in love:

Because a vail was placed over our remembrance of the time before we came to earth, we may not be completely aware of the reasons that these choices were made. And we, like Job, will be very much puzzled until the Lord elevates our understanding and speaks to us from the whirlwind. But, consider the following scripture.

PRO 18:14 The spirit of a man will sustain his infirmity; **but a wounded spirit who can bear?**

If there is a wounded spirit, then there must be one who inflicts the wound and one who receives the wound. And we know little of what happened in the spirit realm of the heavens, but those who wounded the spirits of others in the heavens may not have been chosen in the election. And those spirits not elected may have played the roles of the pharaohs and Esaus in the earth. For souls of those not elected had difficulty in submitting to the spirit man.

1TI 5:24 Some men's sins are open beforehand, going before to judgment; and some men they follow after.
25 Likewise also the good works of some are manifest beforehand; and they that are otherwise cannot be hid.

Verse Seven

TO HOLD MY PEACE WHILE MEN SUFFER WILL BE AMISS

AM I CALLED TO THE KINGDOM FOR SUCH A TIME AS THIS?

WILL THE KING HOLD OUT HIS SCEPTER WHEN I ENTER THE DOOR?

WHAT SURPRISES AWAIT ME OR HAVE I BEEN THIS WAY BEFORE?

LO, I COME TO DO THY WILL, O GOD

EST 4:11 All the king's servants, and the people of the king's provinces, do know, that whosoever, whether man or woman, shall come unto the king into the inner court, who is not called, there is one law of his to put him to death, except such to whom the king shall hold out the golden sceptre, that he may live: but I have not been called to come in unto the king these thirty days.
12 And they told to Mordecai Esther's words.
13 Then Mordecai commanded to answer Esther, Think not with thyself that thou shalt escape in the king's house, more than all the Jews.
14 For if thou altogether holdest thy peace at this time, then shall there enlargement and deliverance arise to the Jews from another place; but thou and thy father's house shall be destroyed: and who knoweth whether thou art come to the kingdom for such a time as this?

In the theatre, there is a tradition, that no matter what happens that the play must go on. And for this reason, in addition to the main actors and actresses, there are understudies. And should an unexpected illness or accident occur, the understudy has been trained to step in and play the role.

And now we wrestle with the concepts of what happens when those whose volume of the book calls for a certain choice and they choose to make other choices. Does God have understudies who will step in and fulfill the mission?

> EST 4:13 Then Mordecai commanded to answer Esther, Think not with thyself that thou shalt escape in the king's house, more than all the Jews.
> 14 **For if thou altogether holdest thy peace at this time, then shall there enlargement and deliverance arise to the Jews from another place**; but thou and thy father's house shall be destroyed: and **who knoweth whether thou art come to the kingdom for such a time as this**?

And we must learn not to presume upon God that because we are called to a certain role, that we have an automatic guarantee that we will always have that role.

> EST 1:17 For this deed of the queen shall come abroad unto all women, so that they shall despise their husbands in their eyes, when it shall be reported, **The king Ahasuerus commanded Vashti the queen to be brought in before him, but she came not.**

Queen Esther played her role because the previous Queen Vashti was replaced. And so it was that Esther was placed in a strategic position with access to the inner court in a time of a terrible trial for her people. But this placement also presented a dilemma to her. If she went into the inner court without being called, she risked death if she was greeted by the king's displeasure. On the other hand, Mordecai told her that she would not escape the decree against her people if she did nothing. So, as she walked she pondered what to do. Was she called to the kingdom for such a time as this?

Then Esther summoned up her courage and made a decision - if I perish, I perish - I will go into the inner court and intercede for my people.

> EST 5:1 **Now it came to pass on the third day, that Esther put on her royal apparel, and stood in the inner court of the king's house**, over against the king's house: and the king sat upon his royal throne in the royal house, over against the gate of the house.
> 2 And it was so, when the king saw Esther the queen standing in the court, that she obtained favour in his sight: **and the king held out to Esther the golden sceptre that was in his hand**. So Esther drew near, and touched the top of the sceptre.
> 3 Then said the king unto her, What wilt thou, queen Esther? **and what is thy request? it shall be even given thee to the half of the kingdom.**

And you know the story of how Queen Esther brought deliverance to her people.

And there is the story of another who brought deliverance to His people. And you might think that His decision would have been an easy decision, since it had been planned for all eternity. But He had a choice, and the choice had to be made. Did He come to the kingdom for such a time as this?

> JOH 12:23 And Jesus answered them, saying, The hour is come, that the Son of man should be glorified.
> 24 Verily, verily, I say unto you, **Except a corn of wheat fall into the ground and die, it abideth alone: but if it die, it bringeth forth much fruit**.
> 25 **He that loveth his life shall lose it; and he that hateth his life in this world shall keep it unto life eternal**.
> 26 If any man serve me, let him follow me; and where I am, there shall also my servant be: if any man serve me, him will my Father honour.
> 27 **Now is my soul troubled; and what shall I say? Father, save me from this hour: but for this cause came I unto this hour.**

If Jesus struggled with His soul in the garden of Gethsemane, we can expect a struggle also.

The wedding of the spirit and soul

Note in the illustration above that the man has a bride in his mind which represents the soul. Paul said that our mind was to be presented as a chaste bride.

2CO 11:2 For I am jealous over you with godly jealousy: for I have espoused you to one husband, **that I may present you as a chaste virgin to Christ.**
3 But I fear, **lest by any means, as the serpent beguiled Eve through his subtilty, so your minds should be corrupted from the simplicity that is in Christ.**

Note also in the illustration above that the woman has a bride in her mind or soul. So she, too, has the battleground of the soul in the garden - even as Jesus struggled with His soul.

JOH 12:27 **Now is my soul troubled**; and what shall I say? Father, save me from this hour: but for this cause came I unto this hour.

LUK 22:42 Saying, Father, if thou be willing, remove this cup from me: **nevertheless not my will, but thine, be done**.

It may seem strange for a natural man to have a feminine soul (Greek - *psuche*) in his mind - but how else can he **conceive** thoughts. And besides, is it not true that Christian men desire to be part of the bride of Christ? The soul or the mind is espoused to Christ.

But, let us look further at the illustration. Note that the woman has an inner man in her heart. Is this not rather strange? And yet consider what was said about Sarah by the Apostle Peter.

1PE 2:25 For ye were as sheep going astray; **but are now returned unto the Shepherd and Bishop of your souls**.

3:1 Likewise, ye wives, be in subjection to your own husbands; that, if any obey not the word, they also may without the word be won by the conversation of the wives;

2 While they behold your chaste conversation coupled with fear.

3 Whose adorning let it not be that outward adorning of plaiting the hair, and of wearing of gold, or of putting on of apparel;

4 **But let it be the hidden man of the heart, in that which is not corruptible, even the ornament of a meek and quiet spirit**, which is in the sight of God of great price.

5 For after this manner in the old time the holy women also, who trusted in God, adorned themselves, being in subjection unto their own husbands:

6 Even as **Sara** obeyed Abraham, calling him lord: whose daughters ye are, as long as ye do well, and are not afraid with any amazement.

The above verses clearly show that Jesus is the Bishop, Shepherd and Bridegroom of our souls. His spirit resides within our meek and quiet spirit as the "inner man". It is Jesus in this inner man that is the bridegroom of our souls. And it makes no difference whether in the natural we are male or female, we, as Christians, still have the Christ in the inner man of the heart. And as we accept the work of Jesus in our heart and the ministry of the Holy Spirit in our minds, our spirit and soul are married together and we walk as one with our Savior for His purposes and according to His will.

For the difficulties began in earnest in the garden when the feminine soul was separated out from the human spirit and was given a choice of who it would love.

2CO 11:2 For I am jealous over you with godly jealousy: for I have espoused you to one husband, **that I may present you as a chaste virgin to Christ**.

3 But I fear, lest by any means, **as the serpent beguiled Eve through his subtilty**, so your minds should be corrupted from the simplicity that is in Christ.

4 For if he that cometh preacheth another Jesus, whom we have not preached, **or if ye receive another spirit**, which ye have not received, or another gospel, which ye have not accepted, ye might well bear with him.

Jesus struggled in the garden of Gethsemane with problems of the soul and so we, both natural men and natural women, struggle with problems of our soul. But, in finality, our soul is wedded to the inner Christ man in our human spirit and we are part of the bride of Christ. And then the feminine soul will be subject to the spirit (husband) and the soulish voice will no longer be heard in the church.

1CO 14:28 But if there be no interpreter, **let him keep silence in the church**; and let him speak to himself, and to God.

29 Let the prophets speak two or three, and let the other judge.

30 If any thing be revealed to another that sitteth by, let the first hold his peace.

31 For ye may all prophesy one by one, that all may learn, and all may be comforted.

32 **And the spirits of the prophets are subject to the prophets**.

And why did God permit the soul to have a choice separate from the spirit? Think of all the suffering that would have been avoided if the soul had to automatically follow the spirit. The parents of teenagers have often thought that it would be much simpler if their children were programmed like robots and would obey their every order. But, in the final analysis, is this what the parents really want? Because, by taking the gift of choice away, the children would never reach the potential desired for them by the parents. And, so God took a risk, and the creature was subjected to vanity so that ultimately the creature might come into the glorious liberty of the children of God.

Verse Eight

TO HIS OVERCOMERS ALL THINGS WORK TOGETHER FOR GOOD

AS THE AUTHOR AND FINISHER OF OUR FAITH KNEW IT WOULD

FOR HE AND WE FOREKNEW OUR MANIFEST DESTINY

FORGOTTEN AND VEILED, YET TO IT WE DID ONCE AGREE

LO, I COME TO DO THY WILL, O GOD

Scribe's Ink Pen

HEB 12:1 Wherefore seeing we also are compassed about with so great a cloud of witnesses, let us lay aside every weight, and the sin which doth so easily beset us, and let us run with patience the race that is set before us,
2 Looking unto Jesus the author and finisher of our faith; who for the joy that was set before him endured the cross, despising the shame, and is set down at the right hand of the throne of God.
5 And ye have forgotten the exhortation which speaketh unto you as unto children, My son, despise not thou the chastening of the Lord, nor faint when thou art rebuked of him:
6 For whom the Lord loveth he chasteneth, and scourgeth every son whom he receiveth.
7 If ye endure chastening, God dealeth with you as with sons; for what son is he whom the father chasteneth not?

EPH 3:14 For this cause I bow my knees unto the Father of our Lord Jesus Christ,
15 Of whom the whole family in heaven and earth is named,
16 That he would grant you, according to the riches of his glory, **to be strengthened with might by his Spirit in the inner man;**
17 **That Christ may dwell in your hearts** by faith; that ye, being rooted and grounded in love,

The inner man in our spirit is part of the sonship of God and will, as a son, go through trials, chastenings, and testings. But, these trials and testings are not without purpose, for they are designed to bring us to perfection.

ROM 826 Likewise the Spirit also helpeth our infirmities: for we know not what we should pray for as we ought: but the Spirit itself maketh intercession for us with groanings which cannot be uttered.
27 And he that searcheth the hearts knoweth what is the mind of the Spirit, because he maketh intercession for the saints according to the will of God.
28 **And we know that all things work together for good to them that love God, to them who are the called according to his purpose**.
29 **For whom he did foreknow, he also did predestinate to be conformed to the image of his Son**, that he might be the firstborn among many brethren.

And yes, all things do work together for good to them that love God, and are called according to his purpose. But God's purposes have a balance. We must avoid the fatalism of simply saying that we did some erroneous deed simply because it was written in the volume of our book and then continue in the same deeds. There is a balance between God's judgement and grace. The concept of the volume of the book is not an excuse to transgress the will of God. Instead, it presents choices to us, that when the right choice is made, we will do His will.

And doing His will has its' grade school, high school, and college. Consider these very difficult tests in the senior year of college of God's will.

We will look at the difficult tests given to Abraham and to Moses in the college of God's will.

GEN 18:22 And the men turned their faces from thence, and went toward Sodom: **but Abraham stood yet before the LORD.**
23 And Abraham drew near, and said, **Wilt thou also destroy the righteous with the wicked?**
24 Peradventure there be fifty righteous within the city: wilt thou also destroy and not spare the place for the fifty righteous that are therein?

EXO 32:9 And the LORD said unto Moses, I have seen this people, and, behold, it is a stiffnecked people:
10 **Now therefore let me alone, that my wrath may wax hot against them, and that I may consume them**: and **I will make of thee a great nation**.
11 **And Moses besought the LORD his God, and said, LORD, why doth thy wrath wax hot against thy people**, which thou hast brought forth out of the land of Egypt with great power, and with a mighty hand?

One of the toughest tests of the senior year is graduation from servanthood to friendship with God. Did not God pose to Abraham that He would wipe out everybody in Sodom and Gomorrah - even Lot? Did not God propose to Moses that He would completely wipe the Hebrew nation off the face of the earth and instead raise up offspring from Moses? The servant would have stepped aside as a robot, but the friend is honest in searching the deep truths of the heart and enters into a dialog with God to find His true will. Lo, I come to do thy will, O God. Our understanding of the will of God changes as we mature in Him and fulfill the volume of our book.

JOH 15:15 **Henceforth I call you not servants; for the servant knoweth not what his lord doeth: but I have called you friends; for all things that I have heard of my Father I have made known unto you.**

JAM 2:23 And the scripture was fulfilled which saith, Abraham believed God, and it was imputed unto him for righteousness: and **he was called the Friend of God**.

Verse Nine

HE SENT MY SPIRIT FROM HEAVEN TO EARTH AND LO!

FOR OF HIM, AND THROUGH HIM, AND TO HIM WE GO

FOR THE AUTHOR WROTE FOR US A WONDERFUL STORY

OF HOW THE FIRSTBORN LEADS SONS AND DAUGHTERS TO GLORY

LO, I COME TO DO THY WILL, O GOD

The Transfiguration

HEB 2:9 But we see Jesus, who was made a little lower than the angels for the suffering of death, crowned with glory and honour; that he by the grace of God should taste death for every man.
10 For it became him, for whom are all things, and by whom are all things, in bringing many sons unto glory, to make the captain of their salvation perfect through sufferings.
11 For both he that sanctifieth and they who are sanctified are all of one: for which cause he is not ashamed to call them brethren,

ROM 11:33 O the depth of the riches both of the wisdom and knowledge of God! how unsearchable are his judgments, and his ways past finding out!
34 For who hath known the mind of the Lord? or who hath been his counsellor?
35 Or who hath first given to him, and it shall be recompensed unto him again?
36 **For of him, and through him, and to him, are all things**: to whom be glory for ever. Amen.

It seems that our spirits have come upon a long journey from the heavens to the earth and we, like Jesus will complete the circuit back to the Father's throne.

ECC 1:6 The wind goeth toward the south, and turneth about unto the north; it whirleth about continually, and **the wind returneth again according to his circuits**.
7 **All the rivers run into the sea; yet the sea is not full; unto the place from whence the rivers come, thither they return again**.
8 All things are full of labour; man cannot utter it: the eye is not satisfied with seeing, nor the ear filled with hearing.
9 **The thing that hath been, it is that which shall be;** and that which is done is that which shall be done: and there is no new thing under the sun.
10 Is there any thing whereof it may be said, See, this is new? it hath been already of old time, which was before us.

What is the mission that is recorded in the volume of our book? What is our purpose for having come to this earth? Each of us, like Jesus, will come to an understanding of these questions.

JOH 18:37 Pilate therefore said unto him, Art thou a king then? Jesus answered, Thou sayest that I am a king. **To this end was I born, and for this cause came I into the world, that I should bear witness unto the truth**. Every one that is of the truth heareth my voice.

And every one that is of truth will witness to His voice and the truths that were given before the foundation of the world.

2TI 1:9 Who hath saved us, and called us with an holy calling, not according to our works, **but according to his own purpose and grace, which was given us in Christ Jesus before the world began,**
10 But is now made manifest by the appearing of our Saviour Jesus Christ, who hath abolished death, and hath brought life and immortality to light through the gospel:

And how shall we know the deep things and the hidden glory that was ordained before the world was? Is it not revealed to us by the Spirit of God?

1CO 2:7 **But we speak the wisdom of God in a mystery, even the hidden wisdom, which God ordained before the world unto our glory:**
8 Which none of the princes of this world knew: for had they known it, they would not have crucified the Lord of glory.
9 But as it is written, Eye hath not seen, nor ear heard, neither have entered into the heart of man, the things which God hath prepared for them that love him.
10 **But God hath revealed them unto us by his Spirit: for the Spirit searcheth all things, yea, the deep things of God.**

And now, El Elyon - Most High God, we come to you in the name and through the shed blood of Yashua, our Savior. We ask that because Jesus made the way, that the Holy Spirit would remove the seals and reveal the deep things of God to each one seeking to fulfill the volume of their book. Father, we ask that they may return to your throne and that You would tabernacle within them. Amen.

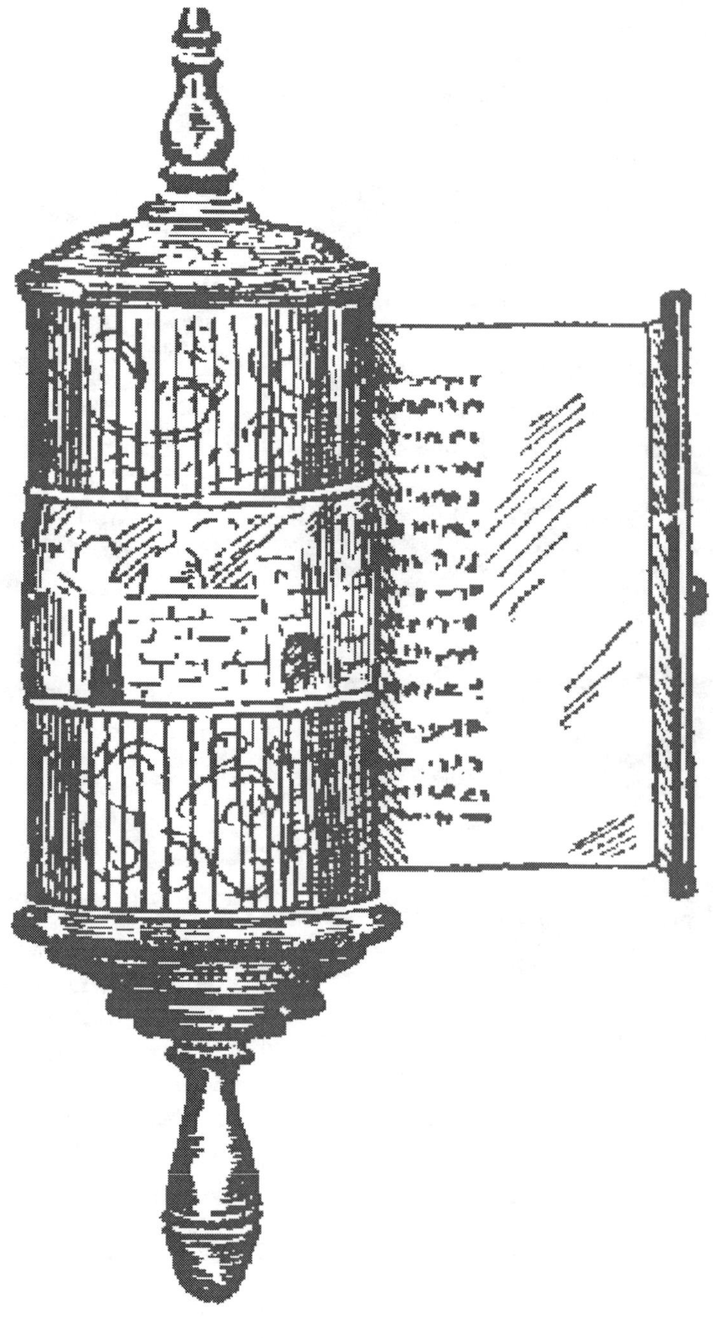

Hebrew Manuscript

A beginning, an ending, and a new beginning.

Songs of the Ancients

Contents of The Songs of the Ancients available at

http://www.TheAncientChest.com/Destiny

The Volume of the Book

Verses

1. A long time ago when with my Savior face to face
I did agree to the volume with his help and grace
The vails are being broken and I see his throne
The dawn breaks through and I will know as I'm known
Lo, I come to do thy will, O God

2. Was I there when Pleiades and Orion were made?
Was I there when the foundation of the earth was laid?
When into the empty place the earth he hung
And the sons of God shouted while the morning stars sung
Lo, I come to do thy will, O God

3. A great mystery sealed into which no one could look
Until the lamb and lion of Judah opened my book
Comforter, sweet spirit of life, reveal so preciously
Sweet remembrance of all that my Savior said to me
Lo, I come to do thy will, O God.

4. For lo, he did command and sift among the nations
His sons as golden grain, the windows of salvation
Amongst every kindred, tribe, and people they were given birth
Not knowing that they were kings and priests to reign upon the earth
Lo, I come to do thy will, O God

5. In the book were all my members written long ago
Before He formed me in the womb, he loved me so
My spirit to earth came from palaces of Ivory
He breathed and Lo, the breath of Life entered my body
Lo, I come to do thy will, O God

6. He put my tears in bottles at my Gethsemane
Why did I agree? For now thy vows are upon me
My life I had planned and my race i began to run,
Until, not my will but thine be done
Lo, I come to do thy will, O God.

7. To hold my peace while men suffer will be amiss
Am I called to the kingdom for such a time as this?
Will the King hold out his scepter when I enter the door?
What surprises await me or have I been this way before?
Lo, I come to do thy will, O God

8. To his overcomers all things work together for good
As the author and finisher of our faith knew it would
For he and we foreknew our manifest destiny
Forgotten and veiled, yet to it we did once agree
Lo, I come to do thy will, O God

9. He sent my spirit from heaven to earth and lo!
For of him, and through him, and to him we go
For the author wrote for us a wonderful story
Of how the firstborn leads sons and daughters to glory
Lo, I come to do thy will, O God

The Volume of the Book

Song is copyrighted.
Permission is granted
to print sheet music.

Anon. / Rita Livingston

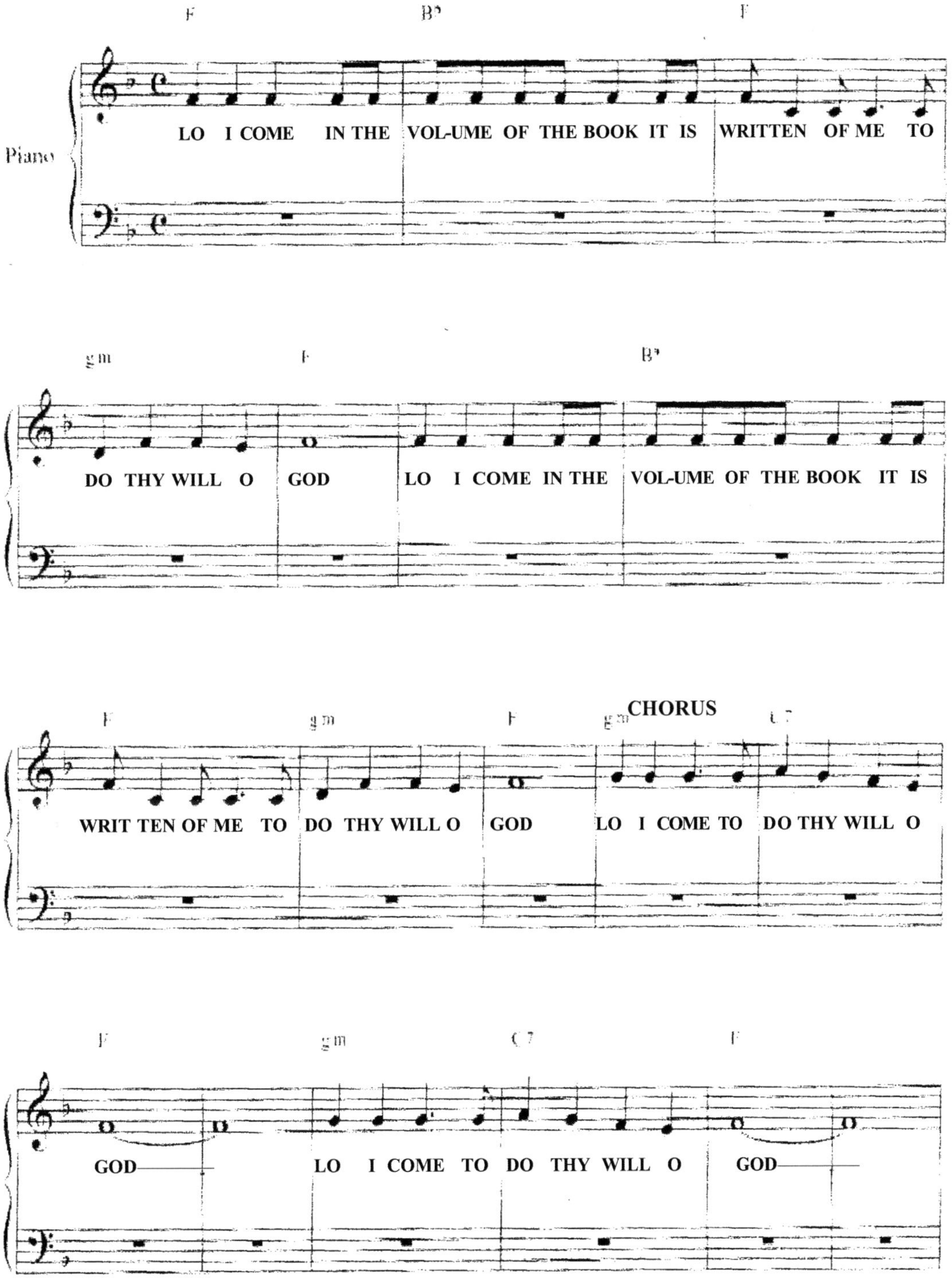
Piano
LO I COME IN THE VOL-UME OF THE BOOK IT IS WRITTEN OF ME TO
DO THY WILL O GOD
LO I COME IN THE VOL-UME OF THE BOOK IT IS
WRIT TEN OF ME TO DO THY WILL O GOD
CHORUS
LO I COME TO DO THY WILL O
GOD
LO I COME TO DO THY WILL O GOD
F
B♭
gm
C7

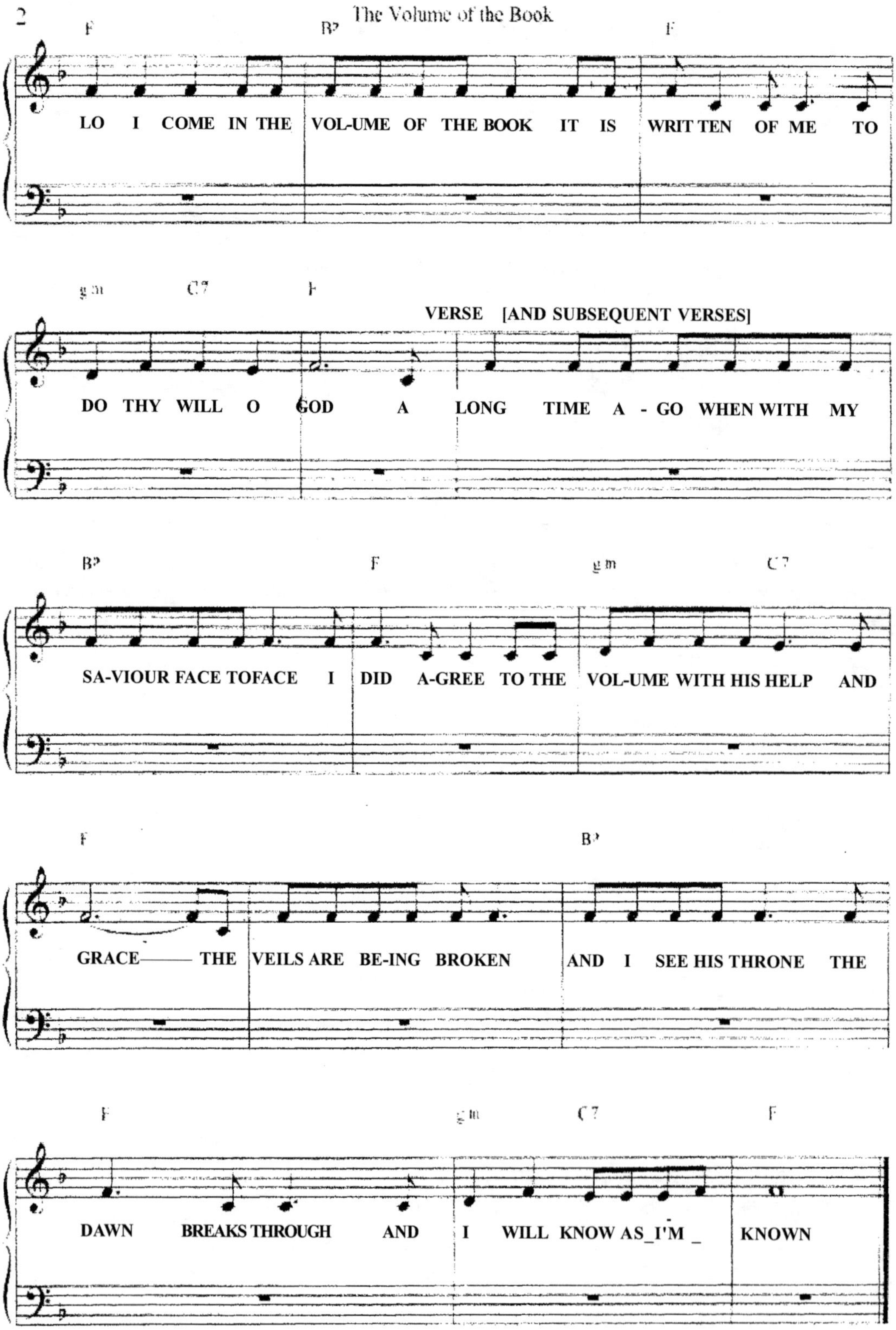
2
The Volume of the Book
F
B♭
F
LO I COME IN THE VOL-UME OF THE BOOK IT IS WRIT TEN OF ME TO
g m
C7
F
VERSE [AND SUBSEQUENT VERSES]
DO THY WILL O GOD A LONG TIME A - GO WHEN WITH MY
B♭
F
g m
C7
SA-VIOUR FACE TOFACE I DID A-GREE TO THE VOL-UME WITH HIS HELP AND
F
B♭
GRACE—— THE VEILS ARE BE-ING BROKEN AND I SEE HIS THRONE THE
F
g m
C7
F
DAWN BREAKS THROUGH AND I WILL KNOW AS_I'M _ KNOWN

Candidates for the Priesthood

THE SONG OF MELCHISEDEC

A Melchisedec Order Decree

Psalm 2:7-8

Music by Rita Livingston
Lyrics by A. Branch (tran.)

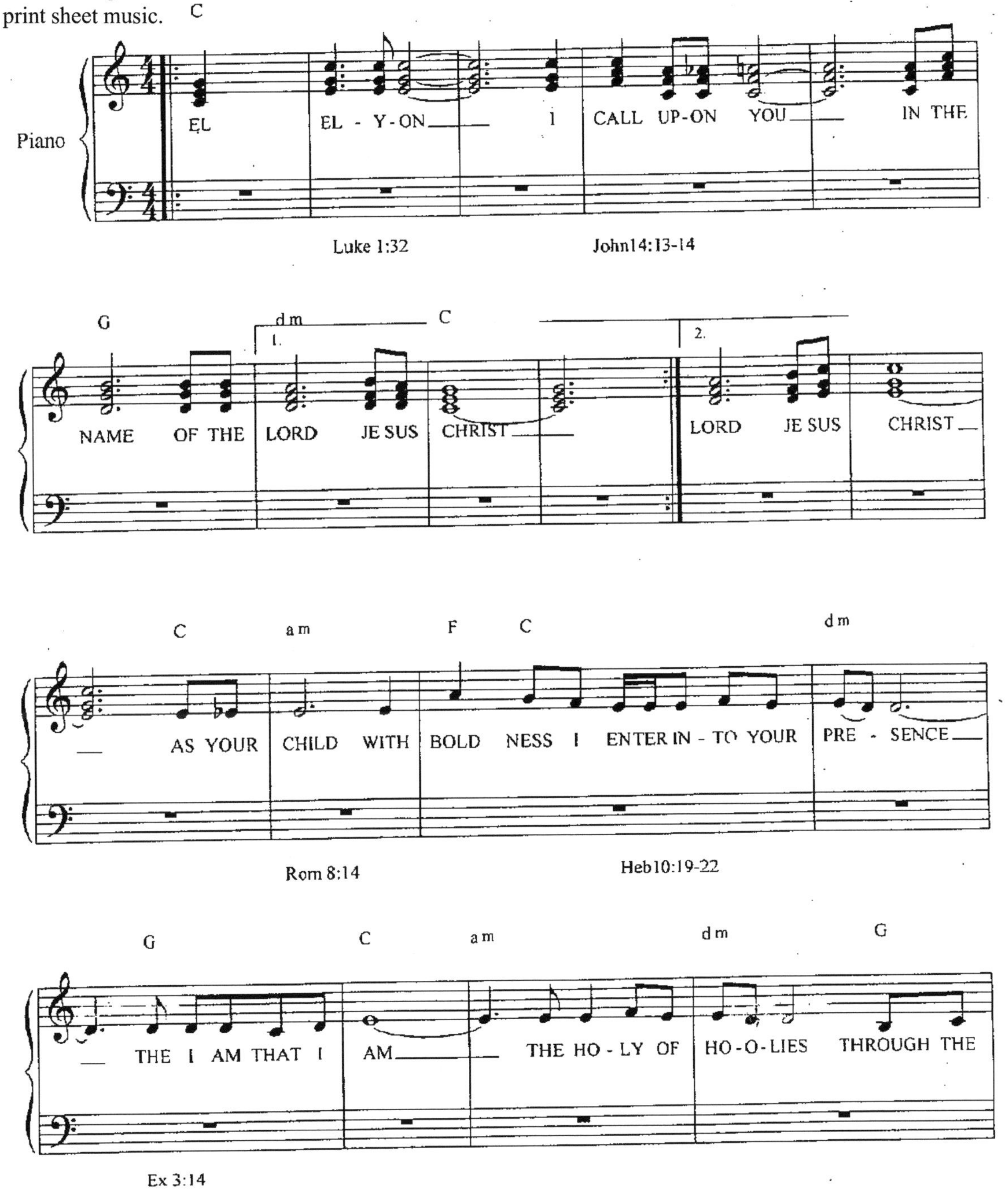

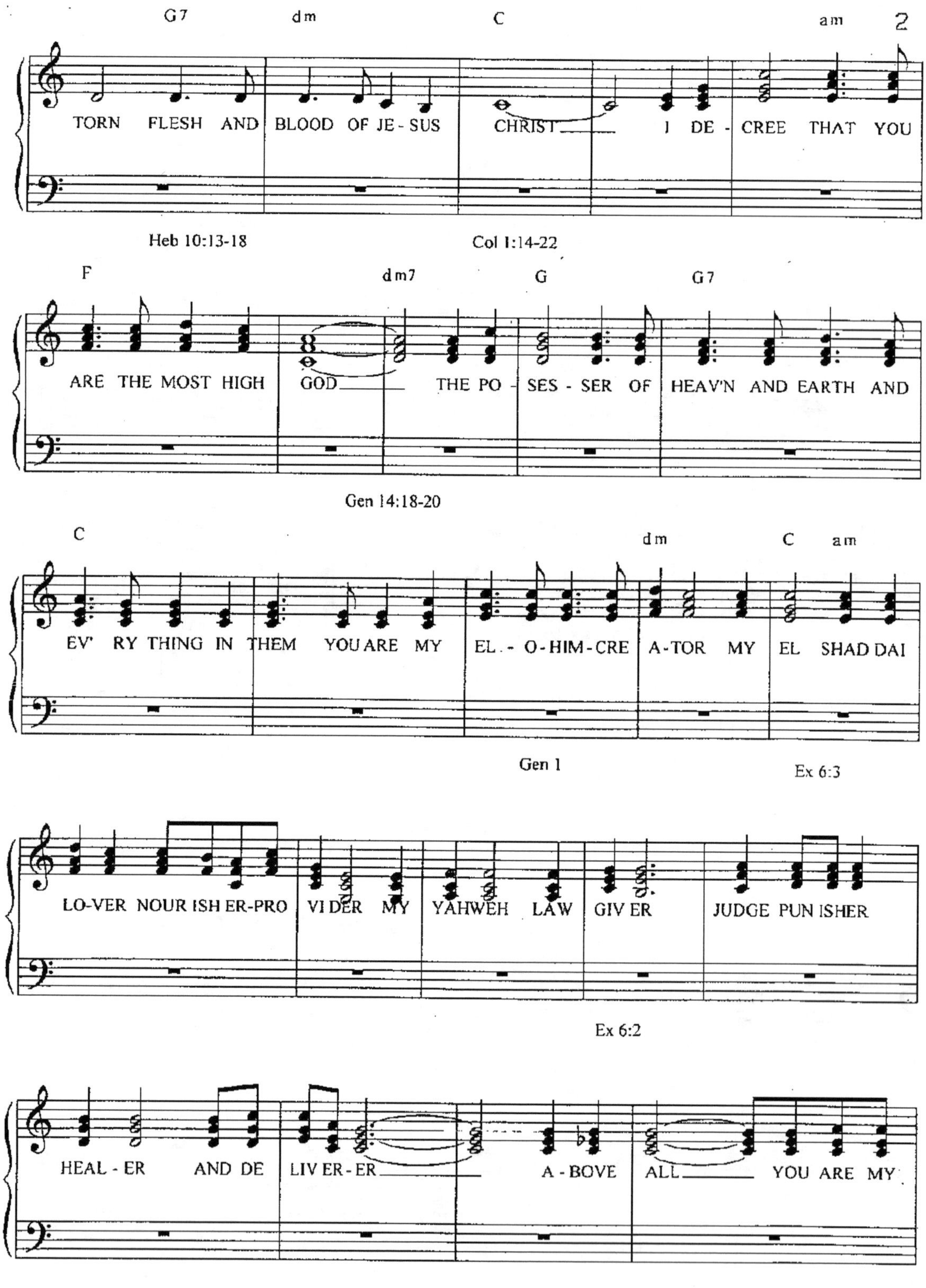
G7 dm C am 2
TORN FLESH AND BLOOD OF JE - SUS CHRIST I DE - CREE THAT YOU
Heb 10:13-18
Col 1:14-22
F dm7 G G7
ARE THE MOST HIGH GOD THE PO - SES - SER OF HEAV'N AND EARTH AND
Gen 14:18-20
C dm C am
EV' RY THING IN THEM YOU ARE MY EL - O - HIM - CRE A - TOR MY EL SHAD DAI
Gen 1
Ex 6:3
LO-VER NOUR ISH ER-PRO VI DER MY YAHWEH LAW GIV ER JUDGE PUN ISHER
Ex 6:2
HEAL - ER AND DE LIV ER - ER A - BOVE ALL YOU ARE MY

3

[Composer]

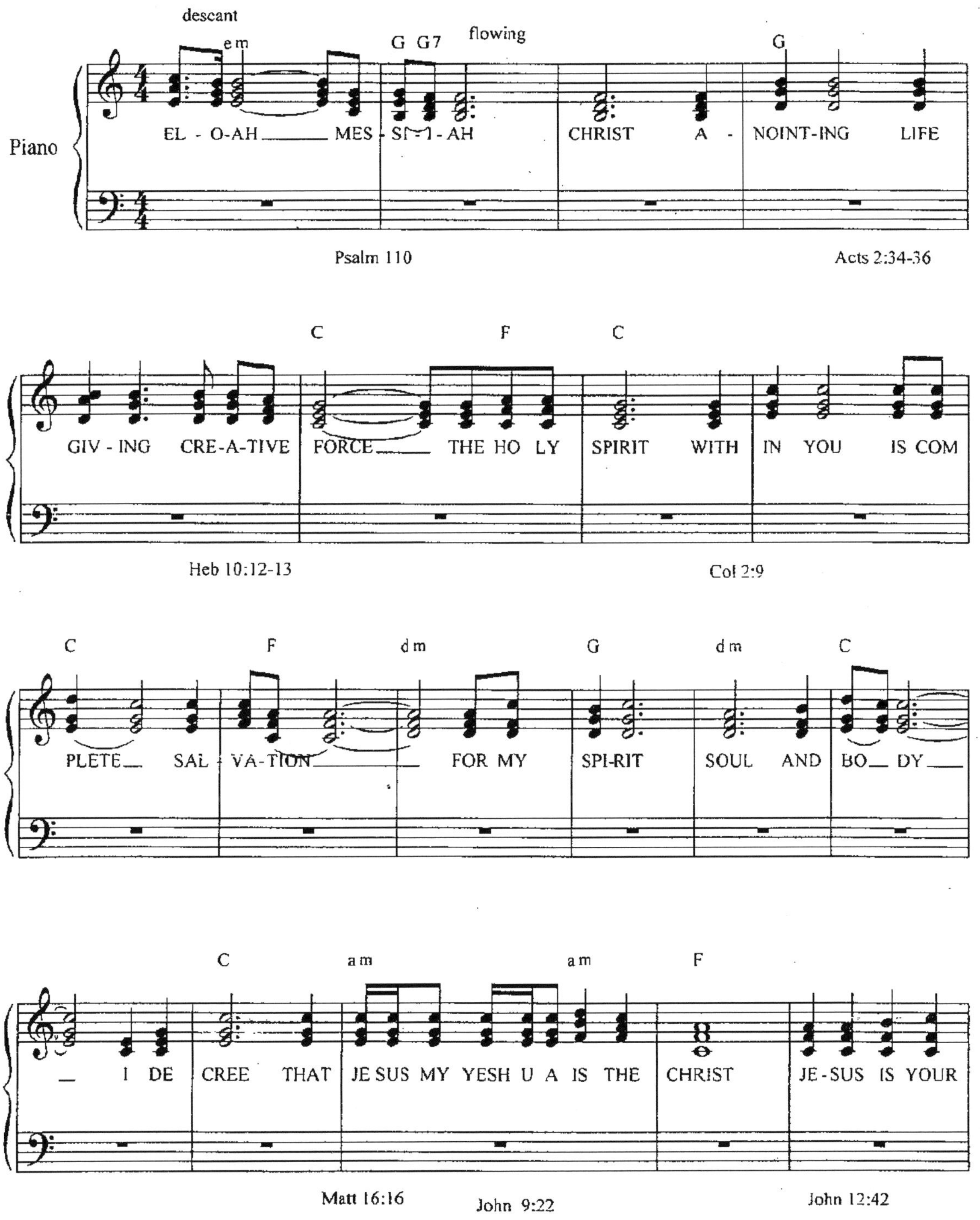
descant
em
G G7
flowing
G
Piano
EL - O-AH MES - SI - AH CHRIST A - NOINT-ING LIFE
Psalm 110
Acts 2:34-36
C F C
GIV - ING CRE-A-TIVE FORCE THE HO LY SPIRIT WITH IN YOU IS COM
Heb 10:12-13
Col 2:9
C F dm G dm C
PLETE SAL VA-TION FOR MY SPI-RIT SOUL AND BO DY
C am am F
I DE CREE THAT JE SUS MY YESH U A IS THE CHRIST JE-SUS IS YOUR
Matt 16:16
John 9:22
John 12:42

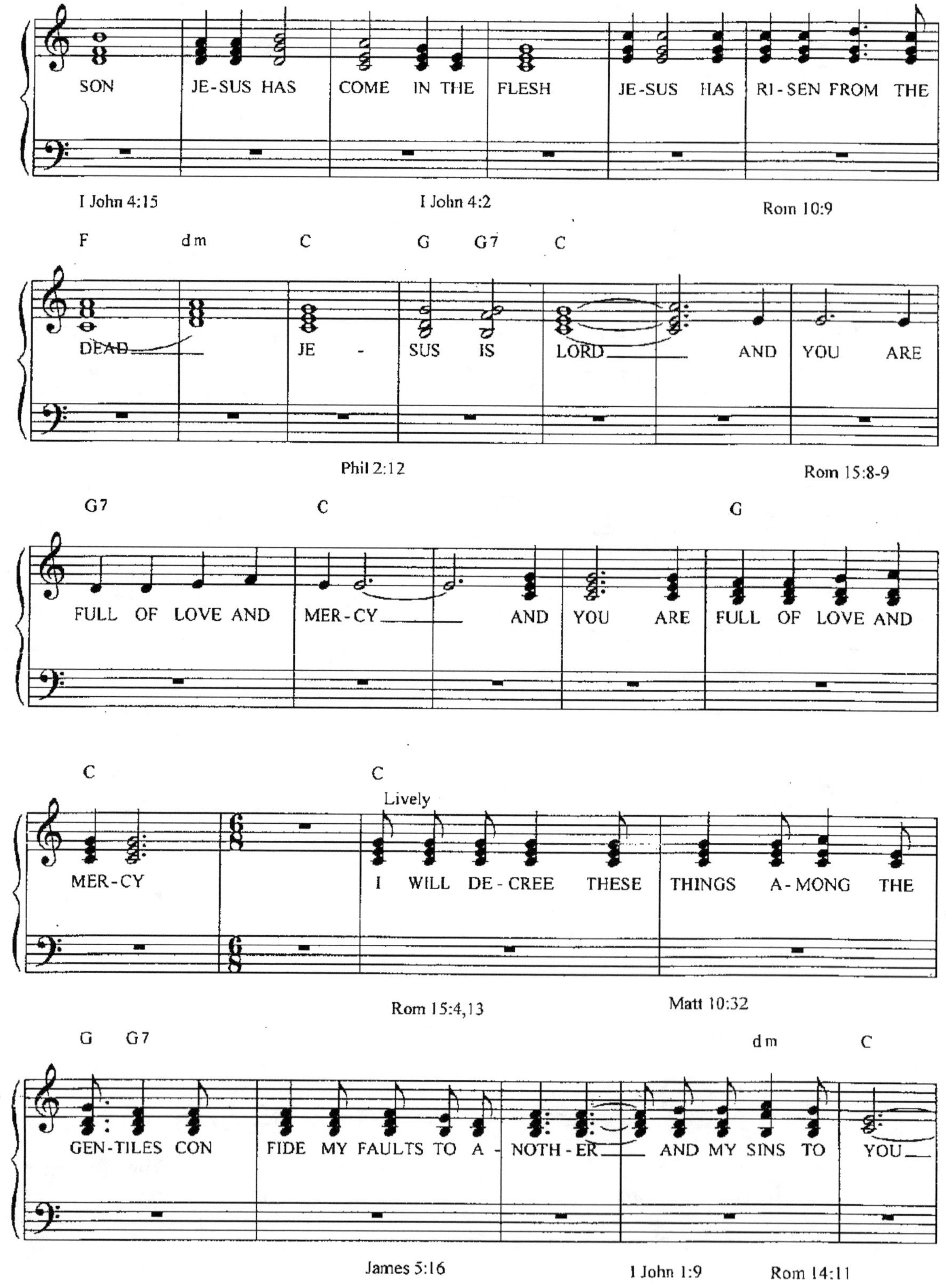
SON
JE-SUS HAS COME IN THE FLESH JE-SUS HAS RI-SEN FROM THE
I John 4:15
I John 4:2
Rom 10:9
F dm C G G7 C
DEAD JE - SUS IS LORD AND YOU ARE
Phil 2:12
Rom 15:8-9
G7 C G
FULL OF LOVE AND MER-CY AND YOU ARE FULL OF LOVE AND
C C
Lively
MER-CY I WILL DE-CREE THESE THINGS A-MONG THE
Rom 15:4,13
Matt 10:32
G G7 dm C
GEN-TILES CON FIDE MY FAULTS TO A - NOTH-ER AND MY SINS TO YOU
James 5:16
I John 1:9
Rom 14:11

5

[Composer]

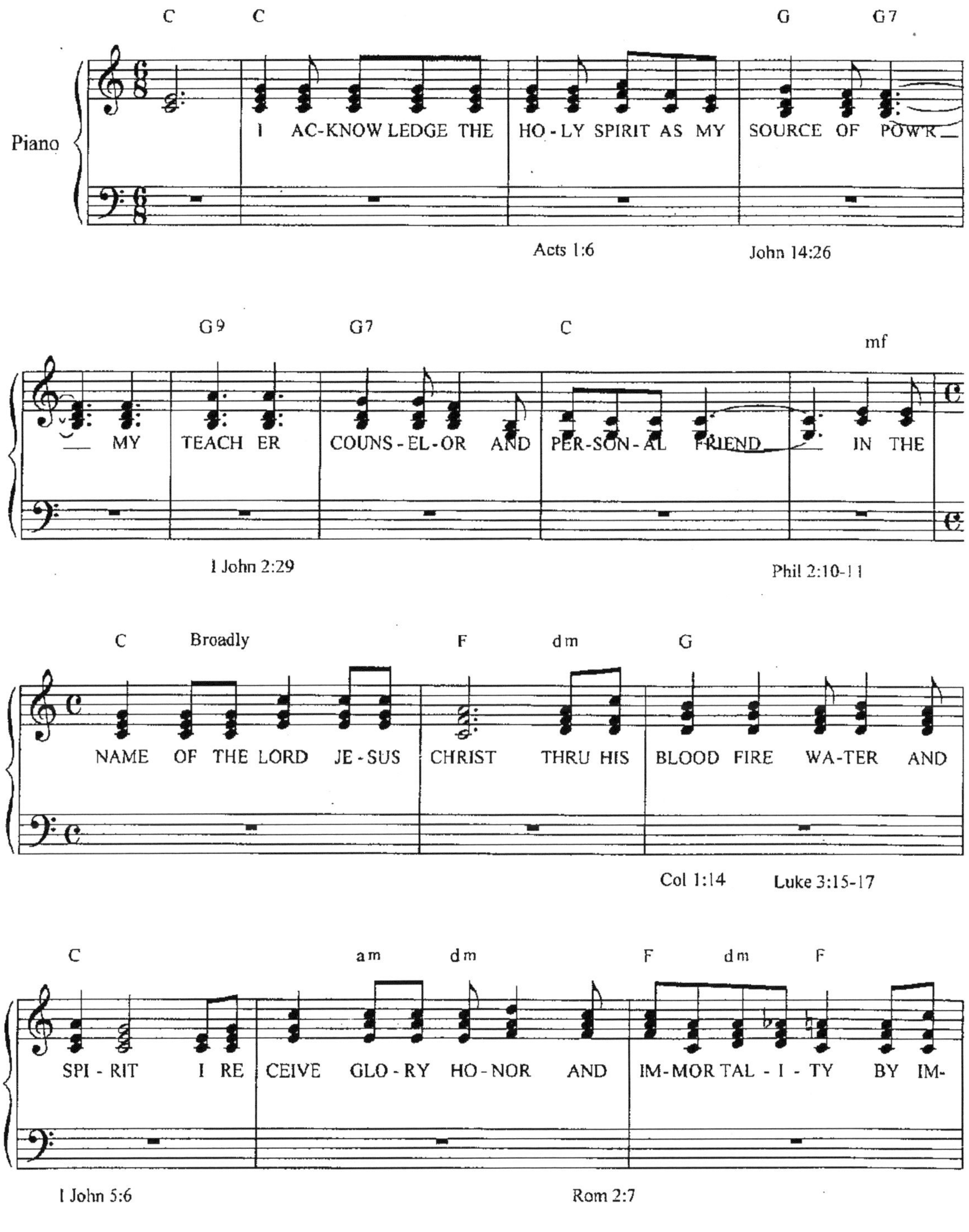
C C G G7
Piano
I AC-KNOW LEDGE THE HO - LY SPIRIT AS MY SOURCE OF POW'R
Acts 1:6
John 14:26
G9 G7 C
mf
MY TEACH ER COUNS - EL - OR AND PER-SON - AL FRIEND IN THE
I John 2:29
Phil 2:10-11
C Broadly F dm G
NAME OF THE LORD JE - SUS CHRIST THRU HIS BLOOD FIRE WA-TER AND
Col 1:14
Luke 3:15-17
C am dm F dm F
SPI - RIT I RE CEIVE GLO - RY HO - NOR AND IM-MOR TAL - I - TY BY IM-
I John 5:6
Rom 2:7

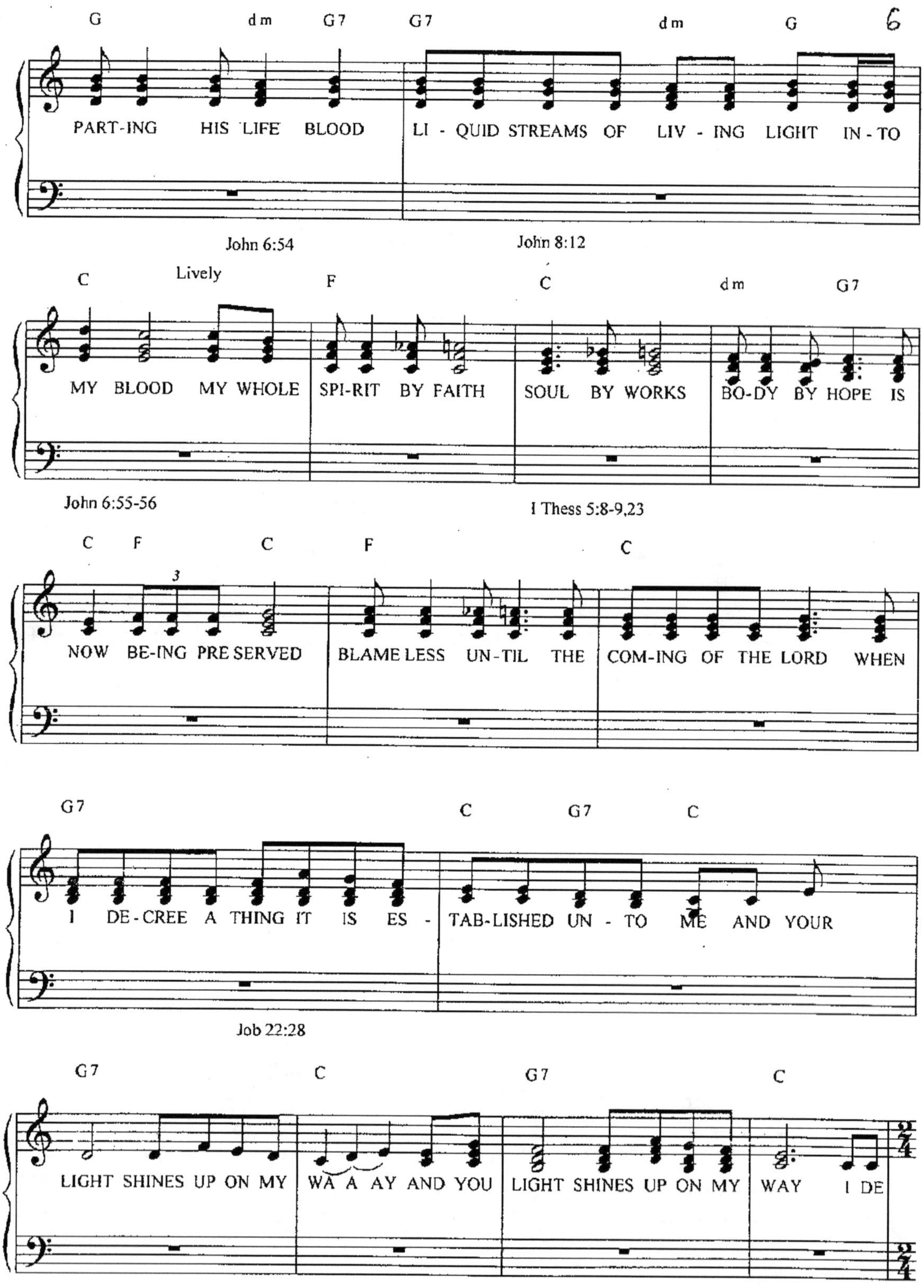
G dm G7 G7 dm G 6
PART-ING HIS LIFE BLOOD LI - QUID STREAMS OF LIV - ING LIGHT IN - TO
John 6:54
John 8:12
C Lively F C dm G7
MY BLOOD MY WHOLE SPI-RIT BY FAITH SOUL BY WORKS BO-DY BY HOPE IS
John 6:55-56
I Thess 5:8-9,23
C F C F C
NOW BE-ING PRE SERVED BLAME LESS UN-TIL THE COM-ING OF THE LORD WHEN
G7 C G7 C
I DE-CREE A THING IT IS ES - TAB-LISHED UN - TO ME AND YOUR
Job 22:28
G7 C G7 C
LIGHT SHINES UP ON MY WA A AY AND YOU LIGHT SHINES UP ON MY WAY I DE

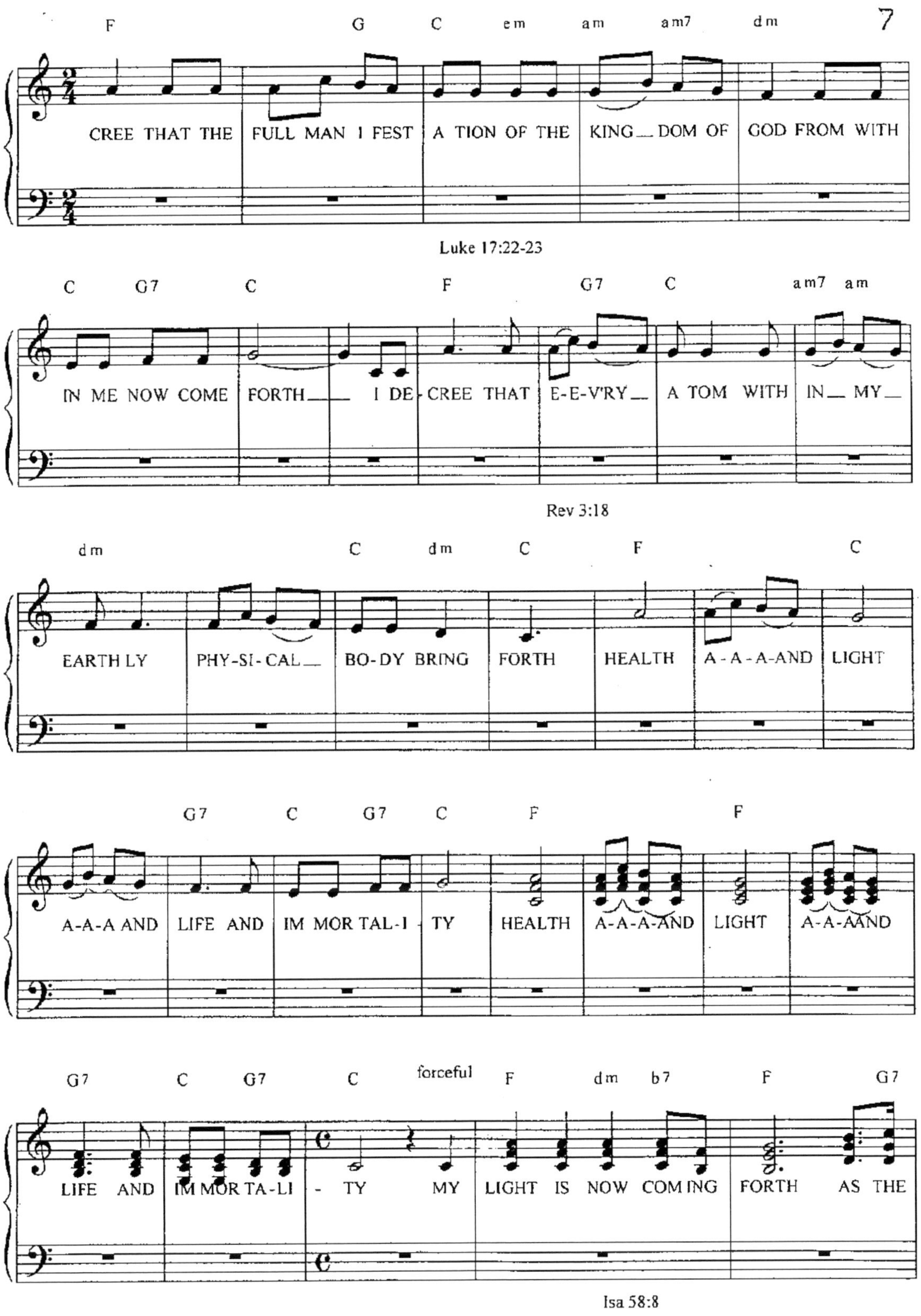
7
F G C em am am7 dm
CREE THAT THE FULL MAN I FEST A TION OF THE KING DOM OF GOD FROM WITH
Luke 17:22-23
C G7 C F G7 C am7 am
IN ME NOW COME FORTH I DE-CREE THAT E-E-V'RY A TOM WITH IN MY
Rev 3:18
dm C dm C F C
EARTH LY PHY-SI-CAL BO-DY BRING FORTH HEALTH A-A-A-AND LIGHT
G7 C G7 C F F
A-A-A AND LIFE AND IM MOR TAL-I TY HEALTH A-A-A-AND LIGHT A-A-AAND
G7 C G7 C forceful F dm b7 F G7
LIFE AND IM MOR TA-LI - TY MY LIGHT IS NOW COM ING FORTH AS THE
Isa 58:8

8

[Composer]

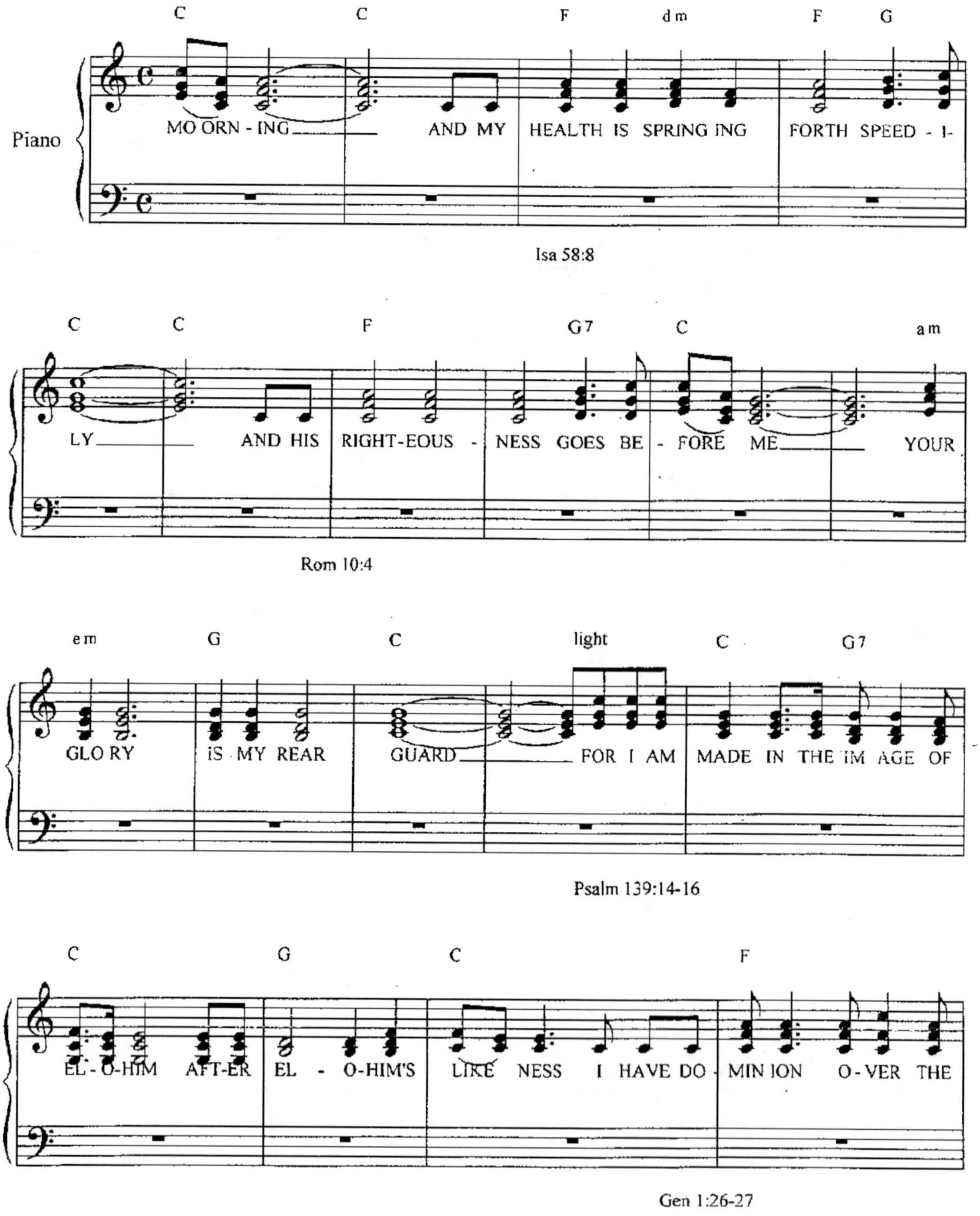
C C F dm F G
Piano
MO ORN - ING AND MY HEALTH IS SPRING ING FORTH SPEED - I-
Isa 58:8
C C F G7 C am
LY AND HIS RIGHT-EOUS - NESS GOES BE - FORE ME YOUR
Rom 10:4
em G C light C G7
GLO RY IS MY REAR GUARD FOR I AM MADE IN THE IM AGE OF
Psalm 139:14-16
C G C F
EL - O-HIM AFT-ER EL - O-HIM'S LIKE NESS I HAVE DO - MIN ION O-VER THE
Gen 1:26-27

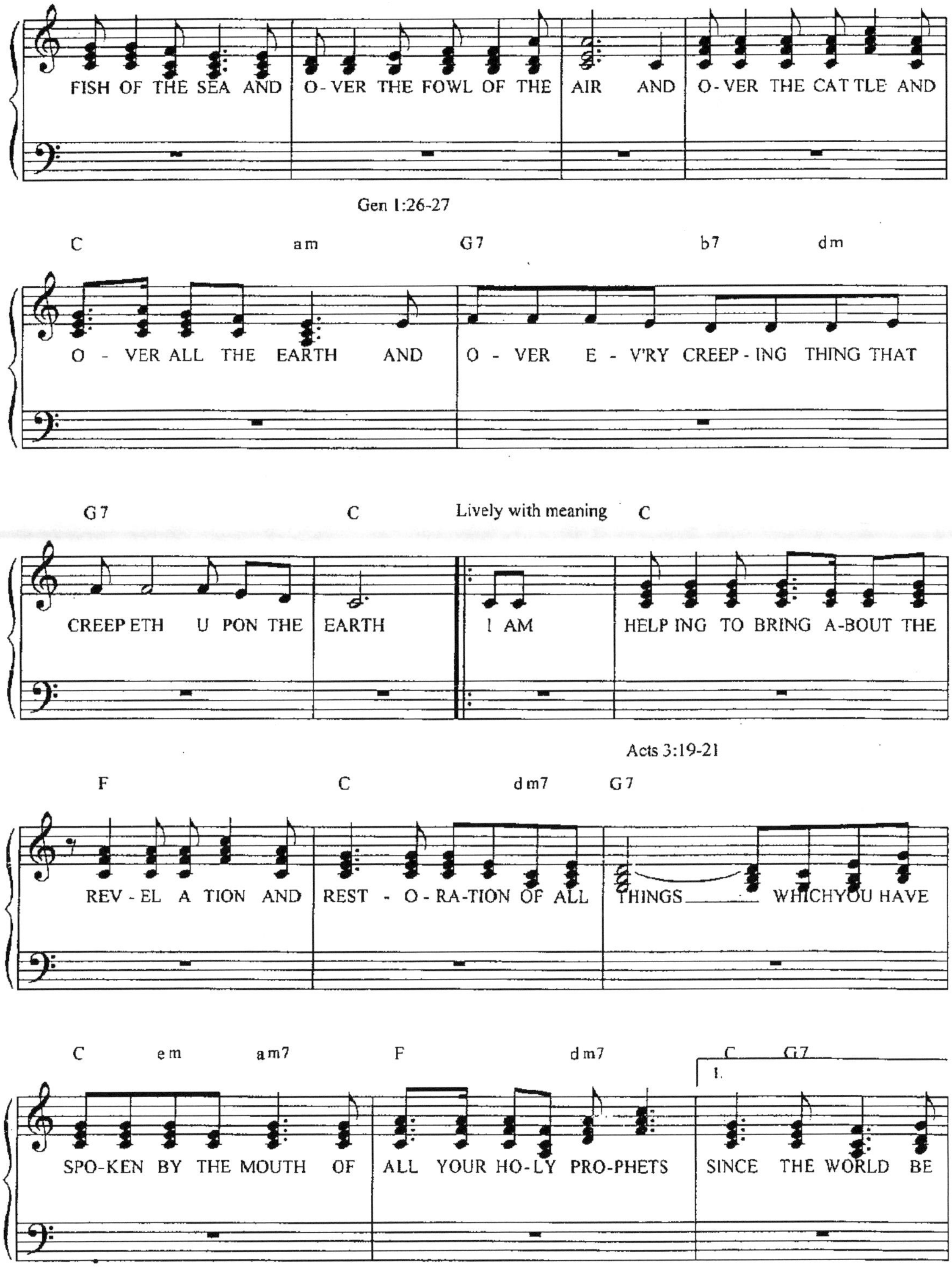
FISH OF THE SEA AND O-VER THE FOWL OF THE AIR AND O-VER THE CAT TLE AND
Gen 1:26-27
C am G7 b7 dm
O - VER ALL THE EARTH AND O - VER E - V'RY CREEP - ING THING THAT
G7 C Lively with meaning C
CREEP ETH U PON THE EARTH I AM HELP ING TO BRING A-BOUT THE
Acts 3:19-21
F C dm7 G7
REV - EL A TION AND REST - O - RA-TION OF ALL THINGS WHICH YOU HAVE
C em am7 F dm7 C G7
1.
SPO-KEN BY THE MOUTH OF ALL YOUR HO-LY PRO-PHETS SINCE THE WORLD BE

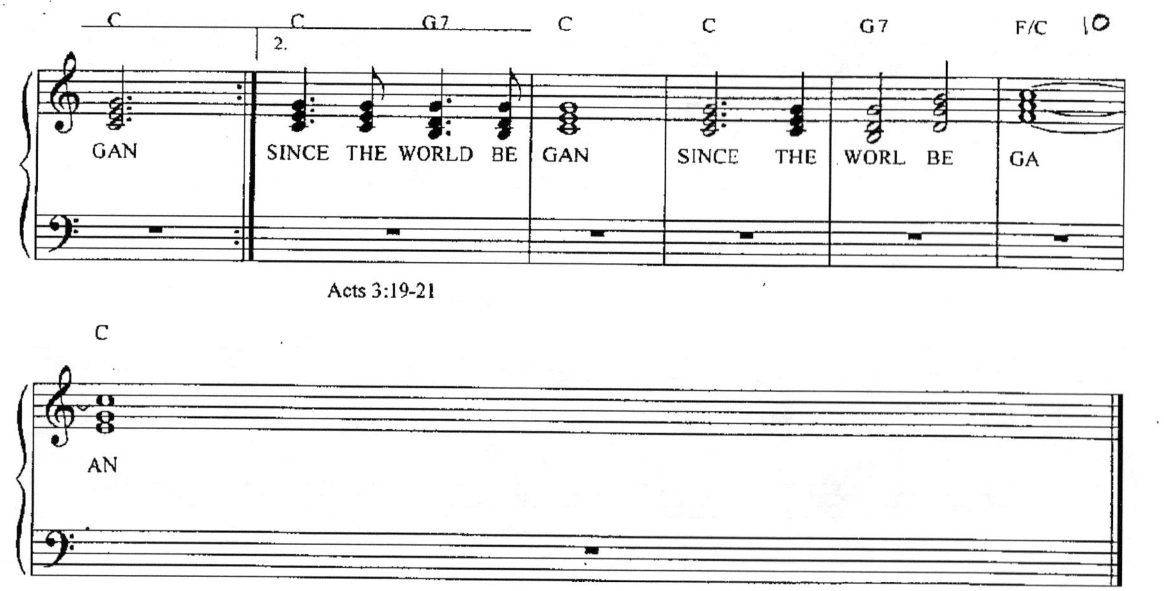
C C G7 C C G7 F/C 10
2.
GAN SINCE THE WORLD BE GAN SINCE THE WORL BE GA
Acts 3:19-21
C
AN

About the Author

Chatan N. Kallah is a herald pointing to a new generation of sons and daughters that is coming forth. Modern day Nebuchadnezzar's will tell this generation that *thou canst make interpretations, and dissolve doubts.** These sons and daughters, like young Daniels, will be schooled in the scientific knowledge of the modern world, but will possess extra dimensions of insight into the spiritual world. They will bring healing of many controversies as underlying truths are revealed. *The wolf and the lamb shall feed together, and the lion shall eat straw like the bullock ... They shall not hurt nor destroy in all my holy mountain, saith the LORD.**

Chatan has a passion for a ministry that Isaiah describes as being *The repairer of the breach, The restorer of paths to dwell in.** This involves the repairing of the ongoing breach between the scientific world and the spiritual world. Kallah goes on to describe other breaches that must be repaired, such as the breach between the right and left brain and between man and woman. This repair is not a 'quick fix' but is rooted in discovering truth, *and the truth shall make you free.** Chatan N. Kallah calls this romance of repairing the breach: The Dove Code

**Daniel 5:16b / Isaiah 58:12b and 65:25 / John 8:32b*